SAIGON
LAUNDRY

SAIGON LAUNDRY

a novel

BY HUGHES KEENAN

This book is a work of fiction. Names, Characters, places and incidents either are products of the author's imagination or are used fictitiously. Any resemblance to actual events or locales or persons, living or dead, is entirely coincidental.

Design by AAD: www.arthuradesign.com
Author photo by Mark McDonald: www.markmcdonaldphoto.com

ISBN-13: 9780615907963
ISBN-10: 0615907962
LCCN: 201392013

L'etranger Books, Austin, Texas

DEDICATION

To my sister, Anne, and my aunt, Mary Lou,
who gave shelter to a wandering soul

THE TEN COMMANDMENTS OF THE CODE OF CHIVALRY

by Leon Gautier
1891

    I Thou shalt believe all that the Church teaches, and shalt observe all its directions.

   II Thou shalt defend the Church.

 III Thou shalt respect all weaknesses, and shall constitute thyself the defender of them.

 IV Thou shalt love the country in the which thou wast born.

  V Thou shalt not recoil before thine enemy.

 VI Thou shalt make war against the Infidel without cessation, and without mercy.

VII Thou shalt perform scrupulously thy feudal duties, if they be not contrary to the laws of God.

VIII Thou shalt never lie, and shall remain faithful to thy pledged word.

 IX Thou shalt be generous, and give largess to everyone.

  X Thou shalt be everywhere and always the champion of the Right and the Good against Injustice and Evil.

ASH WEDNESDAY

He may his life unfold, that he may better know
How his soul may be saved, when he from hence shall go.
Shrived was he surely there-he shewed his misdeeds all,
Or less they be or more, and did for mercy call.
—The Pearl Poet

CHAPTER 1

Sheets of blowing rain beat against the bedroom windows of the apartment with some urgency. Each gust tapped big drops against the glass with a watery rush, reminding him it was time to get up though the throbbing in his head coaxed his eyes closed.

It was late February of what had been an abnormally warm winter. The rainstorm was a welcome relief for a parched landscape that had seen little moisture since fall. There was more light in the morning now, and spring wasn't far off.

He lay on his left side, facing the window. That he was in a position to be looking at the window with such proximity fully woke him, and the accompanying hangover. Jack Muerce was on the wrong side of the bed. He lay still as he pondered the situation, sluggishly recounting the previous night.

Cautiously, he rolled over and his eyes focused on the naked woman next to him. He breathed in the scent of her perfume. She smelled nice—a unique floral scent. It was pleasant. His eyes adjusted to the faint, storm-cast light, then took a tour of the naked woman that started at her ankles, and travelled up her legs. He rested his eyes at the top of the curve of her hip to admire the round crescent of her buttocks before gently following the plunge to her waist. His gaze then made the long, gentle climb toward her shoulders. Tresses of soft, tussled brunette hair covered her upper body, and the nape of her neck.

On the nightstand next to what was normally his side of the bed, was an empty bottle of champagne, and two glasses. The events of the night returned to Muerce's memory with every throb of his hangover. The ex-

1

cess of Fat Tuesday had ended. It was Ash Wednesday. The season for atonement and sacrifice had arrived.

They met at a Mardi Gras party. She worked in advertising, at a big agency, or something like that. Although an artsy type, she was some kind of an account supervisor, pitching ideas to clients, overseeing the creative process, and writing the project status reports. He remembered he thought she was sharp, and forward without being too aggressive. She knew how to carry a conversation when it turned awkward, and remain silent when she thought she was starting to dominate a discussion. But mostly, he recalled, she knew how to listen when he talked. He cringed when he remembered how much he had talked. Too much. It was because of her eyes. He had fallen into them halfway through the night. Brown eyes. Muerce remembered she had brown eyes; sparkly, big brown eyes now hidden behind sleep.

The two of them danced, and drank, and ate some awful gumbo, and talked. He couldn't remember what about. She knew him by reputation. Most people did. Then there was her hair. He liked her hair. Whoever did her highlights was the best in the city, and well worth whatever she was paying them. And he liked that she fawned over him without making him feel it was obvious.

The late hours of the night chewed in his memory like moths in a closet of wool sweaters. The two of them came back to his apartment to continue the pre-Lenten celebration, and to talk—more. After they opened the second bottle of champagne she kissed him. He remembered that, and what followed. She complimented his kissing. At first, she giggled when they kissed. As the passion thickened, the giggles turned first to whispered moans, then more pronounced.

He remembered more of that, but what he couldn't recall, despite all his efforts, was her name.

The alarm in his head sounded though the clock on the nightstand was silent. It was time to extract himself from the situation, albeit from his own apartment, as quickly as he could. Very gently, he eased out of bed and made for the bathroom, taking care to close the door as quietly as possible. After turning the light on, he urinated with precision and stealth, aiming for just above the waterline. He bought a little more time to compose himself in the mirror by not flushing the toilet, and washing his hands. Good habits, but if done too soon, they surely would wake his guest. He tried to remember her name.

Muerce looked at himself in the mirror. Not too haggard. Still in damned good shape for a man in his late forties. He spread his hands across the hair on his chest, some of which had started to turn the same gray that now tinted his temples.

"A good color, well earned," he said. He was pleased with himself when he considered the woman in his bed was, probably, in her late twenties. At the most, early thirties. It didn't matter. The self-satisfied moment passed quickly as he played out his exit strategy. It was a weekday, and he—and likely she—had things to do.

He was practiced at the art of dodging out in the morning. Flushing the toilet, then washing his hands, he turned on the shower. All of it accomplished in less than thirty seconds. The commotion would likely wake his guest, but by the time she collected her thoughts, and herself, he would be shaved, teeth brushed, and toweling off in the bedroom. She could then use the bathroom in privacy, and without much conversation between them. That was the plan.

She rolled over to see him standing in the bright, steamy doorway of the bathroom, lifted herself up on one arm, and smiled a big, warm smile. Her sparkly brown eyes were shining as if, Muerce imagined, she were about to give a branding campaign presentation to a client. Muerce saw she was a chipper one in the morning. Even with all they drank last night, she could rally early the next day. As much as Muerce admired women who could do that, he knew all too well that it was a precursor to the one thing he wanted to avoid; her having expectations of him.

"Good morning, Jack," she said, her eyes welcoming him back to bed.

It wasn't going to be as easy as he hoped.

"How are you feeling?" Muerce replied. If only he could remember her name.

She yawned, sat up, and stretched while looking around the room. A trail of her clothing marked a path from the bedroom, and down the hallway that led to the living room. Muerce hoped she would see it as breadcrumbs that got her to the front door, and out of his day. Then he remembered he drove last night, and she was not the type you trundled into a cab early in the morning.

"I'm hungry," she chirped. "How about I make us some breakfast?"

"Sounds great," he said. He had a smug smile. She did not know him well enough to know that was what it was—smugness. He pictured her naked, rooting around the kitchen for a good while before realizing, like Old Mother Hubbard, that his cupboards were as bare as she. In the meantime, he'd be dressed and ready to leave. Yes, he would offer to take her to breakfast since, he would say, he had forgotten to go to the grocery store last week. No, they would not go. *Works every time.*

She had a beautiful body, he noticed, as she skipped around the bed to give him a kiss. When she did, she wrapped herself around him with affection, and an attempt at intimacy.

"Last night was amazing," she said, looking him straight in the eye. "You're a pretty incredible guy."

"Thanks," Muerce said, pecking her on the lips with as little passion as possible. "You are too. Amazing, that is. Not a guy."

She giggled and half trotted down the hallway to the kitchen before turning to ask him how he liked his coffee.

"However you can make it fastest," he said.

Her departure gave Muerce the opportunity to get dressed, fast. He flipped the light on in the walk-in closet, illuminating two racks of suits, sports coats and sundry jackets that were faced by a wall of shoes, and a large selection of starched and folded dress shirts arranged in various cubbies. At the end of the large closet was a dressing mirror and a waist-high shelf that held most of his accoutrements. There were watches, cuff links, and other various items a gentleman possessed as part of his wardrobe. Muerce liked clothes, and clothes liked him. They wore each other well.

As it was a rainy February day with a chill in the air, and that the day carried the solemnity of being Ash Wednesday, Muerce picked out a gray flannel suit, white spread collar shirt, and a purple, four-in-hand silk tie.

As he looped the tie around a second time for a proper knot, the significance of the day triggered a clarity in him that brought relief and satisfaction. Her name was Ashley. *Oh, thank God.*

Ashley, in the kitchen, barefoot and naked, was getting cold in front of the open refrigerator door. She was confused. Despite the large capacity of the expensive double-door Sub-Zero refrigerator-freezer, the only foodstuffs to be found were a small container of Beluga caviar, a tin of *pate de foie gras*, several small bottles of tonic water, club soda, Perrier, and a jar of blue cheese-stuffed olives. There was a set of six martini glasses on the top shelf. On the bottom shelf were two bottles of champagne, and several bottles of various white wines. In the freezer Ashley discovered only two bottles of Stolichnaya.

Shivering, she closed the refrigerator doors and looked about the expansive, mostly stainless steel kitchen. There was an elaborate Italian espresso machine on the far counter, but nowhere could she find coffee beans. In what looked to be a small pantry all she discovered were some toast points, and an open package of stale crackers.

Although having woken up at her fair share of barren bachelor pads before, the paucity of sustenance at Muerce's apartment was shocking, and slightly endearing. She began to formulate a plan to impress him by doing some basic grocery shopping, and cooking for him sometime in the near future. That was her plan.

Having struck out in the kitchen, she made her way back to the bedroom, picking up the trail of clothing along the way. She arrived just as Muerce walked out of the closet, fully dressed, and ready for the day. He was gorgeous, and the sight of him made her chest tighten. She also felt a pull of anxiety as she stood there, naked, makeup from the night before still on, hair asunder, and clutching her wrinkled clothes.

"Um, Jack, you don't have a single thing to eat in the kitchen," she stammered.

"Oh, I forgot," he said, without looking directly at her as he fastened his wristwatch. "Haven't been to the store in awhile. I've been busy. Why don't we grab a quick breakfast somewhere?"

It was a ridiculous offer, and he knew it. She was not about to be seen having breakfast with him, wearing the same clothes she had worn the night before; and without proper makeup, and time spent fixing her hair.

"Okay, let me just pop in the shower and rinse off quickly," she said. "I can run a brush through my hair and wear it back in a pony. Can you grab my purse for me in the living room? I think it's on the sofa."

She disappeared into the bathroom, closing the door. He heard the shower go on.

That didn't play out so well. Plan B.

Muerce checked the battery on his iPhone. It was low. Distracted the night before, he'd forgotten to plug it in. He would charge it in the car. There were no new e-mails, one voicemail and a text message from Eleanor that said, simply: Noon ashes.

He didn't recognize the number for the voicemail, and decided to listen to it later.

Muerce collected the empty champagne bottle, and glasses from the nightstand. He didn't bother with the bed. The maid would get it. In the living room he grabbed the other empty bottle, and deposited everything on the island in the kitchen. He straightened the cushions on the sofa, and found Ashley's purse. It was a medium sized pink Kate Spade that would, he suspected, contain just the essentials. He had an urge to rifle through it to learn more about her, but the thought passed quickly as there was no need to know more about Ashley, like, for example, her last name.

Ashley was showered and toweling off in the bathroom when Muerce arrived with her purse.

"Perfect, thanks Jack."

She wrapped one of his monogrammed towels around her, pulled out a small, folding brush from the purse, and quickly worked her hair back. She stopped once to smile at him with excitement in her face.

Crap, he thought, I'm lingering too long.

He should have shuffled away from the open doorway to the bathroom but, inexplicably, Muerce found himself standing, trancelike, staring at her. He was enjoying watching the young woman named Ashley, without a last name, primp and preen, and on such a tight deadline. *Maybe breakfast isn't such a bad idea.*

She finished touching up her face and lips, slipped on her yellow, lace panties, and hooked her bra.

"Let me throw my clothes on and we can go," she said, grabbing her outfit, which she had draped near the shower to relax some of the wrinkles.

I'll meet you in the foyer," Muerce said.

Ashley scampered behind him, hopping as she put on her heels.

From the hall closet Muerce grabbed a double-breasted trench coat. Sharply snapping the collar up in a ceremonious fashion that caught Ashley's attention, and her chest tightened again. *Too cool.*

Muerce looked at Ashley with a wane smile.

"It's coming down pretty hard out there," he said. "Why don't you borrow one of my coats?"

Ashley batted her eyes a few times and smiled, though with less of a beam than when she first awoke.

He grabbed a Bennet car coat from the rack of jackets hung on cedar hangers, and helped her slip into it. *Not a bad fit. She looks pretty damn cute in it.*

Ashley instinctively made her way to the two double doors that announced the grand entrance to the apartment. Muerce selected a black umbrella with a wood and ivory handle from a large brass container that held a good half-dozen umbrellas, and various canes and walking sticks. He also kept a baseball bat in the stand.

"Where are you going?" Muerce said.

"To breakfast?" Ashley said, her hand on the knob of the large door that led out of the apartment.

"This way," Muerce said, throwing the umbrella over his right shoulder. He pressed a panel next to a long antique reception table, and the wall opened to reveal a small, caged service elevator.

That Jack Muerce was who he was, and did what he did, was impressive and exciting enough for Ashley. But that he had a private elevator? *Way cool.*

"Why didn't we use this last night," Ashley said, then hesitating for a moment. "Or did we?"

Muerce didn't miss a beat.

"Because I wasn't trying to sneak you in last night," he said.

There was an awkward, and momentary silence.

"But you're sneaking me out," Ashley said, trying to soften the hurt in her voice, which Muerce interpreted immediately. He turned, wrapped himself around her, and brought his face close to hers.

"Not at all," he said, kissing her on the lips softly. He let the kiss linger, and brushed their lips together again. "I'm just trying to impress you. Sorry. We can go out the front door, and ring the apartment doorbells all the way down to the garage if you'd like."

Ashley felt she was melting into him, but firmed herself up, smiled, and kissed him back. She withdrew slightly so their eyes could focus on each other.

"Oh, I'm taking the ride on the private elevator," she said. Muerce felt there was more purpose in her statement than there should have been.

Seven floors later, Muerce slid the elevator cage doors open to reveal a small basement garage that had room for only a few automobiles—all his. The building was old, but had been reinforced over the years. Large cement columns partitioned the parking spaces. It was well lit, clean and bright with fresh, white paint. In a back area of the garage were a maintenance room, boiler room and such, and various storage lockers. At the far end was a ramp that led to a heavy steel garage door that opened to one of the side streets next to the building.

"Now, I remember," Ashley said. "We went up a short flight of stairs over there to the lobby. What were we talking about?"

"Rugs," Muerce said. "Very old rugs about to go on display at the museum in a few weeks. You said your agency is doing some of the promotional work."

"That's right," she said, pleased he remembered.

Muerce quickened his pace, and cut in front of her as they rounded one of the large columns by the parking bays. As she cornered the column, there he stood, holding the passenger door open for her. *Thank God for chivalry.*

While the Medieval tapestry exhibit and the free tickets she would get to attend the gala—and how she so badly wanted to ask him to go with her—were forefront in her thoughts, the sight of his car jumped to the head of the line. In the heat of the previous night, she had nearly forgotten about the car. *How much cooler can this guy get?*

Muerce drove a 1972 Mercedes Benz 280 SE with a four-point-five liter engine. The maroon sedan glistened in the bright light of the garage. Its chrome sparkled and pulsed as if it were a living thing. The car was, like Muerce himself, a classic. Smooth rounded lines, a deep, rich color, not too flashy, but not to be overlooked either.

Ashley slid onto the large, black leather bucket seat. In front of her was an expanse of glossy walnut that framed the console. She had never seen so much wood in a car. It was as if the Mercedes were more sailing ship than automobile. Her thoughts were interrupted when Muerce shut the door behind her. It closed with a distinctive *whong* that echoed in the spacious interior; an announcement of class and comfort. It also made her feel like she was sitting in a vacuum. There was only silence as she watched Muerce walk around the front of the car. She admired the hint of soft curl in his hair, his strong face, and recalled, as they lay in bed, how soft the skin was on his cheeks.

When Muerce opened the driver's door it seemed, to Ashley, that a rush of air escaped from both her and the car. He slid the umbrella into the back seat and settled into his, shutting the door with another *whong*. It was a comforting sound.

The engine turned over with a low, throaty roar, and quickly idled to a purr. Muerce plugged his iPhone into its white charger cord, the connection making a distinctive chime when it was coupled.

"Seat belts," Muerce said, without looking at Ashley. She fumbled with the antiquated shoulder belt until Muerce leaned over to help her, grazing his face against her hair.

"Thank you," she said, pleased at his attention to her safety, yet an uncertain nervousness was building.

He fingered the key-shaped headlight switch on the dashboard, which made a *chunk* sound. The wall on the opposite side of the basement garage dazzled in the illumination. Muerce put the Mercedes in gear and exited, slowly, from the parking bay. The tires *squealed* as they turned on the glistening gray floor surface. Muerce reached up to the driver's visor, pressed the button to the garage door opener, and gave the car some gas. Up the ramp they went, and into a driving rain.

A hollowness filled the car as they drove down the rain-slick street. It was that awkward point of the morning-after. They had to get through it as quickly as possible. Like removing a Band-Aid. It was best to just rip it off. He was searching for the right excuse to beg out of breakfast and drop Ashley off, wherever she lived. She removed a Blackberry from her purse, and was busily checking messages, cradling the device in both hands as if she were praying.

"Oh, damn," she said. "I forgot I have a full staff meeting at nine, and I have to give a project update. Can I take a raincheck on breakfast?" *Why am I lying?*

Muerce stifled his reaction. The windshield wipers beat out a happy rhythm at the turn of events.

"It's raining, so why not a raincheck?" he said, sensing she was covering up, and not caring. He didn't think she wanted to have breakfast with him, in the first place. Not in public. Not wearing the same clothes from the night before. If anyone saw her? The shame. Ashley told him where she lived. It was only about twenty minutes away from his apartment. *That might be convenient, he thought, maybe sometime in the future.*

They drove a few blocks in silence as Ashley tapped away at the diminutive keyboard on her phone. Her frantic messaging wasn't about work, but to invite a girlfriend to lunch to tell her about the guy she met the night before. She ended the message with three exclamation points.

"I was wondering," she said as they neared her apartment building.

"Yes," Muerce said, his eyes on the road.

"I have tickets to the gala for the opening of the tapestry exhibit. We could go together."

Muerce let out a deep sigh, but didn't hesitate to answer.

"I already have a date."

His response deflated Ashley, who suddenly felt like she was in high school, and the captain of the football team she'd gotten the nerve up to ask to prom said "no." She could feel her eyes start to water.

Muerce glanced at her, and felt bad. It wasn't the answer she wanted, but it was the truth. Still, there was more truth to it that would, if he wanted to, ease her hurt feelings. But telling her would also be offering a shard of hope. Still, there was something about this Ashley without a last name that attracted Muerce. She reminded him of someone long gone from his life. Someone he had hurt. Someone to whom he owed a great deal to, but never seemed to satisfy the obligation he felt he owed. He decided to risk it.

"It's my mother," he said.

"What?"

"My mother."

"What's your mother?"

"My date is my mother," he said, surprised at the words coming out of his mouth. "She's on the board of the museum, and I promised I would accompany her. She lives for that kind of thing."

"Oh," Ashley said. There was relief in her voice as she looked out the passenger window, wiped a tear from her eye with the palm of her hand, and smiled. She was already drunk when they met at the party the night before, and was in the moment. Some of the pieces were starting to fit together. Eleanor Muerce wasn't just her client, she was Jack Muerce's mother.

"We could meet up, at the gala," he said.

"Okay."

"I want to."

Muerce reached over, and squeezed her hand.

"Do you have a card?" he said.

Ashley fumbled through her purse to find her wallet, and prayed she had a business card on her. She found one sandwiched between her driver's license, and a gold American Express card. The business card was worn, and had her old title, but the contact information was current.

Muerce pulled to a stop in front of her apartment building, and turned off the engine. He was not just going to dump and run. Ashley smiled again, this time showing teeth, and held up her business card. Muerce ignored the card, leaned over, and kissed her. When he pulled away she started to blush. From the inside pocket of his suit coat he removed a small caramel brown leather business card holder, withdrew a card, and exchanged his for hers. She studied it. She could feel how thick the paper stock was. She guessed it to be one-hundred and ten-pound stock. Running her fingers across the, ecru colored stock, her fingertips caressed the ridges of the black Chevalier font, and embossed edges. She flipped it over. The impression on the reverse side of the card confirmed it was engraved. It was slightly larger, and more square than most business cards. The process of its production was as elegant and tasteful as the message it sent. It stated, simply, centered on the front of the card: John Muerce. Below his formal name, in a complimentary, but different font that Ashley did not immediately recognize, was a telephone number.

Muerce looked at her worn, but very artsy and professionally designed business card, and said, "Is the mobile number good for personal contact, or just work?"

"Work and personal."

He nodded and tucked the card inside the small leather case. He hesitated, then retrieved the card, and proceeded to enter Ashley's contact information into his phone. Ashley thought the tightness in her chest was squeezing the breath out of her, and if felt good.

"Wait here while I get the umbrella," he said. "I'll walk you up."

Always the gentleman.

He cradled the umbrella over her as the rain beat heavy, and rolled in a torrent off the edges of the black fabric above them. They moved quickly, getting their feet wet, to the glass doors under the awning of her apartment. Muerce shook the rain off the umbrella, and waited for the goodbye.

"Can I ask you something?" Ashley said.

"Sure."

"Why do you get the private elevator?"

"That's easy," he said. "I own the building."

She was speechless as he bent down and kissed her goodbye. In the next moment, Muerce was trotting to his car, the umbrella giving little protection from the torrent.

Ashley keyed the security code buttons, heard the buzzer sound, and entered the lobby. She turned around to see Muerce drive off when she realized she was still wearing his coat. She lifted one of the lapels up, and could smell his cologne. She had no idea what had happened in the last twelve hours, or what, if anything, would happen in the coming weeks. But what she did know was she had Jack Muerce's raincoat, and his calling card. And that meant something.

Muerce felt like a weight had been pulled off of him when he drove away from the apartment building, though it had been a pleasant heaviness toward the end. Strange in some ways, too. The rain beat persistently on the Mercedes as he turned the car around on the next street. He fumbled with the buttons on the CD player. It was one of the few upgrades to the car he thought was allowable for its vintage, though the iPhone had nearly made CDs obsolete for him. He clicked through the menu, and found what he was looking for.

The opening notes of Stanley Turrentine's "Don't Mess With Mr. T" played soulfully from the speakers as Muerce plied through the sodden city. The music, somber but crisp, elevated his spirit, and seemed to drive the car on its own as Turrentine dialed up the tempo during the sax solo.

Muerce looked at his watch. It was almost eight o'clock in the morning. He was late for breakfast.

Madame Trung was going to be pissed.

CHAPTER 2

Saigon Laundry was owned and operated by the Trung family. They had come to America in two waves after the end of the Vietnam War. The first contingent of the family arrived shortly after the fall of Saigon in April 1975 with Colonel Bao Van Trung, who served in the Army of the Republic of South Vietnam. He had been politically connected throughout the U.S. involvement in the war, and that qualified him to evacuate with the U.S. forces. With him came his wife, who adopted the name Minny to better fit into to their new home in America, their four children, and Colonel Trung's mother, Madame Trung. The second wave of Trungs—made up of the Colonel's brother, Banda, his wife and children, and several cousins—were granted admission to the U.S. in the early 1980s as part of the Orderly Departure Program. That's how Muerce first came to know, and eventually become part of, the extended Trung family. They, in turn, saw him as their guardian angel in a new, strange, and sometimes hostile land. For the Trung family, Jack Muerce didn't just walk on water—he turned it into wine.

Muerce was fresh out of law school, working for a prestigious law firm, when he was assigned a *pro bono* case to help a Vietnamese refugee family navigate the bureaucratic confusion of immigration and commercial commerce laws. He had no idea what he was doing, but jumped into the work with all he had, partly to impress his superiors, partly because of the way he was raised, but mostly because he could help people. He liked how it made him feel. Helping people who needed it the most became more than a compulsion for Muerce. It was his duty, and it was chivalrous.

While working with the Trung family, Muerce learned how to leverage the resources he had been given by birth to get things done. He was intelligent, handsome, charming, and pragmatic. It also helped that his family was socially and politically connected, and very rich. The Trungs also opened a world to Muerce to which he had never been exposed—the world where people struggled each day to survive, whether it was putting food in their stomachs or a roof over their heads. It was a world where warm clothes and dignity were, too often, scarce commodities. What Muerce admired the Trungs for the most, was that they managed daily life with grace.

He also came to know the Trung family at a time in his life when there was a developing relationship with a young woman who would shape Muerce for the rest of his life—whether that was a good thing or a bad thing was something he struggled with daily. Its ending, and the circumstances around it, left Muerce off-balance, and feeling incomplete for a long time.

The heavy rain abated. Now just a few intermittent sprays were blown by rising winds that typically followed a storm to dry everything off. Muerce liked to think of it as Nature's Car Wash where he imagined God and the angels as a crew of minimum wage earners toweling off the Cadillac Escalades, and their chrome rims, like the guys at the Suds Barn just down Canary Street.

He pulled the Mercedes to the curb in front of Saigon Laundry, and turned the engine off. For a moment, Muerce was lost in the silence of the car. He recalled her face, what her voice sounded like. Even though it had been a long time, all of it was as fresh as the rain. He became frustrated when his thoughts kept wandering back to Ashley's face smiling at him from the bed not more than an hour ago.

The Mercedes door closed with a *whong*. Saigon Laundry was his office, and it was time to go to work.

Saigon Laundry was many things besides a two-story business front. The facade of the building was made of light ocher brick, and ornately carved limestone corners and arches. It sat on half a city block. The second floor, which was comprised of a dozen apartments, housed the extended family, and visiting Trung relatives. Over the years, Colonel Trung had purchased the large Victorian home behind the building, which had once been an upscale residential neighborhood. That was before the suburbs exploded, and the term "White Flight" was coined.

The front of the 1920s era building was plain except for a large neon sign Colonel Trung had installed in the late 1980s. The sign proclaimed "Saigon Laundry", which was formed with an elaborate script, and painted in bright yellow with red trim. Within the letters, pink fluorescent tubing spelled out the name of the business when night came. It was, Muerce thought when Colonel Trung first had it installed, a gaudy waste of money. Time had proved Muerce wrong, and the Colonel right. The sign did its job. It brought in business, and the business, like the Trung family, thrived.

Saigon Laundry was actually three businesses. The door to the far right—as you faced the neon sign—led to a large self-service laundromat. It had twenty-two coin-operated washers and dryers lined against pale green walls, and large, faded Formica-covered folding tables in the middle. There were soft drink, snack and laundry supply vending machines as well. What wasn't provided in the Laundromat was seating. The Trungs learned early on that seating became territorial for customers, who would literally fight for their space. The seating went, and the rules sign went up. Rule No. 1: No sitting on the folding tables. Rule No. 2: Bring your own chair, and take it with you when you leave. Rule No. 3: No outside business (which meant no pimps, drug dealers or solicitations of any kind—even Girl Scout cookies—allowed). The rest of the rules were general housekeeping, and common courtesy.

Over the years, and under the Trungs, the laundromat had become the unofficial community center for the neighborhood. On the front wall next to the entrance were large bulletin boards that served as a community information center, and informal mail post. A flyer from the nearby Catholic Church announced a Friday fish fry, tacked next to it was a photo-copy of a missing young girl with a handwritten note from her family pleading for her to return. There were items for sale, as well as the names of bail bondsmen, and posters for various social service agencies. Four times a year, the city health department set up a small table for childhood inoculations. In the fall, flu shots were provided for infants, and the elderly. On Friday afternoons, the local food pantry truck parked outside to distribute meals and food packages to families in need.

Anyone and everyone was welcome at the laundromat, as long as they followed the rules. And anyone and everyone could be found there. It drew saints and sinners alike: from the nuns that ministered at the parish during the day, to the prostitutes who worked the bars on lower Canary Street at night.

The middle door entrance to Saigon Laundry, which was framed by the simple limestone trim, and situated below the neon sign, was the main entrance. It was the second of the Trung businesses—a dry cleaning operation, and tailoring service. The tailoring was done by Minny, who had worked as a seamstress in Saigon before she met and married the Colonel.

It had not been an arranged marriage, or one that was at first accepted by the Colonel's parents or extended family. The Trungs had been very much woven into the fabric of Colonial French culture. The Colonel was educated in Paris, as were his parents. They had a lucrative business in the bamboo and rubber industries, part of which was a specialty subsidiary that produced the finest split-bamboo fly fishing rods in the world. Some of those rods made in the 1950s, now fetched upwards of ten-thousand dollars at auction houses in the United States. Minny, however, came from a poor family that lived in the Cholon District of Saigon. She had met the Colonel while fitting him for a uniform. They fell in love. They still were very much in love, which Muerce admired, and which Madame Trung had begrudgingly learned to accept over the years.

As you entered the dry cleaners portion of the Trung business dynasty, there was a large, arched opening to the right that led into the Laundromat. Along the wall next to the entrance was a long counter with a cash register, and hanging racks of plastic-covered dry cleaning. The dry cleaning itself was done in another building that was connected by a back alley, and located behind the Trung's house. For tailoring, Minny had customers come to a nicely appointed room in the back. That the dry cleaning, pressing, and such were done off site was a concession Muerce had to have the Trungs concede to so they could get the proper licensing for their third business.

Benny Trung was Banda Trung's son. Banda died of lung cancer two years after arriving in the U.S. There was a shrine for him on the wall behind the cash register that was maintained by daily offerings of food and flowers, and the burning of incense. Benny ran the third Trung enterprise on Canary Street. While you were visually greeted by the Colonel's garish sign on the front of the building, and deafened by the constant drumming of washing machines, dryers and loud talk in the laundromat, it was Benny's operation that stopped you where you stood as you entered. The smells made you close your eyes, and anticipate mellifluous, tart, savory, and exotic flavors.

Benny was the chef at Saigon Laundry. The restaurant was accessed through the smaller arched entry to the left, just passed the cash register and his father's shrine. A dark, beaded curtain separated the restaurant from the rest of the business, and most of the gastronomic world.

The bell tinkled when Muerce walked through the front door. One of the Trung grand-daughters was working the dry cleaning cash register. She was immersed in a college physics textbook, her notes spread out on the counter. A white plastic string fell from each of her ears and merged into one that was plugged into the iPhone laying flat next to her notes. Muerce closed his eyes and inhaled. There was the fresh aroma of baked goods, and dark coffee. *Surely, this is what heaven smells like.*

When he opened his eyes the grand-daughter was holding one of the ear buds in her right hand, and looking at him with amusement.

"*ÔNG Ở ĐÂU mấy nôm nay?*" she said, a hint of inquisition in her voice.

"*BẬN VIỆC, Tôi lã ngửởi danh tiêńg,*" Muerce said.

The grand-daughter smiled at Muerce after chastising him for being tardy, and had a wicked thought of what it would be like to be *occupied* with him.

"Well, you're late and she's on the warpath, giving Uncle Benny a hard time," the grand-daughter said, with perfect American pitch and tone. The sound of a breaking dish came from the kitchen in the back, followed by the voices of a man and woman arguing in Vietnamese.

"*C'est la vie,*" Muerce said, shrugging his shoulders.

"*Si dedaigneux pendant qut nous soufrons de votre ralentissmento,*" the grand-daughter said, plugging the ear bud back in, and returning her attention to the textbook. She lifted her swan-like right arm, holding her hand horizontal before waving him with three quick motions toward the beaded doorway that led to the dining area. Muerce liked her sassiness, though if Madame Trung had observed the interaction she would have interpreted her grand daughter's behavior as disrespectful to her elder, and lacking the appropriate filial piety for the family. Muerce winced when he thought of himself as the attractive young coed's elder, and as a possible lover. *Enough. She is family, and too young.*

Saigon Laundry, the restaurant, wasn't particularly big. It wasn't located in any of the ritzy or fashionably hip parts of town, meaning it took real effort, and for some diners, a strong sense of adventure and courage, to journey there to eat. It was more than just the best French-Indochine cuisine you could find. Benny had taken Saigon Laundry to a new culinary level, earning rankings as one of the best restaurants in the world by a number of prestigious gastronomic associations, and publications. With a scant four, four-top tables at which only dinner was served, and a *prix fixe* menu at that (Benny prepared only what he wanted to serve over seven courses), made Saigon Laundry one of the toughest eateries in the world to get a seat. If dinner reservations were a commodity, getting a table at Saigon Laundry was like scoring a moon rock. Friday and Saturday nights were booked a year—sometimes two years for holidays—in advance. Weekday dinner reservations were full for up to eight months, depending on the day of the week.

Compounding the scarcity and exclusiveness of Saigon Laundry was that it was closed every Sunday and Monday—which Benny used to plan and shop for his menu for the week ahead. And there was only one seating per table per night; sixteen meals, eighty total for the week. All dinner reservations were for eight o'clock in the evening, starting with *aperitifs* and light *hors d'oeuvres*. Dinner service generally lasted until eleven o'clock with dessert or cheese and champagne. Diners had no choice in what spirits they were served. Benny matched cocktails and wines with the food. There were no substitutes, save for food allergies, which were addressed when the reservation was accepted, and again when a confirmation call was made the week before the assigned night. If a party cancelled, or did not show within twenty minutes of their reservation, there was a long waiting list of people willing to throw down whatever they were doing, and race to Saigon Laundry for dinner. Muerce couldn't remember the last time he saw an empty chair at dinner, and he would know because he ate there almost every night.

For his relationship with the Trungs, and the legal and financial efforts he had put in on their behalf over the years—including loaning Benny the money to attend both Le Cordon Bleu in Paris and the Culinary Institute of America in Hyde Park, New York—the lone two-topper table wedged against the far wall was exclusively his. It included breakfast, lunch and dinner. He was the only person other than members of the Trung family, to be fed from Benny's kitchen during the day. The two-topper also served as Muerce's tacit place of business.

For what Muerce did, he only needed a phone, a roof over his head, and a good cup of coffee. He had long ago given up working inside the boundaries of a law firm.

The squabbling in the kitchen ceased. Muerce, now sitting at his crisp, white linen-covered table, prepared to be chastened by Madame Trung. She approached him from the kitchen with a silver tray that held a full French press, coffee cup and saucer, and a plate of *beignets* fresh from the oven.

Madame Trung was the third most remarkable woman Muerce had ever met in his life. There was his mother, certainly, and the woman he did not talk about.

Though the Colonel was the Trung patriarch, there was no doubt as to who had the final say in all family matters. Although eighty, Madame Trung looked like she was in her early sixties. Her features, attractive and intact, were ageless. She was medium height, still thin, and the few lines on her face did not hint at her age; the harsh black tint of her dyed hair, however, could not go unnoticed.

Madame Trung wore a dark purple *ao dai*. The right sleeve of the traditional garment was folded and pinned to her shoulder with an antique Tiffany brooch. Madame Trung lost the arm in an automobile accident in France when she was attending university in the early 1950s. She spoke little of it other than to refer to the incident as "The Tragedy." The only details she had ever given to Muerce was that she had been riding in a delightfully sporting automobile, and the driver, a man, a poet, was killed in the crash. She only spoke of it to Muerce once, many years back, when she had consoled him through his own tragedy. He never forgot the sadness in her voice, or his own sadness.

Madame Trung set the tray on the table with an ease that was impressive for someone of her age and impairment. She had compensated for the lost limb with a grace of movement that made one forget what was missing. She smiled as she plunged the French press to the bottom of the glass container, then poured the hot, dark liquid into the cup. As she bent down, he noticed the large, crudely swathed black cross adorning her forehead. She was a true French Colonial. A devout Catholic. Madame Trung had gone to early Mass for ashes.

"*Bonjour Madame Trung, merci beaucoup,*" Muerce said, as she finished pouring the coffee.

"*Bonsoir Monsieur Muerce,*" she replied, dryly and emphasizing the greeting for the latter part of the day. *And so it begins.*

"*Pardonnez, s'il vous plait, mes offenses,*" Muerce said. "It was an active evening, and I did not get much sleep."

Madame Trung arched an eyebrow, and gave a speculative look at Muerce before putting her one hand on his left shoulder, patting him softly.

"*Et ne nous soumets pas a la tentation,*" she said.

Temptation was Muerce's favorite distraction.

He lifted the cup to his face and absorbed the aroma of the coffee and the *beignets*, which held the promise of a hint of maple syrup goodness. The coffee was *Trung Nguyen*. Dark and strong. The first two sips cleared away what remained of the champagne fog. He closed his eyes and savored another sip before biting into one of the warm pastries sprinkled with confectioner's sugar. There was the distinctive maple sweetness that merged with the airiness of the pastry, and made a subtle *crunch* when he chewed. *Perfection.*

"Vietnam style, no chicory," Madame Trung said of the coffee, her hand still on Muerce's shoulder as she turned to address the kitchen, and began yelling. "*CON BÉ DẠI QúA, không cho khăn ăn ngoài náy.*"

"You go to ashes?" she said, returning her attention to Muerce.

"Noon Mass with my mother at the Cathedral," Muerce said.

At Madame Trung's barked command, Benny appeared in an instant with a crisp, white linen napkin he placed on the table.

"*đủ rồi, đũ rồi bà già, để YÉN cho ông ăn sáng,*" Benny said.

Madame Trung removed her hand from Muerce's shoulder, waved it in the air at Benny in a dismissive gesture, and began muttering in Vietnamese as she returned to the kitchen.

"*Cám ỏn,*" Muerce said to Madame Trung as she departed.

Benny clasped his hands together, as if in prayer, and bent down slightly to greet Muerce.

"How is it, Jack?" he said.

Muerce looked up at Benny, rolled his eyes and contorted his face to mimic a moment depicting the peak of sexual passion, and emphasized the gesture with a *moan. Seriously Benny, what do you expect?*

"Excellent, will you be with us for dinner?" Benny said.

"Yes, early though Benny," Muerce said. "What's on the menu?"

"Seafood all this week. The presentation will be a surprise."

"Sounds wonderful," Muerce said, biting into another pastry.

"We missed you last night," Benny said. "Did you find a better place to eat?"

"Not possible, and you know that," Muerce said. "Mardi Gras party. I was obligated to attend."

"Good gumbo?"

"Awful gumbo. But lots of pretty girls who drink too much."

Benny winked at Muerce.

"What time tonight?"

"Early, say six if that's okay," Muerce said. "I didn't get much sleep last night."

"Yes, that was the speculation when you weren't here... at your regular time," Benny said, looking toward the kitchen. "Six is good."

Some kind of ruckus had begun in the kitchen, and Madame Trung was yelling in Vietnamese. Benny put his hand on Muerce's shoulder, and gave him a look of exasperation.

"I've got to go. She's been at it all morning," he said. "More *beignets?*"

"Yes. Sorry for being late." Muerce said, chagrined that his intimate conquests were part of Trung family conversations. *That's how families are.*

Muerce savored the coffee, the *beignets*, and the sudden quiet that settled in the dining space with Madame Trung and Benny back in the kitchen. There was only the gentle *drumming* of the machines coming from the Laundromat.

He surveyed his surroundings. It amused Muerce, that the restaurant side of the business was in such contrast to the rest of Saigon Laundry. While the décor of the laundromat, dry cleaners and tailoring was well suited for the rundown part of the city—although close in proximity to Downtown—the design of the dining room was high-end French Colonial Vietnam. Paris on the Mekong. It exuded a feeling of expensive and ornate furniture slowly decaying in the fetid heat and humidity of Southeast Asia. Two large ceiling fans circulated the air, which was warmed by the busy nature of the laundromat, and the ovens and stoves in the kitchen. It really was a small space. Two of the four-top tables were tucked toward the back of the room with the opening archway leading to the kitchen. Benny liked that the kitchen was somewhat open for viewing. It enhanced the dining experience, allowing customers to see, smell and hear their food being prepared. That way, Benny believed, all of their senses were heightened when the food arrived at their table.

The other pair of tables were nestled partly into each of the two bay windows at the front of the building. Benny had sealed off what used to be an entrance. Along the front window and where the door used to be, was an elaborate collection of plants and flowers that included some of Madame Trung's finicky orchids. In the fall she would swap out some of the containers for mums. In the spring there would be tulips and daffodils. There were also pots of different herbs like basil, rosemary, thyme, lemon grass and mint.

Large colonial shutters framed the front windows. The floor had been renovated with an ornate *parquet* pattern that squeaked when you walked on it. On the walls were gilt-framed antique street maps of Paris, and what was now Ho Chi Minh City. On the wall above Muerce's table was a framed linen napkin. On the napkin was a drawing of an abstract likeness of a young Madame Trung. It was signed by Picasso. Madame Trung delighted in never telling the full story of the napkin, only saying how upset her father was with the friends she had made attending university. Who, Muerce knew, included the dead poet. Madame Trung, Muerce liked to believe, was very wild in her youth.

She was now, however, immune to Muerce's attempts to flirt with her. Nonetheless, he made efforts to on occasion. When he did, she would smile, and dismissively pat him on the head with her one hand.

Briefly lost in his thoughts, Muerce snapped back to reality when he remembered he had a voicemail waiting for him. He pulled the phone from the pocket of his suit coat that he had draped over the back of his chair. He fingered the bottom button that brought the black screen alive with various colored icons, and navigated his way to voicemail with his index finger.

The drawl was unfamiliar, but the name was not. The call was from Tyler B. Squire, the chief executive officer and chairman of the board of what was now referred to in business parlance as one the largest "health-care systems" in the county. To Muerce they were still hospitals. Just a lot of them under one publicly traded umbrella. You went there if you were sick, or dying. Otherwise, you avoided them as best as possible. Tyler B. Squire was originally from somewhere in the South—Texas or Alabama, or something like that. Muerce wasn't sure. As is the custom in the South, the health care executive's name had been shortened to T.B. Squire. Muerce rolled the humor around in his head. Was there irony in a man in charge of a national chain of hospitals being saddled with the name T.B., or was it just a cruel coincidence?

Distracted with the inane amusement, Muerce missed the point of the message and replayed it, this time intent on listening. He had never given T.B. Squire one of his business cards. That the man had his mobile number meant that either someone of some influence had provided it to him, or someone to whom Muerce was indebted had.

T.B. Squire's message was polite, brief and to the point. Would Mr. Muerce please return his call at his earliest convenience as it was a personal matter involving his son. T.B Squire ended the message saying he was giving Muerce his own private mobile number, and not his work mobile number, and that he would be monitoring for his call as to not miss him.

Muerce contemplated the information, and tone of the message. T.B. Squire had a son in trouble. A son he apparently cared about because his voice was heavy with concern, if not a little fear. If T.B. Squire didn't care about his son, Muerce would have picked up on anger beget from annoyance. If that had been the case, Muerce would politely return Mr. T.B. Squire's call, and without asking what the problem was, say he was unable to be of any help. Muerce shied away from favors having to do with spoiled rich kids. He had done enough of those to know that, in most cases, the kid was better off learning from the consequences than being bailed out by Mommy and Daddy. That, and the return favor was rarely honored.

It was unlikely, though, that Mr. T.B. Squire's troubled son was facing a drunk driving or drug possession charge. Either of those could be handled by an army of attorney's the CEO had at his disposal. Muerce also factored in that the call had come very early in the morning—the memory of Ashley naked in his bed flashed in his head again—and the man had gone to the trouble to find an alternative solution to his problem. Muerce was the alternative people turned to before they had to come face-to-face with the last resort—reality. Anyone who knew Jack Muerce knew that you did not share his mobile number freely. Muerce's business card was as rare a commodity as a dinner reservation at Saigon Laundry. You treated either as a divine gift. *Nothing goes down on this, Muerce thought, until I know who gave out my number.*

He poured the last cup of coffee from the press, and took several sips. It was time to go to work. He thumbed the button that returned T.B. Squire's phone call. It rang only twice before it was answered.

"Mister Murse?"

"It's pronounced mercy," Muerce said, disappointed that T.B. Squire hadn't done all of his homework.

"I apologize Mister Muerce."

There was a moment of pregnant silence between them.

"I'm returning your call, Mister Squire," Muerce said.

"Ah, yes. I'm sorry Mister Muerce. I'm not sure how this works."

"How what works, Mister Squire?"

"Well, frankly, as I said in my message, how I go about asking you to, perhaps, help my son," Squire said. "It's Jack isn't it. May I call you Jack?"

Time to set some boundaries.

"My friends call me Jack, Mister Squire. Are we friends? Have I ever been invited to your home for dinner?"

A few fleeting seconds of awkward silence followed.

"I understand Mister Muerce," Squire said.

Good.

"Can you help me, Mister Muerce?" Squire said, subtly pleading.

"I don't know, Mister Squire, can I?" Muerce said. "How was it you came to get my name and number?"

T.B. Squire hesitated. He was a man used to making important, and very expensive decisions at a moment's notice. He knew when to heal a decision, and when to unleash one quickly. This one involved his only child, his son, so he went with honesty.

"Detective Trumbley," Squire said, pausing. "He asked that I not use his name, Mister Muerce. I wanted to respect that request, but I also want to respect yours as well. Although we've never been formally introduced, I have heard of your family, and your... reputation."

Right answer, though you should have asked about proper pronunciation if you say you know of my family.

"I appreciate that Mister Squire," Muerce said. "There will be no repercussions for disclosing Detective Trumbley's identity."

Muerce knew Trumbley well. Nick Trumbley could call him Jack. He could call Jack anything he wanted, and get away with it. Few people could do that. Trumbley was a good man, and an honest vice cop who wouldn't hand out Muerce's name on a whim. He wouldn't refer T.B. Squire to him unless it was a sensitive, or nearly impossible problem. It was Trumbley asking for a favor, and Muerce would do the best he could to fulfill the request, and find out why later.

"All right Mister Squire," Muerce said. "How time sensitive is the problem with your son?"

T.B. Squire felt like he had been holding his breath beyond his capacity. His chest was heavy. He exhaled and took in fresh air that gave him a positive outlook.

"I'm not sure what you mean by time sensitive?" he said.

"I'd rather not talk about particulars over the phone Mister Squire," Muerce said. "Especially cell phones. I'd like to meet, so we can be... properly introduced."

"Ah, yes, I see," Squire said. "There's a little time, a few days."

"Good," Muerce said, reviewing his schedule for the next twenty-four hours, and realizing that he could only fit T.B. Squire in at dinner. "Six o'clock, Mister Squire. Six Twenty Five Canary. Park out front. Go through the middle door. Ask for me. I'll see you tonight"

Muerce pressed his thumb on the red icon that ended the call.

T.B. Squire scribbled the information on a fluorescent orange Post-It note without giving the address any thought. He was a transplant to the city, and was still unfamiliar with street addresses. Particularly addresses in the part of town where Saigon Laundry was located. Given the discourse with Muerce, T.B. Squire was savvy enough to know that he was to come alone. He would have anyway. The trouble his son, Travis, had gotten into was something he wanted as few people as possible to know about. Not for his own sake, but for his son's.

Muerce placed the phone on the table, and rubbed his hands over his face in a massaging motion. Despite the strong coffee, he was still groggy from too much champagne, and too little sleep. He hoped the vigorous motion might alleviate the faint throbbing in his head. Some of the night before started to return to him. He and Ashley had gone at it, rather loudly, for some time. He didn't think they fell asleep until three o'clock that morning. He also began to realize that his pelvic bone was sore. The duration of their carnal activities, and the soreness it left, made him smile. His headache abated some.

Swiveling in his chair, Muerce lifted the empty press up so Benny could see him. Benny acknowledged with the wave of one finger and spoke to Madame Trung, who reacted with a barrage of Vietnamese that Muerce could not make out. Several minutes later, Madame Trung was at Muerce's table with a fresh press of coffee, and another plate of *beignets*.

"*Merci, merci beaucoup*," he said.

"*Vous vous etes top rejouis hier soir,*" Madame Trung said.

"Yes, too much fun last night," he said. "I'm sore, everywhere."

Madame Trung frowned and pressed too hard on the plunger. A spurt of coffee and grounds was ejected from the lip of the container, staining the white, linen table cloth. She shook her head in disapproval, not at the mess she had made but at what she guessed to be Muerce's activities the previous night.

"Good thing Lent come," she said, in broken English. "You no so young no more."

Muerce screwed up his face in a dramatic wince.

"*Mọi sự đêú trung dung. Tục ngữ Viêt NAM,*" she said. "Old Vietnamese proverb."

"It's an old Greek proverb," he retorted. "The Romans translated it as, *Modus omnibus in rebus.*"

"Vietnam older than Greeks," she said. "You older than Greeks, I think."

"*ông lám tổn thương Tôi,*" Muerce said, clutching his right hand to his chest as if he'd been shot.

"You hurt self. You get ashes with your mother. You start atone."

That last word landed like a lance, and the past spilled into his thoughts like the coffee staining the table cloth. The memories were granular, dark, hot, and messy. Her face was as clear as if she were sitting across the table from him. He felt like his flesh was being torn from his body.

A loud commotion erupted in the laundromat, and the face disappeared. Madame Trung and Muerce went to see what it was about.

"You can't leave that baby here," said the Trung grand-daughter, the white cords of her ear buds dangled from her shoulders.

She was addressing a short, pasty-skinned woman with dark hair cropped very close to her head. The woman wore heavy, black eye make-up, which complimented her black, leather mini-skirt. Her outfit was accented by a tight pink blouse hidden under a white, *faux* fur jacket. She teetered on pink stiletto heels. Her wardrobe left no doubt that she was dressed for work, and the look of desperation on her face indicated she was late. Her boss would not be happy, or understanding.

"It's not my baby," the woman said, with a defiant and heavy Serbo-Croation accent. "Is Redzil's. I was just watching it for a few days while she... was away. For work."

"So?" the grand-daughter said. "You're responsible. You can't just leave a baby here. This isn't daycare drop off."

The crying baby was wrapped in an assortment of dingy blankets, and had been placed inside a dilapidated wicker basket. Muerce guessed the infant was, maybe, three months old.

"Red. Redzil, will be here soon," the woman said, her voice becoming more anxious and desperate than defiant. She kept looking toward the front window at a car idling outside. "She promised to meet me here. Just watch it for a little bit. I have to go. I have to go!"

A white Cadillac Escalade with a cascade of gaudy gold trim and gold rims was parked behind Muerce's Mercedes. The drumming of the washing machines and dryers was interrupted by a series of aggressive *honks* from the waiting car.

The darkly tinted passenger window slid down, and a pale hand covered with gold jewelry that matched the trim of the Escalade aggressively motioned for the woman to hurry.

Madame Trung frowned, and looked at Muerce. *Fine, he thought, I'll take care of it.*

"Nobody go anywhere," he said, looking directly at the pink and black dressed woman. "I'll be right back."

The bell on the front door of the laundromat tinkled behind Muerce as he stepped outside and approached the open window of the waiting car. The wind had picked up, lifting his tie over his right shoulder, and the temperature had dropped a good ten degrees.

The ostentatious car belonged to Mikal Delic, who liked to call himself "Pimp Deluxe". He was also known as "Micky D" for his fondness of the Golden Arches. Mikal was in his late thirties and had come to the U.S. in the mid-nineties after fleeing the hostilities and ethnic cleansing in Bosnia-Herzogovina. There was, at that time, and again in the early 2000s, a flow of immigrants, mostly Muslim, into the city, along with a few Christians. The ethnic cleansing from the "old country" spilled over onto American soil in the form of gang warfare. A lot of it played out along the Canary Street corridor. It had been no different for previous waves of immigrants—Nigerians, Vietnamese, Hmong, Jamaican, Cuban, along with the original settlers of the city; the Irish, Italians, and Germans. Most of them, however, had long ago climbed up the economic ladder, and out of the now worn and squalid neighborhoods that made up Canary Street.

Muerce rested his arms on the open window of the Escalade, and leaned inside.

"Micky D, what shakes?" he said.

Mikal flashed a hip-hop smile. His top left, front tooth was encased in gold. A one-carat diamond was set in the middle of the tooth. He reached across from the driver's seat with an open hand, palm up.

"Jock Mur-see, what it is, my man," he said, smiling, his Serb-Croat accent thicker than the pink and black girl's mascara. Mikal's gold chains made a metallic rustling sound as he leaned over. He wore a purple, velour track suit, and a white "wife-beater" t-shirt.

"What it is, Deluxe," Muerce said, slapping Mikal's hand.

"Stock market good," Mikal said. "Bidness been booming. Girls busy for Deluxe. Think economic finally looking up."

"Yeah?"

"Yeah, move everything out of treasuries. Yields crap," Mikal said. "More opportunity in equities. Deluxe not need to be so liquid. You should talk to my broker."

"Smooth, my man."

"How you do Jock?"

"Business is good," Muerce said, pausing to look back into the laundromat, then back at Mikal. "What's the four-one-one inside?"

"Beech is late for work," Mikal said, agitated.

"The baby, Micky D," Muerce said. "What time your girl shows up for work is none of my business."

Mikal pushed his lower lip up his face and made a slight nodding motion with his head, indicating he understood. Mikal respected Muerce. If you didn't, he knew all too well, you could get burned in a way you had never thought of before. Muerce was fair. He knew what was, *was*, and what is, *is*. It was better to work with Muerce than against him. *You don't fuck with the man who's armor shines brightest.*

"Belong to Redzil, Redzil Hadzic," Mikal said.

"She belong to you?"

Mikal nodded his head that she did.

"You know her Jock?" Mikal said. "Maybe she please you sometime? The tall red-head. Pretty face, big lips, long legs. You like the long legs, Jock, yes?"

The description registered with Muerce. He had seen her in the laundromat before. She was pretty, and she did have the kind of long legs he liked, though she, like all the working girls that frequented Saigon Laundry, were, of his own accord, strictly off limits. *Don't blur boundaries.*

"Your girl, your responsibility," Muerce said.

Mikal rolled his eyes.

"I Pimp Deluxe not Montessori," he said. "Besides, it deal Redzil make with beech inside. I not baby daddy."

"The one inside, she got a name?" Muerce said, his voice rising.

"Mirsad. I lose respect fucking around babysit beech's kids."

"You lose street cred too if you don't take good care of your girls, Mikal," Muerce said. "No more Pimp Deluxe. They'll go to someone else, or start freelancing."

Mikal gripped the leather wrapped steering wheel. His knuckles turned white.

"Look, Jock, you do me favor I do you favor?"

"You still owe me favor, Mikal, lots of favor. I want to know what is going on. Now."

"Da, da, da," Mikal said. "Beech inside—Mirsad—say other beech—Redzil—have side deal she not tell me about. Freelancing, like you say. Piss me off. She give baby to Mirsad take care of while she go for weekend. Weekend come and go, no Redzil. I tell beech inside got to get back to work. Fuck Redzil. Fuck beech's baby."

"Mirsad just volunteered that information, did she?" Muerce said.

"I convince her a little," Mikal said. "Not hurt her bad. Just help get to truth faster."

"Maybe I help Pimp Deluxe get to the truth a little faster," Muerce said. "Does this look like an orphanage Mikal? You just drop the kid off in a basket, and that's it?"

"Like I said, Jock. You do Deluxe favor, he do you favor."

Muerce was losing his patience when he felt a tug on the back of his shirt. It was Mirsad. She wanted past him, and into the Escalade. There was no baby in her arms. Muerce glanced back into the laundromat to see Madame Trung holding the baby in her one arm. It had been decided, not by him, that Muerce would grant a favor. But it wouldn't be for Pimp Deluxe, it would be for the baby. Not so much for the baby's mother, Redzil Hadzic, wherever she was. Muerce opened the car door for Mirsad. As she passed he could see bruising on the back of her neck.

"Look at me Mikal," Muerce said, leaning back into the open window as Mirsad fumbled with the seat belt. "When I call, and I will call, you get one ring. If I hear two, I'll hang up. And then I'm going to start twisting you. Very hard. No more treasuries, no more equities, no more liquidity, no more *beeches* for you."

Mikal smiled his pimp smile, and nodded.

"I have a special dentist who owes me a favor," Muerce said. "Maybe you pay what you owe me in gold."

Mikal's smile disappeared.

"When your girl turns up, tell her the kid is in the system," Muerce said.

Mikal put the car in gear, pressed down hard on the accelerator and sped off, kicking up a dirty spray from the wet streets that soiled the back panel of the pearl white SUV. Muerce stepped back from the car as it bolted away, his hands in the air, feeling like he'd just been robbed at gunpoint despite his threat.

The hot, humid air of the laundromat enveloped Muerce like a blanket. He fixed his tie, frowned at Madame Trung, and reached in his pocket for his phone. The baby was quieter in her arm.

"Miriam, it's Jack Muerce," he said into the phone. He reached voicemail, and left a short message. "I need a favor..."

Half an hour later a black-and-white was parked outside. Muerce gave the two patrolmen what little information he had about the child when Miriam Estrada walked in. She was carrying an infant car seat, and a large diaper bag that she tossed onto the laundry table. She waved her Family Welfare credentials at the patrolmen without looking at either them. Her eyes were fixed on Muerce.

Miriam was a welcome sight, and not just because it meant the cops, Muerce and the Trungs could beg out of dealing with an abandoned child. The Welfare Lady, as Miriam was commonly referred to, was a handsome woman in her late thirties. She was tall with dominant Aztec features: dark skin, high cheekbones, and emerald green eyes. She and Muerce had a brief history, once, years earlier. At the time, she was separated. Her husband had been a good cop with a bad problem. He and Trumbley were partners. Miriam's husband was a drinker. A big drinker. When his liver gave out, Miriam took him back, and nursed him until the end. She called it off with Muerce, who understood her decision. Muerce did everything he could, from a distance, to help her care for her dying husband. After he passed, they decided to remain friends, and only friends.

Still, her eyes twinkled whenever she saw Jack Muerce.

"Been awhile Mister Muerce," she said, addressing him in front of the patrolmen. She turned to the senior cop. "You guys got all you need? I can take it from here."

All business.

"Yes ma'am," the cop said, glad they could get on with their day, but disappointed they couldn't linger to gawk at Miriam a moment or two longer.

"I'm sure you two have more important things to do than change diapers," she said, in a tone used to usher them on their way.

When she heard the tinkling of the bell above the laundromat door as they left, Miriam retrieved the child from Madame Trung's arm, turned to Muerce and smiled.

"You look good Jack," she said, holding the baby in her arms. Her eyes smiled in a way that Muerce thought might indicate a change in their agreement to be friends, and just friends.

"Not as good as you look Miriam," he said. The memory of her soft dark skin, and the dimples at the small of her back came to him easily.

"I drop everything to run down here and that's the best line you have, Jack, really?" she said.

Madame Trung barked an order in Vietnamese for her grand-daughter to get back to the dry cleaning counter, and then excused herself. The handful of customers in the laundromat returned to their wash, gossip, and magazines. Miriam turned her attention from Muerce. Cradling the baby in one arm, she spread out a disposable paper blanket on the laundry table, and went about giving the child a cursory examination for any indications of abuse, or poor health.

"Seems healthy, fairly clean and well-cared for," she said, removing the soaked disposable diaper. "Male. Hmm..."

Miriam looked at the child's irregular facial features.

"Not the prettiest baby I've ever seen," Muerce said.

"As if you've ever seen many babies," Miriam said, still examining the infant, who was, she guessed, about three months old.

"I've seen enough of them," Muerce said.

"You mean you've dated enough of them," she said.

"And I thought you were happy to see me," Muerce said. "So, is something wrong with it?"

"Don't know. Could be fetal alcohol syndrome, crack baby, or any other number of congenital or genetic tags," Miriam said. "Or just plain and simple FLK syndrome."

"FLK syndrome?" Muerce said.

"Funny Looking Kid," Miriam said. "It's not a real term, Jack. He got a name?"

"Mother is a prostitute, Bosnian, I think, goes by the name Redzil," Muerce said. "I forget the name but I can try. Her street name is Red. She dumped the kid off with a... co-worker slash friend... for a weekend special, and hasn't shown up. The friend got behind on her work hours taking care of the kid, and decided to drop him off at Madame Trung's Orphanage."

Miriam looked around the room. "This is as good a place as any, if not better. Hell, it's cleaner than any of the fire stations, or police precincts.

"So, he's a John Doe? Or should we call him Jack Doe?"

"Not funny, Miriam," Muerce said.

She put a fresh diaper on Baby John Doe Redzil, and gleefully handed Muerce the old one before dressing the infant in a floral one-piece cotton jumper that was too big. Muerce held the soiled diaper as if it were nuclear waste.

"What do you want me to do with this?" he said.

"Are you really that clueless, Jack?" she said, pulling a wet wipe from a container, and handing it to Muerce. She placed the child in the infant car seat, and secured the straps.

"Throw it in the trash," she said. "You can flush the wipe if you want when you're done."

Muerce dropped the diaper in the trash can next to him, wiped his hands with the wet wipe, and disposed of it with the diaper. Miriam jumped up to sit on the folding table next to the baby, who was sucking on a small formula bottle she had produced from the diaper bag. Some of the customers in the laundromat frowned at her. Rule No. 1: No sitting on the folding tables. But nobody was going to mess with the Welfare Lady, and she knew it.

"Baby Jack is hungry," she said.

"Yes he is," Muerce said. Miriam either ignored or missed his inflection, so he changed the subject. "Do you want some coffee?"

"Nah, too much already," she said. Muerce could make out the faint smear of ashes on her forehead. *A good Catholic girl.*

Miriam had a girlish smile. She averted her eyes from Muerce's, and looked through the archway that led toward the restaurant.

"Last time I was here was for dinner," she said. Muerce didn't say anything.

"I miss that," she said, wistfully.

"Miss what?"

"Going out to dinner."

"It's been, what, two years?" he said, opting to drop the "death" part from the rhetorical nature of the question. "You're an attractive woman."

"With two teenage boys, Jack," she interjected. "You want to go down that road? Get real."

"Doesn't mean you can't go out to dinner every once in awhile," he said.

There was a loud sucking sound that indicated Baby Jack Doe Redzil had finished his bottle. Miriam turned her attention to the child, which let out a loud *burp*. She slung the diaper bag over her shoulder, and picked up the infant seat holding the baby. As she turned to head toward the door, Muerce stepped in front of her.

"Do you want to have dinner sometime?" he said.

"With you?" she said. "Dinner with Jack Muerce is never *just* a meal."

"Is that a yes or a no?"

The tension in her face eased, and Muerce thought he saw a hint of coquet as she batted her eyelashes a few times without looking directly at him.

"Maybe," she said, slightly embarrassed. Then she walked straight out the door, secured the infant seat in her car, and drove away. *Definitely call Miriam.*

Madame Trung stood in the archway, Muerce's suit jacket and raincoat draped across her arm.

"You going to be late for ashes," she said. "You hurry."

He looked at his watch. Now it was his his mother who was going to be pissed.

CHAPTER 3

There was only one parking spot left in the main lot of the Cathedral. Muerce carefully maneuvered the Mercedes into the narrow space. Another round of heavy rain pelted the city. Retrieving the umbrella from the back seat, Muerce squeezed his way out from between the closely parked cars. The door to the Mercedes closed with a weak *whong* that prompted him to look to see if it shut completely. It had. There were times Muerce was sure the Mercedes behaved like a living thing.

The wind blew the rain sideways into his face as he popped the collar of his trench coat up for protection. Opening the canopy of the umbrella into the face of the gale, he made his way toward a side entrance of the looming gothic edifice. The rain poured off the slate roof and flying buttresses, creating wet slash marks on the limestone of the church that made it appear as if it were bleeding.

Upon entering the church, Muerce's senses were smothered. Sight was reduced, and breathing labored in the dark, mouldering and thick atmosphere. The cloying incense that had been burning since early morning mingled with the smell of the faithful who, drenched by the storm, sat or knelt among the acres of wooden pews. The drone of somber organ music that normally resonated off the cold marble statues of dead saints was absent for the season. Replaced only by the sounds of the storm outside, and the congregation inside. The dark and lifeless stained-glass windows looked down upon them. He paused for a moment so his eyes could adjust. Rows of candles burned in the side chapel of the Virgin Mary. Their illumination was weak, and provided little in the way of light for either finding the person he was looking for, or for his immortal soul. There was an element of decay to having blind faith that Muerce found bitter and unpalatable.

There was a great emptiness he felt when he was in church. A void he filled since adolescence by fantasizing about the more attractive women in attendance no matter what their age, or marital disposition. Even the nuns were fair game for is libidinous fantasies, though few ever meet his criteria. Muerce also felt that it was, nonetheless, his duty, regardless of his desire, to attend Mass with Eleanor. His duty, at least, for the major Holy Days of Obligation. *God has more important things for me to do.*

He need not rely solely on his eyesight to find his mother. Even if blind, in church—in any church for that matter—Muerce could always find her sitting in the front pew. It was irritating. He thought she did it to bring attention to herself, which brought attention to him. Muerce didn't like attention. At least, not in church. He also thought she did it so he had fewer visual distractions to entertain himself with during services.

Out of habit, Muerce dipped his right index finger into a brass bowl of holy water, but it was empty. Habits, he remembered, were made to be broken during Lent.

Having arrived with some time to spare, he walked as inconspicuously as he could across the marble floor, down the side aisle, and past the front of the alter to the first pew where Eleanor sat. Whispered conversations, people moving and knocking about, and the clunking of kneelers as they struck the floor, provided some cover for his arrival.

Holding his soaked raincoat and dripping umbrella, Muerce stood at the entrance of the pew, and winked at Eleanor. Glad to see her only child, she smiled brilliantly back at him, and stood up to kiss his cheek. The church seemed a little brighter to Muerce.

Though they were in constant verbal foil with each other, neither would hesitate to throw themselves in front of a train for the other. Afterwards, if such an event were to happen, they would undoubtably argue how long it took the sacrificial to get in front of the train.

Eleanor was as striking a woman at seventy as she was at twenty. Tall and thin, a round, pretty face set off by pale blue eyes. Her ash blonde hair had long ago turned a soft gray that was not too far from the color of the suit her son wore. She moved with elegance, as if floating just above the earth, and spoke with a distinctive regal elocution. One that did not convey haughtiness, or snobbery. Not unless that was her intent. Her tongue, as Muerce knew all to well, was as sharp as a scalpel. *Dr. Eleanor Muerce, Chief of Verbal Surgery.*

"Good morning, Eleanor," Muerce said, as she directed him to sit next to her. He placed the wet coat and umbrella to his left as a buffer to anyone else who might want to park next to them.

"I wasn't sure you were going to make it," she said, without direct eye contact.

"Of course you were," he said.

"Sure that you wouldn't be here on time?"

"Sure that I would make it."

"Hmm, not so sure, really," she said.

She wore a purple Hermes scarf with her outfit, which was an elegant and understated Chanel suit she had bought in Paris a good quarter of a century earlier, but looked like it had just come out the previous season. The scarf was the only accent of color on her.

"The scarf makes a nice statement," Muerce said, making a foray into whatever short conversation they would have before Mass began.

"I certainly hope you would think so," she said.

"Why is that?"

"You don't remember?"

"Remember what?"

"You gave it to me for my birthday," she said, turning to him with a scolding smile on her face.

"No I didn't."

"Yes you did."

"I'm quite sure I didn't."

"I'm quite certain you did," she said, with some finality.

"Umm, no Eleanor, I didn't," he said. "I gave you the Longchamps bag."

Muerce reached over, and held up the leather purse saddled next to her.

"Then it was the year before," she said, fixing her gaze toward the altar.

"Umm, no," Muerce said, smiling broader, and pointing to her wrist. "I gave you that watch the year before. Which, by the way, makes you look over accessorized."

Eleanor closed her eyes tightly, drew in a breath and slowly exhaled. She settled back in the pew, and crossed her legs so that her posture was directed at her son.

"That flannel suit looks elegant on you, John," she said. "You wear clothes so well. Very tasteful. Very well tailored. And that particular shade truly highlights the gray in your hair in such a complimentary way. It really draws attention to what a distinguished, mature man you've become."

And, Muerce thought, the first cut.

"What a kind thing to say, thank you," he said, pausing for a moment. "Though, I'm not quite sure if I've been disemboweled or just nicked. Pardon me while I assess my injuries."

"Oh stop it," she said, pushing his shoulder. "You started it."

"How was that?" he chuckled.

"Accusing me of having Alzheimer's."

"I said no such thing," he laughed.

"Your insinuation was as plain as day," she hissed.

"Have you been outside?" he said. "Believe me, so far there's nothing plain about today."

Muerce silently cataloged what had already transpired since he woke to the rain, and Ashley. And the day was only half over. *God, what's next?*

"I'm worried about you, Jack," she said, looking at him with concerned sincerity.

"So, we're back to Jack," he said. "Worried about what?"

"We're no spring chickens," she said.

"But spring's right around the corner," he said, lightheartedly.

"Oh, good grace," she said, with some exasperation. "Be serious for a moment. I'm an old lady, and you're not getting any younger, you know. No matter how hard you try... whatever distractions you... who was it last night? No, I don't want to know, though I'm sure she was young, attractive, smart, and blindly infatuated with you.

"Of course, they always are. What woman wouldn't be. But then, poof, they're gone. And it's off to the next conquest."

"Somewhere, buried in all of that, I believe, was a compliment," Muerce said. "This isn't really the time or place for your 'age appropriate' speech, is it?"

"Perhaps not, but you're going to have to move on," she said.

"What? Move on?" Muerce said. "What are you talking about?"

"You know exactly what I mean," she said. "It's been more than twenty years. Even Christ didn't carry the cross that long."

The face reappeared in Muerce's memory. Less clear than the previous time, but clearer than earlier in the day. It *had* been more than twenty years, and still he could not go several hours without thinking of her. Even when he was distracting himself. The itching sensation on his forearms started. He could feel the anxiety gnawing just below the hairs. He fought it off with memories of all the distractions he had accumulated. Some of them, he figured, were likely sitting in the pews just behind him, though he dare not turn to look. He hated the front pew.

Eleanor knew she had gone too far, and patted her son's hand. The distressed look on his face was obvious to her, and she felt ashamed for causing it.

"You'll come for dinner Sunday?" she said.

"Yes, I'll come for dinner Sunday," he said. "What are we having?"

"I'll order the Chicken Kiev from the club, and the macaroni and cheese you like so much," she said.

"Made with spring chickens, I hope," he said. "And garlic bread. Don't forget to get the garlic bread. It will keep the vampires away."

"Of course, spring chickens, why not?" Eleanor said, stifling a laugh, and letting a few beats of contemplative silence pass between them.

"So what is your Lenten vow?" she said.

"What it always is," he said. "What's yours?"

"Compassion, I think," she said, squeezing her son's hand. "I could work harder at that. And, apparently, not to over accessorize my wardrobe."

There was some movement, and a squeaky rustling of wet leather and heavy boots at the far end of the pew. A lanky man, holding a wet rain slicker and dressed in the full leathers of a motorcycle policeman made his way toward Muerce and Eleanor. The policeman draped the slicker over the the pew, creating a small puddle on the marble floor, and placed his white helmet next to him. Muerce nodded in recognition. It was Tom Pruitt. Eleanor nodded too, but with a frown. Pruitt, smiled back at her as he ran his fingers through the shock of matted red hair on his head. His cheeks were still red from the elements.

Pruitt lowered the padded kneeler as quietly as he could, made the sign of the cross, and said a quick prayer. When he finished, he crossed himself again, sat back, and turned to Muerce.

"Hey, Jack," he said, then leaning forward a bit. "Hello Misses Muerce."

"I'm not pleased with you Officer Pruitt," she said, not looking at him. Muerce looked at both of them.

"It's Sergeant Pruitt, Misses Muerce," he said. Muerce alternated pointing his finger at each of them in a way that asked—*what the hell's going on with the two of you?*

Pruitt leaned toward Muerce, and whispered.

"Got her doing forty-two in a school zone the other day," he said.

Muerce shot a look of disbelief at Pruitt. *Seriously, you gave her a ticket?*

"I had to make my monthly quota," Pruitt said, shrugging his shoulders. Muerce turned to Eleanor, who didn't look at either of them.

"Forty-plus in a school zone?" he said, scolding her. "Are you crazy? I'm not sure even I can fix that one."

A harsh ringing of bells at the back of the Cathedral shot out, announcing the start of Mass. The congregation rose to its feet in unison. As they did, Pruitt leaned closer to Muerce.

"Heads up," he said. "Lot of squawk on the radio right before I pulled in here. Central Patrol found a stiff a couple of hours ago. They think it might be the hooker whose kid you found at the laundry this morning."

Muerce, his hands folded at his crotch, turned to Pruitt.

"How do you, how do they, know that?" Muerce said.

"Some freaky stuff," Pruitt said. "Coroner's office is looking for you."

"Bhote? Why?"

"Dunno," Pruitt said. "Maybe they figured 'cause of the kid you could ID her."

"That's a bit of a stretch," Muerce said.

"That's all I know." Pruitt said.

"Well, that's a helluva lot for a mounted cop," Muerce said. Pruitt shrugged his shoulder, and looked toward the back of church.

Muerce's ribs began to vibrate, and he reached into the inside pocket of his suit coat as discreetly as he could to peek at the screen. As he did, Eleanor gave him a disapproving look. It was a text message that said: Swing by ASAP. Bhote.

"Told you," Pruitt said, leaning over to view the message.

Muerce slipped the phone back inside his jacket, and leaned toward his mother.

"Can't stay for communion," he said.

"But you'll get your ashes?"

"Yes, Eleanor, I will get my ashes."

CHAPTER 4

"Thanks for coming," Dr. Sonjay Bhote said. They were at the basement security check-point near the Emergency Room *porte cochere*.

It was the county hospital and rows of the sick and dying, and those who thought they were sick and dying, waited in the ER lobby. Headline News barked from a dusty, cathode ray tube television mounted from the ceiling, to which no one paid any attention. Muerce thought this was nothing like the waiting rooms of any of T.B. Squire's hospitals. The faces there were mostly white, middle-class and covered by private insurance that guaranteed the best care possible. Not so here. At what the cops liked to call the "County Gun and Knife Club," doctors were scarce, waits were long, and the coffee was terrible.

"Don't take it personally, but not seeing you is generally a good thing," Muerce said.

"Don't take it personally, but the people I generally see don't talk back," Bhote said. "Follow me."

They passed through a set of double doors leading, at an incline, to the basement annex that housed the county morgue. The walls of the tunnel were covered in a sickly, green tile that reminded Muerce of what bodies looked like when they had been out too long. With each step down the tunnel, Muerce felt more enclosed. The smell of sanitized morbidity was unpleasant, yet better than the stench of actual death.

Bhote kept a clean shop. He was a consummate pro, and despite frustrating budget cuts over the past decade, had managed to run an efficient, if under-resourced department. County was a meat-and-potatoes morgue. There were no elaborate CSI gadgets glorified by popular television shows. Despite an austere budget, Bhote was considered one of the best in his field. He would be missed when he retired, which was only a few months off.

They passed through another set of double doors at the bottom of the tunnel. Instinctively, Muerce, turned left toward the identification room, where a television was setup that let the living view the dead by remote video. It was less of a shock, especially for family members. Bhote liked to keep the drama in his shop to a minimum.

"Where are you going?" Bhote said, running his long, thin fingers through the few gray strands of hair that remained on his scalp.

Muerce pointed toward the identification room.

"Thought I was here to do an ID, though I'm not so sure I remember the victim all that well," Muerce said. "That's if it is who I'm told it might be."

Bhote stuck his hands back in the front pockets of his jacket, and gave Muerce a grave look. He motioned with his head for Muerce to follow him into the examination room.

The examination room contained four long, thin stainless steel tables on which bodies were autopsied. Large surgical lamps were suspended above each of the tables. Two of the tables were occupied, though the remains were covered by white sheets. Behind those tables were two larger, stainless steel square tables, also lit by large surgical lamps. A bank of thirty stainless steel, refrigerated storage lockers took up the entire wall behind the work tables.

Muerce followed Bhote to the far work table covered by a black, plastic tarp. Bhote waited until Muerce was next to him, and with the flair of a matador he flung back the tarp, exposing what lay beneath.

"Jesus," Muerce shrieked, unprepared, and quickly turning away from the sight.

"Unusual, don't you think?" Bhote said, with scant emotion.

"Fuck, Sonjay," Muerce said, gasping, and uncertain if what he saw was real. He hoped it wasn't, but he knew better. "You could have prepared me a little."

"How do you prepare anyone for something like this?" Bhote said. "Do you recognize her?"

"Do I have to?" Muerce said, sarcastically.

"The karmic damage is done," Bhote said. "It can't get any worse than it is."

Just look at the face, Jack, just look at the face.

Muerce turned toward the table, and looked at the face. The red hair was immediately identifiable. He had only seen the woman—a girl, really—less than two or three times at the laundromat. Then he remembered the time he was parking when she was coming out the door with a bundle of clothes. He recollected her legs, the high cheekbones, and the dimple on the left side of her face. She had smiled at him, and he had felt an attraction to her. There was an innocence about her.

He said her name, which he had only learned just two hours earlier.

"Redzil," he said. "Pretty sure."

"Does she have a last name?" Bhote said.

"I'm sure she does, but I don't remember it," Muerce said.

"She is very young," Bhote said. "Too young, really. Such a shame. With a child, too?"

The two of them stared silently at the macabre assembly of limbs on the table. Bhote, as he always did, recited a Hindu prayer in his head.

"If she was a regular on Canary she'd have been booked before, and I'd run her prints," Bhote said as he walked around to the other side of the table. "But as you can see, we don't have that option. That's why I called you. If we're lucky there will be a mug shot.

"Eventually, we'll run a DNA on her, and with the baby you found."

"I didn't find the baby, it just... he got..." Muerce said, his words and thoughts trailing off. He was still in shock.

The karmic damage had been done. There was no erasing the sight of what was spread out below him. Muerce went as cold and as objective as he could about the disassembled horror on the stainless steel table. Redzil's head remained attached to her torso. On each side of it, lay her severed arms. The table was not long enough to accommodate the length of her legs, so Bhote had placed them alongside the detached arms. Given the fractured condition of her body, Muerce expected there to be a lot of blood. There was none.

Bhote read Muerce's mind. It was the same thing he first thought when she was brought in.

"Look closer," Bhote said.

Do I have to?

"Everything was surgically removed," Bhote said. "Very precise. Cleanest amputations I've ever seen."

Muerce paced slowly around the table, his eyes examining the incisions on the torso and limbs. They had been sutured closed, the skin in some places was stretched tight, and looked like it would rip or burst at the slightest touch. Yet, nothing oozed from the closures.

"Notice anything else?" Bhote said, as if leading a dissection class in medical school.

Muerce stood back for a moment, both horrified and mesmerized. It was too much for him to be a sharp observer. He shook his head that he didn't.

"Not just the fingers, but the toes are missing," Bhote said.

Muerce focused on the missing digits at the end of her feet, and hands. The wounds that now formed stubs were sutured shut.

"I also found this in her mouth," Bhote said. He held up an evidence bag. Inside was a coin that Muerce couldn't make out.

"I lied, Jack," Bhote said. "It gets worse."

He looked up, unsure if he wanted to hear what Bhote had to say.

"The vaginal cavity is sewn shut," Bhote said. "And..."

"And, what?"

Look at the wounds on the limbs, and compare them to the wounds on the torso," Bhote said.

Reluctantly bending closer to the body parts, Muerce smelled a moldy, though not unpleasant, scent that triggered a vague memory he couldn't readily associate with his experiences. Ignoring the odor, he focused on what Bhote wanted him to see. As much as he squinted, and tried to adjust his vision, Muerce was lost. He wasn't a detective, or a forensic scientist. This was way beyond his skill sets.

"I have no idea what the hell I'm looking for Sonjay, so just tell me," he said.

"The wounds are clean on the limbs," he said. "While the wounds on the torso have some slight scabbing, and coagulation. There is some minor bruising on her upper rib cage that is consistent with restraining straps.

"There's also a subclavian puncture wound, indicating a central intravenous line was established. I checked her throat and nasal cavities, and there is scarring consistent with intubation."

"I went to law school, Sonjay," Muerce said. "Not medical school like my mother wanted. None of that means anything to me."

Bhote cleared his throat, and waited a few seconds before answering.

"She was alive when this was done to her."

It took a moment for the horror of what Bhote said to register with Muerce.

It didn't make sense to Muerce. Keeping a victim alive to amputate their limbs, then taking the time, effort and the patience to suture the wounds? And the missing fingers and toes, not to mention what had been done to her sexual organs? Muerce wasn't a detective, but it didn't take much of a deduction to start asking what the motive was behind such a debased act, and where it could have been carried out, and by who. This was the work of a professional. A very skilled professional.

There was something to the wounds that caught Muerce's eye, and he leaned closer to look at the suturing at the hip joint on the torso. The stitching was exceptionally elaborate. It looked like a chain.

"This is pretty fancy work," he said.

Bhote went to the corner of the examination room, and wheeled a large magnifying glass that had a light built into it. He positioned the lens about twelve inches above the victim's vagina, which was absent of all pubic hair.

"This isn't just stitching," Bhote said, flipping the light on, and illuminating the genitalia. "This is embroidery. Artistry, if you like."

Through the magnifying glass Muerce saw several rows of brightly colored threads of brilliant blue and deep red. White and gold threads highlighted the pattern that looked to be a flower or blossom of some sort. He studied the finely detailed work, trying not to focus on the female landscape that served as the backing for the needlework. It was difficult to concentrate, but amid the pattern Muerce thought he saw something woven in gold and green thread just above the elaborate embroidery that sutured her labia closed. It was the French word for unicorn—*licorne*.

CHAPTER 5

Pho Mat, whom most everyone called Sammy, was a small man even by Vietnamese standards. He had been Colonel Trung's *aide du camp* throughout the years the Americans were involved in the war. The only family Pho Mat had were the Trungs, who had paid a significant amount of money to buy his passage out of Vietnam several years after they had fled when Saigon fell. Pho Mat walked with a pronounced limp that was the result of repeated beatings during his years in a re-education camp after the North Vietnamese victory. Now a U.S. citizen, Pho Mat was the *majordomo* at Saigon Laundry. He was St. Peter at the Gates of Heaven, with an edge. As impeccably polite and solicitous as Pho Mat was to the customers with reservations, he could be politely, yet indelibly, rude to the ones who arrived unannounced, and unwanted. Due to the intimate size of the dining area, he also had little patience for unruly patrons, and did not hesitate to provide lessons in manners.

He had not been pleased when Muerce arrived shortly before six o'clock, requesting a second place setting for his table, and that only two courses be served—the appetizer and the main dish. Then there was the insult added to the injury. Muerce selected his own wine—having helped Benny order what was stocked in the cellar he was familiar with what vintages were on hand. That put Pho Mat close to his boiling point. His displeasure with Muerce, however, was tempered. Pho Mat could see Muerce was pale, and tired. There was a vacancy in his eyes that Pho Mat knew well. It was the same blankness he saw when he shaved himself each morning. It was the look of atrocity.

Pho Mat barked orders to the kitchen staff pertaining to Muerce's request as Benny was in the cooler with the *sous chef.* Then Pho Mat ambled to the basement, pulled the bottle Muerce wanted from bin 61, and returned to the kitchen to add the bottle to the chill tub. From a side cubby that served as a makeshift bar, he grabbed a smokey brown bottle with a bright red and gold label. He poured the liquid into a small, fluted glass. Muerce, Pho Mat knew, needed something to give him some color.

With his thoughts and appetite still at the city morgue, Muerce didn't notice Pho Mat arrive at his table. Usually, you could hear a light *thump* when his left leg thrust upon the wood floor with each step. Pho Mat wore an immaculately pressed, and tailored tuxedo. It was his winter tux. After Memorial Day, he would switch to a white, silk dinner jacket until Labor Day. *Impeccable.*

"*Apertif, Monsieur Muerce,*" Pho Mat said, placing the drink on the white linen table cloth. The coffee stained one having been replaced earlier in the day.

"*Bon, Sammy, bon,*" Muerce said, quickly downing the contents.

Pho Mat smiled, and waited for the drink to present its influence.

"Another?" Pho Mat said, retrieving the empty glass, and placing it on the small tray he held.

"*Oui,*" Muerce said, still staring out into an unspeakable space. The scene at the morgue kept cycling through his head.

Pho Mat returned with another *aperitif,* and two wine goblets that he placed on Muerce's table. Muerce quickly downed the liquor. As Pho Mat turned toward the kitchen, Muerce reached out and touched him on his jacket sleeve.

"Sammy," he said.

"Yes, Mister Muerce," Pho Mat said, stopping. He kept his gaze, respectfully, just below that of Muerce's eyes.

"Thank you," Muerce said, pointing at the empty *aperitif* glass. "And I apologize for the last-minute change to accommodate my guest."

"Certainly, Mister Muerce," Pho Mat said. "Is no problem for you. May I inquire as to the personage of your guest, so that when the party arrives I may seat them promptly?"

"My guest's name is T.B. Squire," Muerce said, glancing at his wrist watch. "He should be here any minute."

"Excellent, Mister Muerce," Pho Mat said. "May I suggest the crab and gruyere puffs Chef Benny has prepared for appetizers tonight? They would sit well between the *aperitif,* and the entree."

"Yes, Sammy," Muerce said. "Thank you."

Within minutes, the doorbell chimed. There was a brief exchange of conversation as Pho Mat pulled aside the beaded curtain, allowing a medium-sized, somewhat portly and pasty looking man to enter the dining area. Muerce recognized the man from photos and articles he had read in the local business newspaper. It was T.B. Squire.

Muerce stood to introduce himself. They shook hands as Pho Mat disappeared with Squire's topcoat. The weather had turned from driving rain to a bitter cold wind. Wet spots formed into ice throughout the city.

Squire was both entranced to be dining at Saigon Laundry, and humbled by the reason behind the invitation. It was clear to Muerce that Squire, as influential in the business community as he was, and used to getting his way, was off balance. *Good, easier to work with.*

"Let's eat first, Mister Squire, then we can talk about your son," Muerce said.

"You can call me T.B.," Squire said.

There was a squeak, and pop of a cork being extracted from a bottle. Pho Mat poured the wine from Bin 61. Its amber color picked up the light from the votive candle on the table. Their glasses filled, Pho Mat departed from their table as discreetly as he had appeared.

"Let's keep it formal for now, Mister Squire," Muerce said.

"I understand Mister Muerce," Squire said.

"Please," Muerce said, holding his glass up to indicate Squire had the honor of tasting the wine first.

Squire took a generous sip from the glass, swished it around in his mouth to savor the body and bouquet, and swallowed. It was one of the best he had ever tasted, and the expression on his face communicated his approval.

"Good isn't it?" Muerce said. "I came across it in the south of France last fall, and fell in love. Of course, it's hard not to fall in love with anything French."

Muerce had no more begun to turn toward the kitchen to summon Pho Mat, when he realized the *majordomo* was again, having arrived discreetly, at their table-side depositing two plates of puff pastries. Again, Pho Mat retreated as quickly as he had arrived.

"My understanding is these are crab and gruyere puffs," Muerce said, separating one of the delicacies with his fork and knife. "And what looks like saffron."

Muerce ran his fork through a red liquid garnish that adorned the plate in a simple, yet elegant pattern. He brought it to his mouth.

"Chili aioli," Muerce said, finishing the first puff, and washing it down with a sip of wine. "A nice bite to it. Balances the sweetness of the crab."

Squire, as his body indicated, was a gastronome himself. Although having relocated from Texas only four years earlier, he was still on the waiting list for a reservation at Saigon Laundry despite his stature in the community.

"My wife, Mister Muerce, is going to be fit to be tied that I've eaten here without her," Squire said, devouring another puff.

"Women, Mister Squire, as has been my experience, are generally always in a knot about something," Muerce said. "Perhaps it would be best, given the nature of our business, that you not disclose the location of our meeting.

"At least not right away, and not unless I, we that is, are able to find a solution to the problem your son is facing."

Most people let you know what they are within the first fifteen minutes of meeting them. Squire had a simple nobility to him. He didn't bully, and he didn't overstep. At least, not when it was something he needed that involved his family. Squire was a smart and powerful man, but he didn't wave it around like a flag. Muerce respected that about Squire upon meeting him. He expected the same from his son, no matter how much trouble he was in. It was clear to Muerce that the chances were good the son had not fallen too far from the apple tree. Muerce decided he would do the best he could for T.B. Squire, and for T.B. Squire's son.

Anticipating the needs of the table, Pho Mat poured another glass of wine for each of them. As usual, he was as inconspicuous as possible. Service without conversation. *The consummate majordomo.*

"Tell me about your son," Muerce said.

Squire returned his utensils to the table, took another sip of wine and proceeded, as succinctly as possible, to explain the situation Travis had gotten himself into. Travis had all the markings of the ne'er-do-well son. Muerce figured the kid had been a fish out of water the moment the movers unpacked the boxes from Texas. He had been enrolled as a transfer student at Brambleton Day School, which was so notoriously parochial and pretentious that Muerce's own parents opted to send him off to boarding school to avoid that culture. At least—as Muerce remembered his time at Groton—he had been shunned by people with a global view versus those who saw only a few blocks from where they slept.

Travis, as his father explained, struggled through Brambleton, graduating by the skin of his teeth. Despite pulling any number of strings to get his son into a small college, the experience lasted less than a semester. During his short collegiate stint, Travis had picked up a bad habit. He liked to gamble. Apparently, Travis wasn't any good at it. T.B. Squire covered his son's debts at college. But in the months that followed Travis' return, he ran up a twenty-thousand-dollar marker, not including the interest, or vig, on the street. Travis owed large, and he owed Tino Tomaso. *Not good, but manageable.*

"Titty Boy," Muerce said.

"Excuse me?" Squire said.

"Tomaso's street name," Muerce said. The expression on Squire's face was one of confusion. "Tomaso works out of a strip bar he inherited from his father. Used to be called the White Horse. He worked there growing up. That's how he got his name. His father died. Tomaso took over. Times changed, and Titty Boy changed the place with them. Now it's a tranny—transvestite—hangout called Club Unicorn."

As he said the name out loud, Muerce recalled the embroidered vagina of the dead hooker. *Connection or coincidence?*

Muerce could see T.B. Squire's lips moving, but he couldn't hear him. Thinking about the dismembered Redzil caused Muerce to lose his appetite.

"What?" Muerce said.

"I asked you if you know him," Squire said.

"Know who?"

"This Tomaso character," Squire said.

Muerce took a sip of wine, and leaned across the table toward T.B. Squire.

"Titty Boy Tomaso is no character Mister Squire," he said. "This isn't a Scorsese movie. Tomaso is a real, *motherfucker*. A good mood for him is when he's being an unreasonable prick."

Muerce leaned back in his chair, took a deep breath, and another sip of wine. He couldn't get Redzil out of his head, and the death mask of terror on her face.

"So you know him?" Squire said.

Muerce looked at T.B. Squire, and made a number of quick decisions in his head. Then he took another sip of wine, and grit his teeth.

"Can you get the twenty K, cash, by the close of business Friday?" he said.

T.B. Squire nodded to indicate it would be no problem.

"Have it couriered to me, here," Muerce said. "It will be safe. I'll take care of the vig. Travis will have to come with me. He's going to have to stand up for himself."

"Is that safe?" Squire said.

"It's not an option," Muerce said. "It's about respect for Tomaso, and self respect for your son. He needs to know how serious this is. If I take care of this by myself, well, the pattern might repeat itself. I don't think you want that."

T.B. Squire nodded he understood.

"I don't want him driving," Muerce said. "Drop him off here, Saturday, say ten o'clock. I'll get him home. Make sure he wears a coat, collared shirt, and decent slacks. No white-boy, gang banger outfits."

"And Mister Squire."

"Yes, Mister Muerce?" Squire drawled.

"Travis is going to work off the vig with me," Muerce said. "I have some chores for him. Oh, one more thing. Have they reached out to him yet?"

"I don't understand," Squire said.

"Have they tried to collect anything besides the money?" Muerce said.

T.B. Squire grasped the meaning.

"I'm afraid so," he said. "He came home with some sore ribs last week. The boy felt like he went the full eight seconds with a rank bull. That's what started the ball rolling with you."

"Tell him to stay home until Saturday," Muerce said.

"I believe that won't be a problem," Squire said.

Pho Mat was at their table, bearing the night's *entree.*

"Skate," Pho Mat said. "In a pepper curry, lemon grass cream sauce, accompanied by a mango and cherry infused compote. *Bon appetite.*"

The savory aroma of the lightly sauced fish, and anticipated tartness of the compote brought Muerce's appetite back from the dead. After a few bites, he held up his glass. In it he could see his reflection, and the crudely etched ash cross on his forehead. He thought himself ridiculous. *One day out of the year.*

CHAPTER 6

The mail was neatly piled on the antique reception table in the apartment foyer. Muerce returned the umbrella to its place in the brass stand next to the others, and shed his trench coat. As he hung it in the closet the lone empty cedar hanger to the left of the damp trench coat reminded him of Ashley's naked body lying next to him, and how that felt like a long time ago. *Wonder when I'll get that coat back?*

Muerce gathered up the mail, sorted through it as he entered the living room of his apartment, and turned on the lights. It was all junk mail he tossed into the trash compacter in the kitchen. Muerce was not much for recycling. The champagne bottles from the night before were gone. The maid had done her job. In his bedroom, Muerce knew he would find the sheets changed, and the bed made. *Damn, I forgot to get my shirts.*

From the kitchen he retrieved the *Stolichnaya*, a chilled martini glass, and the jar of blue cheese-stuffed olives. Standing at the bar that separated the living from the dining room, he swirled the inside of the cold glass with a splash of *Lagavulin*, then added three ounces of the glaciated vodka directly from the bottle. With a wood-handled bar knife distinguished by its metal bee, Muerce carved a peel of lemon from a small basket of citrus. He spiked the peel with one of a set of brass cocktail picks that were replicas of Medieval swords made in Toledo, Spain. Three olives where then skewered from the jar; one to balance each ounce of vodka.

Muerce swirled the cocktail with the tiny rapier, and took a generous sip. *And that, he thought, is a twisted blue smoke martini.* Most barmen didn't keep their vodkas in the freezer, and tended to bruise it with a vigorous shaking. *Stolichnaya* was tough enough to take the beating, but Muerce preferred bottles rested in a deep freeze.

A second sip later, Muerce looked at himself in the mirror behind the bar. The garish, ashen mark remained imprinted on his forehead. *Idiot. Get that off now.*

Pulling and tugging his tie off, Muerce strode to the bathroom. He threw the tie on the bed, unbuttoned the top of his shirt, and clicked the bathroom light on. When he did, he felt a wave of anxiety. His chest was suddenly tight, and his breathing more rapid. The faces began to run in a circular display in his head, like an unending loop of a short film: Ashley, Mirsad, Miriam, and Redzil. Each time the loop ended with the image of the dead prostitute, Redzil. The look of horror on her face. Her dismembered body laid out on a table like a human puzzle. Muerce scrubbed his forehead with a hand towel as hard as he could as if he could wipe away his thoughts with the ash crucifix. *A Unicorn?*

He threw the washcloth on the marble-topped bathroom counter, opened the medicine cabinet, and retrieved a prescription bottle.

The bottle of vodka had frosted over, and was still cold when he made another cocktail. He finished it in three gulps. But the film loop continued to play in his head. Muerce picked up the stereo remote from the butler's table behind the sofa, and pointed it in the direction the *Bang & Olafsen* in the library.

Muerce settled into one of the overstuffed chairs flanking the sofa, and fumbled with the safety cap on the prescription bottle. *A two Xanax night.*

He popped the blue pills into his mouth, and swallowed them dry. Paul Chambers' bass laid the groundwork for Miles Davis' trumpet. The selection was "So What." Muerce laughed at the irony. *Modality. Sixteen measures of the first followed by eight of the second, and then eight again of the first.*

"So what?" Muerce said out loud twenty minutes later. The medication kicked in. He was smooth. The anxiety passed. He didn't care. The dead hooker was nothing to him. He did the right thing with the baby. He wasn't a cop. It wasn't his investigation. Not his job. Not his responsibility. All he did was ID a body. He didn't even know the girl. That was bullshit of Bhote to bring him in there like that, and get him thinking about what wasn't his business. *Bullshit on Bhote.*

The only faces in his head were now Ashley and Miriam. His memory of making love to Miriam—though it had been a long time ago—was clearer than making love to Ashley only the night before. If he wanted a better memory of being naked with Ashley he would have to create a new one, minus all the champagne. It was an appealing thought. He also liked the idea of creating a new memory with Miriam. But what he really wanted was on old memory to go away. For the face from the past that he couldn't erase no matter how hard, and for how long, he tried to be erased for good.

The pills, and the drinks made Muerce tired. He looked at his phone to see what time it was. Ten after eleven. *Not too late.*

There was a text message: Such a gentlemen. Will return coat if I can make u dinner. Sometime? Ash.

Muerce powered the phone off for the night without responding, and stood up.

"Whoa," he said out loud, losing his balance. It was the Xanax, the martinis, and the rush of blood to his head. And with it returned the old face. *Go away. I want to sleep.*

THE UNICORN

From all uncleanness freed, the flesh they sever there,
The chest they slit, and draw the erber forth with care;
With knife both sharp and keen the neck they next divide,
Then sever all four limbs, and strip off fair the hide.
—The Pearl Poet

CHAPTER 7

The flame from a votive candle flickered and danced, casting jerky shadows across the table. Muerce sat, mesmerized, watching the show, and thinking of women. It was Saturday night, and the tables at Saigon Laundry were full. Everyone was happy they were there, and anticipated the plates of food Benny and his staff were furiously preparing. Exotic smells emanated from the kitchen with a tangy, and steamy feel that mixed with the subtle mustiness of the decor. Muerce appeared immune to the activity around him. There was only one empty seat in the place, the one across from him.

He glanced at his watch. It wasn't even eight o'clock yet. The appointment with Travis Squire was at ten. They would take a short drive to Tino Tomaso's bar—Club Unicorn. But first, Muerce had a dinner date.

Above the din of the room, he heard the sound he anticipated. The beaded curtain rustled as it was swept aside by Pho Mat, who had an uncharacteristically wide grin on his face.

She wore a strapless, black-sequined cocktail dress with black-strap heels that accentuated very long, almost milk chocolate colored legs. She held a small, sequined clutch purse as she elegantly navigated the one step that led into the dining area. She towered over Pho Mat, which was not a hard thing to do, as he escorted her toward Muerce. A fork or two dropped as every head in the room turned toward the last person to be seated for the evening.

Holding her left arm as if he were walking a daughter down the aisle on her wedding day, Pho Mat escorted her to the table. Muerce stood up.

"Your guest has arrived, Mister Muerce," Pho Mat said.

She has, at that.

"Good evening, Miriam," Muerce said. "You look... you are stunning."

She blushed, which was quite an accomplishment for a woman with skin pigment that pre-dated the Spanish Conquistadors. Muerce was sure she was descended from Aztec royalty, though there was an almost Aryan structure to her face. Her fierce green eyes contrasted her dark skin. She wore her sable hair swept back in a fashion he had not seen on her before.

"I love what you've done to your hair," Muerce said as Pho Mat seated Miriam.

"*Madame Estrada,*" Pho Mat said, scooting the chair in for her.

"*Merci beaucoup, Monsieur Sammy,*" she said, with an accent that leaned more toward Marseille than Paris. She had picked up the southern inflection up from the French nuns that taught her in high school. "*C'est bon de te revoir.*"

"*Enchante, Madame,*" Pho Mat said, standing upright by the table, and nodding slightly with his big grin. "It is, as well, our pleasure to see you again. *Aperitif en champagne?*"

Miriam looked at Muerce, deferring to him.

"*Oui, champagne, se vous plait,*" Muerce said.

Pho Mat uttered a quick "*bon*", and disappeared into the kitchen.

"I feel like an idiot," Miriam said.

Muerce laughed.

"Why?" he said, leaning toward her. "You certainly don't look like one."

"Getting all dressed up like this," she said. "God Jack, I can't remember the last time I wore heels this high. I look like one of the girls working Canary."

Muerce reached across the table and put his hand on top of hers, noticing she still wore her wedding band. He made an obvious survey of the room.

"There isn't a man in here who has taken his eyes off of you since you walked in," Muerce said. "And I haven't seen Sammy grin like that since the last time he saw you."

Actually, I have, the previous winter when when I slipped and fell on the ice on the sidewalk outside.

Scanning the dining room, Miriam caught several men, and a few women, sneaking looks at her. It made her glow inside, and glad she decided to buy the dress. *I do miss this.*

"See, I told you," he said.

A champagne cork *popped* in the background. A few minutes later, and to Muerce's surprise, Madame Trung arrived at their table with a tray, and two flutes filled with champagne. She wore a white *ao dai*. Madame Trung rarely made appearances in the dining room during dinner service. That was Pho Mat's territory. After placing the flutes in front of Muerce and Miriam, Madame Trung twice retrieved a sugar cube from a small dish. She made a bit of a show as she dropped them from the tongs into each flute. Champagne had not been offered to any of the other tables, which caused more curious, and envious looks.

"*để được mai-mắng*," she said.

"And why do we need luck?" Muerce said.

"*Đừng làm lộn xộn, Bà là người đàn bà tốt*," Madame Trung said, leaving the table side.

"I don't like it when you do the Vietnamese thing," Miriam said. "What did she say?"

"She said I'm lucky you're having dinner with me," Muerce said.

"Well, she's right," Miriam said, unfolding her napkin.

Muerce raised his champagne, the sugar cube fizzing at the bottom of the flute.

"To having dinner with you," he said.

"To just a meal," Miriam said, clinking her glass against Muerce's.

"I'm glad you called."

"Stupid," Miriam said, swallowing the champagne, and casting her eyes down.

"It's just a meal, Miriam," he said. "We agreed. I have an appointment later, anyway."

"What's her name?" Miriam said, in a matter-of-fact but testing way.

"His name is business," Muerce said. "And the business is at Titty Boys. Do you want to ride along?"

"Uh, no thanks," she said, sipping more champagne. "So what's for dinner?"

Muerce flipped over a small card that lay on the table. It was hand-written. He read off the evening's offering from the kitchen. Madame Trung's penmanship was exquisite.

The appetizer was fresh oysters on ice, accented with with soy, rice wine vinegar, lemon grass, and a dash of *nam pa*—Laotian fish sauce. It was followed by chicory salad with grilled asparagus, spicy quail egg, goat cheese and a *Kimchi* inspired dressing.

"I don't know how he does it, but Benny infuses the quail egg with something that gives them real heat, so be careful with it," Muerce said.

"My blood can take the heat," Miriam said. "You should worry about yourself, *gringo*. What else?"

He continued. After the salad course was an artichoke and lobster souffle with a fresh mayonnaise and bay leaf sauce. Then a palate cleansing with pomegranate and Port wine sorbet.

The main course was filet of sole with lemon butter, *frommage kale*, and a lentil and pineapple compote.

"For dessert, selected cheeses and miniature *bombe au trois chocolate*," Muerce said, handing the card to Miriam.

"*Merveilleux*," Miriam said, perusing the menu.

"*Tres magnifique*," Muerce replied, looking straight at her.

Over the next two hours, they savored the meal and talked about Miriam, her sons, her job, and the baby of the murdered prostitute, who now had a full name for Muerce—Redzil Hadzic. She had no immediate family Social Services were able to track down. Miriam said the infant's name was Radzic Hadzic, which Muerce hoped, for the sake of the child, would be changed by adoption. That the baby was healthy, male and white, put him at the front of the adoption line, if no family was located, or if they were unwilling to seek custody. It was unfair, they agreed, but it was just the way things were.

"If the kid's white, he's all right," Miriam said, taking a bite of the gooey chocolate concoction on her plate.

"If he were brown, adopting couples might stick around," Muerce said.

"But if he's black, they never come back," Miriam said rather glumly. "People can really suck in my line of work."

"In mine too," he said.

Muerce limited himself to one glass each of champagne, and wine with dinner. He didn't want any fogginess when he went to Tomaso's with the Squire boy. In addition to champagne, Miriam had had two glasses of wine with her meal, but they both switched to coffee for dessert. Muerce looked down at his watch. It was almost ten o'clock. He wished the night with Miriam wasn't over, though the look on her face seemed to him to be one of relief when she saw him look at the time.

"Dinner was wonderful, Jack," she said. "It really has been a treat. Thank you."

"I wish I didn't have to bolt out on you."

Miriam, her elbows resting casually on the table, opened her hands, palms facing Muerce.

"Just a meal, remember?" she said.

Looking at her open hands, Muerce remembered how they had a moistness to them that was unique to her. He remembered how they felt on his skin when she rubbed them against him. There her hands were, palms open, and inviting. He wanted her to touch him again.

"*Pardon, Madame Estrada, Monsieur Muerce,*" Pho Mat said. Miriam's hands closed, and retreated to her lap. "A gentlemen says he has an appointment with you. He is waiting by the counter."

Muerce thanked Pho Mat, and asked if he would tell his appointment that he would be just a moment. Pho Mat nodded, and made his way through the beaded curtain.

"Miriam, I'm sorry, I have to go," Muerce said, looking at her with an apologetic longing. "I want, so badly, to stay."

"What are you sorry for?" she said. She let out a deep breath, sat back in her chair, and contemplated what she would say next.

Muerce didn't want to move, but he could see Travis Squire through the beaded curtain; the next phase of the evening beckoned. The young man was pacing, though there was an air of bravado about him.

"Thank you, Jack," Miriam said.

"It really wasn't..." Muerce began to say before Miriam interrupted.

"Really, thank you," she said. "I just needed to get out. I needed to feel pretty without all the pressure of a date. This was exactly what I needed. No strings. No expectations. You came through for me, Jack. So don't feel bad."

Muerce smiled, though her words felt like he'd been hit by a blunt object. There was not, as much as he had hoped, going to be a new memory with Miriam.

"Of course," he said. "You can ask me for anything."

"I ask that you go take care of whatever business you have," she said. "I'm going to finish my coffee, and this sinfully wonderful, and fattening dessert."

Muerce put his napkin on the table, stood up, took two steps toward Miriam, bent down and kissed her on the cheek.

"Thank you, Miriam," he whispered in her ear. He inhaled so she could hear him as he held her scent. "I can't begin to describe how amazing you look, and how amazing you are."

Turning her head so that their noses brushed against each other, Miriam reached up with her hand and ran it down Muerce's neck. Then she kissed him softly on the lips.

"Be careful at Tomaso's," she said, pulling away. "He's a crazy asshole. Now go, and let me finish my dessert."

"I'll have Sammy walk you to your car," Muerce said, standing up straight, Miriam's scent still lingered.

She winked, and took a sip of coffee.

"No need, because nobody fucks with the Welfare Lady, you know," she said, causing a few heads to turn.

Muerce chuckled as he buttoned the top button of his camel hair sport coat, and fixed his tie.

"Goodnight Miriam."

As Pho Mat held open his overcoat, Muerce looked back through the beaded curtain at Miriam. Madame Trung had deposited herself where Muerce had been sitting, and the two of them chatted away as if they had been sitting together all night. One of the wait staff delivered fresh coffee to the table. In a flash, Miriam looked up at Muerce, and waved goodbye.

"You Travis?" Muerce said.

Travis nodded.

"You Muerce? he said.

"No," Muerce said. "I'm Mister Muerce."

Muerce sized up Travis. Twenty, blond, curly hair, a solid frame, but likely not in as good as shape as he should be. He had hazel eyes that were clear, but very cautious. He dressed as he had been told: sports jacket, nice slacks, and collared shirt. Muerce detected the smell of tobacco and breath mints when he offered his hand.

"Mister Jack Muerce," Muerce said.

Travis tried to mask a scowl, and reached across to shake Muerce's hand with as firm a grip as he could muster. *He's not going to shatter any telephone poles, Muerce thought, but he's not afraid to assert himself either. Good.*

"Sammy, do you have an envelope for me?" Muerce said, not taking his eyes off Travis, who also was not taking his eyes off of Muerce.

Pho Mat went behind the counter, passed the racks of plastic-covered dry cleaning laundry, and punched a few keys on the register. The drawer opened with the sound of an antique bell. Pho Mat handed a manila envelope to Muerce, who then tossed it to Travis.

"Count it in the car," Muerce said, turning to Pho Mat. Muerce pulled a twenty from his wallet.

"Can you make sure one of the boys walks Misses Estrada to her car when she leaves."

"No worry, I do honor myself," Pho Mat said, pushing the money away. "No one bother us."

Goddamned right. Nobody fucks with Pho Mat. And nobody fucks with the Welfare Lady.

CHAPTER 8

"How much?" Muerce said.

Travis fanned the bills in his hand with a flourish that indicated he knew his way around a deck of cards, even if he didn't know how to make them win.

"Twenty large," he said, putting the money back into the envelope. Muerce held his hand out, and Travis handed the cash back to him.

"Your father explain the deal?" Muerce said.

"Yeah, I got the four-one-one from the old man," Travis said. "I guess you got some kind of pull to make a deal. We pay the greaser off, and I gotta rake your leaves and take out your trash, do your laundry, or some shit, to pay back the vig you cover."

As fast and as smooth as the sass came out of Travis' mouth, Muerce pulled the Mercedes to the curb, and stabbed his fist into Travis' ribs—the same ones Tomaso's enforcer bruised. Travis screamed once, then alternated loud moans, gasping and sputtering between his efforts to breath. The pain lasted a good minute or two before easing.

"Do I have your attention now?" Muerce said.

"Yeah," Travis bleated.

"Sure?"

"Yes, I'm sure."

"Good," Muerce said. "You have two choices. You can either lose the attitude, immediately, and do exactly, and say exactly what I want you to, the second I tell you to. Or, you can get out of the car, right now. And I keep the envelope."

Muerce paused a moment for his proposal to register with Travis, who coughed through a secondary spasm of pain.

"I'd like to encourage you to go with the first choice," Muerce said. "Just take a look outside."

Travis lifted his head with some effort, squinted and peered out the window into the darkness. There was a hostility and danger Travis couldn't see, but knew was out there.

"We're in North Canary, you know North Canary?" Muerce said.

Travis nodded his head, submissively, up and down. The pain still stabbed at him.

"Even the cops don't get out of their cars in North Canary at night without drawing their guns," Muerce said. "If you decide to go with the second choice, maybe, just maybe, someone might find dogs chewing on a few of your bones a couple of weeks from now."

Muerce pulled a linen handkerchief from inside his jacket, and handed it to Travis to wipe the snot and spit from his face. Travis accepted it, and cleaned himself up.

"I'll do what you say," he said.

"Good, Option One, I'm glad we cleared that up," Muerce said, accelerating away from the curb. He didn't want to loiter on North Canary any longer than needed. *No bullshit. This place is scary.*

"I'm sorry, Mister Muerce," Travis said, a few minutes later. The tone in his voice carried a slight drawl, which Muerce interpreted as the air of a southern gentleman. Travis held up the soiled linen to return it to Muerce.

"I got myself into a deep ditch, and I appreciate what you are doing for me."

"Keep it," Muerce said of the handkerchief. "There aren't any leaves to rake, but you will be handling some of the laundry duties."

"Yes sir."

They were twenty minutes away from Club Unicorn, and passed most of the remainder of the drive in silence. Muerce didn't regret hurting Travis, given the attitude he was projecting, nor did he enjoy it. Brokering a deal with Tomaso wouldn't be easy, and it wouldn't have been any easier with Travis posturing as a smart-ass, rich kid.

"What's the vig?" Muerce said, cutting through the quiet in the car.

"Thirty percent interest," Travis said.

"Hmm, you must have gotten an introductory deal, it's usually fifty percent," Muerce said. "Compounded daily, or weekly?"

"Weekly."

"How many weeks you behind?"

"Two... rolls to three tomorrow."

Muerce did a quick calculation, and figured he'd have to eat the third week to make Tomaso happy. Tomaso knew Muerce was coming, but he didn't know why. Once Tomaso did, he'd smell weakness, and pounce. But Muerce was ready to counter. Tomaso had some sore ribs too. And Muerce would enjoy poking at them, just for fun. *Titty Boy was a mean prick, but he was predictable.*

"She was smoking hot," Travis said, interrupting Muerce's train of thought.

Muerce shot Travis a look. *What are you talking about?*

"The babe... I, I mean woman you were with, at dinner," Travis said. "She was hot, you know, for an old lady."

Old Lady? Miriam wasn't even forty, yet.

"You want me to hit you again?" Muerce said.

"No, no. I'm just saying she was, killer gorgeous."

Travis pressed his eyes shut and tensed his body, waiting for Muerce to punch him again. But the blow never arrived.

"Misses Estrada, yeah, I'd say so," Muerce said. He could still smell the scent of her skin and hair.

"Misses?"

"The Widow Estrada," Muerce said with clarification. "You'll learn, eventually, Young Squire, that the field of killer gorgeous babes from which to choose from increases as you grow older. Beautiful women, come in all ages."

"And Travis."

"Yes, Mister Muerce?"

"You've used up all your questions and observations for the night."

"Yes, Mister Muerce," Travis said, his thoughts focused on the kind of casual sensuality the Widow Estrada had exuded at Saigon Laundry, and the intriguing realm that was Jack Muerce's world.

— —

Club Unicorn grabbed your attention like a Victoria's Secret shopping bag hanging in the branches of the scrubby, leafless trees that lined slurry ponds. Set among an ocean of single-story, light industrial buildings on the north side of the city, the place was lit up with pink and white bulbs that attracted an exotic variety of moths from the *Homo sapien* genus.

The building was a nondescript warehouse of cinder blocks and brick that had been covered with a garish coat of pink paint applied like pancake makeup. A white and red neon marquee in the design of a unicorn was bolted to the roof. The body of the animal was outlined in white, its horn a pulsating and throbbing neon red that looked as if it had been strapped on as a sex toy accessory. The marquee left no doubt about the tastes of the clientele.

Under the ownership of Titty Boy's father, the White Horse was the drinking grounds for blue-collar workers after they had clocked out of their jobs for the day, and before they clocked in at home. The bar came to Titty Boy after the body of Tomaso Senior was found in the trunk of his car at a hotel parking lot near the airport. Titty Boy's father had two serious flaws; he gambled too much, and paid back his losses too little.

The name Titty Boy was bestowed on the junior Tomaso when he was a teen working at the White Horse. He liked to sneak up and tweak the nipples of the strippers before they went on stage. It made for bad employee relations, high turnover in talent, and a falling out between father and son. The senior Tomaso's crew thought the boss's son was strange, and harmless, and stuck him with the nickname at the same time he was banned from backstage.

They were right about Tino being strange. His being harmless was a gross miscalculation.

When the old man was found curled up next to his spare tire with three small-caliber entry wounds in the back of his head, Titty Boy took over his father's operation, which included gambling, prostitution, and some of the street drug trade. By that time, Titty Boy was his own man with his own crew. Within a year of taking control, every one of the Wise Guys who laughingly stuck junior Tomaso with the monicker Titty Boy had died violently. Their murders were unsolved. The coincidences of · their deaths within such a short time frame garnered Tino a reputation of Draconian proportions. It also made the nickname more popular, though it was rarely used in his presence. With Titty Boy, there were always repercussions.

The old ways were gone, and Titty Boy had begun to tweak *la Cosa Nostra* as he had the strippers' nipples. Weaned on movies like "The Godfather", "Goodfellas", and "Casino," Titty Boy and his crew aspired to the psychosis, romance and violence of Hollywood mobsters, but chose to ignore the endings of those films, which were not happy ones for the bad guys.

There was no mafia anymore. There was no code. *Gangsters* with pinky rings, pin-stripe suits and Thompson sub-machine guns had become *Gangstas* with gold chains, velour track suits and TEK-9 machine pistols. Titty Boy and his crew were just punks with a twist, trying to control a small portion of an ever shrinking landscape of illegal activity amid ever growing global competition. And the competition wasn't just rival crime gangs. Gambling was legal, pot was decriminalized, pornography was free, and the slide of moral standards was socially acceptable.

Titty Boy was more *legit* than he would like to admit.

With the advent of private escort services, mom-and-pop strip clubs had become passe. More elaborate shows and gimmicks were needed to attract money through the door. Tino needed a *niche*, which he found it in the transgender/transvestite community. He changed the name of the White Horse to Club Unicorn, and with it the economic quality of patron it attracted. Club Unicorn was a gathering place that catered to, and celebrated, sexual confusion, debauchery and hedonistic experimentation on a grand scale. It was a home for the fringe; one that came with a hefty cover charge.

Muerce pulled up to the valet stand at the end of the pink and white striped awning that led from the curb to the entrance of Club Unicorn. He narrowly missed a man wearing heavy eye makeup, a toga, and sandals as he staggered into the street, and threw up.

The marque on the front of Club Unicorn announced that tonight's event was a costume celebration of "Nero's elevation to Princeps Luventutis." Muerce could see Titty Boy was throwing himself a toga party.

"What does that mean?" Travis said.

"I have no idea," Muerce said. "But Mister Tomaso will probably tell us... more than we want to know."

Muerce left his topcoat in the car, handed the valet the keys, and a hundred-dollar bill as he requested the Mercedes be parked as close by as possible. He wanted it available for a quick departure—if needed. It was a prudent expense, given the potential downside of Tomaso.

"She'll be right out front where I can keep an eye on her," the valet said. "The keys will be with me, and me with the keys. You 'betcha.'"

Muerce nodded to the valet and, with Travis in tow, headed toward the front door.

"Tickets," purred a diminutive, and overly effeminate man wearing a cherub costume. He was flanked by two large, hormone-pumped weight lifters dressed in Gladiator costumes. They were security, but the real muscle hovered in the shadows behind the cherub. Muerce caught the glint of light that bounced off a collection of gold chains that hung from a neck as thick as a tree stump. It was one of Titty Boy's crew. One of the dumber ones, hence his post at the front door.

"If you don't have tickets it's a hundred and fifty cover," the cherub purred, giving Muerce and Travis a come hither look. "But I should charge you more for not adhering to tonight's dress code."

"We have an appointment with Mister Tomaso," Muerce said, looking directly at the hulk in the shadows.

The cherub fluttered his false eyelashes, and swiveled on his padded stool.

"Vincent?" he said, lisping heavily.

Muerce smiled. *Vinny the Guinea. Buffoon Deluxe.*

The shape moved into the pink-cast light that illuminated the awning. Vinny wasn't as menacingly big as he appeared in the shadows. In the light he was just obese. He was dressed like a cliche with a purple silk shirt unbuttoned to his solar plexus, the gold chains catching and tugging his chest hair. Vinny wore an oversized, double-breasted grey sharkskin jacket that looked like it was tailored by a meat cutter.

"What's you're business with Tino, Merc?" Vinny said, putting an excessive and hard emphasis on the last consonant.

That nickname grated Muerce. He tolerated mispronunciations of his name most of his life. But this was more than that. The nickname was a misrepresentation. He was not a mercenary for hire. He didn't do favors for money, and he certainly didn't do them for immoral or illegal ends. They were chivalrous, he liked to think. A feudal duty ascribed by a high position in society. They also were acts of contrition—absolution for the past.

"Fuck you Vinny," Muerce said, indicating with a motion of his head for Travis to proceed inside. "Tino's expecting me. Call him like the good bitch that you are, and let him know I'm here. *Capiche stunade?*"

Muerce didn't give Vinny a second look, or react to the snicker the Cherub made. As Travis reached for the big brass handle of the door sculpted to the form of a naked woman—his thumb pressed on a breast—Vinny made a lame effort to respond.

"*Va fungule,*" he said, making an obscene motion with his hand.

Without looking back, Muerce raised his right hand and gave Vinny the finger as he entered Club Unicorn.

The interior of the club was an affront to all the senses. Sight, sound and smell were instantly saturated. The first attack came to his ear drums, which were penetrated by the piercing volume of the European techno pop blasting from the dance floor. Muerce's eyeballs twitched from the volume, and he could feel the walls, along with his chest, vibrate with each concussive beat. The air was humid with hormones, booze, sweat, and smoke. Strobe lights exploded in the darkness, freezing the costumed revelers on the dance floor in nauseating flashes of grotesque and menacing sexual postures. Glow sticks of every fluorescent color twirled and gyrated with the frantic masses. It was a Roman orgy that was spiritually Caligula, visually Hieronymus Bosch, and commercially all Titty Boy.

The place was a vat of earthly pleasures boiling over with sex and violence. The predominantly missing ingredient in the recipe was female—the kind formed in the womb.

"Ever been here before?" Muerce screamed at Travis, trying to be heard above the music.

"Once, during the daytime," Travis yelled back. *It wasn't like this.*

"Head to the bar," Muerce said, motioning with his hand toward the far end of the dance floor, which was where Titty Boy's private office was located. Muerce wanted to be closer to Tomaso, and get a drink to wash the taste of the place from his mouth. It was also relatively quieter with its secluded private party area. They would wait there for their audience with Titty Boy.

The music surged and pounded as they navigated through the tables of revelers that looked down on the dance floor. Muerce noted the extravagant costumes. He didn't know there was that much chiffon in the city, nor seamstresses to produce such historically correct robes, and gowns. Roman and Greek dress was the fashion for the evening. There were a few rough togas—interlopers Muerce guessed—but for the most part, the quality and style of the costumes was remarkable. There was a hierarchy to the patrons that was apparent.

The true transgenders were clearly the royalty of the place. Beneath them were the transvestites, then the casual cross dressers, who appeared to serve in the capacity of handmaidens and slave girls. The gays, comfortable with their God-given equipment, dressed as they desired—some as goddesses, some as senators, and poets. The aggressive body-builder types, like the two guys at the door, had opted to be Roman soldiers or gladiators—costume choices that allowed them to show off their sculpted physiques.

The hundred dollar pre-event ticket only got you in the door for the revelry. It didn't cover liquor, food, private party booths, or any of the number of illegal substances being sold discreetly, but consumed ostentatiously. Titty Boy owned all the action. Although he was making money, he also had spent a lot to transform Club Unicorn into an extravagant evening in Rome. And like the Roman emperors themselves, Titty Boy Tomaso spent lavishly for spectacle.

Though a one-story building, interior structural changes had been made that created three tiers of elevation. All of the basic infrastructure was painted or upholstered in black. The dance floor was the the concrete base of the warehouse/bar, which could be easily hosed down the next day. A small rise of about three feet that circled the interior of the building was home to the bar, a small stage for a DJ and dancers, and tables. On the back of the level that faced the stage were party booths, the VIP area, and another bar. Above the party booths, was a third level, which was the back wall of the building that had more tables.

The party booths were the exclusive reserve. There were nine vestibules. The middle private play booth was the largest and most expensive. It went for ten thousand dollars per event.

For tonight's celebration, Titty Boy replaced the tables and chairs in the party areas with pillows—large and small—and bed trays. Hundreds or yards of ornate, lustrous fabric hung on the walls of the booths, creating a lavish and tent-like feeling to the spaces. There were hookahs for smoking, as well as small brass receptacles that served as both vomitoriums, and trash receptacles for the condoms that had been sprinkled among the pillows like Easter eggs.

Muerce and Travis had to push and elbow their way past the first private area situated in front of the entrance to the dance floor. The location made it crowded with dancers, and gawkers. Many of the revelers were too stoned to move, and stood silently and trancelike, obstructing any path through. As hard as they tried to push through the zombies they made little headway.

Muerce was frustrated, and becoming uncomfortable and anxious. Amid the din of the music there was a repetitive voice that wandered and weaved through the stolid crowd.

"*Lasciate ogne speranza... lasciate ogne speranza... lasciate ogne speranza...*" the unseen voice cried out, over and over.

It was to Muerce and Travis as if the mantra came from no one, and everyone, and had the effect of giving them a supernatural feeling of impending doom. Muerce's high school Latin was rusty, but he recognized the word *abandon*.

Travis spoke, but Muerce did not hear him.

"What did you say," Muerce said, getting as near to Travis' ear as he could.

"I said this is some weird shit," Travis said.

Muerce nodded in agreement, and cursed himself for not choosing a different time on a different day to meet with Tomaso. There was no turning back, though it seemed uncertain if they would be able to get through the mass of bodies. Not until they were saved by Neptune.

"Get the fuck out of my way," Neptune, a portly, middle-aged man, yelled. He used his trident to poke and prod the crowd aside. "I'm the fucking King of the Seas, brother of Jupiter and Pluto, master of the equine. I command you to get the fuck out of my way."

The sea of drug-addled zombies parted.

Muerce gave a nod to Travis to follow in Neptune's wake, which provided them passage through the limbo of the listless throng that hung between the frenzy of the dance floor and the relative calm decadence of the party areas.

They had no sooner met up with Neptune then he was gone. Swallowed by the ocean of dancers. The path toward the bar, however, was clearer and would be easier to navigate.

As they bobbed and weaved their way through, Travis glanced at the second party area where a beautiful woman lay naked on her stomach. She rested on a square pedestal; her head supported by a white silk pillow; her body partially covered with a white silk shawl. She was turned so her back was to Travis, the roundness of her buttocks and shapely legs apparent to all who passed. Her gaze was on a pair of kneeling maidens across from her who were passionately kissing, and fondling each other's breasts. Travis was mesmerized, and mildly aroused. The scene was a lustful fantasy. The ivory skinned woman on the pedestal sensed Travis, and when she turned her head to look at him she exposed a small breast. She had a lovely face, and smiled at him. When he smiled back the two maidens, themselves caught in passion, raised their gowns to their waists and, with their free hands, began to vigorously fondle and stroke each other's erections. With a laugh, the woman on the pedestal turned herself completely over toward Travis, exposing both of her breasts, as well as her penis and testicles.

Muerce grabbed Travis, his face blank and stupid with the look of shocked innocence, and pulled him away. *Fairly artistic, play acting the Borghese Hermaphroditus.*

"Custody of the eyes," Muerce said.

"What?" said Travis.

"It's a prison term," Muerce said. "It means keep your eyes to yourself when you walk past someone else's cell. In other words, don't stare. Just keep moving."

"Okay, but how, I mean, she, uh he, her, I mean."

Muerce laughed, and kept moving as best he could with Travis in tow. *The miracle of modern medicine.*

The music stopped, but the sexual confusion continued.

There was relative calm at Club Unicorn as the DJ took a short break. The lights came up, but only slightly. Muerce knew the dance floor would begin to clear, and the party level would swell, making it nearly impossible to cross. As he and Travis inched their way toward the bar they passed the second vestibule where a half dozen revelers lay on pillows, and devoured plates of food spread about the space. In the center of the vestibule, a morbidly obese man wearing only a cloth thong reposed on a bed of large pillows. His face and upper torso were slathered with dark sauce, and bits of food. His mouth picked at a barbecue rib. The area smelled of flatulence and fresh bile. Another man, dressed as a Roman aristocrat, came over to the supine behemoth, and began licking the drippings from the fat man's chest.

"You cunt, it's mine," a voice in the fourth vestibule yelled in a campy and dramatic fashion.

"Share bitch, Dog bought the coke for everyone," another voice replied in an equally effeminate and dramatic manner.

Helen of Troy and a very pregnant and out-of-context Virgin Mary fought over a small bag of cocaine.

"Mine," Helen protested.

"No, mine," the Virgin replied.

"You think you're so special, give it to me," Helen said, yanking the cocaine, and the Virgin Mary toward him.

"I'm the Mother of God, cunt, the coke is mine," the Virgin said, pulling Helen, and the cocaine in his direction.

"I launched a thousand ships, slut, it's mine."

"Mine."

"No, mine."

A tall, athletically built black man costumed as a gladiator appeared and, with the open side of his right hand, slapped Helen across the face with enough force to spin the queen around. The Gladiator held out his left hand to receive the cocaine from the Virgin, who sheepishly handed it to him. With a quick and decisive motion, the Gladiator turned and slapped the Virgin with a backhand that caused the Mother of God to fall to his knees.

"I am Dog, bitches" he said. "I own the coke. And I own both of you."

The Gladiator opened the baggie, poured the powder into is hand, and held it at crotch level.

Helen of Troy and the Virgin Mary—a small trickle of blood running from the side of his mouth—eagerly scurried on their knees toward the Gladiator.

And from the hand of Dog they snorted coke.

Muerce and Travis retreated backwards from the greedy spectacle as the DJ, who had returned to his station, cued the next song. The opening chords of "Gimme Shelter" by the Rolling Stones heralded a sudden turning point for the evening, and sent a shiver through Muerce. He instinctively spun around, his fists clenched, to find the scalpel-sharp tip of a Roman *gladius* beneath his chin. The steel was real. The slight prick of the tip broke skin. A droplet of blood formed. Muerce looked down the shaft of the weapon. The hand that wielded the short sword was steady, firm and surprisingly delicate. The Centurion's face, dewey with sweat, was mostly hidden behind an Imperial helmet, chin strap, and wisps of facial hair that outlined tightly pressed lips. A purple scarf covered most of the Centurion's neck. Across the shoulders of Muerce's provocateur was a leopard skin attached to a red *paludamentum*. The cape half covered elaborate chest armor. The soldier also held the tip of a *puggio* to Muerce's ribs, ready to plunge the dagger into him if he moved.

Though the short sword pricked the skin where his jaw met his throat, Muerce felt as if he had already been skewered by the Centurion's eyes, which stared through him, unblinking, with a fierceness and anger that was purposeful, yet harbored a hint of fascination. It was a gaze of hatred and remorse Muerce had seen a long time ago, and it awoke in him a disturbing and perplexing attraction. Only these eyes now threatening him where of a biological aberration that was altogether new to him. The dilated pupils ran like a broken black egg yolk spilling over the bottom of brown and gold-flecked irises. They had a feline appearance.

Behind the Centurion was an entourage of four Roman soldiers, two on each side, brandishing spears and shields. They were body builder types. Their posturing was aggressive, but not as threatening as the Centurion's.

"It's just a shout away, it's just a kiss away," Mick Jagger wailed in the background.

The crowd around the fifth vestibule stood in silence, watching the provocation before them unfold. Muerce, his hands open and arms raised slightly in deference to his situation, remained quiet.

"Brother, yield your weapon," said a wisp of a transvestite costumed Aphrodite.

"We only want to go there," Travis said, pointing to the bar area. "We're here to see Tomaso."

"They mean us no harm," Aphrodite said, addressing the Centurion. "Let them pass Brother."

Aphrodite put his hand lightly on the edge of the sword. The Centurion slowly lowered, and returned it to its scabbard. When Muerce followed the weapon to its resting place with his eyes, they focused on an abnormally large bulge protruding from the front of the Centurion's tunic just below the waist.

The Centurion grunted and abruptly turned away, glancing back at Muerce in a menacingly pouty way. Muerce noted the shape of the Centurion's calves and ankles, and wondered how they would look in heels and a short cocktail dress.

"I know you," Aphrodite said, looking at Travis.

Muerce studied Aphrodite's face, which was framed by an elaborate and expensive blonde wig laced with flowers. Beneath the softly glittering makeup were the same shaped and pursed lips as the Centurion's. Aphrodite's eyes also had the broken pupils, and brown and gold-flecked irises; though there was a softness and frailness in Aphrodite that was not manifest in the Centurion.

Confusion raced through Muerce's thoughts. He was caught by the wholly unexpected arousal he felt after being pricked by the Centurion, who brandished weapons both lethal and carnal. Muerce wanted to chase after the Centurion, and come to blows.

"You said Brother," Muerce said, interjecting himself between Aphrodite and Travis. The tone caused Aphrodite to take a step back, and lower his gaze.

"She is my Brother," Aphrodite said. "And I am her Sister."

The response left Muerce more confused, and angry.

After the punch in the ribs in the car, Travis registered what an upset Muerce looked like before he struck. Travis was learning quickly. He stepped around Muerce, placing himself in front of the wilting Aphrodite.

"From Brambleton," Travis said, emphasizing his drawl.

Aphrodite raised his head and looked at Travis for a moment before recognition registered.

"You were a senior when I was a sophomore," Travis said.

"Ah, yes, the southern boy," Aphrodite said. "What a tasty little corn fritter we thought you were."

Travis affirmed Aphrodite's recognition with a nod, though he was unsettled at being categorized as a something to be consumed.

There was a shriek in the large vestibule behind Aphrodite. Everyone turned to see a bearded man holding a scythe pull a large set of bull testicles from a plastic Ziploc bag.

"Oh, I have to go," Aphrodite said. "It's time for me to be born."

A tall, thin man, wearing a long red wig helped Aphrodite step into a scalloped-shaped tub at the back of the party space. In one arm he held a red patterned silk sheet as Aphrodite undressed. Muerce and Travis watched as Aphrodite, devoid of any body hair, covered his genitals with the end of the blonde wig, and crossing his chest with his free arm, created the illusion of cleavage by squeezing his chest together.

The bearded man held the bull testicles above the small crowd that gathered around the spectacle.

"Your anus," he yelled, and threw the testicles into the sea shell basin, which was partially filled with water. A machine behind Aphrodite began to pump out volumes of foam as the spectators blew on the naked man-Venus, as if they were the four winds.

Muerce's anger eased at the sight of the campy portrayal of myth, and Botticelli's masterpiece. *Enough of this crap.*

"What was that about?" Muerce said, turning to Travis.

"What was what about?" Travis said.

Muerce gave Travis a flat look that he quickly interpreted.

"Oh, that," Travis said. "I'll explain it when we get to the bar. It's complicated." *And very weird.*

As they made their way toward the back bar, they passed the next vestibule. A man dressed as the Pope appeared to be blessing several men dressed as priests as they fondled several other younger men wearing white and black alter boy cassocks.

In the next party vestibule, a fist fight erupted. Muerce and Travis paid little attention to the altercation and kept moving. Nothing, and nobody, was as it or they should be at Club Unicorn. Not this night. Normal conventions—what was considered normal by most people—were bent and twisted for the evening. At least for a few hours, desires and fantasies normally held in check were let out of the closet.

Muerce couldn't shake the Centurion from his head. He had wanted to kiss the pursed lips when he first saw them, and lock into the cat's eyes. He was aroused by the shape of the Centurion's legs in retreat. There was a feminine smoothness to the aggressive features that struck him.

In the eighth party room a phalanx of mirrors had been set up. Revelers preened and postured in front of their reflections—greatly admiring their alter egos.

Muerce was still ruminating about the Centurion when a masculine Sprite of a maiden thrust a hand mirror in front of Muerce's face. At first, he did not recognize himself. He looked heavier, and older. *That couldn't be me.*

"Do you see?" the Sprite said. "Do you see? We are just fraud's to ourselves."

The Sprite danced and pranced around Muerce, taunting him; the surface of the reflection jammed nearly in his face.

"We look but we don't recognize," the Sprite said. "The mirror shows our souls, not what other people see, or what we want them to see.

"Do you see yourself? Do you see? Do you? See?"

Muerce saw that the night was not going as he had planned. Less than an hour earlier he was enjoying Miriam's company. Dinner with a beautiful, smart and accomplished woman. He recalled Miriam's dark and delicate hands, and the fragrance of her open palms, and the feel of her skin so long ago.

Behind him, in the reflection in the mirror in front of him, Muerce saw another face. A familiar face. The face that haunted him. She wore a yellow dress. Muerce spun around to look for her in the crowd. Bounding around Muerce, the Sprite tried to thrust the mirror back into Muerce's face but shrieked when Travis grabbed his wrist and twisted it. Falling to his knees, the Sprite dropped the hand mirror, shattering the glass into hundreds of shards.

"Fuck, my luck," the Sprite said, defeated. "You've ruined my luck."

The girl in the yellow dress had only been a fleeting apparition. Muerce was starting to see things that weren't there.

Travis released his grip on the Sprite, got Muerce's attention, and pointed toward the bar. A Minotaur waved at them. Pushing their way through the last throng of revelers attempting to get to the dance floor as the heavy beat of the techno-pop music began again, Muerce and Travis entered the relatively quiet zone for Club Unicorn. The last, most private, and nearly empty of the party areas was tucked into the corner. This was Titty Boy's domain. The VIP room. This was where you waited to do business.

The Minotaur removed his head. His shaved scalp dripped in perspiration from the headdress. It was Massimo, one of Titty Boy's crew. Muerce had done Massimo a favor several years back. Something he didn't want Titty Boy, or anyone else, to know about. Something Muerce, as he always did, kept to himself. When you brokered in favors, you brokered in confidences.

Massimo, who had an imposing body but worked hard to keep it that way between bouts of pasta and cocaine, gave Travis a wary look. Massimo was Titty Boy's enforcer. He had delivered the sore ribs as a reminder to Travis to pay what was due.

"Hey, Jack," Massimo said, nodding at Muerce though his eyes remained fixed on Travis.

"What's up Massy?" Muerce said. The two of them struck their fists together at the knuckles.

"Busting my ass trying to manage this freak show," Massimo said, turning to survey the debauchery around him. "Can you believe this shit? I think I've lost ten pounds.

"Look at it. The shit gets weirder and weirder. And you don't want to know what the place smells like in the morning. Goddamned medieval if you tell me. Looks like hell, don't it? Like a fucking Dutch painting."

"Bosch," Muerce said, with a hint of condescension.

"You know, I don't need your smug bullshit Merc," Massimo said, aggressively pressing himself toward Muerce. "You think you're so fucking highbrow. The Christian Brothers taught us a few things, too, you know. Hieronymus Bosch. Born 1450. Died 1516. Married Aleyt Gogaerts sometime between 1479 and 1481. Not a shit load more is known about his personality, or private life, but he was a member of an ultra Christian group called the Brotherhood of Our Lady. Probably a real strange fuck, who beat himself with whips and shit. Would have fit in here just fine. The guy's also credited with being one of the first artists in Northern Europe to produce autonomous sketches in his works."

Massimo took a step back from a surprised Muerce.

"The work we're referring to, here, tonight, is a panel that is part of Bosch's triptych referred to as "The Garden of Earthly Delights." I say referred to because Bosch never titled his works. Nor did he generally date his paintings. But I digress. The "Hell" panel of the triptych is probably his best known, and most reproduced masterpiece. Its surreal and psychedelic interpretations of mans' suffering for his sins make it very popular with stoners, and fire-and-brimstone preachers. It's a veritable fucking visual nightmare. Looking at it even scares the shit out of me. And while it appears to have come alive in this crap hole tonight, in actuality, the piece itself currently hangs in the Prado in Madrid.

"But the real poetry here, the Divine Comedy of the night, if you will, has been the sight of you two country club clowns in your baggy Brooks Brothers sports coats, and OCPDs trying to avoid getting ass ripped while groping your way through Tino's nine circles of Hell."

Massimo drew in a breath, calming himself.

"Fucking Virgil and Dante in middle-class drag, so don't get all pretentious on me asshole," Massimo said.

The three of them looked at each other for a moment. The sound of the dance floor was distant and muted in comparison to Massimo's outburst.

"Well, okay," Muerce said, puffing air out if his mouth in mock exasperation. "Sorry I fucking blew up, Massy."

"Ah, man, Jack, I'm sorry," Massimo said, his body slumping on the bar. "This whole event's been a pain in the ass. Tino's spent a ton of money on it, and getting the place pimped out the way it is, the extra security, the DJ flown in from Miami...

"But the topper was this fucking costume I've got to wear. It's crazy shit Tino's got us doing on top of regular business. I can't keep up."

Muerce thought Massy was about to breakdown and cry. He'd seen it before, but in private. Just between the two of them. He suspected Massy was bipolar, and mixing his prescribed meds with street drugs didn't help.

"You need some water Massy," Muerce said. "You're getting dehydrated in that thing. Being a Minotaur is hard work."

Travis, familiar with the side effects common to ecstasy users, anticipated Massimo's need to quench his parched mouth, and passed a glass of ice water he had ordered from the bartender to Muerce, who handed it to Massimo.

"Thanks, Jack," Massimo said, chugging the water. "Sorry about the Merc thing. I've been under a lot of pressure."

Muerce gave Massimo a look that dismissed the offense. Still, Muerce did not like that name.

Massimo and the bartender exchanged words by cupping a hand over each other's ear. Muerce turned his attention back toward the path he and Travis had taken through the party vestibules, and realized how ridiculous he and Travis must look. When Muerce turned his gaze to the dance floor, the Centurion was surrounded by her cohorts, making exaggerated sexual gestures to each other as they performed their frantic ballet. The Centurion, however, was affixed on Muerce. He was targeted by the cat eyes, which focused on him from the moment he arrived in the bar area, and during and after the exchange with Massimo.

Massimo saw the Centurion had noticed Muerce.

"Someone seems interested in you, Jackie boy," Massimo said. "Very interested."

Muerce nodded without looking at Massimo, and stared back at the Centurion.

"That one's bent, Jack," Massimo said. "Really bent. So folded and twisted you don't know where she begins, and where she ends. You don't want to go there."

Muerce was listening, but he didn't hear Massimo. He couldn't take his eyes off the Centurion who lifted her tunic, exposing a large, black strap-on dildo. She grabbed it at its base and, laughing, wagged the silicone phallus at Muerce as she mocked thrusting it at him.

"I told you, bent and twisted," Massimo said, switching subjects quickly. "Tino knows you're here. He's got business with the Dragon right now."

Massimo motioned to the bartender with his fingers that drinks for Muerce were *gratis.*

"On the house while you wait, whatever you want," Massimo said, lifting the Minotaur headdress from the bar. "I've got to make the rounds. Tino shouldn't be much longer.

"But I'll warn you, he's not going to be in a good mood. This Dragon guy's been busting our balls lately."

Massimo lifted the Minotaur head over his own and onto his shoulders.

"Massy," Muerce said, raising his voice so Massimo could hear him through the costume. "Remind me, what is the ninth circle of hell?"

"Treachery, Jack. Treachery."

As he walked past Travis, Massimo patted him on the shoulder.

"Hey man, I gotta do what I gotta do. Just business, you know, nothing personal," Massimo said, his voice muffled by the costume.

Muerce had had enough of the Centurion's obscene play acting, and turned his attention to the bar and Massimo's offer for free drinks. He swore he could hear the Centurion pouting when he turned away.

"Scotch, neat," he ordered.

When the cocktail arrived, Muerce took a long pull from the glass, and let the scotch filter down his throat and fill him with a welcome warmth. His thoughts were still on the Centurion when he realized another set of eyes were upon him. They belonged to a middle-aged man standing at the far end of the bar. He was wearing a three-piece business suit that was well tailored. He was equally out of place as both Muerce and Travis, which meant only one thing—the man also had business with Tino. That the man had an Eastern European look about him led Muerce to conclude he had something to do with this Dragon Massimo mentioned. Muerce had never heard the name before. *Who, or what, is the Dragon?*

At the same time Muerce noticed the well-appointed man at the end of the bar, he saw Travis taking a picture with the camera on his phone. Muerce abruptly grabbed it from Travis' hand.

"What are you doing?" Muerce said.

"Are you kidding?" Travis said, innocently, and with some youthful excitement. "This place is sick. I was going to post some photos."

Muerce frowned and fingered the delete button on the photos Travis had just taken, making sure all of them were erased from the menu. Then he handed the phone back to Travis, and drew closer so he could be heard. *A teaching moment.*

"My business is my reputation," Muerce said. "And my reputation is wholly dependent upon being discreet. Discretion, in this line of work, is power. Power lets me get things done. Like what I need to get done for you tonight. Do you understand?"

"Yes, I got it," Travis said, sheepishly.

"It's okay," Muerce said. "Part of the learning curve. But let's keep the curve to a minimum. We're not on Facebook. For the time being, I'm your only friend. Can we do that?"

"We can do that, Mister Muerce," Travis said.

That Muerce was more tutorial than angry had a much bigger effect on Travis than he first expected. Travis felt Muerce granted him some trust, and Travis liked that Muerce might have confidence in him. Who Muerce was, what Muerce did interested Travis. *I could learn a thing or two from this guy.*

"Now, tell me about the complicated brother and sister Brambleton twins," Muerce said. "What was that about?"

"It's fucked up, Mister Muerce," Travis said. "You sure you want to know?"

Muerce stroked the area where his neck met his jaw. He felt something, and rubbed at it.

"You're bleeding," Travis said.

Muerce grabbed a cocktail napkin from the bar, dipped it into his scotch, and pressed it against the wound. A rivulet of blood ran down his neck, staining the top of the knot of his tie, and a small area on the collar of his shirt. The stinging of the single malt antiseptic made him think of the Centurion's legs, and the strangeness and fierceness in her eyes. For a fleeting moment he wondered what it would be like to kiss those pursed lips, and if they would yield.

"I think I've earned it," Muerce said. "Go on."

"Paige and Price Sharron," Travis said. "That's Sharron with two r's."

"Why do I care about that?" Muerce said.

"They're very emphatic about it. A twin thing I guess, and they pronounce it *sharing*."

"Paige and Price. Which is which?"

"Price is the less aggressive one."

"Go on."

"They are incredibly close, even for twins," Travis said. "I had a huge crush on Paige. Every guy did, but from a distance. And she knew it. She was a senior, and I was a sophomore. It was never going to happen."

Muerce raised his eyebrows at Travis.

"You wouldn't know it by her getup or acting out tonight, but she's pretty damned hot."

Muerce knew she was. The flash of teeth, an exposed ankle, the hint of a long neck line, and just the right amount of exposed decolletage. He'd been undressing women in his head since puberty, and was quite good at it.

"There more?"

"Unfortunately, while I and every other guy in the school had a crush on her, Price had a crush on me."

Muerce raised his eyebrows again.

"Not my thing," Travis said, emphatically.

"And, yet, here you are," Muerce teased.

"This was your idea, Mister Muerce," Travis said.

"So it was," Muerce replied, draining the last of the liquor from his glass, and looking around. He caught the man at the end of the bar staring at him and Travis. The man lifted his glass as if to offer Muerce a refill. Muerce looked away quickly, and with as much disinterest as possible.

"That it?" Muerce said.

"There was a rumor, right before they graduated, that something went down between them and one of the teachers. It was all wild talk of a threeway or something. You know how it goes in high school. It was probably nothing, but the gossip chain exploded into things like whips and chains, and farm animals."

"Farm animals?" Muerce said.

"I'm exaggerating."

"And?"

"We showed up for school the next fall, that teacher didn't."

"And since?" Muerce said.

"They went off to college, but I don't think either of them still go," Travis said. "I've seen them at a few raves, but I keep my distance."

Muerce dabbed at his wound, and tossed the blood-splotched napkin into his empty cocktail glass. Travis pointed to it.

"You can see why I give them plenty of space."

Muerce amused himself with the irony of the double entendre. *I literally got the point.* Still, he could not erase the shape of her legs, or the pursed lips.

"You are Jack Muerce, are you not?"

It was the man from the end of the bar. That the man knew Muerce's name and spoke with a distinctly Eastern European accent presented a new perspective.

"My name is Krzytof Zajak," he said, offering his hand to Muerce.

"I am, as you said, Jack Muerce," he said, reaching out to accept the handshake.

Zajak shook Muerce's hand with the right amount of pressure to communicate friendship and strength without intimidation. Muerce took measure of Zajak. They were both about the same height and same age, but that's where their similarities ended. Zajak's narrow facial features, slim build, long, fine fingers, and thick, dark hair—that was obviously dyed—reminded Muerce of a ferret. Zajak wore an expensive blue silk suit, that despite the excellent tailoring, he managed to make look bad.

"This is, perhaps, a serendipitous meeting?" Zajak said.

"Doubtful," Muerce said.

"I don't, Mister Muerce, doubt it at all," Zajak said with a confidence as firm and balanced as his handshake. "In fact, our meeting tonight is quite fortunate. For both of us. Don't you think?"

"How is that?" Muerce said.

"I have my gypsy roots, Mister Muerce," Zajak said. "We must trust our instincts, and our instincts are born from our faith in who we are and where we are from. Wouldn't you say so?"

Zajak raised his right arm, and motioned toward Titty Boy's VIP booth.

"Please, I would very much like to have you, and your *friend*, join our little party. That would be okay?"

The emphasis on *friend* carried an inference that irritated Muerce. But it did raise the question in Muerce as to what Travis' role was to be, if anything. The words that came from Muerce's mouth both surprised him, and solidified how Travis would satisfy his debt.

"This is Travis Squire, Mister Zajak," Muerce said. "He's not my *friend*. He works for me."

"Ah, Squire," Zajak said, his face intently focused on Muerce. "Of course, what is a knight without a squire?"

"I am pleased to meet him as well. Will you join us?"

The look on Travis' face left no doubt he was flabbergasted and pleased by Muerce's comments. Muerce gave a quick glance to Travis that communicated he should keep quiet and go with it. Travis understood the look. He was beginning to understand Muerce very well. Travis was a quick study. That was an asset Muerce valued.

"We're here on business," Muerce said.

"As am I, Mister Muerce," Zajak said. "Or should I say my employer is here on business. He's with Mister Tomaso right now. We might as well enjoy ourselves while we wait. And we could get to know each other a little better. Don't you think?"

In the short exchange of conversation Muerce was able to deduce a number of things about Zajak, the most important of them being that he liked to end almost every sentence with a question. It was a bullshit trick used to ingratiate the listener. What it really was about was control. Muerce could use that to his advantage, if needed, as long as he was careful, and patient.

"Might I inquire, if it's appropriate, as to your employer?" Muerce said.

Zajak's smile in response to the question made the muscles in Muerce's lower back tighten, and tripped several warnings in his head.

"I should be more declarative with you, Mister Muerce," Zajak said. "I work for Zmaj Brankovic. Most people know him as the Dragon."

-- --

The name hung as heavy as a chlorine cloud as the three of them made their way from the bar toward the private booth in the corner. A large, simian-looking man in his late twenties, and wearing a black leather coat with a sheen that matched the gel in his hair, sat in the booth. The ape-like man's head bounced and swayed to the metallic beat of the music pounding out on the dance floor. He seemed oblivious to the two women that flanked him—and they to him—although every male heterosexual— of which there were relatively few—had their eyes welded on the pair of women. They were not your normal working girls, not even a cut above. They were what the vice squad guys referred to as "collectibles." They were primped, preened, and pretty. What was also obvious besides their stunning looks, and fashionable clothes, was they were somebody's property. The phrase that popped into Muerce's head was what you saw at the pump of a late-night gas station, "prepay inside." "Primo" was the word that sprang into Travis's head. But he was on the other side of youth from Muerce, and as they neared the booth, the next word that came to Travis' mind was "priapism." He began to mouth algebra equations, and visions of dead kittens to suppress the preliminary signs of pressure building in his pants.

Zajak motioned for the man to get up from the couch, which he did obediently with a nod of his head. The man was much broader in the shoulders, and taller than Muerce figured him to be when he was seated. He also seemed relieved to be dismissed from his babysitting duties.

There were no introductions. Zajak directed Travis to sit on the outside of the girl on the right. Her eyebrows were blonde above the heavy eye makeup, as was her shoulder-length hair. She arched her eyebrows with delight when Travis sat next to her. Travis was handsome, and much closer to her age than the men she came in contact with everyday. Travis was a welcome diversion, and she positioned her body toward him in a flirty, and precocious manner. He was flattered, and fell into fast conversation with her. The two of them melted into their own world.

Zajak said something in Croatian to the other girl, who dismissively acknowledged Muerce with a glance that went right through him. She sat upright, as if at attention. Her long legs were crossed and clearly on display, with the aid of a very short and stylishly revealing black cocktail dress that was punctuated by black Manolo Blahnik stilettos. She turned her blank attention back toward the dance floor, and took a drag off of the cigarette she held in her right hand. She made it look like poetry. The curl of the smoke from the cigarette, how she held it with her long fingers, was exhilarating. She tilted her head back when she exhaled, giving a sort of balance to her. The lights from the dance floor backlit the smoke and gave contrast to her dark, short-cropped hair. It highlighted what Muerce thought were the most perfect cheek and jawbone lines he had seen in a long time.

A bottle of champagne arrived at the table. Zajak poured five glasses, and passed them around. The blonde with Travis made a toast Muerce didn't hear, and brushed several strands of hair back from her forehead.

"To good luck in your business tonight, Mister Muerce," Zajak said, clinking the glass flute with Muerce's. "And to our fortuitous meeting."

The stoic brunette consumed the contents of her glass without averting her gaze from the dance floor, clearly disinterested in Muerce.

"A bit presumptuous, but the champagne is very good," Muerce said, holding his hand over his now empty glass to indicate he did not wish a refill. *Enough of the booze. I still have business with Titty Boy.*

"Too much too soon, perhaps," Zajak said. "I don't wish to overstep myself Mister Muerce."

Zajak removed a business card from his coat, and offered it to Muerce.

"I don't expect you to reciprocate, Mister Muerce," Zajak said. "To receive a card from you is not taken lightly. They are earned. I'm thinking more in the future. In the meantime, perhaps, I can do you a favor?"

"Favors are earned," Muerce said. "Or deserved."

"Deals can be brokered."

"I don't make deals," Muerce said, pocketing the card without looking at it.

"Of course you don't," Zajak said, pouring himself another glass of champagne. "Forgive me, your reputation is above that."

Muerce interpreted the comment as condescending, and gave Zajak a disapproving look.

"Perhaps a token," Zajak said. "A token given in good faith."

"And what would that be?" Muerce said.

"To be cautious and sympathetic when you meet with Mister Tomaso," Zajak said. "He is just now receiving unexpected bad news that one of his, shall we say, franchises, is being absorbed. And without any compensation. He will, undoubtedly, be in an unpleasant mood."

"Which franchise?"

"Let's just say Mister Tomaso can still provide condiments, but no longer the meat with which they are served."

Zajak made a motion with his right hand indicating, as an example, the young woman seated by Travis. The dark-haired girl was not part of the equation.

"Clearly, we provide a much higher quality product than what Mister Tomaso has been able to offer."

"And the drugs, I mean condiment business?"

"I suspect, in time, that will change hands as well," Zajak said, crossing his legs, and leaning back into the couch. "Brankovic has no immediate plans."

"But you do?"

Zajak coyly smiled, and sipped his champagne.

"So the Dragon is taking over the prostitution business?" Muerce said. "Or is it you, Mister Zajak?"

"Another token," Zajak said. "I would not use the name Dragon in his presence any more than I would Mister Tomaso's moniker in his. Or yours you."

"And what's yours?" Muerce said.

"I'm an accountant, Mister Muerce." Zajak said. "I'm invisible. I have no name, no reputation. I am what you like to call in this country, Teflon."

"And if the Dragon knew you were talking to me like this?"

"I would be consumed by fire," Zajak said. "That would be, of course, after pieces of me had been torn from my body, and then sewn back together. That is Zmaj's way. His reputation. It is barbaric, but in his time the results have been effective.

"Still, I feel it unnecessary, and ultimately bad for business."

Muerce leaned back into the couch contemplating the brunette, who had worked the cigarette in her hand and mouth as she would a man. When she finished either, Muerce suspected, nothing more than a pile of ash would remain.

"Don't waste your time, she is as invisible on the inside as I am on the outside," Zajak said. "It is her most endearing quality. Of that I am most certain."

There was a dark fluttering about the bar as if a camp of bats had been disturbed, and now swooped and careened from the ceiling tiles as they would the walls of a cave. The music from the dance floor died, and there was only the sound of beating wings. The crowd stood silently. Some grinned, others were slack-jawed in awe of the lighting, and sound effects. All were giddy with anticipation and unsure what would happen next.

Unable to see the stage from the back area of the bar, Muerce flinched when he heard a high-pitched scream blast through the sound system. The voice was female. He jumped to his feet, and looked around. Travis and the blonde were unfazed, and continued their harmless flirtation. Zajak looked up nonchalantly at Muerce as if to ask what was happening. The brunette's gaze forward was unwavering. Her only reaction was to light another cigarette.

A second, higher pitched, screaming female voice joined the first. Then a third, pitched even higher than the first two. The three built to a crescendo. Standing, Muerce could see the spotlight on the trio of women on the stage.

This went on for almost a minute until, just as the voice of the first screamer showed signs of strain the DJ cued "Desire" by the Irish band U2. The song ignited a frenzy of dancing throughout the club. It was an explosion of light, sound and movement that agitated all five senses. The experience was consuming at first, but as the strobe lights subsided, and his ability to discern reality returned, Muerce comprehended the arrival of a tangible malevolence.

Zmaj Brankovic's business with Titty Boy was over. The Dragon now stood across the short table from Muerce. A cigarette dangled from his mouth, which he lit with a unique sterling silver lighter. The flame illuminated a dark, and menacing silhouette.

Muerce had never heard his name until tonight. His first impression was that the man before him had the most convincing costume of the evening—that of Lucifer. As instantly as that impression flitted through Muerce's head it was gone. There was, Muerce realized, no masquerade regarding Brankovic.

At six-foot-seven, weighing about two-hundred and forty pounds, Brankovic's size was imposing, though it was his features that were his most sinister physical aspect. Brankovic suffered from trigoncephaly, a congenital condition caused by the premature fusion of the metopic suture of the skull. That, coupled with an abnormally long jaw line, resulted in an oblong, triangular shaped head, which Brankovic accentuated by framing in shoulder-length hair that had streaks of gray, and formed a kind of mane. Each of his bushy gray eyebrows were trimmed to a point above the outside corner of his eyelids, which were small in comparison to the rest of his face. It could be the poor lighting in the club, but Muerce was unable to discern iris from pupil in the orbs, which did not reflect any light. Brankovic's chin was covered by a graying goatee that compounded the distorted length of his head. Brankovic's mouth was moving, smoke-laden words emanated from it, but Muerce was so fixed on the sharp and yellowish teeth, he did not hear what Brankovic said. There was only the sound of Bono screaming through the sound system.

The man's appearance left no doubt how Brankovic came by his nickname. The brutal reputation that Muerce was only now becoming aware of obviously grew from an unfortunate set of biological circumstances. Still, what had once been a man, was now more creature.

Brankovic, who wore a black leather duster, stood directly in front of Muerce, but acted as if he did not exist. The Dragon was clearly upset at somebody, or something, as he waved his arms in a variety of demonstrative gestures. When he did so, the leather coat flapped as if they were wings, and Brankovic was about to take flight. The violence of yelling that Muerce could not hear, but discerned was being said in Croatian, shot from Brankovic's mouth like flames. There was a smell of something burnt that Muerce detected on Brankovic. He smelled of sulphur.

Muerce turned to Zajak, who was now standing, his eyes cast down toward the coffee table. On the other side of Zajak the brunette also stood, her focus affixed to a point in the distance. Muerce watched her as she took a draw from the cigarette that consumed a good quarter of the tobacco. A large stem of ash fell from the end of the cigarette. Muerce thought she was as frosty as they came until he saw a small bead of sweat trace its way down the back of her face before coming to rest on her ear lobe.

Brankovic swept passed Muerce, who turned his attention to Travis sitting on the couch next to the blonde girl. The look on Travis' face was a melange of surprise, fear and indignation. In the next instant the cause of Brankovic's anger was apparent.

The Dragon grabbed the blonde girl's hair, and violently pulled her up from the couch. Dangling in the air, and unable to support her weight as she struggled to reach the floor with the toes of her knee-length leather boots, the girl began to scream in pain. Her cries went unheard above the music. What happened next froze Muerce.

Brankovic, yelling directly into the girl's ear in Croatian, released her hair. As she regained her balance on the unsteady high-heeled boots, the Dragon lifted up the back of her short skirt, exposing her buttocks. He grabbed the small triangle of her pink, lace thong at the same time he stomped down hard with the heel of his shoe onto the toes of her left foot. He then pulled the thong up her back until it nearly reached the bottom of her shoulder blades, lifting her off the ground. He again grabbed her hair so she did not completely fall forward, and into Travis' lap. Cantered forward, the girl's face contorted in pain. She was no more than two feet from Travis' face. Big drops of tears fell into his lap. Her nose began to run, wetting her mouth and chin as she choked through the pain, and struggled to breath in the panic.

Brankovic pulled the girl away, and with a firm grip on her hair and panties, extended the humiliation by marching her off, and out the back door of Club Unicorn as if she were a marionette. He was followed by two bodyguards Muerce had not noticed standing behind Brankovic when the Dragon made his appearance.

As the initial shock wore off, Travis made a move to bolt from the sofa and pursue, but Muerce waved him down. *This is not our business.*

The bodyguard who was with the two girls when they came from the bar with Zajak quickly followed behind. The brunette crushed out her cigarette, retrieved her purse, and gave an unfazed look at Zajak, who was now standing next to Muerce.

Zajak let the parade exit the club. The U2 song ended, and there was a pause of silence before the DJ played the next selection.

"Remember," Zajak said, whispering into Muerce's ear. "Wherever there is a dragon, there is a dragon slayer."

The violent scene had not gone unnoticed. Paige Sharron relaxed her two-handed grip on the *gladius* as Zajak exited the club. She felt the ache of the muscles of her forearms, wrists and fingers as the blood in her body began to circulate normally, and her heartbeat slowed with the ebbing of adrenalin that fueled her rage. Paige stood at the far end of the bar, watching and waiting to strike if the ferocious monster in the long black coat made a move on Muerce. She had planned her attack, calculating she had about twenty strides in which to pick up enough forward momentum to drive the sword at an upward angle into, and just below the monster's left shoulder blade, through his heart, and out his chest. With the sword plunged to its hilt, she would then snatch the razor sharp *puggio* from its place on her waist belt, grab the monster's mane of hair with her left hand as he stood in shock, pull herself up and his head back as she planted her right foot above his right hip. Then she would have slashed his exposed neck from ear-to-ear.

What Paige didn't know, what she had not even begun to process, was why she was motivated to kill a man she had never seen before—nor wanted to see again—to protect and defend another man she did not know, and whose blood she had spilled within the past hour. She had never killed before, yet she was willing to sacrifice herself for Muerce.

The other thing she didn't know was the only way to kill a Dragon was to cut off its head.

— —

Titty Boy's private office was an oasis of quiet compared to what was happening outside the sound-proofed red door that led to his sanctuary. Despite Titty Boy's temper tantrum and launching items from his desk that landed with crashes around the office, the room was more calming to Muerce than expected—Cosentino, "Tino," "Titty Boy" Tomaso he knew. Dramatic. Mean. Capricious, and oftentimes violent. But predictable. Muerce counted on it as he and Travis stood quietly and patiently as Titty Boy acted out after his meeting with the Dragon.

"Motherfucker," Titty Boy said, throwing and expensive Baccarat crystal bowl full of jelly beans against the wall. It shattered into a thousand shards. "That motherfucking, cocksucking, foreign freak motherfucker. Who the fuck does he think he is telling me my fucking business?"

"Well, who the fuck does the cocksucker think he is?"

The question was directed at Massimo, who had shed his Minotaur head before escorting Muerce and Travis into the office.

"He's a bastard cocksucker boss," Massimo said.

Titty Boy stopped abruptly, looked at Massimo in disbelief, and threw a small desk clock at him.

"*Va fungool, stunade,*" Titty Boy yelled at Massimo. "I wasn't asking you a fucking question. It was rhetorical you shit brain. Jesus fucking Christ, I have shit brains all around me.

"Jesus, Mary and Joseph, have mercy on me. Mercy, mercy, mercy."

"Yeah, I'm here Tino," Muerce said.

Titty Boy's demeanor turned on a dime. He threw his hands in the air, and smiled.

"Fuck you Muerce," he said, rolling the leather desk chair back to its place behind a large, chrome and glass desk. Titty Boy took in a deep, meditative cleansing breath, sat down, and exhaled. He was the picture of calm.

Titty Boy did not look at all like he acted. If he was a cliche, he was the unexpected cliche. Titty Boy was only a handful of years younger than Muerce, but looked like he was in his late twenties. He had a thick head of dark hair with just the right amount of wave and curl to it that women loved. His facial structure looked like it had been carved from marble by Michelangelo. Good genes, and a blessing from God provided Titty Boy with a physique that required very little effort to remain toned and trimmed. And the entire package was wrapped in olive skin so creamy and flawless that Muerce had to wonder if Titty Boy ever had to shave. *Titty Boy the Pretty Boy.*

In addition to his physical attributes, Titty Boy had a sense of style that Muerce found difficult not to admire. The office decor, straight from the best designers in Milan, reflected sophisticated taste. So did his clothes, which he travelled to Italy to be fitted for twice a year. His favorite designer was Brunello Cucinelli.

The Titty Boy panache was evident even as he sat behind the desk, his hair slicked forward in the "Caesar" style, and adorned with a gold-leaf corona. The toga he wore was made from expensive Egyptian cotton, and had been tailored to flatter his body. On his feet were custom Roman period sandals hand-made for tonight's celebration. They had been produced—by special request and at a considerable sum—by the same shop that made the Pope's red slippers.

Titty Boy put his hands, palms down, on the desk and arched back in the chair. He motioned for Muerce to take a seat in one of the two red leather and chrome chairs on the other side of the desk. Both Muerce and Travis moved to take their seats, but Titty Boy frowned at Travis and waved, dismissively, for him to remain standing by the office door.

"So, we have a delinquent delinquent, and you're here to make a bargain," Titty Boy said.

"No bargain Tino," Muerce said, as he sat down. "We're here to make it square."

Titty Boy contemplated Muerce's words.

"You said, *we*."

"That's right," Muerce said.

Titty Boy stroked the side of his face with his forefinger.

"What's the freight Massimo?" Titty Boy said, his eyes glued to Muerce.

Massimo produced a small notebook, and flipped through the pages. Then he fingered his iPhone on, and began to work the calculator application.

"Twenty grand over two stakes," Massimo said.

Muerce removed the envelope with the cash from his jacket, placed it on the desk, and slid it toward Titty Boy.

"And the juice?" Titty Boy said, still staring at Muerce.

Massimo worked the buttons on the phone in quick succession.

"Seven percent."

"How deep is he?" Titty Boy said. He and Muerce were now in a staring contest to see who would blink first.

"Two weeks, so seven percent on top of seven percent."

Titty Boy, still staring at Muerce, mockingly lifted his arm to check the time on a wristwatch that did not exist.

"It's already tomorrow somewhere in the world, so roll seven percent on top of that."

The faintest of smiles crept across Muerce's face.

"The vig is about thirty four hundred," Massimo said.

Muerce's smile pissed off Titty Boy, who decided to retaliate and throw a dagger into the negotiation.

"Let's not forget the ten percent servicing fee for the loan," Titty Boy said. He gave Muerce a victorious and smug look, then averted his gaze.

Muerce, however, did not waver.

"Total bite, five thousand four hundred," Massimo said. "You want to roll it, Jack."

Muerce slowly stood up, his eyes affixed on Titty Boy, who begrudgingly returned his attention to the other side of his desk. Muerce reached into the left front pocket of his trousers, and pulled out a one-hundred gram, loaf-style gold bar that bore the likeness of Fortuna, the Roman God of Fortune. The bar made a distinctive sound, as if announcing the weight of its value, when Muerce tossed it onto a leather folder on Titty Boy's desk. The glass desk rattled when it landed.

"That ought to do it," Muerce said, smiling broader.

Titty Boy pulled the folder with the gold bar toward him.

"Massimo, Google Friday's close for a hundred-gram PAMP Suisse gold bar."

Massimo did, and the answer appeared on his screen far sooner than he expected given the generally poor cellular service inside Club Unicorn.

"Makes us even, boss," Massimo said. "Maybe even a little over."

"Keep it Tino," Muerce said. "Consider it our cover charge for tonight."

Titty Boy stood up and bounced the gold bar in his hand, appreciating the weight of the bullion.

"Style Jack, real style," he said, as he walked around the desk toward Muerce. "But tell me. The *we?*"

"The kid works for me now," Muerce said.

"Jack Muerce, with a partner?" Titty Boy said. "Oh hell, what's the world coming to? Fucking Superman needs help? Or are you human like Batman?"

"No partner, more like a temporary intern who belongs to me," Muerce said. "Call it insurance. Now that he's clean, nobody touches him. And, especially, nobody takes a bet from him. Even if it's for the weather tomorrow."

"Got it Yogi, no more bets from Boo-Boo bear," Titty Boy said. "Hear that Massy? Don't fuck with junior anymore."

"Got it boss."

"Oh you dumb shit, motherfucker," Titty Boy erupted. "It was a rhetorical statement. Get the fuck out of here now before I shove this gold bar up your ass until I can pull it out of your nose.

"And take Tonto with you."

Muerce, his business complete, turned to leave with Massimo and Travis. He was intent on getting out of there without owing Titty Boy any favors.

"Hold up for a second," Titty Boy said, moving closer to Muerce. "I need to talk to you about something."

Muerce felt like he was about to eat a piece of sushi he knew was bad.

Titty Boy moved to such close proximity of Muerce, that he wasn't sure if Titty Boy was going to knee him in the testicles, or kiss him, or both. Titty Boy squinted at Muerce's shirt collar, and poked his head forward before running his finger beneath Muerce's chin.

"Quite the fashion statement," Titty Boy said, rubbing the coagulated remains of Muerce's wound between his fingers. "I didn't think blood was your thing."

"And I never thought I'd see the day when you were caught with blood on your hands," Muerce said.

"You're a funny fuck, Merc," Titty Boy said, a spark of anger in his voice.

Muerce felt his own anger about to get the better of him.

"Not as funny as, say, Titty Boy," Muerce said, slowly and with emphasis.

Titty Boy bit the inside of his lip, then took another deep cleansing breath, and walked back around his desk and sat down.

"How are those Lamaze classes working for you, or is it the yoga?" Muerce said.

"Okay, we've got the personal attacks out of the way," Titty Boy said. "I want to talk about that thing that was in here before you."

"Brankovic?"

"Yeah, fucking Creature from the Black Lagoon," Titty Boy said. "A real monster piece of shit. And he's trying to muscle me."

"That's none of my business," Muerce said.

"You know him?"

"Never heard of him before tonight," Muerce said. "But yeah, he's a real piece of work."

"A monster."

"So have Massy look under your bed before you go to sleep," Muerce said. "What's it got to do with me?"

Titty Boy made several contortions with his face before he spoke.

"One of his whores turned up dead, and I heard you're involved," he said.

"I made an ID on the body, and a call about an abandoned kid," Muerce said. "It's also my understanding she is, was, one of Mikal's girls."

"That retarded pimp? Brankovic owns Deluxe."

"When did that happen?" Muerce said.

"Last year when the freak landed in town," Titty Boy said. "Where have you been? Brankovic is like going to the beach. Sand in fucking everything."

"I guess you'll stop going to the beach, but, again, this is not my business," Muerce said.

"I think he killed her."

"Killed who?"

91

"The whore," Titty Boy said. "Chopped her up and put her back together like Humpty Dumpty. That's his thing."

The bad sushi feeling in Muerce's stomach took a turn for the worse when the image of Redzil's dismembered body flashed in his head.

"Then call the TIPS hotline," Muerce said. "Maybe you'll even get a reward, and your picture in the paper with the Mayor."

"Funny fuck," Titty Boy said, hesitating to use the nickname. "A real funny fuck."

"Yeah, I'm a funny guy Tino, you can catch my act at the airport Holiday Inn sometime," Muerce said, standing up to leave. "Are we done?"

"I'm just saying, Jack, you should look into it."

"None of my business Tino," Muerce said.

"You will, you're too nice a guy," Titty Boy said. "You can't help yourself. It's who you are."

Just as he was about to open the door to leave, Muerce turned to Titty Boy, who had a distant look in his eyes as he bounced the loaf of gold in his hand.

"We're straight?" Muerce said.

The question interrupted Titty Boy's thoughts. It took him a second before answering.

"Straightest thing there is around here tonight."

— —

A half an hour passed in the car after they left the club before either spoke a word.

"Excuse me for asking, but what the hell just happened tonight?" Travis said.

Muerce laughed. It was after midnight, and the air had turned colder and damper. Muerce fiddled with the defroster controls on the dashboard of the Mercedes to clear the thin film of fog that crept up the inside of the windshield.

"For starters, you're off the hook with Tomaso," he said.

"That's the only part that makes sense to me," Travis said. "Was I tripping? Did you spike my drink with acid or something?"

"No."

"And now I work for you?"

"Yes," Muerce said. "Are you good with that?"

Travis shook his head, amazed, pleased, and intrigued.

"Yeah, I'm good with that," he said. "Is every night like this with you?"

"You kind of liked it didn't you?" Muerce said, amused.

"Kind of did," Travis said.

Muerce spent the next quarter of an hour as they neared the Squire residence outlining the scope of Travis' duties. He would be required to run menial errands, like picking up his laundry, and all that entailed with the Trungs, but the majority of his responsibilities would be done in research. Most of that would be accomplished by computer, which would be set up by Muerce's IT guy. As a joke, Travis thought about asking Muerce if he should get a tattoo of a dragon, but given what happened in the bar at Club Unicorn, he decided against it.

Travis was to arrange to be dropped off at Muerce's apartment by nine in the morning on Monday. Muerce would provide him with a car for the errands, and explain the rest of his duties then.

Muerce pulled up the cobbled circle drive in front of the Squire home—a massive brick Georgian with white trim and large, black plantation shutters.

"No," Muerce said, leaning down to catch Travis' attention as he exited the Mercedes.

"No what?"

"No, every night isn't like tonight."

Travis leaned back into the car.

"Too bad," he said. "See you Monday morning Mister Muerce."

CHAPTER 9

Muerce collected the mail from the table in the foyer. The door to the private elevator closed with a catch that he noted should be addressed with the building superintendent. Muerce leafed through the mail without paying any attention to it and gave up, clutching the small bundle under his arm. He was aware of the sound he made walking across the marble floor, and how the dull click gave way to a soft brush when he transitioned onto the thick pile carpet of the living room. There was a residual shrill ringing in his ears. The inevitability of age. His thoughts were in overdrive, and bounced from one image of the night to another. He tried to fit them all together into a complete collage. But he couldn't.

Muerce was tired. He needed a drink. He needed some sleep. He had the feeling he had been pushed into a rushing river, and was being swept downstream in the current, and there was no way to make it to the bank. He would take a Xanax to quiet the voices in his head. He was home. He was safe. This was his castle. His refuge.

Fumbling through his pockets, his fingers stumbled on Zajak's business card. It was a clever design that he thought Ashley's marketing firm might have come up with. The card was made from clear plastic on which Zajak's business information—with the exception of a title—appeared etched, as if on glass. The name of the company amused Muerce. ACME Glass Company. The name was as generic and plain as Zajak himself. *Mr. Teflon indeed.*

Distracted, Muerce didn't notice the light in his bedroom was on as he fetched ice, and a small bottle of cold club soda from the kitchen. He mixed it with scotch. Taking a big gulp of the cocktail, he savored the flavor and muted burn in his throat as he swallowed. The coldness of the glass felt comforting, holding it to his forehead. *Time for bed.*

The mail fell to the bedroom floor, scattering like Autumn leaves. The shock of what greeted him caused Muerce to swallow the swig he took from his drink the wrong way, and he began coughing.

"Aren't you going to offer me a drink?" Miriam said. She was lying naked in his bed, the covers pulled back as a direct invitation. The small lamp on the nightstand next to her was the only illumination in the room, and bathed her body in a warm light that complimented her rich complexion.

Muerce regained his composure. Grinning, he tugged his tie loose as he walked to the side of the bed where Miriam lay. All the voices and images of the night disappeared in an instant. Miriam was better than Xanax.

"You can have mine," Muerce said, sitting on the edge of the bed. He offered the cocktail to her.

"Oh God, this is awful," she said. "How can you drink it?"

Muerce leaned over and kissed her, tasting her lipstick, and the scotch. He pulled his mouth away from hers, pressed their foreheads together, moved his hand to the back of her head, and gently massaged the nape of her neck.

"To what do I owe this very, very pleasant surprise?" he whispered.

Miriam wrapped her free arm around Muerce's neck, and drew him closer. She kissed him passionately several more times.

"Don't you know?" she whispered in his ear as she nibbled on the fleshy lobe. "Dinner with Jack Muerce is never just a meal."

Muerce laughed as he sat up on the bed. He took the scotch and soda from Miriam, and drank the remaining contents. As he did, Miriam saw the swatch of blood on his shirt collar, and followed it up to the small wound on his neck. Alarmed, she bolted upright to examine it.

"You're bleeding," she said, using her motherly voice. "Did that crazy bastard do this to you? I told you to be careful with him."

"It happened at the Unicorn, but it wasn't Tomaso," Muerce said, standing to remove his shirt. "I'm fine, really."

Miriam frowned as she stared at him, waiting for more details. When it was obvious he wouldn't be forthcoming with them, she got up and headed toward the bathroom.

"I'm going to clean that up before it gets infected," she said. "And while I'm in there where are the..."

"They're out here in the nightstand drawer," Muerce said, kicking off his shoes, and dropping his trousers and underwear to the floor.

She returned with a bottle of hydrogen peroxide, some cotton swabs, and a box of band-aids.

"Tilt your head back, and stand still," she ordered. "Not that one."

"Yes, ma'am," he said. "Sorry, ma'am."

Miriam jabbed him in the ribs, causing Muerce to flex his body forward, and bang his chin on the top of her head.

"I told you to stand still," she said, dabbing the wound with a cotton swab. "Honest to God, Jack, your a disaster. I don't even know why I'm here."

"Which brings up a good point," Muerce said, gently grabbing Miriam's arm to stop her from attending his wound, and forcing her to look at him. "How did you get in here?"

Miriam could lie with her sharp, green eyes but her face confessed as the golden brown skin on her cheeks turned bright red. That someone with such dark skin could blush as brightly as Miriam could, was more than quaint to Muerce, it was arousing. An embarrassed Miriam caused the blood to flow to his extremities.

"Madame Trung," she said, looking down at her feet like a chastised child. "I brought your shirts."

The state of Miriam's embarrassment was brief.

"You seriously need to change the security codes to this place," she said, applying a band aid. "If I had known how lazy you are I wouldn't have had to ask Madame Trung. You haven't changed them since... well, in a long damn time."

Madame Trung? Just fabulous, Muerce thought, I'll never hear the end of this.

"After tonight, I may never change them," Muerce said, pressing himself against Miriam so that she could feel how much he wanted her.

"After tonight," Miriam thought as the moist tip of Muerce's intentions rubbed against her bellybutton. There would be no "after tonight" after tonight. This would be it. A last time with Jack Muerce.

Miriam pushed Muerce to the bed, opened the nightstand drawer, removed several packets, and opened one before turning the lamp off. Muerce, squirming beneath Miriam who was now astride him and unrolling the contents of the package, reached to turn the light back on.

"No," he said. "I want to see you."

"You want to see my stretch marks, the wrinkles around my eyes?" she said, bending toward the lamp to turn it off.

Muerce grabbed her hand and clasped it with his, intertwining their fingers. They were almost face-to-face on the bed, and he was in a position to slide himself inside her, which he did. Miriam closed her eyes, let out a deep sigh, and smiled as if she could taste the sensation.

"You win," she said, sitting upright on top of Muerce. She grabbed both his hands, and directing them to her nipples. "Work them hard."

Miriam's face broke out in a blush several more times in the next few hours until, exhausted, they fell asleep in each other's arms. She turned the light off, and whispered into Muerce's ear that she had to leave by six in the morning, but he was deep asleep, and did not hear her.

— —

Staring at her body in the bathroom mirror, Miriam brushed her hair back into a small pony tail after a quick shower. She had been as quiet as possible. Muerce's rhythmic snoring was undisturbed when she entered the bedroom. She pulled a change of clothes from the overnight bag she brought with her. Without making a sound, she slipped on clean underwear, a sweater blouse, jeans, and black patent-leather flats.

Sitting silently in one of the chairs by the bedroom window, Miriam stared at the slumbering Muerce for a few last moments. She promised her sister she'd pick the boys up before eight. Her plan was to take them to eight-thirty Mass, and then out for breakfast. Then she would tell them.

Miriam carefully cradled one of her breasts made delightfully sore by Muerce only a few hours earlier. She concentrated on how they felt to be worked in that way, and the resulting waves of pleasure when she reached climax. She did not want to forget that feeling. She wanted it to stay with her as long as she could hang on to it.

She was fond of Jack Muerce. She admired and respected him. He was a good man, who did good where he could. She liked him, but she didn't love him. She knew it was dangerous to love him. Dangerous because he was in love with someone else, and had been for as long as she had known him.

Miriam snatched up the overnight bag, and shouldered it. When she got to the marble-tiled foyer, she was careful to walk across it in a way that made no sound. She remembered how much noise the private elevator made on the way up the night before, and decided to leave through the front door. She unlatched the locks with quiet clicks, opened and then shut it. Standing in the hallway, Miriam was suddenly overcome with fear. She had never felt so scared and alone before. Not even when her husband made her a widow with two small children to raise. She reached up to feel one of her breasts. As she did, tears began to well up in her eyes, and she fought back the sobs that were building inside of her.

It had been her decision. Given the size of the two tumors that were found, and her family history—her mother and an aunt died of breast cancer—Miriam opted for a precautionary removal of her healthy breast, in addition to the cancerous one. The double mastectomy was scheduled for Thursday.

Miriam regained her composure, and wiped the tears from her face with the back of her hand. She still had two teenage boys to raise. She was strong. Strong enough that she didn't need Jack Muerce's help.

CHAPTER 10

The strumming of electronic banjo music played somewhere in the back of Muerce's head, waking him from one of the better sleeps he had had in some time. Eyes closed, he reached for the phone on the nightstand. He thumbed the sound off, and went back to sleep. As he drifted back into the shroud of dreams he made a mental note to change his ringtone. Soon, he was back at Club Unicorn, and maneuvering past the private party booths. Now, though, they were occupied by familiar faces. Madame Trung was serving coffee to Eleanor, who wore a black mantilla, and held a rosary in one hand. Miriam wore a Centurion costume, and clutched a sword to her breast. Behind her was Ashley, wearing nothing but the car coat he had lent her. Paige Sharron pranced around, looking like what Muerce thought she would look like naked, and acting like he would want her to with him. She taunted him to come to the bar. She reached out her arm, and with the curling of her finger enticed him closer: to follow her; to do whatever she told him to do. Beyond Paige, standing behind the bar, he saw her. The face he worked so hard to forget, but haunted him relentlessly. He couldn't go an hour without thinking of her. She wore the same pale yellow dress that she wore the last time he saw her. He moved closer to her. Light radiated from the dress. Like Icarus, he flew closer to the sun than he should. Then the ground began to shake and vibrate in intermittent spasms.

Muerce started from his sleep. A wave of anxiety swept over him, and his skin felt wet and clammy. Seeing the face and the pale yellow dress out of context gave him a fright. Muerce hoped he had not cried out in his sleep, waking Miriam. When he looked to see if he had, he saw the other side of the bed was empty. Her overnight bag was gone. His laundered shirts, covered in the flimsy dry cleaners plastic, hung on a knob on the armoire across from the bed.

The vibrating continued. His phone moved on the nightstand, its screen lit up. Muerce didn't recognize the number, but decided to answer the call. As soon as he touched the "Answer" icon, he wished he had pressed "Ignore" instead.

Muerce croaked out, "Hello."

"Muerce, Trumbley," he said, pausing after identifying himself. "Did I interrupt something, Jack?"

"No," Muerce said, rubbing his face to get the blood circulating. "What time is it? And when did you get a new number?"

"Ten o'clock, Sleeping Beauty," Trumbley said. "Another typical Saturday night in the life of Jack Muerce? It must be good to be you."

"No and yes."

"No and yes what?"

"No, it was far from typical, and yes, it's good to be me," Muerce said. "Unless you're calling to say you're on your way up with coffee, leave me alone."

"I need a favor," Trumbley said.

"You're all out of favors," Muerce said, as he stretched out on the bed. "In fact, you're giving away favors you don't have. We still haven't talked about the call I got from T.B. Squire."

"How did that go?" Trumbley said.

"Taken care of."

"Good. Thanks. Let me buy you a cup of coffee," Trumbley said.

"Fine," Muerce said, rubbing his head, and wishing Miriam were still in his bed. "Where?"

"County Morgue."

"What?" Muerce said. "Is Bhote part of this?"

Muerce could hear Trumbley pull the phone away from his mouth to speak to someone nearby. "Muerce says good morning, and asks if you can make a fresh pot of coffee. He's on his way.

"See you in about twenty, Jack."

"Depends on traffic, and how long I have to wait to get a decent cup of coffee before I get there," Muerce said.

He fell backwards into bed, and reached for the pillow on the side where Miriam had slept. He drew it to his face so he could smell her scent, but no trace of her remained. He lay there, the pillow over his head, encased in darkness. In his head the pale yellow dress beckoned to him from behind the bar at Club Unicorn.

The smell, no matter how antiseptic and sanitized the environment, was unmistakable. It came at you in two ways, depending on the cause of death. Burn victims got a pass because they had their own distinctive stench. So did floaters, those bodies found in water after several days. They were the worst. Floaters were pure putrid, especially after they were pulled from the water, and lay in the sun until the guys from the morgue came to haul them away.

For all the other dead there was the first stage of smell as bodily fluids and solids were released when muscle function ceased. Urine and fecal matter. And as hard a Bhote tried, or what he and his staff used, those smells always lurked in the corners and crevices. The smell of death was their fact of life.

After that, there was the second stage when the dead began to decay, and reeked of a sickly sweet smell that adhered itself both physically and mentally. Once you inhaled that unmistakable and fetid odor, it was with you forever. Most of the bodies that passed through Bhote's morgue were fresh. The burned, the floaters and the long dead, but recently discovered, were less frequent. Muerce hoped what he was being brought down to see, which was still a guess, was the former. He also hoped he wasn't about to see what he saw days before.

It had been a busy and violent Saturday night in the city, and the hangover was at the morgue. There had been four victim identifications, so far. The first was a stabbing at a bar. The other three were from an automobile accident in which a drunk father had driven his car, along with his two small children, into a bridge abutment at high speed. Two uniformed policemen led the wailing ex-wife and mother from the identification room when Muerce walked through the double-doors. She was hysterical, and screaming in Spanish. Muerce looked away, and gripped the tall paper Starbuck's coffee cup so hard the lukewarm liquid ran out of the plastic cover onto his hands. The coffee stained his khakis, and starched white shirt. He looked down at the spots, and cursed himself.

The screaming continued, though more distantly as Muerce made his way down the hallway toward the examination room. He noticed there were six gurneys, each with a full black-plastic body bag, lined up against the wall. They were waiting for their turn in the identification room. *A very busy night in the city.*

Past the doors that led into the examination room where he identified Redzil's body days earlier, Muerce expected to find Trumbley and Bhote. He was was displeased to find homicide detectives Ash and Maple.

It was immediately clear to Muerce that he was interrupting a pissing match between vice and homicide. Muerce did not like Ash and Maple. Given the history, they reciprocated the dislike. Muerce had, on two separate occasions, delivered on favors that uncovered the innocence of defendants charged with murder on cases built by Ash and Maple. On each of those occasions, the two detectives received reprimands, but managed to keep their jobs, and remain in homicide.

They were as dense, both intellectually and motivationally, as the trees whose names they bore. They were, Muerce felt, the most dangerous kind of cop there could be—stupid and lazy.

"What the fu... ?" Ash said, turning to Bhote. "What the hell is Merc doing here?"

Muerce detected a lift in the corner of Trumbley's mouth. It was one of those "this is going to be fun" smiles. Muerce smiled back, showing his teeth, and his disdain for Ash and Maple.

"The only way I want to see you come through those doors is in a bag," Maple said. "What do you want?"

"Well detective... it is still detective isn't it?" Muerce said, sipping his coffee. "I have to tell you I'm really relieved right now. When I was walking down the hall I thought Doctor Bhote and his staff were getting lax around here. But seeing you two. Now I know the source of the shit and piss smell.

"Detective Shit, Detective Piss, how are you this morning?"

A flat smile broke across Bhote's face, and Trumbley began to snicker.

"You're a real fucking comedian aren't you Merc," Maple said. "A real smart-ass funny guy."

"You know, I hear that a lot," Muerce said, taking another sip from his cup. "But I don't think there's anything funny about the smell of shit and piss on a Sunday morning.

"By the way, which one of you is Shit, and which one is Piss. You're like twins, I can't tell you apart."

Maple took a step toward Muerce. It was aggressive, but there was little behind it to worry Muerce.

"All right, everyone knock it off," Trumbley said. "Muerce's here on something unrelated. Just bad luck the three of you ran into each other."

"You got what you need?" Bhote said, addressing Ash.

Ash looked at Maple, then back at Bhote and Trumbley. Ash flipped a page on his pocket notebook. Then he looked at Muerce.

"Yeah, I guess, for now," Ash said, looking back at Maple to see if he had any questions, which he didn't.

Ash and Maple stared at Muerce as they walked by him in a childishly intimidating manner.

"Have a great day detectives," Muerce said, moving his head back and forth with a jocular, and bobbing motion.

When they were gone, Muerce turned to Trumbley with disgust.

"Must be bobble-head giveaway day at the ballpark," Muerce said. "What are dumb and dumber doing here?"

"Same thing you are, Jack," Trumbley said.

"Whoa, you said unrelated," Muerce said. "What am I doing here, Nick? Hell, what are you doing here?"

Bhote approached Muerce with a fresh pot of coffee that he offered. Muerce flipped the lid of his cup off, and let Bhote give him a refill.

"We have a second," Bhote said.

"This is only my first," Muerce said, misunderstanding Bhote's words.

"No, a second victim," Bhote said.

"Second, you've got them lined up outside like an airport runway the day before Thanksgiving," Muerce said. "A Second?"

"A second, like the last time you were here," Bhote said.

Bhote's answer registered with Muerce just as the hot coffee scalded his tongue. He leaned forward, spitting some of the liquid on the floor, but not on himself.

"Sonjay, we seem to be repeating the same conversation," Muerce said, averting his gaze from the large examining table where Trumbley stood, and that was covered by a black tarp. "I made an ID last week. That's all. Whatever this is about, it has nothing to do with me. And I don't think it has anything to do with you, Nick."

Muerce forced himself to look toward Trumbley without focusing on the tarp.

"What is vice doing in homicide's business?" Muerce said.

"God gave us free will," Trumbley said. "When He did that, vice became the root of all evil. And from what I've seen so far, this is evil like I've not seen before."

"Again, I repeat, what am I doing here?" Muerce said.

"I wanted you here," Bhote said. "I called Nick, and I asked him to call you. As a favor."

Muerce mulled it over. Bhote was asking. The circumstances had changed. Bhote needed help.

"When I found out Ash and Maple were assigned to the case, well, I knew a different perspective would be needed," Bhote said. He stood by the examining table. "This is bigger than them. I'm afraid it might be bigger than me."

Bhote looked at Muerce, hoping to snare him with intrigue, and perhaps a little guilt.

"Are you ready for this, Jack?" he said, reaching for the corner of the tarp, but not lifting it back to reveal what lay beneath.

"Do I have a choice," Muerce said, looking at his cup of coffee without taking a sip.

"We all have a choice," Bhote said.

"Do we?" Muerce said. "Is this part of Nick's 'free will' speech? Well, it's not like I haven't been to this freak show before. Go ahead, but gently this time."

Bhote pulled back the tarp. It was much like what Muerce saw before. The arms and legs had been removed, the wounds sutured closed. There was no blood. Muerce was shocked but not repulsed, and approached the table with a detached interest.

"Same thing?" he said.

"Yes, and no," Bhote said. "Let me go through the similarities, and discrepancies."

A trigger clicked in Muerce's head when the body was undraped. It was the same moldy scent he noticed on Redzil's remains.

"Do you smell that?" Muerce said, looking at both Bhote and Trumbley.

"Smell what?" Bhote said.

"My nose was shot years ago... menthol cigarettes," Trumbley said.

"What is it, Jack?" Bhote said.

"Kind of musty, perfume, oily smell," Muerce said. "I thought I smelled the same thing with the other one."

The look on Bhote's face was blank. He didn't smell anything. Trumbley didn't either.

"Maybe an association?" Bhote said.

"It's nothing," Muerce said, dismissing the odor. "I must be imagining it. Go on Sonjay."

What was similar, Bhote said, stopping at times to fill Trumbley in on the previous victim, was the condition of the two bodies. Also, both were female. The precise, surgical removal of the limbs, and subsequent suturing and cursory healing—at least to the still functioning torso at the time of amputations—of Victim Two was consistent with Victim One. The stitching, especially in one area, was again exquisite craftsmanship, and accomplished with fine silk thread of the same radiant colors used on the previous victim. Both, Bhote said, had been intubated and kept alive, albeit likely unconscious during the procedure. The toxicology reports would help determine that, he added.

That's where the similarities ended, and the differences began. Victim Two showed signs of bruising at the intubation site, which Bhote suspected was due to the age and physical condition of the victim, who had been identified as a fifty-seven-year-old woman. That was accomplished because her fingers had not been removed. Nor had her toes. The victim had a name that Bhote did not use. He said she was a known homeless person, and alcoholic, with a past record for prostitution, though it had been some time since she was last picked up for solicitation.

Victim Two's digits and sexual organs had been spared. Her mouth, however, was sewn shut. During his initial examination, Bhote had extensive photographs and X-rays taken of the victim's oral region before he snipped the embroidery to examine inside the cavity. He handed the photos to Trumbley and Muerce.

"The victim's tongue has been removed," Bhote said. "Location unknown. And I found this."

He held up a small, sealed plastic evidence bag that contained a coin similar to the one found in the mouth of Victim One. *Consistency.*

"What kind?" Muerce said.

"Ancient Roman coins," Bhote said. "They are very common, easy to acquire, and almost impossible to trace. And not worth much."

"It cost her quite a bit," Trumbley said, looking over the police report made by the first officer responding to the scene. "Says she was found on a traffic island off the freeway near the museum about four-twenty-seven this morning. What do you put as the time death?"

"For the torso?" Bhote said. "Maybe only forty minutes earlier. The morbidity on the limbs goes back a few days, maybe. It looks like they were refrigerated so I need to do additional testing. It's going to take a little time. You can see we're busy."

Muerce focused on the photos of Victim Two's mouth, and the delicate work of the embroidery that sealed the lips closed. The stitching made a floral design, with pink and white silk threads illustrating what Muerce thought were the petals of a flower backed by lush green and blue silk threads representing the leaves and stems. To give the leafy background some depth and richness, gold thread had been laced throughout.

"A lot more time was spent on this than on the previous victim," Bhote said.

"Less canvas for the artist to cover," Muerce said.

"Artist?" Trumbley said. "There is nothing artistic about this at all."

"It is to the perpetrator," Bhote said. "Jack makes a good point. One we shouldn't dismiss."

"We?" Muerce said. "What's this 'we' business? This doesn't involve me. And I sure as hell don't want to be near those clowns Ash and Maple. And neither should you, Nick."

"I'm not worried about them," Trumbley said.

"Look, right now I just need a different perspective," Bhote said. "You two get along, and you've worked together before without any, well, without any professional issues.

"I need a favor. Just give me ideas. Nobody else needs to know. Ash and Maple won't have a clue."

Trumbley shrugged his shoulders in tacit approval.

"I'll think about it," Muerce said. "Can I take this photo with me? There's something about it that bothers me."

"No," Bhote said. "It's evidence."

Muerce frowned, and put the picture—a closeup of Victim Two's mouth—on the empty examining table next to where he was standing. He took out his phone, and with the built-in camera took a picture.

"That okay?" he said to Bhote.

"I didn't see anything," Bhote said.

"We done?" Muerce said.

"For now," Bhote said. "I'll let you know if there's anything else when the test results get back."

"Where was the first victim found?" Trumbley said.

Muerce thought it was a good question, one he should have asked, but it hadn't been any of his business. It still wasn't. He was still thinking about it. Bhote went to his office, and returned with the report on Victim One—Redzil Hadzic.

"On a playground merry-go-round in Founders Park, almost the other side of town," Bhote said.

Neither Muerce nor Trumbley thought there was a connection. *Random.*

"I'll let you know if I think of anything," Muerce said. "But don't hold your breath. This is water I don't normally swim in. Okay?"

"I just want you to think for me," Bhote said.

"And listen," Trumbley said. "You usually hear things long before we do."

Muerce nodded.

— —

Muerce and Trumbley stood at the bottom of the incline of the hallway that led from the morgue up to the main hospital building. Muerce took several test sips before taking a big gulp of his coffee. It had cooled, and tasted terrible. He spit it back into the cup.

"Let's talk about T.B. Squire," Muerce said. "I assume that was a favor for a favor?"

"Yup," Trumbley said, no more information was forthcoming.

"What for what?" Muerce said.

"Private," Trumbley said. "But you got his kid taken care of, right?"

"Yeah," Muerce said, lifting his head, exposing the small bandage on his neck. "But I had to spill more blood than I expected, so dish it out. I don't need details. I just don't want to get bit in the ass by surprise."

"You won't," Trumbley said. "A friend is having surgery and I wanted… them… to get the VIP treatment is all. The timing just kind of fell in place when he called me about his kid being heavy into Tomaso for the bite. Did that slick prick do that to you?"

"No, a woman," Muerce said.

"Gee, no shit, Jack Muerce hurt by a woman," Trumbley said. "When does that ever happen?"

Nick wanted to take back the words as soon as they came out of his mouth, and say he was sorry. But he let it slide, and Muerce let it slide as well. *Some wounds never heal.*

CHAPTER 11

It was Sunday. Monday was trash day. Muerce almost hit one of the large, green plastic tubs a homeowner placed too far into the road for the next day's collection. It was more likely, though, the driving wind and rain blew the receptacle from its usual spot because it wasn't packed full of refuse. The homes along Crest Drive, which snaked its way up the hill, were owned by the very wealthy, who tended to either have few children, or were empty nesters. They had little in the way of garbage, although many homeowners along Crest Drive paid to have an extra one or two of the large receptacles, most of which now were scattered along the narrow, and poorly lit serpentine road.

Crest Drive was the main route to the top of the hill, which was Muerce's destination. It was one of six other geologic features that formed a kind of natural semicircle barrier for the city that stretched across the plain below as it sloped toward the water's edge. The seven hills were more mountain than promontory. They were known as The Districts, and each was named after one of the Seven Hills of Rome. Crest Drive was in the Palatine District, which was the second tallest of the seven hills, and looked directly over the downtown skyscrapers. There was a well-circulated joke in the city that one didn't live in the Palatine, one achieved it.

Muerce cursed as he swerved to avoid another empty trash container that tumbled across the road. The wind began to increase in intensity the higher up the Palatine. There were, luckily, fewer homes bunched together as the car ascended, which meant fewer wind-blown obstacles to avoid in the darkness.

Muerce was hungry. He had only coffee all day, and was slightly queazy from the sloshy, queasy feeling in the pit of his stomach. But he was on his way to have Sunday dinner with Eleanor, who lived at One Crest Drive.

The security gate closed behind the Mercedes as he pulled the car round the large crushed stone driveway area in front of the main entrance of the house. It was lit up in such a way to highlight the grounds and architecture of glass, steel, and sweeping white walls and arches. The crunching sound the car made as he turned on the surface was comforting. So would be the food and company waiting inside.

Growing up in Eleanor Muerce's home was something between living in the Guggenheim Museum, and on the set of the original "Star Trek" television series. There were times, as a boy, Muerce half expected to be greeted by a tour guide when leaving the bathroom, or find Captain Kirk and Mr. Spock in the living room, navigating their way through some galactic adventure.

By the time he was a teen-ager, Muerce often greeted Eleanor for breakfast with a "beam me up, Scottie" when he sat down in one of the Eero Saarinen designed "tulip" chairs. They, along with other furnishings by Saarinen, Charles Eames, Edward Wormby and Harry Bertoila, populated the Muerce home, as they did, in time, a plethora of museums—and in the case of the "tulip" chairs, the Starship Enterprise.

The house was built from an unauthorized, and undocumented architectural design that had been a clandestine collaboration between Saarinen and Eames. It was similar to work they had done on Entenza House. The Muerce House, however, incorporated additional elements seen in Saarinen's work on the Miller Home, and the soaring arches that gave the former TWA terminal flight with their grace and serenity.

Eleanor lived above the fray of the city. But she did not live alone. Keeping her company were Miro, Klee, Picasso, Rothko, Pollack, and a host of others, including Salle and Close, whom she rotated on a seasonal basis. Muerce's favorite was the Kandinsky that hung in the living room near the baby grand piano. Most of the collection was housed in the main space of the front entry to the house that was a mini TWA terminal. It provided ceiling space for a pair of mobiles, and a large central wall where arrivals and departures had given way to the Pollock.

Muerce was soaked when he got inside and stood, for a moment, looking up at the large black and white painting that dripped more than he.

"Don't move," Eleanor directed. "I just had the floors waxed. Here, give me that. And why aren't you wearing that nice car coat I bought you?"

She stuffed Muerce's raincoat into a white, plastic garbage bag that matched her outfit; a pair of white, wool slacks, and a creamy silk turtleneck adorned with a single gold chain that hung to just below where her shoulders merged with her chest.

"I'll hang this in the shower to dry," she said.

"Seriously?" Muerce said.

"Oh stop it," she said, kissing him on the cheek. "The gala is next Saturday, and I'm having a private reception here Wednesday for the board. And another Thursday for select patrons and donors. I don't want water stains on the floor.

"You haven't RSVP'd to either. Are you coming?"

"To the gala Saturday, yes. I'm picking you up. Remember? To the board meeting, and the other thing, no. I'm not on the board. And you know I avoid the private soirees because I can't duck out of the inevitable one-on-one 'can you do me a favor?' requests, which are usually a traffic ticket, or something stupid they could do on their own, but they never want to bother with themselves. Did I ever tell you one of your board members asked me to score them some drugs?"

"Well then, enough of that, let's eat," Eleanor said, directing him with a wave of her hand to follow her to the kitchen. "I got your favorite."

Muerce's stomach rumbled with anticipation. He followed Eleanor, and was greeted with the aromas of comfort. Chicken Kiev, garlic bread, and the Brie Cheese Macaroni from the kitchens of the country club. The empty plastic containers sat on top of the counter. He whisked his finger inside one of them to collect the cheese sauce that hadn't been scraped out.

"Oh my God, that's wonderful even cold," he said.

Eleanor disappeared to hang his drenched raincoat in the bathroom. Muerce opened the refrigerator doors, and scanned the contents to find what he was hoping would be there. *Pairing the drink to food was essential.*

"Rolling Rock, excellent," he shouted just as she arrived back in the kitchen. "Thank you, Mommy."

"I got you Rolling Rock," she said, not noticing that he had discovered her surprise.

Muerce took a long slug of the ice-cold beer, quieting the sounds coming from his abdomen. With an empty stomach, the beer buzz would hit him sooner, which he welcomed. He held the bottle of beer up for her to see.

"Oh, you found them," she said. "And I got some lottery tickets, too."

Still talking, Eleanor slipped oven mitts over both her hands, and stepped back to avoid the burst of heat when she opened the oven door to remove two orange enamel dishes she then placed on trivets.

"It was simply the most charming little out-of-the-way bodega," she said, scurrying around the kitchen to retrieve plates, utensils and napkins. "Such delightful clientele. I'm thinking about getting inked, myself."

"Lovely, mother, perhaps a dragon on your shoulder with a tail that runs around..." Muerce said, then hesitating as his train of thought changed rails. "Wait a minute."

Muerce walked around the kitchen island, and opened a small drawer from which he pulled out a pack of gold-wrapped cigarettes. He held them up, and scowled at Eleanor.

"When did you start up again?" he said. "We talked about this."

Eleanor was defiant.

"You see it's not open, I haven't had one," she said.

"Not yet," he said. "Why at all?"

"With the gala I'm stressed out," she said. "It helps. And besides, in lieu of having any grandchildren, I'm allowed some vices."

"Oh, let's not go there again," he said, taking a pull from the bottle of beer. "Grandmother Eleanor, indeed."

"I prefer *Granmere*, thank you," she said.

"Oh, how pretentious, especially for someone sneaking around out-of-the-way bodegas to buy cigarettes, and lottery tickets," Muerce said, opening a bottle of beer for her. "If the blessed event ever arises, which at my age is becoming increasingly unlikely, and even more unwanted, I think we'll go with Captain Grandma.

"And if you're so stressed out take a Xanax."

Muerce winced the moment the word left his mouth, and hoped she had not heard him.

"Let's do go there, John," she said.

Dammit.

"Fine," he said. "But can we eat first? Then you can have a cigarette, and we can talk. That okay?"

Eleanor smirked, sat down and said a quick prayer that her son did not join in with her, although he made a weak effort at the back-end of a Sign of the Cross. Dinner was then served on plain, white china. The utensils were the Danish block design, which brought back childhood memories of his father teasing his mother about how she was making them eat with "bars of metal" that prevented him from getting the portions of food he wanted. It was, she would reply, her way of keeping him trim.

Muerce gulped down several forkfuls of the rich macaroni and cheese before cutting into the chicken. When he did, a lava flow of cheese and butter was unleashed. He blew on the helping stuck at the end of the boxy utensil, and popped it into his mouth. It was still hot, and Muerce slurped beer from the bottle. Despite the temperature, there was enough flavor that burst in his mouth, eliciting a sigh of contentment.

"Good?" Eleanor said, having taken only one bite of the chicken as she was too busy enjoying watching her son eat. What made it that much better was that he was eating at home. It was an event that was not altogether rare, but rare enough at her age that she wanted to relish the moment.

Muerce served himself a second helping of the macaroni, and a second beer. The buzz settled in his head as the food had in his stomach. Eleanor allowed him to eat in relative quiet, at least for the moment.

"Did you go to Mass today?" she said, ending the moment.

"Guess," he said.

"Of course you didn't," she said, brushing the hair from the side of her face. "I don't know why I even bothered to ask."

"Nor do I," Muerce said, swallowing more macaroni without looking up at her. "God, this is good. But so rich, I don't think I can have anymore."

"In an hour you'll want the leftovers," she said. "Well, at least I can usually get you to go to the High Holidays."

"High Holidays, are we Jewish now?" Muerce said, teasing her.

"You know what I mean."

"What you say and what you mean are almost always diametrically opposed to each other," Muerce said, finishing the last portion on his plate, and wiping his mouth with his napkin.

"You have a duty to God," she said, seriously.

"I have a duty to you," he said, more seriously.

"Where is God in your life?"

"Usually on break, having a cigarette."

Eleanor huffed in frustration.

"He is always present, you rarely stop to look," she said. She had switched to her calm, motherly and religious mode. Next, Muerce knew, she would segue back to his *duty*, which meant his obligation to use the many resources God—and his family—had provided. He did good, and she always lost the argument, though there was some strength in what she said about the underlying motivation behind his acts of good. Or were they acts of absolution, or acts of atonement? Selfish in nature? If they were the former than he was playing God, and Jack Muerce was not God.

That, he knew for sure. If they were the latter—acts of atonement—she would argue, then he had long ago atoned for his "self-inflicted and self-perceived transgressions."

The "favors" as Muerce liked to refer to his duty, his obligation of privilege, were a combination of both. Regardless, Eleanor knew the root cause of the suffering behind her son's endeavors, and it pained her to see it in him.

"There needs to be a balance—between the reckless pursuit of earthly pleasures, and one's *duty*," she said.

"A gentleman's private life is just that, private," Muerce said. "Just as a lady's private life, is private as well."

"You know damn well I'm not trying to pry into your escapades," she said, sharply. "Good God, it's enough that I get all the gory details of your latest conquests every time I go to the hairdressers, or worse, to a board meeting.

"Honestly, at your age. Where do you get the energy?"

"Good genes," he said, draining the last slug of the beer from the bottle.

"Don't try and turn this on me," she said.

"You're only responsible for half," he said, with more tease than accusation. Muerce got up from the table to get another beer from the refrigerator.

"You're Father and I gave you a lot of things, but what you do with them is your responsibility," she said.

"And I do, and have, always taken responsibility for my behavior," he said. "Are you saying I haven't?"

Except the one time, he thought.

"No, but you're dancing around the subject," she said.

"I think the subject of this conversation got lost awhile back, so let's change it," Muerce said, opening the bottle, and making a motion to Eleanor to see if she would like another. She shook her head that she would not. "Will there be dancing at the gala Saturday night?"

"Yes," she said.

"Then you will do me the honor?" Muerce said, eliciting an internal blush in Eleanor, and some motherly anticipation.

"Does that charm work on every woman?" she said.

"Dad said it always worked on you, and I figure since you are on a plain above all other women that if you fall for it, then mere mortal women could never resist," he said, giving Eleanor a flash of his smile to emphasize his charm.

"And I thought this food was going to be too rich for me," she said. "You're enough to give me gout."

Muerce reached into the small drawer, and pulled out the pack of cigarettes along with a plastic, disposable lighter that bore the name of the bodega where the cigarettes, beer and lottery tickets had been purchased.

"Smoke?" he said, holding the pack up for Eleanor to see.

"You're terrible," she said.

"I'm my mother's son," he said.

"Get me a Diet Coke from the fridge," she said. "I love Diet Coke with a cigarette."

The dishes were quickly put away in the dishwasher, and the leftovers covered, and placed in the refrigerator for later consumption. The two of them retreated to the comfort of the sunken living room that faced the large bank of windows overlooking the pool. It, in turn, overlooked the city that was shrouded by the storm. The rain pelted the windows, having gone from a downpour to an almost spray carried by the wind. The visibility was so poor, Muerce could barely make out the ends of the house that flanked the pool, and reached out toward the precipice beyond.

The stereo was tuned to a classical station. Vivaldi's "Four Seasons" gave a civilized cadence to the storm outside. Eleanor finished half her cigarette, and flicked the ashes into a crystal ashtray she cupped in her hand. It was the only one in the house, and she kept it in the small drawer in the kitchen with the occasional pack of cigarettes.

John "Black Jack" Muerce, her husband, and father to her son, died of lung cancer. After his death she quit smoking, and forbid anyone from doing the same in her home. She threw out all the other ashtrays, and didn't smoke for over a decade until, one day she found the ashtray in a box in the garage. It was engraved with the logo of her husband's fighter squadron—the 354th—and had been given to him as a gift at a reunion after the war. It was the one he kept in the garage on the workbench where he tinkered with broken household appliances that he never was able to resuscitate back to working order. Eleanor knew her husband had the mechanical skills of a debutante.

"I just flew the damn things," he would say when she asked in frustration why he was able to shoot down more than a dozen Luftwaffe pilots, but couldn't get her toaster to work. "I didn't fix them."

The tinkering, she knew, was his excuse to smoke a cigarette, drink a beer, smell the smell of gas, oil and solvents, and retreat, if only for a brief moment, into his own world that was not about fine art, high finance or social or familial responsibilities. He was a man in his cave, Eleanor would say to him, long before the term became either fashionable or acceptable.

The nicotine, the music, the cold beer, and the Diet Coke let Eleanor drift into her thoughts, coaxed by the occasional brush of a sheet of rain against the windows. She looked at her son on the other side of the sunken, wrap-around couch. His eyes were closed, his hand cradling a half-full bottle of beer. He was as relaxed as she had seen him in some time. Lost in the soothing music. Eleanor saw her husband in him, and the memories fell on her as the rain outside. She missed her husband, still, tremendously. She felt a chill, and thought about going to her bedroom for the white silk scarf he wore as pilot. On occasion, when she was alone, Eleanor wore it around the house, remembering the first time she had seen him in the scarf. It was at the bar at the Ritz in Paris during the spring of 1946. She was a young girl, and had travelled to Paris with her father on business. Black Jack Muerce, although still attached to the military, was there on business with her father.

To herself, Eleanor recited the two family histories, and their business together. Both hers and the Muerce families could trace their lineage back through the centuries of French nobility. Hers led to the Court of Aquitane, which was how she was given the name Eleanor. The Muerce name led to the Bourbons.

Shrewdness and luck allowed both families to circumvent the fate history bestowed on much of French aristocracy. The two families managed to hold on to their heads, and their titles—though the titles were rarely ever referred to after each line came to America in the Eighteenth Century. Both families also held on to their wealth, and the responsibility that accompanied it.

Eleanor's family was in banking and, by the onset of World War II, had branches throughout the world, including Switzerland. The Muerce's were in finance. Their bond and investment business took a cautions, and conservative stance in the years that led up to the Great Depression, so that when the bottom fell out of the market in 1929 there was little pain for them, or their investors. The majority of whom were European, and Jewish. Only a few of the Muerce's American investors had opted to go the riskier route of speculating on the ever upward spiral of Wall Street during the 1920s. They did feel the pain.

But for those who followed the Muerce's advice, and also banked with Eleanor's family, there developed a level of trust that was tested when Adolph Hitler came to power in 1930s Germany.

When it became evident the Nazis were intent on stripping Jews not only of their wealth, but their lives, a consortium of Jewish families, and businesses in France and Germany, transferred their financial interests to the Muerce firm, and the banks run by Eleanor's father.

For both families it was not a matter of business. It was their duty to responsibly handle the trust that was given them. For the Jewish families that managed to escape from Europe and the Holocaust, their holdings were transferred back to them, with accrued earnings and interest, as quickly as the war was over.

In the spring of 1946, when Eleanor first set eyes on the handsome and charming fighter ace in the bar at the Ritz, her father had begun the difficult, and usually grim task, of tracking down the survivors of families that had been sent to the concentration camps. Black Jack Muerce was about to be released from his military duty, and with his father recently passed away, he was in charge of running the Muerce investment firm. The position would, in the short term, involve Muerce remaining in Europe to locate missing or relocated families, and return their wealth to them. Neither the bank nor the investment firm charged a fee for any of the work they had done for their "dislocated" customers during the war. To profit on such calamity, Eleanor remembered the conversation at the Ritz, would be indecorous.

It was their obligation as nobility, to do the right thing for the people they served. It was, in part, how the man, her son, now sitting across the couch from her had come to be the man he was.

"Have you been sleeping well?" she said, rousing Muerce from his thoughts. He was thinking there was something in the stitching around the mouth of the body he viewed earlier in the day that still bothered him, yet he was unable to determine what it was.

"Sleeping well?" he said.

"Yes."

"Depends."

"It depends on what?" Eleanor said.

"Where are you going with this?"

"Are you still seeing Doctor Riley?"

Muerce hesitated for a second, then answered truthfully.

"Yes," he said. "As a matter of fact, I have an appointment this week."

"Are you still using the pills?"

Muerce looked at Eleanor, displeased.

"I told you I would go there tonight," she said.

"Yes, you did," he said, resigned. "And we are there, finally, thankfully, for you."

"And?"

"I hadn't for awhile," he said, shifting his weight on the couch. "The last two weeks have been kind of rough. I'm sort of working on something, and it's not pleasant."

Eleanor took a last drag from her cigarette. She looked at her son, then released the smoke from her lungs into the living room.

"After all this time," she said. "You have to forgive yourself, and forget."

"It's the forget part I have trouble with," he said, averting his eyes from her. He knew what would come next.

"Emily Benoit was a long time ago, a lifetime ago," she said. "You need not bear that standard any longer."

He had not heard the name spoken out loud for some time. And time had not lessened the pain he felt when he heard it.

The two of them fell silent, listening only to Vivaldi, and the storm outside. Eleanor stamped out the cigarette in the crystal ashtray, and finished her Diet Coke. When the music stopped there was only the rain on the windows.

"It's awful out there," she said, getting up from the couch. "Why don't you stay tonight?"

"That would be nice," he said, staring at his reflection in the distant window.

"Then I'm off to bed," she said, making her way up the three steps that led from the sunken living room. "I'll have coffee ready."

Muerce nodded his head, told her he'd be up early as well, and wished her good night. Eleanor retreated quietly, unsure if she did more damage than good by mentioning the Emily subject.

While time may not have lessened the pain of Emily Benoit, it allowed Muerce to move quickly from those sad thoughts to what was in front of him. And what was in front of him now was his phone, on which he keyed in the four-digit security code, and fingered the sunflower "photos" icon on the screen. His index finger paged through the pictures, stopping at the close-up he took at the morgue. He turned the phone sideways, and using his thumb and index finger, expanded the image so he could study the stitching on the mouth.

Muerce stared at the screen for several minutes, trying to make sense of the gruesome yet beautiful handwork that had sealed the victim's mouth. He thought about the killer. Little made sense to Muerce. He was not trained for this type of thing. But that was what Bhote wanted. An untrained, but curious mind. Muerce let ideas reel through his head as he moved his finger across the lips on the screen to adjust the view of the photo.

Then he stopped. It was there, on the right edge of the victim's mouth, almost hidden among a field of embroidered flowers. Stitched in a combination of gold and silver silk thread, barely discernible from the pallid flesh was the French word for monkey—*singe*.

SPRING FORWARD

The curtains all of silk, and hemmed with golden thread,
And comely coverings of fairest cloth o'er spread.
Above, of silk, so bright, the broideries they were,
The curtains ran on ropes, with rings of red gold fair.
Rich tapestries of Tars, and Toulouse, on the wall
Hung fair, the floor was spread with the like cloth withal.
—The Pearl Poet

CHAPTER 12

"Goddammit," Muerce cursed, spilling hot coffee as he spun the large steering wheel of the Mercedes to make a tight corner on one of the Crest Drive switchbacks. He nearly hit a green trash container obstructing the road.

He slept well the night before, but woke with unicorns and monkeys on his mind. The lidless mug of coffee didn't help. The Mercedes was vintage, and as such, there were no cup holders.

If he timed it right, Muerce could make the ribbon of freeway that ran in the valley between the Palantine and Esquiline districts, and beat the rush-hour traffic. There was plenty of time before Travis was to meet him at the apartment, though an accident on the freeway could constipate the commute for hours. The weather had cleared, and Muerce could see the museum at the top of the Esquiline; its white marble, freshly washed from the storm, glistened in the morning sun. So did the swath of foliage that blanketed the hillside, which had started to green up with the moisture, and the approaching Spring Equinox.

It was a fresh start to a new day, a new week, and a new season. Muerce liked fresh starts because they were rare.

— —

He was toweling off after a long shower when the doorbell gonged three times. Slipping into a robe, Muerce was surprised when he answered the door. It was a delivery service with two packages sent by his IT Guy. There was a half hour left before Travis was to arrive. Muerce signed for the packages.

A note attached to the smaller of the two boxes said the order was complete, and if he had any questions he should call—anytime. Inside the large box was a new laptop loaded with appropriate search software, access permissions to various city, state and federal databases, as well as encryption protocols, and directions on how everything worked. *Secrecy, Snooping and Stalking for Dummies.*

The smaller box contained a mobile phone, also programmed with encryption protocols, and several "special" apps that the new "user" would be instructed how to use at a later date. Muerce detected a hint of jealousy in the last line, and made a mental note to explain to IT Guy what Travis' role would be, as well as the duration of the relationship. Muerce began to formulate a life plan for Travis Squire, unbeknownst to him. The plan itself was somewhat a surprise to Muerce himself, but he was impressed at how Travis handled himself at Club Unicorn. Muerce also thought he would need some additional feet on the ground—or, more importantly, fingers on the keyboard, and eyes on the screen—to assist in Bhote's request.

Muerce put the packages in the spare bedroom that served as an office before changing into casual clothes for the day.

The sun shone brighter through the front windows of the apartment than it had the last few months. He flipped open the louvres of the large plantation shutters to take full advantage of the natural light. The rays were an auspicious sign that winter was waning, even if current events in his life were waxing toward uncertainty.

— —

At exactly nine o'clock, the doorbell broke the quiet of the apartment. Travis was on time. Muerce derived some satisfaction from it, but not as much as Travis did. For the first time, Travis felt like he was going in a direction that suited him.

"I'm here like you said," Travis said.

"Yes?" Muerce said.

Travis stood in the hallway outside Muerce's door, waiting for some further direction and, perhaps, a positive response from Muerce. Instead, there was only an uncomfortable silence.

"You told me to be here at nine and, well, I'm here," Travis said.

"Yes?" Muerce said, making no movement.

"Well?"

"Well what?" Muerce said. "I said nine and you're here at nine. So what? This isn't youth soccer. I don't hand out participation trophies just for showing up. I tell you to be somewhere at a certain time, you're there. I tell you do do something by a certain date, you do it.

"Just doing what is expected doesn't make you special."

Travis' spirit began to puddle around his feet, along with any confidence and enthusiasm he had when he rang the doorbell. He stood, blinking, and feeling very small and stupid.

"I don't like cats Travis," Muerce said. "Do you know why I don't like cats?"

Travis shook his head back and forth. He had no idea why Muerce didn't like cats.

"I don't like cats because they expect you to hold them in your lap, stroke them, and tell them how pretty they are," Muerce said. "And for what?"

"I don't know," Travis said.

"For nothing," Muerce said. "Do you know what I do like?"

"No."

"I like dogs," Muerce said. "Want to know why I like dogs?"

"Yes."

"Because you can train a dog to do things," Muerce said. "Train a dog the right way, and he'll fetch things for you, or do tricks. A trained dog will sound an alarm. A really well trained dog will kill for you.

"Do you know what dogs have that cats don't have?"

"No."

"Loyalty," Muerce said. "Dogs are loyal. Cats, on the other hand, are sneaky little shits that don't give a fuck about their owners. They run away at the first sign of danger. Thus, the term, 'scaredy-cat.'"

Muerce's point registered solidly with Travis, who felt a little taller than he had a moment earlier.

"Are you a cat or a dog, Travis?"

"I'm a dog Mister Muerce," Travis said, his lips tightly pursed, suppressing the smile about to erupt.

"Good boy," Muerce said. "Come on in, and let's start your training."

"Yes sir," Travis said. *Muerce may not like cats, but he sure likes pussy.*

— —

Travis had a sharp mind for numbers, and tasks. It wasn't that he was bad at cards—it was that he had been cheated.

Beyond the cursory tutorials Muerce gave him regarding the electronic equipment—and the cheat sheets IT Guy provided—Travis knew far more about navigating and manipulating them, and the raft of information they provided, than did Muerce. What Travis payed special attention to when Muerce was talking was what the man wanted, and by when he wanted it. He especially listened to *how* Muerce wanted him to operate. What he found especially intriguing and fascinating, what he most wanted to learn from Muerce, was the man's style—his code of conduct. There was an aura about Muerce, a sort of noble light Travis gravitated toward. *I, too, will make a difference.*

Travis captured the tasks and drop-dead timelines like he watched a dealer with a deck of cards. He was a born card counter, who had yet to get the opportunity to hone the skill in a fair stakes game. The cards lost some of their appeal after the rib crunching from Massimo.

Muerce had Travis setup the new laptop on the large, well-worn oak desk in the spare bedroom. The desk had been Muerce's Father's. The room would become the base of operations for their investigation, although the laptop did have secure wireless access, and Travis was allowed to take it home. IT Guy had established a tight firewall in the apartment, and also came once a month to sweep the place of any listening or video devices. He had never found any, but as Muerce explained, he'd rather the place always be secure from eavesdropping. Muerce reiterated the point about discretion he made at Club Unicorn.

Travis keyed his way through various setups, including the wireless printer, scanner, fax machine, and punched in his own security codes, and passwords. IT Guy had already activated the phone, and Travis texted Muerce.

"What are you doing?" Muerce said, looking at the "test" text message on his phone.

"Texting is more secure than voice," Travis said. "Just respond you got the text and we're linked."

Muerce shrugged, and responded. What he didn't know, and what Travis didn't tell him, was that IT Guy had loaded an application on the phone that allowed Travis to download another phone's contacts when they responded to one of his texts. Travis now knew who Muerce knew. At the very least, Travis knew how to contact the people Muerce knew. *This could come in handy.*

"Put that down," Muerce said, pointing to the large magnifying glass attached to an elk antler handle that Travis was spinning around.

"Antique?" Travis said, intrigued by what he suspected would be a good story behind the object.

"No, I just don't want you to break it," Muerce said.

"So this wasn't like something that belonged to Arthur Conan Doyle or J. Edgar Hoover that you bought at auction in London or something?" Travis said.

"No, Restoration Hardware," Muerce said, paying little attention to Travis. "My interior decorator thought it would go with the theme of the place. I doubt it's even real."

Travis's disappointed did not last long. Muerce handed him a set of keys, and a slip of paper.

"Keys to the apartment, and the car you'll be using," Muerce said. "And the security and access codes to the apartment, alarm system, and the private elevator."

"What car?" Travis said, suppressing his reaction to the private elevator. *Way, way cool. James Fucking Bond cool. Jack Fucking Muerce, license to kill, cool.*

"Not the Mercedes if that's what your thinking," Muerce said. "Come on, I'll show you, then you can get started. Follow me."

Travis followed Muerce into the master bedroom, and then into the large and impressive dressing closet.

"*Pleased to meet you, hope you guess my name,*" Travis sang under his breath.

"What was that?" Muerce said, opening up the laundry hamper, and pulling the draw strings closed.

"Nothing, just reminded me of a song," Travis said. *A man of wealth and taste... do, to, do.*

"Laundry every Monday morning," Muerce said, pausing. "Well, go ahead. Get it. It's Monday."

The canvas laundry bag slung over Travis' shoulder made him look like a sailor shipping off to sea. The grin on Travis' face reflected in one of the large brass plates inside the private elevator made it clear the boy was excited to be shipping out. Muerce went over the list of research he wanted completed by Friday as the elevator clanked toward the basement. On the top of the list was everything he could uncover about Zmaj Brankovic—The Dragon.

The elevator gave a small lurch when it reached its destination, and Muerce muscled the gangly metal gate open. He remembered the catch in the elevator, and reminded himself to have the service people out to take a look.

Travis spotted the Mercedes in one of the car bays toward the back of the garage. In a bay behind it was another vehicle covered in a gray protective cloth. He couldn't discern the make of the shrouded car, but knew it was smaller than the Mercedes, and looked much faster.

"This way," Muerce said, walking in the opposite direction of the Mercedes.

"Is that one yours?" Travis said, pointing to the shrouded phantom next to the Mercedes. Muerce didn't answer.

"This is what you're responsible for," Muerce said, standing next to a dark blue 2000 Jeep Cherokee. The paint on the engine hood and roof was faded, and there were a few rust spots on the body work. Through the windows Travis could see the interior had been patched in places with duct tape. However, the tires looked relatively new, and had good tread.

"Get in and pop the hood," Muerce said. Travis did, then exited the car on Muerce's hand signal for him to come around to the front.

"You're thinking what a nondescript piece of shit, right?" Muerce said.

"Definite POS, yeah," Travis said.

"That's the point," Muerce said. "Nobody looks at this car twice on the street, or parked down the block. That's what counts on the outside. This is what counts on the inside."

Travis whistled when he looked inside the showroom-clean engine compartment.

"Replaced the six cylinder with a Chevy V8," Muerce said. "It took my guy a lot of refitting, and tuning time to get it to work. But believe me, it works."

"Damn," Travis said.

"Not that you're going to need this kind of power," Muerce said, slamming the hood down. "I wanted you to know what you're in charge of so you don't do anything stupid, by accident... or on purpose."

"Got it," Travis said, as he decided which long stretch of road on his way to Saigon Laundry he would floor the beast to see what it really could do.

"Perkins," Muerce said.

"What?" Travis said, a look of shock on his face.

"You're thinking Perkins Avenue, say, between thirtieth and twenty-sixth street," Muerce said. "If you catch the lights just right this time of day."

"How did you... "

"Know? Are you kidding? Take Levritt Avenue. The lights are in sync. The cops work Perkins this time of day. And don't forget; laundry, research. You can come and go here during the day as you please, just call, or text, to let me know what you're up to. Garage opener is on the visor."

"Got it Mister Muerce," Travis said, shutting the Cherokee's door with a *clank*. Muerce was already entering the elevator, and closing the metal grate behind him when Travis turned the ignition key. The engine jumped to life with a growl Travis felt in the seat of his pants.

Perfect, he thought, *and I've got permission to see what it can do.*

The peerless moment was corrupted when Travis automatically, and without looking at the dashboard, fingered at the controls searching for the stereo. Instead, his hand found a gaping hole in the console where a stereo should be. *Crap. Going to have to do something about that.*

As the elevator made its way to the penthouse, Muerce pictured Travis looking for tunes, and laughed out loud.

CHAPTER 13

The voicemail Muerce left for Bhote regarded his discovery found in the photo of the second victim's mouth. What it meant, Muerce had no idea. He only wanted Bhote to confirm what he found, and to let him know if there were any other details the examination, or forensic tests might have uncovered.

Then he called Trumbley's direct line at the Downtown station. Trumbley's recorded greeting said he would be on personal leave for several days, and gave his cell phone number in case he needed to be reached in an emergency. Muerce thought it strange Trumbley wouldn't have said something at the morgue about taking time off, and figured it was an old message waiting to be changed.

He didn't hesitate to call Trumbley's cell, which rolled right into voicemail. Muerce left a message about the word embroidered on the mouth of the second victim. Unsure how he and Trumbley were supposed to coordinate on their unofficial investigation, Muerce thought it best to keep the lines of communication open.

Next he called the florist, and had flowers sent to Miriam, at her office. As an afterthought, Muerce placed a second order for flowers for Ashley. Doubling the number of stems. He would, he figured, see her at the gala Saturday night. The flowers would, he hoped, alleviate any awkwardness, and possibly keep the door open for the night. Miriam remained a mystery to him.

There was one call left to make, but he stared at the screen of the phone until it went dark. Muerce was in a momentary daze, deciding if he should make the call or not. But he promised himself after lying to Eleanor about it. He had to make the call.

The number was still in his contacts, and he pressed his thumb to the screen. Dr. Riley's voicemail answered, and Muerce requested a "first available" appointment.

By the afternoon, Dr. Riley returned his call, saying she had an opening for early afternoon the next day. That worked for Muerce. He would see her. Afterwards, he would go to the club for a massage, and a steam. Then he could relax with a nice, quiet dinner at Saigon Laundry.

— —

Tomaso let out a satisfying groan as he ejaculated into her mouth. His hands tightened their grip on the arm rests of his chair as she finished him, careful not to cause a mess on his slacks. She knew not to leave any saliva or semen when she was done, and wrapped her blouse around the base of his groin while most of him remained in her mouth. Slowly, she pulled away after swallowing, and drew the blouse over his fading erection. Just as he left her mouth, Tomaso jerked his knees hard against her shoulders, causing the top of her head to strike the underside of the glass desk. Tomaso laughed. She winced at the pain but did not cry out, or make eye contact with him. She knew better.

Backing out from beneath the desk on all fours, she grabbed her rain slicker draped over one of the red chairs, and stood up. Straightening her skirt, she put the raincoat on over her bare torso. Without speaking, she walked toward the door, stuffing the stained blouse into her purse, and snatched a pair of hundred-dollar bills Massimo held in his raised hand as she made her exit.

"Nothing better than a blow job to clear your head," Tomaso said, standing and zipping his trousers closed. He adjusted himself, and sat back down.

There was a light knock on the door. Massimo looked through the peep hole, opened it, and accepted a cup and saucer of espresso from one of the bar boys. Massimo brought it to Tomaso, who dropped a cube of sugar into the dark, rich liquid, twisted a peel of lemon, and stirred. He clinked the spoon against the white porcelain cup three times.

"That's it" Tomaso said. "St. George."

"What are you talking about?" Massimo said.

"Saint George, the dragon slayer," Tomaso said, downing the espresso as if it were a shot of whiskey.

"And patron saint of the Boy Scouts, too," Massimo said. "But he's Mister George now. The church stripped him of his sainthood along with Christopher."

"Oh, who gives a fuck what the church does, that's not what I'm talking about," Tomaso said. "Our Saint George is alive and well... connected."

Massimo looked puzzled.

"Jack Muerce," Tomaso said. "Saint Jack Muerce. He's going to kill the Dragon for us."

"Muerce kill someone? I don't think so."

Tomaso began pacing as he calculated his options, and opportunities.

"Figuratively, perhaps," he said. "Maybe not actually, although actually would be better. I don't like the prick. I don't like him at all."

"Muerce?" Massimo said. "He's done some solids for people."

Tomaso stopped pacing abruptly and stared at Massimo in a way that conveyed he knew something Massimo didn't want him to know. It made Massimo uncomfortable.

"*Stunade*," Tomaso said. "I'm talking about Brankovic."

Tomaso resumed his pacing, and calculating. "The Skeleton," Tomaso declared.

"You're talking in code Tino," Massimo said. "What are you saying."

"Brankovic's accountant," Tomaso said. "He looks like a skeleton. He was here Saturday night. With those two girls. Right?"

"Right. Plus Brankovic, and those freight trains he has for muscle."

"You said Muerce was with them?"

"I wouldn't say he was with them, but they had some drinks together waiting for you," Massimo said. "In the VIP booth. Mostly it was the accountant talking to Muerce. The spooky girl smoked, stared and didn't talk. The blonde was getting all up with the kid Muerce was with. She got her ass beat over that."

"Bitch didn't know her place," Tomaso said. "The spooky one does. I want the Dragon prick dead, but you have to respect that he values the power of respect."

"Fear."

"What?" Tomaso said.

"Fear not respect. They're all scared shitless of him," Massimo said. "The skinny on the street says for good reason, too. He's hundred-proof motherfucker. Real Code of Hammurabi type of shit. Steal, you lose a hand. Lie, you lose your tongue. Fuck the wrong person, you lose your dick. Has serious rep from the Bosnian war. Hitler-shit. Genocide stuff. Nothing proved though. But they wanted that cocksucker bad back there.

"And he liked to take trophies. Hands and feet."

"Like that dead hooker?" Tomaso said.

"Yeah, could be," Massimo said. "Could be."

"Could be is good enough," Tomaso said. "I tried to get Muerce hip to that."

"But it was none of his business, right?" Massimo said.

"Classic Muerce," Tomaso said. "No fair maiden to be saved. Because she was already dead."

Tomaso continued his nervous pacing.

"Muerce's the key," Tomaso said. "I just don't know how to get the key into the lock, and make him turn. For now we have to get fucked in the ass by Brankovic, and like it. But not too much. And not by Brankovic.

"We'll let him think his accountant is fucking us. Something's going on with him, and Muerce."

"The accountant probably just wants season tickets to the opera," Massimo said, laughing.

"I don't think so," Tomaso said, readjusting his scrotum. "Set up a meeting with the Skeleton. Private. Just him and me to talk about about the... transfer of business."

"I'll take care of it right away," Massimo said, pulling Zajak's business card from his pocket. "I've got his number. Hands these out like Tic Tacs."

Tomaso took the business card from Massimo's hand.

"Hmm, transparent," Tomaso said. "But I see you. Yes I do."

Tomaso looked at the card again. There was no title under Zajak's name. Just a phone number. Massimo turned to leave the office.

"Massy," Tomaso said. "Let's go old school. A steam at the City Athletic Club. Tomorrow afternoon if he can make it. And schedule me for a massage."

"Done," Massimo said.

Standing in the bar area of Club Unicorn, Massimo looked at the empty dance floor; glad he didn't say anything to Tomaso about Paige Sharron's fixation on Muerce. The girl had a hard-on for the guy. Massimo saw her with the dagger, ready to go after Brankovic if he raised a hand to Muerce. It was obvious to Massimo, who knew Muerce was a tool when it came to damaged women. *Damsels in distress*. But it was none of his business, and it need not be any of Tomaso's either. Massimo had his reasons. *I'm doing you a solid, Jack.*

— —

A ribbon of molten glass passed over large rollers behind Brankovic as he held aloft the left hand he had just severed by ax from the man writhing, and screaming on the sand and ash-covered factory floor. Brankovic nodded, signaling his two simian-looking bodyguards to lift the man from the ground, and brace him tightly. Once on his feet, Brankovic slapped his victim with the the man's detached hand to get his attention. Then using the hand, he steadied the victim's head by placing it under his chin.

"You steal from me I take from you," Brankovic said. "You understand?"

The victim was in shock, and didn't respond.

"Now we fix you up, take you to hospital," Brankovic said, patting the man on the cheek with the hand.

Holding the handless arm, Brankovic led the victim, with the assistance of the bodyguards, toward the moving ribbon of molten glass. The heat radiating from the orange slab blew Brankovic's hair from his shoulders. His eyes reflected the intense light, and heat of the slab. Fire was his element. Firmly grasping the victim's handless arm by the elbow, Brankovic thrust the stump on top of the molten sheet, instantly cauterizing the wound, and creating a black streak that moved in the same direction as the ribbon. The man began to howl in bellows that could be heard above the noise of the furnace, and found the strength to push back, and out of the hold of the men that restrained him. He staggered backwards several feet, holding the smoldering stump in front of his face in disbelief, before falling to the ground in convulsions.

"Dump him down the street from the hospital," Brankovic ordered, picking up the severed hand from the dirty factory floor, and brushing the soot and sand from it. "Let him walk, or crawl the rest of the way."

The bodyguards did as they were told. Brankovic turned to make his way toward the complex of offices that overlooked the factory floor. As he passed the large furnace that melted the aggregate that was turned into sheets of glass, he nonchalantly tossed the hand about twenty feet into the cauldron.

Zajak, wearing a respirator that covered his face, met Brankovic outside the large doors that led through a environmental safety room into the factory offices, and factory control rooms. Beneath the mask, Zajak wore a look of disapproval.

"What is it they say Zajak?" Brankovic said, a broad smile breaking the angles of his long face. "Nothing but net?"

"I find little humor in it," Zajak said. "That run is ruined, and will have to be recycled and redone. It will cost us more than what the man stole. On top of that, he was one of the better producers, and now he'll be out for at least six weeks. If he comes back at all."

"He will be back," Brankovic said. "If he still wants to breathe. And much sooner than six weeks."

They did not speak again until they made their way into the labyrinth of offices that overlooked the massive factory floor. Although it was not quite the middle of March, and there remained a seasonal chill, the air conditioning in the office was on high to offset the heat from the furnaces.

The cold made Brankovic uncomfortable, and irritable.

Mikal, dressed in a lime-green velour track suit, but minus most of his gold chains, rings and watches, stood next to one of the large windows that overlooked the factory floor. He was shaking. He had seen everything that had taken place, and suppressed the urge to vomit when Brankovic approached him.

Brankovic stared at Mikal, but spoke to Zajak.

"This is a quick meeting, I have other business," Brankovic said.

"Zmaj, we should go over the books and bank accounts," Zajak said, irritated.

"All is in order as we have discussed before, yes?" Brankovic said, his eyes did not leave Mikal.

"Yes, of course, everything remains in order," Zajak said. "You would know if it wasn't."

"Yes, I would know," Brankovic said. "Which is why there is no need to go over the accounts, right now."

"As you wish," Zajak said. "But there are some other opportunities that we should discuss."

"Mikal, yes?" Brankovic said, ignoring Zajak.

"Da," Mikal said.

"You see?" Brankovic said, turning his head toward the factory floor.

"Da."

"A valued co-worker has been injured on the job," Brankovic said. "We need you to step in for him while he recuperates. Cover his sales territory."

"Da."

"Good," Brankovic said, putting his hand on Mikal's shoulder. "We can count on you then. Do well, and you will be rewarded."

"I won't disappoint," Mikal said, wanting to get away from Brankovic as quickly as possible. He would have agreed to do anything for the Dragon just to get away from him.

"Good," Brankovic said. "Work-related accidents are disruptive to our business.

"And what of the new girl I sent you. She will work out well?"

"Da," Mikal said. "Once the swelling..."

Brankovic frowned at Mikal.

"She will be a good earner," Mikal said. "Very quickly our best earner."

Brankovic looked at both Mikal and Zajak, then turned and walked down the hallway to the elevator. He said nothing when he left. Mikal, uncertain what to do, stood in silence. Zajak stood quietly, and watched until the elevator doors closed. Then he turned to Mikal, surprised the pimp was still there.

"Idiot," Zajak said. "Get out of here."

"Da."

The sound of Mikal making his exit down a side staircase was interrupted by a buzzing inside Zajak's suit coat pocket. He removed the Blackberry, and looked at the screen. The phone number was unlisted, but he took the call. It was Tomaso's lieutenant, Massimo. The one they called Massy. He said Tomaso would like to meet with him to talk about the business transfer. Zajak agreed to the time, and meeting place. It would be just himself and Tomaso.

The pretty but severe brunette that had been at Club Unicorn with Zajak made her way behind him as he talked on the phone. She wore a conservative, but stylish blue pinstripe business suit with white silk blouse, and pumps with short heels. As Zajak finished his phone call, she lit a cigarette. The lighter produced a flame like a blowtorch, and sounded like it was tearing the air around it.

"Who was that?" she said, exhaling the first draw from the cigarette.

"You can't smoke in here," Zajak scolded.

The girl laughed, spun around, and with the cigarette, pointed at the furnace and ribbons of molten glass below them.

"I would think this is the one place I can smoke," she said.

"New city health codes," he said. "No smoking in public places, including the workplace. And you are in management so you have to lead by example. No?"

"So rich the irony," she said, tossing the cigarette to the floor, and stubbing it out with the toe of her shoe. "I would never have thought Hell would be smoke-free."

Zajak got close to her, put his hand on her shoulder, and brushed her hair back.

"My dearest Amelie," he said. "You smoke too much. I don't want it to kill you. I need you around for a long time."

Amelie dropped her head onto Zajak's chest, and rested it there comfortably. There was no one around to see them.

"His brutality is without reason," she said.

"You saw?"

"Yes," Amelie said. "So unnecessary."

"It is," Zajak said. "And unnecessarily reckless in this country. It brings too much attention."

Zajak played the words he just spoke through his head again, and then again. Filtering them in such a way that they presented a new possibility.

"Then again," he said, reaching to hold her face with both his hands. "More attention might work in our favor."

Amelie recognized the look Zajak had when he conceived a new idea. It made her wary.

"Who were you talking to?" she said.

"It was destiny calling," he said, kissing her on her forehead. "I believe the last of its kind will soon be extinct. And we can go about our business without distractions."

CHAPTER 14

"Luther, what's up?" Muerce said. He was parked in front of a nondescript three-story glass office building surrounded by acres of asphalt dotted with brown islands of zoysia. Each of the islands in the sea of parking spaces had a small tree wired to wooden stakes. Light snowflakes struck the windshield of the Mercedes, and instantly turned to droplets of water.

"You getting snow where you are?" Muerce said.

"Nah, just spitting now and then," Luther said. "Still cold though. Thought we beat this weather for the year."

"The last gasp of winter," Muerce said. "Some flakes here, but they won't last long. Too warm."

"Where are you?" Luther said.

Muerce hesitated to respond.

"Past the hills," he said. "In the land of little trees."

"The burbs?" Luther said, chuckling. "Be careful not to stay too long. You might get a rash."

"So what's up my man?" Muerce said.

"Got everything you wanted, and walked the kid through the different programs," Luther said. "He's pretty sharp."

"Uh-huh," Muerce said, more interested in the snowflakes than what Luther had to say.

"Do you still want me for the usual de-bug?" he said.

"Uh-huh," Muerce said, rolling down the window of the Mercedes to capture errant flakes in his hand.

"You know you're ready for some technical upgrades on most of your equipment," Luther said. "Do you still need me?"

"Uh-huh," Muerce said, focusing back on Luther. "What?"

"Do you still need me?"

"What the hell are you talking about Luther?"

"I asked if you still need me," Luther said. "You've never taken on a partner before, and this kid is pretty hip on the tech side. I just figured."

"Relax," Muerce said. "I'm not taking on a partner. He's more like an intern."

"Oh."

"He doesn't know it yet, but he'll be back in school in the Fall," Muerce said. "Besides, you're my IT Guy. Why would I need someone else?"

"Well, thanks, Jack."

"I should probably say it more," Muerce said. "You're the best, my man."

"Ah hell, Jack, does this mean we're going steady?"

"Sure Luther, tell you're wife it's over," Muerce said. His hand wet from the snow flakes. "We can run off to Vermont, and get married."

Luther laughed until he sputtered.

"Hey, Luther," Muerce said, looking at his watch, and feeling more mortal than he had in a long time. "Teach the kid everything you can. We both have to pass the baton sometime."

"Roger that," Luther said. "Just let's hold on to the baton a little longer."

"Let's," Muerce said, ending the call.

Muerce closed the window. Gripping the steering wheel with both hands, he drew in a deep breath before slowly letting it out. *Here we go.*

— —

Dr. Sheila Riley sat in the chair across from Muerce, opened a notebook, and brushed the blonde-turned-gray hair from her face. She smiled, glad to see him. They had a long history together. A long doctor-patient history. Their relationship was strictly professional, and was well defined by unspoken yet clear boundaries. Over the years, she was a refuge Muerce did not have with any other woman—with the exception, on some levels, of Eleanor.

Muerce turned his phone off, and slipped it into his pocket. For the next hour he was unreachable.

"I was glad when you called," Dr. Riley said. "I had been thinking about you. So how are you doing?"

Muerce spent the next ten to fifteen minutes catching Riley up on the progressions of his life since their last session. He talked about Ashley,

Miriam, the murders, and his minor role in the investigation. He focused, for awhile, on the evolving, and curious relationship with Travis. He did not mention Paige, or the face from the past.

"How are you sleeping?" she said.

"Shitty, mostly," Muerce said.

"And how are you doing with the Xanax?"

Muerce paused, looked away from Dr. Riley as a child about to receive a reprimand might, then looked her straight in the eyes.

"I hadn't taken any in months," he said. "Since, maybe, a day or two after our last session. After the morgue, seeing that girl, and what had been done to her. I took some."

"Some?"

"Two."

"Alone?"

"I was alone, yes."

Dr. Riley frowned.

"Oh, I see what you mean," Muerce said. "I took them with alcohol. Two drinks. Two strong drinks."

Dr. Riley rested the pen on her notebook, and sat back in the chair.

"Given what you had seen that day," she said. "I'd have probably done the same thing. Minus the alcohol. That had to have been really awful. And then again this past Sunday?"

"Yes," Muerce said. "A second victim, not a second round of Xanax."

"That's really terrible, Jack," she said. "About the women. And from what I'm hearing, you are involved in the investigation, but not involved? How does that work?"

"I don't know," Muerce said. "I really don't. There's a fascination to it I can't explain. Almost like it's an obligation. I'm afraid I'm in way over my head. I have no formal investigative training, no forensic background, no authority, and, well, limited experience in psychotic killers."

"As I understand it, you've just been asked to look at it from your perspective, without all the professional attachments," she said. "From the point of view of a beginner's mind, and not an expert."

"Yes, that's fair to say," Muerce said.

"Kind of like Travis' relationship with you?" she said.

Muerce contemplated her words.

"You put in a lot of hard work to get off the Xanax," Dr. Riley said. "I want you to be careful. Given how you've described the condition of the bodies, and the ritual nature of the dismemberments and treatment, placement and, I think, timing, it's likely there will be more."

Dr. Riley uncrossed her legs, put her knees together, and leaned forward to emphasize what she was about to say.

"Jack, your role is as a consultant; to just think about what the facts are, and report what you think back to the authorities," she said. "You haven't been asked to go after the killer. And you shouldn't. You're not qualified, or empowered to do that.

"I want us to understand each other on that, okay?"

"No, I get it," Muerce said. "Believe me, I wish I wasn't involved. But a friend asked a favor."

"And you feel obligated to do favors for friends, and others," Dr. Riley said, shifting her weight back into her chair. "So, let's talk about Emily if we're talking about favors."

"We've talked that to death, don't you think?" he said.

"Have we?"

"I think so," Muerce said, looking away from Dr. Riley in an effort to show disinterest in the subject. Still, it hurt just thinking her name. He couldn't remember the last time he had even said it out loud. Eleanor had, but he didn't want to. It hurt too much.

"Do you enjoy the suffering?" Dr. Riley said.

"That's not fair," Muerce said.

"Sure it is," Dr. Riley said. "You've held on to it for so long that I have to ask if you enjoy it. Until you assign some meaning to it, it won't stop. Do you think your work, all the women, the Xanax, are maybe just distractions?"

"It still hurts, Sheila," he said, his voice straining. "After all this time. It's still there."

"Of course it is, it always will be, Jack," Dr. Riley said. "Until you can grow from it, survive and thrive, you will continue to suffer. That's why I asked if you enjoy it."

"I don't enjoy it," Muerce said. "I want it to go away."

"It's not going to go away," Dr. Riley said. "So why not try and embrace it? Consciously make it a part of you, because it has been, and always will be a part of you.

"One of my favorite lines from the teachings of Buddha is that we are the cause of our own suffering."

Muerce attempted to digest what Dr. Riley said, what The Buddha said. It resounded with him on a basic level, but he knew it would take time to fully absorb the meaning. Integrating the words, the suffering, into his life seemed out of reach.

"So I should start burning incense, and take up yoga?" Muerce said.

"If it helps, sure," Dr. Riley said. "But try and lay off the Xanax. You don't want to go back to where you where. And definitely don't mix them with alcohol, please. You see what happens in the news all the time."

"I'll be careful," Muerce said, giving his most engaging smile.

"Please do," she said. "Do you want to schedule another session, or play it by ear?"

"Kind of both," Muerce said. "Do you mind if I call for an appointment in the next few days. Everything feels like it's up in the air right now."

"Sure," Dr. Riley said, walking Muerce to the back door of the office. "I'll wait a few days, and I can call you if I have a slot that opens up."

"Perfect," Muerce said. "Thank you."

"Jack," she said, holding the door open as he stood in the hallway. "Remember, you're not a cop. Be careful."

Muerce smiled, and nodded a thank you as she shut the door behind him.

— —

The phone exploded with a barrage of text messages, and voicemails when he powered it on. The text message that grabbed his attention first was a headline that had been pushed out by the local newspaper, and heralded the possibility that a serial killer may on the loose in the city. *Crap. It's out.*

The second text message was from Travis, and said simply that he was at the apartment. The research was going well, and that he had found some "sick shit" on Brankovic.

Muerce ignored the rest of the text messages, and decided not to listen to any of the voicemails until after his steam, and massage. He always felt a little lighter after a session with Riley, and wanted to hold on to the feeling for as long as he could. The steam and massage would extend the lightness he felt.

He called Eleanor, and left a message that he had seen Dr. Riley, and that he would pick her up Saturday night in plenty of time for them to be at the museum for the VIP reception.

When he thought of Ashley he reviewed his text messages one more time, and found one from her.

Her text said: Got flowers. Made me blush. Thnx. Ash.

The message from her gave Muerce the stirrings of an erection.

CHAPTER 15

"Do you think it's possible to sweat out sin?" Tomaso said.

"No," Zajak said. "The physical indiscretions we inflict upon ourselves are temporal. They aren't sins. Just bad choices. Sins, on the other hand, are footprints we leave on our souls. And only God can wash our souls clean."

"So we can only be absolved through atonement?" Tomaso said, standing up and wrapping a towel around his waist.

The white-tiled steam room at the City Club was empty except for the two of them. The hissing steam vent ceased and the heavy, hot clouds of moisture settled. The air was a little easier to breath. The colorful blue and green accent tiles that depicted various mythical sea creatures were visible amid the vaporous and torpid atmosphere.

Zajak moved himself and his arrangement of towels to the highest of the three benches in the steam room, situating himself in the corner where the heat and moisture tended to accumulate its intensity. He had more than a high tolerance for heat—he had a need for it. And it came in different forms for Zajak. There was the heat of the glass furnaces, the Dragon, and the burning of his own faith, and the direction it had given him.

Brankovic had gotten too hot, too dangerous, too unpredictable. In his time, Brankovic had been useful to Zajak. But circumstances had changed. What was acceptable in the Balkans, was not in America.

Brankovic was what he was; the last of his kind, a mythical creature born and nurtured in the sinister and sadistic dark Middle Ages of the Soviet Empire. When it fell, and the Eastern Bloc dominoes along with it,

Brankovic survived amidst the ethnic cleansing of the Bosnian War. He was the brutal and senseless anarchic procurator of evolution.

A cold finger of memory traced its way down Zajak's sweating back as he recalled the trophies of hands and feet, ears, tongues and noses, Brankovic took during the war. He remembered the crudely stitched wounds of the victims who were allowed to live to serve as testaments to Brankovic's power. Zajak shivered at the thought of them, and wrapped a towel around his shoulders as Tomaso ladled a plastic cup of cold water over the thermostat to coax more heat into the room.

Zajak's soul was covered with bloody footprints, but they were for a cause. He asked for forgiveness every day during prayers, and as part of his atonement he told himself he would become an agent of change. Global change. Allah would prevail. In the meantime, Brankovic had to go, but it was not easy to kill a dragon. Certain customs had to be observed. The head of a dragon had to be severed, and no blood of a dragon could be spilled on the ground as the Earth would not accept it. And not just anybody could kill a dragon. Certainly, Zajak knew, he could not kill a dragon. Only someone with a pure heart could slay such a beast.

Jack Muerce, Zajak believed, had been delivered for the task. It was the will of Allah.

"Your request for absolution must be sincere," Zajak said, as the hissing of the steam jets gained momentum. "You must repent, and ask for forgiveness."

"Ask from who?" Tomaso said, dropping the towel from his waist to the floor before settling back down on the lower bench. He leaned back and looked up at Zajak, who disappeared in the cloud of steam.

"From those we have transgressed," Zajak said. "Which is not always possible. And from Him."

"And how do we know we've atoned, been forgiven?" Tomaso said.

"When we feel better about ourselves," Zajak said.

"Well, I'd sure as fuck like to feel better about what your boss is doing to me," Tomaso said.

"And you will," Zajak said, bemused but slightly irritated that Tomaso was slipping back into more earthly and immediate issues than the spiritual line they were following.

Zajak's plans for the glass factory were to run it as a legitimate business for as long as needed. It would become a source of civic responsibility and ingenuity when the glass recycling arm of the business was introduced later in the year. *Civic pride was the best front, Zajak thought.* At the heart of the scheme, though, the plant was the base of a sophisticated international money laundering operation. The funds were slated to underwrite the software development operation in India. The pieces were falling in place. There was just the one obstacle.

Brankovic knew of the plan that had come from Moscow, though he had little interest in it. Instead, the Dragon wished to remain firmly planted in the areas of crime that allowed him to exercise his penchant for violence—drugs and prostitution.

It was a matter of comfort level. Tomaso was no different than Brankovic in that regard. Zajak did not think Tomaso a stupid man. In fact, he thought Titty Boy, was much more of an intellectual than he let on. He knew Tomaso was a man of good taste, an avid reader, and someone who absorbed history and appreciated philosophical and spiritual banter. What Tomaso wasn't, Zajak knew and counted on, was ambitious. Tomaso liked what he had, and didn't want anymore than that. Complacency was the mark of the Middle Class; truly American, and classically *petite bourgeois*. As far as Zajak was concerned, Tomaso could have all of the drug and prostitution business in the city. *Opiate of the Masses*. Being involved in those vices would bring attention to ACME Glass, the wrong kind of attention.

Zajak wanted nothing more than to hand back over to Tomaso what was already his. In exchange, all he wished in exchange was whatever, if any, influence Tomaso might have with Muerce, which did not appear to be much.

Jack Muerce was an instrument sent by Allah. Zajak was sure of that. How that instrument was to be used, Zajak didn't know.

"The key to repentance is that it must be done with humility, and with no outward displays," Zajak said.

"Yeah, on the down-low, that goes without saying," Tomaso said. "But to be clear about what we are saying, and we won't say it again, Brankovic goes, and I get what's mine."

"Your world would be one again," Zajak said. "You would be free to go about your business, as usual."

"Did he do it?" Tomaso said, referring to the pair of amputation murders that were about to be the lead story on the local evening television news shows. "It sounds like his thing."

Zajak reviewed his thoughts and memories. *Probably, maybe. I don't care.*

"Does it matter?" he said.

"No, not to me," Tomaso said. "But I'm not sure how Muerce fits into all this. I already tried to steer him in that direction, before you and I came to an agreement, but he blew me off. Not his business."

"I'm not sure, quite yet, how he fits either," Zajak said. "But he fits. I know he fits.

"The two detectives working on the case? Do they have any suspects?"

"Who, Dumb and Dumber?" Tomaso said with a slight laugh. "Not yet. But they will. The street is a noisy place. Full of rumor and innuendo."

"Be patient," Zajak said. "Let it play out a little more. No outward displays. I think we still need to see how Muerce might fit into any... act of contrition."

"Okay," Tomaso said.

"In the meantime," Zajak said. "Do as I do. Roll over for Brankovic. Give him his offering so his attention goes elsewhere."

Loud voices outside the fogged and dripping glass door to the steam room interrupted their conversation. A short, plump man entered. He pontificated to another man, older, thinner and taller with the remnants of silver hair that formed a crescent around the back of his head.

Zajak threw a towel over his head, retreating almost unseen into the upper corner of the steam room. Tomaso unabashedly stood up from the bench, full frontal nudity exposed to the pair of men. The fat man quit his political pontifications, and frowned at Tomaso.

"Good afternoon Mister Mayor, Judge Naylor," Tomaso said, then wrapping a towel around his waist and exiting. "Have a nice sweat."

"This club has gone all to Hell," Judge Naylor said. The opening and closing of the glass door had allowed enough cold air to circulate, which stimulated the thermostat into generating a rush of steam that screamed from nozzles on the floor. Zajak was invisible in his corner.

"A member in good standing, pays his dues, I guess," the Mayor said. "He's never been convicted of anything, so we can't throw him out. It's America, after all."

The words had the effect of making Zajak want to laugh aloud, which he stifled. *It's America after all.*

— —

Muerce wrapped a large, white cotton towel around his waist, slid his feet into a pair of black-and-white striped athletic slides, slammed his locker door shut, and made his way to the steam room. He didn't see Titty Boy laying on one of the massage tables nearby.

Upon entering the cavern of steam he was recognized.

"Jack Muerce, just the man I want to see," the Mayor said.

The afterglow Muerce had from the session with Dr. Riley, and the text message from Ashley, was gone. Muerce squinted through the cloud of steam and identified the two men sitting on the lower bench. He could only make out that there was a third man on the upper bench, covered and obviously otherwise engaged in wanting to enjoy a quiet steam. A quiet steam was all Muerce wanted at the moment, too.

"Your honors," Muerce said.

"Jack," Judge Naylor said.

"Jack, can we talk for a moment," the Mayor said, patting the empty spot next to him.

Muerce reluctantly sat next to the Mayor. The Mayor was, in Muerce's eyes, a political buffoon. He was neither very effective—or he would have made the move long ago to the governor's mansion—nor was he very harmful. All the man ever wanted to be was mayor, and all of his actions in life were toward that end—to gain and keep his position in City Hall.

"Thank God there aren't term limits here," Muerce recalled the man once saying. "That means I can live forever."

It also meant, to Muerce, that a long line of favors could be exchanged with such a man. Muerce, sitting down next to the overweight and profusely sweating man, grinned when he recalled the first "discreet" favor he did for the Mayor, who was then in his first term. His honor had, at the time, a very attractive and very wayward wife. As a couple, they both had a series of marital indiscretions. However, the now former First Lady was rumored to be entangled with a serious lover. Dalliances were acceptable, if discreet, but love outside marriage was not. The Mayor asked Muerce to find out who the man was and persuade him, in no uncertain terms, to break off the affair with his wife. It was, in Muerce's career of doing good, the only time he consented to intervening in spousal discord. Within the week, the man had broken off the relationship with the Mayor's wife, who agreed to remain married, and by her husband's side through his re-election. That was, if the Mayor would grant her a divorce afterwards. And that is what transpired, and the Mayor remained enamored, and obligated to Muerce ever since. What Muerce didn't divulge to the Mayor was that the conversation he had with the man who was sleeping with his wife was conducted in the bathroom mirror of Muerce's apartment.

Thinking about it gave Muerce a lift as he situated himself next to the corpulent masthead of the city.

"How may I be of service to the city your Honor?" Muerce said, assured his dripping sarcasm would be mistaken for moisture falling from the ceiling.

"You've seen the news?" the Mayor said.

"Weather or sports?" Muerce joked.

"The serial killer," the Mayor said.

The lift Muerce got thinking about the Mayor's ex-wife stalled.

"Two murders don't make a serial killer," Muerce said.

"I believe three is the magic number," Judge Naylor said.

"The condition of those poor women, what was done to them, well it's pretty clear we're probably going to see more," the Mayor said.

"It's a helluva thing he did to them," Judge Naylor said.

Muerce leaned forward and gave the judge a "what the hell do you know about this" look, which the Mayor instantly interpreted, and to which he responded to diffuse any misunderstanding, or breach of protocol.

"Well, I know is just the inside scoop," the Mayor said. "Nothing's out on the wires. Keeping a lid on it."

"Well, it's none of my business but if you ask me it sounds like you need to keep a tight lid on this or the killer might disappear and you'll never find him," Muerce said.

"Him?" Judge Naylor said.

"Or her," Muerce said. "Whichever. But it's none of my business."

The steam jets hissed more scalding air, hushing the conversation until the hot veil passed.

"But it is your business, Jack," the Mayor said. "I talked to Bhote. He told me he asked you to serve as a kind of consultant. I agree. That's what I wanted to talk to you about. I'm in favor of it."

"I'm not consulting, I'm just doing a friend a favor," Muerce said.

"And I'm asking you the same favor," the Mayor said.

"And it's not even an election year," Muerce said.

The Mayor let the barb slide. Judge Naylor began to laugh then cleared his throat to cover it up.

"Look, very few people know this right now, but we're putting together a committee to develop a pitch to get a Summer Olympics here," the Mayor said. "It's a big deal—for the city, and..."

"And for your legacy?" Muerce said.

"Yes," the Mayor said. "And I don't want some Jack the Ripper to fuck it up."

Judge Naylor stood up and collected his towels.

"You'll excuse me gentlemen," he said. "But I can't take the heat any longer."

"Just keep doing what you're doing for the Coroner's Office, that's all," the Mayor said.

"Nick Trumbley in vice is part of this deal," Muerce said. "Anything I think of I share with him and Bhote. I won't consult with those two homicide clowns—Ash and Maple. And I'm not reporting in to you. Bhote is your source of anything I might come across."

"I understand," the Mayor said.

"You'll let the Chief know?" Muerce said.

"Yes, right away."

"One last thing," Muerce said. "I get to fill a spot on your Olympics committee with a player to be named later."

"Now I can't take the heat in here any longer," the Mayor said, standing up to leave. "Fair enough. I trust you Jack. You'll pick the right person."

"And find this loon or there won't be any committee to talk about."

Soon after the Mayor left, Muerce couldn't take the heat any longer either. He hadn't given as much thought to a possible pattern as he should have. He would wait and see what Travis came up with, but he would ask him if he could speed it up by a day. Thursday at lunch at Saigon Laundry.

Muerce draped a towel over his head and ruminated for a few more minutes, oblivious to the other man in the steam bath sitting silently above him.

"What the hell are you getting yourself into, Jack," Muerce said aloud and, he believed, to himself. "Let's go get that massage."

Zajak expected Muerce to turn around at any moment and confront him, but as quickly as he had appeared and the conversation with the Mayor had taken place, Muerce was gone.

"Praise Allah," Zajak whispered. He had heard every word between them. Jack Muerce was hooked, and would be the uncertain means to Zajak's ends. He tolerated the heat another ten minutes before slipping out to the visitor's lockers, showering and leaving the building by a back staircase.

— —

LeRoi the masseuse finished Tomaso's rub down just as Muerce arrived for his. Tomaso wheeled, sat up on the table, and faced Muerce.

"Big Jack," Tomaso said. "What a surprise."

"Tino," Muerce said.

"Want to grab a quick bite after LeRoi finishes with you?" Tomaso said.

"I've already had lunch, thanks," Muerce said. His good mood completely shot.

"Didn't think so," Tomaso said, getting up from the table. "Well, the least I could do was get it warmed up for you."

"LeRoi," Muerce said.

"Yes, Mister Muerce?" LeRoi said.

"When you wipe down the table check it for lice," Muerce said.

"You're real fucking funny, Merc," Tomaso said.

Muerce was in no mood either, and was getting ready to spit out a "Titty Boy" when LeRoi intervened.

"Mister Muerce, Mister Tomaso," he said, getting their attention. "This is a gentlemen's club!"

Tomaso backed off, and left.

LeRoi sprayed the table with disinfectant and wiped it down. In a few minutes he was working Muerce's shoulder muscles, which felt like large strands of hard rubber.

"Mister Muerce?" he said.

"Yes, LeRoi?" Muerce said.

"You can relax now," LeRoi said. "Mister Tomaso is gone. Take a deep breath and let it out slow."

Muerce did as he was told, but it wasn't Tomaso he was in knots over.

CHAPTER 16

Lutheran Mercy Hospital was situated in the Caelian District. Its VIP rooms had soft pastel colors on the walls, elegantly framed watercolor paintings of gentle pastoral scenes, subdued lighting, and a view of the perfectly manicured hospital grounds that led to the city's Botanic Garden.

None of that mattered to Miriam, who was scared, and a little bit hungry. She had to fast ahead of the surgery, and had not eaten since dinner the night before. She thought of the uncomfortable quiet around the table as she and her boys ate the spaghetti and meatballs she made. The boys had been good with her, trying their best to be funny and relaxed. But she knew they were scared, too. They lost their father. They didn't want to lose their mother, and she didn't want to lose them.

There was a light knock on the blonde-wood door.

"Settling in?" Trumbley said, arriving with a vase of flowers. "Thought it'd cheer the place up a little."

"Nick, that was so sweet of you," Miriam said, putting the last of her nightgowns into a chest of drawers by the sitting area in the corner of the suite near the window.

Trumbley put the flowers on the table by the divan, looked out the window, and whistled.

"Whew, nice view," he said.

Miriam came up behind him, and put her hand on his shoulder.

"Thank you," she said. "But I still don't feel right about this."

"I called in a few favors is all," Trumbley said. "My own kind of bonus miles. It's not that big of a deal."

"On my salary and crappy benefits, it is a big deal," she said. Her voice trailing off as she looked at the clock on the wall. Surgery was scheduled in just over and hour.

"These are the best people around for... " Trumbley said, halting before the words could spill from his mouth.

"Cancer," Miriam said. "It is what it is, as much as I don't like to say it either."

There was another knock at the door, this time much louder and authoritative. A husky, middle-aged woman with frizzy red hair, wearing blue scrubs and pink plastic clogs stood in the doorway with a smile and a clipboard. Both of her arms were canvassed with a tattoos.

"Miriam Estrada?" she said.

Miriam replied with a nod, and a nervous smile. The woman approached, holding out her hand.

"I'm Elonide Lysaught," she said. "Everyone calls me Lonny. I'm your primary nurse while you're here. You're probably thinking what's up with this rough biker chick, but you and I are going to become best friends in the next few days.

"And we're going to kick some ass."

Miriam liked Lonny on the spot. Having someone like Lonny in her corner gave her hope. It was the most relaxed Miriam felt since getting the original diagnosis. Even more relaxing than Jack Muerce. *Oh God, I hope Jack doesn't find out and show up here. Not with Nick around.*

Lonny turned and looked at Trumbley. *I've been to the Barrio, and you don't look like no Mr. Estrada.*

"I'm Nick Trumbley," he said, as if he was under interrogation. "I'm a... a... a family friend."

Lonny smiled, crossed the clipboard across her chest, and looked at her watch.

"Well Nick Trumbley, family friend," she said. "Miriam's in my hands now, and we have a lot we have to get done before surgery."

"Right," Trumbley said, pushing his hands into his pockets, unsure what to do next.

Miriam looked at her new best friend with her big, green and watery eyes, and Lonny understood straightaway.

"Two minutes," she said, sliding out of the suite, and closing the door behind her.

Miriam approached Trumbley. They embraced awkwardly at first, then Miriam reached her face up to his and kissed him on the lips. It caught Trumbley by surprise at first, then he kissed back, and held Miriam as tightly as he could without hurting her. She squeezed back as hard as she could.

"We should have done this a long time ago, Nick," Miriam said. "You're a good man. You've always been there for us. Always waiting. I'm sorry if I made you feel, ignored."

"I can't say I didn't want to, Miriam," Trumbley said. "But it was always a little weird, you being the wife of my partner. Even after he died, it was always, somehow, strange."

"I know," she said.

"Where from here?" he said.

"No more waiting, no more weirdness," she said.

Miriam stood back a step from Trumbley. She mockingly and sorrowfully cradled her breasts.

"Bad timing," she said. "I'm so sorry about this."

"Oh no, don't even go there," he said, reaching out to draw her closer. "You are complete to me no matter what. No matter what."

Miriam fell forward, and began to sob into Trumbley's chest.

"I'm not going anywhere, Miriam," he said. "I'm not going anywhere."

Lifting her head over his shoulder, Miriam could see the Japanese gardens in the distance. The cherry blossoms would be blooming in a few weeks. She wanted to lay beneath them, smell their scent, and feel the delicate petals touch her face as they floated to the ground.

— —

"Detective Trumbley."

"Mister Squire," Trumbley said, standing up to shake hands. Trumbley moved the styrofoam cup of coffee from his right hand to his left, and reached out to T.B. Squire. "Thank you for everything you've done, but you didn't need to drop by."

"Hell yes I did," T.B. Squire drawled.

"Well, that's awfully nice of you."

"How is she doing?" T.B. Squire said.

"Nervous, scared, uncertain," Trumbley said. "And so am I."

T.B. Squire continued to hold Trumbley's hand as a comfort. T.B. may not be a doctor or a nurse, but he always considered himself a health-care provider, and as such, it was his duty to provide care and compassion when needed. Standing in the waiting from, it was clear Trumbley needed both at the moment.

"That's understandable, and to be expected," T.B. Squire said. "That's why I specifically requested Lonny Lysaught. That dog can hunt. Most fearless woman in the place. Hell, even the surgeons are afraid of her.

"There will be no question as to who the team leader is for Misses Estrada. May I call her Miriam?"

"It's fine with me, but you'd better ask her first," Trumbley said. He smiled when the thought about what a hard ass Miriam could be.

"Yes, that would makes sense, she has quite a reputation, our Misses Estrada," T.B. Squire said.

"*Our* Misses Estrada?"

"She's family now," T.B. Squire said. "As are you detective."

"I understand things have worked out well with your son?"

"Exceedingly so," T.B. Squire said. "Mister Muerce has taken him under his wing. My wife and I have not seen such verve and drive in the boy, ever. He's always been a sharp one, but rather listless with his gifts, until now.

"He even beat me out of the house to work this morning."

"Jack's a good man," Trumbley said. "Doesn't put up with much bullshit, though. I'm sure your son has gotten that message.

"I'm glad it's worked out."

"As am I," T.B. Squire said. "But Misses Estrada is our priority now, and I want you to know she is in the best hands there are. Doctor Liu is one of the top surgical oncologists I've ever seen. And we're lucky to have *the* best reconstructive plastic surgeon in the country on staff.

"Doctor Sharron will take charge of the follow-up reconstructive surgery when she's cleared. Usually takes several months after the initial procedure. But, I'll warn you. He's a strange one. But he's good at what he does. They call him The Transformer."

CHAPTER 17

Travis' mouth was overwhelmed with flavors, textures and temperatures he had never experienced before when biting into something he held with both hands. He sat at the family table in the back of the Saigon Laundry kitchen. It was lunch time, and he was served as family.

"*Banh mi*, you like?" Benny said, walking past with a large stainless steel tray of marinated squab slated for Thursday night's seating. The activity in the kitchen was starting to build as the prep work for the various courses was underway.

It was loud, hot, dramatic and aromatic in the confines of the kitchen.

Travis, his mouth stuffed, expressed his delight with his eyes. As he did, Pho Mat placed a tall plastic cup in front of Travis that had a creamy, chocolate-looking liquid served over ice.

"*Cafe sua da*," he said. "You will like. Wash down *banh mi*. You like?"

Travis munched enough of the doughy and crunchy sandwich to allow a swig of the drink in his mouth, and took a sip.

Sweet Lord in Heaven, I like. I like a lot.

The strong coffee, laced with sweetened condensed milk, melted the remnants of the sandwich coddled in his mouth.

Before taking another bite, Travis snuck a peak inside the *banh mi*, identifying cilantro, some kind of bean sprouts, thinly sliced carrots, cucumbers, and a sort of spiced barbecue pork. There was a bright orange smear of condiment on the bread.

"*Nuoc mam*," Madame Trung said, appearing behind Travis without drawing his attention. "Fish sauce. Old family recipe. From Minny's side of the family. Not Trung."

"Yes, ma'am, very good, thank you," Travis said, ever overly polite to Madame Trung, whom he imagined carried a whip, and knew how to use it despite having only one arm.

"I not your 'ma'am', you call Madame Trung," she scolded. "You go now. Mister Muerce at his table. Wait for you."

"Yes, ma', Madame Trung," Travis said.

He started to collect what remained of the sandwich and *sua da* while attempting to shoulder a large canvas messenger bag when she stopped him.

"I bring food," she ordered. "You go now. He wait."

Rushing, Travis nearly ran into Pho Mat, who was making Muerce a latte in the service alcove between the kitchen and the dining room. Muerce was at his table, reading the newspaper. He read the latest article speculating on the killings. Muerce frowned when he saw the ridiculous quote Ash had given the reporter for the story.

"Sorry I'm late," Travis said, breathless despite only having travelled less than thirty feet.

"What are you talking about?" Muerce said. "I knew you were in the kitchen having lunch. Why the hurry?"

"But Madame Trung," Travis said.

Muerce was amused.

"I can't say you'll ever get used to her barking, but you will come to understand it," Muerce said. "In time.

"So, what do you have?"

Travis looked down at the two-top table, and could see there wasn't going to be enough room for his presentation on Zmaj Brankovic.

"Quite a bit, actually," Travis said. "Can we move to a bigger table?"

Muerce looked up at Travis as if he had upset the balance of the world, and just as Madame Trung arrived with the remnants of Travis' lunch. Pho Mat stood by with Muerce's latte.

"No," Muerce said. "Sit down and give me the fifty thousand-foot version."

"I'll give you the thirty thousand-foot version," Travis said, sitting down and unhooking the messenger bag from his shoulder. "Otherwise, it wouldn't make any sense."

Muerce nodded that he was good with that, and sipped his latte. Madame Trung and Pho Mat returned to their duties. Muerce's business was Muerce's business.

"I put together a report and all the supporting documents," Travis said. "The supporting documents are pretty thick, they're all back at the apartment, but I brought my report."

Travis pulled out two-inch thick, comb-bound document with plastic cover, index tabs, table of contents, prologue, and summation. Muerce was impressed, if not a little overwhelmed by the effort. And that Travis did it, if you took Monday out as a training day, in two days. *Impressive.*

"First, I have to say, the database software is amazing," he said. "It's incredible the access I had. Second, I can't take credit for most of this. Mostly, I summarized the file on Brankovic from the ICTY, the International Criminal Tribunal for the Former Yugoslavia, in The Hague."

"The World Court?" Muerce said.

"Yeah, basically, UN court, war crimes, Bosnia," Travis said. "They wanted him bad. Really bad. Tons and tons of anecdotal stories about Brankovic, but not a single shred of hard evidence. He was into some heavy medieval shit, Mister Muerce. Torture and amputations. Sick stuff. Super sick stuff. But they couldn't get a single victim to testify. Nobody would talk. At least, nobody alive.

"His file reads like Hunter S. Thompson wrote it. A kind of 'Fear and Loathing in Ethnic Cleansing'."

Travis gulped down half the *sua da*. He hadn't slept much in days, and craved the espresso buzz he was getting from the drink. The pressure of wanting to do well for Muerce kept him up, but the sadistic imagery of the horrors Brankovic was accused of, and having had an up-close and personal experience with the Dragon only days before, instilled a fear of sleeping in Travis. *No dreams, only nightmares. The kind that were real.*

Muerce sipped his latte as if to say "go on", and on Travis went, gaining momentum.

"The Hunter Thompson line, that's kind of the log line for Brankovic, if we were trying to make a movie about his life," said Travis.

"But we're not," Muerce said.

"Uh, no. Anyway, let's stick to the chronology. So, first, this guy is Romanian, not Bosnian. That kind of threw me for a loop. He's never what you think he is. But that was one of the great things about the Hague file. It contains Brankovic's military file. Russian military file."

Muerce's eyes widened with interest.

"See what I mean? He's never what you think he is. Russian Army. But not just Russian Army—Soviet Medical Service. He was in the field as an aid. Their version of a corpsman. He did a stint in Afghanistan. Got some real blood-and-guts training there."

"And probably learned how to traffic in drugs," Muerce said. "I remember reading that during the Soviet occupation there, heroin was smuggled out in the body cavities of dead soldiers. Their Vietnam."

"Okay, maybe, I guess so," Travis said. His heart began to race. "It doesn't come right out and say it, but Brankovic's military service stops dead in Afghanistan." Travis stopped to finish the rest of his coffee, and feeling like he was building a momentum as he spoke, he continued. "One day he's like superman with the bandages, practically doing surgery for the docs. Commendations, some award. Then, all of a sudden, he's discharged without any reason, and sent back to Romania. The file gets a little trippy after that. Only because there's a notation, and a stamp."

Travis opened the report to a page tabbed with a red plastic notation. On the page was a photocopy of the last entry into Brankovic's Soviet military file. At the bottom of the page, in Russian, is a handwritten notation and a stamp with the initial K, half a capital T and the number 6.

"KGB," Travis said. "Russian alphabet. Roughly translated, the note says the file was transferred to the KGB when Brankovic was discharged from the service. But let me keep it chronological, and go back to his childhood."

"The thirty thousand-foot view," Muerce said.

"Right. I just love the details though. Anyway. So, not surprisingly, right after he's born, Brankovic gets dumped into an orphanage because of his condition. And an orphanage in Romania at the time—it still is now, just not called Romania anymore—anyway, the place—orphanage—is basically a mental hospital. Well, it was, is. Every freak of nature in there, along with your basic, abandoned kids. Man, you just have to wonder what mom thought when he popped out. You've seen him. Freaky. Only way we know the diagnosis on his biological malfunction is because the Russians find that stuff important when you go into their Army, especially the Medical Services. Key file, that one. Anyway, that he survived his first few years of life in one of those Romania orphan shit holes is a miracle. I mean, Nicolae Ceausescu was a piece of work, himself. No abortion, no birth control allowed in the country. Kind of scary when you listen to what the Republican candidates for president say when they talk about Roe Wade. Jeesh."

"Let's get some altitude here Travis," Muerce said. "Out of the weeds and back up to thirty thousand. What's wrong with Brankovic? Physically, I mean. I think we've got a pretty good picture on the mental side."

"Oh, right. Sorry. Trigoncephaly."

"What?" Muerce said.

"Trigoncephaly. Premature fusion of the metopic suture. It's more common than you think, but he's got a pretty extreme case of it. I think he plays on it with the beard and hair *schtick*. Probably first thought to go shaggy to cover it up. But now it's taken on a whole new thing. I mean, you've seen the guy. He looks like he's going to sprout wings, and breath fire. Anyway, add his size and that he's also a pretty smart slick—streetwise—he's done pretty well for himself considering. No doubt he's a straight-up sociopath with some heavy sadomasochistic bents. But you've got to give him some credit. The medical training, and crime lord thing."

"You afraid of this guy, or in love with him?" Muerce said. "Because, I'd be afraid of him."

"No, no, he scares the living crap out of me," Travis said, coming back down to earth, and remembering Brankovic's display of anger at Club Unicorn.

"Then filter the enthusiasm a little, and keep going," Muerce said.

"Okay, I'm good," Travis said. "After he gets shipped back to Romania he drops off the radar. He pops up in an INTERPOL report every now and then as "an associate" or "possible suspect" in various Eastern bloc crime syndicates and crimes. But really, it's a front for the Russian mob. I'm sure the real dirt on that is in the KGB files, but we don't have access to that, and I'm not quite ready to hack into theirs or the NSA's main frames to try and sniff around."

"Skip to war crimes," Muerce said.

"Skip to war crimes," Travis said, taking a deep breath before launching back into his report. "The wall falls in the late 80s, and pretty soon so does the Eastern Bloc. The Baltics especially. Romania, *phwet*. Czechoslovakia, *phwet*. Yugoslavia, *phewt*. Hell, even the Soviet Union, *phwet*. The Commies are out, the criminals are in. Maybe hard to distinguish from either. At least from a historic perspective. Anyway, just conjecturing based on the scant INTERPOL material, Brankovic has kept himself pretty busy learning a new trade in the years since Afghanistan. Drugs, sex slaves, arms, cigarettes, blood diamonds, stolen exotic cars... you name it, Brankovic's talon marks are on it. According to the ICTY file, he surfaces in the early 90s in Sarajevo. And get this. He's not in the Bosnian Serb Army, he's working as a consultant for them. His specialty? Medical services. He's an angel of mercy. That's his line of defense against the ICTY allegations. That, and there's nobody who will testify against him. He might as well have "fear me" tattooed across his head."

"He does," Muerce said. Travis hiccuped a laugh.

"I can go into all the gross details of what he's accused of doing on the torture side, but I'd rather not. It's all in the pages back at the apartment for your late-night reading pleasure."

"I'll take a look at them," Muerce said.

"Let me warn you Mister Muerce," Travis said. "There are pictures in the file. Graphic ones. Death camp kind of stuff."

"How did Brankovic end up here?"

"Well, that's where it gets interesting," Travis said. "Technically, he's not really here. At least, not as far as Immigration and Naturalization is concerned. No visitor visa, no student visa, no work permit, no social security card, no library card, no COSTCO card, not even a coupon to get ten percent off his next oil change. Nothing."

"Just another illegal alien," Muerce said.

"Yes and no," Travis said.

"What does that mean?"

"Luther taught me a few tricks," Travis said. "They know he's here. They just aren't doing anything about it."

"Who is they?"

"The FBI is keeping a file on him," Travis said. There was excitement in his voice. "At the request of the CIA. It was in an e-mail. A low-priority e-mail."

Muerce was not happy that Luther had turned Travis on to snooping on the FBI. *Note to self. Hit Luther in the back of the head to wake him the fuck up.*

"One more interesting thing," Travis said. "Probably just coincidence, but Brankovic was in the same ICTY detention center in The Hague as Slobodan Milosevic, the former president of Serbia or Yugoslavia, or whatever they were calling it, when Milosevic died of a heart attack. That was in 2006. They were all there, including General Ratko Mladic."

"So?" Muerce said.

"So, some of the files had entries that hinted at a senior level defendant possibly agreeing to testify against Brankovic. Milosevic, who had a history of heart disease, dies. Ten days later Brankovic walks."

"And, what, six years later he shows up here?" Muerce said. "Lucky us."

"About five," Travis said. "FBI files have him on U.S. soil in late 2010—let the fun begin."

Travis thought how unlucky the cute blonde girl was who flirted with him. He also realized how tired he was when he reached for the empty container of *sua da*, and spilled ice all over the table. Muerce grabbed Travis' report, and scooted back in his chair to avoid the mess.

"You look like crap," Muerce said. "Go home and get some sleep."

"Did you get what you want?" Travis said.

"More than I expected." Muerce said. "You did a good job. Very thorough. Just one thing."

"Yes, Mister Muerce?"

"Stay out of the FBI's business no matter how untraceable Luther says what your doing is. Okay?"

"Okay."

——

The bell at the front door of Saigon Laundry *tinkled* when Travis left. Muerce heard the engine in the Jeep as Travis wheeled onto Canary Street and, hopefully, back home for some sleep.

"You want another latte?" Madame Trung said, pulling at the soiled table cloth. "Boy make mess."

"No on the latte, yes the boy make mess," Muerce said. "What do you think of him?"

"I think good boy," Madame Trung said, lifting Muerce's empty cup and saucer from the table. "Not man yet. Polite. Respectful. Work hard? Yes, I think work hard."

"He make eyes at granddaughters. But he young. They young. You not so young. Not make eyes at young girls any longer."

"I may not be young, but I'm not dead," Muerce said.

"Not dead yet, but maybe soon," Madame Trung said. "My son feel better, wish to see you in office in house. You go now. He impatient."

"I think you're the impatient one and just want to get me out of here so you can clear the table," Muerce said.

Madame Trung's reaction was to slap Muerce, but her one hand was occupied so she threw her other shoulder forward, and snapped her head at him. Muerce got the message, got up and made his way through the kitchen, which smelled of Vietnamese cinnamon being cooked with scallions and lentils. With the fresh smell invigorating his gait, Muerce exited through the back door, and to the Trung's house on the other side of the alley.

——

Colonel Trung was recovering from a bad bout of flu that put him down for over a week, and away from most of the family so they would not contract what ailed him. His days were mostly spent in his office in the front room of the old Victorian house that served as the Trung family's base of operations. He had long ago passed the day-to-day operations of their various family businesses on to other—and he felt more capable—members of the family.

Colonel Trung, however, still poured over the bills, taxes, income statements and trusts, and held weekly meetings with the heads of the different family businesses to assure the security of the Trung fortune they had built in America.

During those meetings, and through his interactions with other community leaders, the Colonel cultivated what he thought was the most important element of business, what he was most skilled at doing—gathering information. Colonel Trung kept his nose out the business of others, but kept his eyes and ears tuned to everything that crossed his path.

What he heard about the customer from the laundromat who had been savagely murdered, her child abandoned, the second and most recent murder, and the territorial changes among the thugs they lived among were unfortunate, but they were just part of the pattern of life. These things happen. Suffering was inevitable. You did what you could to avoid it. And you dealt with the consequences if you couldn't avoid it. Colonel Trung knew there was strength in being flexible. It was much easier to survive the storms of fate by being resilient. It was so when it came to family. Colonel Trung had received and processed quite a bit of information over the past month on the man called Dragon. He had even gone as far as reaching out to old friends from before the fall of Saigon, who had taken different paths after the war and were the heads of powerful crime syndicates in Asia, Europe and America. Colonel Trung made no moral judgement of his friends. They were his friends, and in some cases, they, too, were family.

Jack Muerce was family. Close family. And as head of the family, Colonel Trung was concerned for Muerce.

The Colonel knew about the incident at the bar at Club Unicorn with the Dragon, and a young prostitute who worked for him. He knew Muerce was there. He knew why Muerce was there. He also knew that Muerce had been asked, informally, to look into the two murders. And like a small, but quickly growing circle, they appeared to be leading to Brankovic.

The flu had put him down, but he was up for their talk. Only he wasn't sure if Muerce would listen.

A rap at the door to his office announced Muerce's arrival. A middle-aged cousin of the Trungs named Pa Binh bowed to Colonel Trung as she waved Muerce in for his audience.

"Mister Muerce here," she said.

"You look much better, Colonel," Muerce said.

"Feel much better," Colonel Trung said. "Good see you Jack. Sorry I sick and we have not had our usual talk. Please sit down. Coffee?"

"No, thank you, I've had plenty."

"Nothing for us Pa Binh."

Pa Binh bowed, and shut the office door behind her. Muerce took one of the cushioned seats in front of Colonel Trung's desk. The top of it was covered with ledgers, mail and community newspapers printed in Vietnamese that Colonel Trung had mailed to him from major world cities with large Vietnamese communities.

The office itself was a study in contradiction. It had a high ceiling, and heavy oak paneling consistent with an old Victorian house. But the decor was Asian *kitsch* with porcelain elephants, stylized buddhas, ornate and vibrant silk tapestries, and the hint of decaying bamboo. There also were dozens of framed pictures of Colonel Trung with celebrities, civic leaders and his family, as well as Chamber of Commerce awards, and other distinctions gathered over his years as a business leader. The one photo that always stood out to Muerce was a black-and-white portrait of the Colonel in his military uniform.

Colonel Trung was in his early sixties. Still slim-framed, but balding with gray hair. The uniform he wore nowadays was a light-blue dress shirt, khaki pants, and tan slip-on loafers.

"Benny tell me he blackmailed into catering museum party tomorrow? Your mother very persuasive woman."

"As is yours," Muerce said, slightly embarrassed. "I've assured Benny, and told her, this would be the first and last time."

"Maybe not," Colonel Trung said. "Could be profitable business. We see."

"I don't believe that's why Benny became a chef," Muerce said.

"Oh, Benny no run it," the Colonel said, stacking loose papers as he moved around his desk. He sat down in the cracked and worn leather chair. "Oversee recipes and quality. Use name. That's all. We see after tomorrow night."

"Fair enough," Muerce said.

"Everything okay with you?" Colonel Trung said. Muerce knew when he was probing.

"You seem bothered," Muerce said. "Still feeling down, or is it something else."

Colonel Trung frowned and pressed his left hand to his forehead. Muerce could tell he was formulating something, something that was painful for him to say. Colonel Trung, he knew, ruminated for days before taking action on a matter he considered of great importance. Particularly when it concerned his family.

"I tell you story I not tell you before," Colonel Trung said. Though his English was broken at times, his words were always measured.

"I young man during war. Officer Army intelligence. Some, this you know. No big shot. Mostly I watch and listen. Do what I told. CIA in charge. ARVN just stupid yellow man. Flunky. Number ten. No number one. Sometimes, big VC official or officer in North Vietnamese Regular Army get caught. Bring to Saigon. Interrogate. Bad thing they come to Saigon. Interrogate. No bring to headquarters. No want record. No paper."

The Colonel waved his hands toward the piles of paper on his desk to illustrate a paper trail.

Then he continued: "Bring to old Chinese laundry in Cholon District. Do bad things make them talk. Do evil make them talk. Think. Okay do evil. I fight for my country. Justified. I be forgiven. I see they fight for their country, too. They no talk. Do more evil. No talk from evil. Get no 'actionable' information. CIA say must get something from evil. Big laundry vats in building. Fill with industrial bleach. Must wear mask. Chlorine very dangerous. Chop arms and legs off. Throw in vats. Let steep like tea. Why you no see me drink tea. Soon. Yellow skin man become white. Purify. Wrap them in white bed sheets like spring rolls. Tie up with string. Fly helicopter late night over VC village and throw out. VC call this Saigon Laundry."

Colonel Trung stopped before taking a deep, cautious breath.

Then he continued: "I want make bad name good again. Help family. Help friend. Help community. Purify myself before I die. War make man sin. Make man do evil. Both sides. After war. Most man want atone for sin. For evil they see. Or evil they do. Some man. No. Evil become part of soul. No can atone. Only God forgive when die.

"Jack Muerce not God. No can forgive evil in soul of such man. You think you know such man. You do not. I tell Jack Muerce. Be careful. Too much sin. Too much evil in such man."

When Colonel Trung was done he did not move. His eyes, soft and empathetic, were locked on Muerce. The air in the room smelled like bamboo, and Vietnamese cinnamon. Muerce digested what the Colonel had said. He saw Saigon Laundry in a different way; more diffuse and monochromatic. Colonel Trung liked to speak in generalities that guided the listener to find their own path. Muerce saw his.

"Brankovic?"

"Yes," Colonel Trung said.

"I'll be careful," Muerce said.

"Not your strength," the Colonel said. "This your challenge."

— —

After Muerce left, Colonel Trung called for Pa Binh to summon Pho Mat from the restaurant. Ten minutes later she appeared, along with Pho Mat. They bowed in unison, then Pa Binh excused herself, and closed the door behind her.

"You wish see me, Colonel?" Pho Mat said.

"Pho Mat, my old friend," Colonel Trung said. "I have job for you. I afraid family member may be in trouble. My ears hear, but now I want eyes that see. You be eyes. We are one on this."

That Colonel Trung used the name Pho Mat instead of Sammy conveyed not only the weight of what was being discussed, but also the manner in which he was to carry out the Colonel's orders. *The Old Ways.*

"Yes, Colonel," Pho Mat said. "Who in family?"

"Jack Muerce."

"Then I be our eyes," Pho Mat said. "We are one."

"You start right away," Colonel Trung said. "Madame Trung do duties in dining room. I tell Benny. Want you to help him at museum Saturday. Muerce be there. Good for us to see.

"After Saturday night, you sick with flu. Only I come see you everyday. Nurse my old friend back to health. Share what we hear, what we see."

Pho Mat affirmed his orders with a bow and click of his heels, but loitered to indicate he had a question regarding the parameters of his assignment.

"What is it Pho Mat?"

"If danger great for family member?" he said.

"Purification," Colonel Trung said. "Do what is necessary to protect body and soul of all family."

CHAPTER 18

Friday menus at Saigon Laundry were always a challenge during Lent. Madame Trung was adamant meat not be served. Colonel Trung was indifferent, but in some things his mother had the final say. "Fine," Benny said at the time, "We serve macaroni and cheese, fish sticks, and peanut butter and jelly sandwiches." No such thing ever happened. After an hour of pouting and throwing pots and pans around the kitchen as the staff either cowered or smoked cigarettes in the back alley, Benny didn't just embrace the challenge, he elevated it to edible art.

That was the first year the restaurant was open. Now, Lenten Friday's were part of Saigon Laundry's gastronomic lore; and of those menus, which included Ash Wednesday, the all vegetarian—although not all-out vegan—evening was the most digestibly creative. It was also one of the hardest nights of the year to get a reservation, and despite the Trung's tight control on seats, it was not uncommon for seatings to be traded, or sold by patrons. Such an exchange was quietly tolerated by the Saigon Laundry staff—specifically Pho Mat and Madame Trung—if a donation was made to the original reservation-holder's favorite charity.

Such an arrangement was to be validated as soon as the surreptitious reservation holders arrived for their seating, and usually elicited either a frown from Pho Mat, or the incredulous look on Madame Trung's face as she arched her eyebrows.

"We are here in place of the fill-in-the-blank's on behalf of the fill-in-the-blank-charity," was the expected response. Anything else, and the party would be politely turned away, and the next name on the waiting list called.

Of the four tables, not including Muerce's single two-topper, three of them were populated for the night under the reservation transfer agreement.

Muerce arrived later than normal for dinner. He spent a better part of the day reading Travis' report on Brankovic, and most of the early evening hours regaining his appetite. He didn't feel he had much to report to Bhote or Trumbley, who had been silent since Sunday. It was still gut feelings rumbling around Muerce's intuitional innards. Nothing solid. Nothing concrete. Not even a good hunch, although whenever he thought of Brankovic as the potential killer he felt his skin begin to itch like he were walking through poison ivy, but had yet to brush up against any. *Not so much if, but when.*

He thumbed away on the screen of his phone, standing just inside the front door of Saigon Laundry, and hardly noticed which of the younger members of the Trung family was working the coat check for the night. She helped him remove his topcoat in exchange for a paper valet ticket. As she walked his coat to the closet she thumbed her phone, no doubt texting a friend. It was still cold at night, but the earthy smell of approaching spring held promise.

Muerce hit the *send* button on the screen, and the text message to Eleanor informing her that he had arranged a car for them for Saturday flew across the ethernet.

When he looked up, he was greeted by Madame Trung. She wore a black, silk *ao dai,* and vintage scowl.

"You late," she said.

"I'm touched, you were worried about me," Muerce said, bending down to kiss her on the cheek. Madame Trung pushed Muerce away with her one arm.

"*Đi chỗ khác, đi đi,*" she said. "Too young girls, now too old women. I not need nonsense from you. Too hard work tonight."

Muerce looked at Madame Trung, then at the busily texting granddaughter who was working the coat check, and who had never worked the restaurant side before. He also noticed the unmanned reservation table by the beaded curtains that led into the dining area. A small lamp illuminated the reservation book on the stand, as well as the empty space where Pho Mat normally stood, conducting the evening.

There was an entirely different tone and tempo to the night that Muerce was only now starting to grasp. There had been personnel changes in his favorite orchestra that were not apparent until the music started. He felt the whole evening was going to be off-key.

"Where's Sammy?"

"He not feel well," Madame Trung said. "He help Benny with museum catering, but I think he have what my son have."

Off-key for sure. As long as Muerce had known Pho Mat, he had never been ill. Going through his memory files, the only time Muerce could remember him missing a day of work was when he became a naturalized citizen; and as a surprise, Colonel Trung took Pho Mat on a trip to see the one American icon that he had dreamed of visiting his entire life—Mount Rushmore in South Dakota.

"*Aperitif?*" Madame Trung said.

"*Oui, champagne*," Muerce said.

Muerce paid little attention, at first, to the diners in the restaurant who were well into their second course of the night. He made straight for his table. The room was loud like a bistro. Above the din he heard Hindi being spoken at the front left table by the window. Madame Trung barked an order to one of the wait staff for Muerce's *aperitif*, then handed him the menu for the evening, which Benny had autographed for the occasion.

"*Est-ce que ce vin vous plaît, ce soir?*" Madame Trung said. Muerce heard a cork pop in the background as he perused the menu, and the wine pairings. The dishes looked perfect, as did the wine selections.

"*C'est magnifique*," Muerce said. "Compliments to Benny."

A flute of champagne was placed in front of Muerce, along with a small plate that had three, thumb-sized spring rolls that were not on the evening's menu.

"*BENNY nói là để ông nếm thử*," Madame Trung said, gesturing for Muerce to eat. "Appetizers for tomorrow night. He want know if you like."

Each of the petite spring rolls was tied like a package with a single rice noodle fashioned to look like the string on a parcel. Muerce hesitated, remembering Colonel Trung's story.

"Saigon Laundry," Muerce whispered.

"Yes, Saigon Laundry, where you think you are?" Madame Trung said. She was not, it was clear, going to leave Muerce's table side until he tried the appetizers. Benny was waiting for Muerce's review.

Muerce thought of a low-flying helicopter as he put the first spring roll into his mouth, felt the crunch of the cucumber as if it were bone, and then a squirting explosion of liquid he imagined blood, but was really *hoison* sauce mixed with honey. The flavors in his mouth battled the visions in his head. By the third spring roll, Muerce's taste buds won out.

"These are fantastic," he said. "How did Benny get the sauce to hold like that?"

"He tell you when he come out," Madame Trung said, obviously pleased. "I get wine, and first course."

The night felt like it was starting to bounce a little better, and he waved for another champagne, and discreetly looked around the dining room to see if he recognized any of the patrons.

Sitting at the table directly in his line of sight was the famous adventure novelist Joseph South Tree. With him was his wife, a raven-haired, blue-eyed French actress whose name escaped Muerce, but whose beauty did not. They were dining with a couple Muerce didn't recognize, but deduced were good friends of the artisan couple. They appeared to be having a good time.

The table across from the South Tree party, was the source of the spoken Hindi. The two seats on the far side of the table facing Muerce were occupied by two middle-aged Indian businessmen. One was more dark skinned than the other, and heavier. Each was dressed in a conservative gray suit, and white dress shirt worn in a casual way, without necktie. The other man at the table had his back to Muerce. He wore a well-tailored blue pin-stripe suit on a skeletal frame. Muerce watched the man gesture with bony fingers as he spoke, although he could not be overheard above the conversations from the other tables and the noise from the kitchen. The man had a bald patch Muerce couldn't immediately place. Not until, that is, he recognized the woman sitting next to him. She spoke Hindi like she smoked a cigarette—with calculated determination.

It was the Spooky Girl from Club Unicorn. The man with her tonight was the man she was with then—Zajak. *Brankovic's Boy.*

Nowhere in Travis' research, not even in the ICTY file on Brankovic, did Zajak's name ever come up. Not once. Muerce pulled out his phone and texted Travis with a new research assignment. Subjects: ACME Glass and Krzytof Zajak. By Wed. next.

Muerce put the phone away as a chilled bottle of *Pouilly Fume* arrived at his table, along with Benny and the first course of the night.

"Cucumber and pickled beet Kimchi galette with an accent sauce of saffron yogurt," Benny said, pouring Muerce a glass of wine. Benny sat down in the empty chair, and waited for Muerce's first-bite response.

"Excellent," Muerce said, the crispness of the wine perfectly complimenting the sweet and sour creaminess of the galette. He took two more bites before resuming conversation with Benny.

"What did you think of the appetizers?" Benny said.

"Didn't Madame Trung tell you?" Muerce said.

"Yes, but she's my grandmother, and she knows how fragile I am over this event, so I need reassurance," he said.

Muerce laughed at Benny's culinary insecurity.

"They're going to be a huge hit," Muerce said. "Eleanor will be ecstatic."

"Ecstatic?" Benny said. "Well, if she is ecstatic then I can't hope for better. I don't know about this catering business, Jack. It's a lot of work."

"I'm sorry, I should have told Eleanor no from the get go. I've told her that this is the first, and last time."

"Maybe not," Benny said. "It's a lot of work, but it's a lot of money, too. Maybe for select events."

Muerce nodded. Perhaps Colonel Trung was right. It could be a lucrative line of business for the family. Benny only had to put his name, and recipes behind it. Someone else in the family could run it. *God knows there are enough Trungs to do it.*

"How did you do the dipping sauce inside the spring rolls?" Muerce said. "What a great surprise when you bite down."

Benny explained how the concept was easy, but the execution was time-consuming. First he made a plum sauce from hoison, honey and sesame seeds. Then using a large kitchen syringe he injected the sauce into common plastic straws, sealed each end with clips, and froze them. Once frozen, he snipped each end of the straw off with scissors, and used a wood dowel to push the tube of sauce out of the straws, cutting them into inch-long pieces. The cylinders of sauce were quickly wrapped in rice pancakes, the ends sealed, and then refrozen. When the spring rolls themselves were made, a frozen vial of the sauce was added with the rice noodles, shredded cilantro, carrots, cucumber and red cabbage. The sauce became viscous again during refrigeration, and by the time they were served at room temperature the condiment was near liquid.

"Jesus, that is a lot of work," Muerce said.

"But the payoff is worth it," Benny said.

"Most definitely," Muerce said.

"I've got to get back to the kitchen," Benny said, standing up.

"By the way," Muerce said. "Where did you get the idea to wrap them with a noodle like a little package?"

"Oh, that was Sammy's idea."

Of course it was, Muerce thought.

As he placed the last bite of the Kimchi galette into his mouth, and washed it down with wine, the spooky girl with Zajak turned in her chair to look over at Muerce. He looked back. Her makeup was less harsh than the previous time he had seen her. Overall, her appearance was much softer, though there remained a chill about her. She was far more attractive than Muerce first thought when Zajak introduced her at Club Unicorn. Tonight, she wore a stylish, though somewhat subdued, red cocktail dress. Club Unicorn had been a blur, and Muerce tried to remember if he thought her body shapely. While he could recount with detail how she consumed a cigarette, he couldn't remember if Zajak had given out her name.

Madame Trung appeared with the next course; a bowl of onion and garlic butter pottage with diced turnips, leeks and noodles. It was Benny's Asian twist on a classic European staple—a Medieval *Pho*. It was accompanied with a chunk of dark rye bread, and a small glass mug—the kind A&W used to serve with kids meals and were now collector's items—of dark ale.

The ale, Madame Trung explained as part of the presentation, was for flavor.

As Muerce concentrated on the pottage course the Spooky Girl returned her attention to her table, and was speaking to the two men across from her in Hindi. Muerce dipped a corner of the bread into the pottage, and chased the sopping morsel with half of the ale. The sweetness of the onion and turnip was in sharp and agreeable contrast to the bitterness of the ale. He repeated the process until the ale was gone.

Between the next course—a chard and sorrel cole slaw that served as the salad—and the palate cleanser before the main courses—a *mojito* sorbet with emphasis on the mint—a feminine cackle of laughter erupted at the table to the left and behind Muerce that sounded more male than female. Muerce discreetly turned, an empty wine glass in his hand as if to signal he needed service at his table, to look.

At first, he thought the table was made up of four men. The man directly across from him he recognized as one of the top arts patrons in the city, Hector Eduard Bennefeld. Muerce didn't know him personally, but Bennefeld served on several arts boards with Eleanor. He was, Muerce recalled, from oil money; he was well-educated, well-mannered, well-received; and, well, openly gay. He was also—Muerce had an epiphany in the moment—Neptune at Titty Boy's Roman debauchery the week before. The instant he connected the dots with Bennefeld, Muerce recognized the pretty young man across the table from Neptune. It was Aphrodite—Price Sharron—who had intervened with the nasty little Centurion with the nice calves, fierce feline eyes, and very sharp sword. Muerce stroked his neck. The scab was gone.

A third man at the table, also young, Muerce didn't recognize. The three of them were dressed in casual, preppy chic. *Very Ralph Lauren.*

When the fourth man, who was shorter than the others, and dressed in a sort of tuxedo with open collar, turned in profile, Muerce understood there were only three men in the group. Her short blonde hair was slicked back into a ponytail that was tucked up behind her left ear so that, from Muerce's angle, she appeared more man than woman. As she continued to twist her body toward the kitchen, Muerce saw her strong jaw and a long, elegant neck line. Her tuxedo shirt was unbuttoned to her solar plexus, allowing, at that angle, a glimpse of her breast. She didn't make eye contact with Muerce. Without a Centurion costume, and because the helmet and *faux* facial hair had obscured most of her face at their last encounter, Muerce didn't recognize her.

Had Paige Sharron worn a dress, stood up and walked across the dining room, Muerce would have known her calves instantly. So too, her eyes, if she had locked them on his, which she intentionally avoided doing since he entered the restaurant.

Madame Trung interrupted Muerce's eavesdropping with the first of the two main courses. She was very careful to put the plate in front of him. Behind her came another of the wait staff with a bottle of *Domain de Valmoissine* burgundy from the Latour vineyards that Madame Trung poured into a clean goblet.

"*Bon appetite,*" she said, leaving the bottle.

Muerce took a sip of the burgundy, and rolled it around his palette. The bouquet of the open bottle filled the environment around his table like freshly cut spring flowers. Glass in hand, he sat back in his chair, and taking another sip, marveled at the dish before him.

Using the tender top halves of alternating green and white blanched asparagus, Benny formed a kind of vegetable crown roast that was elaborately wrapped, and held together with rice noodles dyed in bright red, green, blue and gold. The noodles gave the colors an iridescence that looked very much like the filament used on the two victims Muerce saw on the autopsy table at the morgue.

The fortress of asparagus protected a wild rice, and dried apricot stuffing. The culinary structure was surrounded by a moat of sauce made from a red wine and rosemary infused reduction.

"If you pierce the bow with your knife the meal will unfold itself on your plate," a female voice said.

Muerce did as he was told without looking up, and the asparagus dropped, and fanned out toward the back of his plate as if choreographed. The rice stuffing tumbled forward, and soaked up the moat of sauce.

"Superb," Muerce said. He looked up at the woman standing by his table. It was the Spooky Girl.

"I am Amelie," she said. "We've met. I work with Mister Zajak."

She had a very crisp and clear accent with a hint of French. Her voice was distant, and businesslike. She was not, Muerce detected on the spot, flirting with him.

"May I sit down, for just a moment?"

Muerce lifted himself halfway out of his chair, and motioned with his hand that she was welcome to sit with him.

"Mister Zajak would like to buy your dinner," she said, studying Muerce's face.

Muerce looked over at Zajak's table. Zajak looked back, smiled, and nodded his head at Muerce.

"That's very kind of Mister Zajak, but my meal here cannot be purchased."

"Then perhaps a drink?"

Madame Trung appeared at Muerce's table and, as she adeptly poured another glass of burgundy for him she spoke in a politely calm, but sarcastic tone.

"*Est-ce que je dois mettre une autre place pour la conquete de ce soir?*" she said.

Muerce grinned uncomfortably at Amelie before unsheathing his tongue, and correcting Madame Trung. That the attractive, if distant, young woman across from him spoke fluent Hindi, and undoubtedly any number of other languages, including English, with a Parisian accent, provided Muerce with enough evidence to bet the farm that she was well versed in Madame Trung's second language. Muerce responded accordingly.

"*Je crois fortement que Mademoiselle Amelie comprenne admirablement le francais. Ainsi, je sens que doive faire des clarifications et lui faire vos vegrete. Il ne faut pas la conquerir. Pas ce soir, ni n'importe quel autre soir. Non par moi-meme, et non par n'importe quel autre homme.*"

He turned toward Amelie.

"*Je demande pardon pour l'insulte, Mademoiselle,*" he said.

"*Ce n'est pas necessaire de demander pardon, M. Muerce,*" Amelie said. "The insult was not yours. But you are correct. I won't be conquered. Not

171

tonight, and not by you. I apologize if I have upset the balance of your evening. I only wished to convey the offer of a favor from my superior."

Madame Trung's shoulder slumped forward as she lowered her head toward Amelie, and bowed to indicate her personal humiliation, and as a request for forgiveness.

"Let me return the offer," Muerce said. "If memory serves me, I owe your boss a drink."

"*lám ỏn cho một chai rừởu Sam-banh nỏi bán của họ,*" he said, addressing Madame Trung.

"Oui, champagne," Madame Trung said. She bowed apologetically once more, and retreated to the kitchen.

"Perhaps you were too brusk with her?" Amelie said.

"You were a guest at my table," Muerce said. "That's all that should have mattered to Madame Trung. Besides, she's on me constantly. Especially when it comes to very attractive women."

The Muerce charm had the same effect on Amelie as a BB thrown at a battle tank. The only sound he heard after flirtatiously tossing out the compliment was the weak *pling* the imaginary projectile made when it hit the dining room floor.

"I should return to my table Mister Muerce," she said, standing up. "Thank you for the champagne."

Muerce stood up as she excused herself.

"Amelie," Muerce said. "The girl that was with you. The one who was talking to my young friend. Is she okay?"

Amelie looked straight through Muerce without expression. Her face was as solid as granite. After what seemed like a silent count of three, she turned her back to Muerce, and returned to her table. Zajak put his left hand on her shoulder, exchanging words with her. He turned, nodded, and smiled as the bottle of champagne, compliments of Jack Muerce, arrived at the table.

Muerce returned his attention to his meal, determined to block out the other diners, and enjoy his plate. Engaged in the food, he didn't notice that Paige observed the short visit by the Spooky Girl.

Paige remembered her from Club Unicorn. She remembered the monster, and how she felt, and what she was prepared to do if any violence came to Muerce.

Paige returned the steak knife next to her plate. She had kept it hidden beneath the table, and at the ready, when Muerce was approached by the Spooky Girl. The sharp, serrated knife came with the second main dish of the night: a large, grilled Portobello mushroom accompanied with Creole sauce and eggplant whipped like mashed potatoes. Paige had clenched the knife so tightly during the interchange between Amelie and Muerce that the joints in her fingers hurt when she released her grip.

She had been watching Muerce from the moment he passed through the beaded curtain, coy and careful not to let him see her. It didn't appear to Paige that he recognized her the one time he looked over. Flashing her breast distracted him. It seemed to work. What confused her were her feelings for Muerce. They were unfamiliar, and very complex.

Her actions, however, had not gone unnoticed. Price, too, had kept his eye on Muerce, but only because his sister was watching. Price was her twin. He knew her looks, her thoughts, and her feelings. He knew when she was in a predatory mode. What was different and what he observed at Club Unicorn, was that for the first time in their intertwined lives, Paige was oblivious to Price. She was venturing out on her own. Alone. Without him. Price was pleased, if not a little jealous.

Maybe, he thought, *at least one of us can find a little normalcy; a little happiness.*

Price didn't see the set of eyes behind the carved-wood partition of the small bar and service area leading into the kitchen. The eyes watched all that unfolded in the dining area. Pho Mat made a discreet appearance in the kitchen after receiving a text that Muerce was there for dinner. Pho Mat observed, and heard. He knew who Zajak was, and that he would be dining with the two businessmen from India. He knew who the businessmen were, and what their real business was with Zajak.

What Pho Mat didn't know was why the petite blonde woman with the fierce eyes, and dressed like a man, snatched her steak knife as one would a weapon when the woman with Zajak visited Muerce's table. That Pho Mat didn't know, troubled him.

CHAPTER 19

His tuxedo was impeccable. It was a Tom Ford. Muerce needed a few minor alterations that Minnie executed flawlessly. Muerce tied, adjusted and fidgeted with his bow tie for a good ten minutes before he was satisfied it was the perfect knot. He buttoned the black satin button, snapped down the jacket snug on his shoulders, and took a moment to admire himself in the mirror of his dressing room.

Fishing through a polished walnut valet box, he chose a black, alligator-banded Patek Calatrava for the evening, and strapped it to his wrist. He looked at the face of the watch, making a mental note to remember tonight was the night everyone lost and hour. *Spring Forward.*

There was a buzzing vibration in the bedroom. Muerce adjusted his white linen pocket square, slipped his wallet into his back pocket, and pocketed a gold Calibri lighter, though it was doubtful it would be used. Still, he recalled the words of his father: a gentleman should always have the means to offer a lady a light. The phone buzzed and rattled again on the nightstand.

It was the limo service. The car was waiting outside.

Before turning off the lights, Muerce looked back at the bed and asked any greater force in the universe that might be listening that he not wake up alone the next morning. He also asked that the night go by as quickly as possible.

--

"I hate these things, you know," Muerce said, holding the limousine door open for Eleanor.

"Yes, I know," she said, indifferent to her son's whining. "We all know. So why don't you do Mommy a favor. Grow up and and act like the good host you were raised to be. You might even surprise yourself and have a good time.

"Who knows, there could even be a pretty girl there who might find you charming. But not if you're pouting."

It was like Junior Dance Cotillion and he was twelve again, and Eleanor had just fixed his tie and yanked on his ear to snap him into line.

"Just don't kiss me on the cheek," Muerce said, settling himself in the back seat next to her.

"What?"

"Just don't kiss me like you did before the Dance Cotillion," he said. "There was lipstick on my face most of the night until one of my friends told me. Every girl I asked to dance that night turned me down, then ran off giggling and laughing to her friends. It was horrible."

Eleanor held her clutch purse to her mouth, and began laughing into it. "Oh you poor thing."

"It scarred me for life, you know," Muerce said, with mock seriousness. Soon, he too, was laughing as hard as Eleanor.

"It's not funny," he said.

"No, it's not, it's just... just horrible," she said, removing a tissue from her clutch, and dabbing at the tears of laughter on her face. Muerce caught the driver looking at them in the rearview mirror to see what the commotion was about, perhaps even to get in on the joke.

"Awful, just awful, and it got worse," Muerce said.

"Oh, dear, how could it have been any worse?" Eleanor said, starting to regain control of herself.

"I went to the men's room to wipe the lipstick off my face," he said.

"Yes?" Eleanor said, feeling a peel of giggles starting to build.

"When I came out, somehow, and unbeknownst to me, a long strip of toilet paper had become affixed to the sole of my shoe."

Eleanor erupted in laughter, and decided to make no further attempts to salvage her makeup until they arrived at the museum. Muerce, too, began to laugh out loud.

"Then what happened?" Eleanor managed to say between chortles.

"A lot of pointing and merriment at my expense," Muerce said. "It was unmerciful. Even some of the chaperones were laughing at me. Friends of yours, by the way. I felt like I had no clothes on. Until... "

Muerce paused, and stared out the window at the reflection of light on the wet pavement outside the limo.

"Until what, dear?"

Muerce's laughing ceased. There was a wistful mix of joy and melancholy in his voice.

"Until, the prettiest girl in the room walked up to me and put her hand on my shoulder." he said. He sighed. "Then she leaned forward and whispered in my ear, 'Vous avez relevé vagabond.'

"Her eyes were violet, and she smelled like lilac. I remember she bent down, collected the toilet paper into a wad, and tucked it into the sash around her dress. When she stood up she asked me to dance with her for the rest of the night. And we did."

Muerce turned to Eleanor and saw streaks of tears running down her face. The tissue in her hand was wet and useless. He removed the pocket square from his tuxedo jacket, and offered it over.

"Emily Benoit," she said.

"That was the first time I met her," he said. "The first time she rescued me. We didn't see or talk to each other again until law school."

There was a long silence in the back seat of the limo for several blocks.

"I never put that together," Eleanor said, composed. "It makes sense to me now. She spent several months with extended family, the Fouchards. Away from that... well, that sadness in Paris. They had girls her age, your age. The Fouchards. Of course she would have attended the Cotillion.

"And you were off to boarding school only some weeks later. Correct?"

"That's right," Muerce said.

The rain had picked up, and the driver turned on the wipers. They made a soothing distraction as they rhythmically swept back and forth across the windshield.

"I don't know why I never told you that story before," Muerce said.

"And now you have," Eleanor said. "Do you feel better?"

"No," he said, looking out the rain-streaked window.

Nor do I, Eleanor thought. Dabbing at her face with the handkerchief, she marshaled her emotions, and pushed the memory of Emily Benoit aside.

— —

The Gilmont Center was built on seven-hundred-fifty acres purchased by the Yves R. Gilmont Trust, and was located on the summit of the hill that made up the Esquiline District. It was the tallest of the seven hills overlooking the city. The museum, covered mostly in travertine marble from Bagni di Tivoli, Italy, shone day and night like a pristine beacon of culture.

Gilmont was a Belgian petrochemical industrialist, who began his career in the United States as an electrical engineer. He parlayed several patents for oil rig pumps into a vast fortune of holdings that originated in squeezing oil from the ground, and ended by squeezing money from Wall Street. In business he was obsessive and ruthless. With his family he was stingy and cantankerous. When it came to art, however, he was a patron who gave new definition to generosity. When he was in his late nineties, and nearing the end of his life, Gilmont became one more thing—sentimental. That was when he was introduced to fellow art patron, Eleanor Muerce.

He was in his last years and, at the time, his legacy was about to be handed over to his Trust, which was run by a board he considered nearsighted, at best. Eleanor, on the other hand, understood exactly what Gilmont's intentions were. He had a duty to better the lives of as many people as he could reach. And he wanted to do that through art; his roots in the past, and his belief in the future.

When he died, the first action in his will was to sack the chief executive officer of the Trust, and name Eleanor interim CEO and board member in charge of the search for new "leadership" of the Trust. In essence, Eleanor was tasked with finding the right people to do the right things to carry out Gilmont's intentions to improve lives through the appreciation of art. Within six months, a new CEO was named and half the board replaced. Everybody at the Gilmont was focused, and on mission.

That was over twenty years ago. Since then, the Gilmont Center had been built, its collection expanded, and satellite art centers focused on education and community art exhibits were opened in both poor and middle-class neighborhoods throughout the city.

Tonight's exhibit gala represented the zenith of Eleanor's work for the Trust. It had taken over a decade of preliminary discussions, grueling travel, and hard negotiations just to secure the agreement with the *Musee de Cluny*—officially known as the *Musee du Moyen-Age*—that would allow the most famous works in its collection to come to the United States for exhibit. The agreement in place, it took another two years to work out all the logistics of insuring, transporting, and environmentally storing and exhibiting works of such delicate and massive size. Additionally, there was the security, conservation and cost associated with every element of the exhibit. Eleanor had been at the forefront of all of it, especially the consortium that put together the financial sponsorship of the show.

The gala fundraiser would be the only cost associated with public viewing of the exhibit. For the remainder of the exhibit it was free to the public.

— —

"What's the problem?" Muerce said.

"Traffic, sir," the driver said. "It looks like the exit is backed up for a good quarter of a mile. It's slow, but it's moving."

"How's the time?" Eleanor said. Muerce looked at his watch.

"We have a half hour before we're supposed to be there," he said.

"Goodness, could this all be for tonight?" she said. "This early?"

Two of the west-bound lanes on the freeway that sliced through the valley between the Palantine and Esquiline districts were illuminated by a river of red taillights that ran all the way to the museum exit. Everyone in those lanes were trying to make their way through the rain and traffic to the parking structure at the bottom of the Esquiline. From there, most would take the tram to the museum at the top of the hill. The Muerce's limo, however, would be allowed past the security gate, and up the narrow, winding road that would deposit them at the entrance to the Gilmont Center complex.

"The private reception starts at seven, right?" Muerce said.

"Yes," Eleanor said.

"And that's a pretty small affair. Two, maybe three dozen people?"

"If that."

"What were tickets going for? Fifteen hundred each?"

"Twenty-five hundred... each."

The driver whistled in surprise.

"Jesus, did I pay that?" Muerce said.

"You will," Eleanor said.

"Excuse me sir, madam, I didn't mean to eavesdrop," the driver said.

"Are you kidding?" Muerce said. "You expressed what I was thinking. Good grief, Eleanor. An event of a thousand people—not including the VIP pre-party. That's two-point-five million."

"Which should just about cover Benny's catering costs," Eleanor said.

"Oh please, they're losing money on this deal. And tonight has been sold out for awhile?"

"For several months, I believe."

"That's some pretty damn good promotion."

Eleanor thought so. In fact, she had been very impressed with the marketing of the event, though it was not an area in which she had had much to do.

The line of cars backed up on the freeway moved quickly. That was due to the additional police traffic units hired for the event, and the excellent vehicle flow design into the parking structure/tram station. The parking garage itself was a brilliant architectural piece with its own sculpture garden, reflecting pool and environmentally friendly, and eye pleasing elements like a "green roof", and solar panels that looked like wings.

At the security gate, Eleanor identified herself by showing her museum board credentials, and the limo was waved onto the roundabout outside the garage that led up the twisting access road that paralleled the tram. Muerce saw a tuxedoed and gowned crowd of socialites and wannabe socialites milling about the covered areas of the station, and adjacent sculpture garden. Several museum employees handed out beige umbrellas.

"Oh dear, we might have to start letting them up the hill earlier than we thought," Eleanor said. "I'll have to talk to some of the board members and the staff as soon as we arrive."

"In other words, you're going to abandon me the minute we walk through the doors," Muerce said. "Thanks, again, Mommy."

Eleanor patted Muerce on his hand as if soothing a child.

"Get a hold of yourself," she said, not looking at him. "You know almost everyone who will be there."

"Exactly," he said. "My mother is knowingly throwing me to the wolves."

"You'll survive," Eleanor said, chortling. "You always do."

As the limo pulled to the bottom of the flight of marble steps, now slick with blowing rain, that led to the entrance hall, several museum staff members armed with umbrellas jogged toward the car.

"One more thing," Eleanor said, turning to her son as he pulled the latch to open the car door. "Let's not be found entertaining guests in the coatroom."

"Mother, the only part of me that's ever been in a coatroom is my coat," he said.

"There's always a first time," she said.

"Please, I have some decency at my age," he said, flipping up the collar of his topcoat, and taking an open umbrella offered by a staff member. Another staff member held an umbrella for Eleanor, who secured the small wrap that matched her cream, silk Versace evening dress that, as she said, was "age appropriate" because it covered her shoulders, and upper arms.

Quickly, and without incident they made their way up the slippery eight flights of steps from the Arrival Plaza to the Entrance Hall. As they did, Muerce contemplated the lie he told his mother about the coatroom.

— —

The rain was relentless, and beat down on the large glass awnings that swept over the main entry into the museum. The awning provided only scant protection from the storm. Once inside, Muerce's senses were deluged by the cyclone of activity swirling through the cavernous space. Spotlights fixed on the large Chihuly glass sculptures hanging from the ceiling appeared to explode in loud, cheerful bursts of orange, red, yellow, green and blue. The high-intensity lighting gave the glass-spoked orbs the impression of fixed fireworks glittering and splashing their display above the crowd.

The damp, fungous smell of wet hair laced with expensive Chanel perfume, and doses of designer aftershave, lingered in the air as the crowd skittered, strolled and, in some cases, floated across the black marble floor. It was like a dark lake—soon to turn into a churning ocean—navigated by tuxedoed men, who were either rubbing against, or trying to avoid, the many sharp-pointed icebergs of women gowned, jeweled, and frosted for the evening.

The buzz of polite conversations and perfunctory greetings was accentuated by the clinking of wine and cocktail glasses, and muffled notes of chamber music. The air was cool from the storm, yet Muerce sensed the approaching swampy atmosphere accumulating strength from the body heat of the guests just as a hurricane found its energy from tropical waters. And this was just the VIP pre-party. What was sticky now, would be torpid once the crowd gathered at the tram station at the bottom of the hill made its way into the Entrance Hall.

It would be insufferable. But what would be even more intolerable would be the lines at the bar. Muerce took advantage of the moment, and the open bar at the far end of the reception area, and ordered two scotches—neat. He finished the first just as the second was handed to him by a cute girl tending bar. There was a end—or possibly beginning—of an elaborate tattoo on the left side of her neck that depicted both feathers and scales. Muerce envisioned her naked in the coatroom, and what mythical creature he might find that inhabited her skin. He smiled at her.

She smiled back, and winked. He stuffed a twenty-dollar bill in the tip jar, and walked away, nursing the second scotch. *Focus Jack.*

The chamber music eased his carnal thoughts, and soothed some of his anxiety. He gravitated toward the source of the music, following the sharp harpsichord notes like a compass. Muerce weaved through the guests, politely acknowledging those who acknowledged him as well as discreetly ignoring those to whom he did not wish to notice.

A deep, bellowing voice erupted to his right, commanding immediate attention. It had a familiar ring he thought he recognized.

While maneuvering past a cluster of socialites and civic leaders, one of the group, a city council member, tugged Muerce's sleeve with a sense of desperation. He leaned into Muerce: "I need to talk to you. It's important."

Muerce knew of the matter the Councilman referred. It wasn't important, not to Muerce. It was another in a long line of peccadilloes involving loan fraud that entangled the councilman, and had been in the news for a week.

"The best of luck to you, Councilman," Muerce said. His response was as noncommittal as his expression. The Councilman had his answer.

Simultaneously, one of the women in the group standing near the Councilman tugged on Muerce's opposite sleeve, and whispered in his ear. She was matronly, yet, around her rounded edges, she still carried some of the beauty of her youth and breeding. "You look delicious," she slurred.

Switching the cocktail glass from his right to his left hand, Muerce hooked the woman's arm, brought the top of her hand to his mouth, and politely kissed her plump knuckles.

"Too much, too soon," he said. "*Bon soire, Madame.*"

He reflected the same expression and the same delivery proffered to the Councilman. She, too, had her answer. *I hate these things.*

The deep voice again bellowed, Muerce slipped closer to within range of its source, and to the strains of the chamber group performing nearby.

Muerce had no idea why he was drawn to the voice. There was a curiosity about it that distracted Muerce like an itch that could not be reached. It, like the evening, so far, was an irritation to him. But he was obliged—to Eleanor, and to Ashley. There was an undercurrent of calamity within him like a building fever. Perhaps, he hoped, solving the mystery of the voice might assuage the anxiety. It was one of several itches he wanted to scratch, badly.

The voice bellowed in laughter. Muerce was closer. From the tone and tenor he figured it belonged to an African American man. Navigating around a cluster of socialites who nodded and smiled at Muerce as he passed, he came upon the source. The baritone did come from an African American man. A large man who, despite what Muerce could see was a well-tailored tuxedo, did not wear the outfit well. What did fit well on the six-foot-six athletic frame of the man was a football uniform. And for sixteen games a season, that is exactly what he wore for the city's professional football team.

Kiron Kinson was an All-Pro middle linebacker with a reputation for delivering vicious hits on wide receivers and running backs. His specialty, however, was the damage he delighted upon quarterbacks. To date, Kinson was infamously—or famously in some sports circles—credited with ending the careers of three quarterbacks, of which he boasted by having their numbers tattooed on his right forearm. The most recent of the three unscheduled retirements occurred during the last season. The hit resulted in Kinson being suspended for two games, and fined over six figures by the League. He had blatantly blindsided the passer well after he had released the ball. The incident only enhanced Kinson's reputation, and led to an extension of his contract despite the team's abysmal won-loss record for the year.

Muerce's itch had been scratched. He felt sated for the moment. The relief was not because Muerce was a pro football fan, and had recognized one of the game's hero/villains; the satisfaction came from connecting the voice to the man, and relating both to a different time and a place.

Kinson's nickname was Dog. And when he brought a ball handler down on the field in a particularly brutal way it was known as being "Touched by the Hand of Dog."

Though Muerce didn't by nature pass moral judgements on others—lest they pass judgement on him—he found it amusing such machismo exhibited by Kinson on nationally televised games masked his predilection for having another man gnaw on the Dog's bone.

Muerce nursed his scotch and hovered, alone, several yards from Kinson and his entourage, which included Kinson's wife—a tall, leggy, bottle blonde who wore a strapless sequined gown that clung to her spectacularly augmented breasts like wet tissue paper. *What a delightful cliche. Wasted on her husband.*

There was another eruption of Kinson's bellowed laugh as he unfastened his cufflink and pulled back his jacket and shirt sleeves to show the small, but enamored crowd around him the numbered tattoos. The scotch built a warm buzz in Muerce's head, and his thoughts matriculated to contemplation of whether it might have been appropriate to force German officers convicted of war crimes during World War II to be tattooed with the same numbers they ordered scribed on the arms of concentration camp prisoners. Muerce's drift into non-linear thought was interrupted by T.B. Squire.

"Good evening Mister Muerce," he said, offering his hand.

Muerce reciprocated. He had begun to like the man through his son. These were solid people. They were honest, and they worked hard. They earned the privilege and title they possessed. And with it, Muerce hoped, Travis would, in time, do some good for people who needed some good done in their lives.

"Please, call me Jack," Muerce said.

A mixed look of surprise and achievement radiated from T.B. Squire as they shook hands.

"Jack—that very well may be my biggest accomplishment of the evening," he said.

As the largest underwriter of the exhibit, the corporate logo of the health care system T.B. Squire ran was emblazoned on all the advertising and marketing materials used to promote the tapestries exhibit. T.B. Squire was the reason they would be viewed by the public for free.

"I hardly think so," Muerce said, pointing to the logo that adorned one of the floor-to-ceiling banners hanging in the Entrance Hall.

"That's just honey on the biscuit," T.B. Squire said, modestly averting his eyes as he took a sip of champagne. "Respect, on the other hand, especially between gentlemen, endures."

"With respect, then," Muerce said.

The two of them toasted.

"Oh, Mercy," T.B. Squire said.

"I did say you could call me Jack," Muerce said, lightheartedly.

"Yes, indeed," T.B. Squire said. "I meant mercy in the sense of "oh crap.'"

"And how is that?" Muerce said.

"Kinson."

"The football player?"

"Yes."

"What about him?"

"The company is a big biscuit and we spread a lot of honey around," T.B. Squire said. "We used to ladle it on thick with signage, and two luxury suites at the football stadium."

"Used to?" Muerce said. He took a short sip from his glass, and noticed he was nearing the end of the drink. "Should I be expecting a reference to drawing more flies?"

T.B. Squire grinned in response.

"Something like that," T.B. Squire said. "You know the man's reputation on the field?"

"I dare say his reputation both on and off the field," Muerce said. "But let's stick with on the field."

"Football is a game of aggression, we all know and accept that," T.B. Squire said. "Regardless of whether you approve of how Kinson plays the game or not, as sponsors we were not appreciative of his post-game comments after taking out that quarterback last season. Do you remember it?"

Muerce nodded that he did, though he had only a vague recollection of it.

"He made it clear he was doing his best to support the team's corporate sponsors by sending them customers," T.B. Squire said. "It was a huge PR nightmare for us. We tried to go back channel with the team's front office—even called the League commissioner—to get Kinson to make a public apology."

"I assume that didn't happen."

"Of course not."

"So?"

"We're pulling all of our sponsorship from them for next season, and not renewing our contracts for the luxury suites."

T.B. Squire threw back the remainder of his champagne like it was a shot of bourbon, and grabbed another full glass from a passing waiter. He finished that glass off without haste.

"I gather there's more to the story," Muerce said.

"Hell, I love football," T.B. Squire said. "Now I can't go watch it. And..."

Muerce cocked his head towards T.B. Squire, anticipating the next statement.

"That *sumbitch* played for Oklahoma."

"I'm not following."

"I'm from Texas," T.B. Squire said so that everyone within earshot could hear him. "Hook 'em."

Muerce wasn't sure how to reply, but the awkwardness of his non response was saved by a new glass of scotch that appeared before him.

"You will have to forgive Daddy's passion for the pigskin Mister Muerce," Travis said. "I took the liberty of retrieving a fresh cocktail for you. Glennfiddich? I hope that meets with your satisfaction."

Travis was almost unrecognizable to Muerce. At first, what threw Muerce off was his mere presence at the event—but it made sense when he processed the fact of who Travis' father was, and the social circles in which he ran. Then it was Travis' appearance. He wore a very tasteful white dinner jacket, with shawl collar, that fit precisely. It had all the signs of a bespoke suit. Generally, Muerce had previously observed, Travis dressed appropriately, though slightly preppy for his age. Still, Travis tended to be on the more wrinkled side of presence. He wasn't just a not bad looking young man, but one who could, if he wanted, shuffle through most of the women in the room like he did a deck of cards. *Cut with handsome, Eleanor would say.*

The most unrecognizable element to Travis was the grace and civility with which he carried himself. There was the genteelness of his words, but it was the unspoken carriage of the young man that stood out—obvious despite its understatement. It was, Muerce knew, the best kind of armor a man could wear. T.B. Squire rather beamed as Muerce accepted the drink, and Travis removed himself, for the moment, to cater the empty glass away. Muerce, too, rather beamed.

"His mother and I are indebted to you," T.B. Squire said.

"No, sir, Travis is indebted to the both of you," Muerce said, pausing to contemplate the carmel-colored bottom of his glass. "He does clean up well."

T.B. Squire's humorous snort was interrupted by a twittering peel of laughter, and an unwelcome bellow. Kinson, his wife, and a handful of the entourage had interjected themselves into T.B. Squire and Muerce's conversation. Kinson's large, and unwanted, paw patted T.B. Squire's shoulder.

"Yeah, I know you from somewhere," Kinson said, addressing Muerce.

"I don't think so," Muerce said, keeping his focus on T.B. Squire, who was making great effort to hold his anger in place. Kinson knew who T.B. Squire was, the related ruckus associated with his comments, and the request for a public apology. Kinson thought apologies were beneath him. He was, after all, a superstar.

"Nah, I recognize you from somewhere, I'm sure of it," Kinson said. He stopped patting T.B. Squire, but kept his unwelcome hand on his shoulder. Muerce thought Kinson's behavior both inappropriate and impolite for the setting.

Travis returned, recognizing Kinson, and the tension. He discreetly placed himself just behind, and between his father and Muerce.

"Nah, I never forget a face and I remember yours," Kinson said.

Since Kinson wasn't going to let it go, and Muerce had two scotches under his belt inside of ten minutes, and was working on a third, he decided to waive the polite conversation expected of the evening.

"Given the number of games you lost last season I'm sure you would recognize the ten or twelve fans who bothered to show up," Muerce said. "Mine, fortunately for me, was not among them."

Kinson's wife snickered, causing her breasts to lift and fall in successive breaths.

"A comedian," Kinson said. His voice less jocular, and more aggressive. He looked at his wife in such a way that she and her breasts became as still and cold as a concrete bunker.

"Not really," Muerce retorted.

"Nah, I'm damn sure I know you," Kinson said.

If Kinson wanted to push, then Muerce would push back, and he decided to do so in a manner that would put an end to the conversation. As he began to speak, Muerce caught a flash of gold and blonde out of the corner of his eye that, like Kinson, he recognized but couldn't place. It was a momentary distraction that he would follow up on after finishing off Kinson.

"Come to think of it, I believe you are right," Muerce said. He took a sip of scotch before continuing. "It's a matter of context. This is neither the right location nor are we among the right people for proper context.

"If, perhaps, Helen of Troy or The Virgin Mary were present, we would then likely have the proper context for you to recognize me."

Of those listening to Muerce, only three people knew what he meant. A fourth, Kinson's wife, only suspected. Of the four, only one reacted to what Muerce said—Kinson. Muerce returned his attention to the scotch, then looked about the Entrance Hall for the golden apparition that flashed before him a moment earlier. The stare from Kinson's wife tightened on her husband with the same emotion that T.B. Squire had first felt at the start of the awkward encounter. Travis caught Kinson's attention and, with his eyes, directed the behemoth to remove his hand from his father, which Kinson did.

Done staring at his cocktail, Muerce gave Kinson a look that if he wanted to respond, now would be the time. If not, Muerce's look said, then it was best for Kinson and his entourage to excuse themselves. The veins in Kinson's thick neck popped and pulsed like ebony garden snakes.

The look on his face, however, gave the appearance of having been caught playing with himself.

"You're right," Kinson said. "We ain't never seen each other before."

"Muerce, Mister Kinson," Muerce said. "My name is Jack Muerce. In case we should run into each other again."

Without comment or ceremony, Kinson walked away, followed by his groupies. His wife trailed behind them, obviously lagging on purpose, and stewing.

"I don't know what that was about, but I'm glad it's over," T.B. Squire said. "Damn Sooners."

He looked at his shoulder, then at his empty champagne glass.

"I need a shower," T.B. Squire said. "But I'll settle for a real drink. Jack?"

There was a half finger of scotch left in his glass, which Muerce didn't want to finish. He regretted drinking as much as he had in so short a time. And he was having regrets about the exchange with Kinson.

"I'm done for the evening, thank you," he said.

"Travis?'

"Go ahead Daddy," Travis said. "I have to catch Mister Muerce up on my chores."

T.B. Squire excused himself.

"Chores?" Muerce said, swirling the remaining scotch around the inside of the glass.

"It's not my place to say, Mister Muerce," said Travis.

"But?"

"Kinson's an asshole, but lesson number one you taught me was to be discreet. Well, really, that was lesson number two."

Travis recalled the punch to his ribs in the car.

"What was lesson number one?"

"Regarding Misses Estrada."

"Ah, yes," Muerce said. "Actually, lessons number one and two are interchangeable. But you're right. And lesson number three is Jack Muerce is fallible."

"To err is human..."

"But to forgive is divine," Muerce said. "Yes, Travis. You sound like my mother now. And I don't want you sounding like my mother. Now tell me about your chores."

"I had some of the autopsy photos enlarged, and have categorized the research, put together bullet points on some of the more salient information, and had them blown up too," Travis said. "I thought it would be easier to focus on it in a larger format. I re-arranged the setup in the bedroom for better display. I don't know if you saw any of it when you were getting ready for tonight. I hope that was okay."

"No, I didn't," Muerce said. "And, yes, it's okay."

"The images that size are a little shocking at first but you can really see a lot more of the detail," Travis said. "It's actually kind of amazing when you think about it. That kind of skill, and that it was live flesh."

"I don't know if amazing is quite the word I would use," Muerce said.

"Well, sick, for sure, but interesting. And, from what I've read. Pretty hard to do. I also dug up a little more on Brankovic's business dealings. When would you like to go over it?"

Muerce looked at what was left of his scotch, and handed the glass to Travis. The sight of Mrs. Kinson's heaving breasts, and the flash of gold, stirred Muerce's carnal thoughts. Then he remembered Ashley, whom he promised to seek out. It was her turn for his attention.

"Maybe later tomorrow afternoon," Muerce said. "I'll let you you know. Also, did I see..."

"Yes, you did," Travis said. "She's here."

"Paige, right?" Muerce said. Muerce was not a big believer in coincidence.

"She was over by the bar by the band," Travis said, pointing to Muerce's right. He looked at Muerce with hesitation.

"What is it, Travis?"

"With all due respect, lessons one, two and three might best be considered when it comes to someone like her."

The scotch buzz had settled in Muerce's frontal lobes, delightfully clouding his judgement, and enhancing his anticipation of the possibilities the evening still held.

"Lesson number four," he said, looking towards the bar in hopes of spotting Paige. "We're single, we're at a gala, and we're wearing tuxedos. There's free food and booze, and a room full of beautiful women. Under these circumstances, lesson number four is, forget lessons one, two and three.

"And Travis? It's called a chamber group, or ensemble, not a band. That ain't Eric Clapton up there playing the lute."

"Sting, maybe," Travis said.

Muerce smiled, arched his eyebrows, and made his way toward the bar by the music. Travis deposited Muerce's cocktail on one of the high-top tables, before drifting around the room in a semi-circle path. He would keep close to Muerce, but not so close he could be seen. *Tonight is Jack Muerce babysitting duty.*

There were two other sets of eyes fixed on Muerce as well—Paige Sharron's and Pho Mat's. But only Pho Mat—the watcher watching the watchers—had the vision to see the bigger picture.

— —

Muerce didn't make it very far before he was snagged. When he turned to see who had him, his chest tightened in a way he hadn't expected. It made him giddy. *The prettiest girl in the room.*

"Gotcha," Ashley said. Her smile was more brilliant than the spotlights illuminating the chandeliers above them, and her eyes sparkled with their reflection.

"Don't move," he said. "I want to remember you at this moment, in this place, for the rest of my life."

Her heart skipped a beat. She stiffened her legs when she felt them start to buckle at the knees. The rest of her body went soft, and her cheeks brightened with the blush of a woman at the first moment she is taken by love. Curiously, she was sure she could smell the aroma of cut lavender, and the taste of honey.

"If ever there was a work of art in this building, it is you," Muerce said. "You are priceless."

And she was. In keeping with the theme of the evening, Ashley had planned and saved—a considerable amount she fretted about almost daily—to have one of the top designers in the city create her outfit. Her hair was coifed in an "up-do", and rolled in the back to accommodate a small, rose-colored linen *crepine* from which a short veil of the same material fell to her shoulder blades. Ashley's delicate, long neck melded into a red velvet surcoat that had a prominent collar in the back but opened in the front, partially baring her shoulders before plunging to her chest. It allowed a for a hint of *décolletage*, as well as some freckles, and a small mole. Ashley was of medium breast size, but the surcoat and accompanying external corset—also made of red velvet, and elaborately beaded with small pearls and gold stitching—highlighted her shape, giving the impression she was more ample than what nature had provided her. The velvet sleeves of the surcoat surrendered at her biceps to the same fine rose linen cloth adorning her head. The sheer fabric highlighted her arms, and had the same bead work as the corset. The sleeves opened at her wrists, and were cuffed with a band of elaborate embroidery. The corset was kept in place by a silk busk embroidered in the same manner as the cuffs of the surcoat. The busk also gathered more of the red velvet cloth that draped to the floor like a stage curtain. It opened in the front to expose more of the rose-colored and beaded linen that was backed with a slightly darker shade of rose.

Muerce dressed and undressed Ashley several times over with his eyes.

I don't even know where I'd begin, Muerce thought.

The response elicited from Muerce made the expense of the gown worth the money. Ashley did a mock curtsey, lifted her gown slightly from the floor and proffered her right foot, exposing her leg to mid shin. It was covered with rose-colored silk hose.

"Ferragamos," she said, drawing Muerce's attention to her shoes. "Aren't they fabulous? I can't believe I found them to match the dress."

Muerce admired the footwear, and her well-turned ankle. The shoes were a dark, almost purple, suede, high-heeled sandal. There were five lace points on the top of the shoe, a covered heel and a small cap in the front encasing Ashley's toes. The matching lacing was more ribbon than string, was bordered in gold, and was tied off in an big bow at the top of each shoe. Muerce knew he liked them, and that they were—if a woman wore shoes correctly—the beginning of a journey that led up a long pair of legs that ended in a place of fruitful delight. What Muerce didn't know was that they cost more than thirteen hundred dollars, and were the biggest *coup* of Ashley's outfit. The Italian designer wasn't going to unveil the shoe until the Fall Fashion Show. Ashley's designer had pulled some strings.

"They are *perfect*," said Muerce, with an emphasis all women wanted to hear about their shoes.

Ashley let out a little giggle then gave Muerce a seriously sultry look, and motioned with her finger for him to come closer so she could whisper in his ear. He obeyed.

"There are more surprises underneath," she said, in a warm and moist breath. She took a quick nip at the lobe of his ear and pulled away.

A sharp static voice erupted from Ashley's head. When she stuck a finger in her right ear, Muerce noticed a clear plastic gadget attached to the appendage. With her other hand she adjusted something hidden behind the busk at her waistline.

"Okay, I'll be right there," she said. Ashley was wired for the evening.

"Work?" said Muerce.

"Work." said Ashely.

"My guess is they want to let the main crowd up the hill," he said. "It was getting a bit soggy down there."

A blast of rain splattered against the large bank of windows on the west side of the Exhibition Hall, which led to the courtyard.

"Makes sense," Ashley said, switching gears back to her duties as the person in charge of the event's marketing and public relations. Muerce watched the expression on her face as she contemplated something. She pulled her mobile phone from the folds of fabric held by the busk, and looked at the time. Then she pressed her ear again and said she would be over in several minutes.

"Come with me," she told Muerce, grabbing his hand.

Leading him through the milling crowd of VIPs, past the large doors that led into the Exhibition Pavilion, they made their way down an empty corridor.

Ashley turned to Muerce as they approached another set of doors that led into the main room of the Exhibition Pavilion.

"Close your eyes," she insisted, with delight.

"This will take your breath away," she said.

"You've already done that," Muerce said as Ashley led him into the room.

"I plan on doing it a few more times, too," she said.

There was a noticeable change in the temperature as they entered. It was slightly warmer, and less moist than the Entrance Hall. The air was soft, with a mustiness that reminded Muerce of the morgue.

He knew the immensity of the hall, having been in it many times before for exhibitions, but now there was something that felt confining about the place.

His sense of sound was altered in a way he couldn't distinguish. Silence itself seemed to be absorbed. There was only the soft sweeping their feet made as they walked over thick carpet, and it too, was fleeting. It was as if they had entered a vacuum—one that not only swallowed all sound, but altered all sense of time.

Most of all, Muerce felt like he was being watched—and judged.

"Just wait," she said, stopping, and giving Muerce a quarter turn to his left.

"Okay, now," she said, directing him to open his eyes.

For the second time of the evening, Ashley had taken his breath away.

The size of the tapestries gave Muerce a start, and he rocked back on his heels as if hit by a strong wave. Then their brilliance hit him.

The colors of the six tapestries were sharp to the point of being emotionally expressive. There was an instant response Muerce felt was wrenched from of him. He had never reacted to art in such a way before.

The vibrancy of the colors jumped from the tapestries in their hues, tints, shades and tones with a physiological and psychological force that was indelible, and delicate.

The color that spoke to Muerce with the strongest voice was the vermillion red that dominated the background of the assembled work. It shouted blood, and when he heard it he shivered, and felt the skin on his forearms and the back of his neck get prickly and tight.

"What do you think?" Ashley said.

"Intimidating, and slightly frightening," he said.

It was not the reply she expected. Mulling Muerce's response, she concluded his reaction was more impassioned and heartfelt than she would have given him credit for despite his intelligence and cultural upbringing. Muerce was, she realized, more emotionally vulnerable than she suspected. *Now I'm intimidated and slightly frightened—of falling helplessly in love with an unattainable man.*

A voice crackled again from Ashley's earpiece. Muerce was too consumed by the tapestries to hear her response.

"I've got to go," she said.

He looked at her without understanding what she had just said. Muerce was still overcome by the exhibit.

"Jack, I've go to go," she said, wondering where his focus had turned. "Are you okay?"

Muerce snapped to attention when he realized Ashley was addressing him.

"Yes, fine, just, this was so unexpected," he said. "Hard to explain, really."

He rallied quickly.

"Any more surprises that will take my breath away tonight?" he said.

Ashley winked, and flashed a mischievous smile that promised future intent.

"Only if you're a good boy," she said.

There was another crack of static in her earpiece, which made Ashley's eyes grow wide with surprise, and a tinge of panic.

"Is everything all right?" he said.

"That was your mother," Ashley said. The color left her face as she checked the receiver hidden in her waist. "Tell me she didn't hear that."

"Doubtful."

"That she heard me?"

"That she knows who you were talking to," Muerce said. "I'm sure she heard you."

The panicked look firmed on Ashley's face.

"I'm kidding," he said. "Besides, Eleanor has much more on her mind tonight than your personal life."

"Except my personal life tonight involves you," she said.

"Relax," he said. "Go do your job."

"You're right," she said. "I'm over thinking it."

"Yes, you're over thinking it."

"It was just kind of freaky that it was your mother."

"Which makes me think you better get going, and quickly."

"You're right," Ashley said. She turned to leave, then turned back to Muerce. "You'll be okay?"

"Yeah, I'll be okay," he said. "I promise I won't break anything."

She glowered at him in a lighthearted manner.

"One more thing," he said.

"Yes," she said, drawing the word out in a way to indicate that she was in a hurry, and he need be quick about it.

"I'd like to come to an agreement that it's *our* personal life, not just yours or mine," he said.

For the second time in less than a quarter of an hour, Muerce made her heart skip a beat. If he were to do it again tonight, Ashley hoped, it would be when they were both naked.

— —

Muerce's reaction to the tapestries was strangely intimate, and curiously ominous. They were much larger than he expected; almost daunting. The size and the nature of their composition absorbed most of the sound in the room. It was a suffocating silence, warm and moist. They breathed, and when they did Muerce felt like they sucked the air out of the room, leaving only a faint musty breath.

Muerce approached the first of the tapestries, lured by the rich colors and lustrous texture of the dyed wool and silk strands meticulously sewn by artisans in the *mille-fleurs* style. Thousands of flowers populated the background of each of the six hangings, blanketing the earthly realm of the cartoons.

Their medium and execution was so forceful the depiction of subject matter was momentarily lost to him. His senses fell into the fabric itself. The nearer he approached, the more he wanted to reach out and run his fingers across the surface of the weaves, as if he could touch time itself, and be absorbed into fifteenth century Flanders. In the space between the mingled threads were the hands of ghosts, stained by vibrant dyes, stiff and sore from their splendidly tedious work.

The reminder popped into Muerce's head. Eleanor taught her son that when it came to experiencing art, you were to use all of your senses except one—touch. *Keep your arms behind your back at all times to avoid the temptation.*

Muerce recalled the stinging slap she delivered when he was a boy as he reached across a rope barrier to touch the heavy application of oil paint on a Van Gogh landscape. Ever since, when in the presence of art, he kept both hands locked behind his back as if in bondage. Eleanor raised him to appreciate fine art. He did not, however, love it. His apartment testified to that. The walls were devoid of anything that could be identified as more than than visual fodder to fill a void.

He cared only for the Kandinsky that hung by the grand piano at One Crest Drive. And only because it reminded him of Emily Benoit, and the two of them seated on the piano bench, playing side-by-side.

Muerce visually caressed the tapestry before him. He was so close he didn't see the depiction of a seated maiden holding a mirror in her right hand, which reflected the image of a unicorn. The mythical beast rested its front hooves gently on her lap as it bent down on its rear haunches in supplication.

"It's a progression," a voice said.

The voice startled Muerce, who wheeled defensively toward the source with his arms rising in anticipation of either defending himself, or taking the offensive. Muerce was, however, surprised when he surveyed the source that disturbed his solitude.

The man standing behind Muerce was nondescript. He was of medium height with a slight build, and a rather pallid skin tone. He was balding on top, and what was left of his graying hair he let grow slightly longer, though it was well kept. On his chin was a meticulously trimmed goatee, also gray, that despite the attention it obviously received still had a greasy appearance. Physically, he was not a threat. Muerce tried to relax and recover his composer.

"I startled you," the man said.

Muerce did not reply as he continued to size up the man, who had a bland, yet disquieting quality to him that triggered an alarm in Muerce. But the mixture of scotch and absorption of sound in the room dampened the warning.

"It's a progression," the man said, sweeping his head around the room like he were giving a guided tour.

"What?" Muerce said. The response was awkward, and Muerce felt self-conscious as if he were blinking uncontrollably, and drooling at the corners of his mouth. *What is going on with you Jack?*

"The tapestries," the man said, pausing to give Muerce a diagnostic look. "They have a beginning, and they progress to an end. Are you not familiar with such a perspective?"

"So, they tell a story?" Muerce said, with little conviction in his reply.

"Something like that," the man said. "More like a divine roadmap, I prefer."

"A timeline?"

The man crooked his head and smiled, as if he had the power to lift the roof from the building, and summon the storm inside. The color of the man's irises were indistinguishable from the black coal points of his pupils.

"Very possibly, Mister Muerce," the man said as he turned, and strolled toward the second tapestry.

It bothered Muerce the stranger knew him. He decided to pursue the apparition, whose hands also were locked behind his back as Muerce's had been. They stopped in front of the third and middle tapestry, which marked the halfway point of the exhibit.

"We don't know each other," Muerce said.

The man turned and nodded his head toward Muerce.

"I believe most everyone here tonight knows who you are," the man said.

"But I don't know who you are," Muerce said.

"Ah, yes, how impolite of me," the man said. "I am Doctor Merchant Sharron."

Muerce immediately saw the resemblance of Paige and Price reflected in Dr. Sharron's face, which had the same feminine appearance as his offspring.

Muerce formally offered his hand as introduction.

"I'm Jack Muerce," he said.

Sharron didn't reciprocate, instead, keeping his hands locked behind his back.

"You'll excuse me Mister Muerce," Dr. Sharron said, looking at Muerce's gesture. "My hands are my profession, and I protect them accordingly."

It was clear Muerce didn't understand Dr. Sharron's meaning.

"I'm a surgeon," Dr. Sharron said. "The reconstructive kind."

"Plastics," Muerce said.

"Precisely," Dr. Sharron said, his gaze fixed on the artwork. "The tapestries of flesh, and bone."

There was movement behind Muerce, who turned to find Pho Mat offering a tray of hors d'oeuvres.

"These do look delightful," Dr. Sharron said, taking a napkin from Pho Mat in one hand, and removing an hors d'oeuvres from the tray with his other. The tray was then offered to Muerce, who was displeased by the idea he was being followed, and showed it on his face.

"I was under the impression no food or drink was allowed in here," Muerce said.

"Take tray to Entrance Hall," Pho Mat said. "See gentlemen, and offer first taste."

Muerce looked around the Exhibit Hall for a doorway he knew didn't lead to a catering kitchen as Pho Mat smiled innocently.

"A little off course, Sammy," Muerce said.

"Mister Muerce wish appetizer?" Pho Mat said.

Muerce looked at the spring rolls tied with rice noodles that resembled miniature laundry packages. As he did, there was a sharp *crunch* as Dr. Sharron bit down on one. It sounded, to Muerce, like bones being crushed.

"You should try one Mister Muerce," Dr. Sharron said. A drop of the dipping sauce dribbled from his mouth onto his beard. "They have a nice surprise to them."

"No thank you," Muerce said, looking at Pho Mat. "I've had enough surprises for the evening."

"But the evening is still young," Dr. Sharron said, unaware of the droplet on his beard. Pho Mat offered another napkin for Dr. Sharron, and motioned it to indicate he clean himself with it.

"Heavens," Dr. Sharron said, understanding Pho Mat's meaning. "Excuse me, I've been somewhat messy."

He dabbed at his goatee with the napkin until he was certain the stain was removed.

"What are these called?" Dr. Sharron said.

"Saigon Laundry—a delicacy popular during the war," Muerce said, addressing Pho Mat. "Messy, to be sure."

Pho Mat bowed to Muerce and Dr. Sharron, and removed himself from the Exhibition Hall. Muerce turned his attention back to Dr. Sharron, who had wandered toward the last of the six tapestries. It was the widest of the series. The maiden in the center of the tapestry stood before a tent, and wore a gown very similar to what Ashley had designed for the evening.

"The progression, Doctor Sharron?" Muerce said.

"Leads us here," Dr. Sharron said, his gaze fixed on the last tapestry.

"And where is here?"

"*A Mon Seul Desir.*"

Muerce easily made out the motto emblazoned on the top of the tent behind the maiden, who appeared to be placing a necklace into a chest held by a maidservant standing by her side. The two women were framed by a crouching unicorn and a lion, each holding an end of the maiden's rose-colored train, and a banner. On both banners were three dry moons.

"It's pronounced *sharing*, isn't it?" Muerce said.

"What, the tapestry?" Dr. Sharron said, looking quizzically at Muerce.

"Your surname, doctor."

"The correct pronunciation is CHAR-*ing*," Dr. Sharron said. "My children prefer to soften it. As is their nature."

"Paige and Price," Muerce said, feeling like he finally had an edge in the conversation. "I've come across them."

"I dare say, Mister Muerce," Dr. Sharron said, his attention still riveted on the tapestry before them. "Quite a few people have."

An uncomfortable silence followed Dr. Sharron's response as Muerce wondered if there was an intended innuendo.

"How do you interpret that?" Dr. Sharron said.

The question caught Muerce by surprise, until he believed Dr. Sharron was referring to the phrase emblazoned on the tent depicted in the tapestry.

"Something along the line of my one or only desire," Muerce said.

"No Mister Muerce, not the phrase," Dr. Sharron said. There was a hue of anger, and arrogance in his voice. "The action depicted in the design."

Muerce took a moment to consider the scene playing out in front of him.

"She's retrieving her necklace," he said.

"Not returning it?" Dr. Sharron said.

"In my experience, women tend to take jewelry, not return it."

"As I understand your reputation, it's quite the opposite when it comes to their clothing," Dr. Sharron said. "Your experience?"

"*En garde* prior to the parry would have been appropriate," Muerce said, his voice clipped, and stern. "For a gentleman, that is."

"Touche," Dr. Sharron said, bowing his head in mock defeat. "Point taken."

"Under the circumstances, only a *carton jaune* would be required," Muerce said. "The verbal fencing aside, the progression has led us here, but I've missed much of the route."

"Ah, yes, we did arrive here rather haphazardly, didn't we," Dr. Sharron said. "You see, the first five tapestries depict each of the human senses: taste; hearing; sight, smell; and touch.

"The sixth tapestry, which if you look closely, is slightly bigger than the others, and was completed in a subtle and slightly different style. There have been a number of interpretations. However, in the one to which I'm partial, the maiden, overwhelmed by the passions of all five senses, is returning the necklace as a renunciation of earthly pleasure. It's an act of atonement, of absolution."

"But is it of her own free will?" Muerce said. "The lion looks rather menacing. And it and the unicorn appear to have her in bondage."

"*A mon seul desir*," Dr. Sharron said. "By *my* will alone."

"And what of *her* will?" Paige said, approaching behind Sharron and Muerce. "It doesn't look to me that she has much of a choice in the matter at all."

An unease swirled around the three of them, producing a cold hush that was swallowed by the density of the tapestries. Muerce sensed he had been suddenly forced to hold his ground in a field of eggshells. Dr. Sharron and Paige, however, were clearly adept, if not strangely comfortable, at dancing around the fragile hazards.

"I don't know about *hers*, but *your* will, Sister, has once again bulldozed all manners aside," Dr. Sharron said. "You've interrupted me and Mister Muerce."

"Disrupted a rare and genuine moment of male bonding?" Paige said. "Doubtful. But I don't really care, now, do I?"

Dr. Sharron made a disapproving sound as if he could clear his throat and Paige's rudeness with a single stroke. Muerce was still stuck on Dr. Sharron addressing his daughter as sister.

"We've never been formally introduced," Paige said. She moved towards Muerce but did not extend her hand, instead using her eyes as introduction. Muerce imagined he heard the crunch of the eggshells as she progressed toward him.

Paige had piqued Muerce's interest the first time he saw her. He remembered the shape of her calves, the uniqueness of her feline eyes, and the curve of her breast. In their previous encounter she was fiercely becoming.

Tonight, she was alarmingly beautiful. She stopped only after penetrating his personal space, positioning herself directly in front of him with inches separating their bodies. Her closeness was inappropriate for the setting, but exhilarating to Muerce.

The gold flash he saw by the bar earlier in the evening had, unmistakably, been Paige. Her evening gown and white-blonde hair radiated warning, and enticement. The dress was gold Lame made from silk and metal yarn produced in Lyon, France. The fabric was cut on a bias and formed a stunning sweep of movement from a twist of fabric at her waist that reached all the way to the floor. Its halter neckline of sunburst pleating bared her shoulders, and accented the long lines of her neck. The delicate fabric and cool temperature of the room left no doubt the shimmering fabric was all that covered her body. Those details, however, were soon lost on Muerce who was drawn, again, to the flecks of gold that sparkled within the brown in her eyes. He remembered her unique pupils. For the moment they were the eyes of a cat, and not those of the lioness.

"You heal quickly," Paige said, adjusting her head slightly to the left as she looked Muerce's neck over. She arched one of her eyebrows, which Muerce realized also were white-blonde. Her coloring—or lack of—was God given, and likely consistent over her entire body.

"I'm not a big bleeder," he said.

"But I bet you bruise easily," she said, retreating from inside his personal space. "Aren't you going to introduce me to Mister Muerce, Father?"

Dr. Sharron cleared his throat.

"I assumed the two of you already *know* each other?" he said.

Paige, her eyes still attached to Muerce, formed a wicked smile that her father, standing behind her, could not observe.

"Mister Muerce and I only *know* each other by sight," she said. "As far as the reputation of my other senses, they remain intact."

"Mister Muerce, may I introduce my daughter, Paige Sharron," he said, emphasizing his pronunciation of their surname. "Paige, this is Mister Jack Muerce."

Paige extended her right hand. She wore soft, black suede evening gloves that ended at her wrists. He accepted her hand, and bowed.

"Pleased to make your acquaintance Miss, Sharron?" Muerce said, using her father's pronunciation.

"It's Share-ing, Mister Muerce," she said. "But please call me Paige."

"Before a week ago I'd never heard of you, and now we've run into each other two times," Muerce said.

Three, actually, Paige thought.

"And your point?" she said.

"I believe it was your point, at which we first met," Muerce said. "That still begs an explanation."

"Maybe you're running with the wrong crowd," she said.

"I don't think so."

There was a surge of air as the large doors to the Exhibition Hall opened, admitting the crowd of gala attendees into the room to view the tapestries. The boisterous nature of their arrival turned to appreciative gasps, then silence as their eyes focused on the magnificent artwork for the first time. The pace of the crowd slowed as they shuffled across the carpet and around the exhibit, unaware of Muerce and the Sharrons.

"Younger, perhaps?"

"That wouldn't be altogether *different* for me," Muerce said.

"So I understand," she said.

"That's enough Sister," Dr. Sharron said. "Please excuse my daughter's rudeness Mister Muerce. I've tried to do my best without her, their mother."

"Oh yes, Mister Muerce, the best he could," Paige said. "Poor, Mommy."

"Unfair," Dr. Sharron said. "You've never wanted for anything."

"Want for anything," Paige said, leering at Muerce. "Father never missed an opportunity to *tuck* us in. Me and Brother."

"Your manners, please," Dr. Sharon said.

"I think, Miss Sharron," Muerce said, using the elder Sharron's pronunciation of the name that drew immediate irritation from Paige. "You wouldn't be recognizable without it."

"Without what?" she said.

"Propriety," Muerce said. "The lack of it, that is. Your signature, perhaps?"

"When I pricked you, Mr. Muerce, you could feel my sword," she said. "Is your prick only to be heard? Though, your tongue inflicts a deeper wound in me."

As she turned toward Dr. Sharron, Muerce was distracted by the outline of her leg beneath the delicate fabric of her gown.

"It seems Mister Muerce and I have only three senses left to experience together," she said. "But you are right, Father. Enough, for now.

"Truce Mister Muerce?" she said, wheeling back toward him. Muerce nodded in agreement. Though it was not an outright apology from her, it lessened the tension.

"I did escort someone tonight, and should attend to my responsibilities," Muerce said. "Please excuse me. Doctor Sharron, Miss Sharron."

Dr. Sharron bowed his head in deference to Muerce's request for an exit.

"Your mother?" Paige said, as Muerce turned to leave.

"Yes, this is *her* evening," he said.

"Will you at least escort me to the bar?" Paige said, not waiting for an answer, and hooking her arm inside his to be escorted away.

"Mister Muerce," Dr. Sharron said.

Muerce stopped to turn. Paige's attention remained somewhere between the doorway and the closest bar.

"Spring Forward tonight," Dr. Sharron said, caressing his goatee. "We lose an hour. You wouldn't want to miss any appointments would you?"

Instinctively, Muerce looked at his watch, but caught himself. He felt like he'd been given an order. Muerce looked at Dr. Sharron, whom he thought an arrogant ass. Whatever the Sharron family dynamic was, Muerce wanted nothing to do with it.

Muerce turned and left with Paige attached. He would deposit her at the nearest bar.

Dr. Sharron watched as they disappeared through the double doors. Some of the crowd milled about him, commenting on the sixth tapestry. One in particular broke off from a small group, sidled up next to Dr. Sharron, and curled his arm inside of his. Dr. Sharron took the young man's hand in his, and stroked it.

"How much did you observe?" Dr. Sharron said.

"Everything, Father," Price said. "As always."

"You were correct, Brother," Dr. Sharron said. "Sister has an affection for him that I've not seen before. I didn't think she was capable."

"Jealous?" Price said, both mocking and teasing.

"Surprised," Dr. Sharron said. "Outside of each other, I didn't think either of you felt anything for anyone."

Dr. Sharron threw off the embrace with Price abruptly, and checked the time on his watch. Price looked wounded, yet relieved.

"She's confused about Mister Muerce, but that confusion could be useful," Dr. Sharron said. "I have an appointment."

He turned back to Price, and cupped his face in his hands. Price was trained. The cycle of giving and withholding attention was a familiar pattern for Price. Hate and love, love and hate. Price wanted to break free of the man as desperately as he desired his love.

"Stay close to Sister," Dr. Sharron said, "Muerce has no interest in her. She'll be fragile. Take care of her."

"As always," Price said.

Dr. Sharron kissed Price's forehead, then caressed his face with the backs of his fingers.

"Brother," Dr. Sharron said, patting his son on the top of his head as he would the family dog. He turned and walked away, leaving Price drained and uncertain.

— —

"I love champagne," Paige said, emptying the glass handed to her by the tattooed bartender who had earlier intrigued Muerce. "Aren't you drinking with me, Mister Muerce?"

Muerce motioned to the bartender, who smiled at him, for a second glass for Paige, but not one for himself.

"No, I've had quite enough for tonight," he said.

"Of the booze or me?" she said.

Muerce looked at her with an answer he did not want to verbalize. *A spoiled brat. A drunk, spoiled brat.*

"Oh, I see," Paige said, sipping the fresh glass of champagne. "Your eyes cut as deep as your tongue."

"You're reading to much into me," he said.

"Am I?" Paige said, noticing the bartender had her eye on Muerce as well. "If so, then I believe that would make me and every other woman here illiterate."

"How so?" he said.

"Because, Mister Muerce, you are the cover on the fairytale we all dream will be the story of our lives," she said.

"And what's that?" he said.

"You're the Knight in Shining Armor," Paige said, taking another sip. "Prince Charming sweeping us off our feet and whisking us off to your castle where we will live happily ever after. You're handsome, rich, powerful, kind, considerate and..."

Paige broke off the end of her sentence to finish the bubbly liquid. Muerce saw in her eyes a continence that surprised him. She was more intriguing than he first allowed, though there was her reputation and previous behavior toward him to consider.

"Another?" he said, ready to motion to the bartender who had removed herself from earshot of them.

"No, Mister Muerce, I've had quite enough, too," she said, staring out at the crowd, which had grown larger as the tram brought more of them up from the parking structure, and out of the storm.

"You were saying," Muerce said.

"I was saying what?"

"About the cover of my book," he said. "Your description dropped off in mid-sentence."

She turned and focused her eyes directly on his with intent that was hard, and penetrating.

"Handsome, rich, powerful, kind, considerate, and mature," she said.

"Ouch," Muerce said, motioning to get the bartender's attention. "Now I do need a drink."

Paige hit the right nerve and a devilish smile cinched up the corners of her mouth as she parted her lips slightly.

"Now you're misreading me," she said.

"What, that I interpret *mature* as old?" he said.

The bartender handed Muerce a glass of champagne with a wink that Paige caught, but which Muerce missed altogether. The bartender saw that he was oblivious to her come-on, deflating her. Though not an out-right rejection, Paige felt pleased the flirtatious bartender was hurt, and that Muerce's attention remained focused on her.

"I meant it as a compliment," Paige said.

"How so?" he said.

Paige knew the male ego was a delicate thing. Jack Muerce, she had just proved, was no different than any other man in that regard. He was vulnerable. Now, she knew, was the point at which she had to bolster his confidence and build his trust in her.

"No woman, Mister Muerce, wants to be with a boy," she said. "And most of the men in this room, whether they are wealthy or famous, and many are both, are just boys.

"Maturity isn't about age, it's about confidence."

"Call me Jack," Muerce said.

The request was greeted with a haughty laugh from Paige, which left him puzzled.

"Oh, Mister Muerce, I don't think so," she said, drawing herself closer to him. "I was raised to treat my elders with respect."

Paige's mercurial exchange conversely agitated and enticed Muerce further. She was frustratingly distant and, yet, so near. The conflict and contrast of her words and actions became even more baffling when she reached down to the front of his tuxedo trousers, and cupped his genitals in her hand.

"Confidence shouldn't be confused with cockiness," she said, running her tongue across her bottom lip. "Though I prefer to have one of the latter in hand."

The grope, which caught Muerce off guard, was interrupted almost as soon as it happened.

"Trust me my dear," Eleanor said. "The bird in hand has nested in many a, well... let's just say if you're looking to catch a pair, there are fowl afoot much closer to the age of your shrubbery."

Eleanor gently pressed the tips of her fingers on Paige's right shoulder. Without missing a beat, Eleanor took a sip of champagne from the glass she held in her right hand, and gently coaxing Paige away from her son, continued the conversation.

"I adore your ensemble," Eleanor said, her smile wide, bright and sarcastic. "Let me take a look at you, *child*."

Eleanor's tongue cut much deeper into Paige than her son's. With the pain, Paige felt the anger build inside her.

"Yes, I'm sure I loved it on the runway last season," Eleanor said, half turning Paige in a way that detached her from Muerce, and allowed her dress to be seen. "How novel of you to resurrect the look for tonight. Mixing the old, with, the old."

Muerce detected a small vein on Paige's temple begin to plump and bulge.

"May I introduce Paige Sharron," Muerce said, using the softer *sharing* inflection. "Paige, this is my mother, Eleanor Muerce."

Eleanor, still smiling, curtseyed with a slight nod of her head.

"Dame Muerce," Paige said. The lack of emotion and solicitude in her voice was unmistakable.

"It's *madame*, Miss Sharron," Eleanor said. "The proper pronunciation is more *Am* than *Damned*. I assume your test scores placed you in the Spanish and not French language classes in school. Quite understandable."

The cute bartender with the intriguing tattoo issued a barely audible, but conceited laugh at the exchange. Paige, her face flushed and eyes wide, gave the bartender an intense look meant for Eleanor that matched the infernos of Hell. Eleanor expected Paige to hold her breath, stomp her foot, and run away. Paige collected herself quickly.

"*Madame* Muerce," she said, indicating her intention to excuse herself. Then she turned to Muerce. "Mister Muerce."

With no further gesture, Paige abruptly walked away, followed only by the sound of her heels sharply striking the marble floor.

"Kids these days," Eleanor said, calmly taking another sip from her glass.

"Very tasteful, Eleanor," Muerce said.

"Honestly, what do you expect?" Eleanor said. "Her display with you was undignified. I agree. I rather did navigate that with the right amount of firmness."

"I meant the champagne," he said. "I can handle these situations by myself, you know. I am, as you don't hesitate to remind me, a big boy now."

"Sometimes I wonder, John," she said. "And it isn't about their age, you know. It's their sense of propriety."

"Their sense of propriety? Why are we having this discussion?" he said.

"Decorum," Eleanor said. "It's one thing to desire, it's quite another to act on it, here, in front of everyone... I know..."

"And, we're back to you," he said.

"Be fair," Eleanor said. "This is my night, isn't it?"

"It is," Muerce said. "And to be fair, I was just as surprised as you were. I only met the young woman tonight."

"Mmm, I believe that about as much as I do your lack of experience in a coatroom," she said.

"It's true," Muerce said. "The part about only being introduced to her tonight. We've run into each other in passing recently. But that's all."

"As far as women are concerned, you haven't asked for, and I haven't solicited, my approval or disapproval in a very long time," she said.

"And yet?"

"What I just saw in that girl wasn't the infatuation, confusion or passion of youth," Eleanor said. "She's a predator."

It wasn't the first time Muerce heard the warning, and he suspected it wouldn't be the last.

"I'm a big boy," he said.

"Who would make a big meal," she said. "But that's not why I was looking for you."

"And here I thought you just wanted a drink."

"That, too," she said. "Now, this is going to seem completely contradictory of me, but it's my prerogative as a woman, and your mother. I want you to come over to the table so I can introduce you to the most marvelous girl. I'm very taken by her. I think she's splendid."

"Eleanor-dot-com, the new Internet dating service?" Muerce said.

"At least meet her," she said.

Muerce discreetly rolled his eyes so only Eleanor could observe him. It indicated he would swing by, in his own time, and be introduced to the woman.

"I'm sure she's age appropriate," he said. "Recently divorced, and angry."

"Sometimes I surprise even myself," Eleanor said, finishing her drink. "Make an effort, please. See you in a bit."

"I need to adjust my makeup first," Muerce said.

Eleanor smiled, patted Muerce on his cheek, and gracefully glided away from the bar.

"Champagne?" the bartender said.

"Yes, please."

As she poured his champagne, Muerce anticipated she was about to say something, and he diverted his attention to the traces of her body art that wound around her neck above the stiff collar of her uniform. The bartender smiled and began to open her mouth to speak when she was interrupted.

"Hit me too," requested a female voice that had a hoarse quality Muerce easily identified.

It was Melinda Claussen-Downey-Breen, the ex-wife of the Mayor. She wore a strapless, black sequined floor-length gown, and was draped in David Yurman jewelry. Melinda was a middle-age, attractive brunette with a few touch-ups around the eyes and edges of her lips that gave her the slightest hint of trout mouth. *Time to stop and age gracefully, Melinda.*

"Hello, Jack," Melinda said.

"Misses Downey-Breen," Muerce said, holding his glass up to toast. "How are you?"

"Soon to be just Melinda Claussen again," she said, taking a sip from her glass.

"I'm sorry to hear that, Melinda," he said.

"Don't be," she said. "As hard as I've tried, I've finally reached the point where I know I'm not very good at matrimony, at least what happens after the cake is gone. And it's not them, it's me."

"How very insightful," Muerce said. "You've always been a step ahead of me. Or two."

Melinda laughed from deep in her diaphragm. It was a genuine laugh; one Muerce always liked about her. If anything, Muerce knew Melinda Claussen soon not-to-be Downey-Breen, to be honest about herself, and a woman who had a healthy appetite for sex. The two of them stood shoulder-to-shoulder looking over the growing crowd of the city's finest social climbers, enjoying their champagne together. Muerce spotted the Mayor in the distance. He was flanked by his latest wife, and several council members.

"Tell me, Melinda," Muerce said. "Does His Honor know who dishonored his honor?"

"Oh Jack, really?" she said. "After all this time?"

"Never mind."

"Oh, I don't mind if you don't mind."

"Why would I mind?" he said. "I asked didn't I?"

Melinda moved closer to Muerce so she could not be overheard.

"You did ask," she said. "But I don't want to hurt your feelings."

"Haven't you heard? I don't have any feelings. At least when it comes to women."

"That's so far from the truth, it's laughable," she said.

"Well?"

"You're a wonderful guy, Jack. Fun, exciting, handsome, dangerous, rich, mysterious. Everything a woman looks for... in a fling."

"What's bad about that?"

"You're the secret we all keep. Like the naughty toy we hide in a shoe box in the back of our closet. We only bring it out in the dark, when nobody else is around."

Melinda let the words settle before she looked at Muerce's face. When she did, she saw what she felt bad for putting there—hurt. Now, she wished she had lied to him, but it was too late.

"I'm sorry," she said. "I went too far."

Muerce swept the room with his eyes, trying to identify the women he had slept with. The number was fewer than he first thought, but more than he wanted at that moment. For the first time in a long time, he felt ashamed, and empty. He buried the emotion as quickly as he could.

"I asked. You answered. Thank you."

Melinda was uncomfortable, and uncertain what she should say next. She had not meant to be hurtful.

"As far as his Honor goes, your honor is intact," she said.

Muerce shrugged off the regret, bent down, and kissed Melinda on the cheek. When he did, he noticed there was something different about her that he couldn't readily identify.

"What you said was insightful, and sadly true," he said, his eyes affixed to her.

"Oh, I *know* that look," she said. She took a step back, arched her shoulders behind her slightly, and turned her head from side to side as if she were a runway model.

"So what do you think?"

Muerce looked at her from head to toe. He felt like a game-show contestant searching for the right vowel. When she pushed her shoulders forward slightly the answer popped into his head.

"They look spectacular," he said. His gaze was blatantly set on her breasts.

"Oh, they are," Melinda said. "Trust me. And they were spectacularly expensive, and worth it. Next to age, gravity is a girl's worst enemy."

"Well, bravo then," Muerce said, giving a slight bow.

"My most recent marital disengagement will be completed in the next few weeks," she said. "If you're interested, I could give you a tour."

There was a trace of the previous wound from her words on Muerce's face that made Melinda wince.

"I'm sorry," she said. "Not trying to be pushy Jack. And I would never hide you again, I promise. Maybe just dinner, or lunch."

A voice above the crowd called out Melinda's name from a distance, and she responded with a wave. Melinda, Muerce recalled, had an attention span that could be measured by blinks.

"I've got to go," she said. "Let me know if you want to. You know how to reach me."

In a moment, Melinda was gone and Muerce stood, alone, in front of the bar, recalling her words, and still feeling rejected as the room swirled with the mingling and flitting crowd.

"Excuse me," the bartender said.

Muerce turned and smiled at her in a manner that gave permission to speak her mind.

"It's not my place to say," she said. "But you're a pretty complicated guy."

"Yes, apparently so," Muerce said.

"I'm sorry, but too complicated for me," she said. "I'm out."

Muerce shrugged his shoulders, and chuckled.

"You're the wisest person in this room," Muerce said. "And don't let anyone tell you any different."

"Don't worry, I won't," she said, winking at Muerce as he walked away, heading for the men's room.

— —

The lavatory was large, tiled in the same stone as the exterior of the museum, and completely empty despite the crowd just outside the black, granite doors. Muerce stared at the pattern in the stone in front of his face as he relived himself into the flush-less urinal. He was deep in his thoughts, replaying Melinda's description of how women regarded him. Then he thought about the strange encounter with Paige, Dr. Sharron, and the polite rejection by the bartender. He finished, and shook himself off. Ashley was on his mind as he collected himself, and zipped the fly closed on his trousers.

When he turned away from the wall to wash his hands, Muerce nearly wet himself from the shock. Standing not a foot behind him was Kinson. The look on the man's face was full of rage. His eyes bulged out of their sockets, and Muerce could see the man was tense and about to take some action. Muerce considered how he'd play out getting the living crap beat out of him by a celebrity athlete in a public bathroom during a high-society event. He figured he'd keep it quiet, let the injuries heal before he went out in public again. What he wasn't sure of in that nanosecond of thought, was how he'd explain it to Eleanor.

Muerce tensed his body, and waited for the first punch to land. But nothing happened. Kinson stared at Muerce for a few seconds longer before relaxing his face. Muerce looked up and into the man's eyes. Though the pupils were dilated, and the whites of his eyes bloodshot, Muerce could see what was behind them—fear. Muerce had seen it all too often in his own line of work. It was the continence of a man on the verge of doing something very stupid, or very smart. Kinson was at an emotional tipping point, and Muerce was in the position of sending him in one direction, or the other.

"I'm fucked up," Kinson said.

"Too much to drink?" Muerce said, in a measured voice. "Are you okay?"

"I'm fucked up," Kinson said.

"It happens," Muerce said. "Do you want me to get someone? Your wife?"

"You're not hearing me, man," Kinson said. "I'm really fucked up."

It wasn't a statement, Muerce realized, as much as a cry for help.

"I hear you, now."

Kinson's shoulders slumped as he bowed his head. Muerce knew what was coming next—the confession, the regret, the shame, and the request. Muerce knew, too—having just been dealt a dose of reality himself—that he would help the man.

"I'm really fucked up," Kinson said. His voice was low, and cracked between words. "I'm up high on coke, and on the down-low. I pimp myself on and off the field. I ain't got no respect for no one. Not myself, not no one.

"I'm fucked up, Mister Muerce. Physically, emotionally, and spiritually. I ain't just losing it, I've lost it, man."

"I'm going to wash my hands, Mister Kinson," Muerce said. "But I won't wash them of you. Understand?"

Kinson nodded. He wiped a few tears from his face. Muerce rinsed and soaped his hands in the bathroom sink, and toweled them dry as he talked to Kinson. All the while, looking at Kinson in the mirror.

"What do you want, Mister Kinson?" Muerce said.

"I know your rep," he said. "You help people. Quiet like."

"And you want me to help you?"

"Yes sir, I do."

"When I help people, they help me in return," Muerce said. "You understand that?"

"I do."

"I'm an attorney Mister Kinson, but I'm not going to be your agent. And I'm not going to be your bondsman. And I'm certainly not going to be your therapist."

"Anything, Mister Muerce. I need help."

"First thing, Mister Kinson, from what I've observed, you've got to get clean. Without that, nothing else can be fixed. You've got to be in front of that. Do you understand?"

Kinson shook his head, affirming Muerce's words.

"I don't care what anyone does behind closed doors as long as nobody's getting hurt. You know what I'm talking about, right?"

"Yeah."

Muerce reached his hand inside his tuxedo jacket, pulled out one of his cards and a pen. He scribbled a phone number on the top of the card, and handed it to Kinson.

"Call that number tonight. You'll get voicemail, but leave your name, your number and say that I said it was an emergency. You'll get a call back within the hour. This isn't life threatening so you won't get an appointment until tomorrow afternoon. That's when the work starts."

Kinson stared at the card like it was a multi-million dollar contract extension. He knew what the card meant.

"How fucked up are you right now, on coke?" Muerce said.

"Manageable."

"Flush what you've got left, or don't, that's up to you," Muerce said. "But the favor for a favor part starts tonight, okay?"

"I'm good with that," Kinson.

"I hope so," Muerce said. He stuck his hands in his trouser pockets, and leaned back against the edge of the bank of sinks. "The Squires are personal friends of mine. You're going to suck it up, find Mister Squire, apologize to him, and tell him you're going to make it right. And then you're going to make it right. Right?"

"How?"

"You've got to figure that part out on your own," Muerce said. "That's the first half of the favor you owe me."

"What's the second half?" Kinson said.

"I don't know yet, but I'll let you know when I do," Muerce said. "You good with that?"

"I got to be, don't I?"

Muerce nodded.

"Squire's a fair man," Muerce said. "He may hate Oklahoma, but he loves football. You do the work, you'll get through it."

Kinson held Muerce's card with both hands as if it were a newborn baby.

"Then get your wife, go home, and start the work."

"Thank you, Mister Muerce. "I promise I'll make it square."

"Right now you owe yourself more than anyone else," Muerce said. "You'll have to get there on your own, but you won't be doing it alone. As far as the rest of it with me... there's no deadline."

Kinson looked at Muerce's card and pulled a mobile phone from a leather holder clipped to his cummerbund. His expression changed from fear to nervousness as he fumbled with the phone in a hand that was the size of a youth baseball glove. He took a deep breath, and slowly exhaled. He alternated staring at Muerce and the screen on the phone, wanting to make the call that very moment. Yet, he was unsure if he wanted Muerce there because he didn't think he'd be able to hold it together, even if he were only speaking to a recording on the other end. Muerce understood.

"I'm going to step outside," he said. "And cover the door."

Kinson rocked his head back with gratitude in that way men communicate to each other without words. Muerce, his hands still in his trousers, exited the bathroom by using his shoulder to open the door. No one approached the lavatory for several minutes as he guarded Kinson's privacy. Muerce took the opportunity to call Dr. Riley, and give her a heads up about Kinson, and that he would be indebted to her. More importantly, though, the man needed help.

━ ━

Muerce loitered outside the men's room for several more minutes. Kinson either made the call or didn't. That was his decision. Muerce divorced himself from that aspect of the favor. What he did want was to make sure Kinson had enough time to make his decision. And to do so by himself. At the very least, Kinson would have a moment to regain his composure. No one approached the door, and Muerce quietly slipped away, observed, at a distance, only by Pho Mat.

━ ━

The solitude and relative calm of the black marbled hallway that led to the restrooms, and the coat check, gave way to the noise of the gala, which had turned into an alcohol fueled celebration of the city's *creme de la creme*—at least for those who considered themselves lucky or connected enough to have secured tickets for the evening. It was a sort of imaginary masked ball, Muerce joked to himself, and the masks were images most of the crowd created for themselves—elaborate facades that existed only inside their psyches.

Muerce wanted another drink, but waved himself away from the closest bar, and headed toward the back of the Entrance Hall where several dozen VIP tables had been set up away from the main crowd. There he would find Eleanor. He would also likely find this woman she wanted him to meet. He was partially indisposed at the prospect of the setup, but also somewhat intrigued. Eleanor rarely interjected herself into his personal life. That she pressed for him to meet someone, especially a woman she liked, had happened, he recalled, only once before. The memory was as fresh as if it had happened only minutes earlier. Emily Benoit stood by the pool, wearing a yellow dress, and looking homesick for Paris. The apparition left as soon as it had appeared in his head, leaving Muerce feeling empty again.

A gaggle of thirty-something social climbing women in rented designer gowns honked loudly as they paraded in front of him. He overheard them admiring one woman's new diamond tennis bracelet that had been gifted to her by her husband in exchange for the promise of twice weekly acts of oral sex.

"He'll be lucky if he gets it once a month," she said, laughing to her friends. Her eyes locked on Muerce's when she realized she had been overheard as the group rustled past him. She frowned at Muerce, and he frowned back.

In prison it was what Muerce once heard referred to as custody of the eyes. When walking down a cell block, Muerce remembered hearing, one didn't peer into another inmate's domicile. In prison, privacy was a precious commodity to be respected. For social occasions like tonight, Muerce wanted to invoke custody of the ears. He did not like overhearing other people's conversations, and tonight he was doing his best to avoid it.

Muerce tugged at the cuff of his tuxedo shirt to expose his wrist to see if enough time had passed so he could leave. He was disappointed when he saw, for both the sake of propriety and Eleanor, he would have to stick it out for at least another hour. It was also a reminder for him to change the time. He would lose an hour, one he'd prefer spending in bed with Ashley.

The VIP tables were at the back corner of the Entrance Hall, tucked beneath the soaring staircase that led to the North Pavilion of the Gilmont Center. Eleanor sat at the first table, close enough to watch the event and acknowledge all the right people, yet discreetly distant to avoid all the wrong ones. She waved for her son to join her. The gesture was more command than invitation.

Two other board members sat at the opposite side of the large circular table where Eleanor held court. They were locked in conversation, but nodded and smiled respectfully at Muerce. He reciprocated their gesture, and they continued back into their conversations without paying much attention to him, and Eleanor.

"Oh, good, I was looking for you," Eleanor said.

"But not in the coat room?" he said.

"How charming," Eleanor said, pausing for affect. "Why? Would I have found you there?"

Muerce laughed.

"Certainly not," he said, pausing. "At least not for another half hour."

Eleanor continued talking, but Muerce dialed her out when he glanced toward the bar where the girl had been. She was gone. A shift change, or a cigarette break? It didn't matter. Muerce felt a tinge of disappointment at what might have been, on another night, but the feeling subsided quickly when he spotted Kinson shaking the hand of T.B. Squire, who was both pleased and perplexed. It looked to Muerce as if Kinson wiped several tears from his face when he turned, his posture stooped as if his back were broken, and left the gala with his wife. She had her arm around him in a compassionate manner that denoted love. Muerce felt a sort of forlorn envy that usually ended with him resurrecting the past.

"Have you heard anything I've said?" Eleanor said.

"What?" Muerce responded, without turning to look at her, but glad his thoughts were interrupted. "I'm sorry. Excuse me. I was distracted for a moment."

"About the person to whom I want to introduce you," she said to the back of her son's head. "I've been very impressed by her. And surprised. She isn't at all age appropriate for you, but I'm really taken by her. I'd even say she reminds me of myself when I was her age.

"Are you listening to me?"

"Yes. Of course. Every word," Muerce said, not listening in the least as he scanned the crowd.

"In addition to asking her if she'd have my grandchild with you, I've offered her the job of running the marketing department here," Eleanor said, fully aware her son heard nothing coming out of her mouth. "She wants the job but has no interest in bearing your child. In fact, she thinks you're an impossible bore."

"What was that you said?" he said over his shoulder. "Runny marmalade, and bears?"

"Exactly," Eleanor said. "I'm going to pour runny marmalade over your head so the bears eat you."

Eleanor had an urge to reach out and slap the back of her son's head. Then she realized the woman she was talking about was standing next to her with a pained look of embarrassment that parlayed a strong desire to come back at another time.

Eleanor cocked her head toward the woman standing next to her, indicating frustration with a spoiled child, and would the newly arrived guest be patient for a moment longer? Eleanor tapped Muerce on the shoulder.

"My dear, I'd like you to meet..."

The genteel tone of Eleanor's voice triggered Muerce's social graces. He was being formally introduced by his mother to a woman she likes, and who, very likely, would be of no interest to him whatsoever. And he would, reluctantly but politely, engage in conversation. After which, he would gently, but clearly, find a way not to see or speak to the woman again.

Muerce took in a deep breath and stood up to introduce himself. As he did he smartly snapped each cuff of his tuxedo shirt in such a way as to straighten his jacket.

"Ashley?" Muerce said, surprised as he turned around.

He was as giddy as Eleanor was astounded when he embraced Ashley in his arms, and kissed her on the mouth. Ashley, however, wasn't sure how to play the situation. Here was the man who makes heart skip, and he was kissing her in front of his mother, who was about to become her boss—if she accepted the job, which she knew she would. Unless, Ashley cringed, Muerce had just blown it. The blush of her cheeks nearly matched the crimson of her dress.

In a gesture absent of decorum, Eleanor rolled her eyes so all could see, if they wished.

"I bought tickets for the wrong lottery," she said. "Of course you know the prettiest girl in the room."

Muerce bent down and kissed his mother on the cheek.

"I know both of them."

Eleanor learned to control girlish blushing long ago, though she could feel the scarlet of a son's compliment well up inside her. She also could see Ashley's discomfort at what had just transpired.

"Don't worry dear," she said, standing and taking both of Ashley's hands to reassure her. "It won't be held against you. The job offer more than still stands.

"My son tends to be an indiscretion most women find irresistible. But in this instance, I'm happy you didn't resist. In fact, I'm rather pleased."

"But there might be an appearance of..." Ashley said.

"Of what?" Eleanor said.

"Impropriety," Ashely said, tripping over her words. "Of me, and Jack, um, well. It's not quite nepotism. We're not, well, really, well, to..."

"Together?" Muerce said.

"Well, yes," Ashley said. "Well, I mean, I don't know."

"Well?" Eleanor said, addressing her son.

"What we are is needing a drink," Muerce said.

"Classic male obfuscation if ever there was," Eleanor said, turning to Ashley. "Men are such nonsense, sometimes. My son being at the front of the line."

Ashley appeared at ease, almost relieved at what Muerce had said. She was unexpectedly pleased with the uncertain nature of her relationship with him, but sidelined the feeling to focus on who she still hoped would be her new boss. Still holding Ashley's hands, Eleanor motioned for them to sit down, leaving Muerce standing by himself.

"I offered you the position before I had any inkling about you and my son," Eleanor said. "There is no way you could have used him to get to me. I know better, and *he* certainly knows better. You were given the offer on your own merits. Your concepts, planning and execution for this event far surpassed what I, or any of the other board members thought was possible. It's been quite impressive."

"Thank you, I..." Ashley said.

"I'm not finished," Eleanor said, cutting Ashley off, and eliciting a laugh disguised as a cough from Muerce, who knew better than to interrupt an Eleanor rant. "What you may lack in hands-on institutional museum experience is far outweighed by your creativity and energy, let alone your taste. I haven't even begun to lavish praise on your gown. It's so splendid for tonight. An original. I could take it apart at the seams just to see how it was done."

"Indeed," Muerce said.

"Oh, hush, you're not part of this," Eleanor said, turning her head sideways toward, but not looking directly at him. The distraction allowed Ashley, who was entertained by the push and pull style between mother and son, to wink at him.

"I've lost track," Eleanor said. "Regardless, you're the person for the job."

"Thank you, Misses Muerce," Ashley said.

"Call me Eleanor, please."

"Eleanor," Ashley said. "Your praise is very generous."

"And well earned," Eleanor said.

"It has been a pleasure, a life experience really, and very exciting working on this project. And I can tell you now, without hesitation, that I very much want to continue the work I've started with you, and with the center."

"You're certain?"

"I've never been more certain of anything before," she said, glancing at Muerce.

"Wonderful, then it's settled," Eleanor said. "I'll let some of the board know tonight. We can work out details on Monday. In the meantime, do tell me more about your gown. Who did it for you?"

The two of them chattered away about the gown, leaving Muerce bemused, and still standing as if he were let adrift at sea.

"Well then, I guess that leaves me to plan the celebration," he said.

"Yes, you're good at that sort of thing," Eleanor said, waving her son off as Ashley detailed the finer elements of her costume.

Undaunted by the brush off, Muerce slipped his hands, thumbs out, inside his jacket pockets, and scanned the room. A bright-white dinner jacket weaved through the crowd toward him. At a respectable distance,

Muerce caught Travis' attention, and waved toward him. When he arrived, Muerce slipped his arm inside Travis' to lead him away from the table where Eleanor and Ashley were still enmeshed in *haute couture.*

"I have a task for you," Muerce said, whispering the details of the assignment into Travis' ear while slipping several large bills into his hand.

"I'm on it," Travis said. "Give me fifteen minutes, and it will be there."

Muerce was pleased. The evening was turning out better than he anticipated despite the lingering discomfort left by the interchange with the Sharron's, and Kinson. There was a banality to Dr. Sharron that Muerce was sure hid a malevolence of uncertain nature. As for Paige, she had the attraction of an electric fence. He knew touching one resulted in pain, possibly death, but he had the primal urge to feel the buzz, and tingle at least once.

And there were the tapestries. Old, elegant, and mysterious. They manifest a code, and a time. He tried to concentrate on the animals and the composition of each work; the detailed threading wove their way into his head. But there was little clarity in his thoughts for the moment. There was the sounds of the chamber music, random voices in the crowd, and the anticipation of the carnal pleasures that waited underneath Ashley's dress. There was more for Muerce to anticipate than to worry about. He set aside the more errant and troubling ramblings in his head.

Rejoining Eleanor and Ashley at the table, Muerce interjected himself as they chatted away like a pair of long-lost sorority sisters.

"Ladies," Muerce said.

"Oh goodness," Eleanor said, looking at her watch. "It's later than I thought, and this was the last bit of business I wanted to take care of tonight. I might leave early, if that's okay with you?"

"Why don't you take the car," Muerce said, looking at Ashley. "I think I can bum a lift elsewhere."

After exchanging good-byes for the evening, Eleanor slowly waded her way through the crowd.

"Come with me," Muerce said, taking Ashley's hand. "I want to show you something."

Leading her through the exit behind the VIP tables into the museum courtyard, they passed in front of the large bank of curved windows that framed the courtyard-side of the Entrance Hall. The crowd, if it cared to, could have seen a couple holding hands as they dashed past the linear fountain. The long pool was lined with Mexican cypress trees that led toward a blue-veined marble boulder that looked like a large chunk of Maytag blue cheese resting in a bowl of water near the West Pavilion. Inside the Entrance Hall, the crowd was indifferent to the escaping couple. All except two separate sets of eyes. One set, with curiosity, watched the other set, which belonged to a young woman dressed in a shiny gold dress. Pho Mat recognized the face from the night before. The woman turned away from the windows with a scowl, and disappeared into the crowd. Pho Mat draped a white linen cloth over his forearm, and grabbed two champagne glasses. Cradled in his opposite arm was an ice bucket, and a chilled bottle of *Dom Perignon*.

The rain had stopped, giving way to a faint breeze that swept up the hill toward the Gilmont Center. The lights of the city reflected off the low, swiftly moving clouds, casting an orange glow that moved like a river above them.

"Where are we going?" Ashley said.

"To celebrate, alone," Muerce said. "Trust me, you'll like this."

He led them through the breezeway that separated the Entrance Hall from the Exhibition Pavilion, down a ramp, and up four short flights of stairs near the Research Institute before turning left at the Plaza Level Restaurant.

"Everyone goes to the Promontory, but this is my favorite view," Muerce said.

A square arch made from the same travertine marble that graced the center's edifices, framed a view of the glittering city below that was washed clean of its sin by the rain, if only briefly.

"Wow, as much as I've been here, I've never taken the time to really explore," Ashley said. "The view is incredible."

She let her hand slip from Muerce's and walked slowly, as if in trance, toward the white railing at the far end of the precipice. Muerce followed behind her. When she reached the railing, Ashley grasped it with both hands for support.

"It's like the world is upside down," she said. "The stars glitter below, and the earth spins above us."

Muerce moved up behind her, drawing his arm around her waist. She turned into him, and wrapped her arms around his neck.

"Impressive," she said.

"You have no idea," he said.

There was an intent delicacy to their kissing, which was interrupted by the sharp sound of a cork popping nearby.

"*Pardon Monsieur Muerce*," Pho Mat said. "You wished champagne, yes?"

"*Champagne, oui*," Muerce said, surprised to see Pho Mat.

"*Monsieur Travis*," Pho Mat said, responding to the look of inquiry on Muerce's face. Pho Mat poured a glass, and offered it to Ashley.

"*Mademoiselle.*"

"*Merci,*" Ashley said.

"Ashley, this is Sammy," Muerce said. "The *maitre de* at Saigon Laundry, who seems to be everywhere this evening."

"*Enchante mademoiselle,*" Pho Mat said, handing a glass to Muerce. "Will there be anything else?"

"No, thank you," Muerce said. "Nothing, else."

"Then I wait just down way in case," Pho Mat said.

"I'm sure Benny might appreciate your services inside," Muerce said. "We won't be needing anything further from you this evening, thank you Sammy."

"Yes, of course Mister Muerce," Pho Mat said. The words were delivered through Pho Mat's teeth, which Muerce knew was his way of indicating displeasure, particularly with him. Pho Mat disappeared as quickly as he had appeared. *What is up with Sammy?*

"He seems very, dedicated," Ashley said.

"Strangely so," Muerce said.

Ashley looked perplexed.

"Nothing," Muerce said. "We're here to celebrate. A toast. To the new Director of Marketing. Well done."

They clinked their glasses together, and Ashley finished her drink in one long swallow.

"So, good," she said. "More. I need to catch up."

"Not too much," Muerce said. "You're driving."

He poured another glass for her.

"Am I?"

"I certainly can't," he said. "Eleanor and I came together. I gave her the car. Remember? Besides, I've had, and intend to have, more than my quotient of alcohol."

"Aren't you the responsible one."

"No," he said, striking his glass to hers. "You are."

"Well, it's my intention to be irresponsible at some point tonight," she said, sipping. "Very irresponsible."

Muerce smiled, and drank more champagne.

"Another toast," he said. "Good luck with the boss."

"The boss?" Ashley said. "Oh, your mother."

"Having Eleanor as a mother is one thing," he said. "Having her as a boss is quite another."

"I'm not worried in the least," Ashley said, sipping her champagne more evenly. "She and I are on the same wavelength... about a lot of things."

She gave Muerce a false glower, and raised one of her eyebrows.

"I'm not sure I like that," he said. "Two women in my life on the same wavelength."

"Two women in your life?" Ashley said. "Don't get ahead of yourself Mister Muerce."

Muerce raised is arms in mock surrender.

"So to where am I driving you tonight, sir?" she said.

"My place."

"Then let's go now," she said. There was an insistence in her voice as she pressed herself against him, putting her mouth to his ear. "Because I don't think I can restrain myself much longer."

Her tongue darted into his ear, before her teeth playfully bit his ear lobe. Breaking away from their embrace, Ashley tossed her champagne glass over the railing, and began walking quickly toward the Entrance Hall.

"Are you coming, or what?" she said.

— —

Ashley was as aggressive behind the wheel as she was in bed. Muerce wasn't sure if it was her natural style, or if passion was the impetus for her shooting in and out of freeway traffic, which she did with the precision of a professional race car driver. Her driving skills skirted the edge of control, which impressed him. They talked very little. When there was a stretch of freeway free of traffic, Ashley would place her hand on Muerce's thigh, and hold it there as a reminder. Those brief interludes of contact aroused him.

The drive was short, but provided Muerce the opportunity to get some insight into Ashley. When he thought about it, he really didn't know much about her at all. There had been no first date, and that sharing of personal information that accompanies such relationship milestones. It would be too awkward to jump into twenty-one questions at the moment, and he didn't want to risk taking her attention away driving. So he relied on observation. How someone kept their car could say a lot about them. One of the least emotionally stable women he had ever been with kept her car in immaculate shape—obsessively so. He might wonder what ever became of her, but she didn't warrant his thoughts, so he continued taking mental notes on Ashley.

The car was one of the higher end Volkswagen sedans. Black, with a powerful engine. It was a feminine muscle car that Muerce figured she could only afford as a lease. It was clean. Not overly detailed. A temporary museum parking pass for staff was wedged in the lower left windshield. The chord to the charger for her Blackberry was draped across the center console. There was a bottle of fingernail polish in one of the cup holders. It was the same color Ashley was wearing, indicating it had been applied in a hurry, in the car, right before the gala. That made sense, she would have been rushed. She was in charge of a big event and had a million things to do.

In the back seat were several stacks of brochures, media folders, and several hardcover books about the history of the tapestries. Again, that all made sense given the night's event, and her role. On the floor of the back seat was a medium sized Louis Vuitton duffel bag. Likely, he deduced, to contain her backup clothes, and makeup bag. She got dressed at the event, and tossed what she had been wearing into the duffel. The tan leather handles on the bag were more worn than he would have thought for a woman her age. They were almost black at the apex of the arched grip. *Probably her mother's, or bought used, on-line.*

What Muerce couldn't pinpoint was the faint smell of coffee. It she were a big coffee drinker there would be spill stains on the console, or a stylish insulated stainless steel mug resting in one of the holders. The aroma in the car would also be more stale, and permeate the car, and her breath. When they kissed there was no tell-tale flavor of spearmint. Ashley tasted clean—like a crisp stalk of celery.

The coffee Muerce smelled was pungent, and fresh. It was a question to which he was unlikely to get an answer without asking, and it didn't seem to be that important to ask. Certainly it wasn't when he realized they were a block away from his apartment. Ashley had a good memory, and a sense of direction. She had not once Asked Muerce for directions. His attention turned to the matter at hand, getting them up to his apartment as quickly as possible. He produced his phone from his pocket, and slide the image of the security bar to punch in a code.

"Take a left here and pull onto the apron just past the large yew at the back of the building," he said.

He fingered an application icon on his phone that bore his monogram, which produced a menu that allowed Muerce to operate a number of electronically programmed functions in his apartment that included the security code to the garage door. He also touched one that sent the private elevator to the basement garage so it would be waiting, doors open, for them when they arrived.

As Ashley pulled her car onto the apron the garage door opened, and lights along the ramp that led into the basement went on.

"Take it slow or you'll bottom out when you hit the incline," Muerce said. "When we get to the bottom of the ramp just pull into the empty space on the right."

"How did you do that?" Ashley said, very much impressed.

"My IT guy built a special app for my phone," Muerce said, holding the phone up for her to see. "He's calls it a "locked app", which means it's totally secure or something, and can't be downloaded or ferreted out. It's pretty cool."

"It's good to be Batman," she said. "Always be Batman."

"Just without the tights," Muerce said. "No man looks good in tights."

Enthralled with Muerce's *savior faire,* and near frantic to get upstairs and naked with him, Ashley's last detail was to remember to get her her overnight bag out of the back seat. She pulled into the empty space, reached back behind her to grab the bag and was opening her door when she realized Muerce sat silently, staring at her.

"Oh, there was no way I was leaving here tomorrow in the same clothes I arrived in," she said.

"Commendable," Muerce said. "Might I suggest you turn the car off and take the keys with you?"

Ashley bowed her head, mildly embarrassed.

"If I were a blonde I'd say I was having one of those moments," she said. "But I'm not."

"You're not what?" Muerce said.

"A blonde."

"No, you're enthusiastic," he said.

Muerce reached over and turned the key in the ignition to off, silencing the hum of the engine. He leaned into Ashely, and kissed her. She did taste like fresh celery, and a hint of champagne.

"I'll take enthusiasm over experience any time," he said.

Ashley felt as if all her organs dropped to her pelvis, producing a strong urge to spread her legs. She broke away from their embrace and nodded her head toward the elevator doors, which had just opened with their clanging invitation. Shouldering the overnight bag, she gave it a soft pat. There would not be a repeat of her last overnight visit to Muerce's apartment. In addition to the change of clothes, was a half pound of fresh ground French Roast coffee, a can of cinnamon rolls, a container of yogurt, and fresh strawberries.

The doors to the elevator had no more closed, and the lift started moving, when she dropped the bag to the floor, and they grabbed each other and began kissing with a furious desperation. They clawed and pulled at each other's clothing with a heady frenzy.

When the elevator reached its destination, Muerce and Ashley spilled into the foyer. Without looking, he kicked her bag across the marble floor and the two of them rolled in each others arms against the wall, knocking the umbrella stand over. Ashley ended up with her back against the wall as she tore at Muerce's tuxedo jacket. He moved his hands across her gown, searching for every clasp, button and zipper he could unfasten.

It was a complex outfit that he needed help removing. She reached behind herself with both hands as he kissed and stroked her neck with his lips, and untied the sash covering a set of hooks that held most of the skirt together. When she let go of the waist belt and returned her hands to Muerce's shoulders and her mouth to his, the skirt fell away to her knees. Muerce moved his hands to Ashley's waist and felt the warmth of her bare skin, and the silky stretch band of a garter belt. He coaxed each leg up and out of the lower half of the gown. Like the overnight bag, he kicked the dress out of their way.

Their kisses were deep and wet. Ashley managed to shed Muerce's jacket from him, and popped the shirt studs open with enough force to send one of them flying across the room, hitting the marble floor with a light metallic sound that signaled a deeper need within her. She tugged and pulled at his undershirt, and felt his ribs and back. For a man almost twice her age, he was in excellent shape. Her hands massaged the firmness of the muscles around his shoulder blades gently, then she pressed her fingernails into his skin and ran them down each side of his spine. She reached around to the front of his trousers, but the cummerbund hid the clasp and top of his zipper, and she was, momentarily, uncertain what to do next. Muerce sensed it in her breathing, and he knew he was in control.

From then on, it was all Muerce. He knew what he wanted to do with her. Moving his mouth to her long neck, he lingered in the pulse spots, alternating hot breaths with his lips pressed firm enough that he could feel each beat of her heart, and the surge of blood as it rushed to her head.

Unbound from the restraint of his jacket, his shirt loosed, Muerce moved his attention lower. He fixed his stance with his feet slightly apart from a direct alignment with his shoulders, and lowered himself into a squat. As he did, he stopped at Ashley's belly button and repeated what he had done to her neck, introducing his tongue that he used to mock penetration. Tickling and teasing the orifice. At the same time, he lifted her left leg over his shoulder so that the heel of her shoe barely touched the floor. He lingered at her belly before moving his mouth lower. His lips skipped over the garter belt waistband, passed her lower abdomen an onto the soft mound of flesh atop her labium.

He was close to where they both wanted him to be. Adjusting his weight on the lowered stance, Muerce draped Ashley's rose-covered right leg over his shoulder. She leaned back so that most of her weight was on her back and supported by the wall even though both her feet were firmly on the floor. As he moved his mouth and tongue over and inside her, Ashley felt as though she were floating. The first stirrings of pleasure began to build between her thighs. Taking in a deep breath, she exhaled slowly, and closed her eyes.

Muerce methodically kissed and licked every centimeter between her thighs. She was moist, and receptive. As he explored each fold with his tongue, Muerce placed his right index finger on her perineum. When it flexed and contracted, he knew his tongue was in the right spot. Ashley moaned, squeezed her legs around his head, then bit down on her lower lip as she grabbed a handful of Muerce's hair. With her other hand she grasped and clutched at the wall as someone drowning would for a life preserver that was just out of reach.

Without taking his attention away from the spot, Muerce firmly gripped Ashley's hamstrings with both hands. He straightened his back, and with the power in his legs, he lifted her off the ground and toward the ceiling, increasing the intensity and pressure his tongue and mouth had on her.

Ashley released the grasp she had on Muerce's hair, and with both hands began clutching for something to hold onto besides the bare wall. Her hands thrashed until they found stable handholds in the elaborate molding that joined the wall to the ceiling. Her first thought was that she was thankful the apartment had high ceilings; her second thought was she hoped Muerce had the strength to hold her up long enough to finish her off. She was enjoying what was being done to her. Ashley's third, and final, thought before she drifted back into the delirium of pleasure, was however great her gown was, the best investment she had made for the night was a Brazilian wax.

Once up and stabilized, Muerce knew he could support Ashley's weight with his arms and shoulders for as much time as she needed to reach climax. She weighed, at the most, just under one hundred and twenty pounds. He benched more than double that at least twice a week. Tonight's clean and snatch, he mused as his tongue swirled in a counterclockwise rotation, was a benefit of his regular regimen at the gym.

Once the right rhythm was established with his tongue, it took little time for Ashley to come. She held onto the sensation as long as she could, until she surrendered in a sharp scream as each wave of her orgasm washed over her. When she was done, Muerce carefully lowered her to the floor where she settled into the pile of clothes. He held her and kissed her as she lay limp, drifting in an out of a dreamy state of satisfaction.

"Tell me that wasn't it," she said.

Muerce looked at his watch as he cradled her.

"It isn't even midnight," he said. "And like they say, nothing good happens after midnight. And I want to be really bad tonight."

"You're really good at being bad," she said.

Ashley reached her hands up, and cupped Muerce's face with them.

"And you're really good at being good, too."

He smiled, and kissed her again. Then he picked her up, and carried her into the bedroom.

CHAPTER 20

"Answer it."

"What?"

"Answer it."

"Answer what?"

"Your phone," Ashley said. "This is the third time it's rung, and you've been getting text message beeps too."

Muerce rolled over to retrieve the phone from the nightstand. This time he was on his side of the bed, and he felt more comfortable.

"God, I thought I was having a dream," he said.

Muerce was groggy, but well rested. They had made love on and off all night until they were exhausted, and a little sore. He wasn't sure what time it was when they fell asleep. Ashley was entering the bathroom as he fingered the screen of the phone alive, scanning the caller and text message IDs. There were two calls from Trumbley, and a voicemail, and one call from Bhote, and a voicemail from him. There also were a string of text messages from Trumbley, and one from Travis. Muerce viewed the texts before deciding not to listen to either of the voicemails.

The comfort of his bed was lost when he saw who all the messages were from, and the urgency with which they were sent. There was little doubt about what the calls were about. What got Muerce's attention instead, was the aroma of something baking in the apartment. It was fresh, and smelled like cinnamon.

Ashley emerged from the bathroom wearing only his tuxedo shirt, and headed toward the kitchen.

"How long have you been up?" he said.

"Right before the first call," she said. "I was in the kitchen when your phone started to explode. About fifteen minutes ago."

"What are you doing in the kitchen?" he yelled at her as she made her way through the living room.

"Making sure I get some breakfast before I go to work," she shouted back. "A girl could starve to death in this place if she doesn't look out for herself."

"Work?" he said.

"Yes. The exhibit opens to the public today, and I have to be there for the media."

"When?" he said.

"In about forty-five minutes, and that's cutting it close," she said. "Have you not looked at the time."

Muerce looked at the clock next to the lamp on his nightstand and then at the time on his phone, which automatically changed. There was an hour difference. *Shit, Spring Forward.*

The text messages from Trumbley all said the same thing: Call ASAP. The one from Travis asked if they should get together today so he could go over the additional research he had done on Brankovic and Zajak. Not yet, at least. Muerce skipped past Trumbley's voicemails, but listened to Bhote's. It confirmed what Muerce suspected, and added that Bhote would be waiting for him at the morgue. Muerce put is finger on the "Call" icon under Trumbley's last voicemail.

Trumbley picked up on the first ring. Muerce could tell from the background noise that Trumbley was outdoors. There were voices, the squawking of police radios, and the beat of helicopter blades in the distance.

"Nick," Muerce said.

"Where the fuck you been?" Trumbley said. "I've been calling all morning."

"Well, good morning Little Mary Sunshine," Muerce said. "May I speak with Detective Nick Trumbley please?"

"Oh, fuck off," Trumbley said. "I suppose you're with some fresh pastry right now."

The smell of cinnamon grew stronger in Muerce's apartment. He appreciated the irony of Trumbley's statement.

"And that's why you're the detective," Muerce said. "Quit being so dramatic. You only called and texted me in the last half hour. I could have been shaving and showering for all you know."

"Yeah, right," Trumbley said. "You got any idea what time it is?

"An hour later than it should be," Muerce said. "Spring forward and all that. I hate this time change crap. Fill me in."

"Third time's a charm," Trumbley said. "We got us an official-like serial killer now."

"I didn't think you wanted to know what I was having for breakfast," Muerce said. He took a breath and exhaled through his nose. Trumbley could hear the tone of it through the phone.

"You still there, Jack?" Trumbley said.

"Yup," Muerce said, drawing out the pronunciation. "What do you know so far."

"Little," Trumbley said. "Forensics is processing the scene. They'll probably remove the body in the next hour. No ID on the vic yet. A woman. Tweedle Dee and Tweedle Dum are here, fucking everything up. And..."

"Yeah, Nick," Muerce said.

"The media's here," Trumbley said. "Television crews, everything. Ash and Maple are talking to them like they have their own cable series, and they're working the crime of the century."

It was a crime of some century, Muerce just wasn't sure which one. Not yet. But he had an idea.

"What about the condition?" he said.

"Of the body?" Trumbley said. "Same and different. This time the eyes are sewn shut."

"Okay," Muerce said, mulling over the patterns, similarities and coincidences that popped into his head. "So we'll know more when Bhote takes a look at her, and there'll be damage control with the media. We'll have to figure that out later. See how it plays. At least it's a Sunday so the news cycle is shorter. Still, it's going to be a zoo."

"Yeah," Trumbley said. "I'll talk to the Chief and see how he wants to handle it. I'm sure the Mayor will be in on this, and the City Council, and everyone else from the Sisters of St. Joseph to the Girl Scouts. Shit, what a mess."

"It is what it is," Muerce said. "I'll meet you at the morgue in about an hour and a half. Try and keep a lid on Tweedle Dee and Tweedle Dumb-ass if you can. I suggest calling the Chief now. He can squeeze them quiet."

"Calling the Chief on a Sunday morning, how fun," Trumbley said.

"Oh, Nick," Muerce said. "I'll be plus one at the morgue."

The silence at the other end of the phone told Muerce that Trumbley wasn't comfortable with an extra person. It wasn't like Muerce had an official role in the investigation. Trumbley himself was out of his assigned element.

"An associate," Muerce said. "He's been doing research for me. Trust me. It's okay. Very discreet."

"Jesus, for a minute there I thought you were bringing a date," Trumbley said. "When did you start the Jack Muerce internship program?"

"It's a favor," Muerce said. "The appendage of your favor."

"Enough said," Trumbley said.

"One more thing," Muerce said. "What are you doing this afternoon?"

Trumbley was planning on going to the hospital to visit Miriam, but he wasn't about to get into that with Muerce.

"See a friend, maybe," he said. "Why?"

"If I think what I think is going on, we might need to go on a field trip to the museum so I can explain my theory," Muerce said. "I think we might be able to answer the how and the what."

"How long do you think that'll take, at the museum?" Trumbley said.

"Must be some friend," Muerce said, joking. "You got a girlfriend I don't know about, Nick?"

"Fuck off," Trumbley said. "I'll see you at the morgue."

Three short beeps indicated the call had been cutoff. Muerce had hit a nerve with Trumbley, but the smell of cinnamon rolls overpowered his interest in Trumbley's love life. Muerce was more curious about what was going on in his kitchen. He got out of bed, slipped on a robe, and sought out Ashley.

"How does this thing work," she said. She stood in front of the chrome Italian coffee maker, confused by all the knobs, dials and switches.

"What do you want?" he said.

"Coffee," she said. "Good old-fashioned coffee."

Muerce took the folded bag of ground coffee from her hand.

"What kind?" he said.

"French Roast," she said. "Is there any other kind?"

"Yes, but if you can only have one, this would be it," Muerce said. "Let me make it so you can get back to your Easy Bake Oven."

"They need another ten minutes," Ashley said. "I'm going to take a quick shower and change. Okay?"

"Okay," Muerce said, working on making the coffee.

Ten minutes later a bell that Muerce did not know was there went off on the massive stainless steel range. He was about to take the rolls out when Ashley appeared, dressed in a white silk blouse, jeans and black Tory Burch flats. Her hair was pulled back in a pony tail. She grabbed an oven mitt, and removed the tray of cinnamon rolls from the oven, then poured the small container of glaze on top of them. She ran her finger inside the container when she was done, and looked up at Muerce as she licked the sweet, sticky mixture from her finger.

"How do you want your coffee?" Muerce said, laughing at her sexually suggestive gesture with the frosting. He turned around to get two cups from the shelves above the coffee machine.

"Like the perfect cocktail dress," she said. "Hot, black and fast."

The quip made Muerce's heart skip beat. *Clever girl.*

"Actually, do you have a 'to go' mug?" she said. "I've got to get to the museum."

Muerce was a little disappointed that she was in a hurry to leave. When he turned around, she was looking at her watch, a small silver timepiece encrusted with diamonds. The band was made from a string of pearls.

"That's lovely," Muerce said.

"I'm sorry Jack, I want to stay but I really have to be there ahead of the news crews," she said.

"I meant your watch," he said.

Muerce didn't offer to tell her that most of the news crews she expected were already covering a bigger story than the tapestries going on public display at the center. If he were correct, he'd explain to her later that she should switch into crisis mode for public relations concerning the exhibition.

"Oh, I thought maybe you'd miss me," she said.

Muerce poured coffee into one of a half dozen various "branded" insulated coffee mugs he had accumulated over the years, and snapped the lid down tight. He handed her the coffee, and snatched up one of the cinnamon rolls. After swallowing his first bite he put his arm around her.

"Of course I'll miss you," he said. "I didn't factor the time change, and you did say you had to get going."

He lifted her arm by the wrist, admiring the watch.

"And it is a lovely watch," he said.

"What if I told you it was a gift from a former lover?" she said.

"I'd say he has exquisite taste," Muerce said, kissing the inside of her wrist. "And I'd be jealous of every minute you'd ever spent with him."

A cunning little smile formed on Ashley's face. She wasn't about to tell Muerce that the watch was her grandmother's.

"Maybe I'll forgive you," she said.

"There's a lot for which I need to be forgiven," Muerce said.

She looked at her watch. Plenty of time.

"Well, I'm not leaving here again without eating something, and having a cup of coffee," she said. Ashley took a roll from the baking sheet.

The two of them sipped and munched on the rolls, and spoke about nothing in particular until Ashley looked at her watch again. *Time to go.*

"Can I ask a favor?" Muerce said.

Ashley gave him the *sure-you-can* look.

"You'll be at the museum all afternoon?" he said.

"Yes, and probably into the evening," she said. "Busy day, and I need to get my ducks in a row since I'm giving the agency my notice tomorrow."

"I'd like to bring one or two people by this afternoon," he said. "Can you break away to give us the nickel tour. Just a brief history of the tapestries. Fifteen minutes at the most."

"Sure, that shouldn't be a problem," she said. "Just text or call. Give me a half hour heads up if you can."

"Not a problem," he said. "Thanks."

Ashley retrieved her overnight bag from the bedroom. She had earlier scooped up all the parts of her gown, and placed them in a white plastic bag to take to the cleaners, though she knew, like a wedding dress, she'd probably never wear it again. Muerce followed her into the foyer, and pressed the elevator button.

"How does the garage door open?" she said.

"It's automatic from the inside," Muerce said. "Just drive up the ramp slowly. I'll come down with you."

She looked at her watch again.

"No, no, that's okay," she said, tapping on the face of the watch. "Besides, you have to be somewhere and you're still in your robe."

"You're sure?"

"Yes, I'll be fine."

The elevator door opened, he pulled back the gate, and Ashley stepped inside, looking at Muerce. Should she, or shouldn't she? *Trust, she thought.*

As the door to the elevator began to close she kicked the safety bumper so the door would recycle open. Muerce looked at her with question.

"It was my grandmother's," she said, holding up the wrist with the watch attached.

CHAPTER 21

As he had done previously for Muerce, Bhote dramatically flung back the black plastic tarp that covered the dismembered remains of what was the third victim. The reaction Muerce saw in Travis' face was one of curiosity. He approached the table with fascination. Once he thought about it, it made sense. Travis had been looking at blow-up pictures of the previous two victims, and had been studying the condition of the bodies for days. He wasn't just prepared for the sight, he was looking forward to it.

Trumbley was unfazed. He'd seen it all before despite the unique treatment of these victims.

Bhote's demeanor was one of disappointment. But he moved on without missing a step, and began to articulate, in forensic terms, the condition of the body. The legs and arms had been surgically amputated, the wounds all sutured in an ornate and decorative manner, much the same as the first two victims. The difference was the eyelids of this victim had been sewn shut.

"One of the first things we do when we get a body in here is run X-rays," Bhote said. "With this one, we found metallic objects behind the lids."

Muerce suspected coins.

Bhote was gloved, and picked up a pair of suture scissors and small forceps. He swung the large magnifying glass over the victim's face.

"Everything's been photographed, but I wanted you and Nick to see it before I started snipping," he said.

Muerce reluctantly bent over, and looked at the victim's pallid face through the magnifying glass. Her right eyelid was sutured shut with gold, green and blue thread that spelled out the word *lapin.*

"Rabbit," Muerce said. Bhote nodded his head in agreement.

Muerce stood back to let Bhote cut the stitches.

"So we have..." Trumbley said.

"A unicorn, a monkey and a rabbit," Travis interrupted.

Trumbley frowned at Travis.

"Chinese calendar?" Trumbley said.

"Let's see what's behind door number one," Bhote said, cutting the delicate threads that held the eyelids shut.

"In French?" Travis said.

"Not very Asian," Muerce said. "More Medieval is my guess."

"Ah, I was right," Bhote said. He opened the eyelids and exposed the foreign objects picked up by the X-rays. "Here, take a look."

"Oh, that's just creepy," Travis said.

The victim's face gave the appearance of life as they looked down at her. As Muerce stooped closer, he saw his reflection in her eye sockets. A shard of broken mirror had been inserted where her eyeballs once resided.

"Windows to the soul," Muerce said.

"No," Bhote said. "A window would let you see the soul. A mirror only reflects the soul of the person looking into it."

"No coin?" Muerce said.

"No, we've got a coin," Bhote said. He was standing on the opposite side of the table and bent over, opened her mouth and, using the forceps, removed a coin similar to the ones found in the previous two victims.

"So she got passage," Muerce said.

"Appears she did," Bhote said.

"What about the eyeballs?" Muerce said.

"Missing," Bhote said.

"Nothing at the scene, but I'll double-check," Trumbley said.

"So we're missing a set of eyeballs, a tongue, and ten fingers and toes," Muerce said.

"Trophies?" Travis said.

"Maybe," Muerce said. "Sonjay, anything back from the tests on the other victims?"

"Yes, but inconclusive for the most part," he said. "They were clean. Scrubbed clean, in fact. No prints, no foreign skin or other DNA substances."

"No semen in the first victim?" Trumbley said.

"None at all," Bhote said. "She was not sexually assaulted. And given her line of work, she certainly would have required her customers to use condoms. But there weren't any traces of latex either. She, and the others, were surgically clean. There were only the traces of the drugs used to induce and maintain them in a coma, and keep them hydrated through the procedure. There were traces of narcotics, likely to minimize pain.

"The killer wouldn't want them thrashing about while he was performing the amputations, and there wasn't any tearing around the stitching. Still, there was some bruising—especially on the second victim—where restraints had been used."

"Anything exotic in regard to the pharmaceuticals?" Trumbley said.

"I'll give both of you copies of the reports," Bhote said. "But no. All of it is very common. In fact, you can find any of it on the street if you want."

"Who was she?" Muerce said.

Trumbley flipped open a small black notebook.

"Margaret Nace, Maggie," he said. "We got a hit on prints. She used to be a newspaper photographer and was registered as working media, which meant she was fingerprinted to get her credentials from us. That was a long time ago."

"What's she been up to since," Muerce said.

"Wedding and portrait photography," Trumbley said. "For the past ten or fifteen years. She's got a studio in the Quirinal District."

"Bohemian chic," Travis said.

The Quirinal District was an old warehouse section of the city that had undergone gentrification before the bottom of the real estate market dropped out. Most of the old brick buildings and townhouses had been renovated, but the prices remained depressed, making rents still affordable for artists. The area was slowly starting to recover, and Muerce had been to several of the newer restaurants that were opening in the Quirinal. There was a sushi place of particular note that he liked. Benny didn't do sushi at Saigon Laundry so Muerce was always on the lookout for things he couldn't get there. Benny also didn't do hamburgers or pizza, for which Muerce had the occasional craving. His stomach began to growl. Coffee and a cinnamon roll had not sated his appetite. And he had avoided most of the *hors d'oeuvres* at the gala the night before.

"I suppose Ash and Maple have people canvassing her neighborhood," Muerce said.

"I'll send you what they come up with," Trumbley said. "Which probably isn't going to be much."

"So what are you thinking, Jack?" Bhote said.

"A hooker, a drunk and an artist," he said. "All women, all caucasian, all dismembered and crocheted."

"What I think is we go look at some old rugs for answers."

Bhote, Trumbley and Travis all looked at Muerce with no understanding of what he was talking about.

"We're going on a field trip to the museum kids," Muerce said.

Only Travis appeared to grasp what Muerce was saying.

"I can't go, too much to do here still," Bhote said. "Explain it to me later."

Muerce had no issue with Bhote remaining behind. He turned to Trumbley and Travis to motion they start off for the museum.

As they gathered their jackets, and a fresh styrofoam cup of coffee, Bhote spoke out loud to Trumbley.

"How is Misses Estrada recovering?"

Muerce spun on his heels, and looked sharply at Trumbley, who looked at Bhote like he wanted to slug him. Trumbley stood silently, hoping the question would disappear if he ignored it. But he knew he it wouldn't go away, and he waited for Muerce's response.

"What the hell is he talking about?" Muerce said.

Bhote realized he had divulged something he thought Muerce would have known about. Bhote knew Miriam, though not closely. He had known her late husband, and Nick, as his partner. And he knew Muerce had helped her out in the past when her husband was sick. He assumed Muerce was aware of Miriam's surgery. And now, he knew, he was wrong about his assumption.

"Look, it was Miriam's call," Trumbley said. "She didn't want you to know."

"Know what?"

"She has breast cancer," Trumbley said. "She had surgery."

"When?"

"Last week."

Travis could see Muerce was angry, put his cup of coffee down on a desk, and moved closer to Muerce and Trumbley, thinking he might have to place himself between the two of them. Travis sensed it was a territorial argument. And when those kinds of arguments happened over a woman, it rarely ended well. It was almost comical: a macho death match in the morgue.

"You should have told me, Nick," Muerce said.

"No, Jack, Miriam would have told you if she wanted you to know," Trumbley said. "She told me not to tell you. She asked *me* for help."

Trumbley looked at Travis, and Muerce understood the favor.

"I want to see her," Muerce said.

"I'll ask her," Trumbley said. "Look, I'm sorry. I'm just doing what she wanted."

If a woman didn't want to see you, you had to respect that wish no matter how much it hurt. Muerce knew as much. It wasn't worth arguing about. He also knew he lost his appetite, though he had to get something in his stomach. They agreed to meet at the museum in the next hour. The three of them would go in their respective cars. When he got to the parking lot outside the hospital, Muerce texted Ashley the time they expected to arrive, and if she'd like him to pick up lunch for her. She texted right back that she'd be waiting for them in the Entrance Hall, and that she didn't need anything to eat.

He reached for the ignition to turn the engine over but stopped, and sat back in his seat. He thought about the night with Miriam, and how she slipped out before he woke. And then this secret of hers. And Nick was taking care of her? Muerce felt used. *Perhaps turnabout is fair play.*

CHAPTER 22

The crowds at the museum were far larger than had been expected. Traffic along the freeway was backed up for several miles. The exhibition, although free to the public on a first-come, first-served basis, was essentially sold out for the day. Ashley, and museum officials, were scrambling to amend the ticket policy while dealing with the large crowd on hand. Going forward, tickets could be reserved for free by going online. The public was limited to four tickets per request, unless arrangements were made through the Group Sales Department.

It was a mess. But it was not one that anyone could have anticipated. How popular could a bunch of old carpets hanging on a wall be? Distressed by the mayhem at first—and worried the offer made by Eleanor the night before would be pulled—Ashley was relieved when several members of the Board of Directors called to congratulate her on the success of the exhibit, and how excited they were that she would be a permanent fixture at the museum. She was told there had not been that much public interest when the center first opened.

Ashley's greatest strength was that she remained calm under pressure, and could find practical answers to challenging questions at a moment's notice. She was the epitome of grace, and she would find the time to fulfill Muerce's request for a private presentation while juggling all the unexpected demands of the day. The main hall was too crowded for her to give a private tour, so she decided to use the multi-media presentation in one of the teaching rooms. She called the presentation PowerPoint on crack, and used it to get news organizations and potential benefactors hooked on the exhibit. It lasted less than ten minutes, after which she could cut

Muerce and crew loose to view the tapestries by themselves, and she could get back to work. *This girl don't dick around.*

Travis arrived at the traffic jam on the freeway first and called Muerce, who decided it was better if the three of them—he called Trumbley after talking to Travis—meet up at a shopping center parking lot two exits away. Muerce called Eleanor, who made arrangements for them to be cleared past the security gate at the bottom of the Esquiline, and allowed to park in her spot in the staff garage at the top of the hill.

Still, it took a good half hour to make the five-minute drive past the security gate up to the museum itself. The small, winding road that ran parallel to the tram was partially blocked by television satellite trucks, lesser dignitaries with "opening day" but post-gala VIP passes, and others who had cajoled or finagled their way onto the most exclusive stretch of asphalt of the day. Muerce was surprised by the strong media presence, and wondered if they had made a connection.

There was little small talk in the Mercedes, and the subject of Miriam was not brought up. Certainly, not in the presence of Travis. Muerce moved from shock to anger fairly quickly, and now he was transitioning into the bargaining phase of Miriam's situation. He would wait until he and Trumbley were alone.

"Where have you been?" Ashley said. An earpiece dangled from her right ear. The receiver was clipped to her belt—black alligator leather with a brass logo buckle that matched the one on her flats.

"Trying to get past all the party crashers," Muerce said. "The Arrival Plaza looks like Disney World during Spring Break."

"As if you've ever been there," she said. He had, actually, once with Eleanor when he was ten. He remembered being incredibly embarrassed because he liked getting kissed by Cinderella after a private lunch in the castle.

Ashley introduced herself. Travis shook hands, giving her a look of recognition from the night before. When Trumbley introduced himself, she turned and raised her eyebrows at Muerce. She would wait until later to ask. *Why are the cops here? And why are you with them?*

It was an easy read for Muerce.

"I'll explain later," he said.

She led them to the presentation room she had setup, and gave a short introduction on the history of the museum and the tapestries themselves. Since Ashley had seen the show too many times to recount—which she could recite word-for-word since she wrote and designed it—she excused herself, promising to remain just outside the door if there were any technical problems, or questions. The break would give her time to maintain her orchestration of all the players that had become part of her day.

Over the next ten minutes—with the aid of modern technology, excellent animation, and high quality photography and sound effects—the three of them were introduced to the fascinating and dazzling world *La Dame a la licorne*, the *Musee du Moyen-Age*, Flanders, Medieval cartoons, the import of silk to Europe, and the production of dyes. They met Jean Le Viste, the sponsor of the tapestries whose crest of arms was displayed in the works, King Charles VII, and the novelist George Sand, whose novel *Jean* helped bring public attention to the tapestries in the latter half of the 1800s after they had been discovered moldering in a rundown French hotel. Muerce envisioned several famous Van Gogh's hanging cockeyed and dust-covered in the breakfast lobby of a Days Inn somewhere in Indiana.

Then the presentation reached the part that Muerce was waiting for—the symbolism of the tapestries.

The narrator—a famous Shakespearean actor best known for playing the French captain in a popular science fiction television series—detailed each of the tapestries by their titles: Touch; Taste; Sight; Hearing; and Smell. All five senses were represented. The sixth tapestry, as Muerce had been given a cursory primer on only the night before, was *A Mon Seul Desir*—the meaning of which the narrator said remained open for interpretation despite the numerous explanations given over the ages, and which he described each in detail.

The sixth tapestry—and the most compelling of the set—derived its title from an obscure motto, which had been assigned various implications such as "by my will alone", "according to desire alone", "my one, or sole desire", "love desires only beauty of soul", "to calm passion." The last of the examples resonated with Muerce in an uncomfortable way.

In the tapestry, the narrator went on to say, the Lady at the center of the work is presented an open chest by a maidservant standing to her right. The Lady, whose costume Muerce realized Ashley had had copied for the gala, is framed by a unicorn and lion, which are holding the train flowing from her headdress. She is placing a necklace into the chest. The same necklace, the narrator points out, she wears in the other five tapestries. Muerce remembered seeing it the night before, and the association he had with it, and Dr. Sharron.

The conclusion, presented in a dramatic tone by the narrator, left an opening for doubt. He went on to say that by returning the necklace to the chest, the Lady is performing an act of free will; by her renunciation of the passions aroused by the other senses, she has won the struggle between earthly desires and duty to God.

It was, as Muerce saw, an act of atonement—something he too desired, yet had not mastered for himself. *There was, after all, Emily Benoit to consider.*

The narrator went on about how the exhibit itself had been put together, and how it had only been out of France once before for an exhibit in New York several decades earlier. Muerce did not hear a word of that part as he was fixated on the necklace for reasons he could not explain. When he envisioned Emily putting the necklace into the chest, the face of Paige Sharron popped into his head.

"Jack, JACK!" Trumbley said.

Muerce returned to the present when Trumbley shouted.

"You back with us?" Trumbley said.

"Yes, sorry, I was just thinking," he said.

"So?" Trumbley said. "All very interesting. So what do you think we have?"

Muerce could tell by looking at Trumbley and Travis that they got it. There was an eagerness about Travis, while Trumbley seemed more concerned than before.

"I think we've got the what and the how," Muerce said. "We're probably close to getting the when, but we won't know the why until we find the who.

"So here's where we are. Victim one was a prostitute. Fingers and toes removed, her genitals sewn shut but apparently not used for any sexual purpose by the killer. We have touch. Victim two, an overweight alcoholic. Her tongue removed and mouth sewn shut. We have taste. Victim three, a photographer. Her eyeballs removed and the eyelids sewn shut. We have sight. All three bodies dismembered—surgically while they were still alive—in the same manner with the exception of, let's say, the signature artwork. Why he kept them alive, I don't know. But all three are the killer's tapestries. It isn't stitching, or suturing, or sewing; it's embroidery. Very elaborate embroidery done in the same way as the tapestries, in the *mille-fleurs*—thousand flowers style. Their bodies were his canvas—working on the assumption the killer is a man."

Muerce turned to Trumbley.

"And, Nick, I'm basing the part of the killer being a man on all the detective shows I've watched on television because, and I don't mind hesitating to remind you, I'm not an expert in any of this. Hunting down serial killers is not my forte. Look, I know how to change the oil in my car, but I don't do it. I pay someone else to because I don't want to spend the time, or deal with the mess. I like hobbies that don't leave dirt under your fingernails. This would be a good time to call in the pros. The FBI has teams of people that are experts in this kind of thing."

"You want me to call the feds in on this?" Trumbley said.

"I think we're well past ego at this point," Muerce said. "You're a vice cop. I'm a lawyer, who doesn't even practice that much any more."

"You're a resource, a discreet resource." Trumbley said. "So am I. That's why we've been asked to take a look at it from the edges. The Chief asked me. Bhote, and I know the Mayor, have asked you."

It was a favor. And Muerce did not walk away from favors. He would remain faithful to his pledged word, though he knew this was beyond his experience.

"From the edges Jack," Trumbley said. "No dirt under your fingernails."

Muerce didn't mind getting his hands dirty if it was the right thing to do. He wouldn't hesitate again. He hadn't in a long time. He'd put it all on the line. He would because he regretted that he hadn't when he should have for Emily. Everything he'd done since then was to make up for not being more decisive. Maturity came with a curse; the memory of what you weren't when you were younger.

"So the when," Trumbley said. "If we crack that we might have the who, and put an end to this before we lose the last two senses."

"Six," Travis said. "There are six tapestries. Free will is the last of the series."

"This guy's only halfway done," Muerce said. "And we're not even halfway there.

"Can you get your hands on whatever you can from the crime scenes?"

Trumbley shook his head, indicating he'd do the best he could given the fact he wasn't officially on the case any more than Muerce, and there was Ash and Maple to get around.

"There might be something in their reports that will help," Muerce said. "And there are the coins, the animals, locations, maybe some commonality in the victims' lives. The timing is strange. A Wednesday and two Sundays. Get what you can and send it over."

"I can't," Trumbley said.

"You just said you could," Muerce said.

"I can't just send it over," Trumbley said. "I can get originals you can look at, but only, maybe, for two hours. And I can't make copies. The copy machines are monitored these days. We all get codes we have to use, and there can't be a trail. And it isn't going to look so good if I'm at the Office Max making copies with Official Police Records stamped on them."

"But enough time for us to scan them?" Muerce said.

"I can get you two hours," Trumbley said.

"So how do I get them from you?" Muerce said.

"I'll figure it out and let you know," Trumbley said. "Sometime tomorrow morning."

Muerce swiveled in his chair to address Travis.

"Does that fax/printer/scanner thing in the office you set up work?" he said.

"Of course it does," Travis said.

"I'll give you a call after I get coffee tomorrow. You can fill me in on whatever else you've found out," Muerce said. "I'll call you. No more texting on this subject."

"Yes, Mister Muerce," Travis said.

When Muerce thought of all the research files, charts and blow-up photos of the first two victims Travis had arranged in the apartment office he shuddered at the thought of Ashley—or the maid service—unexpectedly walking into what had become a Den of Death. Awkward for him. Frightening and unsettling for anyone else. He could explain it, but he wouldn't believe it himself. Anyone else would think they had stumbled into a sociopath's trophy room. Then he realized he owed an explanation to Ashley as to why he showed up at the museum with a cop. It looked like the murders were tied to the exhibit, if only symbolically, and the media would eventually pick up on it. The details of the condition of the victims were too salacious for them to resist. Ashley did Muerce a favor, and he owed her the favor of forewarning a possible public relations crisis. He cringed sympathetically for Ashley, and himself. The timing for her, professionally, was awful. The timing for the both of them, personally, was even worse. It meant he'd have to trust her, and Muerce didn't like to trust too many women. The problem with trust was that most people didn't. Muerce was trustworthy. He'd spent most of his life focused on the tenants of chivalry. In doing so, he'd developed a pretty good network of people he did trust. The thought of trusting Ashley pleased him. There was something different about her. What made him uncomfortable was that he was having to trust her so soon. Two weeks ago, they didn't know each other.

Travis was out of his chair, and waiting for Muerce and Trumbley.

"Why don't you go ahead," Muerce said, handing Travis the keys to the Mercedes. "Bring the car around. I need to talk to Nick for a minute."

"Okay, Mister Muerce," Travis said. "I'll be out front."

When Travis left the room, Muerce could see and hear Ashley just outside the door talking on her phone. When the door closed there was an awkward silence.

"I know what you're going to say," Trumbley said. "But Miriam was very specific about you."

"Why?" Muerce said. For reasons he had not yet sorted out, Muerce felt betrayed by Miriam.

"I don't know," Trumbley said. "I asked her but it was clear she didn't want to talk about it. And, honestly, I was glad."

There was an inkling in Muerce about Miriam, and Trumbley, and himself.

"I've had it bad for her for a long time," Trumbley said. "That isn't any secret. But I've been stuck in the 'friend zone', until now."

"And now, you two?" Muerce said.

"I hope so," Trumbley said. "I've been patient, a gentleman. You know?"

Muerce knew it meant they weren't lovers. Not yet. He knew Trumbley was a gentleman, and while Miriam may not have been completely lady-like with him, she was a woman who typically got what she wanted. There was nothing wrong with that. Muerce understood. He and Miriam were alike in that way. He was a last fling. It made him feel a little honored, lessening some of the sting. *Besides, he thought, you don't fuck with the Welfare Lady.*

"I asked her to marry me," Trumbley said.

"Whoa, I wasn't ready for that," Muerce said, stunned. It made sense to him, though. Miriam needed someone stable. She had the boys to consider.

As hard as he tried, Trumbley couldn't avert a lopsided smile.

"But how is she?" Muerce said.

"You know, good, really good considering," Trumbley said.

"What can I do?" Muerce said.

"You're already doing it, and more," Trumbley said. "With the kid. Miriam's got the best there is. Squire made sure. A good guy, actually. Checks in on her everyday."

"I still want to see her," Muerce said.

"I'll ask her," Trumbley said. "She's going to be pissed that you know, but I can blame it on Bhote. It was dumb to think you wouldn't find out eventually. Nothing personal, huh Jack?"

"With women it's always personal," Muerce said. "It's not like Miriam and I are a thing."

"Sure, of course," Trumbley said. "I'll ask her. Hell, I'll tell her."

Muerce lifted his index finger into the air to gesture a warning.

"Yeah, I know, the Welfare Lady," Trumbley said. "Come on, let's go. "

Trumbley got up, checked, as he always did, his service revolver, and walked out. Muerce was right behind him. Trumbley nodded to Ashley, who disengaged herself from her phone.

"Do you want to see the exhibit?" she said.

"No, but thank you for everything," Trumbley said. "We've seen what we needed for now. I have to be someplace else, and Jack is my ride."

"Nick, I'll be just a minute," Muerce said. "I'll see you outside."

Without going into the more macabre details, Muerce gave Ashley an overview of what they were working on, why Trumbley was with him and that, as far as he knew, so far, the museum was only indirectly involved because it was hosting the tapestries. He also told her that he'd only made the connection to the exhibit before asking to come over. He also told her that the media was onto the story, and with three victims the headlines would likely be led with "serial killer", and that she deserved a heads up. He also told her not to poke her head into the office at his apartment next time she was over unless she wanted to be creeped out.

Ashley—who liked the idea of there being a next time at Muerce's apartment—mulled the information over with a calculated look. Muerce was sure he could hear her brain clicking away like a finely tuned machine. It was sexy, and made him want to lead her into the coatroom just down the hallway.

"As far as PR, it's an easy response," she said. "It's an ongoing investigation so we refer all comment to the authorities. Simple. Just so long as it doesn't involve any of the staff, or sponsors."

"Not as far as I can tell," Muerce said.

"Good," she said. "We'll just have to wait and see how the media plays the connection to the exhibit. We'll either have to increase or decrease our advertising. The board will have to make that decision. Can I tell the board?"

"No, this is just a heads up for you," Muerce said.

"Not even..."

"No, not even Eleanor," Muerce said.

"That's fine so long as they never know I knew before them," she said. "I'll throw together a plan that looks like I pulled it out of my back pocket if, or when, it does break."

"You'll look like a genius," he said.

"But only if..." she said.

"No one will ever now, I promise," Muerce said. "I'm sorry this happened. The timing."

"That's the way these things go," Ashley said. "I may look like this is my first trip to the rodeo, but I've been around long enough to know that for every blow job the media gives you—and they've been giving this exhibit a lot of them—you get kicked in the balls twice.

"I'll start wearing a cup."

Muerce laughed, and thought she looked even sexier than she did the minute before. Ashley put her hands on Muerce's chest in a way that restrained, and created a space between them.

"Jack, I'm up to my neck in it right now," she said. "I don't want you to think I'm not interested. I really am. But I'm giving two weeks notice to the agency tomorrow, and still have other clients to tie up strings with, plus juggle the new job with this added twist. I don't know when..."

"That's not an issue for me," Muerce said. "Busy times for everyone. It will happen when it happens. You know how to find me. We okay?"

"Yeah, sure, we're okay," she said. "Thanks, Jack."

Muerce leaned over and gave her a fast kiss on the lips that left Ashley with the sense that they weren't okay, and she may have just let him slip past. But she was busy. This was her career, and there would always be guys that had to wait. She wasn't about to be the woman who held her breath. Not even for Jack Muerce. *You'd turn blue and pass out if you did.*

THE FEAST OF
SAINT PATRICK

With many maiden fair she cometh from her place,
  Fairest was she in skin, in figure, and in face.
  Of height and colour too, in every way so fair
That e'en Gaynore, the queen, might scarce with her compare.
  She thro' the chancel came, to greet that hero good,
  Led by another dame, who at her left hand stood.
    —The Pearl Poet

CHAPTER 23

The siren caught Muerce's attention before the red and blue flashing lights lit up the rearview mirror. Muerce glanced down at the speedometer to check himself. He was doing the speed limit. Just under it, actually. *Crap, what's this about?*

He wasn't four blocks from Saigon Laundry and his morning coffee before he was stopped. The bag of *beignets* Madame Trung packed up for Travis rested on the passenger seat were still warm, and filled the car with their aroma. Muerce pulled the Mercedes to the side of the street where a group of black teens were huddled. It was chilly. Their gathering looked to be more for business than mutual warmth. The street corner meeting broke up when the white man in a Mercedes pulled up next to them, trailed by a motorcycle cop. As they melted into the urban landscape, one of them in a leather athletic jacket flashed Muerce a three-finger gang sign, and mouthed the words "Po Po, Suck-ah."

Muerce checked his side mirror as the cop dismounted and approached, flipping open a leather traffic citation folder. Muerce rolled the window down. The air was damp and cold, and the city smelled fetid like an offshore breeze carrying in the stench of low tide. Still, there was a hint of spring in the folds of the breeze, and buds on the trees had begun to form. The cop bent down to address Muerce.

"Morning, Jack," Pruitt said.

"Good morning Sergeant Pruitt," Muerce said, his voice heavy with sarcasm.

"Damn it smells good in there," Pruitt said. "Saigon Laundry? Can I get one?"

"Depends one what I'm getting in return," Muerce said.

"A speeding ticket," Pruitt said. He scribbled haphazardly, and ripped the citation from the pad.

"You wrote that up faster than I was driving for God's sake," Muerce said. "I was under the limit."

"I wrote it out an hour ago to save time," Pruitt said, unzipping his jacket and removing a bulky manila envelope that he handed to Muerce. "And it comes with this. Trumbley says you have two hours. Says to give it back to me. I'll be on the same corner at eleven. Same routine."

"A second ticket, seriously?" Muerce said.

"I want to make quota early this month," Pruitt said. "My kids have time off before Easter, and I want to spend it with them."

"Motorcycle menses," Muerce said. "A couple of days a month you guys get all cranky and break out the pads. You want some cranberry juice with your pastry, Tinkerbell?

A deep laugh erupted from Pruitt that elicited a smile from Muerce, who was amused by his own joke and realized the two of them hadn't been out drinking in awhile, and needed to do so again, soon. Pruitt, like Nick Trumbley, was a real guy. Real guys cut through all the bullshit. They were honest. They were smart. They were tough. They knew when to be inappropriately funny, and when to be intransigently serious. They knew the tenants. And they always covered the backs of the guys in their circle. Muerce was in Pruitt's circle, and Pruitt was in his. *Was Nick? Sure, guys give guys the occasional pass when it comes to a woman. Just don't abuse it.*

"But I look so good on the bike," Pruitt said, waving the citation pad in the air. "Fight it in court. Look at the date on the ticket. Same one I'll be off with the kids. So how about one of those sweets in the bag?"

Muerce grabbed the package of *beignets*, and opened it to let Pruitt retrieve one of the pastries. Pruitt ate while still hunched over the open window of the Mercedes.

"Mmm, bayonets," Pruitt said, savoring the treat.

"*Beignets*," Muerce said, correcting the mispronunciation.

"Whatever, you fag," Pruitt said, lifting one of his pinky fingers in the air.

"Don't you have cop-cam on your bike?" Muerce said. "You don't want to show up on the Internet, or some dumb-ass show about dumb-ass cops eating donuts after giving dumb-ass speeding tickets to white trash like me."

"Technology, fucking thing keeps breaking down," Pruitt said. "Why, just this morning it crapped out again. Weird, huh?"

Pruitt licked his fingers after finishing off the last bite of the *beignet*, and put his riding gloves back on.

"Hey, you going to the Saint Paddy's day parade Saturday?" Pruitt said. "I'm working it to pick up some overtime. I can get you a good spot. Hey, O'Keeffe's is sponsoring a float. Padraig will let you ride with them. They'll have a keg on it."

"There's white trash, then there's Irish white trash like you, Pruitt," Muerce said. "I can't say I've given it much thought," he added, closing his eyes and gripping the Mercedes steering wheel with both hands. "There, I've thought about it. No."

"Fine, Jack. Two hours," Pruitt said, zipping up his jacket and tucking the citation folder back into the holder on his belt.

"Tommy, you know my Jeep?" Muerce said.

"Yours, yeah, why?" Pruitt said.

"Pull it over in two," Muerce said. "There'll be a kid driving. Travis Squire. He's helping me and Trumbley on this. Okay?"

"No problem," Pruitt said.

"Same court date," Muerce said.

"Ah, Jack, I gotta make my quota somehow," Pruitt said, strolling back toward the motorcycle. "I don't owe this kid any favors. Two hours."

— —

Travis scanned and printed off hard copies of all the documents in the manila folder within the first half hour of Muerce delivering them back to the apartment. He was careful not to get powdered sugar from the *beignets* on the originals. Muerce made several phone calls in the other room while he waited for Travis to finish. The first call was to Dr. Riley regarding the referral he made for Kinson, and if she could spare some time Tuesday to discuss something he was working on that would not be a personal session, but a consultation. The second call was to Eleanor, who was brief and, in the course of the conversation, verified that Ashley had officially accepted the job at the Gilmont Center, and had given her two-week notice to the agency. The third call was to the florist to order flowers to be delivered to Ashley's apartment as congratulations for the new job. There were no messages from Trumbley, who promised to talk to Miriam.

Muerce went back into the makeshift spare bedroom/war room as Travis sorted the documents. Travis took a sip of coffee. It was cold and he discreetly spit it back into the cup, and ate the last of the *beignets*.

"I hope you don't mind," Travis said. "I found some coffee in the cupboard, and used the French press. I had to clean it out. I also ate the last of the cinnamon rolls in the fridge."

"Madame Trung asked if you'd be by later, for lunch or dinner with the kitchen staff," Muerce said.

"I hadn't planned on it," Travis said.

"You'll be there for lunch," Muerce said. "After you get these back to Trumbley."

Muerce explained the document handoff procedure Trumbley had arranged. Travis appeared intrigued and amused by the stealthy exchange system, though another speeding ticket on his record might jeopardize his license, let alone the cost of his insurance.

"Oh, I almost forgot," Travis said, pulling the money Muerce gave him to arrange for the champagne Saturday night. "Sammy wouldn't take it."

"Hold on to it for expenses," Muerce said.

"It's funny, though, Mister Muerce," Travis said. "I thought Sammy was supposed to be sick, but he was there Saturday night."

That hadn't occurred to Muerce, who remembered Pho Mat wasn't at Saigon Laundry for breakfast earlier, either. Monday mornings was usually when he helped Benny prepare for the week when the restaurant was closed. When Muerce asked about him, Madame Trung avoided eye contact and said he was still sick. She had waved her arm to indicate she was done speaking on the subject. Muerce decided he'd ask again, at dinner, if Pho Mat remained absent. He was worried about Pho Mat, if he were really sick. He didn't appear to be Saturday night when he was hustling *hors d'oeuvres*, or when he appeared at the West Promontory with the champagne. *Curious.*

Travis checked the e-mail account he had set up to receive correspondence from various organizations regarding the research he was conducting from Muerce. The e-mail account was secure, but not foolproof. A new message arrived while Travis stared at the laptop screen. It was from Bhote, and had three pdf files attached. Two of the attachments were official coroner's reports on the first two victims. The third was a preliminary toxicology report on the third victim.

"Mister Muerce, Doctor Bhote just sent this over," Travis said, angling the laptop so Muerce could see it. Muerce bent over close to the screen to look, which Travis knew from watching his parents read the newspaper meant Muerce's eyes weren't what they used to be. Muerce was a candidate for bifocals or, at the very least, reading glasses. *A chink in the armor.*

"Print them for me," Muerce said.

Travis fingered the arrow over the print icon, and the printer on the desk clicked and whirled as it spat out the copies.

"I thought we were supposed to be on the down low with this," Travis said. "I mean, now Doctor Bhote is e-mailing us inside stuff. That toxicology report isn't even official yet."

"That ship just cleared the lighthouse," Muerce said, scanning the reports.

There was a look of confusion on Travis' face, that Muerce quickly understood had gone right past his new assistant.

"Analogy; the proverbial ship that has left the harbor," Muerce said.

"Well, duh, yeah, I get that," Travis said. "No, what I was asking is what's changed?"

"We reached the magic number," Muerce said. "Three graduates whoever our perpetrator is from just a *killer* to a *serial killer*. He's in the big leagues now. He's got everybody's attention. It's not just us, or, God help us, Ash and Maple's investigation. The feds are going to get involved. They're probably already on it. And the state cops, too. And then there's the media. If they make the connection we think we've made... this is sexy."

"The tapestries," Travis said.

"That's the hook, for sure, but I think we're the only ones on to that, for now," Muerce said. "Women, prostitutes, surgical dismemberment, elaborate mutilation—the embroidery that is—and there's a lot of symbolism we haven't figured out."

"Only two of them were prostitutes," Travis said, glancing over the copies of the police notes Trumbley had temporarily loaned them. "And of those two, only one had an arrest for solicitation in the last two decades. Victim One was active on the streets in the past year. It looks like Victim Two retired some time back. She had a couple of arrests for drunk and disorderly that go back to the mid-nineties. But that's it. And the latest victim has no police record at all."

"So other than being women, they have no commonality?" Muerce said, speaking out loud more to himself than Travis.

"No, they're not even close in age," Travis said. "One was just seventeen, Three was in her forties and Two near sixty."

It had not occurred to Muerce before that Redzil was so young, and with a child. It was a sad fact. He shuffled through the copies of the reports and photos taken at the crime scene. The locations where the bodies were found were spread out over the city in no discernible pattern. Redzil's body was found on a merry-go-round in Founders Park.

The second victim—who had several aliases, but most often went by the name Rose Stanley—was found on a traffic island at an intersection just off the freeway near the Gilmont Center. Muerce remembered he must have driven past it with Trumbley and Travis on their way to the museum for the slide show. Margaret "Maggie" Nace, the photographer, was found on a floating dock at the end of a pier in a remote, and seldom used area of the harbor. The locations appeared to be abstract and disconnected to Muerce, who continued to sort through, out loud, the information at hand.

The coins were easy. Too easy. Greek myth. All three victims had them—although ancient Roman ones that were virtually impossible to trace—placed in their mouths. They were payment to the ferryman of Hades as toll for passage across the rivers Styx and Acheron. Having suffered martyrdom in life, their killer showed them each a kindness in death. Their souls would not have to wander for a hundred years.

The coins were cliche. "Taunting us, perhaps," Muerce said. *But, he thought, it was the least the killer could do for them.*

Muerce wasn't sure what to make of the shards of mirror placed in the empty eye sockets of the photographer. That was something he wanted to ask Doctor Riley about.

He picked up the copies of the two autopsy reports and compared them to the official toxicology reports with the preliminary toxicology report on the third victim. In all three victims there were varying amounts of midazolam loruzapam and diazapam. Next to those compounds Bhote had handwritten that they were commonly used for sedation. Atropine, succinylcholine, phenobarbital and ketamine had handwritten notations that they were consistent with use for intubation. Next to morphine Bhote wrote "pain management." The last handwritten message from Bhote simply stated, "all are available on the street."

"What do you make of this?" Travis said. "Victims One and Three have traces of estrogen and progestin. Victim Two's toxicology shows neither, but high levels of ethyl alcohol."

"Birth control. One and Three were on the pill," Muerce said. "Two was a drunk."

"Oh," Travis said, with a sheepish demeanor.

"That's okay," Muerce said. "Look at everything."

Before Muerce arrived at the apartment, Travis had printed off color copies of each of the six tapestries and taped them to a large white, dry erase board that was propped against the mirror of a dresser. Muerce looked at each of tapestries, focusing on the fauna.

"They're from the presentation we saw yesterday," Travis said. "You can download it off the museum's website. I'm having the print shop enlarge them so we can get more of the detail.

"They're more impressive up close."

Licorne, singe and lapin. What did the animals mean?

"We have Touch, Taste and Sight," Muerce said.

"Just missing Sound and Smell," Travis said.

"Probably not for long," Muerce said, stopping to think about the timeline. The first victim was found on a Wednesday. The other two on the following Sundays'. All three were discovered early in the morning.

"Let's not forget *Desir*," Muerce said. "Or the choice not to, depending on how you look at it.

"Let's change the subject. You said you found out something more about Brankovic."

"It's a combination of what I found, and what I didn't find," Travis said.

Go on, Muerce thought.

"Kind of an odd thing," Travis said. "You know how Brankovic was raised in an orphanage? Well, the particular one where he got dumped was kind of famous, in a way. I guess the kids were a little higher functioning. This place made wineskins out of pig bladders, and covered them in leather. Bota bags. The fancy kind you see gypsies with in movies. They also made gypsy shirts. All of it for export. It's like the original Eastern Bloc sweat shop for kids."

"Hardly original in the history of child labor," Muerce said.

"I get that, it just sounds cool," Travis said.

"Unless you're one of the child laborers," Muerce said. "So?"

"So, the wineskins, shirts and blouses," Travis said. "They were all embroidered by hand. Really intricate stuff. It's what made that orphanage famous—notorious, would be better."

"That gives Brankovic a skill, not a motive, necessarily," Muerce said. "So what didn't you find?"

"The Zajak guy," Travis said. "Doesn't exist. He's a ghost. Not a driver's license, passport, immigration documentation, birth certificate, nothing."

"What about the business card he gave me," Muerce said. "I gave that to you, right?"

"That's the only piece of paper on him," Travis said. "When I looked up the company background, officers, registrations, all that, his name never comes up," Travis said. "It all traces back to a holding company registered in the Caymans."

"That's not overly surprising," Muerce said.

"Then there's the Spooky Girl," Travis said.

"Amelie," Muerce said.

"Yeah, Amelie, something or other in French," Travis said. "I've got her last name written down here somewhere. Anyway, she's got an interesting story. Born in France. Single mother I guess because there's no father listed. They're mailing me a copy of her birth certificate. It hasn't been digitized yet."

"How did you get that?" Muerce said.

"It's amazing what you can get from admissions departments," Travis said. "They're mostly staffed by kids working financial aid who could care less about privacy issues. Anyway, she graduated from the Sorbonne in Paris. Got an MBA from Wharton. Which was kind enough to promise me a copy of her birth certificate, which she needed as a foreign exchange student to enroll there.

"After Wharton she worked a few years as a trader for a London-based hedge fund. She had a Linked-In profile she deleted, but I hacked into their system, and the original information is still there. Then she does a short stint in Geneva, trading for an East Asian company."

"Then?" Muerce said.

"Then she's here?" Travis said. "Mister Muerce, I may be a college drop out, but my daddy didn't raise no fool. This chick's got serious CV. Like rock star status. There isn't a house on Wall Street that wouldn't hire her. And she gives all that up to be what, head of sales and marketing for a company named ACME? That makes glass? That dog just don't hunt."

It was puzzling to Muerce, who took a slow and contemplative breath before looking at his watch.

"You better get going," he said, still thinking about Amelie. "Bundle up the originals. Let's get them back to Trumbley."

Travis pulled all the files together in the order they came in the packet. He shutdown the laptop, closed it and slipped it into a leather messenger bag he tossed over his shoulder, and started toward the hallway.

"Travis," Muerce said.

"Yes, Mister Muerce?" Travis said.

"Don't forget the laundry."

Before he left the room, Travis turned at the doorway and looked at Muerce, who stood, staring at the images of the tapestries.

"Have you ever done anything like this before?" Travis said.

Muerce paused, and pushed his hands into the front pockets of his trousers.

"Like this, exactly, no," Muerce said. "But something similar. A long time ago."

Travis could tell it wasn't the right time to ask a follow-up question. There were only fifteen minutes before he had to be at the intersection to be stopped for speeding, so he fetched the laundry from the master bathroom, and left without saying anything more. Muerce, his hands still in his pockets, walked over to the window, and stared out at a cloudy sky. When he looked down at the street he saw Travis drive away in the Jeep. He wasn't much older than Travis when that all happened before. He remembered Emily and the bright crimson spots of blood on the yellow dress, and the look of horror and disbelief on her face. It had been springtime then, too.

On the official coroner's report, Bhote classified the deaths of the two women as homicide. The cause of death was "heart failure with underlying circumstances." *Heart-break*, Muerce thought, *with underlying circumstances*.

CHAPTER 24

Miriam was tired of laying in bed. As unrealistic as it was, she was sure she was developing bed sores. *That's crazy, she thought.* Her surgery was less than a week ago. She was healing well. Everything was exceptional, considering the circumstances. She couldn't get any better care in the world than what she had. *God bless Nick, she thought.* What Miriam was, was bored. She had too much time to think. When she rested her thoughts, fear always crept in. *What if, what if... she thought.*

She missed her routine. With two teenage sons at home she was used to having early starts to hectic days, which had not let up since she graduated from college, gotten married, and had kids. She had been, for most of her adult life, the responsible one, taking care of everything before the sun came up, and until long after it went down. Even when he was well, her late husband hadn't been much help around the house, or with the boys. Very little in the way of Miriam's daily routine changed when he died, other than there was one less person for whom she felt responsible.

Now, *she* was being cared for, and that made her uncomfortable. She was physically and mentally fragile despite the attention, meds and positive post-op comments from the medical staff. Miriam knew she'd been a wreck since getting the diagnosis. She had made several mistakes when her guard was down, and was angry at herself. She ticked them off in her head: forgot to sign the spring athletic participation form for Carlos; forgot to tell the neighbors to watch out for the house because the boys would be staying with her sister; forgot to get those last six cases sitting on her desk at work processed; forgot to send her second cousin in El Paso a birthday card; slept with Jack Muerce.

"Just stupid," Miriam said out loud. Miriam saw a nurse's aid walk by the open door to her room. The young woman cowered her shoulders, thinking Miriam was addressing her for something she'd done wrong. The aide quickly skittered away down the hallway.

"Oh my God, I didn't mean you," Miriam said, though the poor girl was already at the other end of the ward, and could not hear the apology. "I meant me. I'm stupid. I'm so sorry, I'm so sorry, I'm so sorry…"

By the third *sorry* Miriam crumpled into one of the recliners in her room, and began to sob uncontrollably.

"Hey, girlfriend, what hell do you want to raise today?" Lonny said, not seeing Miriam distraught. "How 'bout we go to the cafeteria and flash some ass at the cute interns."

Lonny had blasted into the room as she always did, full of confidence, energy, and strength. She knew that was what her patients responded to best. *Get 'em up, get 'em well, and get 'em out.*

It was her chosen profession. She loved her work, but she hated hospitals. They were full of the sick and dying. She felt best when her patients were discharged. It meant they were well.

Putting the blue tub that contained everything needed to get Miriam's daily blood samples at the end of the bed, Lonny saw Miriam wasn't having a gold star day, and dialed back her approach so her gauge was tuned to *compassion*. It was natural for patients like Miriam to cycle through depression after surgery. Lonny was good at the ballsy, cancer ass-kicking, tattooed nurse bitch/pal routine, but it was her tenderness that was valued the most.

Lonny turned a latch that flipped on the Do Not Disturb sign, shut the door, and walked over to Miriam. Lonny bent down, softly stroked Miriam's hair and pulled out some tissues from a small package she always carried in the top pocket of her Grateful Dead scrubs. Miriam wiped her eyes, blew her nose, and curled up into a tighter ball. Lonny gave Miriam all the time she needed to get the tears out of her system.

After awhile, Miriam settled down with only intermittent convulsions of sobbing. She looked up at Lonny.

"I'm so scared," Miriam whispered.

"I know honey, I know," Lonny whispered back. She wrapped her arms around Miriam, who reached out both arms, and held onto Lonny as tightly as she could.

"I screwed up," Miriam said.

"Honey, you didn't do anything wrong," Lonny said. "It was done to you. Mother Nature can be a real bitch sometimes. I'm pinning this on her, because God makes me think of men, and a man doing this to a woman, well, it turns me into Ultra Bitch."

The reply got a smile out of Miriam.

Lonny rocked back on her heels. Twisting her body at her waist, she grabbed her right wrist with her left hand, and flexed her large and muscular right bicep. The move directed Miriam's attention to the tattoo that dominated Lonny's arm. The artwork inked into Lonny depicted a hospital bed surrounded by large red roses. In a scroll underneath the colorful image was the word *Life*.

Miriam erupted in laughter, as did Lonny, and continued until they were crying with a shared joy. Lonny dispensed more tissues, wiped her own tears, then blew her nose.

"Let's get you back into that bed of roses so I can do my Dracula thing," Lonny said. For a woman of Lonny's size, Miriam was a delicate thing. Squatting on her feet, Lonny scooped Miriam up in her arms, and carried her over to the bed.

"I really did screw up," Miriam said, as Lonny prepped her right arm to take blood.

Go ahead sister, Lonny thought, get it all out. I've got your back.

In one long, lunging run-on sentence, Miriam explained her relationship with Nick, whom Lonny had begun to know through his daily visits, her past history with Jack Muerce—his relationship and history with Nick and her late husband—and her dinner with Jack; that dinner with Jack Muerce was always more than a meal; and that Nick didn't know about dinner with Jack, and Jack didn't know about the cancer.

"So what do you think?" Miriam said.

Through her own personal lifestyle, Lonny didn't like cops. She was a biker chick, and pigs were pigs. *Five-O.* But many of the girls she worked with at the hospital were married to cops, and she didn't mind partying with them when the badges and service revolvers were tucked away in a dresser drawer. She'd even made it with a couple of mounted cops because they spoke the same language. Nick seemed stand-up. He obviously cared deeply for Miriam, and doted on her when he was around. She didn't know this Jack Muerce character, and wasn't sure she would even if she met him. But he must have been something if Miriam chose him for her last fling.

Lonny was about to open her mouth when the door opened, and a doctor in a white coat attempted to stroll in as if he were royalty. It pissed Lonny off to no end.

"Don't they teach you how to read in medical school?" Lonny barked. "Wait outside until we're done."

The physician glared at Lonny, and stood his ground. Lonny wheeled around Miriam's bed, snapping her plastic gloves as she removed them to emphasize her order.

"It looks to me as if you've completed your duties, nurse," the doctor said. His voice was authoritative, if a little effeminate. Despite his posturing, there was a blase, bland quality to the man that Miriam found mildly disturbing. Lonny pulled her shoulders back, walked to the door and stared straight into the doctor's eyes as she closed the door, forcing him to retreat to the hallway.

"Thank you for waiting outside, doctor," Lonny said. "I'll be just a minute."

"Who was that?" Miriam said. Lonny returned to her bedside to record her blood pressure.

"That's Doctor Transformer," Lonny said, making notations of Miriam's vitals on an electronic tablet.

"Doctor who?" Miriam said.

Lonny chuckled when she realized Miriam wasn't hip to the nicknames the nurses gave the doctors.

"Your plastic surgeon," Lonny said. "You know, like the kids' show? He can change shapes."

"Oh, I know Transformers," Miriam said. "I took my boys to see Transformers on Ice at the arena once. I can't believe I sat through the whole thing. Awful. Of course they loved it, and had to have every one of the action figures. Tell me it isn't like that."

"He can be a pretentious little prick," Lonny said. "But he and God both know he's the best skin guy in the business. Can't promise you a centerfold in *Playboy*, but you'll wear a two-piece to the beach this summer, for sure.

"Somebody sure pulled some strings. He has surgery privileges here, but he spends most of his time overhauling rich bitches at his clinic in the Caelian District."

"No really, tell me what you really think?" Miriam said, with some sarcasm.

"I think you're a lucky girl," Lonny said. "You got an early diagnosis of the cancer, the Queen of England suite, the best doctors there are, an attentive fiance, and me."

"What about how I screwed up," Miriam said.

Lonny pondered Miriam's predicament.

"Stick with Nick," Lonny said. "This Jack guy, he was just a one-night stand, right? You don't have the same feelings for him, right? And he doesn't have those feelings for you, right?"

"He's not the kind of guy you settle down with," Miriam said.

"Just a boy in a man's suit?"

"No, not that," Miriam said, unsure exactly how to describe him, or who she thought the *real* Jack Muerce was, or if she or any other woman would ever really know.

"Complicated, huh?"

Miriam bobbed her head up and down.

"And he and Nick are friends?" Lonny said. "It's complicated all right. And you don't think he'd spill the beans to Nick. But at the same time you feel bad not telling this Jack what was up with you?"

"That's pretty much it," Miriam said.

"You trust this Jack guy?"

"Yes, very much," Miriam said. "He wouldn't hurt Nick. And he knows I'm in here, and hasn't said anything."

"Well, I definitely wouldn't say anything to Nick," Lonny said. "But if the other guy keeps asking Nick if he can see you, that might open a can of sorry ass you don't want to eat."

"Yeah, it sucks," Miriam said. "I really fucked it up."

"No you didn't, honey," Lonny said. "You just wanted to get your freak on with the twins one last time. Ain't nothing wrong with that if it feels good. And it did, right?"

"Yeah, pretty much," Miriam said.

With that kind of grin, Lonny thought, I definitely want to meet this Jack Muerce dude. At least, she's smiling again.

"If you trust the guy to keep his mouth shut, and it wouldn't be unusual for him to visit you, I figure you can explain yourself and make it right," Lonny said. "At least you'll be straight with one of them. With the cop... I'd carry that secret to my grave."

Miriam pondered Lonny's advice as she left the room, and decided she'd wait until later in the day to make any decision about Muerce. Her mind began to wander back to her boys. She tried to remember if the Deceptacons were the good, or bad Transformers.

Outside in the hallway, Lonny was greeted with a look of holstered malice.

"How dare you address me like that in front of a patient," Dr. Sharron said. "I'm here at the request of the chairman of the hospital for an introductory consultation. I'm very busy. I have a tight schedule today."

"My understanding doctor, is she's not your patient, yet," Lonny said. "Does that sign say Please Interrupt and Disturb? No it doesn't. At the very least, you could have knocked."

"We're all aware of your reputation around here Nurse Lysaught," Dr. Sharron said. "But I'm the surgeon here."

"We're all aware of that," Lonny said.

Dr. Sharron purposely looked at his watch to make a point. When he did, all Lonny noticed by the gesture were his fingernails. They were meticulously manicured, and treated with a light sheen of clear polish. Lonny had to laugh to herself, and thought how long he would last in some of the bars she frequented.

"I'm due in surgery and want to get this consult out of the way while I'm here," Dr. Sharron said.

Dr. Sharron's arrogance put Lonny over the edge. She'd had enough of the effete man, flipped open her tablet, and looked at Miriam's chart. *Doctor Bitch, I'll be damned if I let anybody fuck with my girl like this.*

"Misses Estrada isn't scheduled for surgery with you for at least four months," Lonny said. "If everything goes well for her."

"I'm only in the hospital on Monday's so this was convenient for me," Dr. Sharron said. "I don't have a lot of time here."

"Well doctor, it's not convenient for Misses Estrada," Lonny said, her finger scanning the screen of the tablet. "She's having a rough day today. I'm sure you understand. Tomorrow will be much better for her. Say, five o'clock? I'm sure you'll be done with the life saving work you do at your clinic.

"And I'll be sure to let T.B., excuse me, our chairman, know how flexible you're being. I'm also here at his request, and he asks for daily updates. Oh, heads up. Her fiance's a cop. I don't think you want to piss him off, either."

With that, Lonny curtly turned and walked away from Dr. Sharron, who wasted little time with her words. Dr. Sharron had dealt with rude nurses before. Besides, meeting with Miriam was meaningless chit-cat. His work was done best without conversation. He checked his watch as if nothing had happened, and proceeded in the opposite direction. Dr. Sharron was a busy, and important man, with work to do.

Lonny got to the nurses desk at the center of the ward, and turned around to look for Dr. Sharron, who had disappeared down the back stairwell.

Transform that, Lonny thought, you arrogant bastard.

CHAPTER 25

It was mid-afternoon and Muerce couldn't wait any longer. He called Trumbley's mobile phone to make sure the files had been returned as planned. That was the excuse. What he really wanted to know was how Miriam was doing, and if he could see her.

"Jack," Trumbley said, sounding distracted.

"You get them back?" Muerce said.

"Yeah, no problem," Trumbley said.

There was a long pause.

"Something else, Jack?" Trumbley said.

"Well, yeah," Muerce said.

The light went on with Trumbley, who had been sifting through a pile of unrelated cases that had accumulated over the days his attention was focused on Miriam.

"I haven't heard from her yet," he said. "I called her cell this morning but no answer."

"You didn't talk to her last night?" Muerce said, feeling like he was pushing the issue too far.

"Oh yeah, sorry," Trumbley said, still distracted as he looked at the paperwork spread out on his desk, and the antiquated and rarely useful desktop computer. "She didn't say anything, but I could tell she was thinking about it."

"All right, just wanted to make sure what was yours was returned," Muerce said. He flinched, and hoped Trumbley didn't read something into what he'd just said. "And if there's anything I can do, for you and Miriam, you'll let me know?"

'For you and Miriam.' It was Nick and Miriam. Good with it. Happy even. Just want to get past the awkward part with her. Nick never needs to know.

"Thanks," Trumbley said. "Oh, Jack. No flowers. I know you live for that shit, but she can't have any in her room after the surgery."

"No flowers," Muerce said. "Got it."

The call ended. Muerce thought about the flowers he ordered for Ashley. She wouldn't see them until tonight. The super at her apartment would have them. Muerce scrolled the directory on his phone until he found the number of the florist. He called and ordered a basket of flowers for Eleanor to congratulate her for the success of the gala Saturday night. For the basket, he told the florist to buy two Lotto tickets and add them along with a pack of her preferred cigarettes, and a six-pack of Diet Coke.

Muerce leaned back in the large leather-covered swivel chair that had once occupied his father's office. The antler handled magnifying glass was half covered by copies of the police reports. Muerce picked up the magnifying glass and walked over to the dry erase board to look at the pictures of the tapestries. He alternated between using the optical enhancement and his own vision. There was little doubt. He knew he'd have to get glasses sooner than he wanted.

— —

The back of Saigon Laundry was a typhoon of kitchen prep activity, swirling around Travis as he sat alone at the large white-tiled table in the back. It was where family and staff meals were served. The kitchen was a controlled frenzy that delighted all the senses. There were the sounds of knives slicing, chopping, or being sharpened with slashing cross-hatch motions; talking and shouting was done in a melange of English, French, Vietnamese, Spanish, Italian and Creole. Saigon Laundry's reputation and four stars attracted some of the best apprentice cooking talent from around the world.

Although touch might be considered the least involved of the senses in the kitchen, Benny told Travis, it was just as important as all the others; poking, pressing, pinching, squeezing and fondling everything from fish to spices told a chef about the quality and freshness of his ingredients. In the short period of time he had been exposed to life with the Trungs, Travis had begun to separate and appreciate the power of smell, which could be overpowering at times, and barely discernible at others. He would close his eyes in the kitchen and try to identify with that sense alone what was happening around him. Sitting at the table, very still and out of the way, he would think through his nose. There were cold smells of garlic, cilantro, shallots, parsley, lemons, limes, fish, poultry and red meats as they were delivered, minced, squeezed, cut, cleaned and trimmed. In the afternoon, as the time for the first seating approached, the pace increased and hot smells would dominate. The braising, boiling, baking, sauteing, and searing filled Travis with delight. He could taste, feel, see and hear through the one sense he focused on above the others.

Ultimately, the sense that all of the work in the kitchen was critically dependent upon was taste. It was, as Travis and everyone else who worked in Benny's world at Saigon Laundry knew, the difference between success and failure. There were few other places in the world as currently renowned as Saigon Laundry, but that could come to a shattering and disgraceful ending with only one bad serving. There was little doubt of the intense pressure everyone was under every day.

Travis opened his eyes. When he smiled, a crease formed on his forehead. Though he was new to the Trung family—still an interloper to some—Benny could read the young man Muerce was cultivating. He could tell Travis was absorbing everything he could, and that he was hungry—literally, and figuratively. Travis was a novelty. Never before had Muerce had an attendant.

Benny ladled out a strong smelling, red gravy that had chunks of parsnip, rhubarb and leeks, and poured it over a chicken breast that had been broiled over a spit. It rested on a large plate ringed with basmati rice. There was a sizzling and popping when the sauce hit the chicken that was plated right off the spit. It was the dramatic effect Benny wanted for the presentation. The dish was an experiment for Thursday's meal, and today Travis was his official taster.

Madame Trung passed through the kitchen on her way to the dining room. Benny waved her over, and asked her to serve Travis. The rest of the staff and family had been served *pho* for lunch, with baguettes and a spread made from cranberry and black pepper infused goat cheese. Madame Trung looked at Travis and then back at Benny with a raised eyebrow of disapproval. Benny didn't flinch. In the kitchen, her bark was worse than her bite. Outside the kitchen, she was a pit bull.

"You late," she said, placing the dish down in front Travis. "Benny make special. You try. What you want drink? *Sua da?*"

She was telling, not asking Travis what he wanted to drink. It just happened that was what he wanted. He had become addicted to Vietnamese coffee.

"Yes, thank you Madame Trung," he said. He had learned not to give her direct eye contact, out of respect.

A yellow traffic ticket stuck out from the back pocket of his corduroys. Travis had to circle the block several times at the location where Muerce told him a motorcycle cop would pull him over to make the exchange, and where he'd be issued a ticket in the process. For the sake of appearances. Travis told the cop that he might lose his license with the ticket, but was assured that Muerce would handle it. Favors. Still it bothered Travis. He needed to tell his father, but he'd talk to Muerce about it first. It also made him late for lunch, which was why he was sitting alone, shoveling down Benny's experiment with Indian cuisine. What he was now devouring with zeal, despite burning his mouth, was a Saigon Laundry interpretation of chicken *Tika*.

The chalky, rich flavors basted his mouth. Then the curry detonated inside Travis' nasal cavity just as Madame Trung arrived with a tall glass of *sua da*. His eyes immediately filled with tears, his nose dripped, and Travis was sure there was a ringing in his ears as if the air bag in a car had accidentally triggered in his face. Though he had difficulty breathing, he managed to chew and swallow the tender piece of roasted chicken. His tongue felt like it swelled to twice its size as he gulped down the cold *sua da* to extinguish the fire. Benny, who had a high tolerance for spicy flavors, had been watching to see how Travis reacted to the dish, and was at the ready with an open can of coconut milk. He rushed over to the table.

"I tell you too much curry," Madame Trung said to Benny. There was a hint of sadistic satisfaction on her face. "I get another *sua da*."

Benny poured the coconut milk on the dish, assuring Travis that it would mitigate the heat. There was no apology, just a mental note Benny made to reduce the power in his spice mixture.

The *sua da* helped Travis regain his composure, even though his mouth felt raw. He would, however hard it might be, finish the dish to save face. Some of the kitchen staff snickered in the background, but not so that Benny or Madame Trung could see.

"See what happen you late?" Madame Trung said. She placed another tall glass of iced coffee on the table. "Not always good be Benny's guinea pig."

Goddamned right, Travis made note, never be late again.

"Madame Trung, is Sammy around?" Travis said.

"Sammy sick," she said, abruptly. "Why you ask?"

"No reason," he said, the spices still kindling in his mouth.

"Hmm," she said. "You eat."

After struggling through half the plate, and with Madame Trung busy barking orders in the dining room and noting he was no longer the center of attention in the kitchen, Travis pulled out his phone and texted

Muerce. He typed, purposely, in caps: FYI. MT SEZ SAMMY SIC. NOT AT SL.

— —

Muerce's phone beeped to alert him he had a text message. It was from Travis. It gave Muerce pause for concern. *Sammy is never sick, he thought.*

As he contemplated what could be wrong with Pho Mat, banjo music interrupted Muerce's train of thought, announcing an in-coming call. The area code was from Washington, D.C., though Muerce didn't recognize the number. Usually, he'd let such calls roll to voicemail, but he decided to chance taking it. It might get his mind off Pho Mat, and the macabre photographs of dead women that surrounded him.

"Hello," Muerce said.

"Jack, it's Benedict Pope."

"The Great and Wonderful Oz."

"I'm in town."

"How about dinner?"

"Can't. How about a late drink?"

"Sure."

"Something out of the way."

"Easy," Muerce said. Saigon Laundry was out of the question. "Place called O'Keeffe's. It's a cop bar. That out of the way enough?"

"Perfect."

"Need a ride?"

"Got one."

"What time?"

"Ten too late for you, old man?"

"I'll take a nap and up my meds," Muerce said. There was a chuckle at the other end of the call.

"See you then, buddy."

"Looking forward to it," Muerce said, ending the call. It was either going to be a very late night with Pope in town, or a very short one.

— —

"You want another?" Madame Trung said, offering the bottle of Barrollo to Muerce.

"No thank you," Muerce said, covering his glass with his hand. "I have to meet someone later."

"You pick at food tonight," she said. "You no like?"

"No, it's very good," he said. "Just distracted."

Madame Trung turned when Muerce stopped her.

"How's Sammy doing?" he said. "Feeling any better?"

"Sick," she said. "My son take care of him. He be better, soon."

"Anything I can do for Sammy?"

"You be careful," she said, hesitating for a beat. "Not get bug Sammy got. My son have too. You hear me, you be careful."

"*Oui, Madame*," Muerce said.

It was quiet enough that Muerce could hear Madame Trung's slippers slide across the floor. The sound reminded Muerce of sand blowing through stiff sea grass at the beach. It was the sound of time running away before a big storm approached the shore.

CHAPTER 26

O'Keeffe's was busy. It was, after all, the kick-off week that culminated with Saint Patrick's Day. Muerce told the cute girl dressed in an outrageously short, green-plaid kilt and tight white blouse tied off at her waist that he was expecting a friend, and that he'd wait at the bar until a booth was available. You didn't tip at O'Keeffe's, but a wink could get you a booth if you were a regular.

Muerce settled into a stool at the end of the bar. He'd had a glass of the exceptional Barrollo with dinner, and wanted to pace himself for the night, and the drive home. He ordered a 7-Up with a slice of lemon. Muerce saw the refrigerator and freezer tucked behind the bar under the elaborate mirror-backed display of liquor bottles. The refrigerator/freezer was glass fronted, and he could see a bottle of Stoli gently resting, waiting for his order. He would wait until Pope arrived. Muerce swiveled around to scan the crowd. It was mostly young professionals, and mostly not cops. Fifty-one weeks out of the year O'Keeffe's was a hang out for cops, and for the stream of young men and women from Ireland fleeing—as many of their ancestors did—their home country in search of jobs. The Celtic Tiger ceased roaring by 2007. Five years later, it was a homeless feline living off scraps from the European Union to stave off another famine; its highly educated offspring streaming out of Dublin Airport to take teaching jobs in Russia or Australia, or to hang dry-wall in the United States.

Tonight, it was the party crowd, sprinkled with a few faces Muerce recognized. The evening shift change at Cop Central was four hours ago, and these guys were hammered. Their wives had given them either the night, or the rest of their lives, off to celebrate St. Patrick's. Knowing the faces and personalities that slouched their way back and forth from the bar and the bathroom, Muerce knew that for most of them home life was automatically deducted from their monthly paychecks.

A familiar voice made Muerce swivel back toward the bar. He looked at his watch. The News at Ten had started. Muerce's, and the rest of the eyes at O'Keeffe's, looked up at the large-screen TV to see a haggard, but determined Kinson sitting down behind a forest of microphones. Camera flashes exploded in his face, but Kinson was patient, and waited to speak. A voice-over explained that the press conference occurred earlier in the day, but with baseball spring training not yet in full swing, the NBA season as boring as it could be, and the NHL essentially the Greatest No-show on Ice, Kinson's press conference was the top sports story of the day.

What came next was not unexpected to Muerce. Kinson, with his wife sitting next to him as a show of support, confessed to the world that he used drugs on a recreational basis, but considered himself a drug addict just the same. He said the attitude that got him into drugs off the field dictated his "appalling behavior" on the field. He went on to say that he was entering treatment on his own, but had asked the team for the press conference so he could apologize to his fellow teammates, coaches, the front office, the owner, and especially to the team's sponsors. It was at that point, Kinson broke down. His wife draped her arm over his massive shoulders, and wiped tears from his face, then hers. It was a moment that would be replayed on sports shows for months to come. Kinson recovered quickly, and pulled up both sleeves of a taupe cardigan sweater, exposing his forearms and the infamous tattoos. He said that it was nearly impossible for a black man to have them removed, but he would have the latest in laser technology do what could be done to erase "my embarrassment." What was left—likely keloid scars and discoloration of his skin—would, he said, be a lifetime reminder to "be a good man." Kinson pointed to each tattoo and said aloud the name of the player associated with it, and issued an apology to each man. He also told them that it wasn't enough to do what he was doing on television, "at a distance from a true apology, and honest request for forgiveness." He would, he told the assembled reporters, after he completed rehab, seek out those men for a face-to-face meeting, if they agreed to one.

"Quite an act of contrition," Terry, the barman said. "For a shine."

He looked at Muerce, whose disgust was obvious, as was the look of O'Keeffe's owner, Padraig, who was standing next to Terry.

"What do you want Muerce?" Terry said.

"For you not to be such a racist asshole, Terry," Muerce said. "And for Mister O'Keeffe to take my order for the rest of the night."

"Fook all Tarry," Padraig said in a lilting brogue. He pointed to the far end of the bar where the cheap drunks congregated. "Take the other end now, boy."

Padraig slapped the back of Terry's head with a wet bar towel as he crossed in front of him toward the far end of the bar, and the soupy eyed regulars who paid in change.

"That fooking shine puts butts in the seats hare every Sunday daring the season," Padraig said as Terry passed. "The customers don't want to be haring your racial boo-shit. Now piss off, and get ta work."

Padraig threw the bar towel into a hamper, and grabbed a clean one. Working at a pub in Limerick, Padraig had learned early on that a towel-wrapped fist helped prevent injuries to himself, and to customers when a fight broke out. Saint Patrick's was just days away. O'Keeffe's had doubled its weekly order for bar towels.

"Wive's sister's kid's fooking coosin by marriage, twice removed," Padraig said, wiping down the area next to Muerce. "Family, what are you going to do? You need anything, Jack?"

"Just waiting on someone," Muerce said. "But you know what I want."

Padraig leaned back to look under the bar. Among the small bottles of onions, Maraschino cherries and bitters was one filled with blue cheese stuffed olives.

"All set for you," he said.

After a commercial break, the News at Ten returned with a live shot of a reporter in front of Police Headquarters. The story was about the investigation into "what appears to be" a string of murders in the city that "authorities are hesitant to describe as the work of a serial killer."

Muerce felt a tap on his shoulder.

"What's your theory, Jack?"

Benedict Pope was standing behind him. Jack stood up and they shook hands, then embraced in a hug.

"About what?"

Pope pointed to the television screen, which flashed police mug shots of the first two victims, and a glamor shot of the third that had been pulled from the victim's Facebook page.

"That I need a real drink," Muerce said, holding up his nearly empty glass of 7-Up.

"Whatever you're having," Pope said. "Think we can get a booth?"

Muerce spotted an empty booth by the juke box, and waved to the waitress who was seating people to see if they could grab it. She winked back at Muerce, smiled and nodded her approval. Muerce turned to Padraig, who was drawing a pint of Guinness, pointed to the booth and held up two fingers. Padraig nodded back.

The two of them settled into the booth. They had not seen each other in several years, though they kept in contact by e-mail, Christmas cards and occasional phone calls. The usual updates were made between them, mostly about Pope's wife and kids. Muerce had little to fill in on a personal level. Eleanor was doing well. That was about it.

Benedict Pope and Jack Muerce were classmates in undergraduate. They crewed together, and belonged to the same finishing club. Both of them stayed on to attend law school, were in the same study group, and lived together as three-Ls in an apartment that had a nice view of the Charles, and the Citgo sign across the river. After law school, Muerce went home. Pope went into the government; first at the Justice Department; then the FBI; and the last Muerce heard, he was deputy director of something-or-other with Homeland Security.

Another young, cute waitress with a skimpy kilt, pretty legs and Gaelic lilt arrived at the booth with their cocktails.

"I always wondered why Mr. O'Keeffe kept these glasses in the fridge," she said, placing each in front of the two men. "Not much call for high-end drinks around here. My name's Afric. Will you be needing anything else at the moment?"

"No, darling," Muerce said. "We're covered for now."

Muerce couldn't take his eyes off her as she walked away. Pope shook his head. *Same old Jack.*

Pope raised his cocktail, and they toasted each other without exchanging words. Pope took a sip, and closed his eyes to savor the smoky flavor.

"God, I'd forgotten how good these are," Pope said, swirling the olives. "Who was it that turned us on to these? The torts professor? What was his name?"

"No, Intellectual Property," Muerce said, taking his second sip. "Woollsey."

"Right," Pope said. "Olives balance ounces, and the twist keeps you honest."

They laughed, and ate the first of the olives.

"So, Jack, how's your investigation going?" Pope said.

Muerce didn't flinch. He took another sip and looked Pope straight in the eye. Muerce's lips were flat. His concentration and demeanor serious, as if he were about to propose marriage to a woman, or play a bluff at the poker table.

"I haven't any idea what you're talking about, Ben," he said. "Enlighten me."

Pope wasn't about to ask for a call yet. Not before he got Muerce to raise the ante.

"The murders," Pope said, looking directly at Muerce as he took two generous sips from the martini glass, and another olive. "They've yet to come up with a catchy headline name for them, but they will. So tell me what you think."

"I really don't know much about them," Muerce said. He hesitated before chewing on his second olive.

"Really?" Pope said. He was down to his last olive and ounce of the cocktail. The final sip was the best. The scotch had settled to the bottom with the bits of blue cheese that found their way from their olive encasement. And there was that penultimate, lovely layer of ice cold vodka that preceded the scotch closer.

"Really," Muerce said.

Pope finished his cocktail, and downed the remaining olive.

"Then I suppose you know nothing about a Travis Squire hacking into the FBI's files using a computer bought by you, on a pretty highly secure wireless network paid for by you, and surfing through confidential files and e-mails," Pope said. "Not to mention breeching Interpol, and a slew of other law enforcement and government agencies."

And there was the twist, presented by Pope on the the end of a cocktail spike he dropped with a light clink into his empty glass.

"Well, I don't much use my law degree anymore anyway," Muerce said. "Promise me you'll bring a carton of cigarettes when you visit me in prison? I'll need them for trade."

Pope laughed.

"So I'm not walking out of here with government issue bracelets?" Muerce said.

"You could," Pope said. "But you're not. Favor for a favor, Jack."

"Squire is my responsibility," Muerce said. "He was doing what I told him to do."

"He'll be under my umbrella, but under your direction," Pope said. "Ask me if you need information. But only *you* ask. He stays off the net, and out the loop with me. Better for him. Besides, from what he's looked at already, I think you have all the information you need from our end."

"Fair enough," Muerce said. "So what's the favor?"

"The kind that's like a bad STD," Pope said. "It'll keep popping up at the most inconvenient times, long after you think you're cured."

"Nothing I don't already live with now," Muerce said, finishing his martini. "I never could get rid of you."

"So what are you infecting me with?"

Muerce twirled his cocktail spike before popping the last of his olives into his mouth.

"Keep doing what you're doing," Pope said. "Minus the computer hacking."

"And what is it that I'm doing?"

"Quite unofficially, so I'm told, you're the brainstorming outside consultant on the investigation," Pope said.

"What's your interest in them?" Muerce said. "I don't think whoever's behind them is the least bit interested in taking down the entire country. Just their own little sick piece of it."

Pope removed a mini smart-pad from inside his jacket, and maneuvered is fingers across the screen. He turned it so Muerce could see the images of two men who were obviously East Indian.

"Seen these guys before?" Pope said.

"No," Muerce said. "I don't think so."

There was a familiarity to them that he could not place.

"Sure you have, Jack, think harder," Pope said. His finger scrolled to the next picture sequence. "Maybe this will help. Seen him before?"

It was a grainy picture that had been taken from a distance, then enlarged to show just a face. It was Zajak.

"Brankovic's guy, his accountant, I think," Muerce said. "You want Brankovic?"

"We're not interested in Brankovic," Pope said. He scrolled back to the first image of the two men. "I want them."

Muerce looked closer, and made the connection after seeing the picture of Zajak.

"Don't know them, but saw them at dinner with Zajak," Muerce said, trying to remember when.

"At Saigon Laundry a little over a week ago," Pope said.

"You tailing me?" Muerce said.

"No, you just happened to be there," Pope said. "That got my attention. Then the hits on Brankovic in the system."

"Didn't talk to him that night," Muerce said. "I only met him the week before. Squire, Travis, was in some trouble with a low-life. Gambling debts. I was doing a favor for his father. He's the..."

"Yeah, yeah, we know who he is," Pope said. "We know all about the kid. Off the chart SATs, by the way. Way better than you and me."

That's the first thing about this conversation that doesn't surprise me, Muerce thought.

"That's really all I know," Muerce said. "Honestly, Ben, Zajak comes across as a sniveling *apparatchik* for Brankovic."

"Exactly what he, and the others, want Brankovic to think," Pope said.

"So he's a front?"

"No, Brankovic is the front," Pope said. "He's a brutal, sadistic thug of a front. A war criminal, in fact. In some circles, he's a diplomatic and policy embarrassment. The Milosevic affair. But that's a different story, and way out of bounds for this conversation. Brankovic's just a cut out."

"Do you think he's the killer?" Muerce said.

"Yes, uh, no," Pope said. "Sorry, confused there for a second. He's used to killing on a large scale. These murders would be like appetizers. I don't know. Maybe he misses it, and this is all he can get. It's not like genocide is an everyday opportunity. These murders look like his signature. The Soviet guys miss the old days. So do the Serbs, I guess. It's not what it used to be. He's not what he used to be. His glory is in the past. He has no army, no troops. Only pimps and hookers follow his orders now."

"So?" Muerce said.

"Not to be callous, but we don't really care about the killings," Pope said. "Here's the landscape. My world. Post Nine-Eleven, the guys at the bureau are focused on finding the psychopath who wants to kill a couple thousand people with a suitcase bomb, not the psychopath who wants to kill ten with a knife and a needle.

"They haven't got the resources. The cops might get some help on the lab front, but even then, under the best of circumstances, it takes weeks for the Bureau to process any forensic evidence. Right now, Hollywood's the only place tracking down serial killers with any vigor."

"So where do I fit in?" Muerce said. "I don't see the favor."

"Like I said," Pope said. "Just keep doing what you're doing. Keep an eye on Zajak, and let me know if these two guys show up again. That's it."

"That's it?"

"For now."

Pope looked at the time on his watch. It was a green, plastic Timex of a military design.

"What happened to your Rolex?" Muerce said.

"Ha, sold it so I could buy a mini-van," Pope said.

"Aren't you like a GS fourteen million or something?" Muerce said.

"Have you looked at the cost of college lately, Jack?" Pope said.

"Why would I do that?" he said.

"Come on, there has to be a knock-off Jack Muerce running around the world somewhere, right?"

"So I'm buying the drinks" Muerce said.

"Yup."

"Another round?"

"Nope," Pope said. "Got a plane to catch. I'm wheels up in twenty minutes."

Twenty minutes? The Pope sure ain't flying commercial, Muerce thought.

"Can I ask where you're off to, and how I get ahold of you if anything pops up? And do I need to keep my shades drawn? Listen for clicks on the phone?"

"New Delhi. You've got my cell. No and no. I don't care who you're screwing. Just as long as it isn't me."

Muerce stood up with Pope to leave. One drink was enough. He dropped two twenties on the table. Then put down another ten.

"I wouldn't *fuck* you," Muerce said, halting. "No, really, I wouldn't *fuck* you. You're too ugly."

"Same line you used in college," Pope said. "You ever going to grow up?"

"Why?" Muerce said. "So I can drive a mini-van?"

They walked outside O'Keeffe's where a black Chevy Suburban with dark tinted, bullet-proof windows waited. A young guy whose suit fit his muscular body like a glove exited the front passenger door, and opened the back passenger door for Pope. Muerce could see a second Suburban waiting fifty feet behind them, its window cracked just enough to allow the muzzle of a gun to pass, if needed.

Pope turned to shake Muerce's hand.

"By the way, I sold the mini-van," he said, waving his hand in the air at the SUV. "Keep in touch, Jack."

The two SUVs sped away, and Muerce found himself standing alone in front of the bar. In the distance a siren wailed, and there was the rumbling of a bus as it pulled away from a corner stop. The wind had picked up, and was blowing from the south. It was the first warm air of spring.

Muerce checked his phone. He had three text messages, and he read them in the order they had been sent.

The first was from Eleanor: Basket delightfully inappropriate. Love.

The second was from Ashley: Flowers amazing. Thnx. Vry bz. Tlk sn. Ash.

Ashley's text seemed distant. Muerce thought he might be losing his touch, but at the same time, not having a woman underfoot was best. It wasn't as if they were in a relationship. They'd slept together twice, but hadn't been on a date. Saturday night didn't really count. It was a pre-planned hook-up, nothing more. Muerce let it go. *She'll call if she calls.*

The third text was from Miriam, and lifted his spirits: Srri. Pls call.

Muerce looked at the time stamp of her text, and the time on his phone. He had put it on silence before dinner, and forgotten to take it off. Her text was sent a little after nine. It was now quarter to eleven. Too late. He'd call in the morning. He went through his contacts, selected Travis' number and called.

"Hello," Travis said.

"Listen, don't talk," Muerce said. "Don't use the computer at all. I'll explain in the morning. Eight. Coffee. Saigon Laundry."

"Got it," Travis said.

Muerce ended the call, and walked across the street to the Mercedes. As he pulled away from the curb to head home, the headlights of another car parked a block away came to life, and followed him.

CHAPTER 27

Pho Mat followed Muerce home from the bar, circling the block once before pulling into a parking lot behind the apartment building across the street. He had taken an efficiency studio apartment on short-term lease. It was on the seventh floor of a twelve-story building, giving him a slightly higher but almost direct line of sight into Muerce's sixth-floor, penthouse apartment. Pho Mat's view let him know when Muerce was home, who was coming and going from the building, and what, if anything, was happening on the roof.

When he was in the temporary apartment, Pho Mat never turned the lights on except in the bathroom, and then only when the door was closed. There was little in the way of amenities in the place. He needed little. There were the basics for hygiene—all stored in the bathroom—a coffee pot, cup, two pounds of ground *Trung Nguyen*, a roll-up mat for sleeping, and his perch. Positioned five feet from the window was a large, heavily worn overstuffed chair, and a pair of binoculars. The chair came with the apartment.

For more than a week, when he wasn't following Muerce around town, Pho Mat sat patiently for hours, unseen in the darkness, away from the window. He would sit, on guard, on the top of the chair, his feet on the armrests. He would stay on station until Colonel Trung dismissed him from his duty.

The two apartment buildings were not located among the seven hills of the city. They were in a no-man's land between downtown and the Canary Street neighborhoods. It was known as the Linwood Plain. Eighty years earlier it had been among the best places to live. Close to downtown, the harbor, and the city's arts and entertainment districts, the Plain was populated with some of the best examples of Art Deco architecture in the country—mostly in the auspices of elaborate apartment buildings. They were castles unto themselves, with gated, private parks that lent an air of exclusivity, as well as fortification, from the outside world.

Time had worn on the area. The brick and limestone stanchions that had once been connected with elaborate, wrought iron barricades, and had walled in the sweeping green lawns and tall elms of the various apartment buildings, now stood alone, crumbling and helpless. The iron barriers had either rusted to splinters, or had been stolen and sold for scrap. The lawns were overgrown and weedy. The elms died off by the 1960s, when Dutch Elm disease ravaged them, much as White Flight had the area.

Despite some gentrification in the past two decades since Muerce bought the apartment building, the Plain remained an anonymous part of town. Muerce liked that about the area. Not many people ventured to the Plain just to drop by and say hello. If you wanted to, you could disappear. Even if you didn't want to, you could disappear.

Pho Mat locked his car and was halfway between it and the rear entrance of the building when he realized he was not alone. Once a glamourous address, the apartment building had long ago been converted to low-income housing. The water, heat and electricity in the building was maintained, but little else was. Other than door locks, there were no other security measures to the structure. The light coming through the wire reinforced glass of the back door of the building was the only illumination in the parking area. Pho Mat knew he could be at his watch in less than three minutes, and verify by the lights that went on in Muerce's apartment that his subject was home. He did not want to waste time with any non-essential interactions, and picked up the loping pace of his journey to the back door of the building.

There was the smell of rain in the air that Pho Mat felt in his bad leg, which he now stretched in a longer stride to loosen the muscles and ligaments as best he could. His senses became more acute to his surroundings. He knew where the door was but did not look directly at it so his eyes could be more adapted to the darkness of the parking lot. He shifted his head several times, looking to see what was lying on the ground, next to the wall, near the trash bins, or against cars. He began flexing his fingers, and slowing his breathing. Pho Mat listened as he walked, not for any sound he made, but those made by others.

A light breeze rustled the tops of the barren scrub trees that lined the far side of the parking lot. They made a scratching noise as the branches jostled with each other.

The sounds of nature were broken by the whistling of an object as it flew through the air, then crashed and splintered ahead of Pho Mat. Broken shards of an empty pint bottle settled on the asphalt.

"Hey, little man," a voice said.

Pho Mat did not stop to answer.

"I said hey motherfucker!"

Pho Mat was not going to stop until he saw the shadow of a man partially block the light in front of the door that led into the building. His escape cut off, Pho mat stopped. He could hear the soft crunch of footsteps against the broken asphalt of the parking lot approach behind him. There were two men. Their footsteps were heavy. One set shuffled. Pho Mat identified the other set as slower, and probably more inebriated than the other. The shadow by the door did not move. As he turned to face the two men coming from behind, Pho Mat saw a length of pipe lying next to the trash bin among a pile of wood and plaster that had been ripped from one of the apartments.

Pho Mat was not interested in either what these men had to say, or what they wanted. He did not want to waste any time with them.

"What you want?" Pho Mat said.

They were young, probably in their early twenties, but street life made them look much older. They were black, though the one who shuffled when he walked was lighter skinned. They stopped several feet from Pho Mat.

"What do I want?" the larger and darker of the two men said, gesturing with his hands as if he were on stage, and also to impress his colleagues. It was his way of letting everyone involved in what was about to happen know who was in charge.

"Check it out, the little Korean motherfucker wants to know what *I* want."

"Not Korea, Vietnam," Pho Mat said. He was losing his patience.

"Well excuse me you little gook, slant-eyed motherfucker," the man said, again waving his arms dramatically in an effort to show his dominance.

"I old man, not want trouble," Pho Mat said. "You want money, I have ten dollar."

"Ten dollah, ten dollah," the man said, mocking Pho Mat. "He got ten dollah. Motherfucking ten dollah."

The taunting ended abruptly, and the man took a step closer to Pho Mat.

"What I wanted was your money, but now I want your respect you little yellow turd," he said.

Enough time had been wasted with the men. At first, they were keeping him from his duties. Now they were a threat. In one fluid motion, Pho Mat crouched down on his left leg—the good one—reached to the ground with his left arm, and balanced his weight with his hand and foot while he swiveled and bent his right leg to center. Pho Mat shot his right foot out, extending the leg like a piston, and slammed it into the man's left knee. There was a crunch and a popping noise as the man's leg inverted backwards, sending him to his one good knee. The pain from the injury would cause most men to pass out, but the booze buffered that reaction. It did not, however, alleviate the man's extreme distress, and he began howling like a suffering dog. The man's cries were such that Pho Mat was concerned that attention might arise, and the police called, so he rose from his stance, and fisted the man's larynx to quiet him. What had been a high-pitched wail subsided into a softer, gurgling and gasping sound. The man was suffering, but he did so with less drama.

The lighter skin man next to him froze, but Pho Mat heard fast approaching steps coming from behind. His weight still on his good leg, Pho Mat cartwheeled toward the dumpster and, despite some soreness from the kick, managed to stabilize himself on his bad leg. At the same time, he grabbed the half-inch pipe. It was three to four-feet long.

Stepping away from the trash bin to clear any obstruction, Pho Mat twirled the pipe like it was a baton. The open ends of the pipe made a whistling sound similar to the pint bottle that had been thrown at him. The twirling stopped when Pho Mat was in the proper defensive position. The shadow that had been standing by the back door did not stop, and Pho Mat reacted. He wanted to neutralize his second attacker much faster than the first. He rotated the pipe into high speed, then feigned a strike to the man's leg.

The new attacker saw what had happened to his partner's knee, and reacted instinctively by juking to his left, and putting both arms down for protection. The move left his head an open target that Pho Mat used the opposite end of the pipe to strike. Pho Mat stepped aside as a matador would in the ring, and the man, unconscious, was propelled into the trash bin by his momentum. There was a loud bang as the man's body collided into the metal wall of the bin.

Pho Mat did not wish to linger. He retrieved his keys from his pocket, walked to the door, unlocked it, and went inside the building. The light-skinned man had run away after the punch to the throat of his friend. That man continued to cough and sputter as he crawled—one handed—through the broken glass of the pint bottle, cutting himself as he went. He would live. So would the man lying next to the trash bin.

Two minutes later, Pho Mat was peering through the binoculars. The lights were on in Muerce's living room. Then they came on in the bedroom. Pho Mat was relieved. Muerce was safely home. Pho Mat closed his eyes. He focused internally, and took in a deep breath that he slowly exhaled. His eyes still closed, he massaged the soreness in his bad leg, and smiled. *You don't fuck with Pho Mat.*

CHAPTER 28

The sheets were warm from their bodies. They had lay in bed together most of the night, listening to the wind blow outside between tasting each other; there was the pleasure they felt in that, and the sounds and smells that accompanied their lovemaking. They were at the point of the night where they were delightfully exhausted, and the sweetest effort was in the exchange of words.

Massimo was in love. It had happened easily, like it always did. The flirtatious look, the seductive body language, the invitation, and the assignation. They had been with each other several times in the past two weeks. Massimo felt like they had been together forever. He would do anything to keep hold of their time together. He closed his eyes and fixed on the smell of his lover, who exuded a musty, sandalwood odor that became more potent when their bodies sweat against each other as theirs had. The fragrance they made when they were entwined reminded Massimo of church, and sin. He felt the stirrings in his groin start to tingle again.

"You are so beautiful," he said. He ran his hand across breast and ribs before resting it on the sharp rise of a hip bone.

"You are too," Price said, turning and raising himself up onto his elbow, and kissing Massimo on the lips. "Tell me more."

"About how beautiful you are?" Massimo said.

"Yes, but no," Price said. "About Jack Muerce. Then more about me."

"I've already told you," Massimo said, stroking Price's bangs from his forehead.

"Yes, yes," Price said, looking away from Massimo with a pouty and indifferent affect. "That this Brankovic creature is muscling in on Tino's business, but his, what did you call him, lieutenant?"

Massimo nodded that Price remembered correctly.

"Brankovic's lieutenant and Tino are conspiring to push him out of the way, with Muerce's help. But how, again?"

"Those murders we saw on TV," Massimo said. "Brankovic's a sick fuck. A really sick fuck, that cuts people up, then sews them back together. Tino said this Zajak guy says he did it all the time back in the war."

"Which war?" Price said.

"The Bosnian thing," Massimo said. "Of course, nobody remembers that since the rag heads drove the planes into the towers. Ancient history, like Vietnam or the Civil War."

"You've seen him do this?" Price said.

"No, and I don't want to," Massimo said. "The guy was charged with war crimes. But then he was let go. No evidence. But Tino says Zajak says there were plenty of witnesses. Still are, I guess. Word is he chopped some pimp's hand off last week, too. Sick fuck."

"Do you think he's the one?" Price said.

"Hell yes," Massimo said. "He should get the death penalty just for looking that way. Did you see the guy at the club?"

"At the club?" Price said. "The Unicorn?"

"Yeah," Massimo said. "The night we first talked to each other. Don't you remember?"

"Of course, silly, I'd been trying to get the courage up to talk to you for months, but I wasn't sure... about you," Price said, giving Massimo a longing look. "But I don't remember this Brankovic person. No, not at all. And the way you described him, I don't ever want to meet him."

Massimo pondered the ceiling, recalling the event at Club Unicorn. "No, you're right, it was your sister who did," he said.

"And Muerce was there?" Price said.

"Yes, I've told you," Massimo said. "There was some kind of run-in with Brankovic, and one of his girls. And there was a kid with Muerce."

"Ah, yes, the southern boy, I know him," Price said, playing back the run-in between Muerce and Paige, and his intervention, though unnecessary. *Sister's way of showing affection.*

"You do?" Massimo said. Price detected some jealousy in Massimo's words, which he knew he could use to his advantage in the future, but not tonight. He wanted to know more about Muerce, and Tino's plans for him.

"No, not like that," Price said, caressing Massimo's chest. "We were at prep school together. So what's Muerce like?"

"He's an arrogant, rich prick," Massimo said, but with very little conviction.

"That sounded more like envy than hate," Price said. "Do you want to be Jack Muerce?"

Massimo laughed out loud, falling backward onto the mattress so he lay on his back. His head sank into the pillows as he stared at the ceiling. "Everybody wants to be Jack Muerce," he said.

"Do you?" Price said.

"I wouldn't mind holding all his money," Massimo said. "But I wouldn't want to hold his burdens. No. I don't want to be Jack Muerce. Not at all."

"Mmm, burdens, that sounds delicious," Price said, moving closer to Massimo, and whispering in his ear. "Tell me, tell me."

"Once you drill down past all the bullshit, Muerce's a stand up guy," Massimo said. "He's class. He does what he says he's going to do. There's the widows and orphans, for sure. But he's helped a lot of people out. A lot."

"The gift of mercy," Price said, cuddling Massimo to encourage his talking further. "Does he really hand out cards?"

"Yeah," Massimo said, his memory taking him back in time.

"Have you ever seen one?"

"I've got one," Massimo said.

Price almost jumped up on the bed with excitement.

"You do?" he said. "Jack Muerce owes you a favor?"

"Other way around, my sweet."

Price settled himself back down. He could see suspicion in Massimo's face, and he wanted to draw out more information before the night was over.

"You look so sad," he said, caressing Massimo's face. "I don't want you to be sad, my love. Would it help to talk about it? You know you can trust me with secrets. You already do."

Tino was tolerant when it came to the sexual preferences of his clients and, to a lesser extent, his employees. As long as it didn't hurt either his reputation, or business, whatever you did was fine. Just keep it off the street; don't make it a public lifestyle. Still, in the culture and community Tino and Massimo were raised, homosexuality remained taboo. It was aberrant, and it was against Church teachings. Massimo could handle the wrath of Tino—he did it every day—but he would never risk shame on his family. It was a burden he would take to his grave. Massimo would rather face God when the time came, and ask for His mercy and forgiveness. He would also, when that time came, ask the Almighty why He made him the way He did.

"There was someone who I was in love with," Massimo said. "It seems like a long time ago now. We were in love, but we weren't lovers. He was my guide to this life. He was older, mature, and I was young and confused. He was kind and patient. Introduced me to others, like us. He had these great parties, and everything was discreet."

Massimo turned and looked at Price from his toes to his head, halting his admiration at his face.

"You remind me of those times," he said. "The beauty of youth."

"And what happened?" Price said.

"It fades," Massimo said. "He got sick."

"He had it?"

"Yes," Massimo said, the sadness welling up. "It was when it was a plague. That's hard to understand now. When the sores started, everyone abandoned him. He lost his business, his friends, everything. It was terrible. A different world. Some hospitals wouldn't even take him. Doctors and nurses wouldn't treat him. Hippocratic oath, bullshit for sure."

"So, what happened?" Price said.

"I was still just a street punk, muscle," Massimo said. "Tino hadn't taken over his old man's territory yet. Young Turks. Busting our asses for the Capos. I was doing shakedowns and enforcement along Canary. You hear shit. So I hear about this guy helping out the people that own the laundry. Somehow the place is off limits to my line of work. That came down from the made guys. You know made guys?"

"Yes, I've seen the movies," Price said.

"Well, anything comes down from them like that, I figure it's pretty special. Like they got a piece. But they don't, and it's not like it's a hangout for those guys, or something. I figure, this guy can get things done. Quietly. I was a mess. I'd didn't know what else to do. I didn't have any money, and I sure as shit couldn't turn to the crew I ran with and say, 'Hey, fellas, I'm a faggot and my fag friend has AIDs, and needs help.' That wasn't going to happen."

"So what did?" Price said.

"I go in the place," Massimo said. "It was before there was a restaurant. There's Muerce all suited up like he's going to a board meeting, or something, sitting at a little table in the corner of the laundromat, drinking coffee and reading the paper."

"And?"

"And, right away you know you can trust the guy. I spilled my guts. He listens. No judgmental looks. No smart ass fag comments. Like it's no big deal what was going on. Says to come with him down the street. I follow. We go up to a run down house and knock on the door. Some wiry, white trash guy answers. Muerce introduces himself, but not me. Tells the guy we'll be waiting down the street. If he's not out of the apartment in the next ten minutes we'll be back; if he ever smacks his wife or kids again, we'll be back; if he ever shows up again, at all, we'll be back."

"What happened?"

"By the time we were on the sidewalk, we see the guy running out the back door with a trash bag full of his shit, jumps into a beat up Plymouth Duster, and bolts out of there. I'm getting a chuckle out of it, and Muerce whips out a little notebook, and asks for my friend's name and address. Then he hands me his card and says what just happened was a test. He never says it, but you just know that you owe. Then he says, 'What's between *us*, is between *us*.'"

"And your friend?" Price said.

"The Sisters of Mercy have a convent outside of town where they used to make communion wafers," Massimo said. "He gets set up there that night. They took really good care of him. They let me visit once a week. By my fourth visit the nuns were taking care of more like him. Two months later, it's a fully operational AIDs hospice. No more communion wafers. These sisters had a real mission. Pissed the Bishop off big time, but he never did anything about it. They were fully funded by a private donor. The Bishop figures he looks better if he acted out of compassion over AIDS, than condemnation. Rome made him a fucking Cardinal for it."

"And your friend?"

"There was no fifth visit."

"So the Sisters of Mercy are the Sisters of Muerce," Price said. "He's quite the Messiah."

"What's all this interest in him anyway?" Massimo said.

"Jealous?"

"Of him with you?" Massimo said. "Not in the least."

"Sister has developed quite a desire for him," Price said. "I'm very protective of her, you know."

"Your sister's fucking crazy," Massimo said. "That night at the club I thought I was going to have to slug her. She had a knife out, looking for trouble. And.."

She was looking right at Muerce.

Before Massimo could finish the sentence, Price had a firm grip on his scrotum, tightly squeezing the sack. The shock and pain left Massimo helpless, and confused.

"Never say that about her again," Price said. His words hissed malevolence as he jerked Massimo's package away from his body, and squeezed tighter. "Do you understand me? Never."

The pain made Massimo want to vomit. He could feel Price's nails slice into the delicate skin around his testicles as he struggled to breath.

"So we understand each other," Price said, pressing his mouth and face next to Massimo's. "You are the slave, and I am the master. That's what's between *us*."

Price eased his hold on Massimo, to allow a response. Massimo sucked in as much air as he could, closed his eyes in submission, and nodded his agreement to the dynamic of their relationship. He was in love, and if Price wanted it rough he would submit, and never mention Paige's name again.

"You're finished for the night," Price said. "But I'm not. Now roll over on your stomach, and be as quiet as possible."

— —

As she walked toward the stove, the naked young girl was unsteady. Her knees felt like they would buckle with each step she took across the cold brick floor. The bruises swelling on her buttocks and the backs of her legs ached with every movement. Her head was pounding. She had not been given any narcotics for several hours, and the pang of need was building in her. The shaking and nausea would start soon. She had never taken the drugs willingly before, but now she wished their effect so she could forget what she had just been through.

The floor was cold, but it was hot in the room. Still, she shivered as she passed the man sitting in the chair in front of the stove; his eyes blazed at her when she glanced at him. Averting her look, she bowed her head toward her feet. The searing pain between her legs had subsided to a mild burning sensation. As she approached the blazing window of the stove she noticed a distinct wet tingling on her leg. She looked down to see a trail of blood and semen streaking her thigh. When she bent down to get a small shovel full of coal, a large clot of the discharge dripped to the floor.

"Clean yourself with dirty bed linens," the man said. "Then make bed with fresh ones you were given. Then make tea."

"Da, Zmaj," she said, her voice cracked with fear. She burned her hand on the door latch as she opened the stove, then tossed two shovels of coal into the fire. A wave of the super-charged heat from the stove lashed out, blowing her long hair over her shoulders, and exposing the bite marks the man had made. She wished she could fit through the opening of the stove. If she could, she would jump in so the fire could cleanse her of her shame, and end the misery of the life she knew awaited her after tonight. Her hand was scalded a second time when she closed the latch.

Stripping the bed of the soiled sheets, the girl made a sad assessment of her situation. She had been promised a new life in America. She was to be a nanny for a rich family. They would pay for her to go to school. All the arrangements had been made for her. She was given money to buy a train ticket to Warsaw, and for food for the trip. She would be met at the station by a man who would help her; only she had to leave that night or the opportunity would be lost forever. She could contact her family as soon as she got to Warsaw. She would be given her own mobile phone. She could call her family, and friends anytime she wanted. She had always wanted her own phone; a pink one with the big screen. The older girls all had them. The man who made the offer was a friend of her cousin. She knew his family. She could trust him.

But he lied. The man who met her at the train station in Warsaw told her her new mobile phone was at the apartment where she would stay before she would board a plane for America. So were her passport and papers. He said she must be hungry from the trip, and he took her to eat. They went to a McDonald's near the station so she could get used to American food. It was clean and bright, though the food tasted strange to her. As she finished her soft drink she began to feel very tired. She wanted to sleep. The man took her to the apartment to rest. There was no phone. Only fuzzy dreams.

The days after that were black ones. She dreamt she was handcuffed to a bed in a room that rocked back and forth all the time. There were other girls around her. The rocking made her and the others sick sometimes. In the dream someone cleaned and fed them. The same was true for their bathroom needs. Then she woke up in America, a drug addict. She needed her medicine twice a day. Sometimes it was a pill. Sometimes it was something she would have to smoke. Sometimes she was injected by a needle with it. She also learned how to inhale her medicine through her nose. She found she did not need to eat or sleep as much, or did she care to keep herself clean.

A man with gold teeth who called himself Deluxe told her to start taking care of herself. He asked if she had ever been with a man, she cried, and said no. Deluxe said that was good. She would be special. "But after the Dragon," he said. "You will have to earn."

She was made to bathe, and an older girl dressed in pink and black, showed her how to fix her hair in a new way: and how to apply makeup. There were new clothes for her. She looked at herself in the mirror. She was pretty, and looked older though she did not feel older.

This night, she was told she would be given to the Dragon. *It was an honor.* He would have her as a woman. As a young girl, she had idealized what sex was supposed to be when you were in love, but not what it would be like when you lay with a beast. He took her in many different ways; ways that she did not think were possible, or natural. It went on for a long time. She thought she was to be ripped apart by him; that he would devour her. She tried not to look him in the face because it was that of a monster. While he tore at her flesh with his teeth, hands and loins, he did not put his mouth on hers. There was relief in that because his breath was the most foul she had ever smelled. It reeked of sulphur, and feces. She gagged the first time he breathed on her, and buried her face in the sheets as much as she could.

Now it was over. She would have to *earn* for Deluxe. The young girl made the bed. She cleaned herself as best she could with the stained bed linens, then dressed. As she made tea by the stove on the far wall of the room she took in the place where the Dragon lived.

The darkness when she first arrived hid the size of the space. She remembered Deluxe drove through factory gates. There was a sign—the name of the factory—with big letters that said A C M E. She did not recognize the word after the letters. It was in English. They went past a large building where the windows glowed from what had to be a large fire inside, and there was a strong scent of burnt earth. Surrounding that building were several other small structures—some made of rippled metal—they passed until they reached the one where the Dragon lived. The building appeared derelict except for a plume of white smoke that looked like steam licking at the sky from the top of a tall, brick smokestack. There were no lights outside, and few windows. A large man in a black, leather coat stood guard at the door. He told Deluxe to wait in the car with the engine and lights off. Deluxe handed her and an envelope and fresh bed sheets over to the man. That seemed so far away, now. She was different. Changed. She would be for the rest of her life.

"Tea," she said, her hand unsteady as she offered the cup to the Dragon, who sat in the chair by the stove. He had been fidgeting with something in his lap that she now saw. He motioned her to put the tea on the table next to him, and come around to the front of the chair. When she did he held up what had taken his attention away from her in the bed. She gasped.

It was the most beautiful embroidery she had ever seen. She guessed it was the breast piece of what would become a peasant blouse like her grandmother used to wear. But this work was far more intricate, and colorful than what she had ever seen before.

"Do you like?" the Dragon said.

"Da, Zmaj," she said. "It is very wonderful."

He reached down below the table, and produced a brown paper bag that he handed to her.

"Open," he said.

In the package was a finished peasant blouse, adorned with embroidered motifs of animals, flowers and maidens. It was the most exquisite thing anyone had ever given her.

"Is for you," he said. "Means you have been with me. You belong to Dragon. Respect from other girls. Understand?"

"Da," she said, afraid to disagree with him though she was unsure of his meaning. She hesitated briefly, but felt, with the gift of the blouse, she could ask him a question. "Can you tell me what day this is?"

He pondered her question for a reason behind it, but he did not care.

"The thirteenth of March," he said.

Brankovic settled back into his chair, and turned on the television. She stood silently, holding the blouse to her body, running her fingers against the fine stitching, thinking in disbelief, that such work could be done by the hands of a monster. Brankovic flipped through the channels with the TV remote control before landing on the News at Ten. He watched as the reporter's words were translated into closed captions at the bottom of the screen. The screen expanded with a photograph of Redzil. It was a police mug shot. In it, she wore a peasant blouse decorated with embroidery.

"You, go, now," he said. "Tell man at door to come."

She hurried to get her coat. She slipped the awkward high heels on, and gingerly made her way to the door with the hope she did not fall and twist her ankle.

"Wait," the Dragon shouted. Her heart fell to her stomach as he got up from his chair and walked toward her.

"What is your name?" he said.

"Misha," she said. "My name is Misha."

"Misha," he said, standing in front of her. "What is your birthday?"

"In two weeks," she said.

"No," he said. "Today is your birthday. Like wedding. Da?"

"Da, Zmaj," she said, without looking at him directly.

"Little Misha to be eyes of Dragon," he said. "Da?"

"Da."

He bent toward her, putting his face near hers. He could smell her fear as he moved from one cheek to the other. She clamped her eyes shut, and held the air in her lungs tight.

"Never lie to Dragon," he said.

Misha squeaked out that she understood, and pursed her lips in anticipation of a strike.

"Man with gold teeth, calls himself Deluxe," he said. "You watch for me. Only tell Dragon what man does, who man sees. Da?"

"Da."

"Now go," he said, grabbing the wrist of her hand that held the blouse. "Don't forget meaning of gift."

Outside, she told the man standing guard he had been summoned. When he shut the door behind him, Misha experienced the first, although fleeting, idea of freedom she had since getting on the train for Warsaw. The cool air smelled cleaner, and there were stars twinkling beyond the fast moving clouds. She wanted to run, and keep running, but her shoes would not take her far, and there was nowhere to go. She was alone, and she belonged to the Dragon. If she did run, he would find her. The fantasy of escape ended when a car engine came to life, and the lights flashed at her from across the lot. As she made her way to the car, Misha was determined of two things: she would be the eyes of the Dragon; and today was never going to be her birthday. In two weeks, she would turn fifteen.

— —

Brankovic sipped tea in front of the stove, watching the television. The black bar of words at the bottom of the picture identified Redzil as the first victim of a string of murders. It said she was seventeen. Brankovic did not care that she was dead, or how old she was. What interested him the most was that she was the mother of a three-month old baby boy.

"All good boss?" the man who guarded the door said.

"Da, all good," Brankovic said. "Did weekly takes all arrive?"

"Yes, boss," the man said. "All on time."

"No problems from the Italian?"

"None boss."

"Good," Brankovic said. "Call Zajak, tell him we go over books tomorrow. Also, tell him I have special errand for him. Need lawyer."

"Yes, boss."

"Also, I not trust Mikal," Brankovic said. "Flashy. Big mouth. This girl tonight. Misha. She watch him for us."

"Yes, boss."

"Now go."

Brankovic searched for more news channels with the story about Redzil. He sipped his tea, looked over at the newly made bed, and counted backwards twelve months before reaching for a cigarette. Grabbing the engraved sterling silver lighter from the table next to him, Brankovic flipped it on and off, igniting and extinguishing the flame over and over, as he had as a child when it was first given to him in the orphanage.

CHAPTER 29

In Byzantine Greek the word *souda* means fortress, or stronghold. Knowledge, in the Middle Ages—that period of noble darkness that blanketed Europe between ancient times and the Renaissance—was synonymous with power. Great castles were built to protect that power from what was seen by those who ruled within their walls as the eventual destruction of facts rendered by God if they were allowed to be freely interpreted by outsiders. Those who did not adhere to their code of beliefs were the unbelievers—infidels.

As such, in the 10th Century, an encyclopedia of knowledge was compiled and named the *Souda*. In it, the Acheron River in Greece—both the actual body of water and the mythology that developed around it—is described as, "a place of healing, not a place of punishment, cleansing the sins of humans."

It was from this passage Dr. Sharron derived the name for his life's work—The Acheron Institute. There, using his knowledge and skills as a physician, he performed miracles of healing for those who suffered from grotesque hair lips and disfiguring wounds of war, and for those who—more often and lucratively for the Institute—were agonized by low-self esteem. They found renewal through breast augmentation, rhinoplasty and regular injections of Botox.

Much to his displeasure, Dr. Sharron was given the nickname *The Transformer*. He preferred to think of himself capable of more God-like qualities than that of an animated cartoon character; he possessed the ability to alter human flesh from imperfect form given by God or the actions of man. Though he may not be able to resurrect life from death, he did have the power to manipulate its exterior in a way that had a profound effect on his patients' psyche, and quality of life. Within his hands, he believed, rest absolution.

Four centuries after the *Souda* was written, Dante Alighieri penned his *Inferno*, in which he took a different view of the Acheron. For Dante, it was the river that borders Hell, and across which souls are ferried to Hades. Another four centuries later, Sigmund Freud found intellectual sustenance from the waters of the Acheron, which he considered to be the psychological underworld beneath the conscious mind. In the opening dedication of *The Interpretation of Dreams*, Freud used a Latin quote that translates, "If I cannot deflect the will of Heaven, I shall move Hell."

Architecturally, the Acheron Institute was a modern masterpiece designed by a renowned German architect, who gave the structure balance and life despite its unorthodox shape. The building was circular and somewhat oblong, and was at its most narrow at its base. From there it subtly expanded laterally each story it gained in height until the structure was widest at the third floor. From the fourth to the fifth floor the building sloped sharply inward. The few windows there were were randomly located, and at alternating heights; the little glass there was was dark and provided views from the inside out, but none from the outside in. The facade of the building undulated and curved in subtle, rounded variants, and was clad in durable synthetic, white coating that glistened regardless of the weather. From the aesthetic standpoint of the public the Institute was commonly referred to as the *Brain Building*.

Structurally, the Institute sat atop the ground, or main floor, which was a quarter-acre in size and, from both an engineering and operational perspective, provided support to the soaring edifice above. The ground floor was the body of the Institute. It was where the surgical pre-operation, operation and post-operation facilities were located, as well as the administrative and custodial activities. The staff called it the *Bunker*, but not within earshot of Dr. Sharron.

If not for the oval-shaped entrance to the Institute accessed from street level, a passersby would think the building sat atop a grass-covered hill appointed with low trees, shrubs and various floral plantings. Upon entering the Institute under the lush, turf pediment, patients passed through the Bhodi Ayurveda Center. Dr. Sharron often referred to it as the *bazaar of potions and lotions*—concoctions of herbal remedies mixed with regimens of diet and exercise practiced in India for thousands of years. In Sanskrit, Ayurveda means knowledge of life. For the Institute's purposes, it provided a calming ambience of sights and smells, physical and mental relaxation through massage, yoga and meditation, and had profound marketing appeal to most of the Institute's upscale constituency. It was a spiritual *wow factor* Dr. Sharron wanted for the Institute that projected a soft metaphysical experience of mystical medicine to temper the cold, sharp steel of the scalpel and bleak, sterile landscape of the operating rooms.

While passing through the cosmic crystal of the Bhodi Center—the name an homage to the tree under which The Buddha experienced enlightenment—served to settle and sooth, the Institute's reception area was designed to expand and prepare. A receptionist dressed in a stylish medical uniform stood behind a half-moon teak registration desk—there was no sitting for the Institute's staff; all work, all the time, for which they were paid generously. Behind the registration desk was a circular pedestal four feet high, and clad in teak from its base to its lip. Contained in the pedestal, which had the circumference of a backyard trampoline, was a reflection pool. At five points that formed a circle, a single flame danced on the water. Each of the flickering points of light was fed by a line of natural gas to torches fashioned from stainless steel, and formed to look like lotus leaves floating on the serene surface. Anchored within the five flaming lotuses, and rising two floors from the reception area, was a barren stainless steel tree by the artist and sculptor Roxy Paine. It was titled *Absolution*.

The work's brightly polished branches spread upward and outward into the Institute's atrium, before ending in the sharp spikes of a crown of thorns. The twisting limbs of the sculpture spiraled in every direction, snaking off under and over each other as they reached toward the only source of light in the building—an opaque, circular eye of glass panes designed in the shape of a pentacle, and situated in a false ceiling on the fourth floor. Above it was a small courtyard on the fifth story of the building, which opened to the sky at the cranium of the building.

The architect referred to the source of natural light for the atrium as "the third eye", which was a focus of amusement by the Institute's staff because Dr. Sharron often took his meals in the rooftop courtyard. They felt he was always watching them though the skylight was not transparent. He generally took most of his meals in the courtyard. The fourth and fifth floors of the Institute were the private residence for himself, and his two children, Price and Paige.

It was, for Dr. Sharron, a sanctuary of balance between earthly desires, and divine enlightenment. *A life's work.* The Institute embodied everything he wanted to accomplish—*almost* everything. He was devout, and prayed daily for the direction to complete his purpose. For his devotion, he believed, his prayers were always answered by God, and before those of others. As an anointed, he found purity in impurity, right from wrong, and deliverance from evil; though he be led into temptation, he was forgiven his trespasses.

The tips of his manicured fingers rested on his forehead, thumbs crossed and cradling the rosary beads that gently rocked back and forth in the air; the suspended crucifix swaying like a pendulum as he whispered each prayer in sequence. The polished concrete floor of the courtyard made his knees ache and throb as his lips pursed through an agonizing Our Father. It was through excruciating discomfort—even that of others—he was directed. Suffering without meaning was just suffering, and Dr. Sharron did not subscribe to unnecessary suffering. Applied with skill, pain was a guiding light that could train and educate both the teacher and the pupil. It was the disinfectant for an unclean soul.

As he grimaced through the last cycle of the rosary, Dr. Sharron's meditation was interrupted when Price, dressed in a white silk robe that was open, exposing his nakedness, entered the courtyard. Dr. Sharron, still in prayer, gave notice with his eyes. Price, too, gave notice, and sashayed so his penis swayed from side to side, keeping time with the swinging rosary. Dr. Sharron closed eyes and mind to the mockery, and continued his prayers.

Aside from the loosened drapery of the robe, Price wore a pair of disposable surgical slippers Institute patients were given before procedures. To accentuate the rustling sound they made when he walked, and to cause further irritation, Price slid his feet across the hard surface before stopping in front of the surgical cart that had fresh coffee, assorted fruits and yogurt. He poured the coffee from the carafe into a mug in a way that mimicked urination, causing the liquid to splatter onto his robe and the floor.

"Oops, I had an accident," Price said, pronouncing the words as if he were an innocent child.

Dr. Sharron finished praying the rosary, rose from his knees and looked disapprovingly at Price with silence before making his way toward the trolly. Price situated himself in one of the padded patio chairs and drank his coffee; his legs splayed open and robe falling to his sides. From the cart, Dr. Sharron removed a small tray with hot water, a honey pot, lemon slices, assorted tea bags, a cup and saucer, and sat down at the glass-topped breakfast table across from Price. Dr. Sharron tapped a spoon on the tray to get Price's attention. The disenchantment was visible in Dr. Sharron's eyes as he locked them on Price, who matched the stare. With calm deliberateness, and without blinking his focus from Price, Dr. Sharron proceeded to pour the hot water into his cup, stopping precisely a quarter inch from the rim. He dipped the tea bag into the cup to steep, added honey from the honey pot, and squeezed a slice of lemon—the procedure was flawless, without drips or an errant squirt, and performed as if the surgeon were blindfolded.

After removing the tea bag, and giving the cup three swirls with the spoon, which he then tapped against the saucer to announce he was done, Dr. Sharron broke eye contact with Price, and sipped the brew.

"You can show some modicum of decency," he said. His voice was calm and flat. "We can expect my scheduling nurse any time. I have a busy day."

"Too busy even for me, Father?" Price said.

Dr. Sharron sipped his tea with feigned indifference.

"I have something you want," Price said. He stood up, again exposing himself, and slid his way to the cart to freshen his coffee. This time he poured without the urinary affectation, and turned around to face Dr. Sharron. "Oh, heavens, not that."

Price put the coffee on the cart, wrapped the robe closed and tied off the sash around his waist.

"You're pressing my patience," Dr. Sharron said.

Price returned to the chair, and slumped down in it.

"I've been a good boy and fetched, as you asked," Price said. "It seems some very bad people are very interested in Mister Muerce. Present company aside."

"Go on," Dr. Sharron said, ignoring the last remark.

"It seems these bad people want to leverage him," Price said. "Well, at least his reputation for benevolence and honor. He is cloaked in quite the lore. So genteel, and a very handsome man, if I do say so, not that he has any interest in me. He's very conventional that way."

"It's not his interest in you that interests me," Dr. Sharron said.

"Mmm, Sister?" Price said. "Vetting her suitors, are we? Or just jealous?"

"According to who?" Dr. Sharron said, getting up and making his way toward the cart where he began squeezing several different melons in a large bowl.

"Sibling intuition," Price said. "It's a twin thing. But you know about that yourself, don't you?"

"Muerce, please," Dr. Sharron said.

"Ah, of course, focus," Price said. "According to who? According to my inside man. He's very enamored of me, you know. In love, I'd say, and under my thumb. Jealous now?"

"Their desire for Mister Muerce?" Dr. Sharron said, still fussing over the melons.

"Greed, I gather," Price said. "The swarthy Italian is in cahoots with the Slav."

"I don't understand," Dr. Sharron said.

"The Tomaso person who runs the club I like so much," Price said. "Titty Boy. That's his gangster name, you know. Quaint, isn't it?"

"That Unicorn place," Dr. Sharron said.

"May not be your style, but yes," Price said. "The horrid person I told you about before—Brankovic—has muscled in on the trade in drugs, gambling and prostitution, and the boy of tits is not happy about it."

"And your source..." Dr. Sharron said.

"Tomaso's right hand man, even though he's left handed," Price said. "Unnecessary detail. Anyway, he says Brankovic's own man is looking to extract himself from his employer, and establish a business of his own with no interest in Tomaso's product line."

"And how do they plan to accomplish this with Mr. Muerce's help?" Dr. Sharron said. Interested in a particular melon, Dr. Sharron held it up, and *flicked* and *thumped* at it several times with his finger to test for ripeness.

"I assume you've heard about the murders, it's been in the news," Price said. He bent sideways for a better look at Dr. Sharron's reaction. "Very gruesome."

"Murder is a daily occurrence in the city," Dr. Sharron said, contemplating the melon in his hand. "Unavoidable, I'm afraid. The tariff of sin. What have they to do with Muerce?"

"Well, Tomaso and company are under the impression Mr. Muerce has an interest in them," Price said.

Dr. Sharron, wheeled around and looked at Price with an expression of intent curiosity.

"Really, how so?" he said.

The reaction caught Price by surprise, and made him hesitant.

"They believe Brankovic is the killer," Price said, looking for a reaction.

"Based on what?" Dr. Sharron said. With his free hand he picked up a large knife from a tray next to the basket of fruit and tapped it on the melon, producing a dull *thud* that pleased Dr. Sharron.

"Old habits," Price said, almost stuttering. "He likes to cut things up. People. A butcher of sorts. Torturer. Something about war crimes. Bosnia. And..."

"And what?" Dr. Sharron said. He brought the melon, knife and a small surgical tray over to the table, and sat down across from Price.

"Sometimes he'd sew the pieces... the people... back together," Price said.

"Like the murders?" Dr. Sharron said.

"Yes."

"And having Muerce point the finger at this Brankovic fellow lends credibility to their accusation, and would remove the obstacle for their own immoral endeavors," Dr. Sharron said. "Yes, given his reputation, he would serve their purpose quite well. If there be guilt."

"If?" Price said.

"Truth, for someone like Mister Muerce, is a virtue," Dr. Sharron said. "He would have to believe Brankovic to be the killer. Once that were established, he would not recoil from thine enemy... and would make war without cessation, and without mercy."

Dr. Sharron swung the knife in the air and brought it down with force upon the melon, splitting the cantaloupe in two, and startling Price.

"I see his usefulness more clearly now," Dr. Sharron said. *God has answered me.*

"Why your interest in Muerce?" Price said.

"Absolution," Dr. Sharron said. He peeled back the plastic cover from a hermetically sealed surgical scalpel, and held the blade to the light. "Lent is the season for penitence and fasting. We suffer. Then we are saved. Reborn. Washed clean of our sins."

"Some sins are *never* forgiven," Price said.

After quartering the melon with the large knife and removing the seeds, Dr. Sharron wielded the scalpel. With meticulous and fluid incisions the fruit was sliced and sectioned as if rendering flesh from bone.

"Careful now," Dr. Sharron said. "You wouldn't want me to cut you off."

"From the family?" Price said. "And what a special one it is. Our little dynamic."

"The price we pay for our sins," Dr. Sharron said.

"And Price never stops paying, does he?" Price said, upset. "Remember, *Father*, you may be *our* provider, but I am *her* protector. You're jealous. That's what's behind your interest in Muerce."

"What about Muerce?" Paige said.

"Brother was just saying you are enamored of him," Dr. Sharron said. "Another school girl crush?"

Paige, who wore a robe identical to Price's but no slippers, frowned at Price with displeasure.

"He was being his insistent self," Price said.

"Merely curious," Dr. Sharron said. "I don't wish to meddle in your private lives."

"That would be a first," Paige said. She poured herself a cup of coffee before turning to face Price. "And you, Brutus?"

"Come Caesar, take my slippers," Price said, pushing his slippers off of his feet, and sliding them in front of him. He gestured for Paige to join him by patting his lap with childlike delight. "You look a chill your Highness, come let me warm you."

Paige huffed, throwing back two large gulps of coffee as she sauntered toward Price, the top of her robe open, exposing her breasts. They exchanged kisses on each other's foreheads after she pushed her feet into his slippers and sat in his lap. Paige bent her head closer to Price's and whispered in his ear.

"Where were you last night?" she said.

"With the Minotaur," he whispered. "On a mission from God over there regarding your Mister Muerce."

"Lay with beasts, Brother, you will get fleas," she said, aloud.

Paige was unhappy Price had been tasked to check up on her, but she managed to keep her displeasure to a severe look and a few sharp words. She shot her head up and stared at Dr. Sharron with daggers until her gaze broke his concentration on the dissection of the melon.

"Have you found, Father, a insect whose wings you can tear off?" she said.

Dr. Sharron smiled at Paige, skewered the last bite of melon with the scalpel, and ate it.

"Just craving something sweet, dearest," he said.

"Do you find Muerce sweet?" Paige said.

"From what I know of him I find him to be a bit of a fool," Dr. Sharron said. "One who appears to follow some antiquated code of rules, and is predisposed to favor the fancy of young women, such as yourself. So not just a fool, a lecherous fool; old enough to be your father."

"But he would be a rich, handsome father, Father," Paige said. "Do you not wish your progeny to marry well... Brother and I each betrothed to a Prince."

Paige turned her face to Price with a wide-eyed comical look that caused the two of them to erupt into laughter.

"But only I get to wear Vera Wang," Price said.

Dr. Sharron was patient as his two children had their fun at his expense. He sat back in his chair, folded his hands across his medical frock, and contemplated Paige and her open robe as she giggled. She had the same look as her mother when she laughed, which was seldom, and almost always, as did Paige, at his expense.

"How are you feeling Sister?" Dr. Sharron said.

The comment caught Paige off guard, and caused Price to become rigid with concern.

"I feel fine," Paige said. She uneasily anticipated what might be said next.

"How has your sleep been?" Dr. Sharron said. "Any aches or pains."

"The same," Paige said. There was a hesitation in her voice that Dr. Sharron was looking for. "Why?"

"I noticed your shoulders are more stooped," he said. "Are you favoring your spine?"

"No, I feel fine," she said.

"She says she's fine," Price said. "Leave her alone."

"You haven't been doing your exercises," Dr. Sharron said.

"Because I'm fine," she said.

"Because they hurt, more," Dr. Sharron said. "Don't they?"

"Because I'm lazy," she said.

"Come, let me see," Dr. Sharron said, beckoning her with his hand.

Paige and Price looked into each other's eyes with trepidation, then hers became watery. The expression on her face was if she were asking permission of Price, and then there was the resignation.

"He knows best," Price said, caressing the hair that fell across her face. "Don't worry. I'm here."

Reluctantly, Paige unseated herself from Price's lap, and walked over to Dr. Sharron. Emotionally detached, she stood in front of him as he nodded his head at her in a command she understood well. She turned her back to him, untied the sash of her robe, and let the cover fall to the floor. Her skin reacted not to the cool air that touched her naked body, but to the delicate fingers probing her back.

Starting at the nape of her neck, he traced down each side of her spinal column, pausing at four separate points that were marked by delicate scars. He did this several times, massaging various areas on each side of her backbone for an indication he did not find. When he moved from one spot to another without comment, Paige and Price looked at each other with relief. Dr. Sharron's fingertips settled on the tail of Paige's spine, which was absent any scar. He pressed and prodded for several minutes before making a low humming noise.

"What is it?" Paige said. It was a blurted out with alarm. Price rose quickly and made a step toward Paige before he was stopped by a a raised hand from Dr. Sharron.

"I'm not sure," Dr. Sharron said.

"But there's something?" Paige said. "You found something?"

"I'm sure it's nothing," Dr. Sharron said, continuing to manipulate the area around her tailbone.

Panicked, Price disregarded the order for him to stay where he was, and came over to see for himself.

"Show me," he said. "What did you find? What? Anything?"

"I don't think you're qualified," Dr. Sharron said, settling back in his chair.

Price placed his hand in the spot on his sister's back that was in question, and pressed.

"I don't feel anything," he said.

"You don't know what you're looking for," Dr. Sharron said.

Stooping to the floor, Price picked up Paige's robe and helped her put it back on.

"Maybe we should get a second opinion?" he said. There was an accusatory tone in his voice as he looked at Dr. Sharron.

"Ridiculous," Dr. Sharron said. "When Misses Robbins comes up with the surgery schedule for today I'll have her set an MRI appointment for Sister. If there is something there it's small, and we can take care of it right away, here."

Paige was shaky, and stared off at the far wall. Dr. Sharron rose and put his arms around her, holding her stiff body as close to him as she would allow.

"Don't worry Sister," he said. "We'll take care of it, like we always do." He turned to Price. "She needs some rest now. It will be fine."

"I'm fine," Paige said. "I'll be fine. I'm always fine. Just fine. Stop touching me."

Price put his arm around Paige to lead her away.

"It's nothing," he said. "I know it's nothing. Don't worry. Brother will watch out for you. I promise."

As they were about to pass through the sliding glass doors leading into the living area, Dr. Sharron stopped them.

"Oh, you two might wish to go out tonight," he said. "We're running the incinerator. The weekly burn. I know how it bothers you, but it's been busy, and there's quite a backlog."

The thought of the incinerator in the basement turned Price's stomach. Paige had a higher tolerance for its operation than he did. The knowledge that human fat and tissue, along with other medical waste items, was burning where he lived sickened him. Though it was a highly regulated operation that underwent routine inspections by the County Health Department and the Environmental Protection Agency, Price repeatedly pleaded with Dr. Sharron to have it done offsite, which was refused for what he was told were practical and economic factors. The compromise was to go out the nights of the incinerator operated. In recent weeks, the two of them had been going out a lot.

"Let's get dressed and go now," Price said. Paige was more steady, and appeared to regain her composure the farther they got from Dr. Sharron. "We'll make a day, and a night of it. We can go shopping, lunch, spa... what do you say?"

"Only if you tell me everything you know about Jack Muerce," Paige said. "Everything."

CHAPTER 30

The meeting with Dr. Riley left Muerce with more questions than answers. She was not, as she said from the outset, a criminal psychologist. Dr. Riley had studied criminal science as part of her psychiatric rotation during her medical training, but decided early on that it was not a field she could or would want to pursue professionally. "She saw," she said. "Few positive outcomes with such patients." And it was just "too damn depressing" and "potentially dangerous."

There was a strong tendency within the ranks of sociopaths, borderlines and malignant narcissists to demonize the very people who were trying to help them, and target them for their own special kind of Hell. What they did to the people who loved them, was usually much worse. For the afflicted, the line between love and hate, good and bad, was blurred. Personal and social boundaries were easily crossed, usually resulting in long-term emotional damage for their victims; violence, sometimes leading to death in extreme cases; and serial murders in rare instances.

Muerce mulled what he could remember from the inventory of sociopathic behaviors Dr. Riley outlined—there being no difference between a sociopath and a psychopath as the terms were interchangeable. They were disposed to social influence, stress immunity, fearlessness; were nonconformist to an almost rebellious point, externalized blame, were egocentric to Machiavellian proportions, cold hearted, and the one that made little sense to Muerce—carefree non plan-fullness.

He understood the killer he was following was anything but carefree, and he was meticulous in his planning.

Despite what was under debate in the awaited fifth revision of the Diagnostic and Statistical Manual's (DSM) classification of mental disorders, Dr. Riley subscribed to the spectrum of sociopathy developed by Vienna born Dr. Otto Kernberg. Working from a combination of a patient's case history and direct interviews, how a subject scored on Kernberg's inventory list placed them within one of three ranges of psychotic disorder. On the low range of the scale were those with narcissistic personalities, then came the malignant narcissists in the middle, followed by full-blown psychopathy at the high end.

A horn blared from the car behind Muerce. The light at the intersection had turned green. His foot was still on the brake pedal. *Fuck you, can't you see I'm thinking?*

When he pushed the accelerator down, Muerce's memory recall reengaged the conversation with Dr. Riley. Traffic light. Giving it gas. *Gaslighting.* The recall flashed in his head—projection and introjection of psychic conflicts from the perpetrator to the victim... the transference of painful and potentially painful mental conflicts. Muerce pulled at the string of the conversation still wound in his head. When gaslighted, victims would begin to doubt their perceptions, contributing to ever increasing levels of distress. It was the psychopath's roadmap of manipulation that eventually led to the victim's final destination; the "so-called" nervous breakdown—the death of their psyche.

Dr. Riley expressed surprise that the FBI's Center for the Analysis of Violent Crimes was not, from Muerce's understanding, involved in the case in any significant manner given the treatment and condition of the victims, and the strong likelihood the killer was going to act again. The pattern, she agreed with Muerce, would suggest another victim by Sunday, and one more after that. A sixth victim—based on the theory the tapestries were part of a theme for the killer—was beyond her conjecture, though there was a high probability the cycle of the artistic symbolism had significance, and could represent the crescendo event of the perpetrator's actions.

Two blocks down the avenue Muerce was again stopped for a red light, and mulling Dr. Riley's explanation of the ultimate goal of gaslighting: to get the victim to doubt their memory, perception, and sanity. Muerce was again blasted back to reality by a car horn. He looked up at the light, then into the rearview mirror. It was from the same car that honked at him before. *Wake up Jack.* There was something else in the mirror that he let slide. Two cars behind the one that honked was a Nissan four-door. It was a car that had been following him for almost a week. But that did not register with him. He pushed on the gas and accelerated through the intersection.

What was it she said? He racked his memory, visualizing his brain to be an archaic library reference file. He saw himself rifling through the cards of titles and Dewy Decimal System numbers, looking for the one that would give him all the answers. *What was it?* He almost veered into the inside lane of the three-lane avenue, but caught himself and steered back between the lines, letting the car that had honked at him pass on the outside. Something was bothering him. It was eating at him like the name of a face seen in the supermarket, on an elevator, or on the street. Familiarity without recognition. He couldn't identify what was behind the mental irritation that eluded him.

Again, Muerce's thoughts slipped back to the conversation with Dr. Riley. He could Google most of what she said, and commit it to his head permanently, but he didn't want to lose the initial introduction to the subject matter. She said sociopaths consistently breached social mores, broke laws, and exploited others. *What was the other thing?* "What was the other thing?" he said aloud. That was it. "Yes," he said, looking at himself in the rearview mirror. "Charming and convincing liars who consistently deny wrongdoing," he said. "Of course they do," he continued talking to himself. "Because they aren't doing anything wrong. They are always right. Right?" He questioned himself for the moment. *No, I'm not always right.*

The rearview mirror still bothered Muerce. When he looked at the traffic behind him there was nothing suspicious, still he fixated on the mirror, remembering the ones placed in the empty eye sockets of the latest victim. Dr. Riley wasn't sure what to make of those adornments. They appeared to be an aberration in how the killer treated, or "prepared" the bodies of his victims. The only thing she could come up with was a faint connection to narcissism. Narcissists, she had said, create strong *false selfs* to make up for the poor, and usually shame-riddled, perception they have of themselves. She compared interaction with a narcissist to talking to a mirror; you see and hear only yourself, and not the person on the other side of the reflection.

The air horn from a semitrailer pierced Muerce's ears, startling him from his thoughts, and making him jump in his seat. *Jesus!* It was then Muerce grasped what was bothering him. He'd been going at the case in the slow lane, biding his time and disinterested. He was half-assing the favor for Bhote. It was time to get into gear. A little chagrined, but mostly empowered by the epiphany, Muerce punched the gas and the engine of the Mercedes roared to life. By the next block he had sped past the car that previously honked at him, and honked back. He soared through a yellow light while fumbling with his mobile phone looking for the contact for Luther—the IT Guy. He didn't have all the answers, but he'd do his best to get to them. *Jack was back.*

He began mental box checking. Dr. Riley had thanked him for the Kinson referral, and left it at that. He'd circle back with Kinson after he completed rehab. He left a voicemail with Luther regarding the conversation and the warning about hacking from Pope, and to have the same conversation face-to-face with Travis. The text message warning last night wouldn't suffice. He'd call Bhote for any updates from his end, same with Trumbley, when he got to Saigon Laundry for lunch. The first thing he'd do, though, when he got to his table, would be to call Miriam and see if he could visit that evening.

As he sped through another yellow-turning-red light, Muerce noticed that a row of forsythia bushes fronting a house off the street were starting to bloom. There was just a hint of the bright yellow blossoms bursting on a few of the higher branches. Spring was arriving much earlier than normal.

-- --

Pho Mat thought he'd been spotted when the burgundy Mercedes that had been lackadaisically making its way through traffic suddenly bolted. Despite the strained effort of the Nissan's four-cylinder engine, he could not keep up with Muerce, who was now out of sight. He was not worried for the moment, as they were headed toward Canary Street, and Saigon Laundry was the usual destination. Pho Mat looked at his watch. It was almost lunchtime. He knew where to find Muerce. Pho Mat would park on a side street several blocks away from Muerce's route, then report to Colonel Trung. He would need another vehicle for his assignment. Today had been a good lesson. *Easy to find Muerce now, he thought, maybe not so easy in the future.* He needed a faster car to keep up with the Mercedes if there were an emergency. Colonel Trung would agree. It was a prudent precaution. For all Muerce knew, Pho Mat took the bus to and from the restaurant everyday, and probably didn't even think Pho Mat had a driver's license, let alone a car. Certainly, he wouldn't have connected the silver Nissan to him. He knew Muerce could be oblivious to the more mundane activities that went on around his everyday life, and now counted on it. To Muerce, Pho Mat was Sammy, the *major domo* at Saigon Laundry. Maybe not completely mundane, but pretty close, and that suited Pho Mat for the task at hand. Muerce knew of the relationship between Pho Mat and Colonel Trung during the war, but only on a very surface level. Colonel

Trung had opened the door only slightly to Muerce, and only recently. For Pho Mat, Cholon was never far away in his thoughts.

-- --

Luther listened to Muerce's voicemail twice, and cursed. He swiveled around in his large ergonomic chair, and began hammering away at the keyboard of one of a half dozen laptops he had up and running in his workshop. In a few keystrokes and clicks of the mouse, he had remotely accessed the laptop given to Travis for research. Luther could see Travis was busy working in an Excel spreadsheet. He was making updates to a file named Brankovic. Luther banged a few more keys and was immediately into Travis' search history. *Aha, Luther thought.* Travis hadn't followed all the protocols for clandestinely searching the FBI database, and was easily traced. Luther uploaded the history and transferred it via a backdoor connection that would bounce his activities around hundreds of unrelated servers located globally in a chain that would frustrate the best hackers, and ware the patience of anyone snooping on him. After several days of server handoffs and satellite exchanges, the trace would land in a bank of secure servers that belonged to the U.S. Postal Service. He liked the irony. Whatever went in there, would never get delivered.

Lines of code began to cascade down the computer screen. He keyed a few lines in to give the appearance Travis' snooping days were over, per Muerce's direction. He did, however, leave some gateways open for the boy, who Luther found to be very bright when it came to analytics, but he'd keep the open gateways a secret for the time being. Travis was talented, but hadn't been cautious. Eventually, Luther would have him trained. He saw real potential in Travis. Someone he might even bring to Las Vegas with him for his yearly splurge at the poker tables.

The cascade stopped abruptly at a short line of code. He cut and pasted the line into an instant message that he sent to the laptop on the far end of the long table. He took a large swig from a twenty ounce plastic bottle of Mountain Dew as he propelled himself on the rolling chair to the far end of his workspace. The instant message flashed on the computer screen, and he cut and pasted the code again, and ran it through a series of encryption software programs he had written. Before he could take another sip from the bottle the answer he was looking for popped up on the screen.

"Hello," Luther said. "My, my, we are playing with the big boys."

The line of encrypted code showed National Security Agency computers had been tasked to watch Travis' activity. Luther wheeled back to the first laptop and clicked away, entering several new lines of code where the cascade had ended. He wanted to know what Travis had done to trigger the NSA into action.

"You guys think you're so tricky," Luther said, taking another drink a soda. "But you *so* aren't, are you?"

Twenty seconds later a small line appeared. Luther repeated the cut and paste routine, and returned to the laptop on the far end. Cut, paste, run through encryption breakdown program again and *bang*, Luther had his answer. The search term "Brankovic" got their attention. As he contemplated the name, which had no meaning to him, the screen on the first laptop exploded with lines of code that dripped from page into page. The volume of data coming in set off an alarm that got Luther's attention.

Panicked at first, he quickly realized he wasn't being hacked. The NSA was, and its acres of classified, state-of-the-art mainframe servers were fighting back, furiously. He banged at the keys of the laptop to setup a series of standoff firewalls that allowed him to watch the cyber battle from a safe, and untraceable distance.

Page after page of code streamed on the computer. Some from the NSA, some from the attacker. Luther stared at the cyber swarm on the screen as the seconds turned to minutes, which was an eon for such a war. As he stared he began to see patterns in the code. Specifically, he saw a small line of code that repeated itself in evolutions. It was coming from the attacker. With a pen and paper he wrote the snippet of code down. He had seen enough and shut down his observation post. Curious, he punched in the code he had written down into the laptop on the far end, and ran it through the encryption program. The hard drive on the laptop whirred as if it were in overdrive and might explode. Then it stopped.

"Gotcha," he said.

He looked at the screen with puzzlement. Knowing does not always equate to meaning. The software was able to decode a small fragment of the information. Luther ran it through a location filter program. In less than a nanosecond a small blue screen appeared within the window on the computer with the name of the attack program, and its likely country of origin. The program was called Ganesh, and it originated from an unknown server located somewhere in India.

— —

A jet of steam screamed with furious insistence, filling the tiled room with heat and moisture. Zajak flailed at his body with fresh birch branches, opening his pores to take full advantage of the cauldron. The earthy smell and tingling sting of the sodden leaves and bark was invigorating. He sat on the highest bench to absorb more of the heat. It was mid-afternoon. The lunch crowd from the club had left. Zajak and Tomaso, who rested on the bench below, baked undisturbed. It was an excellent location for them to conduct their business. The torpid environment was hostile to modern technology. Listening devices were delicate things. While their capabilities for quality and range had become exceptional, they were still fragile, and worthless in the damp and corrosive environment of a steam bath. The steam jet settled to a hiss, leaving only the sound of an occasional water droplet falling from the ceiling. Tomaso toweled his face of sweat, and slicked back his curly, black hair. Zajak offered him a birch branch.

"No," Tomaso said. "I've had enough of a beating from you this week."

"Patience," Zajak said. "The weekly payments will soon come to an end. I am more certain of it each day. When they do, I have promised you your money back."

"With interest?" Tomaso said.

Zajak chuckled, and slapped the branch across his back.

"No," he said. "You must consider it the cost of doing business."

"You fuckers," Tomaso said. "The cost of doing business to get my business back."

"However you wish to look at it," Zajak said. "Again, I caution patience. Brankovic is satisfied, for the moment."

"Explain to me again how a hooker gets pregnant," Tomaso said. "In this day and age, really?"

"Simple," Zajak said. "She was not a prostitute when she was impregnated. Just a naive little girl, like so many where I come from, wanting a better life. Don't we all?"

"And how is this 'fortuitous' for us?" Tomaso said.

"It's the *pozzolan* we've been looking for," Zajak said. "Act of God or fate, doesn't matter. The ingredients are there. We only need to mix them the right way."

"What the fuck are you talking about?" Tomaso said.

Zajak was disappointed in Tomaso, and frowned at the Italian. He had expected more from him, but noted for future reference the man's weaknesses. Zajak leaned forward, as teacher to pupil.

"It is the difference between the Pantheon and this steam room, Mister Tomaso," Zajak said. "Look closely around you. There are new tiles and old tiles. You can see by the grout. I can spot at least a half dozen patches. Fairly recent ones, I'd say."

Tomaso did as he was instructed, and quickly spotted several patched areas. Then he recalled the steam room being down at least several days every few months for repairs, either to the pipes, or for the tiles.

"Combine calcium hydroxide with silica and you get common plaster," Zajak said, sweeping his hand around as if giving a tour of the steam room. "Throw in some silica that has trace amounts of alumina and iron oxide, and you get an empire.

"We work with what's around us. Sustainability is the popular term now. What the Roman's had around them was plenty of volcanic ash—*pozzolan*. We only need a little."

The expression on Tomaso's face told Zajak that his example had registered.

"I won't bore you with the chemical interactions that give Roman concrete its endurance," Zajak said.

"It's some strong shit," Tomaso said. "That's my people."

"Yes, 'strong shit'," Zajak said. "But aren't you of Sicilian descent?"

"Yeah, Sicilian, Italian," Tomaso said.

"Sicilian, Italian, but not Roman," Zajak said.

"They're all the same thing," Tomaso said.

A Roman, Zajak thought, would disagree. He chose not to respond, and waited for Tomaso to change the subject.

"So, let me get it straight," Tomaso said. "Brankovic's a pedophile freak. Knocks this Balkan teen queen up. She manages to pull her weight on the street—pregnant. Keeps it quiet. Who knows? She wasn't careful at first. Baby Daddy could be any of a couple hundred guys. Nine months later, out pops the kid, which she keeps—to her credit. The runt's kind of weird looking. Brankovic eventually figures it's his. Gets pissed and does one of his slice and dice jobs on her. It brings back fond memories and he cuts a few more to cover up the first one, and, well, let's face it, he just likes the rush. Meanwhile, Satan's offspring ends up with Muerce, who hands it over to welfare.

"So, boss man, what's the *pozzolan* in this?"

"I'm merely an accountant," Zajak said.

"Uh hmm, then run the numbers for me, Mister Merely an Accountant," Tomaso said.

"The child is the *pozzolan*," Zajak said. "Brankovic wants his son."

"Someone's got to take over the family business," Tomaso said. The image of his own father lying dead in the trunk of his Cadillac El Dorado flashed in front of him. "It's easy. Make a call. A quick DNA test, and Brankovic is doing a quarter to life in the Capitoline Pen for child sexual abuse. Pin the murders on him, he's got an all day and a night stretch. But for my money, he goes for a stainless steel ride."

"Brankovic must not go to prison," Zajak said. "Brankovic must die."

"And you think Jack Muerce's going to do that for us?" Tomaso said.

"Largess," Zajak said. "It's Mister Muerce's DNA. Widows and orphans."

"And how are we going to make that happen?" Tomaso said.

"As I said before," Zajak said. "We have the ingredients. We just need to mix them. Carefully. We start tomorrow."

The steam jet sputtered at first, then began screaming as it spewed its scalding vapor into the room, ending the conversation. Zajak had the recipe to bond Muerce and Brankovic together. It would help that the mason had a pretty face. *After that, he prayed, it would be the will of Allah.*

— —

Madame Trung brought a large bowl of *pho* to Muerce's table. She placed it in front of him, bowed without saying a word, and disappeared back into the kitchen. Muerce took little notice of her. He was engrossed in his cell phone, reviewing e-mails and text messages that had piled up. He stopped to look at the text message from Ashley from the night before, and debated whether he should respond to her thank you. It wasn't necessary that he did, but if he did she might interpret it as him having continued interest in her. *Maybe too much for right now.*

The pungent aroma of the *pho* wafting up from the bowl broke Muerce's concentration. He put his phone down on the linen tablecloth, and spooned the soup and some of the noodles into his mouth. It was a curry fish *pho*. *Cod, he thought.* Red pepper flakes floated on the oily surface. After the first spoonfuls, his mouth began to tingle with the spicy heat of the meal. Muerce broke a piece off the small baguette that came with the soup. It was crisp and chewy. Pieces of the crust fell into the *pho* as impromptu croutons. Muerce fished some cilantro from the bowl with his spoon, and chewed on it with his front teeth. The herb neutralized the burning in his mouth.

As he reached for the water goblet, the phone began to buzz and slowly rotate in a quarter circle on the table. The caller ID told Muerce it was okay to answer. Still, he held his breath as he touched the button to accept the call, and pressed the phone to his ear. It was Danny Turko, the last full-time city columnist for the newspaper. He was one of the few reporters with whom Muerce still had a relationship. Most of the others had left long ago. The smart ones knew the industry hit an iceberg, and found lifeboats. Others were thrown overboard by management. A select few, like Turko, were determined to go down with the ship.

"Jackie boy, it's Turko," he said.

"You calling me looking for a job?" Muerce said.

"I'm still in the game, man," Turko said. "Don't you read the paper?"

"Does anybody?" Muerce said. "Oh wait, let me get your web site up on my phone."

"You're killing me, Jack," Turko said.

"What are you looking for Turko?" Muerce said.

"Looking for what you know," Turko said.

"About what?" Muerce said.

"The Death Weaver," Turko said.

There was a long, awkward pause in the conversation. The tip of Muerce's tongue was burning. He took a sip of water that could be heard on the other end of the call.

"Got to go Danny," Muerce said.

"Talk soon, Jack," Turko said.

Muerce knew that it was only a matter of time before the media sunk its salacious teeth into the story. He told Ashley as much at the museum. Now the killer had a public name. One for the headlines. Catchy. *Definitely Turko's work.* At least the nickname wasn't directly connected to the tapestries. Not yet. For the time being, Muerce hoped, Ashley and the museum would be out of the limelight. He would talk to Turko, eventually. They both knew that. That's why Turko's response was so matter-of-fact when Muerce brushed him off.

Just when Muerce thought he was getting control he could feel it slipping away. He had bought some time with Turko. But not much. With Turko, Muerce had a new chess piece he had to account for in the game. He thought about the next move as he worked his way through the *pho.* The burn in his mouth made him think better.

Muerce picked up his phone and texted Trumbley: The Death Weaver?

With little delay, the electronic bell sound on the phone chimed to announce an incoming text message. It was from Trumbley: I know. See you tonight.

"Shit," Muerce said, loud enough that Madame Trung poked her head into the dining room to see what was wrong. *I want to talk to Miriam alone, first.*

315

CHAPTER 31

The reception desk and nurses' station in the VIP wing of the hospital was a jumble of noise and activity that Muerce floated into unnoticed.

"Excuse me," he said, getting the attention of the nurse behind the desk when she hung up the phone. "Can you direct me to Miriam Estrada's room?"

"Estrada?" the nurse said, motioning with her head over her shoulder. "You'll have to talk to Nurse Lysaught."

There were several women in various styles of nurses' scrubs standing, drinking coffee from styrofoam cups, and talking to each other. Muerce noticed two of them giving him flirtatious looks when he arrived, and hoped the cute brunette was Nurse Lysaught.

"Lonny," the seated nurse said. "This gentleman is here to see Miriam Estrada."

The muscular nurse with frizzy red hair who wore a brightly colored flower patterned outfit that clashed with just about everything and everyone in the hospital except the tattoos on her arms walked toward Muerce. In addition to the outlandish outfit, she was wearing a frown. It was obvious and unfortunate, Muerce discovered, that Nurse Lysaught was not the cute brunette. Muerce's first instinct when she made her way around the reception desk was to ready himself to take a punch.

"Who are you?" Lonny said. She gave him the once over. Expensive clothes. Trim body, decent shape. A little gray in the temples. Tall enough. Delicate hands with fingernails that haven't seen dirt under them since he was a kid. *So this is the guy?*

"A friend," Muerce said.

"What kind of friend?" she said.

"Apparently, the kind that needs either a warrant or a note from his mommy to visit," Muerce said. "Is there a problem?"

"No," Lonny said, backing down a little. "I'm in charge of Misses Estrada's care."

"I doubt that very much," Muerce said, laughing. "I've known her a damn long time, and ain't nobody in charge of Miriam, but Miriam."

Damn right, Lonny thought. This is the guy. Kind of a smart ass. Well, Miriam, I can see it. You go, girl.

Muerce thought he detected a small crack in Lonny's veneer. Still, he wasn't going to be surprised if she tried to throw a punch.

"Follow me," she said.

"You don't want to know my name?" Muerce said, trying to thaw Lonny a little.

"Guys like you all have the same name," she said, leading him down the hall to Miriam's suite. *Trouble.*

"Here you are," she said, standing in front of the door.

"Thank you," Muerce said.

Before turning to make her way back the way they came, Lonny burrowed her brow at Muerce.

"She's a tough broad," Lonny said. "But this can put anyone on their ass for a little bit. She doesn't need any grief right now. No drama. Got it?"

"We're on the same page," Muerce said. Her comment confirmed what he suspected. Lonny knew exactly who he was. *Girls talk.* Though she may not think much of him, Muerce liked Lonny. She was protective of Miriam.

Lonny nodded warily before walking off. Muerce waited until she was halfway down the hall before knocking softly on the door. He heard Miriam's voice invite him in.

When he entered, Miriam was folding and packing her suitcase. She looked surprised when she first saw him, and her face flushed with color.

"You going somewhere?" Muerce said.

"Oh, I didn't expect you so... I've got to get out of here... I mean... checking out," she said, fumbling through her words. "Wait, I didn't mean it that way. I mean, damn, I had this all thought out, and you show up early."

"Sorry," Muerce said. "I thought it best if we talked alone first, before..."

"Nick got here," she said, putting down the gown she was folding.

"Best I think," Muerce said, nodding his head a little, and squinting with one eye.

Miriam stood on the other side of the bed and exhaled loudly, letting her shoulders slump and chin dip slightly. She looked, Muerce thought, more vulnerable than the day she buried her husband as their two boys clung to her legs, terrified.

"I'm so sorry Jack," she said. "We shouldn't have... I shouldn't have... It wasn't fair to you... I should have been honest... With you... With myself... With..."

Muerce stepped quickly around the bed toward Miriam as she rambled through her broken apology and list of regrets, and put his hands on her shoulders for reassurance. In the moment, he wanted to hold her close to him in friendship, but he was hesitant to fully embrace Miriam because of her surgery.

"I'm sorry," Muerce said, looking at the hospital bed then around the room. "This wasn't fair. Not for you. Not after all you've been through."

Taking her chin in one hand, Muerce lifted Miriam's face toward his.

"But Nick is..." Muerce said, continuing. "He's a good man."

"He is," Miriam said. Her eyes softened and glistened.

"If I had known," Muerce said. "I wouldn't have."

"I only knew when this all happened," Miriam said. "It's been so... fast."

"Give yourself some time," Muerce said. "And for God's sake, don't beat yourself up. Listen, I love you, and I love the boys, and I love Nick. And I would never do or say anything to hurt any of you."

"I know," she said. She looked at Muerce appreciatively. "I need a hug."

"Can you?" Muerce said, looking to her chest.

"This is such a pain in the ass," she said. "I just need to lean into you with my shoulders."

Miriam rested herself sideways on Muerce's chest, and they both wrapped their arms around each other, swaying lightly back and forth for a quiet moment.

"Jack," Miriam said, talking into his chest. "I want you to stop beating yourself up."

"It was just dinner, Miriam," Muerce said. She pushed herself away, and playfully beat at his chest with her fists.

"I'm serious," she said. "You're a good guy, too. There's someone out there for you."

"I don't know, Miriam," he said. "You know me."

"Oh, I do, you're so frustrating," she said, throwing up her hands in mock exasperation. Muerce smiled. "I've got to finish packing."

She looked at the clock on the wall.

"Nick will be here soon," she said, folding her clothes at a faster pace than when Muerce first entered the suite. "Talk to me while I get it together."

She practically dashed into the bathroom, and Muerce could hear the clanking and clinking of cans and bottles being stuffed into assorted makeup and toiletry bags. He stuck his hands in his front trouser pockets, and walked over to the large picture window. The days were getting longer, and the faint, pink light of sunset painted the landscape outside.

"Is that that Botanical Garden?" he said. "This is a helluva view."

Miriam returned to the main room of the suite, and packed all she brought from the bathroom.

"It is, and yes, it's a helluva view," she said. "I forgot to thank you for it."

"Don't know what you're talking about," he said, still admiring the landscape spread out before him.

"Right," she said. "Nick told me you called in some favors to get this. They had to be pretty big ones."

"It was all Nick," Muerce said. "My end was nothing, really."

"Not from what I heard," she said.

"Trumbley's gaming you," Muerce said. "Classic flatfoot trick. Wants you to think he's all modest and suave by giving all the credit to someone else so he can build up trust. But he's the guy with the juice."

"*Tsk*," Miriam said. "You're gaming yourself. T.B. Squire was in here everyday checking up on me. That man acts like you parted the Red Sea."

Coming up behind Muerce, Miriam slid her arm inside of his and stood, admiring the view with him.

"I'm serious," she said. "Thank you."

"You're welcome," he said. "You can stay longer if you want."

"I'm going stir crazy here," she said. "I've stayed longer than I need to. My doctors cleared me days ago. Besides, Carlos and Miguel miss me, and I miss them. And God knows what kind of trouble they're getting into at my sister's.

"And work. Crap. There's an avalanche of paperwork sitting on my desk, and we're down four case workers because of all the budget cuts. Those kids need someone, too."

Miriam inhaled deeply. Her chest was still tight from the stitches, and she experienced a few minor pangs of pain when she stretched her lungs. But the deep breathing made her feel alive. Captivated by the late day's light, they did not hear a knock at the door.

"You can see the Japanese gardens from here," she said. "Another week or two and the cherry blossoms will be blooming. I love walking through them when that happens. When a breeze hits them it's like pink snow-flakes falling around you."

"With such an early spring we're having, there's always the chance a frost will kill the blossoms before they fully develop," a voice behind them said, surprising both Muerce and Miriam.

"Did I startle you?" Dr. Sharron said. "I suppose you didn't see me coming." He pointed at the large picture window. "My reflection," he said.

"We didn't," Muerce said. "You should make your presence known."

"Oh, my work speaks for me, Mister Muerce," Dr. Sharron said. "I must say, I'm quite surprised to find you here."

"I can say the same," Muerce said. Miriam sensed irritation in his voice, and felt his arm tense as he spoke to the doctor.

"Excuse me for the intrusion, Misses Estrada," Dr. Sharron said. "I tried to come by yesterday, but Nurse Lysaught said you were resting. I just wanted to introduce myself. I'm Doctor Merchant Sharron. I'll be doing your reconstruction."

The convent education in Miriam took over, and she walked straight-away to Dr. Sharron to shake his hand.

"Miriam Estrada, I'm pleased to meet you Doctor Sharron," she said. "How can I help you."

"It's I who am tasked with helping you," Dr. Sharron said.

"Call me Miriam," she said. "I assume the two of you have met before."

She glanced back at Muerce with a look that conveyed she expected him to behave himself.

"We have," Dr. Sharron said. "Just recently. At the opening of the new exhibit at the museum. Remarkable work, wouldn't you agree?"

"The scale is a bit dramatic for me," Muerce said. "More shop than studio. But skillful yeoman's work, I guess."

"Ah, yes, more of a post-modernist man," Dr. Sharron said. "A cultural skeptic, but one, I sense, with a moral foundation firmly rooted in the past."

Dr. Sharron turned his attention to the open, and partially packed suitcase on the bed.

"I didn't mean to interrupt," Dr. Sharron said, reaching into the pock-et of his white physician's smock. "I can see you are being discharged so I won't linger. I just wanted to introduce myself.

"Here is my card. I believe we have your contact information. My of-fice will call and schedule a preliminary consultation. Usually, we wait for these kinds of procedures for four to six months, but I think we can move that forward some, if all progresses well."

"Thank you, Doctor," Miriam said, taking the card.

"Perhaps, next week sometime," Dr. Sharron said. "For the preliminary exam."

"Yes," she said. "That would be fine." She turned to Muerce to signal he should be courteous, and shake Dr. Sharron's hand before he left. Muerce understood his orders.

"Doctor Sharron," Muerce said, extending his hand.

"Again, a delight, Mister Muerce," Dr. Sharron said, reciprocating the gesture. Muerce thought Dr. Sharron's grip that of a four-day old mackerel, flaccid and slimy. "I look forward to the opportunity to discuss art with you at greater length sometime, soon. Until then, good evening."

After leaving the suite, Dr. Sharron stopped halfway down the hallway, and checked the schedule on his electronic tablet for openings the following week. *Perfect, he thought, Friday afternoon.* The word for what he was feeling was one he rarely used, and had some difficulty recalling at first. It was a silly word, but it was accurate for the situation. The encounter with Jack Muerce was, for Dr. Sharron, serendipitous.

CHAPTER 32

T he *brioche* was just out of the oven when Madame Trung plucked a trio of them from a baking tray before the morning kitchen staff could transfer the golden pastries to a cooling rack. She placed the hot bread on a medium-sized plate with a dipping bowl of orange and lime marmalade, deliberately excluding butter as a condiment option. The *brioche* at Saigon Laundry was rich enough without the added butter cream. Carefully folding a crisp linen napkin around a set of utensils, she tucked a single violet blossom into a fold, and set the package on a serving tray next to the plate of rolls. An empty cup and saucer were added. Satisfied the serving was properly framed, she turned to the stove, and with a kitchen towel wrapped around the handle, lifted a large kettle from a back burner. The bracing aroma of fresh coffee fused with the smell of the fresh-baked *brioche* as she poured steaming water into a French press. It went on the tray after the plunger was affixed to the glass *carafe*. With her one arm, she slid the tray to the edge of the kitchen prep table, bent her knees slightly and, balancing the tray on her hand, briskly made her way to the dining area with the fluid steps of a ballerina.

Muerce was busy tapping away at his phone when breakfast arrived. He was engrossed, but took the time to look up at Madame Trung, and smile in a manner that conveyed his thanks. She smiled in return as she placed the tray on the vacant side of Muerce's table, then removed all its contents and laid them before him. Leaving him to his work, she whispered a *bonjour*.

By reflex, Muerce slowly pushed the plunger to the bottom of the carafe, and poured himself a cup of coffee without looking up from the screen of his phone. He took several sips of the dark, rich brew and let the perfume of the drink work its charms. It was only when reaching for a *brioche* he became alert and attune to his surroundings. Prodded to get ahead of the game, Muerce arrived for breakfast earlier than normal, and caught Madame Trung unprepared, which was a rarity. Muerce liked that. He also liked the *brioche* as a change up from *beignets*. Their crust was golden brown from the egg wash, and adorned with large sugar crystals. It was more confection than bread. When Muerce pulled one apart a hint of steam wafted from the two halves. He took a bite of one, savoring the delicate flavor and puffy texture. Then he dipped what remained of the portion into his coffee cup, and popped it into his mouth where it melted instantly. Onto the other half, Muerce knifed a dollop of jam. He took his time nibbling on it and the chewy citrus rinds. The tart spread complimented the rich, slightly sugary bread. With no hesitation, Muerce finished the other two *brioche* on the plate, scraping the last of the jam from the dipping bowl with his finger.

"You get fat, eat like that," Madame Trung said, arriving at Muerce's table with a plate of two more *brioche*. Muerce held up the empty jam container.

"I'll go on a diet when Lent's over," he said. "More jam, please."

The front door to the dry cleaning area opened, striking the bell above it to announce there was a customer.

"I have to cover laundry counter this morning too," Madame Trung said. "Grand-daughter has mid-terms. You wait for jam."

As she turned toward the beaded doorway leading into the central corridor of the building, Muerce raised his hand toward her back to stop her, though she could not see him.

"How is Sammy doing?" he said. She did not answer, and he returned his attention to his coffee, and the messages on his phone.

There were two municipal court hearings in his schedule over the next few days. Muerce had agreed, as a favor, to represent a teen-age girl arrested on a charge of being a minor in possession of alcohol. That was an easy fix. Her father owned a manufacturing business, and would return the favor with a healthy donation to a charity of Muerce's choice. Muerce would also ask the man to sit on the board of the charity, replacing the spot he held. He was tired of attending board meetings, and this was the last one from which he had to extract himself. The other hearing was in chambers to discuss consolidating Eleanor's numerous speeding tickets, agree on a fine to combine all the penalties, and suggest she be given community hours. The prospect of the meeting made Muerce laugh. He could get her off with just the fine. The community hours was his idea to teach her lesson. He finished another half a cup of coffee before deciding which agency would be graced with Eleanor's presence for eighty to one hundred hours. *Ma mere, indeed.* He'd ask that she be assigned to a day-care center for underprivileged children; with the infant's so she could change diapers to her heart's content. *Maybe that'll cure her.*

The bead curtain rustled, followed by the distinctive clicking of high heels as they struck the parquet floor. The cadence indicated confidence, the measurement grace, and the pattern aristocracy. Whoever approached him did so regally. Muerce counted out a two-four beat in his head before turning to see if he guessed right. He was surprised when he looked up.

"Pardon me, I was dropping my cleaning by and saw you here," Amelie said. She wore large, round black-framed Channel sunglasses. "I thought maybe I could speak with you?"

Muerce rose to his feet.

"Please, join me," he said, motioning with his hand toward the chair across the table. Amelie nodded appreciatively, and thanked Muerce as he moved behind her to hold the chair for her as she sat down. Catching Madame Trung's attention through the beads, Muerce indicated there would be a second at his table. He detailed Amelie's ensemble. She wore a smart, well-tailored dress suit; black with simple lines along the lapels and pockets, a white silk blouse with a kind of Russian collar that was clasped with two buttons that matched the fabric. The hem of the pencil dress was a hint higher than five inches above her knees. The suit, he guessed, was a Donna Karan. The shoes, black cap-toe heels, were definitely Jimmy Choo. A business professional. Not at all like the Spooky Girl he first saw at Club Unicorn. But he also knew more about her than she him. He would keep that to himself.

Muerce took his seat as Madame Trung approached. He was encouraged by her demeanor that there would not be a repeat of her last exchange when Amelie sat across from him.

"*Cafe?*" Madame Trung said, addressing Amelie. There was no greeting as they had just spoken at the dry cleaning counter.

"*Oui, cafe negro, s'il vous plait,*" Amelie said, taking her sunglasses off.

"*Bon,*" Madame Trung said, bowing before making her way toward the kitchen.

The sun was bright springtime light that flooded through the front window of the restaurant. The colonial shutters had been opened for the herbs and orchids. Amelie turned sideways to remove her jacket, and the sun reflected off the whiteness of her blouse, creating an aura around her. When she turned to look at him, and brushed the bangs of her jet black hair from her forehead, Muerce's chest constricted sharply as if the air had been sucked from them. His heart did not beat so much as pound, pumping to the point that it throbbed in his ears.

"Are you alright?" Amelie said, a look of confused concern on her face. She turned to look behind her, believing there was someone or something threatening she had not seen a moment before.

"I'm okay," he said, trying to hide the deep breath he took to calm himself.

"You look like you saw a ghost," she said.

"Your eyes," he said. "They are, unique."

"It's the light," she said.

"I've only ever seen eyes like that once before," he said. The memories beat at him like waves driven against a cliff by a gale.

"Violet?" she said.

"Yes."

"They're actually blue," Amelie said, removing a compact from her purse, and using the mirror to look at her eyes in the sunlight. "It's a question of melanin production in the irises. In the right light, they look violet."

"Genetic or congenital?" he said.

"True violet eyes only occur in rare forms of Albinism," she said. "Typically that's congenital, though there can be some genetic overlap. From what I know, mine are the result of winning the genetic lottery."

Madame Trung arrived with a fresh carafe of coffee, and a refill of the the jam Muerce requested. She placed them on the table, and looked at Amelie then the press. Amelie nodded her approval, and Madame Trung slowly pushed the plunger to the bottom of the carafe. The tray was half on the table, and the other half balanced on Madame Trung's right leg that she raised slightly as she poured Amelie's coffee. She placed the French press back on the table, tucked the serving tray underneath her arm, and politely backed away from the table. The bell on the front door announced another customer, and Madame Trung swooshed by them, and through the beaded curtain after depositing the tray on a nearby table.

"Please pardon me Mister Muerce," Amelie said, watching Madame Trung. "I thought you were a bit harsh with her when I last saw you."

"You thought I was rude?" he said.

"Yes," she said, taking a sip of her coffee.

"Pardon me," he said. "But the company you keep... can be... unpleasant."

"The company I keep is my business," she said, replacing her cup on the saucer with a loud clink. "They are who they are. But from you, I expect more."

"You sound like my mother," he said.

"Then she must be very intelligent and courteous," Amelie said. "I think I would like to meet her sometime. We would have a lot in common."

The light made Amelie's eyes appear more vibrant and purple than before, resurrecting the rapid heart beat in Muerce. His response was to look away.

"*Brioche?*" he said, pushing the plate toward her.

"No thank you," she said. "I do have a figure to watch."

Ridiculous, Muerce thought. Figure to watch? Young woman like you. Hell, you and Ashley are the same age. You're old enough to be my..."

The thought railed him. For the first time in his life, Muerce realized he was sitting across from a beautiful, smart and sophisticated woman to whom he was not sexually attracted. Quite the opposite. A protective, almost paternal feeling came over him that he was unable to grasp.

"Why are you here?" he said, abruptly.

"I was dropping my cleaning off and thought..." she said.

"Nonsense," he said, cutting her off. "I'm in here almost every morning. You've never brought your cleaning here before."

Amelie, who had the cup to her mouth, stiffened in her chair. She took a sip and returned the cup to the saucer. She folded her hands in a professional manner, and put them on the table.

"You're right, Mister Muerce," she said. "The laundry was an excuse. I came specifically to talk to you."

"All right," Muerce said, settling back into his chair. He lifted his cup to his mouth while looking directly into and past the color of her eyes. "Talk."

"It's a matter of some discretion and privacy," she said. "It concerns a child. The one you found here. The one who's mother died."

"Murdered," Muerce said. "Rather brutally."

"Yes," Amelie said, averting her eyes. "My employer, Mister Zajak, you remember. The community, Croatian community in the city, like others, is close. Mister Zajak has been in contact with someone who may have an interest in the child."

"How do you mean, interest?" Muerce said.

"This person believes they have a familial relationship with the child," she said. "They would like to explore the possibility of gaining custody."

"Custody or adoption?" Muerce said. "If they're family all they have to do it contact Child Welfare, and prove it. It's not that complicated. I can give you the name of a couple of family law attorneys that specialize in it."

"No, Mister Muerce, not adoption in the traditional sense," she said. "Or legal."

Her caginess pointed Muerce to a more exact scenario.

"So Daddy was a regular?" he said. "Probably married with a family and a good job; giving her support money on the side, maybe a little trade in return every now and then? But not enough to keep her off the streets. Doing the right thing, huh?

"Redzil, by the way that was her name, had the misfortune of running into, let's just say, a very unpleasant end. I'm sure you've seen it on the news. Now, burdened with guilt, and wanting to avoid publicity, Papa wants baby back?"

"I don't know all the details," she said, her hands remained diligently folded in front of her.

"I don't do white, black or gray market adoptions," Muerce said. "Besides, the kid is in the system. There's very little I could do even if I wanted to."

"You know the case worker?" she said.

"Yes, I do," Muerce said. "And you don't want to go there."

Pursing her lips, Amelie reached down for her black leather valise.

"Then you won't help?" she said, pulling a business card from the valise.

"No," Muerce said. "I'm sorry."

"You would be paid well," she said, sliding her card across the table. "In case you change your mind."

Muerce laughed as he picked the card up to look at it. The printed information said:

Amelie Bertrand

Chief Investment Officer

Why does a company that manufactures glass need a chief investment officer? Muerce recalled Travis' observation regarding her previous career track compared to where she was now.

The sound of Amelie scooting her chair back to leave snapped Muerce to attention, and he stood for her as she slipped her jacket on, and retrieved her valise from the table. Out of more than just politeness, he offered her his hand, which she accepted. He wanted contact with her, and when they shook he did not want to let go.

"Miss Bertrand, Amelie, what are you doing with these guys?" he said, almost clutching her hand while looking deeply into her eyes.

"My business is my business," she said, breaking the handshake.

Muerce rifled through the inside pocket of his suit coat hanging on the back of his chair as she turned to leave. The sound of her heels caused a mild panic in him.

"Wait," he said, nearly shouting. She stopped and turned as he offered her his business card.

"Really, Mister Muerce," she said. "I'm old enough to be your daughter."

"For you," he said, uncomfortable and straining to find the right words. "In case... you find... you need... a lifeboat."

When she was gone Muerce brooded over his coffee, pushing the plate of *brioche* away. He struggled to make sense of what he was feeling. Muerce had never had such a sensation around a woman before. She was, he felt, someone he needed to shield, and only he should be the one.

Amelie drove two blocks down Canary Street before calling Zajak on her Blackberry.

"How did it go?" he said.

"As you expected," she said.

"Excellent," he said. "Was there anything else?"

"No," she said.

"Come to my office as soon as you get back," he said, ending the call.

Amelie put the phone down on the console, and picked up Muerce's card. Holding it as she drove, she felt the texture of the engraving, and the sturdiness of the paper stock. Amelie tucked it away in the valise where it would be hard to find. It was just for her. She would not tell Zajak about it, as dangerous as it might be not to tell him.

CHAPTER 33

The whining sounds of air ratchets and pneumatic wrenches reverberated in the garage when Pho Mat walked through the open bay doors at the front of the building that was Diablo Racing. Inside, the smell of motor lubricants and aerosol paint made him want to hold his breath. The caustic atmosphere of the garage reminded Pho Mat why he was glad he worked at Saigon Laundry. Restaurant kitchens could be noisy and hot environments, with tempers to match, but the aromas and flavors they generated made up for any short comings.

Colonel Trung had called ahead. Pho Mat was to ask for Diablo's owner, Cong Ly van Banh, a Trung cousin. As a business owner, Cong Ly was known as Ding Banh. Diablo Racing had started out as a body shop for automotive bumps and bruises, but with the rising popularity—mostly within young Asian American urban culture—of transforming late model Japanese imports into Rice Rockets, Ding made the switch to customizing. Diablo creations were regularly featured in hot rod and racing magazines, and web sites; souped up four-cylinder engines in cars with outrageous body enhancements, and electric, sparkly flamboyant paint jobs. In the last two years, Ding's business added an export component. There was a strong demand among China's growing middle class for Ding's custom jobs.

Ding employed more than fifty people in the shop. They were mostly a mix of Mexican and Vietnamese, some of the younger employees were Asiacans. Within the shop a *patois* of Spanish, Vietnamese and Hip Hop was spoken. A cultural and visual spectrum of body art and piercings were also on display. Just below the din of the pneumatic tools and high pitch of revving engines Pho Mat could feel the repetitive thumping of

Rap music. Ding, who was approaching middle age, but looked to be in his late twenties, presented a hip and laid back appearance, but ran his shop like the Trung's operated Saigon Laundry. Behind what seemed to be the snarling chaos of the garage was an iron fist, hidden behind a smile. The tenant of *filial piety* was the backbone of Diablo Racing.

Pho Mat knocked on a grease-covered door with a sign that said "Manager's Office." Below the title was a large decal of a white elephant. He opened the door after a voice on the other side beckoned. When he entered, Pho Mat clasped his hands together, raised them to his forehead, and bowed. Ding rose from a beat up metal swivel chair and reciprocated the gesture. He offered Pho Mat coffee, which was declined. They exchanged a few pleasantries, mostly updates on the Trung and Banh families when it became clear to Ding that Pho Mat did not wish to waste time at the garage.

Ding turned his attention to a large white dry erase board that listed the makes and models of several dozen vehicles, and the status of each car. At the top of the list were automobiles nearing makeover completion. Columns on the board listed power plant, electrical, frame, body, interior, sound, paint, and other elements Pho Mat did not understand. At the bottom of the list were automobiles assigned to "Area 51", which was the razor-wire topped cyclone fence parking lot behind the garage. Ding looked at the board, then reached for the phone on the desk. He keyed the intercom, which projected his voice throughout the shop at a level that cut through the clatter.

"Quan to the office," he said. "*Di di.*"

A minute later the door to Ding's office opened. Pho Mat was confused when the name on the coveralls of the boy who walked in said Elvis instead of Quan. Pho Mat guessed the boy to be no more than eighteen from the acne on his face. Quan's greasy and stained coveralls were cutoff at the shoulders, exposing sleeves of tattoos on his arms. The words *Amor de Ray* were inked on Quan's right forearm—Love to the King. The sides of Quan's head were shaved, though he sported a four-inch pompadour that a heavy application of hair putty helped to defy gravity. A large black curl of hair adorned Quan's forehead. The boy's appearance began to make some sense to Pho Mat. What came out of his mouth, however, did not.

"*Ese*, I heard the Lurch," Quan said. "You rang, massah?"

"What are you rolling on right now?" Ding said, still looking at the board.

"Prep stripping the Yoda fodor to frame in the a.m.," Quan said. "Got motor work left on the Bishi for the after."

"Where are you on the Supra?" Ding said.

"Put all new binders and boots on yesterday," Quan said, looking at Pho Mat suspiciously. "Once the fill is dry, off to paint. Gonna hit it up with some sick cannonball. That bucket be primo when Estefan is done."

"Let's take a look," Ding said. "You got the keys?"

Quan reached into his coveralls, lifted a set of keys in the air and jangled them like they were wind chimes.

In one of the bays at the far end of the shop was a 2002 twin turbo Toyota Supra. About half of the original black paint remained, and was worn and scratched. The other half of the Supra was splotched with gray body putty that either masked dents and dings, or melded the old lines of the car into ground effects moldings that had been added to the bottom front and sides. The rear of the vehicle was adorned with a six-inch wide flying fin that reached skyward four feet higher than the roof of the car, and was more show than practical aerodynamics.

"Car work?" Pho Mat said.

"Grandfather asking me if the car work?" Quan said, looking at Ding with sarcastic disbelief. "Paint be crusty, nasty, but the bitch is the shat batch."

"What he say?" Pho Mat said, addressing Ding. "He speak English?"

"Yeah I speak En-grish, Grandpa Ho," Quan said, gesturing at Pho Mat to suggest he was ready to fight him. "And I'm standing right here. I got game, you want?"

Pho Mat dismissed Quan's childish bravado with a frown, and another quick glance back at Ding, who walked up to Quan and pulled him aside for a private conversation.

"Hip up fast Quan" Ding said. There was insistence and warning in his voice. "This man Pho Mat. You call, Sammy. He works for Trungs at Saigon Laundry. Work for Colonel Trung during war. Sammy old school. Got game you never have. He's the OG. Make BTK boys look shit. Got game like Call to Duty Five. Game you never have. You *comprende?*

Quan bobbed his head that he understood, though he didn't believe it.

"Sammy use car for awhile," Ding said. "Show him."

Shrugging his shoulders, Quan composed himself, and begrudgingly walked over to Pho Mat.

"You know how to drive a stick?" Quan said.

"Learn to drive with stick," Pho Mat said. "Citroen. Before your father born."

"Yeah, I bet you win all the Vietnamese Drag Races," Quan said.

"Quan!" Ding said. "Answer up."

"Get in," Quan said, addressing Pho Mat after bowing his head toward Ding. "I'll show you the Double-O-Seven."

Quan opened the passenger door and held it for Pho Mat, then jogged around the back of the Supra and got in the driver's side. He slipped the keys into the ignition, and the engine came to life. After revving the RPMs up several times, he turned the car off.

"The engine's all new," Quan said. "Dual fuel injectors. You can do a buck fifty, no problem."

Flipping open the console between the driver's and passenger's seat, Quan exposed a box with a red button.

"This is your NOS system," Quan said.

"What is NOS?" Pho Mat said.

"Nitrous Oxide," Quan said. "Hit the button to prime the system."

With his hand, Quan showed a line of tubing that led to a small tank bracketed in the compartment behind them. Then he brought his hand to the steering wheel.

"Hit it and you're Buzz Lightyear," Quan said, making a rocket sound. "To infinity and beyond."

"I not understand you," Pho Mat said.

"Press the button and nitrous oxide is fed into the fuel mixture," Quan said. "Big boost like kick in pants. Do a buck ninety. I don't think you'll use it."

Pho Mat understood. He liked the idea that the extra power was there if he needed it.

"Good," he said. "I take car. It have gas?"

Quan looked at the indicator on the dash board."

"Not much," he said. "It was going to paint."

"No paint," Pho Mat said, getting out of the car. "Good as is. I get gas."

The unfinished black and gray scheme of the Supra was perfect for Pho Mat's needs. It was urban camouflage. He would blend in with the other traffic, yet have the speed to keep up with Muerce, if needed. Walking around the car, Pho Mat hesitated at the spoiler attached to the rear of the Supra. It was the one element that was not discreet.

"Too much," he said. "Must remove."

"Oh, hell no," Quan said, turning to Ding. "I got love in this car. No way I'm taking it off. No way."

Ding appreciated Quan's passion for his work. Though he did not question Colonel Trung for the reason for the loaner, he also understood the look on Pho Mat's face when he watched Quan protest.

"No problem," Pho Mat said, walking over to Quan to get the keys. He stood close to Quan, calculating the boy's height in relation to the airfoil on the car. "I handle."

"Fine," Quan said, handing over the keys, and pleased he won the argument.

"I no want be seen," Pho Mat said. "I leave by alley. Have car back, I think, few weeks."

Ding nodded to Pho Mat that he was okay with the timeframe.

"Quan, get the back door," Ding said.

The sound of the Supra's engine mingled with the rattling of the pull chain Quan worked to open the large metal door at the back of the garage. It led into the alley, and an empty gravel lot that was next to the fenced car storage area.

Pho Mat reversed the Supra out of its bay and positioned it to face the door Quan was opening. When the bottom of the door reached the level of Quan's pompadour, Pho Mat gunned the Supra's engine and released the clutch causing the tires to squeal and smoke before they gripped the garage floor. Alarmed by the sound, Quan stopped pulling on the chain, and turned to look back just as the car passed by him and through the opening. The next sound Quan heard was a loud crunch as the airfoil of the Supra was decapitated. It fell to the garage floor where it rattled and swayed at Quan's feet. Pho Mat spun the Supra on the gravel ninety degrees, and, when the small cloud of dust settled, found a break in traffic, and drove away.

Ding shook his head at Quan, and grinned. He knew. *You don't fuck with Pho Mat.*

— —

A sonar *ping* resonated from Muerce's coat pocket. At Travis' suggestion, he had set up an Internet account to alert him to any news stories or web postings that related to the killings, or the three victims. He read the headline on the screen of his phone.

COPS STITCH CLUES IN CITY'S
SADISTIC DEATH WEAVER SLAYINGS

The story was bylined by Danny Turko. Muerce scrolled through the text, cursing under his breath. When he had read enough, he called Trumbley.

"Nick, Jack," he said. "Have you seen Turko's column today?"

"No," Trumbley said.

"So much for keeping a lid on Ash and Maple," Muerce said. "Apparently, CSI now stands for Can't Speak Intelligently."

"How bad is it?" Trumbley said.

Muerce read through Turko's column again.

"Not horrible," he said, glad the two errant detectives had said nothing about possible suspects, nor mentioned any direct or symbolic connection to the tapestries. As far as Muerce knew, they had yet to make any connection to the tapestries at all. He thought of Ashley and her new job at the museum. *She can take care of herself on that front.* He let the image of her naked in his bed snap through his head before refocusing on the article. Still, Muerce bemoaned, Ash and Maple talked about the condition of the victims' bodies, the mystery of the sequence of the killings, and the locations of where the remains had been found.

"But more than they should have," Muerce said.

"It's a big story now—Death Weaver," Trumbley said. "The buzz is picking up around here, too. A lot of talk of the Feds jumping in."

"That may not be a bad thing," Muerce said. They were, after all, the experts at this. But he felt invested in it now, and a little possessive.

A short silence passed between Muerce and Trumbley.

"Fixable?" Trumbley said.

Muerce mulled the situation over. Trumbley could hear him breathing into the phone.

"Possibly," Muerce said. "I can buy a little time with the news. As far as Brankovic... there might be a string I can pull on to see if anything unravels."

"I've got nothing," Trumbley said. "What do you think? Sunday?"

"Hopefully, not," Muerce said. His gut told him that a fourth victim would surface somewhere in the city early Sunday morning. At that point, he was certain, a collective panic and hysteria would take over the city and the investigation, and when that happened, any control or influence he had would be lost. He knew, if he didn't pick up the pace there was little he could do about it.

"I can't put a tail on Brankovic," Trumbley said. "Even if I knew where he was, it would have to go through Ash and Maple, who'd fuck it up."

"You can't, but I can," Muerce said. "I've got to talk to some people. I'll let you know if anything comes together."

The call clicked dead. Muerce thought about what he'd do next. He'd call Turko and set up a meeting for Saturday. For the moment, Turko was driving the story, and the other news outlets were taking his lead. If Muerce could get him to go along, he'd lure Turko into playing down the story for a few days in exchange for everything—*not quite everything*—he knew. It would buy a little time. Anything past Sunday and a fourth dismembered body, Muerce knew he wouldn't be able to manage as far as the media was concerned.

It would be a long weekend for Travis. He would be going on his first stakeout. Muerce decided to have him sit on Brankovic, but from a safe distance. Travis only need report Brankovic's comings and goings, particularly late Saturday night. No tail, just a watch. Muerce felt it would be a relatively easy assignment. First, they needed to know where Brankovic was. Muerce knew who to talk to about that, but he'd have to wait for breakfast the next day.

Was the Death Weaver really a Dragon? Muerce pondered the question before dialing Turko. Regardless of the answer, there was a beast somewhere to be slain.

CHAPTER 34

"Jock, my man," Mikal said, waving his hand toward the yellow-padded plastic bench seat across from him in the booth. "Come, sit."

Mikal was easy to find. He ate breakfast everyday at the home of the Golden Arches. Store number six hundred-sixty-six was located at the corner of Canary and Ricketts Avenue. His eatery of choice was how Mikal first acquired the street name Mickey D: aka, Deluxe; aka, Pimp Deluxe. It was also where he conducted most of his business. His girls would assemble there in the morning, and be given their assignments for pre-arranged customers, or the location of the street corners and low-rent motels they'd work. It was also the one free meal they could get for the day. Depending on how hard they worked, he might treat several of them to a late-night hamburger when he collected their daily earnings.

Four girls sat in the booth across from Mikal. Behind them were another two, applying bright orange nail polish to each other's fingers. Muerce recognized one of them as the girl who dropped Redzil's baby off at Saigon Laundry. She chatted away with the other girl, giving Muerce no notice. The four across from Mikal were mostly silent, and picked at the food in front of them with little enthusiasm. They had defeated looks on their faces, and appeared depressingly resigned to what the day would unfold for them. One of the girls, whose breakfast sandwich looked untouched in its wrapper, caught Muerce's attention. She was absorbed in a pink encased smart phone that she tapped and scrolled on without looking up. She wore a puffy peasant blouse adorned with bright, embroidered patterns and figures. Though her blouse and the innocence it suggested stood out from the suggestive outfits the other girls wore, it was her face that caught Muerce's interest. She was barely out of puberty. *Still a child, he thought.* He could allow himself to get infuriated, maybe even do something about it, but he needed information at the moment, not confrontation.

"You want?" Mikal said, holding up a medium-sized cup that was half-full of a putrid green frozen mush. "Shamrock Shake—seasonal special. They awesome. Off the menu next week."

"No thanks," Muerce said, sitting down.

"My treat?" Mikal said, taking a long slurp from the straw. "I get you coffee?"

"Sure," Muerce said.

Mikal, who wore a lime-green, velour track suit with "Deluxe" embroidered in gold on the zip top, swiveled in place and motioned at one of the nail polish girls to come to him. It was then Muerce recognized her as the blonde girl from Club Unicorn that flirted with Travis. Her reply to Mikal was a look of exasperation, and she held her hands up, nails facing him, to indicate the polish was drying. Mikal frowned and pointed toward the girl with her; the one Muerce recognized from Saigon Laundry. The friend of Redzil. When she approached their booth, she nodded at Muerce as an acknowledgement she remembered him.

"Get large coffee," Mikal said, handing her a five-dollar bill. She winked at Muerce, and attempted to walk away but was stopped short when Mikal did not release the bill to her possession.

"Bring change," he ordered. She rolled her eyes at him, and he slapped her rear as she turned. The points of her heels tapped against the tiled floor as she walked away. Muerce turned, watching her as she left, and wondering if she might be a back-up source of information. Mikal noted Muerce's interest.

"Maybe, you order something else off menu?" Mikal said.

"Not today," Muerce said, swiveling to face Mikal. Muerce feigned a smile to indicate he might have an interest in the proposition at some later time, but it was only to soften Mikal's defenses so he could learn whatever he could about Brankovic.

"Then you come to Deluxe for favor, da?" Mikal said.

"I come to *Mikal* for favor," Muerce said.

The remnants of the Shamrock Shake were sucked up the straw with an obnoxious sound. Mikal wanted to make sure he got it all.

"I love this," he said. "All of it. This what makes America great. You know why?"

"No, I don't," Muerce said.

"Reliability," Mikal said. "You know reliability?"

"Tell me," Muerce said.

"Is trust, loyalty," Mikal said. "I come here I know food best quality, price same, service same, bathroom clean. Safe place to hang, you know?"

The gastronomic opiate of the masses. But Muerce understood and, looking Mikal straight in the eye, dipped his head in a gesture of agreement.

"America is great country," Mikal said. "Land of dreams. We all have dreams, yes?"

Again, Muerce, his eyes locked on Mikal's, motioned his approval with a slight movement of his head.

"America not my dream," Mikal said. He swept his arms up and around as if to grab the entire building. "This my dream." With his left arm outstretched toward the booth with four of his girls he said, "This... bad dream."

Mikal folded his arms and pushed his body against the bench seat, fixing his eyes on Muerce to study him.

"You want to know my dream?" Mikal said.

"I do," Muerce said. For the first time he was genuinely interested in Mikal. Private lives were never completely private, not even for pimps. Behind the street bravado and flash of Pimp Deluxe was Mikal from the former Yugoslavia. Mikal who knew Wall Street like an investment banker. Mikal who was classically trained to play the violin. Mikal the poet. Mikal, who buried his soul beneath layers of gold jewelry and gaudy velour athletic wear. Mikal who was hard, but fair with the girls who worked for him.

Muerce had heard talk of this Mikal, but he'd never bothered to find out if there was anything to it.

"You know Dubrovnik?" Mikal said.

"Yes," Muerce said. "Once. Many years ago. Before the war. There was very good wine, back then."

"Da," Mikal said. "You know what Dubrovnik not have?"

"No," Muerce said.

"This," Mikal said, sweeping his arms up in the same gesture he made earlier. "No McDonalds. Have brother in Dubrovnik. Move there after war. Owns two fish and chip restaurants. Does good tourist business. Is honest. Not pimp criminal like Deluxe."

Mikal clutched at the gold chains draped around his neck, and leaned toward Muerce.

"This," he whispered. "All bullshit. Fake. Buy knock offs, clothes, shoes. Gold teeth fake. Caps. Even car buy used." He motioned with his head toward his girls. "Use girls to barter for tinted windows, rims, and bling. I save cash. Invest. Even pay taxes under real name.

"Have money to buy franchise. Be silent partner with brother."

"But?" Muerce said.

"Not easy buy franchise," Mikal said. "Even with brother as front man, must have connections, like sponsor. Hard thing to do in Europe. EU. Fucking Germans."

"And if you're dream came true?" Muerce said.

"Leave this shit," Mikal said. "Be, what you say, *legit*. Run store with brother. Have quiet life. Maybe marry Greek woman. Get old and fat. This dream."

Finished, Mikal sat back in the booth and stared at Muerce, who stared back while he absorbed and calculated what had been said. Muerce reached inside his jacket and removed the leather case that contained his business cards. From it he pulled a single card, and placed it on the table in front of Mikal. Though the presence of the card portended the possibility of a life's dream coming true, Mikal was cautious. The card was on the table, but it had not been offered.

"Maybe, Jock Muerce help Mikal?" he said.

"Maybe," Muerce said. He tapped on the card with his right index finger. As he did they were interrupted by a husky Serb with spiky hair. Muerce put him at the front end of thirty. He wore a greasy black leather coat, and smelled like breath mints and antiseptic. It was when the man awkwardly set a brown plastic tray that held a pancake and sausage breakfast, hash browns, and a large cup of orange juice Muerce noticed the white gauze bandage where the man's left hand used to be. As he slid the tray in front of Mikal with his one hand, he pocketed the stub in his jacket.

"Take seat in back," Mikal said. As the man did, Mikal poured three containers of syrup over the pancakes and sausages, and attacked the meal as if there was a time limit on it.

"Love this shit," he said, looking up at Muerce, and wiping his face with a flimsy paper napkin.

Muerce said nothing, but looked over Mikal's shoulder and, with his chin, pointed toward the man sitting in the back of the restaurant by himself.

"Brankovic," Mikal said, shoveling another plastic fork-full of syrup-drenched pancake into his mouth.

Muerce tapped his finger hard on the calling card when Mikal said the name. It caught Mikal's attention. Now he understood Muerce. It also caught the attention of the young girl sitting across from them. The one thing Misha was able to hide from Brankovic, Mikal, and most of the girls who had taken her under their street smart tutelage, was how well she understood English. She knew, for the time being, her survival depended on Brankovic. She would do as she was ordered, and carefully listened to the conversation between Mikal and the American, who did not seem interested in buying any of the women.

Mikal took another large bite of his meal, wiped as much of the stickiness from his face and fingers as he could, and pushed the tray away.

"So, is deal?" Mikal said.

"All you know in exchange for your dream," Muerce said.

"Jock Muerce can do that?"

"If I have to fly to Oak Brook, Illinois, myself," Muerce said. "And one more thing. I inherit your girls when you leave. I'll help the ones who want off the streets. The others can do as they please."

"You can have beeches," Mikal said. "Pain in the ass, this business. Drama, drama, drama. Like reality show everyday."

Muerce slid his card across the table to Mikal, who covered it with his hand.

"Brankovic," Muerce said.

"This very dangerous," Mikal said. "Dangerous for me, for you. Brankovic bad man."

"Enough with the disclaimers," Muerce said. "Get to the point. Where can I find him? How many people does he keep around him? What's his routine?"

"He used to move around a lot," Mikal said. "Now spends most night in old boiler plant near glass factory. You know glass factory?"

"I've got the address," Muerce said. "Go on."

"Two bodyguards, sometimes more," Mikal said. "Depends on what is shaking with business. Hard to know. Not like we friends on Facebook."

"What's his day like?" Muerce said.

"Not same every day," Mikal said. "But once week, someone bring laundry—sheets, clothes, stuff like that. Now and then, bring girl. Must be virgin. Hard to come by. Very rare. Have to go young to find them. Most import. Not Amber Alert where they come from."

Mikal turned his head toward Misha.

"Like that," Mikal said. Misha's eyes focused intently on the blank screen of her phone, but her ears took in all that was being exchanged across from her.

340

"You in the import business Mikal?" Muerce said. "If you're trafficking this deal is done, and I'll drag you to Hell myself."

"No, not me," he said. "Sometimes give to me to bring to him. Show up with laundry. I wait in car, get leftovers for Deluxe posse. Only two times. Tell truth Jock Muerce. Honest. They big pain in ass. Cause trouble with other beeches."

"Why's that?" Muerce said.

"Bride of Dragon," Mikal said. "Think they are special. Lots of lip from them.

"You see blouse she wear?"

Mikal motioned to Misha with his cup of orange juice. It was painful for Muerce to look at Misha but he did. She was just a kid. *Maybe not so innocent anymore, he thought, but just a kid.* However it played out with Brankovic, serial killer or not, Muerce promised himself he'd get her, and the others off the street. He'd get them back home if they wanted.

"Is like gang colors," Mikal said. "She not work right away. But soon enough. Other beeches show her ropes. Get used to routine."

"She's still too young," Muerce said, letting some of his anger out through the tone of his voice.

"What you want me to do, Jock?" Mikal said. He put the nearly empty cup on the table, and raised both hands up toward Muerce while throwing his head back in the direction of the one-handed man behind him. "You see what Brankovic does. I like to keep my hands, and my head."

"Just following orders?" Muerce said.

"Da," Mikal said. There was resignation and shame in his reply.

"You said twice," Muerce said. "The other?"

"Was Redzil," Mikal said. "Now get to part of best information."

"What's that?" Muerce said.

"Brankovic want baby," Mikal said.

Amelie's violet eyes were the first image to flash into Muerce's head. Her surprise appearance at Saigon Laundry, and her cryptic conversation, became clearer to him. Then he thought of Miriam.

"Go on," Muerce said.

"Is ask around about baby," Mikal said. "Who has, how he can get."

"So he thinks it's his?" Muerce said. "Redzil was one of your girls. How did that happen?"

"Not show for long time," Mikal said. "She keep secret. Too late for scrape. She work hard. Good earner. She want to keep baby. Her business as long as she earn. Deluxe good to his beeches. Take care of them."

"Yeah, you're a real prince," Muerce said. "You never suspected it was his?"

"Not then," Mikal said. "She young. Not show right away. She swear it was mistake with customer."

"And Brankovic never suspected?" Muerce said.

"No," Mikal said. "They with him only once. He not care after."

The Dragon had a child. And he wanted it. For every beast He created, God allowed for weakness. Muerce was sure he discovered Brankovic's.

"That it?" Muerce said.

"Wants baby, bad," Mikal said. "By any means."

The child was somewhere in the system. If it was Brankovic's he could submit a DNA test and claim custody. But to do that, he'd have to emerge from his cave and become part of the civilized world. To become, *legit*. That, Muerce knew, wasn't about to happen. Brankovic would work outside the framework to stay in the shadows. A few payoffs, some threats, a little muscle, and he would get what he desired—the child's location, and the child. What Brankovic didn't know, and Muerce did, was the baby's advocate—his gatekeeper—Miriam. Getting past her would be no easy task. There were rules. *Rule Number One: You don't fuck with the Welfare Lady.*

CHAPTER 35

Have you ever heard of a scumbag shylock named Genero Blanco?" Miriam said.

The phone call caught Muerce off guard. First, because it was Miriam, who had checked out of the hospital only days earlier. Second, because the noise in the background indicated she was back at work.

"Well?" she said.

"Well what?" Muerce said.

"Have you ever heard of him?" she said.

"No," Muerce said. "Is that even a real name?"

"If it wasn't I wouldn't be asking," she said. Muerce detected irritation in her voice.

"So why are you asking?" Muerce said. "And why aren't you at home, resting."

"Sitting around the house drives me crazy," she said. "There's nothing to do."

"Read," Muerce said.

"I'll do that when I'm old," she said. "So no help on Blanco."

"I'm blanco on Blanco," Muerce said. "What did he want?"

"Pushy little jerk," Miriam said. "One of those voices that you just know he's a small man in every way."

Whatever he had said to Miriam, Blanco enraged her to the point Muerce knew she would go out of her way not to be of assistance. Whoever Mr. Blanco was, he broke Rule Number One.

"So what did he want?" Muerce said.

"To tell him where the baby is," she said.

"What baby?" he said.

"Baby Jack Doe Redzil," she said. "Remember?"

Muerce sat up straight in his chair, and snapped his fingers to get the attention of Travis, who was looking at a Google Map of the grounds around ACME Glass. Scribbling Blanco's name on the back of an envelope, he tossed it over to Travis and gestured with his fingers to mimic typing to communicate he wanted him to do a fast search. Travis immediately typed in the name, and started reading the search result headlines. The printer began to whir as it warmed up in anticipation of spitting out copies of what Travis found to be relevant information regarding Blanco.

"Miriam, tell me exactly what he said," Muerce said. There was a hesitant silence. "It's important."

The call had been very short, she said. Blanco was rude and demanding from the moment she said hello. He identified himself as being hired to represent a client who he would not identify, but had custodial rights to the child. Blanco commanded her to hand over the child to him by the end of the day; that she provide the address of the location where the child was being cared for, and he would go himself. She could meet him there, if she wanted, or not. He didn't care what she did as long as she gave him the address. He threatened lawsuits on numerous and frivolous grounds if she did not do as he instructed.

"I told him to sue, and hung up," she said. "It didn't sound at all like he knew anything about family law. Prick."

Travis shoved several printouts in front of Muerce, who scanned them quickly.

"That's because he's an ambulance chaser," Muerce said. "Slip and falls, medical malpractice, auto... and he's a parasite at that. Jumps in on class action suits after another firm has done all the work."

"Um, I might have said something to him in French," Miriam said. Muerce laughed as he imagined what she might have said. Given Blanco's surname and his clientele, he likely had a good understanding of Spanish. Even if he knew some French, he would never have understood Miriam's Marseilles accent pounded into her by the nuns.

"I think you're okay on that front," Muerce said.

"What's going on?" she said.

"Is the baby in a safe place?" he said.

"Yes, of course, but I'm going to move him to another home just in case," she said.

"Don't," Muerce said. "Not if you don't have to. Secure all the paperwork and computer files with the address if you can."

"I locked all that down as soon as I got off the phone," she said. "And I have all the case files. Nothing was done with them while I was gone."

"Good," he said. "I'll be in municipal court later today for a minor in possession. I'll swing by the clerk's office in family to see if Blanco files anything. I doubt he will. Not on this one."

"You haven't answered me," she said. "What's going on?"

"I need you to trust me on this, Miriam," Muerce said. "Okay?"

"Of course," she said.

"Just stay clear of it for awhile," he said. "If Blanco calls again with the same threats and demands, notify enforcement, and then let me know."

"This is getting a little scary, but okay," she said.

"Whatever you do, don't make any home visits today," Muerce said. "In fact, go home and rest. You should be doing that anyway."

"Now it's getting super spooky," she said.

"Just being cautious," he said. "You and Nick going out tonight?"

"Pizza and a movie at home with the boys," she said. "Carlos has a basketball tournament tomorrow."

"Sounds good," Muerce said. "Let me know if you hear from Blanco."

The next call Muerce made was to Trumbley, who confirmed that Miriam knew nothing of their unofficial investigation into what was now heralded across the city as the work of the Death Weaver. Muerce filled Trumbley in on his breakfast with Amelie at Saigon Laundry, and the download from Mikal. They both agreed they should keep Miriam at as much of a distance as they could from what looked to be unfolding with Brankovic and Redzill's baby. Miriam's first reaction was to relocate the child to what she thought would be a safer refuge. It was a natural thing for a case worker, let alone a mother, to do. Both Muerce and Trumbley suspected Brankovic and his people were thinking the same thing, and would have a tail on her. Once located, they would force their way in and take the baby, who would disappear into Brankovic's dark world. Blanco was just a well-paid errand boy. Trumbley said he'd get Miriam to play hooky in the afternoon, and he'd be with her and the boys the rest of the weekend. If he spotted a tail, he'd make a call and stop that nonsense right away. A broken taillight, some priors; whoever it was would sit the weekend out in the city lockup.

"It's getting pretty edgy around here," Trumbley said. "It's Saint Patrick's Day tomorrow. We're expecting a half million people at the parade. More if the weather stays good. Nothing like a cultural excuse to go on a daylong drunk. Fights, DUIs, urinating in public... just general obnoxiousness."

"So what's new?" Muerce said. "You guys live for that crap. It's like Christmas for vice."

"Because on top of it we've got the Death Weaver," Trumbley said. "Hell, Jack, the precincts all have pools. And they're not about *if* there's a victim the day after tomorrow. The money is on what time the body will be found, and where."

"And all the overtime is focused on the parade," Muerce said.

"The fucking Feast of Saint Patrick," Trumbley said.

"Ever wonder where all the snakes went?" Muerce said. "Now we know."

At least tomorrow night, Muerce thought, somebody would be keeping an eye on the reptile he wanted to banish.

CHAPTER 36

The green plaid scarf he wore was appropriate enough for Muerce to blend into the crowd at O'Keeffe's for his meeting with Turko. The sun was bright, and the sound of birds in the trees announced the advent of spring despite the cold chill in the air. The zipper on Muerce's hunting coat was broken so he shoved his hands in the front pockets, and crossed them to close the jacket as he turned into the slight breeze. A teenage boy, supported by a traffic light pole, threw up into the gutter as his friends stood nearby on the corner, taunting him. The group was adorned with every shade of green found in nature, and other hues that Muerce suspected came from nuclear waste, or alien spacecraft.

After spending a quarter of an hour looking for a parking space, and finding one a half dozen blocks from O'Keeffe's, Muerce cursed himself for not proposing a different location when Turko suggested the bar. O'Keeffe's on Saint Patrick's Day. Right after the parade ended. *Bad idea.*

The crowd at the bar spilled outside and was congregating on the street. Muerce opted to cut through the alley, and enter by way of the kitchen. The pungent smell of boiling cabbage hit Muerce like a punch in the nose. It was Saint Patrick's Day. Corned beef was being sliced and served on plates with floury mashed potatoes. None of the kitchen staff looked at Muerce twice when he walked passed them.

Turko was where he said he'd be, at the end of the bar nursing a bottle of domestic beer. They waved at each other across the sea of drunken humanity. Muerce pushed his way through the boisterous crowd, and squeezed his way between two giant men who spoke in slurred brogues before he arrived next to Turko. Muerce raised his eyebrow at Turko's bottle of beer.

"You think I'm going to drink that green shit?" Turko said. "What do you want? One of your pussy martinis?"

Muerce smiled and shook his head. It took some effort to hear above the shouting and singing. Too much. The two of them looked around and agreed, without exchanging words, that it was not the best environment for their meeting.

"I need a smoke," Turko yelled. "Let's go outside."

Muerce motioned with his hand they should go through the kitchen. As they jostled their way through the revelers one set of eyes were stuck on Muerce. Paige had spotted him the moment he emerged from the kitchen. His warm face and the hint of curls behind his ears was set off by the scarf and the rustic jacket. The sight of Jack Muerce made her work for breath. There was a tightness in her chest, and a urgent looseness between her legs. She wanted to giggle when she saw him, but controlled the urge. She was not, however, able to stop the blush that painted her cheeks. Any interest she entertained in the guy who had been flirting with her, and buying her drinks for the past half hour, evaporated.

"What's your name again?" she said, without looking at the young bank branch manager in front of her.

"Bradley," he said.

"Well Bradley, I just saw the guy I'm going to fuck tonight so I'm leaving," she said. She pushed her plastic cup of green dyed beer toward him. "You can have the rest of this."

Before he could form a thought to put into words, Paige was swallowed by the crowd.

Turko bummed a light from one of the Mexican kitchen workers copping a smoke in the back alley, and sucked hard on the cigarette. The cherry ember glowed red hot. He exhaled like a long-distance runner finishing a marathon, and coughed.

"I can't believe I still do this," Turko said.

"Then quit," Muerce said.

They were standing next to a stack of empty aluminum beer kegs.

"I did," Turko said. He flicked the cigarette to the pavement, and squashed it with his shoe. Then he removed a pack of nicotine gum from his pocket and popped one into his mouth.

"You sound like the priest who's proud of himself because he's cut back on fondling altar boys to only once a week," Muerce said.

The laughter that erupted from Turko triggered a short coughing spell.

"You sound like my wife," Turko said. "Well, ex-wife."

"Which one?" Muerce said, laughing.

"All of them," Turko said.

"How the hell do you afford that?" Muerce said. "What is it. Four?"

"Five," Turko said. "But I use the old Jack Muerce trick. Never have kids."

"That I know of," Muerce said. "Seriously Danny, marriage is like investing in a timeshare. You never enjoy your time in the place, and you always end up losing money on the deal. "

"Yeah, next time I get the urge to marry I'll find a woman I can't stand, and buy her a house."

"I suggest looking to rent," Muerce said.

"Houses?"

"Hell no," Muerce said, putting his hand on Turko's shoulder. "Women."

"I need another beer," Turko said. "But I've got a column to write."

The two of them searched each other's faces for the direction the conversation would go.

"So what am I writing about, Jack?" Turko said.

"The Saint Patrick's Day parade," Muerce said.

"That's for the Metro desk," Turko said. "Right now my column's empty for the Sunday edition."

"And you want to fill it with the bodies of mutilated women?" Muerce said. "Here's a catchy headline: Saint Turko Sews Up City's Slayer."

"It's news, Jack, not conjecture," Turko said. "I only report the facts. The pieces of three women are lying in the morgue. All cut the same way. All stitched up the same way. Some variation in patterns and wounds, but it looks to be the work of one guy. Fancy work at that."

"Your Death Weaver," Muerce said.

"Not mine," Turko said. "Yours from what I hear."

"From who?" Muerce said.

"Give me a break."

"Yeah, yeah, sources," Muerce said. "What do you want to know?"

"What you know," Turko said. "You can read what I know."

"I know you know more than you want me to know," Muerce said. "You hear more than you can write about. '*Off the record.*' What about Ash and Maple?"

"Those two scabby testicles?" Turko said. "They should have been castrated a long time ago. At least the Chief keeps them in the same sack."

"Touch a nerve?" Muerce said.

Turko clucked out a *tsk* of disdain between hard chomps on his nicotine gum.

"Did you forget I started at the paper working the cop shop?" Turko said. "I remember when they were walking beats. They haven't got the brains between them to figure out which knob turns on the hot water. Even if they got lucky, they'd be stumped to find the cold. And they're dirty as shit."

"Still?" Muerce said.

"I'm not up on current events," Turko said. "But when they were working vice... Titty Boy owned them."

"Titty Boy," Muerce said. Muerce stuck his hands back in his coat pockets and paced back and forth in front of Turko, thinking. "Look, Danny, I'm just doing a favor for someone."

"Bhote," Turko said.

"Yeah," Muerce said. "I'm not even going to ask how you know that. I'm just a fresh set of eyes. A different perspective is all. I don't even know what I'm looking for."

"That's usually the best vantage point," Turko said.

"I tell you what," Muerce said. "I'll do a confirm or deny. Deep background. You can't use any of it."

"Doesn't give me much," Turko.

"I haven't got much," Muerce said. "Shoot."

"Each victim has a clue embroidered in them?" Turko said. "A word?"

Muerce nodded yes.

"The name of an animal?"

Again, Muerce nodded yes.

"You going to tell me the name of the animals?"

"Confirm or deny," Muerce said.

Turko pursed his lips in frustration, reached into his pocket and popped another piece of nicotine gum into his mouth.

"One victim had her fingers and toes removed, another her tongue, and another her eyes," Turko said. "Those parts haven't been recovered yet."

Muerce bobbed his head in agreement.

"They were alive during the amputations?" Turko said.

"Alive, but probably not conscious," Muerce said. "I hope they weren't."

"So the killer's got some skill sets, he's not just a butcher?" Turko said.

"There might be precision in his process, but he's still a butcher," Muerce said.

"I haven't seen any autopsy photos," Turko said. "But I'm told the stitches, or whatever you want to call them—it's pretty artsy stuff. It took some time to do it."

Muerce squinted his eyes, and nodded yes.

"Like the tapestries at the Gilmont?" Turko said.

There was hesitation in Muerce's face that Turko thought gave him a momentary advantage.

"Favor for a favor, Danny," Muerce said. "Tread lightly with that. For now."

"Why?" Turko said. "Your mother?"

"Yeah," Muerce said, thinking of Ashley. "There's no direct link to the tapestries. Some coincidental symbolism, but that's it."

"Don't screw with me Jack," Turko said. "The Death Weaver's got three of the five senses covered. I don't just write for the paper, I read it too. Even the arts section."

"The animals?"

"Confirm or deny," Muerce said.

"Oh for Chrissake," Turko said.

"It's a leap for me right now," Muerce said.

"Oh, come on," Turko said. "Do I need to make up a list of all the beasts on the rugs, and go through it with you so you can 'confirm or deny' each one?"

Muerce nodded his head to indicate yes. Turko spit the large wad of gum in his mouth across the alley.

"What about the pattern?" Turko said.

"What pattern?"

"When the bodies were found?" Turko said.

"A Wednesday and two Sundays?" Muerce said. "It's shaky at best."

"Jesus, Jack," Turko said. Disbelief erupted from him. "Only *the* Wednesday in the Christian calendar. Then every Sunday after? Might as well call him the Lenten Killer."

"Coincidence at this point," Muerce said. "There hasn't been any religious connection. Not even with the clues."

"Unless another body pops up tomorrow," Turko said.

"Even then," Muerce said. "Like I said, Danny, I'm not the pro here. It's just a favor."

"Some favor," Turko said. "But you think there'll be another body tomorrow?"

Muerce frowned. Maybe not, he hoped. If Travis saw anything suspicious at the Dragon's nest he was to call him. He'd give a heads up to Trumbley, who could send a patrol car. If it looked particularly ominous, Travis was to call 911 himself. The cops were jumpy enough to respond right away if there was a report related to the slayings. It was then Muerce realized it wasn't a good plan. The police were understaffed for the night to compensate for the parade overtime, and Turko's headlines and the television news coverage had stoked enough interest in the case to fuel all the paranoids and crackpots in the city. The 911 switchboard would be a mess. He thought about taking Travis' place on watch.

"If the pattern holds," Muerce said. "But there will be eyes out there tonight."

"So there is a suspect?" Turko said.

Muerce nodded again.

"I haven't got a name," Turko said. "But the inside line is some foreign national crime boss."

"Does that make sense to you?" Muerce said.

"No," Turko said. "I'd want to keep a low profile if I were him."

"Me too," Muerce said. "Unless I wanted to send a message."

"If it is," Turko said. "It's the wrong message to the wrong people at the wrong time."

"Then I'd consider the source," Muerce said. "What does he have to gain... or lose?"

The two of them looked at each other then smiled when they realized they were talking about the same source—Titty Boy. Muerce had a name, but Turko didn't. They were being played. Muerce giving up Brankovic's name to Turko was the third-party validation Titty Boy wanted. *Who didn't trust Jack Muerce?* Armed with the information, Turko would bait the name in interviews with the cops. For Ash and Maple, it would be a nice, plump wriggling worm they couldn't resist. The hook would be set, but the fish would be a Dragon. The two homicide detectives would slam around the city like a pair of bowling balls in a crystal boxcar looking for Brankovic, who would have to disappear for awhile. Good for Titty Boy. *And good for Zajak, Muerce thought.*

After a couple of rounds of Q&A with the cops, the idea of Brankovic the Suspect would change hands, and Turko would be able to source the police in any story about the Death Weaver. It was a tight trick. *Kudos to Titty Boy.* It was a clever ploy, but too clever for Titty Boy.

"I think we just got our nipples tweaked," Muerce said.

"Does that sort of thing give you pleasure, Mister Muerce?" a voice behind them said.

Turning toward the back door of O'Keeffe's, Muerce and Turko had been joined by Paige. She wore an Aran turtleneck sweater, green tartan plaid slacks that fit tightly like leggings, and brown riding boots with a slight heel that rose to just below her knees. Her hair was pulled back in a ponytail, but loose strands hung in front of her ears to mid-neck in an elf-like fashion. A breeze blew the golden wisps of hair across her face, the sun highlighting their color. She wore a charcoal tweed cap that was more feminine than masculine, and made her look more innocent than predatory. In each hand she held a fresh pint of Guinness. In her eyes she held Muerce.

"Not in back alleys, Miss Sharron," Muerce said. "And not with this ugly mug."

It took Turko a nanosecond to size up the situation. The young woman arrived with only two beers, and her gaze hadn't wavered from Muerce since she interrupted them. Neither had Muerce's gaze broken from her. Turko knew when an interview was over, and how best to exit with grace. He cleared his throat, garnering Muerce's attention from Paige. Muerce made a quick introduction. Turko smiled and blinked at Paige, who made no effort to reciprocate.

"I think my column tomorrow will be about the excesses of the Feast of Saint Patrick," Turko said. "Of course, nobody will read it because they'll be too hung over. Or unless there's breaking news. In which case, Jack, we'll need to talk again."

As the two of them turned to shake hands, Turko leaned into Muerce and whispered, "Seriously, talk."

Then he turned and addressed Paige.

"If I can't interest you in a timeshare Miss Sharron, I'd love to buy you a house."

She gave Turko a perplexed look. It was the first time she acknowledged that he was even there. Her expression provided Turko with the satisfaction he wanted.

"I'll let Jack explain it to you," he said, winking at Paige as he walked past her and back into O'Keeffe's. "Top of the day."

"What was that about?" Paige said.

"It was a marriage proposal," Muerce said.

"Strange man," she said.

"Very," he said. "But a good one."

"And they're hard to find?" she said.

"Are they?"

"Very," Paige said, offering one of the pints to Muerce, who looked at the time on his watch. It was well past noon.

"Why not?" he said, taking the glass of chocolate colored stout. With his free hand, Muerce grabbed two white plastic yard chairs that were used by the staff at the bar for smoke breaks, and moved them out into the alley away from the back entrance to give he and Paige some privacy. With his hand he swept the seat of one of the chairs clean for her.

They sat down, and *clinked* the glasses together.

"*Slainte*, I think it is," Paige said.

"I don't know," Muerce said. "I'm not good with the Irish."

Paige sipped the stout, which left a mocha cream mustache on her upper lip that she removed by slowly and seductively licking with her tongue.

"But you French good?" she said.

"Not quite as well as you innuendo," Muerce said, taking a drink from his glass, and mimicking her Guinness mustache removal but with a quicker swipe of his tongue. When she laughed at his gesture Muerce saw a warm sparkle in her eyes he had not seen before. He liked it.

"Oh, Mister Muerce, I'm shocked," she said.

"I very much doubt that," he said, taking a long, aggressive pull from the glass. "Since we're drinking together, why don't we drop the formalities. I'm Jack."

"I was raised to respect my elders, Mister Muerce," she said, matching Muerce's intake of stout.

"I don't believe in coincidence," Muerce said. "So why don't we cut through the bullshit. What do you want?"

"To cut through the bullshit," she said. Paige reached up and gently caressed Muerce's face with her fingertips. He didn't resist. Then she moved her hand to the back of his head, and slowly twirled the curl of his hair around her index finger. She thought he was beautiful, and strong. He had the confidence to keep silent as she touched him, and not look away from her. It gave her the fortitude to do what she had wanted to when she held a knife to his throat. It was what she desired every time she saw him.

Lifting herself from the chair, she leaned up and into Muerce's face, and brushed her lips against his before pressing into them with a demure kiss. It was quick. When it was done she glanced the tip of her nose against his cheek, and held it there. His skin was soft and warm, and she did not want to leave it.

Paige sat back down in the chair, unsure what Muerce's reaction would be, but glad she had kissed him. There was an innocence to the moment. It was something she had never felt before, and it came with an uneasiness of being vulnerable. It was, strangely for her, comfortable to lower her defenses around him.

Muerce was not altogether surprised by Paige's kiss, though her motive was still suspect. Still, he was intrigued, attracted, and even a little enchanted by her. He had seen her dark side. Now there was a delicacy and frailness about her that he craved. He was standing on the edge of a cliff, overlooking the expanse of a turquoise sea. Unsure of how deep the water below him was, Muerce couldn't resist the thrill of the jump.

The two of them sat, silently staring ahead at the building across the alley, and drinking. It was a relaxed quiet that passed between them as they listened to the sounds of the city, and absorbed what little heat the afternoon sun generated. After a time, Muerce held his glass up to the light and swirled the last swallow of stout and foam.

"Paige."

"Jack."

Muerce squinted as he looked at the bottom of his pint, and ran a hand through his hair.

"You want to get drunk?"

"With you?" she said, letting the question float. "Hell, yes."

She drained the rest of her pint, pivoted toward him and grinned with a fresh, velvet Guinness mustache.

"One rule," Muerce said, reaching for her face. "We can talk about anything except each other."

He wiped the stout frosting from the top of her lip with his finger, and put it in his mouth.

-- --

The Saturday night crowd at The Monastery was more subdued and mature than the swill and spill throng at O'Keeffe's. The sound of jazz from a bootleg recording of an old Monterey Jazz Festival performance caressed the oak and green-velvet draped bar where Muerce and Paige had set up camp for their day of inebriation. Thelonious Monk played. With his fork, Muerce tapped out the beat on the table, and checked the time on his watch as the waiter delivered a third round of twisted blue smoke martinis. It was just past five o'clock, and he and Paige were well into their cups. They had stuck to their plan. After couple of rounds of beers to accompany a late lunch of lobster bisque and fish tacos, they took a break for espresso and shots of Red Bull and vodka. A platter of delicately sliced smoked salmon, kobe beef carpaccio, and a selection of artisanal *frommage* and dried fruits, accompanied the third round of martinis. They were pacing themselves. Drunk, but not so sloppy. The buzz they put on was still light and breezy, as were the topics of their long-running debates and discussions. They talked about anything and everything, except themselves. Muerce was surprised to find Paige much sharper and balanced in her opinions on politics, art and history. When religion crept into one of their circular conversations, she cocked her head at him as a reminder of their accord, and he adroitly switched subjects.

The combination of booze, bar and Paige's *tout ensemble* had the effect of softening Muerce's first impressions at the same time they accreted his desire for her. For Paige, the long afternoon that had turned to early evening was confirmation of her own craving.

"Delicious," she said, sipping the fresh martini.

"Dangerously so," Muerce said, lifting his glass in a toast.

"To the risk," Paige said. She took another sip of the cocktail and put it down. There was a polite urgency in her demeanor.

"I need to excuse myself," she said, standing. "Which way to the... whoa..."

Paige teetered precipitously when she stood up, and wavered slightly causing Muerce to spring from his seat. He experienced the same sensation, and grabbed the edge of the table to steady himself.

"Whoa is right," he said. "Are you okay?"

"Yes," she said, taking the opportunity to draw herself closer to him as she used his arm for a brace. "But I think it's time to move the party."

They were three olives from being sloppy drunk. Paige brushed the long strands of hair from her face, and licked her lips as she squeezed his arm before letting go to make her way to the bathroom. Muerce was wired, but not so much that he couldn't reel it in, though it was Paige who set the hook.

He motioned to the waiter for the tab as he sat down, and pulled his phone from the hunting jacket draped on the back of the chair. Muerce fingered it on. There were no messages. He was both relieved and disappointed there was nothing from Ashley. There were no messages from anyone. It had been days since he had heard from her. *Fine, he thought, she's moved on.* In his wistful intoxication Muerce took the technology silence as a sign of heavenly approval for the day's, and soon to be evening's, indulgences. To ratify the thought, Muerce called Travis, who answered on the third ring.

"You set?" Muerce said.

"Yeah," Travis said. "No sweat."

"Remember what we discussed," Muerce said, avoiding any slurring of is voice. "Watch from a distance. Anybody looks at you twice, even if you imagine they do, get out of there. Text me. Anything looks fishy. Get out of there. Text me. Anything..."

"Looks criminal, get out of there, call Trumbley direct," Travis said. "And text you. I've got it. We've been over it a dozen times. Trust me. Don't worry."

"It's not you I'm worried about," Muerce said.

"Well, thank's a lot," Travis said.

"Get over it," Muerce said. "Even if nothing is going on, just..."

"Text you," Travis said. "Relax already. Why don't you go see a movie, or something. It's not too late, you can still catch the Grand Slam Special at Denny's."

Muerce responded to Travis' smart-ass by ending the call without comment. That was comment enough. He put the phone away, signed the bill when it arrived, and waited for Paige to return from the powder room. They were both over the limit to drive. He checked his cash. There was enough to give the valet a big tip to keep the Mercedes in a safe spot overnight. Since they'd cab it, Muerce decided he still had the capacity in him to finish his drink, and the reserves to both start and finish Paige. Several times if need be. They had the rest of the night. The booze was like gasoline to the bonfire of passion. The more he thought about it, the bigger it got.

"What are you smirking about?" Paige said, arriving back at the table.

"You," he said.

She pushed what was left of her drink off to the side, reached across the table—stealing the last of Muerce's spiked olives—and inserted it and the spike that impaled it into her mouth. As she chewed it slowly, Paige pressed the plastic spear against her lower lip with a coquettish flourish.

"Pace yourself," she said. "You'll need the energy."

— —

Pho Mat almost missed Muerce when he and the woman with him got into a green-and-white taxi.

Too much drink, he thought. Muerce go home now. Easy night for Pho Mat. Easy morning, too.

Turning the engine over, he geared the Supra into first, let out the clutch, and smoothly pulled a U-turn after the traffic behind Muerce's cab cleared.

From Downtown, it was only a few miles to Muerce's apartment. Traffic was light, and Pho Mat kept a three-car distance from the taxi. The traffic lights were agreeable, and the trip took less time than normal.

As the taxi pulled away, Pho Mat saw the woman lift herself to her toes and wrap her arms around Muerce as they kissed in front of the entrance to the apartment. The display elicited a smile from Pho Mat as he pulled into the dreary, broken-glass speckled parking lot of his watchtower apartment. The sky was lit with the faint orange of a departing sunset.

— —

No words passed between them in the back of the cab. They exchanged, instead, furtive looks. Between the anticipatory glances, Paige tucked her lower lip into her mouth and softly clamped her teeth together as she imagined Muerce biting into her flesh. She was flushed and hot under the heavy knit sweater, which scratched the skin on her arms and shoulders, as they entered the lobby elevator. Arriving by cab, the apartment's public elevator was the best option to make the trip to Muerce's penthouse. Given the amount of alcohol they had consumed, and the sexual tension swelling between them, the stairs were out of the question. Muerce tapped the code for the top floor into the security keypad on the brass control panel, positioned himself against the elevator wall opposite Paige, and leaned back so the lower half of his body angled away from her. As he did, he pushed the front of his coat open and behind him, and clasped his hands behind his back. The lift jerked alive, and began to ascend as the blood flowing into his groin also caused an increase in elevation that did not go unnoticed by Paige. She spread her arms open, firmly grasping the brass hand rail that wrapped around three-quarters of the inside of the conveyor with both her hands. When she relaxed her head backwards against the wall, her tweed cap slid low over her forehead in a vampish fashion. Paige's eyes were fixed on Muerce's as she cocked her right leg up and pressed the foot of her boot against the wall just above her left knee. The folded leg swayed back and forth, opening a little wider each time they passed another floor. Glancing at the elevator indicator, Paige made an obvious show of pinching her upper lip between her teeth as she directed her gaze to Muerce's aroused inseam.

The elevator gave a slight shudder when it arrived at its destination, and the door made a *clunking* sound as it slid open. The hallway air that crept into the elevator was fresh, warm and slightly moist. They did not move. As the door began to close, Muerce jammed his foot against the bumper, and it retracted with another *clunk*.

"Think we can make it inside?" Muerce said.

"We can make it," Paige said. "Wherever you like."

The subtle laugh that Muerce coughed out was less of humor, and more like the rolling of eyes. He took Paige by the hand, and led her in a half run down the hallway to the door of his apartment. They were breathing hard with anticipation as Muerce, facing the entrance, patted over himself for his keys. Paige pressed herself against his back, and thrust her hands into the front pockets of his trousers where she found the key ring with one hand, and the ring of the key of his carnal intention with the other.

"Which one?" she said, dangling the former in the air while plucking with her fingertips on the ridge of the tip of the latter.

"The one that opens the door," he said.

"And which door do you want to open?" she said.

That was enough conversation for Muerce. They could talk more, later. In a flurry, he spun around, reached under Paige's sweater, grabbed her by the waist and spun back around again so she was against the door. The tweed cap fell to the floor as he forcefully grabbed her arms and raised them so they were above her head. He snatched the key ring from her hand, selected the correct one, and plunged it into the lock. The door swung open with the combined weight of their bodies, and crashed against the wall with a *boom* that sounded like the door had come off its hinges as they fell forward into the foyer. Muerce pushed Paige against the wall next to the table that held the day's mail as he punched in the code on the security system keypad that disarmed the alarm. He reached back with his leg, catching the edge of the open door, and flipped it shut with another, but less alarming *boom*.

Paige grabbed the lapels of Muerce's coat and yanked the jacket down to the top of his biceps, locking his arms in place, then pulled his mouth lower toward hers. They kissed with a starving abandon, devouring each other as the famished would a full banquet table. Their mouths pressed hard with violent passion, their teeth striking with a delicious pain as wet tongues slashed and stabbed at each other with intense attacks. Neither retreated or gave ground. The alcohol lust gained momentum as the pace and sound they made breathing through their nostrils increased. With each inhale came a wave of pheromones and the scents of perfume, cologne and warm flesh. Every exhale was felt on the soft skin of their cheeks like a hot summer wind. As they consumed each other with their mouths, Muerce tried to wrap his arms around Paige, but was frustrated by his lack of movement.

Well past the booze, Muerce was drunk with primal desire. It had taken him over, but not completely. There was, somewhere deep inside him, a dark region of reason; a free will that existed only for the moment. What he wanted in the moment was control. Complete control. Paige had his arms pinned. She had him bent, and was feeding on him. *She* was in control. Like the talking, he had had enough. He wanted what he wanted, and he wanted it right now, regardless of the consequences.

He was overtaken with animal desire. He disregarded all precaution.

There was anger in his action, and in his eyes, as he heaved and bumped his chest against Paige, breaking the controlled embrace, and sending her backward into the wall. Muerce flung off the hunting jacket, which he grabbed with one hand and threw to the floor in a gesture of dominance. He breathed harder, but slower as he stared at Paige with sexual intent. A silent shock registered on her face as she stared back at him. She sized him up with each flare of his nostrils.

She knew what he wanted, and she wanted it for him, and for herself. Their lips, which only seconds before were wild and inviting, were pursed shut. They stood, breathing long, slow and audibly through their noses, and stared at each other. As their blood rushed to engorge their groins, a tingling, crawling sensation crept up their arms to their necks. Muerce felt the itchiness settle behind his ears as it merged with the interior pounding of his pulse.

Paige subtly parted her lips as she dropped her gaze from Muerce's eyes to his feet in consent. Control had been passed. Muerce responded by kicking his shoes off, and tearing the shirt from himself. Several buttons bounced and scattered across the marble floor. Paige followed Muerce's disrobing frenzy, and shimmied out of the sweater, under which she wore an emerald green silk camisole. There was a hint of redness where the sweater had irritated the bare skin of her shoulders and arms. Muerce was down to his boxer shorts when he saw Paige was having difficulty getting her boots off. Anxiously, he squatted and, alternating legs, grabbed behind each knee with one hand and the heel of a boot with the other, and pulled hard to remove them. He helped her tug and tussle her pants off, along with a pair of lace panties that matched the camisole.

Muerce did not linger in the position, and as he rose, he tucked his fingers inside the camisole, and lifted it up and off of Paige's body. Freed from her clothes, she dropped her hands down and pulled the front of his boxers toward her so they could slide to his ankles without getting hung up.

Their hands feverishly coursed over their naked bodies, never stopping for more than a squeeze or pinch before they wrapped their arms around themselves in a tight embrace, and merged their mouths in arduous kissing. Again, they tasted each other deeply and furiously. Muerce cupped Paige's face in his hands, kissing and brushing his lips over her eyelids, brows and temples as he worked his way toward her ears, down the side of her neck to the top of her shoulder, and back up the front of her throat. Reaching behind her head, he rolled the black elastic band that held her ponytail together until it fell to the floor. He ran his hands through her loosened hair, threading it between his fingers as his tongue worked in partnership with hers. He gripped at her scalp and bent his knees slightly so he could more easily enter her.

Paige felt him between her legs, opened her stance and raised up on her toes so Muerce could rub against her wetness. As he did, she began to part in acceptance. Muerce bent his knees lower, ready for penetration when he felt Paige push him away.

"No," she said. Pulling her head back, and without looking at him, she put her hand to her mouth and deposited as much saliva as she could onto her cupped fingers. She reached down and rubbed the spittle on Muerce's bulb. Then she quickly spun herself around, placed her hands against the wall, arched her back and thrust her rear toward Muerce as she lifted her left leg up and off to the side.

"Like a boy," she said, twisting her head as best she could toward Muerce as if she were giving him an order.

The look on her face was insistent and defiant. It enraged Muerce. Both passion and anger drove him into her. She was a beast to be tamed, to be controlled, to be humiliated into submission. He grabbed a handful of her hair and pulled hard, causing Paige to yelp then moan as he opened her up. He paused, and felt the tight ring of her anus spasm as if it were trying to strangle the neck of his shaft. The muscle soon surrendered and Muerce probed deeper. With a firm grip on her hair, he turned her head sideways against the wall so he could look at her. Her mouth was wide open, breathing deeply in readiness for his next thrust. The look in her eye was submissive.

Paige began to slowly rock herself up and down on Muerce, who reached around her waist with his free hand. When their action intensified in speed and ardor, Muerce released the grip on her hair and controlled Paige's body with both his hands on her hips. She was loud and descriptive as he had her, causing Muerce to build to a climax much sooner than he anticipated.

As he approached the point of sexual crescendo, Muerce pushed deeper and harder into Paige. She cursed and moaned her encouragement louder. They had both begun to sweat. An earthy perfume was generated by their sex, and reminded Muerce of the way the air smelled before a thunderstorm. Then he thought of the faint, musty smell of the victims in the morgue. His thoughts were drowning in a pool of alcohol and sex. What they were doing was a sort of death.

Muerce was nearing his end, and he reached for a handful of Paige's hair that he balled into his fist. Her hands were splayed open against the wall, her knuckles white. As Muerce made his final and deepest intrusions into her, he focused on a bead of her sweat that began to roll down through the downy blonde hairs at the back of her neck. Each time he stabbed at her the drop moved. It was then he noticed a small scar on the middle disc of her cervical vertebrae. It was dark, almost like a tattoo, and no wider than the width of two fingernails. It looked to be something written in Sanskrit, but Muerce didn't know Sanskrit. It was Hindi, but Muerce didn't know that.

Again he went deeper into her. She moaned, and the bead of sweat dropped down her spine. There looked to be four more small scars along her backbone. One each in the thoracic, lumbar, sacral and coccygeal regions. They were not discolored or appeared to be words in some Near Eastern language like the one that was, at the moment, near his eye level.

He welcomed the familiar tight squeeze beneath his testicles. He was about to lose all control and instinctively thrust deep one last time. As he released himself into Paige in successive convulsions, he concentrated on the two dark dashes with squiggly lines on the back of her neck. When he was spent, so was his interest in the strange skin adornment on her neck. Drenched, drunk and exhausted, they both slumped to the cold marble floor.

Paige in his arms, Muerce drifted off in his after glow, forgetting about the scar, and delightfully ignorant. He did not know they were the words *yauna iccha*. Hindi for sexual desire.

— —

Travis had a smug grin on his face as he played with the night vision binoculars he bought with the petty cash Muerce gave him for his work. He tucked the receipt into his pocket, and fiddled with the various knobs and intensity settings on the field glasses.

It was dusk. He had found a discreet spot to park behind a large, industrial rubbish container that afforded a clear view, albeit through a chain link fence, of the front of the building where Muerce said Brankovic was living. Travis jumped into the assignment with the zeal of youth. It was the kind of field work he romanticized doing for Muerce, and not the daily routine of errand boy and computer snoop, which sometimes left him feeling like he was more stalker than investigator. He didn't like the idea of creeping the Internet. *The Information Age, he thought, was too easy, too open, and too much.* The experience had caused Travis to reassess his own presence on the net. He purged everything he could to ghost himself—doing what he could to close Facebook, Twitter and other social media accounts, and contesting the few Google images of him that were out there. Still, there was no putting technology back in the box. It wasn't the Middle Ages. There weren't monks cloistered in fortified monasteries busily pointing and clicking their way to divine enlightenment. But what if there were?

Three hours later, Travis was still kicking the concept of a sequestered Internet around in his head when the realization struck him that he was bored. Terribly so. His butt was sore from sitting practically motionless for so long, and he had to go to the bathroom. He looked at the empty mayonnaise jar lying on its side in the front passenger seat. He had read about it somewhere, but had not actually done it. Sure, he had peed into a cup for various standard medical tests—and for some drug testing his parents had forced on him in the past year. But those were for samples, and were given in the environs of sparkling clean lavatories. This was different. Sitting in a car? He unscrewed the blue metal cap of the jar, and moved the container around his crotch for practice. He didn't see how it would work without contorting his body in such a way that couldn't be perceived as an act of perversion. There also was the risk of spillage. The thought of being soaked and sitting in his own urine for the rest of the night was unappealing. So was the idea of having a jar of warm piss swilling around next to him.

He was going to have to do something soon. His bladder felt like the size of the Hindenburg, and it was about ready to explode.

"Screw it," Travis said to himself. He reached up to the roof light of the car, pried open the plastic cover with a pen knife, and removed the light bulb. He grabbed the keys from the ignition switch so the open door warning wouldn't go off, and exited the car.

The night air was cold enough to produce a hint of steam as Travis urinated behind the dumpster. He didn't care. It would dissipate before he finished zipping his pants closed, and he was good for another couple of hours if he laid off the Thermos of coffee he brought.

As he was adjusting himself and feeling more relaxed, in the distance he heard the sound of car tires as they crunched over broken glass and gravel. He peaked around the corner of the large dumpster. A large vehicle was entering the grounds of the steam generator building. Out of caution, he slipped into the car through the passenger side, and awkwardly climbed over the center console. He saw headlights approaching the large brick structure that was Brankovic's lair. Even in the dark, the structure was an easy spot. The silhouette of the massive chimney that rose from the back of the building was a landmark for the area.

Activating the low-light field glasses, Travis adjusted the focus. Through them, the world was a hundred shades of green. It was a monochromatic scheme, but one that provided excellent detail. The car was a Chevy Suburban. Travis adjusted the light setting so the headlights of the Suburban were less brilliant. He made a second adjustment when a door opened, and more light spilled from inside the steam plant that had once fed more than a dozen factories in the nearby area with heat and power. As part of his preparation for the stakeout, Travis found old maps and schematics of the building. There were dozens of tunnels that were part of the derelict plant's delivery system. On paper, it looked like a spider web that ran under most of the industrial area. There were six tunnels alone that fed into the ACME Glass Company factory.

The lights of the Suburban died, but Travis could see the engine was still on. A thin cloud of vapor puffed out of the exhaust pipe. The brightness of the open door that led into the steam plant framed a large man. He had shoulder-length hair. Travis pegged the figure as Brankovic. It had to be. The driver's body language indicated subservience. The long-haired man in the doorway pointed to the back of the Suburban, and the driver—who was bald—responded by retrieving something from the trunk area. Travis saw the two back doors swing open. The driver removed what looked like a large bag. It was long, and appeared to have some weight to it. As the man brought the bag into the building, disappearing behind the figure Travis believed to be his subject for the night, the passenger door opened. The figure that emerged was small, also with long, but light colored hair. It was a woman. A young one, though Travis could not make out her features. She approached Brankovic. She was talking to him. He was listening. When it looked like she was done, Brankovic leaned over and kissed the woman on the top of her head. She got back into the Suburban, and shut the door. A small flame erupted inside the car and quickly disappeared, leaving a pinpoint of light that danced nervously in the air. *Cigarette, Travis thought.* That the little cherry inside the Suburban moved as much as it did without any noticeable increase or decrease in intensity indicated to Travis that the woman was not a smoker. It was for show.

The light from the doorway suddenly decreased when the driver emerged and stopped next to Brankovic. They stood, side-by-side, staring straight ahead. Travis could not make out if they were talking to each other. The longer they stood there, the more Travis became uncomfortable. The two men had not moved. It was as if they were staring straight at him. He dropped the binoculars from his eyes, thinking if he stopped looking, they would stop looking back. Travis went rigid as he processed his situation. He was sure he was in a safe place. Still, if he could see them, they could see him. *Paranoia.* Travis picked up his phone, but did not activate it out of concern the light from the screen would be seen. Slowly he raised the binoculars back to his eyes. As he did, the lights of the Suburban alighted, flooding the the field glasses and Travis' eyes. The sudden brightness made Travis squint. When he adjusted them to account for the illumination, the car was pulling away. The door to the building was closed. There was no one outside. Travis cursed himself. He didn't know if Brankovic was leaving in the Suburban, or if he was back in the building. Travis followed the car with his binoculars until it disappeared around a building.

For the next half hour, Travis debated whether to text Muerce. Something happened, but it wasn't strange. Certainly, it didn't warrant calling Trumbley, or the emergency number. There was no emergency. He also didn't want to explain to Muerce that he wasn't sure if Brankovic was still around. For all he knew, Travis was watching an empty building. *God it's going to be a long night, he groaned.*

Just as he was anticipating the tedium, Travis heard a *crunch* outside the car. There was a flash of dark movement he caught when he looked at his door mirror the same moment the window by his face exploded in a shower of glass. Simultaneously, Travis felt tremendous pressure accompanied by sharp pain near his temple. There was another shower of glass, this time they appeared to be electric sparks, and traced lines of light in the air. Travis tried to reach out and touch them, but he couldn't move his arms. He couldn't keep his eyes open, either. He thought he heard the dinging of the car warning to let him know that he had left the keys in the ignition. Or was it a bell announcing the end of a boxing round? He wasn't sure. He felt like he was being pulled. He was laying on the ground. He closed his eyes again. More pain, though not as sharp, poked at different points on his body. His lower back. His arm. His stomach. Then higher in the middle of his back. Dull thuds accompanied each point of pain. Then faded. He opened his eyes again when he felt something in his hands. He was holding onto something. It wriggled and moved. He was holding onto it as if his life depended on keeping it in his grasp. Travis could barely see. It was dark. The light was very low. *Where were those bin-*

oculars? He squinted. It was a heavily booted foot he held in in his hands. A big foot. There was a crash. The mayonnaise jar. *Thank God I didn't pee in it, he thought.* Travis saw the foot again. It was no longer in his hands. He had let go of it. There was more pressure. This time on the top of his head. Travis felt tired, so he closed his eyes and fell asleep.

— —

Paige was still wired and couldn't sleep. After they had recovered from the foyer, she and Muerce opened a bottle of white wine and drank some of it in the shower. They had sex twice more, and in more traditional form, before Muerce fell asleep in the bed.

The apartment was quiet as she walked around the place naked. She rooted around in the kitchen, finding very little to eat or drink. From the refrigerator she took a small bottle of Perrier water, unscrewed the cap, and took a sip. The fizzy bubbles made her feel less drunk.

As she wandered through the living and dining room, she stopped occasionally to pick up an item and look at it. She was precise in how she returned each object to its place. There was little that interested her. It was hard for her to concentrate anyway. She decided to return to the bedroom. As she walked down the hallway, sipping the gassy water, she instinctively tried the door knob that led to the second bedroom. The one, she did not know, that had been set up as the repository for his research into what was being called the Death Weaver killings. It was locked. *Everybody has their secrets, she thought, moving on.*

In the bathroom, Paige scanned Muerce's medicine cabinet. *A bathroom can tell you everything.* His only told Paige that he was a man. One with good taste, and expensive grooming tools and products. She pushed the vials and tubes, brushes and razors around in the cabinet. For Paige, it was not to snoop, but so she could connect with Muerce—Jack—more than just physically. There was more to him, and she wanted to know it.

"What have we here?" she said, finding an amber-colored plastic container. It was the only prescription bottle in his cabinet.

Paige read the label. Dr. Riley. Alprazolam. 50 3mg tablets. Paige pinched the safety cap, twisted it off and looked inside. There were seven left. He was low. Shaking one out of the bottle, she popped it into her mouth, and chased it with the Perrier.

Twenty minutes later, Paige was fast asleep next to Muerce.

— —

Pho Mat relaxed when the bedroom light went out in Muerce's apartment. He had been on edge since remembering where he had seen the woman Muerce was with. He recalled the night at Saigon Laundry, and again, a week ago, at the museum. She was beautiful, but skittish and unbalanced. He did not know enough about her to be at ease. At least for the night, Muerce appeared safe.

Pho Mat lit a cigarette in the dark, and stared out the window. In the late-night stillness, he could hear the insistent scream of sirens in the distance.

CHAPTER 37

Cradling his head in his hands as he sat on the edge of the bed, Muerce wasn't sure he'd make it to the toilet. Even if he did, he wasn't sure what he would do, and in what order, once he got there. He opted, instead, to remain as still as possible and count the heartbeats pulsing in his temples. Slowly, his nausea faded, and he could move his head from side to side without the room spinning, but he did so cautiously. Twisting himself around, Muerce looked at the body in the bed behind him. Paige lay covered by a single sheet, her head buried under a pillow. A leg was exposed, showcasing one of her perfect calves. *Oh, the sex.* Recalling the previous night, Muerce's shame was as colossal as his hangover.

A gray, dingy light flooded the bedroom. They had been too drunk and engaged with each other to close the drapes. Standing up, Muerce didn't bother to draw them when he heard the birds singing their announcement of Spring. The incessant chirping was enough to make him retreat into the silence of the bathroom. Like the drapes, he did not bother to shut the door. From the looks of Paige's condition, Muerce guessed he could run a chainsaw in the shower and she wouldn't wake. Propping himself with one arm against the wall behind the toilet, he emptied his bladder. Given what he felt like doing when he woke up, it was a good start for the day. When he was done, he lingered in the same position. The cool tile felt good on his hand and feet. He continued to prop himself up with his right hand. Looking down at himself, he thought of the chainsaw again.

Might as well cut the damn thing off now.

"Stupid, Jack," he said, out loud. "Stupid, stupid stupid."

After splashing his face with cold water, he noticed a half empty bottle of Perrier on the counter. From the medicine cabinet he grabbed a bottle of Extra Strength Tylenol, and shook two out. There was some fizz left in the water that produced a short, but refreshing interlude as he swallowed the pills.

Rummaging through the kitchen, Muerce gave boundless thanks to Travis when he came across a full bag of ground coffee in the cupboard above the elaborate coffee machine. Next to the coffee was a box of biscotti, and a half eaten package of Chips Ahoy. He ate two cookies as he started the coffee brewing. There was nothing breakfast-like in the refrigerator except a slight chill as Muerce stood naked in front of the open doors. The concept of a shower appealed to him. Maybe it would help wash the guilt and shame that clung to his skin like rancid oil. It would make him feel better, and he could mentally prepare for the awkward conversation that awaited him.

The shower only reminded Muerce of the night before when he walked in to turn the water on, and almost kicked the empty bottle of wine over. There was a full goblet of wine on the shower floor, and an empty one next to it. He couldn't remember which was his as he poured the remnants down the drain. Paige had not moved on the bed. She was so still, Muerce wondered if she were alive until he heard her snoring softly beneath the pillow.

He showered, put on a robe and returned to the kitchen for coffee. As he did, he spotted the pile of their clothes on the floor in the foyer. *Stupid, stupid, stupid.* He also remembered his phone was in his jacket, and that he had put it on silent mode. Muerce collected the clothes and dumped them on the living room couch. Postponing the inevitable for at least a few more minutes, he slipped the phone into the pocket of his robe, went to the kitchen, and put together a tray of cookies and coffee that he carried back into the bedroom.

Paige tried to blink away the fog as she looked up at Muerce from beneath the pillow. At first, she wasn't quite sure where, or who, she was with, but the smell of coffee put things back on track. Muerce could see she wasn't a morning person, and they wouldn't be talking until she warmed to the day. Without asking, he went to the bathroom, and got two more Tylenols.

Paige sat up, chased the pills with coffee, and stared at her feet. The post Xanax grogginess helped ease her hangover, but came with a gauzy next-morning perspective. She took a cookie from the tray, and crossed her legs so Muerce could sit next to her. With a refill of coffee, she was ready for light conversation.

"Good morning," Muerce said.

"Thanks," Paige said, referring to the cup of coffee in her hand. She took another sip. "Some night."

"Yeah," Muerce said. "Whose idea was wine in the shower?"

"Yours," she said.

He had a vague memory of the suggestion.

"It was *my* idea to get drunk," he said.

"Oh yeah," Paige said, dipping a second cookie into her coffee and eating it. "You could have said 'let's rob a bank' and I would have gone along with you."

"I didn't see any loose cash laying on the floor," Muerce said. Paige looked up from her coffee, and toward the door as if she were walking her eyes into the foyer and asking Muerce a question at the same time.

"I put everything on the couch," he said. "Do you need something?"

Paige shook her head at him, indicating that she didn't, and finished the cookie. Muerce casually lowered himself onto the end of the bed, facing Paige, and propped himself on his right arm. She sat, crossed leg, Indian style, naked, sipping coffee, and allowing Muerce to see whatever he wanted to look at.

"This is kind of awkward," he said.

"Okay," Paige said. Uncertain and apprehensive of the subject Muerce was about to raise, she set her coffee on the nightstand and braced herself.

"We didn't really have *that* talk last night, before," he said.

"Before what?" she said. "Before we fucked?"

"Yeah, before we *fucked*," Muerce said. He emphasized the last word that came out of his mouth to match Paige's abrupt and nonchalant delivery, but it only made him feel prudish and stupid.

Paige could read it all over him, and it made her smile. Jack Muerce has a weakness, and she knew what it was. She leaned forward onto her hands and knees, and kissed him on his forehead. Then she looked into his eyes.

"I'm not the slut you think I am," she said. "And I don't want your baby. If you test positive for anything, it didn't come from me."

She rocked back on her heels, sat upright, fluffed two pillows to lay back against, and retrieved her coffee and another cookie.

"Should I be worried?" she said, wiping the crumbs from her mouth.

"No," he said. "I'm sorry. I could have been more of, well, a gentleman."

Paige smiled at Muerce again, bigger inside than out.

"You're cute when you're vulnerable," she said. "That doesn't happen very often, does it?"

"Being cute?" he said. Muerce was surprisingly comfortable with Paige's observations. She was more mature than he expected, and not nearly the spoiled brat he thought her to be.

"Being vulnerable," she said.

"No, I suppose not," he said.

"Good," she said. "Kittens are cute. Do you like cats?"

"I hate the damn things," he said.

"So do I," Paige said.

"What do you like?" he said.

"For you to be as angry with me as you were last night," she said. "Without having to get drunk."

— —

The screen on Muerce's phone detonated with icons that screamed at him for responses. There were thirteen missed calls, seven voicemails, and as many text messages. Almost all of the phone calls and voicemails were from Trumbley and Bhote. There were two calls and one voicemail from Turko. He didn't need to listen to them to know what they were calling about. The text message headline alert from the newspaper told him what he didn't want to know.

Death Weaver: Fourth Female Found on Float Following Feast

"Who won the pot?" Muerce said.

"Someone over in the Tenth Precinct, I think," Trumbley said. "You listen to my messages?"

"No," Muerce said. "I just called. Give me the Cliff Notes."

"Feds are here," Trumbley said. "They've taken over the crime scene. Same at the morgue. Apparently, they're here to *help* us. They've locked everything down. Bhote says to meet him in the hospital cafeteria. He'll download what he can."

"Who's case is it now?" Muerce said.

"You know damn well who's running the case, now," Trumbley said.

"Good," Muerce said. "Let them. I'm out."

"The hell *you* are," Trumbley said. "The hell *we* are."

"Nick," Muerce said. "Let's get some perspective here. It was a favor for Sonjay. He asked for an outside perspective when he found out Nit and Wit caught the case. Same with the Mayor and the Chief. Like it or not, the FBI has bigger dicks than ours."

"That are only good for fucking up and pissing all over the place," Trumbley said.

"Doing what they're best at," Muerce said.

"Sonjay still wants to meet with us," Trumbley said. "Deal's a deal. Favor's a favor."

Muerce drew in a deep breath, and exhaled slowly as he considered Trumbley's words.

"Fair enough," Muerce said. "When?"

"He's up to his eyeballs in G-men right now," Trumbley said. "Let's say two hours. The cafeteria. I'll let him know."

"The coffee is shit there," Muerce said, relieved he could ignore replying directly to Bhote. "By the way, did you get any messages from Travis?"

"No, why?" Trumbley said.

"I had him watching Brankovic's place last night," Muerce said. "Guess nothing happened."

"You didn't do it yourself?" Trumbley said.

"No, why?" Muerce said.

"Is he really ready for that kind of thing?" Trumbley said. "He's only been under your wing, what? Two weeks?"

"Were you when you were his age?" Muerce said. "He's a sharp kid. A lot smarter than us."

"I'm just saying," Trumbley said.

"What's with the guilt?" Muerce said. "It was a squat and watch. I told him that if even the wind changed direction he was to get the hell out of there, and call me."

"Like that would have done any good," Trumbley said. "I called you a million times this morning and you didn't pick up. I'm not asking who or what you were up to. Just saying. You're not the most available person sometimes."

"Yeah, yeah," Muerce said. "I get it. I'll call him right away."

"See you in two," Trumbley said, ending the call.

Muerce was going through his contacts list to call Travis when the screen announced an incoming call from Unknown. His instinct was to ignore it, but he took the call anyway.

"Jack, it's Pope."

"Ben," Muerce said. "Where are you?"

"It's tomorrow where I am," Pope said. "I hear things are getting a little more complicated on your end."

"You've got big ears," Muerce said.

"The biggest there are," Pope said.

"I'm listening," Muerce said.

"The First Bunch of Idiots are in from Quantico," Pope said. "The BAU unit. Like I said, I really don't give a shit about the case. You know what I'm interested in."

"Haven't forgotten," Muerce said.

"I need you in the loop, at least their loop," Pope said. "They're not interested in talking to you. That whole territorial thing they have going on, but I made some calls. They'll stay out of your way, if you stay out of theirs."

"I've got no problem with that," Muerce said.

"Favor's a favor," Pope said.

"So I keep being reminded," Muerce said.

"You got anything you want to tell me?" Pope said.

"It's yesterday where I am," Muerce said. "I'm just now waking up trying to figure out what's what."

Muerce waited. If Pope had been watching him he'd say something about the impromptu meeting with Amelie at Saigon Laundry. And there was the Brankovic baby. But nothing was said.

"Call if you've got anything," Pope said.

"Unknown?" Muerce said.

"My regular cell," Pope said. "I'll pick up."

"Ben," Muerce said. "Be careful with the curry. Old man like you. It could really mess up your digestion."

"Get out of bed and put whoever she is in a cab," Pope said. "I need you working. And call your mother."

Three beeps and the line went dead.

Get a cab? Call your mother? Jeez, what does he know and not know?

He thumbed through his phone. No messages from Eleanor. He listened to the voicemail from Turko: "Jack. Turko. It's primetime now. Sorry man. I got to go with what I got. Call me."

In the bathroom, Muerce heard the sound of the shower end. There was the soft rustling of Paige toweling herself off. His call to Travis rolled into voicemail: "Travis, call me. Let me know how it went last night."

During the call to Travis a text message arrived on Muerce's phone that he didn't expect: Hey stranger! brunch today? Ash.

Crap. Muerce froze, looking at the screen unsure what, or whether he should answer.

"Everything okay?" Paige said. She had a towel wrapped around her waist, and used another to towel her hair dry.

"Complications," he said.

"Not from me," she said.

He liked her answer.

"Can I give you a ride?" he said.

"Did you forget?," she said. "You don't have a car."

"Oh," Muerce said. "I've got a car."

— —

It was hard not to be impressed, but Paige suppressed any expression of amazement—as she had done on the ride down to the basement garage on the private elevator—when Muerce snatched off the large cover cloth. He did so with the flourish of a matador taunting the bull with a *muleta*. Muerce did, indeed, have a car. Its brand was distinctively thoroughbred, but it was a bull nonetheless. Glistening before Paige under the harsh fluorescent light of the underground garage was a black 1962 250 GT Berlinetta Lusso Ferrari. It was one of only three hundred and fifty produced, and had belonged to Muerce's father. And it rarely left the garage. It was so beautiful, Paige wanted to take her clothes off and lay on it.

"Let's hope it starts," Muerce said, opening the door for her.

It doesn't have to, she thought. She ran her hands across the dashboard and over the angled console that housed two large, round gauges directed at the driver. She slipped her fingers around the gear shift, then brushed them against the black, leather diamond patterned luggage cover behind her. When the engine turned over, she felt the vibration from deep in her seat up to her nipples. The range of the sound of the engine was low and throaty like a lover whispering promises into the ear of his beloved. The smell of the leather was heavy and primitive. All together, the sensations raised the delicate hairs on her arms and the back of her neck.

"Where do you want to go?" Muerce said.

"Anywhere," she said.

Muerce looked at her with mock annoyance, which disappeared when he saw how hard she was working at hiding what she was really feeling. He wanted her to drop the front, and say what he wanted to hear; what every man wants to hear from a young, beautiful woman who has just left his bed—that she's impressed. The slight tilt of his head, and squint in his eyes conveyed it. Paige figured she'd give some, but not all to him. She would stroke his ego, while keeping his vanity in check.

"The car is cool," she said. "But that doesn't mean you are. The penthouse elevator thing is pretentious. I'm taking points off for that."

"Tough crowd," Muerce said. She was sharp, and sassy. Still very much a mystery to him; an intriguing challenge. He was hooked on her game. "So where?"

"My gym," Paige said. "I keep extra clothes there, and I could use a workout."

"What about your car?" Muerce said, slowly pulling the Ferrari out of its bay and up the ramp as the heavy corrugated metal garage door opened.

"I'll figure it out later," she said, looking out the window and away from him as they pulled onto the side street next to the apartment building. She put her hand over her mouth to cover the grin that stretched across her face.

Then Muerce did something that surprised both of them.

"I need to get some grease in my belly," he said. "I have a few errands to do. How about I pick you up at your gym when you're done, and we grab a late lunch-early dinner?"

Paige did not bother to hide her wonderment.

"Sure," she nearly sputtered through her fingers.

Muerce wasn't sure if it was the coffee or her response that made his stomach flutter. The giddiness, however, didn't last long.

— —

Halfway down the block after dropping Paige off in front of her swanky, upscale gym, Muerce's phone rang. It was T.B. Squire.

"I'm glad you called," Muerce said. "I've been trying to reach Travis."

"That's why I'm calling," T.B. Squire said. His delivery was deliberate and serious, and immediately put Muerce on edge. "I'm at the emergency room at County. Travis is in serious, but stable condition."

"Serious, not critical?" Muerce said.

"That's right," T.B. said.

"I'm on my way there now," Muerce said.

"We're moving him to Lutheran Mercy," T.B. said. "He needs some minor surgery. His face is pretty torn up. It's not that there aren't fine surgeons here..."

"I understand what you're saying," Muerce said, pausing. "He's your son. Do you know what happened?"

"He's not talking right now," T.B. said. He began to crack when he spoke. "Can't. Broken jaw, cheekbone, ribs, punctured lung. He's beat bad. They've got him heavily sedated."

There was an uncomfortable pause in the conversation. Muerce heard T.B. swallow a breath before he spoke.

"I'm afraid the police think he was buying drugs," he said. "They found Travis in a part of town where he had no reason being."

"No, it wasn't drugs, or gambling related," Muerce said, without hesitation. "This is my fault T.B. Travis was where he was because I sent him there. He was doing something for me. This wasn't supposed to happen, but I own this, and I'll make it right."

"Then I'm sure he'll want to talk to you as soon as he is able," T.B. said. "I'm thankful it wasn't about any of those things, but mostly I'm thankful he's alive."

The silence that followed T.B.'s statement was a clear indication that was all he was thankful for as far as Muerce was concerned.

"I'm sorry," Muerce said. "I'll explain it all when I see you."

Muerce pulled to the curb when the call ended. He turned the engine off, and sat silently for several minutes, beating himself up with guilt. He'd gotten drunk, and had sex with a woman he hardly knew. Unsafe, and bestial sex at that. And Travis had paid the price for his wanton behavior. Muerce knew better. He second-guessed himself when he gave Travis the assignment and did't act on it, instead, allowing his passion to overcome rational judgement. He should have gone instead. Even Trumbley knew it. Travis deserved better. Paige deserved better, too. And what about Ashley? Looking out at the gray sky, Muerce vowed to the overcast heavens that he'd do better; he'd be better. His thoughts began to focus on Brankovic, and as they did the sense of shame began to transform into a righteous anger.

The Ferrari's engine roared to life, its tires squealed as Muerce drove off for his meeting with Bhote and Trumbley. He thumbed a call on his phone.

"Nick, Jack," he said. "Can you make some calls before we meet?"

Trumbley said he could, and Muerce filled him in on what had happened to Travis. He also confessed his poor judgement in making Travis his proxy for the assignment. Trumbley told him to let it go.

▪ ▪

The black Ferrari zipped past Pho Mat, who was still annoyed with himself for having missed Muerce's departure earlier. Perched at his watch, he was expecting a taxi when he saw the elegant sports car pass by the front of the apartment. It had snapped around the corner when Pho Mat became alarmed. Only Jack Muerce would own such a car in this neighborhood. He should have suspected Muerce had a spare vehicle sitting around for his pleasure, as he apparently did with women—and as equally fast, and lovely.

With some directional guessing based on gut feelings, he caught up to Muerce just as he was letting Paige off at her gym. Pho Mat ducked the Supra behind a small delivery van, then pulled out when Muerce did.

The Supra had heavily tinted windows that protected Pho Mat's identity while the Ferrari retained its clear glass that came from the factory decades earlier. As he passed, Pho Mat could see Muerce, who could not see Pho Mat.

Muerce was on his cell phone, and when he sped by the Supra he did so with no indication of recognition of the car next to him. It was a relief to Pho Mat, who was unsure if Muerce had spotted the tail when he had abruptly pulled to the side of the street and stopped. The unexpected move had been so sudden, Pho Mat could only drive past to avoid suspicion, and hope to re-acquire the Ferrari down the road.

Guessing at Muerce's destination was elementary. Pho Mat knew Muerce's patterns. And he kept up on current events. The news on the all-talk radio station was exclusively focused on the top item of the day; the early morning discovery of a fourth victim of the serial killer terrorizing the city. If Pho Mat were to wager, which he did on occasion and with great pleasure, his money would be on finding Muerce at the Coroner's Office at County Hospital.

They were headed in the right direction.

— —

The cafeteria coffee was thoroughly awful. Muerce pushed the styrofoam cup away as he sat, waiting for Bhote and Trumbley to arrive. It was late morning, and there were few people around. A television echoed in the background. It was a local news crew, reporting live near the scene where the remains of the fourth victim were found. The body was discovered on one of the floats that took part in previous day's parade. The severed arms and legs were arranged—as if still whole—near the victim's torso. In an exclusive detail to the case, which the reporter and the news channel promoted at each commercial break, the head remained attached to the torso. Authorities, the reporter barked, were not releasing any other details, other than the float was a re-creation of a map of Ireland, and its counties, main cities and famous attractions.

"The one thing I was afraid of," Bhote said. He looked gaunt and exhausted.

"The media?" Muerce said.

"Like maggots on a summer corpse," Bhote said, putting a file on the table so he could massage his temples.

"Thanks for the cream and sugar, but that's not going to make the coffee here taste any better," Muerce said.

"I'm not going to miss either when I retire," Bhote said. "Is Nick coming?"

Trumbley entered the cafeteria as the question left Bhote's mouth. He waved at the two of them as he paid the cashier for a cup of coffee. After taking a sip when he sat down at the table, Trumbley spat the liquid back into the cup.

"This is crap," Trumbley said.

"There's a Starbuck's a few blocks away," Bhote said. "Not much call for a barista here. This is where the dead and dying come."

"Well, they sure as hell don't come for the coffee," Trumbley said. "You look like shit, Sonjay."

"It's been a long day," he said.

"And it's only half over," Muerce said. "How's the FBI? They going to ask you out for a second date?"

"Fucking Bossy and Intrusive," Bhote said. Muerce and Trumbley were amused. Bhote very rarely dropped the F-bomb. "Excuse me. Our visitors from the Bureau are very demanding, and insistent guests. Apparently, you can't go near the body, but I'm allowed to talk to you. Though, they're not too happy about it."

"What have you got?" Trumbley said.

"Asian, female, early thirties," Bhote said. "Chinese. No ID yet. Body the same condition as the others."

"Except," Muerce said.

"Her ears are missing," Bhote said. "The skin from her face was stretched back and sewn to the flap of her scalp."

"Sound," Trumbley said. Bhote nodded in agreement.

"The same kind of Roman coin was found in her mouth," Bhote said.

"And?" Muerce said.

Bhote opened the folder in front of him, removed a large, glossy photo, and slid it across the table for Muerce and Trumbley to see. He tapped at a specific area with his long, bony finger.

The photograph was an enlargement of the stitching used to close the patch of skin that covered the area where the victim's left ear used to be attached. The work was, again, precise, delicate, and morbidly artistic.

Amid a border of colorful flowers and elaborate silk-thread cross knots was the French word *chien*.

"What's that say?" Trumbley said.

"Dog," Muerce answered.

"Chien, Chinese—is there any connection?" Trumbley said.

"I don't think so," Bhote said.

"So no race crime element? Trumbley said.

"The other three were caucasian," Muerce said.

"There's another thing," Bhote said. "He removed a second photo from the folder, and pushed it across the table. "Look at the finger tips of her left hand. They're heavily calloused."

He slid a third photo toward them.

"Her right hand," Bhote said. "Not the same."

Muerce and Trumbley looked puzzled.

"Violin, cello... I think she was a musician," Bhote said. "Love them or hate them, the FBI came up with something we missed."

"What?" Muerce and Trumbley said, simultaneously.

"Our second victim, Taste," Bhote said. "She had a life before the alcohol and drugs. She was a *sous* chef. Trained in New Orleans.

"They were all artists, in their own way."

"Artists who wasted their talents," Muerce said.

God given talents, Muerce thought.

"I don't follow," Trumbley said.

"The prostitute is easy," Muerce said. "Touch for a price. The chef who lost her Taste to booze. Then Sight. The photographer. Don't you remember she won a Pulitzer working for the newspaper? It was part of that series on the war in El Salvador. Once a great photojournalist. These days all she did was shoot weddings, babies and *bah mitzvahs*."

"If I had to guess, Sound was a street musician who had higher aspirations at some point in her life."

"All that's left is Smell," Trumbley said.

"Smell," Muerce said. "And Desire."

"I have to get back," Bhote said, collecting the photographs. "I'll let you know what I can let you know."

"Wait," Muerce said, removing his phone from his pocket. He took a quick picture of the photograph of the wound with the embroidery. "They won't mind."

Bhote sniffed, turned, and left Muerce and Trumbley in the cafeteria.

"What do you think?" Trumbley said.

"I think we're peripheral," Muerce said.

"Looks that way," Trumbley said. "Why do I feel like we screwed up?"

"Because that's how they want you to feel," Muerce said. "It was never ours to screw up in the first place."

"Doesn't make me feel any better," Trumbley said.

"It's not over yet," Muerce said. "Besides, don't you have a wedding to plan? How's she doing?"

"It's Miriam, Jack," Trumbley said, testing the coffee in his cup to see if it was cool enough to drink. "She's too tough to let you know how she's doing. But I can tell. Good days, and bad days. She's recovering the Miriam way. She goes to work."

"Goddamned right," Muerce said.

"Never fuck with the Welfare Lady," they said, in tandem. Muerce and Trumbley broke out in laughter so loud it drowned out the noise from the television.

— —

The meeting with T.B. Squire at Lutheran Mercy had the potential to be very awkward. Whatever might be thrown at him, Muerce felt he deserved, and he'd readily accept the responsibility, offer his sincerest apologies, and do whatever had to be done to make appropriate restitution. As he walked down the hall toward the waiting room outside the surgery suites, Muerce anticipated the worst, but was hopeful in knowing Travis would live. Whatever dread Muerce imagined dissipated when T.B. Squire spotted him approaching, and stood up with a broad smile. Travis' mother was busy in conversation with a surgical nurse. T.B. met Muerce halfway, and offered his hand.

"Thank you for coming," T.B. said, shaking Muerce's hand with warm regard. "It means so much."

"T.B," Muerce said. "You have every right to take a swing at me."

"Not at all, Jack," T.B. said, surprised at Muerce's comment. "Not after what you told me."

"I put your son in harm's way," Muerce said. "I don't know what happened, but he could have been killed."

"But he wasn't," T.B. said.

"I don't understand," Muerce said.

"He was doing a job," T.B. said. "It may have been dangerous, but he chose to do it. He hasn't talked much about what he's been doing for you, but his mother and I could see he loves it. He isn't the boy we used to worry about, he's a man. That comes with risks."

"It can," Muerce said. "But this was a risk I should have taken."

"Maybe, maybe not," T.B. said. "I've heard three good things today since hearing the one bad. The first was my son was alive. The second was you telling me that this wasn't a drug deal, or he owed more gambling debts. And the third was his hands were bruised and skinned.

"He fought back."

Muerce understood. *Good for Travis, he thought.*

As they stood in the hallway quietly comforting each other with Travis' machismo in the face of a severe beating, Mrs. Squire joined them.

"You remember Travis' mother, my wife, Anna Marie," T.B. said.

She offered, and Muerce accepted her handshake firmly in his. It was delicate yet firm, directing Muerce's clasp before relaxing her fingers to indicate the exchange of greetings was finished. She was Old School, Old South—if a blow was to be proffered, then it would likely come from her.

"Misses Squire," Muerce said. "It is my fault your son is here. I offer my apology, even though it sounds hollow to the ears of a mother."

"That is generous of you, Mister Muerce," she said. "But the time for apologies is past. What are you to do about this?"

"I can assure you I will find out who did this to Travis," Muerce said. "And there will be consequences."

"That, Mister Muerce, despite my Christian upbringing is what a mother wishes to hear," Anna Marie said.

"May I see Travis?" Muerce said.

"He's in surgery now," T.B. said. "They had to wire his jaw, and do some cosmetic work on his face. There were some severe lacerations."

"I need to talk to him as soon as I can," Muerce said.

"Not until tomorrow," T.B. said. "But I'm sure he'll want to see you. He kept trying to write your name down before they sedated him."

"It's quite a testament to the effect you've had on him," Anna Marie said. "We do appreciate what you've done for Travis, and we, as he, look forward to seeing you again soon."

"I promise to take better care of your son," Muerce said, directing his words to Anna Marie. "And I will take care of whoever did this to him. You have my word."

"I believe I do," Anna Marie said. "If you'll excuse me."

Muerce bowed slightly as she returned to the waiting room.

"I love her to tears," T.B. said. "But sometimes the woman scares me to death."

"She's frightened, T.B.," Muerce said. "Protecting her offspring. She can be as mean as she wants to me. I don't blame her."

"I suppose," T.B. said.

"You said cosmetic surgery?" Muerce said. "Doctor Sharron?"

"Actually, no," T.B. said. "We weren't able to reach him. His scheduling nurse said he doesn't take Sunday calls during Lent. Strange, I never thought of him as a religious person. Odd man."

Very, Muerce thought.

CHAPTER 38

As agreed, Paige was waiting on the curb outside the gym when Muerce pulled up. He held his hand up for her not to move, jumped out and made his way around the car to open her door. She was dressed casually, in a light cotton sweater, jeans and flats. She had a simple, black Kate Spade purse slung over her shoulder along with a black, leather Dolce and Gabbana duffel. The post-workout glow lit up her face, and highlighted the smile she gave Muerce as he held the door open. He noticed she had taken the time to style her hair instead of pull it back into a pony. There were light touches of makeup. When he slipped behind the wheel and shut his door, Paige's fragrance permeated the confines of the Ferrari. It was a natural scent that had a sweet earthiness like a summer field after a rain, and complimented the rich smell of leather.

"You look great," he said.

"Good enough for a greasy burger?" she said. Paige was flattered by his compliment, and very aware of the small group of women who had been in her spinning class who noticed her getting into the car. She wanted to turn and wave at them, then give them the finger, but instead kept her attention on Muerce. *Bitches.*

"Is that all right?" he said, unsure if he should step it up to match the effort she had put into getting ready for him.

"Are you kidding?" she said. "That's all I was thinking about during spinning class. I'm still a little fragile from last night."

Half an hour later, Muerce was biting into a thick, juicy cheeseburger topped with dill pickle and onion straws that he chased down with an ice-filled glass of Pepsi. Between chomps on the burger, he dragged his sweet potato fries through the puddle of ketchup he squeezed on his plate. His stomach, which hadn't had anything except bad coffee and a couple of chocolate chip cookies, was satisfied. The salt and sugar of the meal also burned off the last rough edges of his hangover. To his surprise, Paige ordered a shot and a beer to start, then chased it with water as she nibbled on her hamburger, hardly touching the side of cottage cheese.

"You don't mind coming back here?" Muerce said. O'Keeffe's was nearly empty, and tired from the previous day's festivities. The televisions were mostly tuned to a NBA game. One channel, with its sound off, continued its coverage of the Death Weaver.

"Back to the scene of the crime?" Paige said, referring to the start of their previous day's debauchery. They had taken a table near the dartboard range, and she stood, focused on the target, casually throwing darts between bites of her sandwich.

"Bad choice of phrase," Muerce said, his attention was focused on the news channel.

"What are you talking about?" Paige said, retrieving her tosses from the board.

"Nothing," he said. So focused on satisfying his hunger, Muerce paid little attention to Paige's activity at the dartboard. He had not noticed that every dart she tossed hit the bull's eye. She was nonchalant and relaxed, taking each throw with casual effortlessness. At times, she swayed her hips back and forth to an internal rhythm that calmed her as she flung the missiles.

"These aren't weighted well," she said.

"What?" Muerce said. There were two, maybe three bites left of his sandwich, but he had had enough, and threw in the towel by wiping his fingers with his napkin, and tossing it onto the plate of food. "What are you doing?"

"Just goofing around," she said. Paige checked the line on the floor, and pumped three darts in a row at the disc five feet, eight inches away. The red, feathered fletching formed a perfect triangle with each point securely within the boundary of the center circle. Muerce had to squint to make out the bull's eye. He sipped at his soda, and watched Paige repeat the feat three more times before she noticed him staring at her.

She blushed when she looked over at him.

"That's amazing," he said. "Can you do that every time?"

She grabbed a loose dart from the holder on the wall next to her, her back to the target, looked over her shoulder at the dartboard, and then back at Muerce. She winked at him and tossed the yellow dart over her shoulder. It landed in the middle of the three red-fletched darts, knocking one of them to the floor.

"That's a hell of a party trick," Muerce said, clapping at the feat.

"Oh, you want to see a trick?" Paige said. Her eyes were sultry and inviting as she swayed toward him. When she got to the table she scanned the room to see if anyone was looking. There was obvious mischievousness on her mouth when she bent toward Muerce. He thought she was about to steal a kiss when she snatched a fork from the table, turned and launched it. The fork impaled the dartboard just above the array of darts stuck to its center.

"The middle's a little crowded,' Paige said, lifting Muerce's drink from the table, and taking a sip.

"Did you grow up in a circus?" he said.

"Hmm," she said. "Just a gift, I guess."

She put the drink down and left the table to retrieve the darts.

Paige was as an intriguing woman as he had ever known. Full of strange surprises, and exotic behaviors that could be as alluring as they were foreboding. He thought of her as both innocent and dangerous. He was quite taken with her to the point he didn't mind ignoring the red flags.

Muerce was so engrossed in Paige's play, he did not notice detectives Ash and Maple when they entered O'Keeffe's. It was not until they sat down at his table, beers in hand, Muerce paid them any attention. Paige continued her dart play.

"You're early," Muerce said. "The garbage doesn't get picked up until tomorrow."

"Fucking funny, Merc," Maple said. "A goddamned comedian."

"Ah, what's the matter guys?" Muerce said. "Lose your jobs?"

Maple stiffened, and cocked his arm back in a threatening pose. Ash nodded at his partner to relax, then took a swig of beer. Maple backed off, and sat back in his chair, spreading his legs open and taking a long pull from his glass.

"We all got big-footed today," Ash said. "Even you, Muerce. Doesn't it piss you off, a little?"

"Not the slightest," Muerce said. "Could be for the best, you know. They're the pros after all."

The three of them looked up at the television carrying the new coverage of the serial killings. A young, good looking and well suited man identified as an agent with the FBI was being interviewed.

"Damn, he's pretty," Muerce said. "Looks like he's got the case solved. You know the FBI."

"Yeah, they always get their man," Ash said.

"Even if it's the wrong one," Maple said.

Muerce snorted, and kept his attention focused on Paige, who tossed more darts at the target, and snuck an occasional glance toward the table.

"I'm actually kind of busy right now," Muerce said, watching Paige. "What do you want?"

"The FBI doesn't know shit," Ash said. "It'll take them weeks to get up to speed. And the bodies will keep stacking up."

"How many more do you figure?" Muerce said.

"The Weaver's just getting started," Maple said. He tried to stifle a belch, but it curled out from the side of his mouth.

"We can break this case," Ash said, looking at the handsome FBI agent still talking on the television. "You know who's behind this."

"I know who's been whispering in your ear who's behind this," Muerce said.

"Same's been whispering in yours," Ash said.

"Lots of people whisper in my ear," Muerce said, staring at Paige. "But I don't let all of them fuck me."

Ash sipped his beer, listened to Muerce, and imagined what Paige looked like naked as he stared at her ass while she tossed darts.

"You're getting worked," Muerce said. "Titty Boy has his own agenda."

"So what?" Maple said. "Brankovic killed hundreds of people. Fucking raped them and tortured them. Does his needlepoint thing on them when he's done. Now he's here, doing the same shit. How the hell did he get here in the first place? I'm telling you the feds are going to let this turd slip down the pipes. It's political. Fucking conspiracy if you ask me."

"Stop checking that out, will you?" Ash said, looking away from Paige's tight jeans, and toward Maple. "This ain't the X-Files just because the FBI showed up.

"Brankovic's good for this. You know it Muerce."

"I know the evidence isn't any harder than your partner can get," Muerce said.

"Fuck you Merc," Maple said.

"You know, the only thing hard about you is your last name," Muerce said, turning to Maple. "I don't know what the hell the force gets out of you, except for, maybe, syrup."

"I've had enough of your lip, Merc," Maple said. Reaching his right arm back. He started to shift his weight to launch a punch when the air was broken with a gentle *whir* that was followed by a distinctive *thunk* that sounded in the region of Maple's crotch. There, on the wooden chair where he sat, an inch from his testicles, stuck a dart. A blink of his eyes later, a second dart landed, pinning the left inseam of his trousers to the seat. Maple froze from the neck down, but looked up to see Paige poised with a third dart at the ready.

Muerce had seen a similar expression on her face before. When she held the knife to his throat at Club Unicorn, and when he was behind and inside her in the foyer the night before. Those had been wild and aggressive flashes that carried an invitation. What was in her eyes as she concentrated her aim on Maple was protective and territorial, and capable of doing almost anything. Muerce had seen a glimmer of it in Anna Marie's eyes at the hospital. Seeing it in Paige both excited, and frightened Muerce. It was not an emotion that could be controlled.

"Good thing she missed," Ash said, standing slightly up from his seat for a better view.

"She doesn't miss," Muerce said, his eyes locked on Paige.

Ash stood up, and raised his hands to Paige to signal concession, and defuse the tension.

"Let it go," Ash said, motioning for his partner to leave. Maple pulled the dart from the chair, and the one from his trousers, and placed them on the table next to Muerce. His sneer was ignored as he got up and headed toward the bar. Before he left, Ash turned to Muerce.

"We could work together on this," he said. "Think about it."

Paige collected the pair of darts from the table after the detectives left, and took another pull from Muerce's Pepsi.

"Promise not to throw anything at me," he said.

"Not unless you like that sort of thing," Paige said.

"I don't," Muerce said. "Ever."

"Who were those apes?" she said.

"Just a couple of monkeys who like to throw shit at people," Muerce said.

Then, for the second time in as many days, Muerce looked at Paige and said something that surprised him.

"You want to help me get the car I left in the garage yesterday?" he said.

"Right now?" she said.

"Tomorrow morning," he said.

"What time?"

"Early," Muerce said. "I'll buy you breakfast, and then we can get your car."

"Sure," she said. "But only if I can spend the night."

ROSE SUNDAY

By my five wits I feel t'is the fiend, in truth,
Who here hath given me tryst, my life he seeks, forsooth!
                    —The Pearl Poet

CHAPTER 39

ACME Glass was perdition. Upon entering it, all unprotected human senses were attacked simultaneously. Heat seared skin, sound shattered ear drums, razor fine particulates in the air cut corneas, and scarred the linings of the nose, mouth and throat before settling in the lungs. An errant heat plume erupting from the primary furnace, which reached temperatures of more than twenty-seven hundred degrees Fahrenheit, could bring instant death. The victim vaporized in a flash from Hell. In the relatively cooler reaches of the factory floor a single breath could stalk a victim for a lifetime, causing a respiratory malady that slowly squeezed the life out of them until they suffocated in painful fits of excruciating suffering.

The factory made float glass. Large sheets of plate glass were produced from abrasive materials that included sand, sodium carbonate, dolomite, limestone, sodium sulfate, and other additives that lent physical and chemical properties to the finished product. A batch of the billowy materials was mixed, creating toxic clouds, along with cullet, and fed into the primary furnace, which was a thirty-by-fifty-yard section of real estate ascended from Satan's realm. In it, twelve-hundred tons of the molten soup was superheated, then cooled to just above two-thousand degrees Fahrenheit, lending it specific gravity. This stabilized the glass so it could be introduced into a three-inch deep pool of molten tin that was thirteen feet wide and as long as half a football field. A mixture of nitrogen and hydrogen created a positive pressure in the tin bath to prevent the buildup of dross on the molten glass.

Once it hit the liquid tin, the molten glass smoothed and flattened across the surface, forming an even thickness. What started as a searing glob was now an orange ribbon of glass, slowly cooling to a more manageable twelve-hundred degrees—less than what it took to vaporize human flesh, but still hotter than a crematorium. The ribbon was then lifted from the bath onto giant rollers that, by calibrating the speed and flow of the glass, various thicknesses and widths could be achieved.

The ribbon then passed over a series of shoulder-high flat rollers for about ten feet before entering a Lehr Kiln. There was a three-foot gap between the last roller and the opening to the kiln that allowed enough space for physical inspections of the machinery during operational down times. During production, the space was a No-Man's Land, the floor below it baked and charred from the heat generated by the ribbons of glass that passed overhead. Just outside the last roller was a small, insulated metal box that controlled the speed of the rollers, and also served as an emergency shut off station. At the bottom of the lever inside the control box it simply said SLOW, at the top it said FAST. Below the lever was a big red button that said STOP. The box was a redundancy. The entire process was computerized, and operated from the environmentally sealed safety of a main control room that looked down on the factory floor from the office side of the massive building.

In the kiln, the glass was gradually cooled so that it could anneal without cracking. When the sheet exited the kiln at the "cold end," machines cut the slab to prescribed specifications. It was there humans began to interact with the finished product, but still with great caution. It was not unheard of for a large pane of glass to shatter unexpectedly, severing limbs, or cutting a man in half.

Zajak appreciated the irony. That this violent and dangerous process resulted in glass through which the world could be seen, and that light could pass, was not unlike his purpose—through destruction he would bring transparency and clarity to the world. He would shape Hell to move man to the will of Allah.

Contemplating his own Hejira, Zajak exited the factory floor into a series of clean rooms that sucked the dangerous micro particles from his white safety suit, and prevented them from escaping into the office environment. In the second clean chamber, he removed the heavy rebreather protecting his eyes and lungs, and hung it on a peg on the wall. Then he pushed back the hood of the suit, removing the ear plugs, unzipping the top of the suit, and placing the plugs in the top pocket of his shirt.

He was satisfied with his inspection of the plant, though it had nothing to do with production. The public face of ACME Glass was about to shatter, and he was quietly initiating his exit strategy. ACME had served its purpose, and would soon die. How it died, and how soon, remained in play.

When the elevator doors opened to let him off at the administrative floor, there was the unmistakable smell of cigarettes and sweat that let Zajak know that Brankovic was in the office. As he exited the elevator, Zajak was eyed by two of Brankovic's body guards on the far end of the large working area that led to his office. Six software writers quietly tapped away at their computers, listening to music as they worked on financial programs and currency transfers; none of which had anything to do with the production of float glass, yet they were the core of his plan. They did not bother to look up from the computer screens on their desks as he passed. As instructed, they remained oblivious to anything outside their cubicles. Zajak nodded at the two large men, proceeded past them, and into his office.

"Zmaj, you are early," Zajak said, looking at his watch.

Brankovic sat on the black leather couch on the far wall of the office. Amelie stood, nervously, across the room from him. They were both smoking. Zajak looked at Amelie with disapproval. She looked back at him with an insincere apology for smoking in the office.

"But Amelie keeps me company while I wait," Brankovic said, slowly exhaling smoke from his nostrils. "She is lovely, yes?"

Zajak went to the small table by one of the windows that gave him a view of the front parking lot of the factory, and the Downtown skyline in the distance. As he poured himself a cup of tea from a carafe, Zajak could see Brankovic's car was not outside. *Good,* Zajak thought, *he is using the tunnels... like a rat.*

"More than lovely, she is very smart, and very clever," Zajak said, turning to look at Amelie. "She has shown you the weekly report?"

"Da," Brankovic said, taking a long drag from his cigarette. "Very clever. But I do not understand the technicalities. The timestamps of bank transfers, and why so many? Some I've never heard of, and others I would think we would be careful to avoid. And there are no Swiss accounts."

"The Swiss, Zmaj, are not what they used to be," Zajak said, sipping as he sat down at his desk. "Do you wish Amelie to explain her system?"

"I wish her to be lovely," Brankovic said, staring at Amelie with menace, and lechery. "Her explanation would only give me headache."

"You have had a lot on your mind lately," Zajak said. "Maybe, too much."

"What is it you say, Zajak?" said Brankovic.

"I see you have no car outside," said Zajak.

"This place is filthy," Brankovic said. "Every time I come I have to wash car."

"Better it's not seen here now, anyway," Zajak said. "Not after Saturday night."

A low grunt emanated from Brankovic as he lit another cigarette.

"That was not wise," Zajak said.

"He was spy," Brankovic said.

"There are spies everywhere, we cannot beat them all," Zajak said, glancing at Amelie. "So we don't show them what they want to see. This spy you beat belongs to someone who could be dangerous to us. Or helpful."

"Muerce?" Brankovic said. "I have seen this man. He thinks he is royalty. Elitist. Soft. Of no use to us."

"Amelie, thank you for the report," Zajak said. "You can go now."

"Must she?" Brankovic said, hissing smoke from between his teeth as she turned to leave.

"Yes," Zajak said.

They both watched as she left the office. Zajak had a paternal, yet professional affection for her. He had recruited her himself, and saw the potential in her. Though Brankovic leered at Amelie, he was not sexually interested, but liked to twist the prospect of his being with her in Zajak's head. She was Zajak's pet, and Brankovic did not like pets. To him they were a sign of weakness.

"Muerce could be of use to us, to you," Zajak said. "You could have killed his associate."

"If I wanted to kill him, I would have," Brankovic said. "How is it this Muerce could help me?"

Zajak put his tea down and reached for Amelie's report. He raised his other hand as if he were anointing the words that were about to come from his mouth.

"Our investors are pleased with her work," Zajak said. "Very few people in the world can do what she is doing. This is the business of the future."

"Good," Brankovic said. "Moscow is happy. I am happy."

"It is more than just Moscow," Zajak said. "Business is growing. We have investors in new markets."

"So I am told," Brankovic said.

"As you should be," Zajak said.

"So?" Brankovic said, smoking and looking away from Zajak with disinterest.

"Your business with Tomaso," Zajak said, holding the report up with one hand and placing his finger on the line that showed the income from drugs and prostitution for the week. "It is more like hobby. Pocket change."

"Who works for who, Zajak?" Brankovic said. His eyes blazed with anger.

"I work for you, Zmaj," Zajak said. "This line item. Is yours. Moscow does not care. I do not care. What I worry about, is your interest in the baby of the prostitute. It is not like you."

"It is *my* business," Brankovic said.

"Da," Zajak said. "I understand. You asked me to look into it. We have an attorney for it now. But also, this is where Muerce could be of help."

"You had your precious pet talk to him, and he said he would do nothing," Brankovic said. "I have my own people too, Zajak."

"Ah, spies everywhere," Zajak said. There was a hint of laughter in his voice. "So why attack Muerce's? And risk angering him?"

"I did not know he worked for this Muerce," Brankovic said.

"Then your spies are no good," Zajak said. He picked up the morning newspaper from his desk and opened it to show the large-type headline about the Death Weaver and his most recent victim. "Should I know why he sent someone to watch you Saturday night?"

"Who works for who, Zajak?" Brankovic said, standing and shouting.

"I need not remind you, Zmaj," Zajak said, with no emotion. "We both work for Moscow."

"Enough of this," Brankovic said. "I'm leaving. Do what you are told."

"I always do, Zmaj," Zajak said, smiling.

Brankovic crushed the cigarette dead into the palm of his hand, threw the butt to the floor, and headed toward the door.

"Tell me, Zmaj," Zajak said. "What do you want with the child?"

"To see it," Brankovic said, hissing between his teeth as he opened the door. "To see if it is mine."

"And if it is?" Zajak said.

"Then to see it die," Brankovic said, slamming the door behind him as he left.

Such dramatics, Zajak thought. He allowed his lips to form a smirk. Zajak leaned forward and pressed the intercom button on his phone.

"Amelie," he said. "Come in."

Zajak motioned for her to shut the door when she entered.

"He is a brutal and ignorant man," Amelie said. "A liability. I will be glad when we are rid of him."

"Soon," Zajak said.

"How soon?" Amelie said.

"If you are patient, you can find certainty in the uncertain," Zajak said. "Be patient."

"How, will we be rid of him?" she said.

"Exactly how, I am uncertain," Zajak said. He scanned the front page story, then opened the paper to continue reading past the jump. "But the answer will be delivered to us, and we must be ready."

"What do you want me to do?" Amelie said.

"Keep the attorney looking for the child," Zajak said. "If he finds it, say nothing. I don't want Brankovic near that child. Ever. Do you understand?"

"Yes."

"We are going to be getting out of the glass business much sooner than I anticipated. Back up all your files. Leave nothing behind. Keep a bag in your office."

"Like Madrid?" she said.

"Yes, but first we disappear for awhile," Zajak said.

"Good," Amelie said. "Just so long as we go someplace where I can smoke in the office."

"I don't think that will be a problem," Zajak said.

— —

The electronic sound of typewriter clicks Travis' iPad made as he hunt and pecked on the screen with bandaged hands distracted Muerce from focusing for too long on the overall appearance of the young man laying in the hospital bed before him. The left side of his head was bandaged, and there were a baker's dozen of visible stitches on his jaw, cheek and forehead that were the result of shards of glass ground into his flesh when the driver's side window was shattered at the start of the attack. Travis' left eye was open, but the whites were mostly red, and the surrounding skin was the swollen bluish purple of what had become a magnificent shiner.

Beneath his hospital gown he was bandaged for the cracked ribs. There was a row of stitches where the Emergency Room physicians had gone in to reposition the broken rib that punctured his lung. The plastic surgeon had not been needed as first thought. Most of the lacerations along the left side of his body and back were superficial, and had been closed with surgical glue and butterfly stitches. Also beneath the gown and bedsheets was a long bruise that ran from just above Travis' left knee to the small of his back. There was, luckily, no damage to his spleen, though he was passing some blood in his urine, and his kidney's remained a concern.

Travis, whose jaw was wired shut, held the tablet up with his right hand for Muerce to see the screen. He pulled back the bandage on his head with his other hand, exposing a garish scar that had been sutured closed with very fine stitches that ran at an angle from the top of his head to just below his left cheekbone. The stitching reminded Muerce of the Death Weaver's work. The difference, besides there being no colored filament, was Travis' wound oozed. He was alive.

On the notes application of the tablet Travis had typed: Chicks dig scars.

"It's a keeper, for sure," Muerce said. It was a moment of levity he needed. "How are you doing?"

Travis typed: Demerol :) Nurses :(Peeing :O

Muerce laughed out loud, causing a painful chortle from Travis.

"Okay, okay, enough," Muerce said. "Your mother's ready to strangle me as it is."

Travis dismissed Muerce's comment by pushing at the air with one hand, and a slight roll of his eyes.

"Look, Travis, I'm sorry," Muerce said. "This is my fault. You shouldn't have been there. It was my job to do."

Travis made an obvious effort to frown, dropped his head, then looked up at Muerce. He pointed to Muerce, and shook his head to say no. Then pointed at his own chest, and nodded yes. Then he began typing on the tablet: My choice. I wanted. Could have said no.

"It was my choice to send you, or not send you," Muerce said. "I was wrong."

Travis typed: Done is done. Cool scar. Cool story. Get laid a lot, now.

"That would happen without the scar," Muerce said. "Do you remember what happened?"

Another frown appeared on Travis' face, and he moved his head deliberately up and down to indicate that he did. He began typing. The bandages on his bruised and lacerated hands made it awkward, and it took some time to finish.

He handed the tablet to Muerce. It read: My fault. Didn't follow gut. Should have left when they saw me. I say to self. No way saw me. Nothing for awhile. Quiet. Then window break. Hit hard. Fuzzy. Hurt first. Then slow motion. Kicked a lot. Think I hit someone. Couple of times. Maybe three guys. Big, big fuckers.

Muerce, who had pulled a chair next to the hospital bed, reached over, and gently raised Travis' hand in the air for him to see.

"You hit someone, a lot," Muerce said, carefully putting Travis' hand down on the bed. "Did you recognize anyone?"

Despite the discoloration in his left eye, both pupils were clear and focused when Travis looked at Muerce. The almost imperceptible nod was expressed as if it were accompanied by trumpets. Muerce understood, and nodded back. Travis began pecking at the tablet again.

He typed: Grabbed headlight knob when pulled out. Lights on. Was on ground after beating. Got rolled over. He was standing in front of car. Face exploded in fire. Then smoke. All shiny in his hand. Recognized it right away.

"Recognized what?" Muerce said.

Travis held his hand up to gesture for Muerce to wait. He continued typing: Never forget it. Saw lighter from Unicorn. Sterling silver. Engraved with a dragon.

"Brankovic," Muerce said.

Travis squinted with his right eye, and nodded to affirm Muerce's declaration. He started typing again: Had a smoke while they beat the piss out of me. Give me your phone.

"My phone?" Muerce said. Travis pointed to a white docking cord on the table next to his bed. Muerce handed it and his mobile phone over to him. There was the distinctive *clunk* when the two devices connected. Travis touched and dragged several screens and icons on the tablet, then typed in a series of passwords. The bar on a blank application box on the screen of Muerce's phone indicated a program was being loaded. When it was completed, Travis disconnected the devices, and had Muerce lean close so he could show him what he had done.

On the phone screen, among the applications for weather, music, and news reports, was a red box with the icon of a dragon. When Travis touched the image a menu screen appeared that listed: Photos; Documents; and Maps. Travis fingered through the first two items to show Muerce what they contained. It was the research he had collected on Brankovic and company, the case files from Trumbley, and autopsy reports. There also were all the updated news stories, both web, print and broadcast. The photos were mostly the ones of the victims provided by Bhote, and the ones taken at the respective locations where each body had been discovered by crime scene investigators with the exception of the latest victim. Travis also included images of the six tapestries from the Lady and the Unicorn series on display at the Gilmont.

"Maps?" Muerce said.

Travis held up two fingers. The first map on the screen was a map of the city. In the center of the map was a pulsating blue dot that gave the GPS location of the phone—and, the reasoning went, the location of Muerce. The second map was an engineering overlay of architectural blueprints of the ACME Glass factory, the surrounding buildings—including Brankovic's steam plant building—and the underground access tunnels that connected them.

"You did this?" Muerce said. "Very cool."

Travis nodded with satisfaction. What he did not tell Muerce was that he was the fourth—and last person—to have the application downloaded to his phone. Nor did he tell him the original idea behind its development came from Colonel Trung. Pho Mat also had it loaded on his phone. Travis did not tell Muerce that they had both been to the hospital early that morning to visit him, or that Colonel Trung had summoned Travis to his office the previous week to suggest creating the tracking system. During that meeting, Colonel Trung was vague about why he had Pho Mat following Muerce, and why Travis must keep the request in trust, until, if needed, a later time. Instead, Colonel Trung explained the meaning of filial piety. The term was rooted in Confucianism. It was an important virtue, he had said, very deliberately, for all members of the family to adopt. It was the primary duty of each member of the family to be respectful, obedient, and to care for one's parents, and elders. It was a matter of honor. Colonel Trung ended their meeting by putting his hand on Travis' shoulder, and telling him that he, in a very short time, had become part of the Trung family. Travis understood, and would obey the Colonel.

How the Trung's knew of the attack, or which hospital he had been transferred to, Travis wasn't sure. It didn't matter. They just knew, and they were there for him, as he would be for Muerce. There was a feeling of belonging in Travis that he had not felt before; a greater purpose that—even better than the Demerol—lessened the pain.

As Muerce got up to leave, Travis tapped at the keyboard, and held it up for him to see. The message said: Cut his head off, and burn him.

Muerce read it without responding. He stopped at the open doorway, and turned to address Travis.

"Cool scar," Muerce said.

Travis had battled a dragon on its own ground. Though he lost, he lived. There was more than just character in what he had done, there was courage, and virtue. Travis was worthy of being avenged.

— —

The sun neared its midday zenith as Muerce navigated his way through the open parking lot. The sound of birds in the budding trees at the far end of the lot that bordered the Botanic Gardens lent some lightness to what had been a difficult visit. The morning, overall, had not been too bad. Muerce woke up next to Paige. They had slept comfortably, and soundly, and without having sex. Perhaps it was because they were exhausted, and still somewhat hungover from the previous night. That was okay with Muerce. The rest was good. They had taken a taxi to the garage next to the Monastery where the Mercedes was parked since Saturday night. At her request, he dropped Paige off at her gym. When he asked why she didn't want to be taken home, she ignored him. Muerce didn't press the issue. Her mood was light and bouncy when she slipped out of his car, and he did not want to change it.

Now he stood, next to the Mercedes, fumbling through the pockets of his pants for his keys. When he felt his phone, without thinking, he pulled it out and checked for messages. There were three. All text messages. All from different women.

The first message was from Eleanor: Did we breakup? Haven't heard from you in some time. Call your mother!

The second was from Paige: Some gentleman. No goodbye kiss.

The third was from Ashley. Muerce winced before he read it: WTF? Nice heads up on the media. Not. What's with us? Ash.

Muerce let out a deep sigh and looked up at the sun, and the bright blue spring sky. There was a faint smell of cherry blossoms in the air. But it was not enough to relieve his guilt. He thought of Paige, and could not answer himself when asked what that was all about. He thought of Ashley, and wasn't sure what that was about either. *Jesus, Jack. What are you doing?*

Muerce selected Ashley's number in his contacts, and initiated the phone call. It rolled to her voicemail, and he waited for her greeting.

"Ashley, it's Jack," he said, stumbling slightly over his words as he thought about what he would say as he was saying it. "I'm sorry. I got caught up yesterday. Well, lately. Things are a little distorted right now. With me. Work. It's, well, complicated. That sounded stupid. Sorry. I'll explain. I promise."

When he ended the call he looked down at his phone, and wondered if he would call her again. *Not very gallant.*

CHAPTER 48

A second carafe of coffee arrived at Muerce's table amid a torrent of commands in Vietnamese Madame Trung barked out over her shoulder to the kitchen staff, and her grand-daughter behind the dry cleaning counter. Muerce, engrossed in the screen of his phone, was oblivious to the commotion around him. Monday night had been a restless night of sleep. He had showered, dressed and arrived at Saigon Laundry earlier than usual. It was another beautiful spring morning. The daffodils Madame Trung planted in various containers, and placed in the front window of the restaurant, were blooming. The sky was crystal blue. The sound of robins and mourning doves masked the droning city traffic, and occasional rumble of aircraft on approach to the airport near the water.

There was little to do today. Muerce had nothing on his schedule. He would make arrangements to have the Jeep towed from the city impound, and the shattered window replaced. Later, he could have one of the Trung grandchildren pick it up from the repair shop, clean it, and deliver it back to the apartment. He would ask Madame Trung to see who was available.

Pushing the plunger of the French press, Muerce watched as the dark fluid rushed and swirled through the filter. As careful as he was not to push too fast, some grounds escaped. There was always a thin layer of sediment at the bottom of his cup. Inevitably, a few large grounds snuck through the filter. Muerce thought they did just to mock him. Something always sneaks by.

Muerce put his phone down, and scanned the room as he sipped. He swiveled in his chair to look into the kitchen, then through the beaded curtain where the granddaughter was helping a customer. Again, Pho Mat was nowhere to be seen.

"Where's Sammy?" he said to Madame Trung.

She looked irritated. As if Muerce had interrupted her weekly high-stakes game of backgammon, and did so while she was losing.

"Not here," she said.

"Yes, I can see that," Muerce said. "That's why I'm asking. Is he still ill?"

"No, better," she said, without giving Muerce eye contact. "Do errands for my son, the Colonel."

"Yes, I know who your son is," Muerce said.

"Then why you bother me Jack Muerce?" she said, rushing away. "I have work to do. No bother me."

"*Pardonnez moi, pardonnez moi, Madame*," Muerce said, halfway raising his arms in mock surrender. *Jeesh.*

After another cup of coffee, Muerce was bored again. He picked up his phone and called Eleanor, and got her voicemail.

"Hi, it's your long-lost son," Muerce said. "I'm calling to see if I can take you to lunch today. Call me back. Cheers dear."

Still bored, he thumbed the application Travis loaded on his phone, and began flipping through the autopsy photos. By the time he got to the second victim, the phone rang. It was Bhote.

"Sonjay, your ears must have been burning," Muerce said. The boredom had spurred a kind of restless jocularity in Muerce.

"I don't know what that means," Sonjay said. The tenor of his voice was serious, causing Muerce's upbeat mood to crash immediately.

"What's wrong?" Muerce said.

A short silence on Bhote's side of the call validated that something was wrong.

"I screwed up," Bhote said. "I missed it."

"Missed what?" Muerce said.

"The FBI figured it out," Bhote said. "They picked it up right away. I've been at this too long. Good thing I'm retiring."

"Figured what out, Sonjay?" Muerce said.

"The smell," Bhote said. "The one you noticed on the bodies. I was going to get to it, but..."

"But you have a million things to do running a understaffed, under-funded coroner's office in one of the most violent and heavily populated counties in the country," Muerce said. "They are focused on one thing, and they have a rich uncle who buys them all the cool toys they want. Who cares who found what, what was found?"

"They picked them up when they ran a UV light over all the remains," Bhote said.

"Them?" Muerce said.

"Crosses," Bhote said. "Applied to the eyes, ears, nostrils, lips, hands and feet."

"Applied with what?" Muerce said. "I didn't see anything."

"They, indeed, do have cool toys," Bhote said. "A portable desorption electrospray ionization machine. Ran the chemical analysis right in front of me. I swear they were grinning the entire time."

"And?" Muerce said.

"Commiphora, cinnamoman, kaneh bosum, and Olea europaea," Bhote said, anticipating Muerce's next question. "In English: myrrh, cinnamon, cannabis, and olive oil. Holy oil."

"Extreme unction," Muerce said. "They were given last rites."

"Exodus, chapter thirty, verse twenty five," Bhote said. "Make these into a sacred anointing oil, a fragrant blend, the work of a perfumer. It will be the sacred anointing oil."

"So the Death Weaver has religion," Muerce said. "Thanks Sonjay. Let me know if the whiz kids find anything else."

Muerce put his phone screen-side down on the table, and swilled the last sip of coffee before gulping it down.

"Holy oil," he said to himself. "There's nothing holy about a dragon."

When he looked at the bottom of the cup, Muerce spotted an unusually large grain of coffee grounds stuck amid the finer particles, and wondered how something that big got past the filter.

— —

The metal surgical tray crashed to the floor with a nerve-jarring clamor that could be heard in the reception area of the Acheron Clinic. The receptionist, and several of the medical staff stopped what they were doing, and glanced up toward the second floor examination room where the alarming sound had come from. They looked at each other, then went about their business, though with a heightened, and edgy demeanor. It was not unusual to hear such displays of anger from Dr. Sharron.

"Has been spending the night with who?" Dr. Sharron hissed through clenched teeth.

"Muerce," Price said. He was frightened by the response, but delighted the news struck a jealous, and painful nerve.

"He is a known fornicator, unclean," he said, glaring at Price. "I don't approve."

"Since when have we needed your approval?" Price said. "Do you think us so innocent, ourselves?"

"She has feelings for him?" Dr. Sharron said.

"Yes," Price said. "It's rather novel for her. She even seems to have a radiance about it. I'm quit envious."

"Hmm," Dr. Sharron said, collecting himself. "Feelings. And I always thought you were the weak one."

"That was mean, Father," Price said. "You know my feelings belong only to you."

"Some bargain," Dr. Sharron said. "Brother would do anything to protect Sister? Wouldn't he?"

"From that, with you?" Price said, focusing his attention on the surgical tools scattered on the floor so it was obvious to Dr. Sharron. "Yes. Anything. I may be weak, but Sister is my strength. As Mother was yours."

"Mother was weak," Dr. Sharron said.

"Strong enough to leave you," Price said.

Dr. Sharron calmly walked to Price, as if to repair the argument. Instead, when he reached his son, he violently grabbed Price by his hair, and slapped his face with enough force to raise welts on each of his cheeks. The blows caused a thin line of blood to form at the corner of his mouth.

Price responded by thrashing, and dropping away. Freed, he scurried across the floor on his hands and knees, picking up a scalpel from the floor. When he reached the near wall of the brightly lit examination room, Price turned and held the scalpel up in defense.

"Tell me again how it was just an accident," Price said, tears wet his crimson cheeks.

"It was," Dr. Sharron said, calmly. "Just... an accident."

"Yes, an accident," Price said, holding the scalpel up higher. "She just *accidentally* cut both her wrists while she *accidentally* took a bath. And Sister and I were just *accidentally* tied to our chairs so we could watch. How old where we? Three?"

"You have no memory of that," Dr. Sharron said.

"No, but Sister does," Price said. "Father... Uncle, Brother. Mother... Aunt, Sister."

"Sister is ill," Dr. Sharron said.

"Your Sister is dead," Price said.

"And yours will be too, if she doesn't have the procedure," Dr. Sharron said.

The look in Price's eyes turned from rage to fear.

"This is the last one?" Price said. "She'll be cured? You promise?"

"Yes," Dr. Sharron said. His voice calm, and soothing as he approached Price. "It's the last of the lesions. She will be free of it, forever."

"And we'll be free?" Price said, crying as he dropped the scalpel to the floor.

Dr. Sharron knelt down and caressed Price's hair, smoothing it in caring and compassionate strokes.

"Yes, we'll all be free of it," Sharron said. "We'll all be free."

"I'll be there," Price said, looking up with a fragile determination. "To make sure."

"Yes, of course," Dr. Sharron said. "Sister will need your help. Your strength. And so will I."

Dr. Sharron began softly kissing Price's head. His thoughts were of Paige when he kissed Price. Of her lips, touching his. Then he thought of her lips touching Muerce's, and the anger welled up inside of him again. He would contain it this time.

"Forgive me," Dr. Sharron said. "I care for Sister as you do."

As the two of them rose to their feet, Dr. Sharron helped Price straighten his clothes. He let his hand stay in place as he tucked Price's shirt into the front of his pants.

"It's Tuesday," Dr. Sharron said. "The incinerator will be operating tonight. You'll remind Sister. How curious that she imagines she can smell it. Impossible with all the scrubbers and filters."

"It's not that there's a smell," Price said. "It's the idea of it that bothers her."

"Just medical waste," Dr. Sharron said. "There's only a small amount of flesh and blood. Far less than what the Lord sacrificed for our souls."

"You like Tuesday nights," Price said.

"Don't you?" Dr. Sharron said.

"Not recently," Price said, aggressively removing his father's hand from the front of his trousers. "I have a date tonight. You still want to know more about Muerce, don't you? Though Sister probably knows more of him than we do."

Not the kind of knowledge I'm looking for, Dr. Sharron thought.

"I am disappointed," Dr. Sharron said. "But you will let me know if anything more turns up with our Mister Muerce, or if Sister turns up with him."

"Of course," Price said, dabbing the blood from the side of his mouth with his tongue. "It's what you want, isn't it? And haven't *we* always given you what you want?"

"Watch your defiance around me," Dr. Sharron said. "You don't want to strain my patience. Go now. And remind Sister.

"Enjoy your *date*."

"Oh, I shall," Price said, leaving the room.

After closing the door, Dr. Sharron got down on his knees and began to pray. God would deliver an answer. He always did. Dr. Sharron had been chosen to deliver unto God what He wanted, and in return he would be granted absolution for his sins. Until that day, prayer had helped him—most times—harness his desires, and focus his anger. Jealousy now tore and wrenched at his emotions like a demon. Dr. Sharron could feel the demon devouring his body and soul. He prayed for an answer from God. He prayed for relief. As he waited in prayer, his mind wandered to the tapestries. He pictured them in his mind as if they hung on the wall of the room. When he did, he saw the face of Jack Muerce woven into the trees. He was hiding in the trees. Looking at the maiden standing before the tent, he saw Paige's face. She was holding the jewels in her hand given to her by the handmaiden to her left. He concentrated on the face of the handmaiden as he prayed.

The intercom of the phone on the wall of the examining room blared, and interrupted Dr. Sharron's epiphany.

"Doctor Sharron, your next appointment is ready for you in Room Five," said the voice of his scheduling nurse.

God had answered him. Dr. Sharron crossed himself, rose from his knees, and picked up the receiver.

"I'll be right there," he said. "I need to change the schedule for later in the week. There's a patient I want to see Friday afternoon."

Muerce would serve a purpose after all. The plan, sent to Dr. Sharron by God, was divine.

— —

Either out of boredom, or the nagging unease that began to build in him over the past few days, Muerce decided to stay in Tuesday night and go over the files related to the string of grisly murders. Bhote's call had stirred a renewed interest in the case, which had been waning since the FBI took over the investigation. And he had promised Pope to keep a watch on Brankovic, who remained the top suspect as far as Muerce was concerned.

Muerce and Eleanor had a delightful lunch at the club. Their conversation turned into a late afternoon that ranged widely in subject matter, but managed to, at times, circle back to that of Ashley, and how wonderful Eleanor thought her. Muerce agreed with his mother on the subject of Ashley, but only with silent nods. He did not feel it worth mentioning Paige, given their exchange at the gala, and his own mixed feelings of guilt about, and desire for her. Eleanor also said that she was considering a trip to Paris. It had been years since she had been back, and she wanted to go "once more before I'm dead." He dismissed the part of her dying with a laugh. As far as him joining her; Paris was the last place on earth Muerce wished to return, and Eleanor knew it was for a good reason. She planned only to introduce the prospect of it to him, and not bring it up again, for awhile.

On his way home from the club, Muerce called Saigon Laundry to let them know he would not be there for dinner. He typically did this, to free up his table. Somewhere in the city, a couple was frantically changing their plans so they could make the coveted eight o'clock seating. Madame Trung, not Pho Mat, had answered the phone. Muerce was used to Pho Mat's absence, and mentioned nothing about it to her. He confirmed he would be there in the morning for coffee, and hoped for *beignets*. Madame Trung said *brioche* was planned for the ovens.

Muerce sat in the bedroom turned War Room, typing an e-mail for Travis asking how he was feeling, and that he'd swing by the hospital late morning. His thoughts were restless, and churned on Brankovic, and what, if anything, connected him to the murders. His mind spun in place. When Muerce tried to clear his thoughts, he heard only the growling of his stomach. He was distracted and hungry when the apartment buzzer sounded, accompanied by a knock on the door.

He wasn't expecting anyone, and that whoever was there got through the front door without being buzzed in was suspicious enough to make Muerce cautious as he entered the foyer. Since he had no plans for the night, Muerce wore an old pair of khakis, and slipped on a faded and worn, gray athletic t-shirt that bore the name of his alma mater, and its crew team. He wore only wool socks on his feet, which made no sound as he walked over the marble floor. When he looked through the peep hole on the door, he was pleasantly surprised.

He unchained, then unlatched the locks on the door, and opened it. When he did, Paige looked at him with forlorn and lonely eyes meant to elicit sorrow. It was the look of a child abandoned on the steps of an orphanage.

"I don't have anywhere to go," she said. Muerce thought she might start crying at any moment.

"Then I'm glad you came here," he said, motioning her inside.

"Are you alone?" she said. Paige was dressed in faded jeans, a green quilted jacket, white t-shirt, and a pair of cowboy boots so beat up it was clear they were her favorite pair of shoes. Muerce could smell food in the bag she carried. It was a large white plastic takeout bag, lined with a brown grocery sack.

"Not anymore," he said.

"I brought sandwiches, chips and beer," she said. "If you're hungry."

"What kind?" he said.

"Of beer?" she said.

"Of sandwiches?" he said, closing and latching the door.

"A large Philly cheese, and Italian sub," she said. "You pick."

"We'll split them," Muerce said. "I'm starving."

When he took the bag from Paige, he bent down and kissed her in a way that invited her to stay the night.

— —

Pho Mat was so busy playing with the application that Travis loaded on his phone that he didn't notice Paige park in front of Muerce's apartment. He could expand the screen to a detail of twenty feet, and, as long as Muerce had his phone on him, Pho Mat could follow him in his apartment.

Like the schematics of the Glass Factory, and the tunnels and buildings surrounding it, Travis had loaded the floor plans to Muerce's apartment building into the application. Pho Mat could see the small blue pulsating orb that gave Muerce's location as it moved from the guest bedroom, through the living room, and into the foyer.

He lit another cigarette as he watched the dot move into the kitchen where it stayed for the next hour, moving only slightly every now and then. When Pho Mat returned to his perch near the window after making a fresh pot of coffee, the lights in Muerce's apartment were off. The blue dot said the phone was in the bedroom. It pulsated, but did not move for the rest of the night. Pho Mat noted the time. It was unusual. Muerce had gone to bed before nine o'clock.

— —

Paige lay on her stomach next to Muerce, who lightly brushed his fingers up and down the length of her spine. They had made love in the darkness. It had been soft and gentle. More intimate than aggressive. After each coupling, they kissed for a long time, and held each other in tight embraces.

Muerce stopped his fingers at each of the scars along her backbone, gently tracing the raised tissue.

"What are they?" he whispered.

"I thought we weren't supposed to talk about each other," she said.

"We don't have to," he said, continuing his exploration of the scarred skin.

"I have a condition," she said.

"What condition?"

"Tethered Spinal Cord syndrome," Paige said. "Something like that. Kind of like my spinal column is being strangled."

"And the scars?" Muerce said.

"Where lesions have been removed."

"Are they all gone?"

"Except one," she said. Her back tensed.

"Where is it?" Muerce said, moving his fingers up and down.

"At the bottom."

Muerce moved his hand to her tail bone and, pressing firmer with his fingertips, searched for the lesion.

"How can you tell?" he said.

"A bump the size of a pea," she said

Taking his time, Muerce massaged his way up her spine until he reached the highest of the scars. He retraced his path to her tailbone, but felt nothing. If there was a pea-sized lesion, he couldn't find it.

"Are you going to have surgery?" he said.

"Yes, soon," she said.

Muerce reached his hand across her hips, bent down, and kissed the bottom of her spine.

CHAPTER 41

For five-hundred dollars, Genero Blanco got the tip he was looking for from a soon-to-be furloughed records clerk who had access to the Child Welfare Agency's Protective Services files. Blanco had a name, and an address of the clandestine foster home where the child he was looking for had been taken for temporary placement. As secretive as Miriam wanted to be to protect the child, she had procedures to follow. There was always a paper trail. Social Services was, after all, a bureaucracy.

For the kind of money he had been promised, Blanco had little remorse if there needed to be a snatch-and-grab. Just as long as he wasn't implicated.

From his legal offices located in a run-down strip mall on the far north side of the city, he was tuned into the streets. He had built his practice on the plaintiff side of slip-and-fall lawsuits, small-time medical malpractice, automobile accidents, and a smattering of immigration and family law services. As a personal injury lawyer, Blanco's clientele existed on the lower tier of society. They were mostly Black and Hispanic; the working poor who made up the bulk of the service industry. And there were those who came to him for legal needs who operated in the shadowy fringes of the city. They made their living in the underground, and illegal economy. Either way, Blanco had access to unusual places and people, and their information, and services.

Those kinds of resources were Blanco's power, and power meant money.

He knew who wanted the baby, so he didn't have to ask any questions. What Blanco needed to figure out was whether he could negotiate a bonus for getting the child by himself, or if the safer route was to provide the information at hand, and let outside muscle take over. Although his only contact for the case was Zajak's attractive finance officer, Blanco knew who she worked for—the Dragon.

He pondered his choices for a good hour before making his decision. He'd play the long odds.

— —

"Jack."

"Miriam," Muerce said. He picked up her call on the first ring. "How are you feeling?"

"Pissed off," she said.

Miriam pissed off was not a good thing, and Muerce hoped it was not at him. He couldn't think why she would be.

"What's wrong?" he said. He could hear the sound of a baby crying in the background.

"I'm in the car, where are you?" she said.

"Having lunch," he said.

"Where?"

"Where else?"

"No bullshit right now, Jack," she said.

She was angry, and upset. Muerce switched into a different gear. She wanted direct answers, and quickly.

"I'm at Saigon," he said. "What's going on? Are you all right?"

"I need a favor," she said.

"You've got it, anything," he said. "Tell me what's wrong, Miriam."

"I've got Redzil's baby," she said. "The system sucks. You know? Sometimes, the system just... it just fucking sucks."

"What do you need me to do?" he said.

She looked at the clock on the dashboard of her car as she pulled onto the freeway.

"Traffic looks light," she said. "I'll be there in twenty minutes."

Redzil's baby had fallen asleep on the way to Saigon Laundry. The boy rested quietly in his baby seat as Miriam recounted the course of events to Muerce as she sipped from the glass of iced tea Madame Trung brought to the table.

"It was that ambulance chaser," she said. "The same one that tried to bully me. Showed up at their door, claiming he represented the biological father, and had the legal right to see if the child was being properly cared for."

"Then what happened?" Muerce said.

"They know the system," Miriam said. "Hell, the husband's a lawyer himself. He was at work. She, the wife, told the guy, what's his name, Blanco? She told him they were between foster children. That there was no baby in the house, and if he didn't leave right away she was calling the cops, and the state bar to file a complaint."

"But she called you instead," Muerce said.

Miriam nodded that that was what the woman did.

"This was a secure place, secure," she said. "These people only take the high-risk babies. Domestic abuse, and possible flight cases. That somebody showed up at their door scared the crap out of her. There aren't but a handful of people in the court system that know about this house."

"Apparently, that's too much," Muerce said. "So she called you."

"Yes, the safe place was no longer safe," Miriam said. "I thought the best thing to do was remove the child as soon as I could, and find a better option."

"And I'm the better option?" Muerce said. Miriam pursed her lips, and nodded.

"Miriam, this is illegal in about a million different ways," Muerce said. "It's essentially kidnapping. I go to jail. You lose your job, and go to jail."

"I'm an officer of the court," she said. "So are you, the last I looked. We have to do what's right for the welfare of the child."

"Which is call the cops," he said.

"Pffft," Miriam hissed. "We'd be right back where we are, only sooner."

"Have you talked to Nick?" Muerce said.

"No way," Miriam said. "I don't want to put him in this position."

Muerce made an incredulous face at her.

"Stop, I didn't mean it like that and you know it," she said. "He'll be in a better place to help when we need him not knowing what we're doing right now."

"You're right," Muerce said. "Some plan you came up with on the fly."

"He just needs to be off the grid for a few days," Miriam said, looking down at the slumbering infant. "Until we get it figured out. I can float the paperwork for that long. So?"

There were several options Muerce mulled over before deciding on the best one. It was, actually, the perfect solution for the situation.

"I'll take care of it," he said. "Leave him with me."

"Thanks, Jack," she said, leaning over to kiss his forehead.

"I want something in return," he said. Miriam sat back in her chair, and waited for his request. "I want you to rest. You need time to recover.

You're running yourself too hard, too soon. Promise me you'll go home, and stay there for a few days."

She smiled, and tilted her head sideways. Muerce wasn't sure if that meant she would, or that she was taking it under advisement.

"Now go," he said.

He waved at Miriam as she passed the front window of Saigon Laundry on her way to her car. She was still smiling when she waved back. Looking at his watch, Muerce dialed the number on his phone. A minute later he ended the call. The arrangements were made. He would drop the child off within the next hour. He was pleased with himself. Nobody could get past this guardian. Not Blanco, not Brankovic, not even a division of Marines.

— —

The phone in Miriam's purse started to buzz as soon as she got into her car. She fumbled to open her purse, spilling some of the contents as she fished for the phone.

"Miriam Estrada?" the voice said.

"This is her," she said.

"Hi, my name is Rochelle Robbins, I'm from the Acheron Clinic," the voice said. "Doctor Sharron apologizes for the late notice, but he said he didn't get the chance to meet with you in the hospital for a consult. There's an opening for four-thirty Friday afternoon. He'd like to see how your recuperation is going, and discuss the various options you have."

"Hmm," Miriam said, pausing.

"Can I be honest, Misses Estrada," the voice said, not waiting for an answer. "It's pretty rare there's an opening in his schedule, and he asked to put you at the top of the list."

"Sure, why not?" she said. Muerce's words that she recuperate were still in her head. *That Nick, she also thought, still pulling strings.*

— —

It took several attempts to figure out how to secure the baby carrier in the back seat of the Mercedes, but Muerce managed to do it without waking the infant. The process distracted him, and he did not notice when the car halfway down the block began to follow him. It was a dingy yellow, late-model Chevrolet Caprice. The driver had been hired by Blanco to follow the Welfare Lady. Where the baby went, the driver was to go. When Miriam left Saigon Laundry without the child, the driver waited, and was rewarded for his patience when Muerce emerged, carrying the car seat, and the baby.

Blanco's bluff at the foster home paid off. He figured his visit would force the Welfare Lady to relocate the child to another location. That way Blanco would know for sure where the baby was. Then he could make his next move. What Blanco didn't figure on was the tail on his tail.

Pho Mat kept a respectable distance from the yellow Caprice. Twenty-six miles later, he knew where Muerce, and the Caprice were going, and he called the Colonel.

— —

Madame Trung went straight to her son after Muerce left the restaurant with the child she recognized from the incident at the laundromat only three weeks earlier. Although an innocent, she thought it was a bad omen the baby was abandoned under the Trung roof on Ash Wednesday. Despite her strict Roman Catholic upbringing, Madame Trung held fast to the ancient superstitions of her native country. Miriam Estrada's sudden arrival at Saigon Laundry, and the handoff of the orphaned baby to Jack Muerce, only fed the fear of her cultural beliefs. There were evil spirits about. Something terrible was near.

Colonel Trung thanked his mother, and told her he would do everything in his power to prevent trouble. They folded their hands in the traditional manner, and bowed respectfully to each other.

When she left, the Colonel sat behind his desk and drank a cup of coffee. He waited patiently for a phone call that came within the quarter hour. It was Pho Mat. After they spoke, the Colonel made several phone calls in Vietnamese. The last call he made was in English, and was a conversation with Benedict Pope.

After he was done, the Colonel went to the shrine for his brother Banda behind the dry cleaning counter. There he lit a stick of incense, and said a prayer. Madame Trung brought a small bowl of rice from the kitchen, and placed it next to the picture of her dead son. She, too, said a prayer.

CHAPTER 42

I confess to Almighty God, and to you my brothers and sisters that I have sinned, in what I have done, and what I have failed to do...

Muerce couldn't remember the rest of the words, or why he was compelled to recite them. Struggling through what he could recall of the Lord's Prayer without the support of a mumbling congregation, he gave up, and took a sip of wine.

It was a 1996 *Corton Charlemagne Bonneau du Martray*. An excellent year, worth keeping. Instead, Benny selected it to accompany the *Le Foie Gras Chaud au Fenouil et Citron* appetizer, and *Rognans de Veau Montardieu Flambe Grand Fine*.

Muerce thought the ripe, well defined fruit flavor of the pairing went well with the seared *foie gras* and fennel, but not so much with the veal kidney flambe.

It was Colonial France night at Saigon Laundry, and Benny was taking the menu old school.

The kidney was perfect and robust of flavor, but Muerce was disinterested in it. The texture in his mouth unsettled him. Thankfully, the plate was small, and he washed down the few bites he took with the white burgundy.

The dining room was, as always, full. But, as usual for a Thursday night, most of the patrons were unrecognizable to Muerce. Tuesday through Thursday seatings were doled out, almost exclusively, to the less *cognoscenti*. Muerce knew no one, and few knew him. It seemed, to Muerce, that was becoming the norm for him. Without Pho Mat to banter with, and Madame Trung busy filling in, Muerce felt out of place. He was distracted, and was drinking too much wine so early in the meal.

Peering out the front window of the restaurant, he was further distracted when a lumbering silhouette flashed by on the sidewalk outside. There was a familiarity to the phantom, but not of a degree that was immediately distinguishable. The shape was big, and menacing. Spurred, somewhat, by the four glasses of the Corton Charlemagne he practically inhaled in the last half hour, Muerce left his table to investigate without his phone, or excusing himself to Madame Trung.

The night air was cool, and still. There was a faint aroma from the blossoming Bradford Pear trees that dotted the neighborhood. Muerce found no one loitering outside the facade of the building. He walked to the corner. As he approached, the sound of glass breaking caused him to react, and spin around on his heels. As he did, he heard a car engine roar to life just as his head exploded in a fantastic shower of sparks. The light show turned to darkness, and Muerce was sure he heard the bells of the Cathedral ringing. They rang so hard, he thought his head would explode.

— —

The image of the Michael Jordan Nike logo came to mind when Muerce began to regain consciousness. His head hurt terribly. He wasn't sure if it was the wine or something else, or both. But he focused on the logo. Muerce felt like he was in the same position as the famous basketball player, soaring through the air, his left leg fully extended, his right arm stretching to its limits. Only, there was no basketball in his hand, no rim as his goal. There was just the pain.

"Are you comfortable?" a growling voice said.

Muerce shook his head to clear his thoughts from the leftover sparks of the light show. When he tried to wipe them away with his hand, he realized his left arm was tied behind his back. It was the least awkward element of his predicament. He was standing on his tiptoes, his left foot was bare. When he tried to settle the weight of his body onto his heels, there was a tearing pain in his right hand. Looking up at the source, he saw he was strung to a metal beam by his thumb.

A pitcher of ice-cold water was thrown into his face, fully waking Muerce.

"Good," the voice said. "You are awake, but you are not so comfortable. This, only to get worse."

Muerce squinted as hard as he could to clear his vision. When he opened his eyes he was face-to-face with Brankovic. Muerce looked around, and realized very quickly what had happened to him, and where he was. Brankovic was much taller than Muerce thought when he first saw him at Club Unicorn. But Muerce had been sitting down then. The Dragon was close to six-foot-seven, and broad. Muerce himself was a tall man at six-foot-two, but not like the hulk standing in front of him.

Brankovic grinned, exposing his sharp, and yellowed teeth as he took two steps backward. He pulled a pack of cigarettes from his pocket. When he lit one, Muerce fixated on the lighter. It was the same sterling silver one he had seen at the club. But what Muerce saw now, that he hadn't seen before, what Travis saw when he was beaten, was the elaborately engraved dragon on the lighter casing.

As he exhaled, Brankovic nodded to someone standing behind Muerce, who lifted him up by his waist. It was one of Brankovic's bodyguards. He had a large bruise below his eye. *Travis.* Muerce smirked. At the same time, the second of Brankovic's body guards pulled the slack taught on the cord tied to Muerce's thumb. He was being positioned, and when Muerce looked down he could see what on.

Wedged between a large crack in the dirty cement floor was a freshly carved six-inch wooden stake. The end of it was rounded enough to prevent the skin at the bottom of Muerce's bare foot from being broken, but peaked enough to cause excruciating pain when the full weight of his body was pressed down on it.

The distress was less immediate than Muerce thought it would be when Brankovic's thugs finished balancing him. He alternated shifting his weight from foot to thumb. Either way, it hurt. He could tear his thumb from his hand, or have the misery of the spike on the arch of his foot.

"I have smoke, give you time to hurt some," Brankovic said. "Then I ask questions. You answer."

"If I don't?" Muerce said. His foot was already beginning to burn from the pain. The agony was coming more swiftly now.

"You will hurt, and you will answer questions," Brankovic said. "I think I have tea with my cigarette."

Brankovic motioned for his bodyguards to join him. Muerce writhed and teetered in pain as he watched the three of them sitting at a large table. He was intent on focusing his attention on them, and away from his suffering. Muerce figured he was in the boiler building on the grounds of the glass factory. The same place he sent Travis, and where Travis was savagely beaten. *My turn, Muerce thought, good.* What doesn't kill you...

He calculated the size of the building, the layout of Brankovic's living quarters. Once he lost interest in staring down the three men having tea,

Muerce looked around as best he could for windows, doors, passageways. Any means for escape if he could free himself. He thought about the app Travis loaded on his phone with the maps. His phone. The pain seemed to multiple when he realized he left his phone, his keys, and his wallet at Saigon Laundry. He should not have left them, or Saigon Laundry.

What would Madame Trung think? What would she do?

— —

Pho Mat sat in the Supra parked down the block on Canary, but within eyesight of the entrance to Saigon Laundry. He had seen Muerce walk outside, and disappear around the corner down the side street in front of the Trung's house.

When he looked at the pulsing blue dot on the screen of his phone, Pho Mat guessed Muerce had re-entered the restaurant through the back alley. Looking again, Pho Mat saw the dot begin to move, slowly.

Muerce eat fast, go home now, he thought.

The dot on the screen, however, was getting closer to the Supra. When he looked up from his phone, and down the street, Pho Mat saw Madame Trung walking toward him, carrying Muerce's overcoat.

She was frowning, and her brow was as furrowed as he had ever seen. The Colonel was behind her.

— —

"You have high tolerance for pain," Brankovic said. "Unfortunate. I speed things up, yes?"

Brankovic cocked his right arm, then struck with a blow to Muerce's left rib cage, leaving him gasping for air. Waves of pain scourged him with each desperate gasp for breath. The full weight of his body was on his foot, which felt electrified with spasms of misery. Muerce's eyes teared, and his nose ran like a broken faucet.

"Now you answer questions," Brankovic said.

"You should have called to make an appointment," Muerce said, with some effort. "I'm busy right now."

"You arrogant pig," Brankovic said, throwing a left hook into the opposite side of Muerce's rib cage. Muerce let out an explosive gasp that flung his saliva and nasal effluence onto Brankovic.

It was a momentary respite from his discomfort, and Muerce laughed.

"Who's the pig?" he said.

Brankovic walked away from Muerce, and toward a small table that was positioned next to a larger, stainless steel flat table. Behind it was one of the large boilers. The doors to the natural gas-fed furnace that operated the boilers was open. His attention drifting from the pain, Muerce thought the intensity of the flames was muted by the subtle blue flames of the burners. Brankovic wiped himself off with a blue surgical towel. Snapping his attention from the boiler back to Brankovic, Muerce focused on the small table next to the Dragon. It was draped with a larger, surgical linen cloth. On the table, as best as he could make out, was a variety of stainless steel surgical tools. Muerce struggled to remain conscious.

"Fine," Muerce said. Brankovic was back, standing in front of him. "You've got my attention."

"Where is child?" Brankovic said. He lit another cigarette. Muerce was sure he could feel the heat of the flame from the lighter.

"Your child?" Muerce said.

"The child," Brankovic replied, blowing smoke into Muerce's face.

"Don't you have an attorney working on that?" Muerce said.

"He says he does not know," Brankovic said. "Only, that you and the pretty, dark-skinned woman do. Social worker, yes."

"You know what they say," Muerce said, grimacing. "About anything a lawyer says."

"You are attorney, too, yes?" Brankovic said. "And I should trust what you say?"

"I haven't said anything," Muerce said.

The cigarette dangling from the side of his mouth, Brankovic placed the small surgical towel in front of Muerce's face to absorb any spray of spit, and punched Muerce in the left rib cage again. Muerce arched his back in a spasm that caused him to fall off the spike, yanking his thumb out of place. Muerce jerked and danced in pain as he dangled until Brankovic motioned for one of the bodyguards to reposition Muerce on the spike.

"Where is child?" Brankovic said, after Muerce was back in place, and his body had stopped twitching.

Muerce was done talking. He only stared back at Brankovic with a malevolent disdain. He would take the pain. As much of it as Brankovic wanted to dispense. After all, Travis was in worse shape than he was. Pain was good for Muerce. It was cleansing. It could be, if God wanted, liberating. He was not totally unfamiliar to it. Emily understood that.

Brankovic knew the look in Muerce's eyes well. A lifetime of torturing trained him to see the signs. He could torture the man's body all he wanted, but he would not break him. Not now. It was time to make his soul suffer. To do that, he would have to keep Muerce alive. Brankovic signaled to his bodyguards to cut Muerce down. When they did, he collapsed to the floor in a heap. Before he blacked out, Muerce managed to form his mouth into a crooked smile.

- -

Paige thought nothing of dropping in on Muerce. They had spent almost every night since Saturday at his apartment. He hadn't said she could come over, but he hadn't said she couldn't. It was late, and there was a rare open parking space on the street corner in front of his building. She pulled into it, got out of the car, and pressed the alarm button on her key chain. In the quiet night air, the chirp sounded louder than normal, and made her uncomfortable. Muerce had a lovely apartment, but it wasn't in the safest of neighborhoods.

She almost tripped and fell over a large bundle of clothes piled in the doorway to the apartment building. It made a noise, and she realized the heap was a person.

"Shit, Jack," she said, alarmed. "What the hell happened?"

He was slightly delirious as she checked him over for wounds. His face was contorted, but there were no visible cuts or bruises. He was disheveled and disoriented, but not bleeding. He was beaten, but not broken.

When she got him to his feet, Paige noticed he was missing the sock and shoe from his left foot. He also favored his right hand, cradling it with his left. The weak hand was swollen, and bruised around the base of the thumb.

"Where's your shoe?" she said.

"Get me inside," he said. He whispered the security code to open the door, and told her where he hid the spare key.

By the time she got him settled in the apartment, Paige had decided that she would start carrying the *puggio* she had with her the first time she met Muerce at Club Unicorn.

CHAPTER 43

Madame Trung could be solicitous in her relentlessness: "Where you go last night? What happened to you? Who drop you off now?"

Before they left his apartment for Saigon Laundry, Paige bandaged Muerce's right hand to immobilize the dislocated thumb. The fingers on the hand operated normally, but with some soreness if he tried to bend his wrist. He limped slightly from the tenderness on the sole of his foot, and he wasn't sure if he had a cracked rib or two, which made deep breaths a painful challenge. As beat up as he was, Muerce was relieved. Brankovic did him a favor. One that could have cost Muerce a lot more.

"Coffee, please," Muerce said, sitting down.

She returned with a full French press, and a plate of *beignets* and *brioche*. After ducking back into the small service cubby that led into the kitchen, she returned with Muerce's overcoat, and placed his phone and key chain on the table. Revived by the strong coffee, Muerce looked up to find she was still standing next to him, and standing next to her was Colonel Trung.

"May I join you?" he said.

With his bad hand, Muerce motioned for Colonel Trung to sit down. Madame Trung slipped away from the table with a soft rustle. She returned with a cup and saucer for her son. The Colonel finished half a cup before engaging Muerce in conversation.

"My mother much worried about you," Colonel Trung said. "She pray. Keep me up most night. I too, worry my friend."

"I should have been more cautious," Muerce said. "I'm sorry."

"Not be sorry, be careful," the Colonel said.

"I didn't have much of a hand in the matter," Muerce tried to joke, holding up his bandaged paw. "What's done is done."

"Not done, I think," Colonel Trung said. "Not think worry over."

"What are you saying, Colonel?" Muerce said.

"You have time I tell you story?" Colonel Trung said.

"Of course," Muerce said. "Although, the last time you did I lost my appetite, and I don't think I'll look at a spring roll the same ever again."

"Not that kind of story," Colonel Trung said, chuckling. "You finish *beignet* just in case?"

Muerce cocked his head, smiled, and finished the last of the *beignets*.

"Please," he said, washing the last bite down with coffee. "Your story. Just don't start it with 'Once Upon a Ti...'"

"There was beautiful princess," Colonel Trung said before Muerce could complete his sentence. He grinned at Muerce, and paused for affect. "Mi Nuong, daughter of Emperor Hung Vuong the Eighteenth." The Colonel hesitated, "I continue?"

Muerce nodded that he should.

"Men come from many country to seek her hand in marriage," the Colonel said. "Emperor wish only most distinguished and powerful man marry his daughter. One day, two men come to palace. They Son Tinh, the Mountain Spirit with armor of eagle, and Thuy Tinh, the Sea Spirit, wear armor of sea dragon. Both equal in handsome, and distinguish. Both powerful. Only difference: Son Tinh, gentle and quiet; Thuy Tinh, bad temper."

Sitting upright in his chair, Colonel Trung pushed what he had left of his hair back with his hand, and took a sip of coffee from the cup he held in his other. "Son Tinh bow head, tell Emperor of his mountain kingdom. Son Tinh reign over all creatures and riches. The beautiful trees, plants and flowers. Son Tinh can summon elephant, tigers, and birds. Son Tinh have power to make mountains grow to sky. Promise Emperor, if he marry Mi Nuong he bring her happiness, and eternal life.

"Thuy Tinh bow head, tell Emperor of his sea kingdom. Thuy Tinh reign over all creatures living in ocean. Own all pearls, coral, and treasures. Thuy Tinh can raise level of sea to mountain top. He able to make rain, and gather great storms. Promise Emperor, if he marry Mi Nuong he make her Queen of the Sea. Build her most magnificent palace."

Colonel Trung paused, and could see Muerce was engaged in the tale. He continued: "Emperor listen both men, but was unsure to choose. Each arrive at same time. Each handsome and powerful. Emperor decide both men have until next day to bring wedding gifts from their kingdoms. First man to return, marry Mi Nuong. Son Tinh rush back to mountain. Tell his men, collect best diamonds and precious stones can find. Fill many baskets with most delicious fruit, and most fragrant flowers. Thuy Tinh tell his men collect best pearls and treasures. Also, most exquisite sea food, and delicious seaweed."

"Who won?" Muerce said.

"Next morning, Son Tinh and many attendants first to come to court," the Colonel said. "Son Tinh bring trays of jewels, baskets of mangos, grapes, strawberries, roses, orchids, jasmine, and much more. Emperor very pleased. He agree to let Son Tinh marry Mi Nuong. She bid farewell to Emperor, and follow Son Tinh to mountain kingdom. After Son Tinh and Mi Nuong leave, Thuy Tinh arrive with men carrying trays of pearls, treasure, and many baskets full of sea food."

"He's the angry one, right?" Muerce said.

"Hmm," Colonel Trung said, correcting Muerce for his interruption. "Yes. Thuy Tinh become very angry. Order his men to follow Son Tinh and take Mi Nuang away. Thuy Tinh has magic sword. Turn all creatures in sea into army. Make heavy rain begin to fall on land, and strong winds to blow. Thuy Tinh raise level of ocean, higher and higher. Big waves and floods wash down trees and houses. Many people killed.

"Son Tinh also have magic sword. He turn all animals into army. Make mountains grow higher in sky as water rise. This battle go on many days. No one win. Many lives lost. Finally, Thuy Tinh give up. Go back to sea. But Thuy Tinh still want Mi Nuong. Every year he gathers storm and raises water up mountain where Son Tinh and Mi Nuong live. Every year, in springtime, when battle between both spirits happen, people and animals suffer, many crops and properties destroyed. Thuy Tinh always battle, but never win war."

Contemplating the Colonel's words, Muerce rested his hands, as best he could, palms down on the table, and sat back in his chair. He was tired and sore, and unsure of what to make of the story. Colonel Trung sensed it in Muerce.

"Is inevitability of life," the Colonel said. "Cannot avoid. Monsoons inevitable. Conflict inevitable."

Muerce looked up at Colonel Trung, and blinked. The Colonel pushed Muerce's phone and car keys across the linen tablecloth to him.

"Take sword," Colonel Trung said. "Raise mountains. Muerce can summon elephant and tiger."

The relief Muerce had felt earlier was gone, replaced with an anxious anticipation that had no clear source, and no certain end. *Inevitability, he thought.*

"I think I'll go for a steam, and ice this down," Muerce said, raising his bandaged hand. "And get some rest."

"You look, need rest," the Colonel said. "I have dinner bring by your apartment?"

"Tell Benny the table is available tonight," Muerce said. "And tomorrow night. I have dinner with the Squires. Travis gets out of the hospital today."

Colonel Trung stood up, clasped his hands together and bowed his shoulders and head toward Muerce, who returned the gesture from his seat.

"Tonight, for one, or two?" Colonel Trung said.

"For one," Muerce replied.

— —

After a long steam, and massage, Muerce plunged his left foot into a bucket of ice, and his right hand into another that sat in the chair next to him. Positioned in the corner of the club's training facility, he grabbed his phone from the top of a bundle of towels with his good hand.

He called Eleanor to check in, and to see if she needed anything. All was fine, and she needed nothing. Likely, Muerce guessed, she had all the diet Coke and lottery tickets she needed. There wouldn't be any cigarettes.

After mulling it over for a few minutes, he called the florist and had an elaborate arrangement of spring flowers sent to Ashley at the museum. There was nothing witty or clever he could think of for the card, so he simply had them write down: Ash, thinking of you, Jack. It was the truth, and it would suffice.

He stared at the contact number on his screen for Paige. He wasn't sure what he wanted to say to her, or in what manner he should deliver his words. Muerce couldn't remember the last time a woman had spent consecutive nights in his bed. He wasn't sure why he let Paige. His feelings for her were uncertain. There was an intense attraction sustained by mystery. They had kept to their rule not to talk about each other. When they were together they had neither a past nor future. Just that moment. The unnaturalness of their relationship puzzled Muerce. The ease of being with Paige hid a darkness in her. Lifting his injured hand from the ice bucket, Muerce held it aloft and gingerly moved his fingers and thumb as the frigid rivulets ran down his forearm. What he was certain of with Paige, was that there wouldn't be a another consecutive night.

He needed solitude to contemplate, and to wait. *How high, he thought, will the mountain need to be raised?*

— —

The covered garage structure of the Acheron Institute was practically empty when Miriam pulled into it. Entering through the back doors, she found only the receptionist behind the desk in the soaring lobby of the building. The thorny tree sculpture that sat in a shallow pool of still water seemed mildly inappropriate to Miriam. It's stark, bare metallic branches was more an icon of pain than beauty.

"Miss Estrada?" the receptionist said.

"Misses," Miriam said.

"Yes," the receptionist said, looking down at Miriam's file. "Let's get you situated in one of the examining rooms. Have you been with us before?"

"No," Miriam said.

"If you can fill out this paperwork while you're waiting," the receptionist said, handing Miriam a clipboard of blank medical forms.

"Do I need to get this validated?" Miriam said, holding up the parking ticket the machine dispensed when she entered the garage.

"Oh, don't worry about that," the receptionist said. "The attendant will be gone by the time your appointment is finished. The gate will be open for you."

Miriam followed the receptionist around the sculpture and up the ramp to an examining room on the first floor. The room was modern, and appointed with furniture that was both stylish and practical for medical evaluations. The lighting was bright, but not overly so; the artwork of colors and shapes was soft and soothing for being so modern. The room was so calming, Miriam did not notice that there were no windows.

"What should I do with these when I'm done?" Miriam said, referring to the forms.

"Just leave them on the reception table," the receptionist said, looking at her watch. "You're the last appointment for the day. I hope you don't mind. I've got to pick my daughter up. First soccer practice of the season. You have kids?"

"Yes, two," Miriam said. "Been there, still doing that." Both the boys were at friends for sleepovers. Trumbley was working overtime on a case. Miriam was looking forward to a night alone.

"There's a gown in the closet," the receptionist said, standing in the doorway. "Go ahead and slip into it. Doctor Sharron will be with you shortly."

She closed the door. Miriam changed, finished filling out the paper-work, and waited for Dr. Sharron.

CHAPTER 44

Saturday arrived with bright sunshine. The forecast called for unseasonably warm temperatures predicted to reach into the high seventies, and possibly low eighties. The air was damp from the wet spring that followed the dry winter. The city was blooming with life.

For most of the regular clientele of Mikal's girls, mid-month paychecks had been distributed the day before. They were now cleared and cashed. Mikal could smell the money burning a hole through their pockets, and into their loins. It would be a busy Saturday, and Mickey D wanted the girls to get an early start. They were all at the Golden Arches for breakfast when Brankovic and two bodyguards walked through the door.

The Dragon's presence had the effect of fingers snapping the dining room to a frightful quiet. The chatter between the girls ceased, and their heads dipped toward the trays in front of them.

Brankovic was not in a good mood. His search remained in progress, and so far, fruitless. He knew time was running out. He was pressing, brutally, and in the process, collecting information from anyone connected to Muerce, who could lead him to the child. Brankovic pointed to Mikal's one-handed man as he delivered Mikal's breakfast tray.

"You, Clubby," Brankovic said. "Take car keys from Deluxe, get girls on street." Looking at the two tables of Mikal's girls, he said, "Off asses, on backs. Start earning, now."

Without a word, the girls hastily collected their things, leaving the trays of food in front of them untouched, and hurried out of the restaurant while avoiding direct eye contact with Brankovic. As Misha passed, Brankovic reached down and gently grasped her by her arm, stopping her in place.

Looking at the one-handed man, he said, "This one, Misha, not work. Stay with you." Brankovic leaned down, and kissed her on the top of her head. His gaze was fixed on Mikal.

"Good girl," Brankovic said, loud enough for Mikal to hear.

As Misha and the one-handed man left, the two bodyguards positioned themselves in the booth behind Mikal in such a way they were practically breathing down his neck. Brankovic sat down across the table from Mikal.

"Is problem, Zmaj?" Mikal said, nervously.

"Is problem?" Brankovic said, putting his large, clenched hands on the table. "You tell me Deluxe."

Mikal could see the knuckles on Brankovic's hands were scraped, and raw.

"You okay, boss?" Mikal said. "You have accident?"

"Da, da, I have accident," Brankovic said. "I go to see my attorney this morning, and accidentally fall into his face... sixteen, maybe seventeen times. Tragedy, yes?"

"Da," Mikal said.

"Give me appetite," Brankovic said, pointing to Mikal's tray of pancakes, sausage and hash browns. "May I?"

"Sure, boss, sure," Mikal said, wiping sweat from his forehead.

"Are you hot?" Brankovic said, removing a set of white plastic utensils from their wrapper. "To be very warm today. Relax, take off sweat top."

"No, I fine boss," Mikal said.

"No, take off," Brankovic said, pouring the plastic container of maple syrup onto the hotcakes. Mikal obliged Brankovic, unzipped the track suit jacket, and removed it. Underneath the jacket, he wore only a wife beater and his collection of gold chains. One of the bodyguards smiled at Mikal, and took the jacket from him.

Brankovic cut into the pancakes, put a forkful into his mouth, and began to chew. Then he ate half a sausage, and swallowed.

"This is terrible food," Brankovic said. "How you can eat this shit. I not think is the weather that make you sweat. Is food. Give you diabetes. I worry Mikal, maybe you have, what they call? The shu-gah."

Brankovic pushed the tray away, licked the fork, and began picking at the tines.

"What business are you in, Mikal?" Brankovic said.

"I'm in your business, Zmaj," Mikal said. His answer caused Brankovic to snap a tine from the fork. "I work for you."

Brankovic snapped another tine from the fork.

"Hmm, I hear maybe you go into business with your brother," Brankovic said. "You bring Golden Arches to Dubrovnik. With help from Jack Muerce."

"What?" Mikal said, with some desperation in his voice. "No, boss."

Another tine was snapped from the fork, leaving a lone spike on the plastic utensil that Brankovic held up.

"Ah, I get upset, look what I do," Brankovic said. "I need another."

Brankovic craned his head toward one of the tables where the girls had left their breakfast trays, and spotted a fork. Leaning over, he retrieved it, and a wet napkin packet. Opening the pouch, Brankovic carefully cleaned the new fork.

"Not know where beeches have been, yes?" Brankovic said. Mikal nodded. "I think, good day for spring cleaning, yes?"

Mikal did not respond.

"I think you open mouth," Brankovic said, snapping a tine from the new fork. "Put in too much of this food. Diet in this country very bad. All sugar and salt."

The sound of a second tine being snapped from the fork punctuated Brankovic's words. He leaned over, poking Mikal's belly with the blunt end of the fork.

"You've become too fat, Mikal," Brankovic said. "I think is time for us to lose weight, yes?"

"I make you good money, Zmaj," Mikal said, pleading, his body tightening with fear. The bodyguards reached over to get a firm grip on Mikal's torso, and secure his arms despite his frantic squirming. "Why you do this, boss? I good earner. I trustworthy. I good. I look for child. I pay your money each week, on time. I not trouble... I... I..."

"Deluxe talks too much," Brankovic said, nodding to his men to hold Mikal's head steady as they wedged the track suit jacket into his mouth. Snapping a third tine from the fork, Brankovic held it up to Mikal. With only one tine remaining, the fork resembled a human gesture; one that uses only the middle finger.

"Fork you," Brankovic said before plunging the plastic dagger into Mikal's eye. The makeshift gag did little to muffle his screams, but it did collect the river of blood and gelatinous vitreous fluid streaming down his face. There was nothing to be done about the violent sounds of his legs beating against the underside of the booth table.

Unable to stand up in the booth, Brankovic scooted himself out, and then stood over the writhing and screaming Mikal with the first fork from which he had clipped three of its four tines. Brankovic did not hesitate, and jabbed it into Mikal's other eye with enough pressure to cause the ocular fluid to squirt across the table. With his thumb, Brankovic collected a swab of blood, and made a sign of the cross on Mikal's forehead.

"Soon you will be in Heaven, Mikal," Brankovic whispered. "But to get there, you must first pass through my Hell."

Brankovic motioned with his head for the bodyguards to remove Mikal from the establishment. Now limp, and in shock, Mikal was easy to handle. They draped the track suit top over his head as they dragged him out the back door, and into the parking lot.

Such disturbances were not uncommon on Canary Street, and the employees remained silent, and intentionally oblivious to the commotion. As Brankovic followed, a young Hispanic employee emerged from the women's bathroom with a mop and bucket, and quizzical look on his face.

"My friend have accident," Brankovic said. "We take to hospital. Sorry for mess. Have nice day."

Blanco lay in the back of the Suburban. He was bound and gagged, and starting to regain consciousness. He had made the wrong bet with Brankovic, though he still held onto the information given to him by his tail on Muerce. It was the one thing that might keep him alive. In his fuzzy state, Blanco figured he could negotiate a deal, if only for his life. As he tried to blink his way to more coherent thoughts, and breath through his nose as his mouth was duct-taped shut, the back doors of the SUV opened, and a body was thrown next to him.

The sight of Mikal's bloody face with two plastic forks protruding from his eye sockets, sent Blanco into a panic attack that caused him to loose control of his bodily functions. As he evacuated his bowels and bladder into his pants, the attorney decided he would tell Brankovic everything he knew as soon as his gag was removed.

Unfortunately, the Dragon would entertain himself first. Despite his feeling of time running out to find his child, Brankovic was certain Muerce's female friend who worked for the Child Welfare office would be found, too, and brought to him. He would get what he wanted, Redzil's baby, and a large chunk of Muerce's soul—if not Muerce himself.

— —

Dinner at the Squire's was relaxed, simple and delightful despite the relative silence of Travis, who was still taking his meals through a straw. They were used to the clicking Travis made on his tablet. It was his preferred method of communication, accompanied by the occasional grunt or groan he made.

Muerce still favored his right hand, but had opted not to wear the bandage to avoid questions. The thumb was sore, but it worked as long as Muerce did not attempt anything too strenuous with it. The same with his foot. Icing helped the recovery of both.

It was a quick evening. Muerce was excusing himself after two hours. He wanted to go home and rest. Without explanation, he would go back to his apartment, fix up two bags of ice, and go to bed early. It was a time for waiting. The odds were, as he and almost everybody else in the city suspected, that Sunday morning would bring a fifth Death Weaver victim. There was, as he drove home, a quiet dread that hung in the air. Temperatures had gotten as high as eighty degrees. There hadn't been a cloud in the sky, and the earth absorbed as much of the sun's radiance as it could. The streets were damp from humidity as darkness fell. It was as if all sound had dipped below the horizon with the sun. Silent until tomorrow.

Standing in front of the bathroom mirror dressed in only pajama bottoms, Muerce knocked his gamey hand against a collection of medicine bottles, facial creams and other assorted toiletries as he reached for the toothpaste. Some scattered across the countertop, others bounced and rolled in the sink until coming to rest.

Muerce cursed silently, as he retrieved the scattered items. The last of them was a prescription bottle of Xanax that he had forgotten about. There were fifty pills. He held the bottle up to the light. He placed the bottle back on the shelf, next to the one that contained a few pills, and did not think about them again.

After brushing his teeth, he iced his hand and foot as he lay in bed. He checked his phone before plugging it into the charger for the night. There were no new messages. He read the last one he had received. Paige's text message reply to his text that he would be very busy with work for the next few days, and unable to see her. Her response was simple: OK. Muerce was sure it was typed with a fair bit of hurt feelings. Though he was not responsible for the feelings of others, he couldn't help but think he was the source of a pain for a lot of women.

By midnight, he was asleep. The bags of ice melted, unwatched, on the bedroom carpet, leaving two large wet spots.

CHAPTER 45

Muerce was deep into a dream. He was running as fast as he could up a mountain to escape a wall of water closing behind him. Running beside him was a unicorn, a monkey, a rabbit, and a dog. At the top of the mountain he saw Eleanor standing next to a lion. She was smoking a cigarette and drinking a Diet Coke. She also had a sword that she held out to him. Eleanor was about to speak when he heard his phone ring. He tried to listen to what she said, but the phone kept ringing loader and louder. Then he woke up.

Fumbling, Muerce grabbed for the nightstand. He yanked the phone charger cord out of the wall socket when he found what he was looking for.

"Yeah," Muerce said, rubbing his eyes awake.

"Mister Muerce," the voice said.

"Yes," Muerce said, removing the charger cord from the bottom of his phone.

"My name is Agent Gabriel, Alexander Gabriel. With the FBI."

"Uh, huh," Muerce said.

"Did I wake you?" Gabriel said.

"You did Agent Gabriel," Muerce said. "What time is it?"

"Just about six a.m.," Gabriel said.

"Smell?" Muerce said.

"Excuse me, sir?" Gabriel said.

"Is there a fifth victim?" Muerce said.

"I can't discuss that right now, Mister Muerce," Gabriel said.

"Then why are you calling me?" Muerce said.

"Doctor Bhote asked that I contact you," Gabriel said.

"Why is that?" Muerce said.

"He would like you to come to the scene," Gabriel said.

"So there is a fifth victim," Muerce said.

"Like I said, Mister Muerce, I can't discuss that," Gabriel said.

"What's the game here, Agent Gabriel," Muerce said, irritated.

"No game, Mister Muerce," Gabriel said. "Doctor Bhote believes strongly that you should be here."

"Where is here?" Muerce said.

"The Botanic Garden," Gabriel said. "Specifically, the Japanese garden. Someone will direct you when you arrive."

"Okay," Muerce said.

"How soon can you be here, Mister Muerce?" Gabriel said.

"I don't know, half an hour, maybe twenty minutes," Muerce said.

"Sooner would be better, Mister Muerce," Gabriel said. The phone call went dead.

At first, Muerce wasn't sure he had just had the conversation he had just had. When he moved to get out of bed, he placed both his feet into the wet carpet, giving him a start. The urgency in Agent Gabriel's voice left little doubt that Muerce would skip a shower. He splashed water on his face, and ran some through his hair. He dressed, and was driving out of the basement garage less than ten minutes after the call. There would be coffee, he was sure, at the Botanic Gardens.

— —

Two dark, unmarked police cars blocked the main gate to the Botanic Gardens. The policemen, dressed in street clothes, checked Muerce's driver's license. One squawked on his radio that Jack Muerce had arrived, and gave directions to the command center. It was a slow and solemn drive through the narrow twisting road that passed through the gardens to the Japanese section. Muerce had not bothered to close the car window after checking in at the front gate. As he drove, he heard the soft crunching of the Mercedes tires on the pavement, the sound of the engine, and breathed in the wet fragrance of a million blossoms that clung in the foggy air.

A cold front pushed through during the night. When it passed over the city, trapping the warm air radiating from the earth, a thick ground fog developed, blanketing much of the city. The Botanic Gardens were located in one of the lowest points of the city, which collected the dense air like a bowl. Visibility was limited to twenty feet. Less in some places.

Red and white lights illuminated the airy blanket in throbbing flashes as he neared the command post. The morning light was only just starting to ease its way through the fog, creating small pockets of visibility through which Muerce could see the silhouettes of trees standing like silent soldiers. He recounted his dream, and Son Tinh. *If I was on a mountain, Muerce thought, I could see over this soup.*

He came upon two long rows of various law enforcement cars parked on the grass along the narrow road. Some were regular black and white squad cars, others unmarked. Most, he realized, belonged to the Feds. Muerce pulled the Mercedes over and parked.

The doors to the large, shiny blue Police Command Center bus were open, and a half dozen uniformed and plain clothes policemen moved about in the bright interior light. A handful milled outside, sipping coffee, and smoking. The lack of conversation was noticeable, even for a crime scene. Passing around the bus, Muerce came upon the open doors of an ambulance, its lights were flashing but it was empty, and there was no one standing nearby. In the distance, just past several other cars, and two vans Muerce guessed belonged to forensics, a bright disc glowed like a burning mound of smoke. The light and fog created a halo effect at the top of ethereal mound. Muerce had no more than seen the light, when it disappeared.

Everything went gray as Muerce's eyes adjusted to the sudden loss of light.

"Mister Muerce," a voice said.

Muerce turned to find a young man, tall, thin, and wearing a dark suit with an even darker overcoat, standing behind him. He had a bony facial structure, and what looked to be short-cropped strawberry blonde hair. Despite the wane light, Muerce was struck by the clarity, and intensity of the young man's gray eyes. He presented his identification.

"Agent Gabriel," he said. "You got here fast. I'm sorry I had to wake you."

"I suppose it was time," Muerce said.

Gabriel did not answer.

"Where's Bhote?" Muerce said.

"Right here," Bhote said. The density of the fog, and the sudden lack of light allowed Bhote to approach without being seen.

"They're just about finished processing," Bhote said, addressing Gabriel.

"Why don't you lead the way Doctor Bhote," Gabriel said.

Muerce could sense they were descending a gentle slope. He felt the gravel of a pathway under his feet. It had a soft crunch to it. At first, Muerce thought the dense air was absorbing all the sound, but when he looked down he could see the ground was covered by a layer of pink cherry blossoms. After a few feet, he saw the pathway was marked with yellow and black crime scene tape.

There was enough morning light for Muerce to see they were walking through a grove of cherry blossom trees. Nearly two-thousand of them, in various varieties, made up the Japanese section of the Botanic Gardens. Because of the poor visibility, Muerce wasn't sure which part of the Japanese garden they were in. The splash of a carp told him they were near water. He knew there was a series of small lakes and ponds in the garden.

The sound of muffled voices followed the splash, and footsteps walking over a wooden structure. Then there was the crunching feet on gravel. Three men, wearing black windbreakers that had FBI printed on them, approached Muerce, Bhote and Gabriel. They stopped just ahead.

"Sir, we're ready to transport the remains," one of the agents said to Gabriel.

"When we're done," Gabriel said.

"We already have an ID," the agent said, with a questioning tone.

Gabriel gave the agent a look of severe disapproval that practically turned the agent to stone.

"When we're done," Gabriel repeated, much softer than his facial expression.

During the exchange, Bhote had not turned to look at Muerce. In fact, Bhote had not looked directly at Muerce at all since he arrived.

"All rather unusual, Sonjay," Muerce said, probing.

"Yes," Bhote said, not looking back at Muerce. "Unusual."

Within a few feet of running into the three FBI agents, they were crossing a bridge. It was a wooden Japanese footbridge, painted red, that was gently arched. It led to a small island on which a lone cherry blossom three stood guard. The tree was, Muerce calculated by looking at shadowy shapes and sizes of nearby trees, one of the largest of its kind. The clunking they made as they crossed the bridge was muffled by a thin layer of blossoms. The contrast of the delicate pink petals against the bright red wood was beautifully striking.

The island remained shrouded by the fog that was thicker near the water. As they passed over the crest of the bridge, Muerce could see the island was blanketed with fallen blossoms. A film of them populated the surface of the pond near the island. What seemed to be four stick men

435

were located at equally distant points on the island. They were the stands for the portable flood lights Muerce saw when he first arrived, and were now off as the daylight began to burn off the top of the mist.

At the far end of the island, an intense pinpoint of light glowed orange, and faded. Muerce could see the dark figure to which the glow was attached was a man. He was smoking. His shape seemed familiar to Muerce, but not immediately recognizable.

"Over here," Gabriel said. "Try and stay inside the tape. We have to wait to blow the blossoms away to see if there are any footprints."

"Careful," Gabriel said, moving around what looked like a large mound of cherry blossoms about a foot high, and four feet long. The top quarter of the mound that was closest to the base of the lone tree had a thinner layer of blossoms than the rest of the mound. There were also smaller piles of blossoms that looked to have been swept aside. Beneath the blossoms Muerce could make out what looked to be a rose-colored shroud, and the shape of a torso and head.

"Doctor Bhote," Gabriel said.

Bhote walked behind Gabriel, and bent down on one knee near the victim's head. He reached with both hands to collect the edges of the shroud, and looked up at Muerce with a pained expression, and rheumy eyes.

"I'm sorry, Jack," Bhote said, carefully pulling back the shroud, and scattering a fresh layer of blossoms.

Muerce fell to one knee when Bhote stopped at her neckline. Several blossoms floated down, and gently rested on the soft, jet black hair. The color of her face had faded some, but the sight of her caramel-colored skin as it was now would stay with Muerce forever.

The itch of anxiety began to crawl up his arms. He felt it tingle in his shoulders and throat before it settled in his jaw, and scalp. There was the heaviness in his stomach. A kind of bulky, dull soreness that hurt. Muerce wanted to kick and scream. If he punched the solid trunk of the tree near him, the physical pain might block his anguish.

He kept it tight and together. Bundling it all as best he could in a neat emotional package. He'd managed too before. He would deal with it later.

"Miriam," Muerce said, leaning closer to touch her face.

"No, Jack," Bhote said, grabbing Muerce's hand. "Evidence." The touch of admonishment turned to consolation as Bhote held onto Muerce, and he to Bhote.

A mixture of sadness and rage began to envelope Muerce. Like the fog, it would eventually burn off, leaving only a cauldron of anger. Mourning would wait. Muerce closed his eyes, listened to the silence, and forced himself to look at Miriam again. When he did, he could see her nostrils had been sewn shut. The embroidery was almost unnoticeable. It was more delicate than the previous work. The threads looked as if they had been chosen to compliment her coloring. The light was too poor for Muerce to see any detail, or find what he was looking for in the embroidery.

"Lion," Gabriel said.

"Yes," Muerce said, closing his eyes to stop them from twitching. When he stood up, Muerce was lightheaded, and nearly fainted. He did not realize he had been holding his breath.

"She was," he said, recovering. The haze was much thicker than it had been a few minutes earlier.

Bhote carefully covered Miriam with the tulle shroud left by her killer. The smell of the cigarette made Muerce want one. He turned, recognizing the figure standing on the other side of the island. It was Trumbley, who Muerce remembered, quit smoking twenty years earlier. As he began to walk towards him, Bhote put his hand on Muerce's shoulder.

"Not now," Bhote said. "Let them be alone."

Without a word, Muerce, Bhote and Gabriel made their way across the bridge. A few steps up the gravel walkway, he turned. The sun had begun to burn through the morning fog, as trails of vapor rose from the surface of the water. Like the tree on the island, Trumbley stood guard over Miriam.

A light breeze caught the branches of the cherry blossom trees, creating an elegant snowstorm of pink flecks that floated to the ground. In a patch of light that lit the far shore of the pond, a blue heron beat its wings, lifted itself into the lone column of sunlight, and disappeared into the fog with a single cry.

— —

The styrofoam cup of coffee Muerce nursed was dreadful, but it was hot, and black. He stumbled through his emotions, feeling like and empty plastic jug that that had been thrown down a flight of stairs, bouncing and banging its way to nowhere. Bhote had disappeared into his work. It was still a crime scene, and soon they would transport Miriam's body to the morgue. Muerce did his best to not think about her severed limbs. He thought about Trumbley, and Miriam's two boys, and her naked body on top of his.

"What are you thinking," Gabriel said, sipping his coffee as he approached Muerce.

"None of your business," Muerce said, then stopping. "Sorry, still in shock."

"You were close?" Gabriel said.

"We are, were all friends," Muerce said. "Close friends. Miriam is engaged to Nick, Detective Trumbley. Was."

"I know," Gabriel said. "Again, I'm sorry. Doctor Bhote thought it important you come here. So did Assistant Director Pope."

"You talk to Pope?" Muerce said. "You're FBI, he's Homeland Security."

"I'm detached to Homeland," Gabriel said. "I'm part of his think group."

"Think group?" Muerce said.

"Like a task force," Gabriel said. "Only smarter. More flexible. Less, bureaucracy. It's my understanding you're part of it, too."

"Am I?" Muerce said. "I wasn't aware I was, so defined, by Ben. Assistant Director Pope. I thought I was doing him..."

"A favor," Gabriel said. "I think we're past the point of an obligation of good will. What will you do now? What do you want to do?"

It was his station. There was only one thing Muerce could do. The only thing that he knew would keep him from disintegrating into self pity, and weakness.

"I shall, Agent Gabriel, make war against who did this," Muerce said, his jaw tight. "Without cessation, and without mercy."

Muerce took in a deep breath, and looked in the direction of Miriam and Trumbley. As he sipped his coffee, his hand trembled slightly, and the twitch in his right eye returned. A soft crackle of static came from inside Gabriel's overcoat, and he put his finger to his ear.

"Excuse me for a moment," he said, taking a few steps away from Muerce. Gabriel looked as if he were talking to himself. Muerce took another sip of the putrid coffee, and poured what remained in the cup on the ground.

"If you give me a lift, I'll buy you a decent cup of coffee," Gabriel said.

"I'd like to see Nick first," Muerce said.

"I think later will be better," Gabriel said. "He's going to accompany, ride with Doctor Bhote."

"I don't know if that's a good idea," Muerce said.

"Maybe not," Gabriel said. "But right now, I'm going to let Detective Trumbley do whatever he wants. And that's what he wants."

Muerce's silence was tacit agreement. *Let Nick have that time.*

"I believe you'll want to go with me," Gabriel said.

"Why?" Muerce said.

"I just got a call," Gabriel said, putting his finger to his ear. "Two more victims have been found."

— —

"Rose Sunday," Gabriel said, taking the *venti* coffee cup Muerce passed to him as he sat in the front passenger seat of the Mercedes. Muerce slowly accelerated out the drive-through lane of the Starbucks they found on the main avenue that led from the entrance of the Botanic Gardens. As he drove, and carefully sipped the hot coffee, Muerce looked at Gabriel with little understanding of what the young agent meant.

"Today's Rose Sunday," Gabriel said.

"That doesn't register anything with me," Muerce said, putting on the left blinker to indicate he wanted to turn onto the freeway on-ramp. They were headed to a car wash on North Canary, not far from Saigon Laundry. If traffic was light, it would take them forty minutes.

"The fourth Sunday of Lent," Gabriel said, careful to sip the coffee, and not spill any on himself, or Muerce's magnificent vehicle. "Also known as Laetere Sunday. *Mi-careme.*"

"Mid-Lent," Muerce said. "*Laetere* is?"

"Rejoice," Gabriel said. "In the Roman Catholic tradition, flowers are allowed to be placed on the high altars, the organ can be played as a solo instrument, and priests have the option of wearing rose vestments instead of violet or purple."

"The cloth over Miriam," Muerce said.

"Rose-colored *tulle* left by the killer," Gabriel said. "The cherry blossoms..."

"Flowers," Muerce said. "*Mille-fleurs.* Like the pattern in the tapestries."

"Yes," Gabriel said. "And the last of the senses."

"Smell," Muerce said.

"Today used to also be known as the Sunday of the Five Loaves," Gabriel said. "It refers to the Gospel reading for the day. Christ's miracle of the loaves and fishes."

"What's the connection?" Muerce said.

"I don't know," Gabriel said. "Maybe none. But we apparently have two more victims."

"The sixth tapestry," Muerce said. "A *mon* seul desir. There are two women pictured in it. The lady and her handmaiden."

"Maybe," Gabriel said. "We'll have to see."

They drove silently for several miles. Gabriel was sure Muerce was still in a state of shock, and capable of exploding at any moment. If he did, Gabriel wanted to point Muerce in the right direction. After waiting to express what he wanted to say when they first met, Gabriel could think of no more appropriate time than now.

"You'll excuse me," Gabriel said, getting Muerce's attention. He was careful with his words. "Detective Trumbley's fiance, your friend. She was treated differently than the others. As if she were special. I had the chance to look at her, in good light. She was handled more carefully. There was, I don't know how else to say it, less decoration. But what there was of it, was more intricate. His best work. And the location, and her preparation."

"I, don't," Muerce said, unsure what Gabriel meant.

"It doesn't fit," Gabriel said. "Unless."

"Unless what?" Muerce said.

"Unless he were trying to send a message," Gabriel said.

"To who?" Muerce said.

"To you, I think," Gabriel said. "Had she, you, put your nose someplace it didn't belong?"

Muerce opened his window and threw his cup of coffee onto the freeway. Gripping the wheel of the Mercedes as tightly as he could, Muerce pressed the accelerator to the floor as if it would fuel his anger beyond where it already was, and leave the sadness that was drowning him behind. He wanted to hurt someone, he just wasn't sure who, yet.

Looking in the side mirror, Gabriel saw the Supra that had been following them since they left the Botanic Gardens as it weaved through traffic, trying to keep up with them.

— —

A three-block radius around the car wash was cordoned off by the police. Yellow crime scene tape flapped in a rising breeze. The fog had lifted on North Canary, and the sun burned through the patchy remnants of mist. Police barriers were setup at all the intersections around the scene, and satellite television trucks were camped just outside them. The news crews were beyond the range of getting film footage of the scene itself. Bright lights shone on reporters doing live reports that gave viewers only speculative information. The air above them reverberated with the thumping of several circling helicopters.

Gabriel showed his ID, and they were waved through the phalanx of police. Little of the circus registered with Muerce, who was numb. His hand trembled slightly.

"Where were all the satellite trucks at the gardens?" he said.

"We've got that on lockdown," Gabriel said.

"You can do that?" Muerce said.

"Not for much longer," Gabriel said. "You're not planning on tipping anyone, are you?"

"Not unless it gets me what I want," Muerce said.

Although he had driven by the car wash thousands of times before, Muerce never paid much attention to the faded, and run-down structure. Only as he pulled the Mercedes to a stop did he realize that each of the four car bays were peaked with sheet metal formed to resemble circus tents.

"Do you see that?" Muerce said.

"See what?" Gabriel said.

"In each of the six tapestries, there's a tent," Muerce said. "Campaign tents. They look like circus tents."

Gabriel looked at Muerce, then at the car wash, and said nothing. An agent wearing an FBI windbreaker approached them, addressing Gabriel. Though Muerce's attention was on the roofs of the car wash, his soul was cut and covered by cherry blossoms on the other side of the city. He didn't hear the exchange between Gabriel and the other agent.

"Mister Muerce, are you alright?" Gabriel said. "You with me?"

Muerce response was a distant stare.

"There were two victims here," Gabriel said. "Each seated in a chair placed in separate bays. One was bound. The other wasn't."

Gabriel turned toward the car wash, and raised his arm. The flash of a camera exploded in the direction he pointed. An FBI agent was taking photos inside one of the bays. When he finished and walked away, Muerce could see a man sitting in a chair. He was motionless. Gabriel's body language indicated Muerce should follow.

Muerce was just outside the bay when he recognized the victim by the gold chains draped around a blood-drenched neck and chest. There had been a lot of blood. What looked like swipes made by a thick magic marker were lacerations from a sharp blade that covered most of the naked body. They were superficial; meant to cause pain, but not death. Large bruises had formed on the fleshier portions of the victim's body before he died, creating a palette of purples and blues complimented by the darkening crimson of coagulation.

Two white plastic sticks protruded from the victim's eye sockets beneath which black streaks gave the appearance of mascara gone awry. The victim's mouth was sewn shut with heavy black thread.

"Mikal," Muerce said.

"You know him?" Gabriel said, snapping on a pair of disposable surgical gloves. He squatted down to examine Mikal's body closer. "How?"

"Goes by Mickey D, and Pimp Deluxe," Muerce said, sure of where the instruments protruding from Mikal's eyeballs had come from. "Works for Brankovic."

"What's this?" Gabriel said, lifting Mikal's arm up. "Looks like he's holding something."

Turning the limb so the hand faced up, Gabriel carefully opened the fingers.

"What is it?" Muerce said.

Gabriel removed the object, and held it up.

"I'd say it's his tongue," Gabriel said. "Must have been talking to someone he shouldn't have. Any idea who?"

"Yeah," Muerce said. He'd seen enough, turned and walked outside the bay. In the one next to Mikal's body there was an empty chair sitting in a small puddle of water. Cut and twisted lengths of bloodied duct tape were strewn on the cement next to the central drain.

Gabriel handed the tongue to an agent, who bagged it for evidence. Another team of agents began preparations to remove Mikal's body to the morgue.

"How did he die?" Muerce said.

"Your Mikal?" Gabriel said, removing the gloves, and throwing them on the ground. "Bled out, maybe. But my guess is heart failure. With what he went through, I'd have given up."

"You said there was a second victim," Muerce said, staring into the bay with the empty chair.

"Hospital," Gabriel said. "He'll live. But not without some challenges."

"What do you mean?" Muerce said.

"He had some bruising like he'd gotten a beating," Gabriel said. "But nothing like in there."

"And," Muerce said.

"And, both his hands were amputated," Gabriel said. "Location unknown."

"Surgically?" Muerce said.

"Hard to tell," Gabriel said. "The wounds were cauterized to reduce bleeding. Very crudely from what I've been told."

"Both were men," Muerce said. "Doesn't fit. Similar, but not the same. Close, but not close enough."

The sensation of being on the edge of a cliff overlooking the ocean, swept over Muerce. Only the water was not so inviting. The cliff was high enough that a leap could end in calamity, but low enough there was a chance to jump safely. He felt frozen, as if he needed a push.

"Is there an ID on this one?" Muerce said, looking at the empty chair.

"Yeah, once they pumped him full of morphine, and he stopped screaming," Gabriel said, looking at the notes that had been e-mailed to his phone. "Blanco. Genero Blanco. Know him?"

Panicked, Muerce felt like he'd just been pushed without warning. As he fell, the cliff was higher than it first seemed. Muerce dialed his phone. Eleanor answered.

"You've caught me at an awkward time, dear," she said. In the background, Muerce heard the distinctive action of a shell being chambered in a shotgun. "I'm going to have to call you right back."

The call went dead.

-- --

Eleanor put the phone down next to an open can of Diet Coke, a box of assorted shotgun shells, and the ashtray which rest on the seat of one of the tulip chairs she'd positioned inside the front door of the house. She took a long drag from the cigarette dangling from her mouth as a black SUV crashed through the front gate. Pressing a button on the panel next to the door, a row of sixteen cylindrical steel posts popped up from beneath the crushed stone courtyard. The SUV, which Eleanor had watched on a small security television screen on the panel next to the door, had backed up to gather momentum to breach the gate. That transpired after she refused entry to the occupants of the car via the intercom outside the gate.

The driver gained enough speed to crash through the gate, unaware of the hidden obstacles in the courtyard, but not enough to overcome the pneumatic posts. The SUV's speed went from just over thirty-five miles per hour to zero as it hit two posts head-on, bending the frame at the point where the engine compartment and windshield met.

Waiting for the dust to settle, Eleanor stepped outside, and fired two rifled one-point-three ounce steel shotgun slugs into the engine block. There would be no retreat. Aiming at the driver, she could see through the spider-web cracked windshield that he was slumped over the steering wheel, unconscious. She stepped back inside the house, shutting and locking the door behind her as the two other occupants in the car emerged, somewhat unsteadily, and began firing automatic machine pistols in her direction.

Eleanor made a silent prayer thanking the insurance company that required her to install the elaborate security system, and blast resistant glass, as part of their offering a policy covering her art collection. The spray of small arms fire coming from either side of the SUV harmlessly spat and skittered on the glass. Taking another drag off her cigarette, and chasing it with a sip from the can of Diet Coke, she loaded two more of the rifled slugs into the twelve gauge.

The two assailants paused to reload, finding cover behind the open doors on either side of the disabled vehicle. Eleanor took the opportunity to step back outside. Her first shot sheared in half the top door bracket on the left side of the car as she faced it. The weight of the door sagged on the lower bracket, exposing and surprising the man behind it. As he stood, dumbfounded, his gun by his waist, Eleanor placed her next shot in his right shoulder. The round lifted, and spun him around, depositing him on the gravel driveway six feet back, and slightly away from where he stood a moment earlier. He tried to lift and fire his weapon, but when he looked at what remained of his shoulder he realized the only thing holding his arm in place was a shredded piece of his leather jacket, and he passed out.

Stepping back inside the house as the remaining shooter drained another clip, Eleanor flicked the accumulated ash of her cigarette into the ashtray, and took another drag. She had one round of the steel slugs in the chamber and, rummaging through the box of ammo, selected two, two-and-three-quarter inch fleshette shells. When the man at the gun shop showed them to her several days earlier, she thought the tiny metal arrows housed in the plastic casing were delightfully cute, and painfully deadly.

His clip emptied, the last of the assailants hid behind the open passenger door on the opposite side of the car to reload. Again, Eleanor used the lull to her advantage, stepped outside and blew the top hinge off the car door with the same result. Exposed, but not hesitating as his companion had, he snapped his gun up to fire. The first blast of fleshettes caught him squarely in the face and neck, blinding him in one eye, and nicking his carotid artery. The impact from of the second shot took out his left knee, sending him to the gravel where he quickly bled out.

Eleanor went back inside, shut the door and reloaded. The shotgun cradled under one arm, she took a long pull on the cigarette, and stamped it out in the ashtray.

"You'd have been damn proud of me today, Jack," she said, speaking as she exhaled the smoke from her lungs. The Jack she spoke to was her husband, who had taught her about many things, including how to shoot, and shoot well.

When she turned her attention back to the courtyard, Eleanor saw a small group of armed men enter on foot through the gates. They were Asian, dressed in street clothes, and their weapons were pointed at the SUV and the two men lying on the gravel. She recognized the man walking behind them dressed in khaki pants, and a light blue dress shirt. It was Colonel Trung. She could hear the scream of police sirens as they wound their way up the hill toward the house.

Waving at Colonel Trung with a surprised curiosity, she placed the shotgun by the door, and went to her bedroom. She bent over the portable playpen set up next to her bed, and lifted the sleeping child into her arms.

"Not to worry sweetie," she said, gently cradling Redzil Hadzic's baby in her arms. "Auntie Eleanor's made all the bad men go away."

-- --

Eleanor finished giving the details of her past quarter of an hour, and was about to explain why Colonel Trung appeared at her house with a small cadre of armed men just after the shootout when Muerce was interrupted by Gabriel.

"Something's come up regarding Misses Estrada's case," he said.

Muerce raised his finger to interrupt Eleanor's chain of conversation as if she were standing next to him. He said: "But everything's fine? The police are there now?" Eleanor confirmed that was correct, and drew in a breath to continue when she was cut off.

"I've got to go," Muerce said. "I'll check back as soon as I can." He ended the call, and turned toward Gabriel. "What is is?"

"A routine patrol came across her car," Gabriel said. Muerce waited for the rest of the information, but Gabriel hesitated.

"You're not going to do anything rash, are you Mister Muerce?" Gabriel said. Muerce's answer was reflected in his face, and body language. The image of the black SUV, and Eleanor's description of the men she shot streamed through his head. His body was tense, and twitchy. The anger in him was more pressure now than heat, building each minute with the grief he suppressed.

"That's what I thought," Gabriel said. "Her car was found a couple of blocks from the ACME Glass factory. Near the old steam generation plant."

There was more Gabriel wanted to say, but he stopped short.

"What else?" Muerce said.

"You don't have a move here, Mister Muerce," Gabriel said.

"Then whatever you tell me won't matter, will it?" Muerce said.

Gabriel's nostrils flared as he formulated what he would say. "There was blood in the trunk of the car. A lot of blood."

There had been nothing promising about the day. The heavy morning fog lifted, but the respite was brief. The clash of rising, warm moist air into cooler descending air now pushing over the seven hills had begun. The sun disappeared behind a dark wall cloud that would soon envelope the city. A bright flash illuminated the approaching bank of wind and rain. Thunder crackled, then rolled and reverberated in the air, rattling windows and drowning out the chop from the circling helicopters as they retreated to safety.

"There's nothing you can do," Gabriel said.

Muerce headed toward the Mercedes, stopped, and turned to address Gabriel.

"I can do, Agent Gabriel, what you can't," he said. Gabriel touched his ear, spoke into the cuff of his jacket, and followed Muerce.

— —

It wasn't unusual to be called into the office at a moment's notice to work on Sunday morning. Long, unpredictable hours were part of the job requirements the IT headhunters emphasized when offering what was a very lucrative contract to do software programming. The contract was to last six months in the U.S., but had been extended by another six months. With the type of programming they were working on, Xerxes Kamal expected another six-month extension. It was sophisticated code. He and the five other programmers, all young, single, bright, and focused as himself, were recruited from Mumbai, India.

The money was, as Kamal joked among his fellow programmers, "stupid big." The problem was they never had time to spend it. The other problem, of which they never spoke, was they were designing software that had nothing to do with making glass. And there was the secrecy, and their employers.

He liked his boss, Amelie Bertrand. She wasn't much older than he was, and attractive in an unapproachable way. As pretty as she was, it was her genius that enthralled him. She was brilliant, and had them writing code for financial trading in algorithms that were part of a bigger puzzle he hadn't yet grasped, but it was culminating. He could feel it in every line of code he typed. Each of the six programmers at ACME were not to discuss or share what their different projects were, but each knew they were all working toward the same end. What that end was, only Amelie knew. While she was their overseer, there was no doubt who the master's were. Hers, and theirs. And when they were in the office, all eyes remained locked on computer screens, no matter what happened around them.

Recently, there was more tension and urgency in their work environment, so the call from the office didn't surprise Kamal. Unfortunately, he didn't get it until he re-charged his mobile phone that ran out of power overnight. He was running an hour behind, and was scrambling out the front entrance of his apartment when two large SUVs with darkly tinted windows pulled up in front of the building. In an instant, he was surrounded by men wearing sunglasses, earpieces, and matching plain, black windbreakers. One of the men asked Kamal who he was, and where he worked. Kamal confirmed the man's inquiry, and was then shown a photo identification, and a badge. The man, whose name Kamal almost immediately forgot in his state of fear, said he was with the FBI.

By the end of the day, Kamal had been transported by military helicopter, then government jet, to a remote facility in the Nevada desert where he underwent a short, and cordial debriefing by a man who did not identify himself as a member of the FBI, or any other government agency. Then Kamal was escorted through a barb-wired fence into a compound of small, recently built bungalows, and told which one was his. In fact, the entire complex looked to him to have been only recently constructed. When he reached down to open the door, he realized there were no locks. Before he went inside, Kamal, now alone, looked back at the security gate through which he just passed, and the soft light of of the stars on the desert surrounding the complex. The attention of the guards, he realized, was focused outside the fence. Kamal wasn't the prisoner, he was the protected.

-- --

The office windows rattled and shook from the thunder, alarming Amelie. She looked at her watch, and the empty desk. One of her programmers had yet to show. She called his number, and left another message. As she did, the elevator doors opened and Zajak, carrying a travel bag and briefcase, emerged. He smiled at her, and indicated she follow him into his office.

"Is everything backed up, as we discussed?" Zajak said.

"Yes," Amelie said, opening her hand that held three thumb drives. "And on my laptop as well."

Her travel bag and briefcase rested on one of the office chairs by the window.

"All of our arrangements are in place," Zajak said.

"What is going on?" Amelie said.

"Precautions," he said. "Zmaj, I believe, has gone too far."

"And done what, now?" she said, irritated.

"Outlived his purpose," Zajak said. "We are relocating, without him. Thankfully."

"How complete a relocation?" Amelie said, stifling any hint of dread in her voice.

"As I said before, complete," Zajak said, stopping what he was doing at his desk to look at her directly, and be assured she was on board.

"You wished to avoid another Madrid," she said, coldly.

"I did," Zajak said, sympathetically. "But I'm afraid we don't have enough time. This is what Moscow wants."

"It will take another six to eight months to rebuild the knowledge base," Amelie said, lighting a cigarette to calm her nerves. "And there's the project execution element that still needs to be recruited, and trained. We will need more resources, and no more interruptions."

"You shall have both," Zajak said. He walked over to Amelie, and placed his hands on her shoulders to comfort her. "I do not wish this either. It's the cost of our association with Zmaj Brankovic. Soon, we will be rid of him, and his barbaric methods."

"How?" Amelie said.

"Fate," Zajak said. "He has upset a balance that existed here. Anomalies always do, you know. Nature must even things out. Whether by its own forces, or that of man."

"Always such philosophical riddles with you," Amelie said, exhaling. "You are too romantic. God exists in the sequence of numbers, not fairy tales."

"Of course He does," Zajak said. "But the numbers for Zmaj have become too much. For Moscow, and for the local authorities, who, if they haven't figured it out by now, soon will. It's my understanding even Mister Muerce is working on the equation. The Dragon desired too much."

"With our complicity," Amelie said, suppressing her remorse, and the building trepidation she had when she thought of Jack Muerce.

Zajak didn't respond, glad that whatever might play out between Brankovic, the police, and Jack Muerce, he would be rid of the Dragon. *It is Allah's will.*

"Not everything is backed up," Zajak said. "I noticed your numbers outside do not add up."

"Kamal," Amelie said. "He called to say he was running late. He should be here soon. How much time do we have?"

"We can wait some for him," Zajak said. "Otherwise, other arrangements will be made. I will make some tea."

Amelie finished her cigarette, and stood by the large window in Zajak's office that overlooked the factory floor. Shimmering plumes of heat billowed from the furnace and ovens below. A ribbon of molten glass rolled slowly across the cylinders that fed it into the Lehr kiln. From a distance, the glowing slab had a lifelike quality that was alive, and anxious.

— —

The wind picked up just as Muerce pulled the Mercedes off the exit ramp that led into the industrial section of the city where ACME Glass, and the steam generation plant, were located about two miles from the freeway. With each block, Muerce drove faster, his grip on the steering wheel tighter, and the determination in his eyes more focused. His rage was palpable.

Gabriel didn't say a word when he got in the car with Muerce at the second crime scene. Muerce didn't care if Gabriel was there or not. They hadn't spoken, even as they weaved in and out of traffic at high speeds. Gabriel wasn't worried about what Muerce might do when they got to the site where Miriam Estrada's car had been found because he was sure they were going to die in a spectacular crash first. The only sound Gabriel made was a grunt when the speedometer reached one-hundred-ten miles an hour. The car was rattling so much, Gabriel thought it was going to fall apart before crashing.

As they sped through empty intersections of the rundown industrial section, ignoring red lights and stop signs, Gabriel began to consider what Muerce might do. A dust devil spun in an empty lot. The brick smokestack of the steam plant rose in the distance. Wisps of smoke licked at the lip of the stack before the gusts of the approaching storm erased them. The windshield of the Mercedes was struck by several errant drops of rain.

The storm was on them.

— —

As fast as the Supra was, Pho Mat struggled to keep up with Muerce on the freeway. Speed was not the issue. Muerce's driving was. He was taking risks, darting in and out of lanes, that Pho Mat was worried weren't calculated. Muerce was operating on pure emotion. And that, Pho Mat knew, was more dangerous than Muerce's driving. Colonel Trung's orders were clear—protect the family member in great danger. If Pho Mat could not help Muerce from himself, then he would support him. *Protect body and soul.* Even, Pho Mat knew, if it required purification.

— —

The rain started just as the Mercedes pulled next to Miriam's abandoned car. It was parked on the street next to a rusted chain-link fence that bordered a derelict, weed-pocked lot. There was no sign of the police cruiser that made the call.

"Where the hell is everybody?" Muerce said. He was upset, and impatient.

"I don't know," Gabriel said. "They were supposed to hold tight until investigative units arrived. No surprise, we beat everyone else here."

Gabriel touched his ear, and lifted his cuff to speak to a dispatcher. Muerce wasn't interested in what Gabriel was saying. He couldn't care less if the federal agent was with him, or not. Instead, Muerce scanned the area. Just as the rain intensified into wave after wave of wind-blown torrents, he spotted a police cruiser parked by the side entrance to the steam generation plant. The front doors of the cruiser were open, but Muerce did not see any cops nearby.

The large metal door to the side entrance was open, too, and Muerce recalled being dragged through it, still flinching and barely conscious, two nights earlier. Remembering his torture, looking at Miriam's abandoned car, its trunk apparently soaked with her blood, and the recollection of the surgical tools in Brankovic's workshop pushed the anger in Muerce beyond any he had experienced before. Brankovic had even gone after Eleanor. And Mikal, his eyes skewered, tongue cut out, and mouth sewn shut. Muerce swiveled around in his seat, sure this was about the same spot where Travis had been attacked.

Muerce's hands and legs began to shake. His thoughts were quick and jagged, lacking any coherence. He was unable to concentrate on them beyond the instant they snapped in his head. Each of the victim's faces appeared to Muerce as if they were being screened for him on the windshield of the Mercedes. The contorted look of disbelief and horror on each of their faces. Each slide washed away by the heavy rain, only to be replaced by the next, until, there was only Miriam's face staring at him.

Flipping the windshield wipers on, Muerce stomped down hard on the accelerator. The back wheels spun and squealed on the wet pavement until they gripped, launching the Mercedes forward. Busy talking into his sleeve, Gabriel was taken by surprise when he was pushed back into his seat as they accelerated toward the steam plant. The heavy downpour obscured most of the building. He was violently tossed up and back when Muerce jumped the curb and drove through a fence. Gabriel spotted the police cruiser. As they got closer, he saw what looked to be two men face down on both sides of the patrol car. Neither was moving.

The Mercedes skittered and slid to a stop, making a quarter turn as it slipped across the wet and broken asphalt. Both Muerce and Gabriel—his weapon drawn—jumped from the Mercedes. They were immediately soaked to the skin by the rain. Gabriel cautiously made his way to the body lying on the ground on the passenger side of the squad car. It was a patrolman with a gunshot wound to his head just above his eyebrow. With his free hand, Gabriel checked the man's neck for a pulse. As he suspected, there was none. The cop was dead. The rain had begun to accumulate, and dilute the pool of blood around him.

Muerce, though unarmed, ran to the body that lay by the driver's side of the patrol car. Without hesitation, he rolled the patrolman over on his back. The blood covering his face was washed away by the rain that pelted them. Rivulets of water dripped off Muerce as he crouched over the man, wiping his bloodied face clean. Muerce saw the head wound was superficial. Then he discovered a second wound. It had struck just outside the patrolman's Kevlar vest, tearing a lot of flesh and shattering the socket of the man's right shoulder. Blood oozed everywhere. Lightening flashed, and was followed by a clap of thunder that startled the injured policeman. He blinked several times, and struggled to breath.

"He's still alive," Muerce said, as Gabriel, having made his way behind the patrol car, kneeled down. His gun pointed toward the open door.

Gabriel touched his ear, and spoke into his sleeve: "This federal agent Alexander Gabriel. Be advised, two uniformed officers down. Repeat, officers down. Dispatch ambulances to my location. Multiple GSW. Two to transport. Have all available units respond. Copy."

Muerce heard the static reply "copy", and within seconds the city erupted with the exigent wailing of every police unit available, and many that weren't. Gabriel had radioed on an open police channel. Muerce looked up at the door to the building, and the darkness inside. Then he looked at Gabriel.

"Wait," Gabriel said, with little conviction. Muerce reached down to patrolman's belt, unfastened the holster, and removed the forty five-caliber service weapon. He cocked the slide, chambering a round, and stood up.

"Me first," Gabriel said, standing up. "Or, I'll shoot you."

The rain pelted them as they cautiously approached the doorway. There was the sound it made as it splattered against their wet clothes, and the soft crunching the fractured asphalt and gravel made beneath their feet. Behind them, in the distance, growing in numbers but still too far to be of help, was the screaming of sirens. Muerce and Gabriel stopped, each on opposite sides of the open doorway. Muerce wiped his eyes dry as best he could. Gabriel nodded at Muerce to see if he was ready. He nodded back that he was, holding the gun with both hands, the muzzle pointed to the sky.

Gabriel ducked into the building so quickly Muerce was unprepared, and followed behind, unsure what to do, or expect, once they were inside. Muerce had been in the large space before, and while his eyes adjusted to the darkness he instinctively pointed in the direction he thought offered the best vantage for an ambush. He remembered the chair, the stove, and the bed and dresser behind it. The first of a volley of shots exploded from the far side of the room, and the direction Muerce's gun was pointed. The crack of rounds passing in the air near him rang in his ears before they struck the brick behind him. One of the hits made a softer sound. Muerce responded to the first shot by squeezing off four rounds in the direction of the flashes he'd seen. One of his rounds made a similar soft impact, followed by what sounded to Muerce like someone tossing and turning beneath bed covers. A shadow darted across the back of the room, and from it came two more shots that Muerce returned with a pair of his own.

Pausing, his eyes acclimated to the dim light, Muerce saw Gabriel laying on the floor next to him, clutching his leg.

"I'm going nowhere," Gabriel whispered as he removed his belt, and strapped it tight around the top of his leg as a tourniquet.

"I think I hit him," Muerce said, also whispering.

"How many do you have left?" Gabriel said.

Muerce looked at the borrowed semi-automatic Glock, then recounted his shots in his head: "Standard clip. I've got seven left."

"Take mine," Gabriel said, holding the Baretta nine-millimeter in his blood-stained hand. "I didn't get a single damn shot off. You've got sixteen to kill him. Anything more than that, improvise."

"You're going to be okay," Muerce said, exchanging weapons while keeping his eyes locked on the far end of the room.

"I'll be fine," Gabriel said.

"I wasn't asking," Muerce said. There was no humor in his voice. Any concern he might have for Gabriel was set aside with the exchange of gunfire. Muerce was resolved to do what had to be done.

"Hey," Gabriel said, getting Muerce's attention. "You're on your own."

Muerce grabbed Gabriel by his arm, and dragged him to the door.

"Better that way," Muerce said, disappearing back into the darkness. Gabriel could hear the cacophony of sirens trumpet their way nearer as he radioed for a third ambulance to be dispatched. Still, they were at least five minutes away. He knew a lot could happen in five minutes.

— —

The downpour made visibility all but impossible for Pho Mat. He kept his distance from the building that he could not see, opting, instead, to pull over and assess what he could from his phone.

The blue pulsing dot on the screen was Muerce, and Pho Mat had seen it jump quickly from the street outside the steam plant to just outside the structure. Now the dot moved slowly inside the building. Pho Mat switched the app on his phone to the architectural schematics Travis downloaded as part of the tracking program.

Pho Mat felt helpless sitting in the Supra, unable to see or hear anything more than twenty feet away in the driving rain, and unsure what was happening with Muerce.

Eventually, the torrent would lift, but Pho Mat wondered if it would be too late. There was an urgency building in him. He needed to make a decision soon.

— —

The small splinter of wood imbedded in Brankovic's left eye rendered him partially blind. The man shooting at him was not good, but was lucky enough to manage a ricochet off the top of the dresser, splintering the wood that sprayed into his face. Despite the heavy tearing, the injury was not so much painful as bothersome.

He had fired back as he dashed across the room to find cover, and assess the eye. Crouched in the stairs that led to the tunnel access to the glass factory, Brankovic first tried to blink away the foreign object. When that failed, he ran a finger over the eyeball to find anything that might be protruding from the orb. He felt nothing, which meant it was probably too small to remove without surgery.

It was, Brankovic realized as he checked the chamber of his revolver, the least of his problems. He was out of ammunition. Peeking over the top of the stairwell, Brankovic could see only the man's feet as he walked slowly toward the dresser. The box of ammo was in the top drawer, and unreachable.

What Brankovic did have was a scalpel. He had pocketed it right before he was about to dispose of the souvenirs taken from the attorney into the fire that fed the boilers. That was when the two policeman knocked on the door. The souvenirs, like the box of ammunition, were on the dresser.

— —

The Baretta cradled in his hands, Muerce spun and pointed at every corner with each step he took as he made his way toward the direction of his last two shots. There was no sound other than the rain beating against the windows, and the muffled scrape of his feet against the concrete floor.

Just past the bed, he was able to see the top of the dresser. There was a fresh gouge in the wood, which was fractured. Next to it lay an object that was out of place. It was a severed hand. *Blanco's, he thought.* Swinging behind the large piece of furniture, Muerce stepped on something, and nearly slipped. In an attempt to catch himself from falling, he knocked over a lamp. The light went on as he stumbled, illuminating that corner of the immense boiler room, and casting macabre shadows on the walls.

It was the opportunity Brankovic was looking for, and he launched himself up the short flight of stairs, and toward the man with the gun.

Muerce sensed movement to his left. When he wheeled toward it, he felt a sharp sting in his right shoulder. A punch to his sore ribs sent him spinning backward, and away from his assailant. Muerce's only thought was to hold on to the gun no matter what, and start shooting.

The muzzle of the gun flashed twice, sending each round splattering off the concrete floor. It was enough to stop Brankovic's attack. Muerce raised the Baretta for his next shot, but the pain in his shoulder was too much, forcing him to drop his aim. During the pause, Brankovic glowered at Muerce, who reciprocated the look. *You are my enemy, Muerce thought, and I will kill you, no matter the cost.*

Releasing the grip of his right hand from the gun, Muerce let the use-less arm drop to his side, and raised the weapon with his left. Brankovic was unarmed. The scalpel imbedded in Muerce's shoulder, the revolver in his hand empty. It was time to retreat, and regroup. Muerce, he knew, would give chase.

Brankovic threw the empty revolver at Muerce as a distraction to buy time for his escape. As Muerce deflected it with his left arm, Brankovic turned and fled, crouching behind the dresser as he sprinted to the stairs that led to the tunnel. Muerce reacted by firing four shots into the dresser, which absorbed the energy of each round.

"You all right?" Gabriel said, laying on his stomach in the doorway. But he was unable to see much in the darkness.

Muerce looked at the handle of the scalpel protruding from his shoulder. The blood stain on his shirt expanded like a blotter absorbing ink. He made a weak effort to see if he could remove the scalpel, but the slightest pressure resulted in an electric shock of pain. It would have to stay in place. He could barely move the arm without a great deal of discomfort. *Useless, he thought. Thank God I'm left handed.*

"Fine," Muerce said. "It's Brankovic."

The sirens sounded closer. He was losing a lot of blood, and time was winding down for Muerce. Whatever was to play out between him and the Dragon needed to happen soon. There was a beast to be slain.

Making his way around the shattered dresser, Muerce saw what caused him to slip laying on the floor. It was the shredded remnants of a hand. Looking up at the top of the dresser, the other severed hand still lay like an ashtray next to the gouged wood. The hand on the floor was splayed open, two fingers attached only by pallid dead skin. One of Muerce's earlier shots had struck it. That was the soft sound of flesh he had heard. What Muerce didn't know, was the same shot had partially blinded Brankovic in one eye. His prey was wounded, but still very dangerous.

From the top of the stairs that led to the tunnel, Muerce could hear the echo of footsteps down a long corridor. He descended, and followed. Twenty yards in, Muerce became disoriented. He didn't know where he was, or where he was being led. Dim light bulbs marked the path, but not clearly. Steam pipes, and years of other detritus partially blocked the tunnel, and obscured any direct view. Still, Muerce could hear movement in the distance.

He remembered the phone, and the application Travis loaded on it that had the map of the buildings, and connecting tunnels. Ducking behind an old crate for cover, and to hide the light from the phone, Muerce set the Baretta down as he worked the phone with his left hand. He tried cradling it as best he could in his right hand, but he could not grip it tight enough to keep the device from slipping in the blood that dripped down his arm.

The blue dot pulsed on the screen. It gave Muerce his location. It was the access tunnel to the glass factory that was about three hundred yards away. He saw there was a cross tunnel about fifty yards ahead of him that Brankovic could use to surprise him. Muerce pocketed the phone, and cautiously made his way to the junction, careful to make as little noise possible. He kept the Baretta at eye level, his finger ready to squeeze of a quick shot.

— —

The torrent of wind and rain began to subside. Visibility improved. Pho Mat now saw the steam building clearly. The Mercedes was parked next to a patrol car. Two men lay on the ground, likely dead. A third, who was not Muerce, sat upright, his back against the door jamb.

The world sounded as if it were about to descend on the site. As best as Pho Mat could determine, the closest siren was only a minute or two away. When he looked at the screen of his phone, the blue pulsing dot was moving. It was no longer inside the building, but moving across the empty field and open parking lot toward the glass factory.

The tunnel. Pho Mat understood, and started the Supra with a rumble. Muerce was on the move, and Pho Mat knew where he was headed. He would meet for him on the other side.

When he pulled into the abandoned parking lot that surrounded the glass factory, Pho Mat saw Muerce was moving faster than he first calculated. It was a quarter of a mile to the factory building across the lot. Pho Mat flipped open the center console, and punched the accelerator down hard. Shifting into third, he revved the RPMs over the redline. The speedometer was almost at sixty, when Pho Mat shifted into fourth, and pushed the red button in the console that initiated the nitrous oxide system.

The Supra's engine sounded like it was about to explode as Pho Mat was pushed back into his seat. As quickly as he accelerated, Pho Mat was working on decelerating the vehicle. Downshifting to a reasonable velocity, Pho Mat gave the steering wheel just a hint of turn to the left as he pulled the lever of the parking brake up while stomping down on the brake pad with both feet. The Supra leaned left and began to slide sideways across the old asphalt, kicking up loose gravel and broken glass. That the surface was drenched from the storm, prevented the tires from overheating, and squealing loudly. The Supra came to a stop, its rear fender facing the side of the building with inches to spare.

Pho Mat jumped out of the car, and ran, as best as he could with his leg, to a side door that led to the factory floor. It had been left open for ventilation.

— —

The tunnel intersection worried Muerce, and he approached it with apprehension. Every sense in his body was alert. His smell was keen, his eyes sharp. He could hear every drip and creak in the tunnels. The pain in his shoulder persisted, but Muerce did not let it bother him. He was focused. He would deal with it later if he needed to; if there was a later for him. Even that thought didn't bother him.

Farther up the tunnel, Muerce heard a crash, and then footsteps going away from him. There was no ambush waiting at the junction. Muerce increased his pace, and concentrated on the space ahead of him. He made the remaining distance without incident.

Emerging from the tunnel, Muerce was certain he had entered Hell itself. His eyes began to water from the irritants in the air, which was stifling hot, and made breathing labored. The ground was covered by a fine layer of black ash that crunched and puffed in clouds with each step he took.

The weekend operation of the factory was almost fully automated. Only the back end of the factory was manned by two workers, who removed and stacked the sheets of glass as they emerged from the cutting machine. They were not only out of sight, but on break.

Past the giant furnace, Muerce saw a figure move between two steel support beams. The long flowing hair billowed from the heat of the inferno. It was Brankovic. Muerce raised the Baretta, and fired a shot that ricocheted off one of the beams, getting Brankovic's attention. The Dragon turned, looked back at Muerce, and scowled before ducking behind another beam.

— —

"What was that?" Amelie said.

Zajak stood by the window overlooking the factory floor. Below he could see Brankovic as he made his way around the blast furnace. Then he saw Muerce, following behind.

"Fate," Zajak said. "Has arrived."

"Is that?" Amelie said, now standing next to Zajak.

"Yes," Zajak said. "The Dragon, and the Dragon Slayer."

"What should we do?" Amelie said.

"Watch," Zajak said, turning to her. "When it is over, no matter what happens, it will be time for us to leave."

Amelie's attention was fixed on the factory floor. Her instinct was to help Muerce, but she couldn't. She still had her role to play. She had her own demon to battle.

"What is that Brankovic has?" she said.

"Some kind of a pipe," Zajak said. "I think they use them to check the molten glass for quality control."

She could see Muerce lift his gun, and take another shot at Brankovic, who ducked behind a bank of ceramic cauldrons used to pour the molten glass into the tin bath. The report of the shot was distinctive, as was the sound the bullet made when it pinged off a metal strap.

"Muerce has a gun," Amelie said, with some relief. "This should be over soon."

"That won't kill Brankovic," Zajak said.

Amelie turned and looked at Zajak without understanding what he meant, and asked for clarification by squinting her eyes.

"Muerce's strength is in his heart," Zajak said. "Not in his hand. Purity is his sword."

— —

Although the first shot caught Pho Mat by surprise, it provided him with valuable information with which he could formulate a plan. Scrambling up a flight of metal steps in the corner of the factory, Pho Mat crept along a second-story catwalk that ran the length of the building. The catwalk was one of three that serviced various air filtration machines, and ventilation turbines. There were also cranes that ran along suspended rails that had once been used to convey sheets of glass, and other heavy machinery across the factory floor.

Chains of varying thickness hung from the arms of the cranes, which reached nearly to the middle of the factory cavern. They were tied off at several locations along the catwalk like rusted drapery strings.

From his vantage, Pho Mat could watch, and follow the two men on the floor below him. He could, if needed, be on the ground in seconds.

— —

The blast of heat that billowed from the open side of the furnace that received the aggregate to make glass was stifling. Muerce tried to lift his bad arm to shield himself, but was able to move it only a few inches before the pain in his shoulder overrode the burning he felt on his face.

He trotted away from the gaping inferno as quickly as he could, ducking beneath a wide metal slide that fed the cauldron of molten glass. As he rounded the corner of the furnace, and into the open flats of the factory floor, he saw Brankovic duck between what looked like enormous espresso cups, framed with thick metal bands. Muerce snapped off a quick shot that missed.

A moment later, he saw Brankovic's crouching body bolt from behind the cups to a bank of gas cylinders and machinery that overlooked a silvery lake of molten tin. Muerce aimed, but did not fire. *Like hunting rabbits with his father, Muerce thought, it can't be this easy.*

Beyond the tin bath, and the machinery Brankovic was hiding behind, were giant rollers. Next to them were dozens of unopened metal crates, some stacked on top of others. Muerce saw Brankovic dart between two of them, and disappear into the maze of crates. At the same time, he thought he heard the sirens in the distance. He was sure the first units were at the steam plant building, and more would be on their way. His time was almost up. Muerce had to flush Brankovic out, and he had to do it now.

Counting in his head, Muerce figured he had about ten rounds left in the clip. Six of them could be wasted by firing randomly as he darted through the crates. Four would be enough to kill Brankovic once he got him in the open. Muerce only hoped he didn't run directly into his prey as he made his way in and out of the maze.

Taking a breath, Muerce did a little skip before hurling himself toward the crates. Five feet from the first open space between crates, Muerce fired down the narrow alley, then reeled behind the maze and the tin bath, and fired again. Ducking between two crates he fired as he headed toward the middle of the loose structure; and took an abrupt right turn, still firing. There was the sound of another person running. *It worked, Muerce thought.* He only need get himself out of the maze.

Juking left, Muerce saw a gap between two crates that led to the large open space beyond the crates, and what he counted on being the killing ground. He fired off two rounds, the sound echoing loudly between the metal containers, just before he emerged.

As he exited the maze, Muerce's peripheral vision caught movement of an object as it swung down, crashing into his injured shoulder, and snapping the handle of the scalpel off. The resulting pain blinded Muerce with flashing strobe lights. His only thought was to hold onto the gun as he stumbled to the sandy, abrasive factory floor. Rolling away on his back as quickly as he could, Muerce lifted the Baretta in the direction of his attacker, and repeatedly pulled the trigger.

He was surprised when he heard only two rounds leave the weapon, replaced by the disappointing clicking of an empty chamber. Brankovic stood over him, grinning. His left eye was bloodshot and swollen. He cocked his head to target with his right eye as best he could as he lifted the large pipe for another swing at Muerce.

Just at Brankovic began his lunge with the pipe, Muerce rolled. The pipe made a ringing sound as it struck the sand-covered concrete. Muerce managed to lift himself up with his left arm, and shuffle walk several steps away from Brankovic before falling down.

Muerce was in worse shape than he thought. Though his legs worked, his equilibrium struggled through spasms of pain. Brankovic followed Muerce as he crawled, lifting the pipe above his head. The sound of a heavy object breaking through the air, caused Muerce to turn, and stiffen. The pipe struck the top of his right thigh, and he cried out more in frustration than pain.

The anger in Muerce regained a foothold. Disregarding what he felt in his leg and shoulder, Muerce sat up, using the momentum to hurl the empty Baretta at Brankovic's head.

The mass of the weapon landed in Brankovic's good eye, temporarily blinding him. He stood, still holding the pipe in both hands, blinking and screaming in protest. Muerce didn't understand the words coming from the mouth of the monster that loomed above him.

Muerce scrambled as best he could across the floor with his good leg and arm. He was almost past the large rollers the sheets of molten glass passed over before being fed into the Lehr Kiln. His head still foggy, Muerce spotted the narrow area between the rollers and the kiln, figuring he might be able to crawl underneath them. *Better, he figured, to be burned alive than slowly beaten to death.*

As he attempted to turn toward the opening, Brankovic blocked Muerce's escape. He shook his head back and forth, clearing his vision. The long mane of hair swept each way as he shook. What Brankovic could see was blurry, and within a narrow field of vision. Muerce lay on the ground, vulnerable. It was all Brankovic wanted to see before he killed him.

"Now, death," Brankovic said, lifting the pipe above his head with both hands, and moving toward the prone Muerce.

＿ ＿

Pho Mat had a gift for conceptualizing time, space, mass, and force. It would work, he thought, if he had enough strength in his arms, but there would be a cost to himself.

Unfastening the chain, Pho Mat hoisted himself onto the catwalk railing, and waited for Brankovic to move into position. When he lifted the pipe above his head, Pho Mat leapt into space. As the slack in the chain went taught, Pho Mat folded his body into sitting position, pointed his legs forward, and extended his arms so they were parallel to the chain.

There was nothing more to do until he reached the low apex of his trajectory. It was a short ride to that point, which if he calculated correctly, would place him two feet above the floor, and ten feet in front of Brankovic's path toward Muerce. Pho Mat said a very quick prayer that his arrival be accurate, unheard, and unseen.

Practically blinded, and focused on finishing Muerce, Brankovic did not see Pho Mat as he swung toward him. Clearing the floor by just under two feet, Pho Mat pulled his body weight up at the moment his trajectory moved upward, having the same effect as a child pumping their body to gain height on a swing.

The heels of Pho Mat's feet landed just below Brankovic's solar plexus. The force compressed both of Pho Mat's knees, severely damaging tendons and ligaments. It also lifted Brankovic off the ground, throwing him almost thirty feet backward, and into the crawlspace between the rollers and kiln. Brankovic hit the rollers, then bounced his head against the top of the kiln opening before falling to the floor. He was stunned, and did not move though he moaned loudly.

Pho Mat lay in a heap not far from Muerce. He felt his legs, but he could not move them. That was the cost. Muerce was speechless at Pho Mat's acrobatic feat. He crawled over to him.

"You okay, Mister Muerce," Pho Mat said.

"Dandy, Sammy," Muerce said. "How are you?"

"No good," Pho Mat said. "Legs gone."

As Muerce helped both of them sit up straight, Pho Mat pulled on Muerce's shirt, and pointed toward Brankovic. He was moving, albeit slowly.

"Sorry Mister Muerce," Pho Mat said.

"My turn," Muerce said, lifting himself off the ground with some difficulty. His left leg and arm still functioned. His right arm was limp and useless, and bloodied. He dragged his right leg with great effort as he moved toward Brankovic. Muerce bent down to pick up the pipe that lay on the ground. As soon as he lifted it, Muerce knew he didn't have the strength to use it against Brankovic. Dragging his leg and the pipe, Muerce limped toward the rollers, and the kiln. He looked around the factory, and saw no one. A horn blared, and a large slab of molten glass was lifted out of the tin bath, and into the jaws of the rollers that would squeeze the material into the desired thickness.

Muerce was out of breath by the time he reached the opening, and slumped against one of the operations panels, smearing it with his blood. He was getting light-headed, and tired. The idea of sleep appealed to him.

Muerce closed his eyes for a moment. When he opened them, Brankovic was on one knee, dazed, but alive and still dangerous. The last of the feeder rollers to the kiln blocked Muerce's line of sight. He lowered his head to see below them, and locked eyes with Brankovic. The Dragon grinned, his yellow teeth smeared with blood. He blinked his eyes, and could see well enough to know Muerce was done. The little man with him was finished too.

"Come on," Muerce shouted, using most of his strength. Leaning against the blood slicked panel, Muerce slipped and fell to his knees, dropping the pipe. The clang was an invitation for Brankovic to strike, and he lifted himself to a crouch.

Taking three deep breaths, Muerce grunted, and reached for the side of the panel to pull himself up. As he rose, he grasped the cover of the control box and nearly fell down again when it swung open, exposing the control levers.

Back on his feet, Muerce leaned against the panel, and looked around the factory again. Still, there was no one around except him, Pho Mat, and the Dragon. To his right, he saw the superheated slab of glass emerging from the press rollers onto the rack rollers. The heat from it was building.

Muerce ducked his head below the roller again, to get Brankovic's attention. The Dragon, still crouched, but slowly rising upright, looked back. His eyes were like black pinpoints of evil, the veins in his forehead pulsed. His nostrils flared as he breathed.

Muerce smiled, taunting Brankovic. Then he shouted, "Your time, is over", and stood up straight. Instinctively, Brankovic, his anger stirred, stood up to match Muerce's posture.

Reaching across his chest with his left arm, Muerce grabbed the lever that controlled the speed of the rollers that fed the molten slab into the kiln, and pushed it to the "FAST" position. The rollers spun at first, then connected with the glowing slab, shooting it forward.

The wood sliver embedded in Brankovic's left eye severely limited almost all of his peripheral vision. He did not react to what he didn't see. He had not taken a step toward Muerce when the leading edge of the slab clipped him mid-neck, slicing through flesh and bone as easily as a hand passing through water, and severing his head from his body. The intense heat radiating from the orange slab instantly cauterized both of the large wounds.

Brankovic's headless body dropped to its knees. Where his head had been attached was now a smoldering scab sealed by intense heat. The large frame teetered before falling forward. The disembodied head rolled and danced on the scalding surface of the slab as it moved beneath, searing flesh, and burning hair. Muerce pushed the emergency stop button on the controls, and watched as Brankovic's head rolled to a stop. The heat quickly boiled the contents, until the pressure found an escape through both eye sockets, which exploded in a ghastly spray turned instantly into vapor. What remained of his skill burst into flames, and was consumed in seconds, leaving a dark spot on the orange slab, and the sickly smell of broiled flesh.

The Dragon was slain, without a drop of blood being spilled.

— —

Amelie watched in disbelief, and relief. Both emotions were fleeting.

"It's time," Zajak said. "Follow behind, and collect the laptops."

He picked up his travel bag, briefcase, and the small semi-automatic to which he attached a silencer. Pausing at the office door, Zajak turned to Amelie, who had her bags slung over her shoulder.

"Use that," Zajak said, motioning to a wheeled mail cart.

Amelie steeled herself, and nodded that she was ready. He opened the door, and proceeded down the row of cubicles where the programmers were stationed. Each wore ear buds, and listened to music as they worked, their attention always focused on the screens of their computers. Zajak systematically stopped at five of the cubicles, shooting each of the programmers twice in the back of the head. Amelie followed, retrieving their laptops—some splattered with blood, and was careful not to get any on her hands.

It took less than a minute to finish the task. It was a "complete" relocation. With the exception of one.

The elevator doors opened, and Amelie wheeled the laptops behind Zajak.

A blast of hot air enveloped them as Zajak opened the heavy, insulated metal door that led to a walkway near the furnace. Metal sheets encased the factory side of the walkway for protection. Halfway down the walkway one of the covers had been removed. Zajak stopped, and began throwing the laptops through the opening where they landed on the chute that fed aggregate into the furnace. One-by-one, the laptops slide down the chute, into the molten glass, and disintegrated. When he was done, he tossed the gun with the silencer into the furnace.

He motioned with his hand for Amelie to leave the cart where it was, and walked to the metal steps at the far corner of the factory. They descended the steps onto the factory floor to a series of three doorways that led to different tunnels that were part of the steam distribution system.

At the entrance to the far tunnel that led to the steam generation plant itself, Amelie saw something shiny on the ground, and went over to pick it up as Zajak entered the middle tunnel. Holding it up to the light, she recognized it immediately. It was Brankovic's lighter, with the elaborately etched image of a dragon. *He must have dropped it, she thought, in flight from Muerce.* She slid it into her pocket, and hurried to catch up to Zajak.

They walked in silence for almost five-hundred yards. It was the longest of the tunnels, and led to an abandoned warehouse several blocks away. When they emerged from the building, a black Lincoln Town Car was waiting. The last of the sirens in the distance went quiet.

Forty-five minutes later, the car deposited them on the tarmac of the nearest airport that catered to private aircraft. A Gulfstream G650 was fueled, and waiting. It had a range of just over eight-thousand miles, and they would use them all, and more.

Amelie followed Zajak up the steps of the plane, stopping before she entered the cabin. She put her hand into the front pocket of her jeans, and felt the texture of the engraved business card she hid inside. She wondered if she'd ever need to use it, and if Jack Muerce would respond if she called.

"Where were you?" Zajak said, when Amelie sat down in the seat across from him.

"What, just now?" she said. The engines of the jet had begun to whirr and thrum.

"At the factory," he said. "At the tunnels."

Amelie slid her hand into the front pocket opposite where she kept Muerce's card, and pulled out the lighter to show Zajak.

"A souvenir," she said.

"That's something to behold," he said, smiling at her. "And you think me the romantic."

Someday, Zajak thought, I might tell you the story of that lighter.

CHAPTER 46

The doctor in the County ER was Amerasian, and claimed to be from a small town in eastern Montana, or was it North Dakota? Muerce wasn't sure, and he didn't care. He'd forgotten the attending physician's name almost as soon as he said it. The doctor swept back the curtain surrounding the bed where Muerce, sitting upright in a hospital gown, was being treated. He held up a baggie containing the remains of the scalpel removed from Muerce as if it were a prize won at the county fair.

"I'd let you have it as a souvenir," the doctor said. "But the authorities want it for evidence."

Muerce's look of indifference and exhaustion said enough to the doctor, who got down to business.

"It was pretty deep, but there wasn't any major damage to be concerned about," he said, examining the stitching on the wound. "You're going to be sore as hell for awhile. Need to keep it immobile until the wound heals. I'm going to give you some antibiotics, and painkillers."

The doctor moved his hands down to Muerce's right leg.

"Nothing broken. Just a really nasty bruise. You'll want to ice it and rest for a few days."

Reaching across, the doctor lifted Muerce's left arm. It was raw from abrasion and speckled black from crawling through the hot ash, and aggregate of the glass factory floor.

"There's walking across hot coals Mister Muerce," the doctor said. "And then there's crawling over them. Some of this will come out on its own. Some of it may be permanent."

Moving to the end of the bed, he lifted Muerce's left foot, and pressed on the arch. Muerce winced, and the doctor stopped.

"Fairly recent, but not in the past hour," the doctor said. "Do you want to tell me about it?"

"I stepped on something I shouldn't have," Muerce said, looking across the room.

"Fair enough. As far as I'm concerned, you can go home," the doctor said. "I'll get you the meds, and you can be released."

"Keep the painkillers," Muerce said. "I won't need them."

"If that's what you want," the doctor said. "Under one condition. Please don't step on anything you shouldn't for awhile.

"Do you have someone who can take you home?"

"I his ride," Colonel Trung said, standing just outside the curtain. He held a parcel wrapped in white paper, and tied with string. The doctor nodded, and left with the scalpel baggie.

"Bring clean clothes," the Colonel said, unwrapping the parcel he placed on the end of Muerce's bed. "Nurse also give sling for you to wear. I take you home."

"Thank you," Muerce said, pausing. "How is Sammy?"

The Colonel chuckled, as he removed a fresh shirt and slacks from the package. "My old friend to get new knees in next weeks. To be better than new, I think. Much pain, but he not say. Also not take pain medicine, like you. Why I have such foolish friends."

"Lucky, I guess," Muerce said, exchanging the gown for the shirt.

"Yes, some lucky," Colonel Trung said. "Some not so."

The Colonel went on to update Muerce on the condition of FBI Agent Alexander Gabriel, who was in stable condition following surgery to repair the damage to his leg. The police officer was in critical, but stable condition, and would live. His partner was dead, but Muerce already knew that. What he didn't know was the police found the bodies of five more people in the factory offices. All of them had been executed. Then there was Mikal. And the lawyer found with him. Blanco was alive, but he would never use his hands to steal from anyone else again.

Eleanor was safe, and well. The child was returned to social services, without any questions of protocol. Repairs were already underway to the house. Colonel Trung insisted a security presence remain for several days, but Eleanor dismissed the offer, assuring him she was capable of taking care of herself.

"Of course she is," Muerce said.

And there was Miriam, but the Colonel did not mention her.

"How long?" Muerce said.

"How long, what?" Colonel Trung said.

"Have you had Sammy watching me," Muerce said, awkwardly pulling up the slacks with one hand.

"Some time," the Colonel said, gathering Muerce's torn and bloodied clothes into the white paper, which he tied off with the string. "Not long. Talk about later. We go now, yes?"

"It wasn't high enough," Muerce said. "The mountain."

"Kingdom was saved, my friend," Colonel Trung said. "Sadness not all creatures survive such storm. Life is fragile. Honor all family, all friends each day. Sadness inevitable. Storms inevitable. Rainy season almost over."

Looking at the spots of his blood that splattered the hospital floor, Muerce knew his body would heal, but doubted his heart and soul would. The blade of the scalpel, he was sure, had pierced more than his flesh. Colonel Trung saw no victory in his friend, only exhaustion and pain.

"Take you home, now," the Colonel said. "Rest."

— —

Before entering the apartment after Colonel Trung deposited him at the front of his building, Muerce removed the emergency key from its hiding place, and pocketed it. Once he was inside, he changed the codes to all the security keypads, and locked down the private elevator. He left the parcel of his bloody clothes on the table next to the mail in the foyer. *Saigon Laundry, he thought.*

In the kitchen he went through the cupboards until he found a glass flower vase that he tucked under his arm. From the bar he removed a highball glass, and a bottle of scotch. All of these things he deposited on the bathroom counter. He filled the vase with water, and set it aside. Then he rifled through the medicine cabinet until he found the vial he wanted. He had to squeeze the safety cap as hard as he could with his right hand as he turned the caramel-colored bottle with his left. When it was open, he spilled the contents onto the counter.

Crushing two of the large blue pills with the bottom of the cocktail glass, he then placed the highball under the lip of the counter and swept the powder into it. Muerce poured three fingers of scotch, swirled the mixture around, and swallowed the contents in two gulps. He poured three more fingers, and drank half of it before removing the mobile phone from his trouser pocket.

On the screen were dozens of texts, phone calls, and voicemails. Muerce finished off the scotch, dropped the phone into the vase of water, and poured himself another drink.

PASSIONTIDE

Thy misdeeds hast thou shewn, and hast confessed thee clean,
Hast borne the penance sharp of this, mine axe-edge keen,
I hold thee here absolved, and purged as clean this morn
As thou hadst ne'er done wrong since the day thou wert born.
                    —The Pearl Poet

CHAPTER 47

Darkness covered Muerce like the violet shrouds cast over saintly icons worshiped in the sanctuaries of the Church. They were kept under wraps for the duration of Passiontide: the last two weeks of Lent, ending on Holy Saturday. For his own sequestration, Muerce draped himself in booze and Xanax.

As each day passed, he worked his way from the dark to clear spirits in the apartment, which he used to wash down the pills. Scotch then bourbon. Whiskey then rye. Vodka then rum. Wine then beer.

He did not eat, or did he bathe. When he remembered, he smeared antibiotic cream on the stitches that held the crusty wound on his shoulder together. His sheets were spotted, and brown from blood seepage, and stunk of sweat and urine.

For every face, struck with horror and fear, he took a pill. For every thought of cherry blossoms and fog, he took a pill. For every memory of a young woman in a yellow summer dress, he took a pill.

Dragons chased him in nightmares through horrific landscapes of fire and brimstone. Running, he was always running. The beast was close behind, its teeth and claws slashing at him. Its great wings beat at the air, creating waves of concussions that smothered all other sounds. He passed the dead as he ran, their eyes torn out, ears severed, mouths agape and hollow. Their limbs were missing fingers and toes, their faces absent of noses.

He had fallen into a Dutch painting. The one Massimo knew well.

By Monday evening, Muerce had ripped apart the guest bedroom, and all its contents, in a rage. The enlargements of the Death Weaver's work lay shredded on the floor. He attempted to burn the images of the tapestries, but failed to get them to ignite. He gave up, took another pill, and passed out in front of the fireplace.

At times, he heard banging. He was certain the beast was just outside his door, ready to break in and devour him as it had the other victims strewn about the apartment. Muerce hid in the shower until the beast went away.

By Tuesday, the vomiting began, and with it came stronger hallucinations. Unable to hold the liquor on an empty stomach, he ate what little there was in the kitchen. Until, there was only a stick of butter in the refrigerator, which he consumed by mashing it with his teeth, and chasing it with gin.

Hours stretched into days, though Muerce had lost all sense of time. He was getting low on booze and pills. Wednesday night he summoned the courage to look at himself in the bathroom mirror. He did not recognize what he saw. It was the beast, naked, caked in dry blood and vomit, with sunken black eyes and pasty flesh. His hair had turned to horns, and his legs were mutating into those of a monster, one at a time. First it was the right, which was purple, blue and yellow. Soon, he feared, the left would follow. Aghast at what he saw, Muerce fell backwards into the shower stall, sobbing uncontrollably until he passed out on the cold tiles.

— —

It took until Tuesday morning for Muerce's voicemail to fill to the point that no new messages could be left. That was when Eleanor became worried, and called Colonel Trung. Once on Tuesday he went by Muerce's apartment to check on his friend, but there was no answer. The security code he had did not work. He assumed he had been given the wrong code by Madame Trung. She had the code for instances when Muerce needed his laundry, or a meal, to be dropped by the apartment. She also knew where he hid the spare key.

Muerce was a grown man, capable of taking care of himself. It was likely, the Colonel conjectured, that Muerce took a short trip out of town to reflect on what had happened. It would not be unusual for him to do. The Colonel called Eleanor, and told her not to worry.

Twice on Wednesday, the Colonel went by Muerce's apartment. The first time he managed to raise the building supervisor, who let him inside to knock on the apartment door. The spare key was not to be found in the hiding place Madame Trung described. Knocking as hard as he could without disturbing any of the other tenants, there was no answer.

Later that afternoon, Colonel Trung made a second visit. The building supervisor asked the Colonel if he would drop off the mail, which had been accumulating since Monday. Normally, the super, who also had a code and a key, would deposit it on the table inside the foyer. However, he told Colonel Trung, the security code to the apartment door no longer worked. Colonel Trung took the mail, and returned to Saigon Laundry for a business meeting.

He was worried. So, too, was Eleanor, who went to her son's apartment three different times over the course of Tuesday and Wednesday.

Unable to sleep, Colonel Trung woke shortly before four o'clock Thursday morning, dressed, and went to his office where he made a pot of coffee. The aroma woke Madame Trung, who also dressed. When she appeared at the doorway to Colonel Trung's office in a black *ao dai*, he asked her to be seated, and offered a cup of coffee.

Then he made two phone calls.

— —

Both Eleanor and Travis met the Trungs at the front of the apartment building, where the super let them inside. They rode the lobby elevator in silence. At Muerce's apartment door, Travis unscrewed the panel to the security system, and clipped a pair of alligator clamps onto two wires he cut. Then he hooked them up to his laptop, and initiated a program disarming the system. The sound of two deadbolts unlocking indicated that only the door knob lock remained secure. Colonel Trung wriggled the knob several times before directing the others to step back.

Standing at an angle to the door, he raised his leg, and kicked the knob toward the jamb. Positioning himself directly in front of the door, he kicked again. It swung open as the broken knob fell, rolling across the marble floor of the foyer before coming to a stop in front of the disabled private elevator.

There was a dark silence in the apartment, and the unmistakable stench of self loathing. Madame Trung held her hand to her nose. Eleanor's eyes filled with tears.

"Must wait," Colonel Trung said, motioning for them to remain in the foyer.

He found Muerce naked and unconscious in the shower. He was alive, but in rough shape. The Colonel found a robe hanging on the back of the bathroom door, and covered Muerce with it. As he did, the lights of the bedroom came on. When he got up to investigate, Colonel Trung accidentally kicked an empty prescription bottle. He picked it up and read the label.

Madame Trung was stripping the bed. Eleanor, stoic despite the teary puffiness of her eyes, retrieved fresh linens and blankets from a hallway closet, as well as a clean mattress pad. She had seen her son like this before.

"Take these," Eleanor said, handing Travis towels and a washcloth. "Help Colonel Trung."

After they cleaned Muerce as best they could, the Colonel had Travis make a phone call to his father to tell him Jack Muerce needed a favor.

— —

It was heaven. The kind where everything was peaceful, quiet, and clean. There was a pleasant fragrance in the air, and sunshine filled the bedroom. In the soft light, he could see there was even a plump faced, red-headed cherub attending to him. He lay on his back in freshly ironed cotton pajamas as the cherub gently stroked his arm.

Rolling his head from side-to-side, Muerce looked around the room. It was his room, with his furniture, and it was comfortable. He looked back at the cherub who tugged at the sleeve of his pajama top rolled over the elbow. As his eyes focused, he could see she was gently coaxing a intravenous needle out of his arm.

"What the hell?" he rasped. The words took some effort. "Where am I?"

"Well, good morning sunshine," Lonny said, retrieving a plastic glass of ice chips she held to his mouth. "Suck on these. You haven't talked in awhile."

Muerce nursed the ice to build enough saliva to speak. The cool refreshment also helped him regain his vision, and his memory. At least, the last thing he remembered, which he wanted to forget.

"I know what happened," Muerce said. "But what happened?"

"The long version or the short version?" Lonny said.

"Short," Muerce said.

"You've been sedated, hydrated, and titrated," she said. "Out like Rip van Winkle."

"What's today?" he said.

"Sunday," Lonny said. The calendar math was too much too soon for Muerce.

"You're Miriam's..." Muerce said.

"Nurse," Lonny said. There was more reflection in her eyes than sadness. She had lost many patients over the years, but none to a serial killer. "Was."

"What are you doing here?" Muerce said, watching as Lonny packed up the IV equipment.

"Doing you a favor, I suppose," Lonny said, holding up a prescription bottle of Xanax. "These belong to me now. Per Doctor Riley, I'm weaning you off them by the end of next week. You're stuck with me until then. After that, you're banned from this shit forever. Clear?"

"Not really," he said, looking at her arm. "What's your ink?"

Lonny smiled, pulled the sleeve of her shirt up, and exposed the tattoo of the bed lying in a field of roses with the word Life. It caused a dry chuckle in Muerce.

"Yeah, no shit," he said.

"You want to try for some solid food?" she said. "Madame Trung has soup in the kitchen."

"Madame Trung is here?" Muerce said. *Oh, just great, he thought.*

"Has been almost the entire time," Lonny said. "She and Eleanor tag team it. Me, I've been here the whole time. Nice bed in the guest room, by the way."

"You mean my mother?" he said.

"Just Eleanor to me," Lonny said. "She bums cigs off me all the time."

"Don't go in on any lottery tickets with her," Muerce said, straining to reach over to the nightstand. "She'll stiff you if she wins. Where's my phone?"

"Last I saw, part of a flower arrangement," she said, getting up to leave. Before reaching the door, Lonny turned and looked at Muerce, who looked back, anticipating a question.

"You know you're kind of a hero today," Lonny said.

"How's that?" Muerce said. He was already tired again, and wanted to close his eyes.

"It's Sunday, and there's no sixth victim," she said. "You got him."

She waited for Muerce to say something, but he didn't. Instead, he looked at the empty side of his bed, and remembered Miriam as she walked into Saigon Laundry for dinner.

"What was it like?" Lonny said. "When you killed him?"

Muerce responded with the first word that popped into his head when he thought about Brankovic, and the factory.

"Hot," he said. "Very, hot."

— —

Paige, like the rest of the city, knew about what happened at the ACME Glass factory, but not how it happened. Few details were released to the media, other than authorities were confident the Death Weaver's work was done. The two responding officers and an FBI agent were the public heros. Muerce's role in the incident was word-of-mouth, which to the best of their efforts was being quieted by federal officials for reasons of national security.

She called and texted Muerce several times, but there was no answer, or reply. The codes to the security system into the apartment building had been changed. She was locked out.

For days she drove by, hoping to spot him. Several times, she observed an older Vietnamese man coming and going. One time, she recognized Madame Trung from Saigon Laundry. Another time, she saw Muerce's mother and a husky, red-headed nurse standing outside, smoking cigarettes.

After almost two weeks of silence, she gave up. The tightness in her back returned, and with it the headaches. This time, they were accompanied by an unsettled stomach. She would have the surgery soon, and would focus on that. Jack Muerce, Paige knew from the very start, was beyond her reach.

— —

As part of his new routine, Travis gathered the mail from the lobby each day, and brought it up to the apartment, along with a wrapped and tied bundle of clean laundry. Lonny insisted on clean linen everyday. Muerce remained in bed most of the time, but had begun venturing out into the living room, and kitchen.

Travis had done the apartment cleanup himself. That first day was the worst. After collecting all the empty liquor bottles and cans for recycling, and sanitizing various places where Muerce had gotten sick, he went about assembling the Brankovic research that had been torn and scattered around the apartment. It went into a black, plastic trash bag Travis kept in the front coat closet. The temporary office had been returned to its previous state as a bedroom where Lonny slept.

Travis' role was quiet, partly because his jaw remained wired shut. The wires would come off soon, after which, he decided, he'd keep his mouth closed as much as possible. Holding his tongue had been a valuable lesson.

During the first week of Muerce's recovery, a package addressed to Travis arrived. It was from the University of Pennsylvania. Specifically, the Wharton School of Business. It contained a hard copy of the records Travis requested weeks earlier. In the package was a thin envelope of papers, among which was a photocopy of Amelie Bertrand's birth certificate.

As he sipped coffee in the kitchen, Travis read the documents. He reviewed the Spooky Girl's birth certificate. Her birthdate made her twenty nine. She had blue eyes, dark brown hair, and weighed three-point-three kilograms. Travis easily converted the weight into pounds—seven-point-two. *Healthy, he thought.* She was born at two-thirty in the morning at the *Hopital de l'Hotel-Dieu* in the sixth *arrondissement* in Paris, France. *Inconnue* was listed for father. Unknown. The name of her mother was listed as Emily Benoit.

The name meant nothing to Travis. He put the papers back into the envelope, and stuffed it into the plastic trash bag he kept in the coat closet as he left for Saigon Laundry with Muerce's dirty linen.

— —

Eleanor scheduled a quiet lunch with Ashley at the Gilmont Center's restaurant. It was a date she made to compliment and thank Ashley for the work she'd done over the past few weeks. Ashley had, Eleanor told her, handled the crisis with aplomb and grace. What Eleanor really set the luncheon for was to ask Ashley to be patient with her son. Privy to more details than were publicly known of what happened at the glass factory, Eleanor explained the circumstances as best she knew them. She was careful to include what transpired afterwards. "Warts and all," she said. If Ashley were still interested in him, which Eleanor hoped she was, the time would come soon for her to reach out.

"He's complicated," Ashley said.

"You should have met his father," Eleanor said.

From her seat, Ashley could see out the window to the arch where they had toasted with champagne to celebrate her new job. It was a night when the world was upside down, and dreamy. Now it was right-side up, and brutally clear.

"Do you love him?" Eleanor said.

Ashley's gaze drifted past the arch into a clear blue sky. "Don't we all?"

CHAPTER 48

Having been homebound for nearly two weeks, Muerce was restless. Lonny was gone, having left the apartment the previous Friday. Her work was done. He was off the pills, and healing. At least, physically. For the first week, Dr. Riley made daily house calls. By the second week, she and Muerce talked in his living room every other day. It helped. He was scheduled to resume office sessions with her the following Monday.

Both the Jeep and the Mercedes were back in the garage. Colonel Trung had taken care of that. The Mercedes, however, had sustained considerable front end damage when Muerce jumped the curb outside the steam plant. It had been fixed, but Muerce was considering retiring the car. *Time for a change, he thought.*

A box from Luther arrived earlier in the day. It was a replacement phone. Muerce instructed him not to save any prior messages, or texts. The phone was a clean slate.

Muerce knew there were calls to make, but he would procrastinate as long as he could. He had no words for Trumbley. In his malaise, Muerce missed the memorial service for Miriam. He couldn't have sat through it anyway. *Nick would understand, Muerce thought.* Ashley, he was sure, was history. He couldn't blame her. *Jack-ass Muerce.* Paige, however unlikely, did not come to mind. Despite her proximity to him in the days leading up to the encounter with Brankovic, his memory of her blurred into the post-dragon slaying nightmare Muerce abused himself into.

"I got lunshh onsa way ack from za hoshital," Travis said, entering from the foyer, and talking through the wires in his mouth.

"What do we have?" Muerce said.

"*Pho*, and aguette," Travis said, slurring his words as he entered the kitchen. A baguette protruded rakishly from the bag.

"You sound like Daffy Duck," Muerce said. "When are you going to get the hardware off so I can understand you? How did the surgery go?" Pho Mat's knee surgery had taken place that morning. Travis gave a thumbs up that Muerce saw through the kitchen arch.

Travis returned with a bowl of Pho, and a broken piece of bread. Muerce motioned for him to sit down. He wanted to talk.

"I've been thinking," Muerce said. "We need to take your apprenticeship in a different direction." Travis nodded, unsure what might come next. "I'll talk to your folks, and make some calls. Come Fall, you need to be back in school, somewhere."

Travis rolled his eyes.

"You'll be doing me a favor," Muerce said. "Understand?"

Travis slurred out a "yesh," figuring it was not an altogether bad idea.

"Is there gas in the Mercedes?" Muerce said.

"Yesh, why?" Travis said.

"I've got an errand to run," Muerce said. "Promises to keep. By myself, thank you. Probably stop off for a drink after."

Travis' face showed alarm.

"I'm kidding," Muerce said. Though he wouldn't order any hard liquor, Muerce craved some night life. Listening to jazz would do it.

— —

There was nothing either significant or appropriate about showing up at Club Unicorn on Good Friday. Muerce had a surprise for Titty Boy, who was not expecting him. The place was nearly empty when he walked in. Massimo was behind the bar, taking inventory of the bar stock for the weekend.

"Jack," Massimo said, surprised and glad to see Muerce. "Jack is back. You doing okay?"

"Hunky dory," Muerce said. "Tino in?"

Massimo nodded that he was, and led Muerce to Titty Boy's office.

"Hey, Tino," Massimo said. "I've got a surprise visitor for you." Titty Boy, who was sitting behind his desk, stood up and opened his arms when Muerce walked in.

"My favorite giant killer," Titty Boy said. "Back down from the bean stock. Sit down, sit down. I want to hear all about it."

"Feel good to be back in business, Tino?" Muerce said, taking a seat across from Titty Boy.

"Are you kidding?" Titty Boy said. "With no encumbrances. Life is good Jack. Life is really good. I should thank you."

"You should," Muerce said. "And you will."

"Fuck, I figured it was too easy," Titty Boy said, his demeanor less upbeat. "How are you going to screw me, Muerce?"

"I had a deal with Mikal," Muerce said. "His girls belong to me now."

"You fucking kidding me?" Titty Boy said. "You're going to run the stable? Never pictured you for a pimp. And they sure as shit ain't going to be your harem. I know your taste. You're uptown, Jack. Why are you slumming now?"

"My girls, my business," Muerce said.

"You even fucking know their names?" Titty Boy said.

"I'll start with Mirsad," Muerce said.

"Suit yourself," Titty Boy said. "I don't give a shit about them. The street ho's are nickel and dime. The money's in the escorts anyway."

"Good," Muerce said, standing to leave. "Then we're done. And you're welcome."

Titty Boy snorted and shook his head as Muerce left the office. "Don't get too comfortable, Jackie. There are lots of monsters in the forest."

Outside Club Unicorn, Muerce stuffed his hands into his pockets, musing about how Dubrovnik would soon get its first McDonalds, and whether it was best for the young girl in the peasant blouse to work there, or return to her family. She shouldn't stay in this city.

— —

"Jack," Melinda said, effusive as she bent down to kiss Muerce on the cheek. "Buy me a drink. I'm celebrating."

"What are you celebrating?" Muerce said.

"Celebrate with me," she said. "Come on. I'm Melinda Claussen again. The divorce became final today. No more Downey-Breen."

"Melinda, I will definitely buy you a drink, and most certainly will celebrate with you, but I'm sticking to club soda tonight," he said. He motioned for the bartender to serve Melinda whatever she wanted.

"Oh, God, that's right," she said, with an empathetic tone. "I read about it. That must have been horrible. Do you want to talk about it?" The bartender hovered for Melinda's order. "A dirty martini, with three olives."

She cocked her head, and squinted as she sized up Muerce's mood.

"I know that look," she said. "You don't want to talk about anything."

"God I love you," Muerce said, causing her to laugh.

"Oh, let's not talk about love," she said. "Let's just sit and listen to the music. I don't need to get sloshy, just a little tipsy."

Muerce toasted Melinda with his club soda when her martini arrived. They each sipped their drinks, and listened to the quartet play a subdued kind of bebop. The Monastery was upbeat for such a somber night. The crowd likely resting before the Easter Sunday festivities went into full swing. Lent was almost over.

The group played two sets, and Melinda had two martinis before speaking.

"Are you free?" she said.

Muerce gave her a look to convey he didn't understand her meaning.

"I'm free," she said, holding up her left hand, and wiggling her naked ring finger. "Are you?" Now he understood.

"I suppose I am," Muerce said. "What are you suggesting?"

The stage lights twinkled in her eyes as she bent down and kissed Muerce on the lips. The first kiss was soft like a makeup brush applying color. Her second kiss was more passionate.

— —

Melinda made a show of removing her blouse and bra as she stood next to the bed. Her breasts, which had been "done up" months earlier, were spectacular. They had not been bad before, Muerce remembered. These, however, were larger, firmer, and practically shouted at him to fondle.

"Bravo," he said.

"Thought you'd like them," Melinda said, shimming out of her skirt so that she wore only her panties. She jumped onto the bed, and invited Muerce on top of her with her eyes. He managed on his own to get his shirt and t-shirt off, exposing the bruised and puffy scar on his shoulder. The sight of it made Melinda swoon.

"I'll be careful," she said.

"I won't," Muerce said, devouring her breasts with his mouth. He ran his hands over the lovely mounds, pressing and gently pinching them with his fingers. He squeezed and kneaded them as his alternated darting his tongue across each nipple. Tracing his fingertips under Melinda's left breast he felt something like a faint bump. He ran his fingers across it again. It felt like a line of bumps instead of a single one.

Muerce lifted his head away from her chest to investigate his discovery. His body language was not subtle.

"Is something wrong?" Melinda said.

"What's this?" Muerce said. The look on his face was more clinical than lustful, and changed the mood in the room, and in Melinda.

"What's what?" she said, slightly self-conscious.

"These," he said.

"Some scarring," Melinda said. "It's normal. I was told it will go away in time. You're not grossed out are you?"

"No," Muerce said. "This is just, I can't explain. It reminds me of something. Can I look?"

"Knock yourself out," she said. "You've killed the moment anyway."

Muerce examined the scarring as best he could. A surgical line where the saline implant was inserted curved at the bottom of the breast just above Melinda's rib cage. Along the line there appeared to be writing that was raised. Muerce's eyes were not good enough to make it out. Then he remembered the magnifying glass with the fake antler handle sitting on top of a stack of art books on the coffee table in the living room.

He rushed out of the bedroom like it was Christmas morning, leaving the nearly naked Melinda on the bed, and starting to fume.

"Bear with me," Muerce said, returning with the magnifying glass.

"I don't know what you think you're going to do with that," Melinda said. "But the only place I want that thing going into is the top drawer of your nightstand."

Muerce ignored her, and bent down to hold the glass above the scar. What he saw was as clear as day. It was a word, delicately formed in the scar tissue. Muerce recognized the writing. It was Greek. *Χαρυν*. Charon. The style of the work was familiar. It was the same he'd seen on the Death Weaver's victims. Muerce began to feel sick to his stomach.

"Who did your surgery?" Muerce said, alarming Melinda.

"What's wrong, Jack?" she said, frightened. "You're scaring me."

"Who, Melinda?" he said, insistently. "Who did the surgery?"

"I had it done at the Acheron Institute," she said, near tears. "Doctor Sharron. Why?"

Jumping up, Muerce pulled his hands through his hair. *Got to think, Jack, got to think.*

"Oh shit," he said, speaking in a staccato. "It's Good Friday. Christ on the cross. He died for our sins. Absolution. Free will. Oh, damn. It's the sixth tapestry. Passiontide, Melinda."

"What?" she said, sitting up in bed. Scared, feeling exposed and vulnerable, Melinda crossed her arms to cover herself.

"Passiontide," he said. "The last two weeks of Lent. They cover all the crosses and statues with purple sheets. Essentially, it's a two-week break. A kind of spiritual vacation. That ends, tomorrow."

Muerce began frantically dressing, looking for his keys. "There's no time. I can't explain. I've got to go."

Melinda was confused and frightened when she heard the elevator door clank shut in the foyer. She tried to examine her breast as best she could, but the angle and size of it prevented a detailed viewing. When she looked for the magnifying glass she noticed that Muerce had been in such a rush he left his mobile phone on the nightstand.

CHAPTER 49

The parking garage at the Acheron Institute was dark and empty when Muerce pulled into the structure. Unfamiliar with the place, and with no plan to speak of, he jerked the Mercedes around until he found the rear entrance, and haphazardly parked the car in front of it.

There was an immediacy he felt to his very core, a sickening ache. On the hurried drive over, Muerce thought of Redzil, and Miriam. There were the five dead found in the ACME Glass offices. There was even Brankovic, who now looked to be a convenient cutout for several people. How high would the death toll go? Mostly, as he stood, staring at the security keypad at the door to the institute, he thought about Paige. *Best, Muerce thought, to call the police now.* When he reached for his phone, he realized it was still back at the apartment. He cursed himself.

Muerce thought it through as best he could. There wasn't time to drive around looking for a cop, or a phone. He needed to get inside as quickly as possible. No matter how unsure he was of what might be transpiring inside the Acheron walls, he was sure Paige was in trouble. He remembered the scar on the back of her neck, and that it, too, had an uncertain meaning. It, like Melinda's, and the five victims, was the work of Dr. Merchant Sharron—the Death Weaver.

There was only one option for Muerce. He would crash the Mercedes into the door. It was worth the risk of alarming Dr. Sharron, it would also likely trigger an alarm that would bring the police. As he was about to turn to get into the car, Muerce had an idea. *Worth a try, he thought.*

He punched in the numbers 3–3–7–4–7–3. Nothing happened. Again he keyed them into the pad. Again nothing.

"Right," Muerce said under his breath. "*Desir* in French."

Muerce poked at the keypad, eliminating the last digit. A green light went on, followed by a low buzz signaling access was granted. Without thinking, Muerce entered the building, uncertain of his surroundings.

Surprisingly, all the lights were on. A small sign on on the wall gave Muerce the directions he needed. There was even an arrow pointing the way to the Operating Suites.

As he made his way around a curved wall, the sight of the Roxy Paine sculpture sent a chill through Muerce's body. The hair on his forearms stiffened. It was a foreboding piece of artwork, wrought with dread. He let the feeling pass when he saw the door to one of the operating suites was partially open. Through it, he made out what looked to be a body on a gurney.

No one appeared to be around as he approached the door. With each step he looked for anything he might use as a weapon—either defensively, or offensively. The hallways were spartan, lacking anything Muerce could pick up with convenience. It was quiet.

Angling himself across the hallway from the suite, Muerce peered across a distance of ten feet. Inside, he could see Price, naked and strapped to a gurney. He appeared to be alive, but unconscious. Maneuvering for a closer look, Muerce saw a second gurney. The occupant's legs were held aloft by a set of stirrups. Muerce recognized them right away. They belonged to Paige, who looked to be unconscious though not strapped down as her brother. On a wheeled surgical table next to her lay an array of instruments, including several scalpels. *They were better, he thought, than nothing*

He was no more than five steps into the operating room when he was stopped.

"Tut, tut Mister Muerce," Dr. Sharron said. "You've gone as far as you can."

Turning around, Muerce raised his hands when he saw the gun Dr. Sharron pointed at him.

"If you'd please, take the seat in the corner," Dr. Sharron said, pointing at a stainless steel folding chair with the gun. Muerce did as he was told, his hands in the air. Dr. Sharron walked sideways to a table set up next to Price, and picked up a white fabric mask that looked like the kind worn when sanding drywall. With his free hand he inserted a wad of loose gauze into the mask, and placed it into a kidney shaped stainless steel surgical dish. Taking a deep breath, which he held, Dr. Sharron unscrewed a bottle containing a clear liquid, and poured a teaspoon of it into the mask.

Stooping to put the dish on the floor, the pistol still aimed at Muerce, Dr. Sharron stood up. In a soccer-style half kick, the dish slid easily across the slick floor, stopping directly in front of Muerce's feet. A strong, caustic smell stained the air.

Dr. Sharron released his breath. "Now, be so kind as to retrieve the mask from the dish, affix it over your nose and mouth, and take a deep breath," Dr. Sharron said. "I promise you the sensation is quite pleasing. Intoxicating even."

"If I don't," Muerce said.

"Rest assured, I will shoot you, and go about my business," Dr. Sharron said. "Family business, Mister Muerce. And, perhaps, tomorrow night I might take an interest in your family. Your mother, Eleanor, isn't it? A lovely woman. A true patron of the arts. I should think I might want to thank her, in person. If it weren't for her, I would not have had the pleasure of seeing the tapestries again. They so rarely travel. Now, please." Dr. Sharron signaled with the barrel of the gun for Muerce to pick up the mask. "I don't have all the time in the world, and you interrupted me in the middle of an examination."

Dr. Sharron nodded his head in the direction of Paige's legs. "This way," he said. "You and I can have more time to get to know each other. I might even let you watch me work, later."

Reaching down without averting his eyes from Dr. Sharron, Muerce grabbed the mask with resignation, and held it to his face. Muerce never experienced ether before. It was intoxicating. By the third breath, he closed his eyes, and dreamily slumped in the chair.

— —

A slap of cold water woke Muerce from his stupor. As enjoyable as it had been, he'd forgotten his dream as soon as he opened his eyes. The water ran down his face, and saturated the top of his shirt. He could not move his arms or legs, having been duct-taped to a padded office chair that had roller wheels. If he squirmed hard enough, he could move an inch or two, but no more.

Another slap struck Muerce across the face. This time it came from Dr. Sharron's hand, and fully raised Muerce to consciousness.

"I'm disenchanted with you," Dr. Sharron said. "Very disenchanted."

Muerce blinked hard to try and clear his vision. He had a thick headache, the kind you got from drinking too much beer. Looking around, he saw he was no longer in the operating suite. They were in some kind of garden room with padded patio furniture. A large hole in the roof was covered by white canvas, which appeared to undulate with the wind. Below it, in the center of the circular room, was a large skylight decorated with opaque panes of glass formed into a pentagram.

Dr. Sharron paced angrily around the skylight. He fidgeted with his hands, shaking them up and down, then intertwining them together. He repeated the gesture as he circled without looking at Muerce. He was manic. It was the kind of behavior Muerce had once seen visiting a psychiatric ward. It was not, Muerce realized, a good sign. If he couldn't talk him down, then maybe he could send him over.

"So tell me Doctor," Muerce said. "What are you feeling right now?"

The words froze Dr. Sharron in place. The pained look on his face disappeared, his shoulders relaxed. He smiled when he glanced at Muerce. There were gears to Dr. Sharron's personality, and Muerce had just switched him back into low. If he weren't already in a dire predicament, Muerce would have been worried by the suddenness of the change.

"You really are quite amusing," Dr. Sharron said. "Ignorant, but charmingly amusing."

"Then enlighten me," Muerce said. "We have time, don't we?"

"Not a lot, but more than we had before," Dr. Sharron said. "It appears, you have unwittingly spoiled my work. God's work, really."

"God?" Muerce said. "I've seen your work. There's nothing Godly in what you've done, or in what you are about to do."

"Did you see my work?" Dr. Sharron said. "Exquisite, don't you think?"

"Pedestrian," Muerce said. "Almost cliched. Like it was outsourced to China."

"Oh, now, Mister Muerce, or can I call you Jack?" Dr. Sharron said. "Jack, you're just being spiteful. We can hardly have an enlightening conversation with you in that frame of mind, can we? Of course not. And I spent so much time with your friend."

Muerce flared his nostrils.

"Goodness, got a rise out of you on that one, didn't I?" Dr. Sharron said. "But that was the plan. I'd like to take credit for it, but like I said, it, like you and Misses Estrada were delivered by God. His plan."

"Why?" Muerce said, trying to calm himself. "Why Miriam?"

"I have to admit, I was perplexed at first, too," Dr. Sharron said. "You see, the work had been a progression. We discussed it at the museum, at the gala. Do you remember? The death of each of the first four senses was an absolution. They had sinned against their particular gifts. Each in their own way." Dr. Sharron folded his hands behind his back, and slowly circled the skylight.

"The prostitute sold her sense of touch. A once promising chef, traded her trained palette for cheap liquor. The eyes of a talented photo journalist, saw only commercial profit through her lens. The virtuoso cellist turned her ear for the symphony for that of the streets. You see, Jack, they sinned against God, and needed to be cleansed."

"And what about Miriam," Muerce said. "There was no sin in her."

"Which was why I was so perplexed," Dr. Sharron said. "I prayed on it at length. I did. But I had no choice. She, and you, were sent from God."

"I don't see anything divine in it," Muerce said. "It was... opportunistic. Dumb luck."

A chortle rose from Dr. Sharron. "Perhaps," he said. "But it served my purpose. How could I not take it? And did the world not profit from it? Did you not profit from it? Are we not rid of a monster? I dare say, you will be rewarded in Heaven for your actions. The Dragon Slayer. Very romantic. Even noble. Maybe you'll be canonized."

"How?" Muerce said.

"The cardinals make those decisions," Dr. Sharron said.

"No, how did you do it?" Muerce said.

"Oh, that," Dr. Sharron said. "It was quite easy. As you can see, I'm well set up here for the procedure. Even disposal. Identifying and acquiring each sense was a matter of research. And, as I said before, Misses Estrada was a quandary to me, at first. Eventually, she delivered herself.

"The complexity with her was, let's say, in the staging. She was to me, as she was to you, special. It was a beautiful location. Challenging. Both from a transportation and timing perspective. But we had a lovely boat ride together before I lay her to sleep."

"And her car?" Muerce said.

"That was tricky," Dr. Sharron said. "There was ample supply of evidence to leave in the trunk of her car. The difficulty was finding a bus in that part of town at such a late hour."

"No, how did you know where to park it?" Muerce said.

"I have a little bird," Dr. Sharron said. "He's lying downstairs. Always do your research, Jack. Plan your work. Work your plan."

"What now?" Muerce said. "You're going to kill you own children?"

"The fly in the ointment," Dr. Sharron said. "This is the cause of my previous agitation, and disenchantment with you."

His hands still locked behind his back, Dr. Sharron winked as he made his way behind the chair, and out of Muerce's vision. Muerce could hear the sounds of a kind of preparation that would not end well for him.

"I must confess, Jack, I have my failings," Dr. Sharron said. "Misses Estrada was, in part, something I acted on in jealousy. One of my many weaknesses. My children and I have a special bond. One that goes beyond being mere parent and child. It is a bond handed down to us from my parents, and their parents. It is God given, and pure."

"You're losing me," Muerce said.

"Yes, quite, and soon," Dr. Sharron said, remaining out of Muerce's visual range. "You see, Jack, as shocking as it might sound to your, what was the word you used? Pedestrian? Yes, pedestrian. Your pedestrian sensibilities. I'm more than Price and Paige's father. I'm their uncle, too. Biologically speaking. Their mother, my wife, was my sister. Twin sister. As were our parents."

"I might use a different word," Muerce said. "Aberrant."

"I don't expect you to understand," Dr. Sharron said.

"How were you jealous of Miriam?" Muerce said.

"Oh, I wasn't jealous of her," Dr. Sharron said, emerging from behind Muerce with a large bottle of ether, and a fresh mask and gauze. "I was jealous of you. Envious even."

Muerce looked puzzled and confused.

"My weaknesses," Dr. Sharron said. "The progression, you see, our family progression, can only be sanctified by God through the absolution of the five senses. My handiwork. All of it leading to impregnation of Paige by Price. And this, Jack, is where I must confess more of my indiscretions. Obviously, and this is entirely my fault, Price is not, shall we say, predisposed toward natural coupling. I'm afraid my urges deviated with his while my own natural but unmet desires for my daughter flourished. It was a temporary bargain Price and I brokered, for her sake."

"*Mon seul desir*," Muerce said.

"It is a bit complicated, isn't it?" Dr. Sharron said.

"Not really," Muerce said, recalling one of the items on Kernberg's sociopathic checklist—carefree non-planfulness.

"I'm afraid Father's Day isn't much of celebration around here," Dr. Sharron said.

"And her condition, spinal twist, or whatever," Muerce said. The bottle of ether Dr. Sharron held to his chest triggered a primal urge in Muerce to buy more time. Dr. Sharron looked at his watch.

"Non-existent," Dr. Sharron said. "A canard used to control both her and her brother."

Gaslighting, Muerce thought.

"How am I the fly in the ointment for your progression?" Muerce blurted out. His anxiety began to press into fear.

"I'm afraid you've run out of time, Jack," Dr. Sharron said. "But what the hey, you deserve to know. Seems we had the makings of a shotgun wedding tonight."

"What?" Muerce said, practically shouting.

"I was about to do a pelvic examination when you interrupted me earlier," Dr. Sharron said. "I'd already pulled her blood, and was running tests. The plan was to impregnate her with Price's seed. Unfortunately, I discovered, she had already been impregnated. Apparently, by you, Jack. You're the fly in the ointment.

"Time's up. Hope you don't mind if I call you son. We truly have gotten to know each other better, don't you think? So tell me, son, what are you feeling right now?"

A rustling, followed by a loud crash sounded behind Muerce, who tried to crane his head to look.

"Looks like we have a surprise visitor, Jack," Dr. Sharron said, taking several steps back toward the skylight. "Have you come to say your good-bye's Sister?"

After stumbling into the table, Paige righted herself. The effects of the ether and other sedatives left her wobbly and disoriented. Pausing at the doorway to recover from her journey from the ground floor to the fifth floor patio, she had heard, unseen, most of the conversation. She did not have to struggle to make sense of the information.

On her way up, Paige stopped twice to rest. One of her stops was in her room where she found her robe, and tied it off tightly in front.

Her presence announced, and struggling to regain her bearing, she shuffled toward Muerce before stumbling into the back of the chair. She righted herself again, and surveyed Muerce's bondage. Her body functioned poorly, but her mind solved the puzzle. With a grunt she rolled the chair, and Muerce to the side with a slight spin. Muerce had seen the look in her eyes before.

"What's this?" Dr. Sharron said, holding the large glass jar of ether higher to his left shoulder.

Paige steadied herself, then stood as upright as she could. As she did, Muerce was able to scoot the chair so he could see both of them. He spotted the *puggio* lashed to her back by the belt of the robe just as Paige reached for it. The move was so swift Muerce did not have time to cry out, though it would only have been for encouragement. Her throw was as accurate as it was quick, landing directly on Dr. Sharron's heart. It was not, however, deadly. The *puggio* struck heel first, and fell to the floor. The damage the toss did was to the container of ether, which shattered, spilling its contents down the front of Dr. Sharron's medical smock.

A look of shock in his face, Dr. Sharron furiously attempted to remove the drenched smock to avoid its effects, but it was too late. The harder he fought to disrobe, the more vapor he inhaled. In his frenzy, he stumbled backwards, tripping over, then onto the skylight. The glass gave way, sending Dr. Sharron hurtling down into the lobby atrium. His fall ended amid the spiked branches of the sculpture. He lay, still alive, but impaled through one leg and his abdomen, gazing up at the shattered remains of the skylight. Paige bent, and peered down at him. Within a second of settling on the stainless steel sculpture, the highly volatile vapors of the ether were ignited by the the flame from one of the gas lotus pedals floating on the surface of the reflecting pool.

The screaming ended just as the building's sprinklers activated. Paige stood on the skylight precipice, watching as her father burned. Something inside of her snapped when the sprinklers went on. She moved unsteadily until she stood directly beneath one of the sprays as if she were showering.

Muerce watched as she unrobed, turning and twisting with child-like delight under the sprinkler. When she stopped to look at Muerce, she could see he was talking to her. His face was emphatic, as if he were screaming, but Paige heard nothing. She watched as he struggled against his bonds. His hands opened and closed like a desperate grapple. Her only response was to smile at him. She was in control. Not the kind manipulated by violence, greed or sex, but self control. A calming peace washed over her with the spray. She looked down, putting her hands on her belly. Then she looked up at Muerce, smiled again, and stepped through the skylight. As she fell, Paige wondered if their child would have had the same soft skin as its father.

CHAPTER 50

With the dawn of Easter Sunday, a new liturgical year was born, though Muerce chose to sleep in. He had spent late Good Friday night, and almost all of Holy Saturday at Police Headquarters.

Rifling through the kitchen, wearing slacks and a bathrobe, he found the pantry bereft of food. For the first time in his adult life, Muerce felt the urge to buy groceries. The phone in his robe pocket buzzed and vibrated. It was a text message from Ashley: Open the door. Ash.

Simultaneously, the doorbell to the apartment gonged. When he answered it, he was greeted by and outstretched hand holding a clear plastic dry cleaning shroud containing the car coat he loaned her the morning after their first night together.

"I got used to wearing it," she said. "So I had it cleaned."

Muerce took the coat from her as she crouched down to grab the handle of two reusable grocery sacks. A third was in her other hand.

"Well, are you going to invite me in?" she said.

He motioned with his arm and a smile that she was welcome, and she made straight for the kitchen.

"You promised me I could cook for you sometime," she said, unloading the groceries onto the kitchen island. "It's sometime."

"Got any coffee in there?" he said.

She removed a gray one-pound bag of freshly ground French Roast, and handed it to him.

"Can I ask you something?" she said, removing the groceries from the bags into their respective places in the cupboards and refrigerator.

"Anything," Muerce said.

"Anything?" she said.

"Yes," he said.

There was a pause in the conversation, but not in their activity. Muerce began to make the coffee as Ashley put the food away.

"Who is Emily Benoit?" she said.

"She was my fiance," Muerce said, without hesitating. "It was a long time ago."

Ashley stopped what she was doing, and turned toward Muerce, who turned toward her, and smiled.

"Do you want to have breakfast with me," he said. "Tomorrow?"

She smiled back.

"I know this little place that makes the best *beignets*," he said.

ACKNOWLEDGEMENTS

I wish to thank the following people and institutions
for their assistance and contributions to this book:

John L. McCabe—French translations

Tom Fox—Vietnamese translations

Denis Greene

Patrick Keenan

James T. Seigfreid Jr.

Musee National du Moyen Age

J. Paul Getty Museum

Nelson-Atkins Museum of Art

AUTHOR

Hughes Keenan began his writing career at The Kansas City Star and was a member of the staff awarded the 1982 Pulitzer Prize for reporting. He has been a correspondent for United Press International, The Associated Press, Reuters and Bloomberg News, covering war, politics, sports and finance. His first novel, *The Harvest Is Past*, was a finalist for the Thorpe Menn Award for Literary Excellence.